"Quinn Yarbro is one of our finest writers, incapable of a slack paragraph or a fuzzy thought. The Count remains a vibrantly original character, one of the greatest contributions to the horror genre."
—Peter Straub

"Yarbro's painstaking research yields a finely wrought tapestry of lives in grim historical context. Those new to the Count, as well as his loyal admirers, will enjoy this richly textured tale of political intrigue spiced with hot blood."
—*Publishers Weekly* on *Communion Blood*

"Chelsea Quinn Yarbro has created the most remarkable and original vampire since Bram Stoker's Dracula."
—*The Bookwatch (Midwest Book Review)*

"Yarbro's latest installment featuring her compassionate and sophisticated vampire hero offers a rich, detailed look at a complex time in Europe's history."
—*Library Journal* on *Communion Blood*

"These solidly researched novels show us a Saint-Germain who genuinely learns and grows from a fiend into a being of great gentleness, wisdom, and compassion. The series is probably the most sustained and impressive treatment to date of extreme longevity."
—*Minneapolis Tribune*

"A heady, intoxicating blend of historical fiction and subtle horror. Yarbro expertly mixes historical figures with fictional characters, paints a vibrant picture of seventeenth-century Rome in all its power, grandeur, and decadence."
—*Voice of Youth Advoc...* ...*d*

"Take time to read one of the ... ...be grateful. You'll also be hook...
— ...News Service

By Chelsea Quinn Yarbro from Tom Doherty Associates

A FEAST IN
EXILE

A Novel of Saint-Germain

Chelsea Quinn Yarbro

A TOM DOHERTY ASSOCIATES BOOK
NEW YORK

This is a work of fiction. All the characters and events portrayed in this novel are either fictitious or are used fictitiously.

A FEAST IN EXILE

A Tor Book
Published by Tom Doherty Associates, LLC
175 Fifth Avenue
New York, NY 10010

www.tor.com

Tor® is a registered trademark of Tom Doherty Associates, LLC.

Library of Congress Cataloging-in-Publication Data

Yarbro, Chelsea Quinn.
    A feast in exile : a novel of Saint-Germain / Chelsea Quinn Yarbro.
        p. cm.
    "A Tom Doherty Associates book."
    ISBN 0-312-87843-5 (hc)
    ISBN 0-312-87842-7 (pbk)
    1. Saint-Germain, comte de, d. 1784—Fiction. 2. India—History—1000–1526—Fiction. 3. Timur, 1336–1405—Fiction. 4. Vampires—Fiction. I. Title.

PS3575.A7 F43 2001
813'.54—dc21   2001042322

First Hardcover Edition: October 2001
First Trade Paperback Edition: October 2002

Printed in the United States of America

0 9 8 7 6 5 4 3 2 1

This one is for

Randall Behr

and

Frank Corsaro,

the opera connection.

Author's Notes

India has a rich history that is not much understood in the West: the population is comprised of a complex mixture of cultural, ethnic, religious, and language groups which, over time, have taken on an uneasy national identity. This is a fairly recent development. Until the mid-nineteenth century, the many divisions were more sharply defined; today the most obvious segmentation of the population is religious—Hindu and Muslim conflicts being uppermost in that sad antagonism. The centuries before any significant European presence in India were filled with social, regional, and ethnic turmoil that shaped the way in which the population responded to everything from visiting strangers to district warfare to trade.

Trade had long been a factor to the Indian subcontinent—trade with China (both overland and maritime), trade with what is modern Indonesia (maritime), trade with Burma (overland and maritime), trade with Himalayan states of Mustang, Bhutan, and Tibet (overland), trade with Arabs (overland and maritime), with Persia (predominantly overland), with Armenia and Afghanistan (overland), with Russia (predominantly overland), with the Mediterranean world (predominantly overland to the Black Sea and then by maritime ventures to markets from Gibraltar to Vienna and Alexandria), and with east Africa (predominantly maritime). With trade came foreigners, bringing ideas as well as goods to the various states of India. Begun in the first century A.D., by the fourteenth century (Western calendar), a small but steady stream of materials and scholarship ran between Europe and India, and a far more active commerce existed between the Arab-controlled Middle East and the Indian subcontinent.

In the north-west region, the Tughluqs held sway from their stronghold at Delhi, and maintained an empire that at one time stretched across most of India; however, by the time of this novel, the real power of Delhi had shrunk to a small wedge in the corner of the Empire. The Tughluq dynasty still held the throne, but Nasiruddin Mohammed bin Tughluq, the Sultan at the time of this story, did not spend much time in Delhi, leaving it to the care of his relatives while he built a series of fortresses to buttress his borders, such as they were. While the various court officials in this story are fictional, they are typical of and drawn from the actual officials of the period. The Tughluq dynasty followed the Persian tradition and did not use the name of the ruling Sultan unless specifically addressing the man himself; otherwise, his title alone was used as a show of respect.

Timur-i Lenkh, the Turko-Mongol conqueror known in the West as Tamerlane, carved out an impressive Empire for himself between his rise to power in 1364 and his death in 1405 at age sixty-eight; his territory extended from the borders of Ottoman Turkey in the west, through all of the old Persian Empire (modern-day Iran and Iraq), to the southern shores of the Black Sea, all but the northern-most end of the Caspian Sea, to his capital at Samarkand, and south to Delhi and the Persian Gulf. Nominally Muslim, Tamerlane spent most of his adult life on campaign, initially warring against his Jagatai cousins, and then against the Ottoman and Mameluke Empires, both Muslim Empires, in the West, and finally against the Delhi Empire, another Muslim Empire, in the east.

His cavalry tactics were especially formidable: he would dispatch cavalry units, each man with six horses, riding one, leading the other five, and as the ridden horse tired, moving to the next and so on. Traveling at a trot, such units could cover an astonishing eighty miles a day; the army itself, with all its support vehicles and personnel, could, in a real push, cover fifteen to eighteen miles a day, depending on the ground being crossed and the time of year, a remarkable accomplishment for animal-pulled vehicles. I should note that in spite of what Tamerlane's opponents said, his cavalry-men did not actually leap from horse to horse while traveling. Not that the soldiers were not sufficiently skilled horsemen for such a feat—they were. But their saddles could not leap with them, and all their gear, weapons, food, and water were carried on their saddles.

With the erosion of the Delhi Sultanate, which in 1340 had a degree of control of almost all but the southernmost portion of India, central and southern India became rife with rebellions and power-grabs from a number of local Rajputs (Princes: literally, rulers' sons). Gujerat was the first successful break-away from Delhi rule; over the next forty years regional conflicts erupted in many places, and eventually settled down into a number of fairly well-defined principalities, but at the time of this story, that process was just beginning. Beragar and its principal city of Devapur are fictional, as is the Rajput Hasin Dahele, but he is typical of the men who strove to grab a portion of the old Delhi Sultanate for themselves. Most of the Rajputs' territories were not sharply defined except by geographic features such as rivers and mountain ranges; where such clear physical demarcations did not exist, the frontiers were a kind of narrow zone between territories where the Rajputs' authorities were as likely to not exist at all as to overlap. The port cities of Cambay and Chaul are both real, Cambay being at the mouth of the Sabarmati River, and Chaul, immediately south of modern-day Bombay. Both were crucial to trade across the Arabian Sea to the Persian Gulf and the Red Sea, and had been for well over two thousand years.

Military expeditions in central and southern India at the time were ponderous affairs, depending on cavalry and elephants for most of the actual combat. Mounted archers were the preferred soldiers, with elephants used to batter down defenses and remove tactical obstacles. Unlike in the West, mules were not much used at the time except for hauling support vehicles, and even then they did not become as utilitarian and ubiquitous as they were in Europe; asses and ponies were generally used as pack-animals in their place.

Because of the many ethnic groups and regional dialects inherent in this period and locales, I have tended to use Saint-Germain as my reference point for such things as the names of clothing and other every-day items in common usage, using the word he would tend to use rather than to try to select the appropriate word for each ethnic and caste group for that time and region, which would result in a dozen different names for a single item of clothing, such as, for example, the kandys (a kind of caftan-like garment); where multiple languages are being spoken, I have tried to keep defined who is speaking what. Sanscrit was the language of education and some religion, much like Latin in the West, but it was not the spoken language of most of the population, and so is not a useful starting point for ordinary regional language.

Europe and the Middle East were divided differently than they are today: in 1398, the now-tiny Baltic state of Lithuania reached all the way to the Black Sea through much of what is Poland, Ukraine, and Romania today; the Ottoman Empire was just beginning to spread out from modern-day Turkey into the Balkan States of what today are Bulgaria, Romania, and Hungary; the Mameluke Empire, centered in Egypt, included much of present-day Israel and Jordan. Cities have changed names, and, in a few instances, locations, since the time of this novel. For example, the trading town of Fustat in Egypt grew into the modern city of Cairo, and Delhi expanded, adding New Delhi to its larger districts.

Among those who provided insight and help on this project, I would like to thank, in no particular order, Spencer Campbell for the astronomical information he provided; Lucy Shelton for the access to her references on trade-routes and the business of trade between Asia and Europe; to James Bentley for information on the cultures, religions, and languages of fourteenth-century Delhi; to Caroline Sagan for providing information about law, tradition, and domesticity in India in the fourteenth and fifteenth centuries; to Palmer McKay for showing me his maps on the ecological history of Asia; to Edward Herriton for lending me two terrific books on warfare in Asia from 1500 B.C. to A.D. 1500; to Jerri Denning for general information on the movements of Timur-i Lenkh's armies; and to L. G. Hoffmann for letting me read his material on India after Timur-i Lenkh. Errors in historicity or fact should be laid at my door and at none of these good people's.

On other fronts, thanks are also due to Eleanor Guzman, Andrew Hawkins, and Sharon Cho, who read the manuscript for clarity; to Maureen Kelly and Sharon Russell, who read it for fun; to Lewis Bruma, who read it for accuracy; to Wiley Saichek, who made sure everyone on the Internet knew about it; to my agent, Irene Kraas, who took care of it; to my editor at Tor, Melissa Singer, who shepherded it through the publication process; to my attorney, Robin Dubner, who protects Saint-Germain; to Lindig Harris, who keeps the newsletter going (*Yclept Yarbro*, P. O. Box 8905, Asheville, NC 28814, or lindig@mindspring.com); to the many independent booksellers who keep Saint-Germain on their shelves; to those Internet bookbuyers who continue to order these books; and, by extension, my readers, who have been so good to Saint-Germain for nearly a quarter of a century (not long from his point of view, but still . . .).

Chelsea Quinn Yarbro
August 2000

La carità è un festin' in esilio.
Charity is a feast in exile.

Venetian aphorism

NORTH-WESTERN INDIA 1400 AD

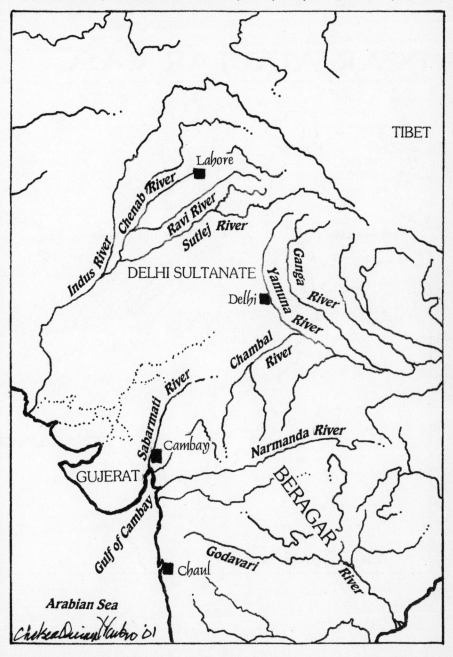

TIBET

Lahore

Chenab River

Ravi River

Sutlej River

Indus River

DELHI SULTANATE

Ganga River

Yamuna River

Delhi

Chambal River

Sabarmati River

Narmanda River

Cambay

BERAGAR

GUJERAT

Gulf of Cambay

Godavari River

Chaul

Arabian Sea

NEAR AND FAR EAST

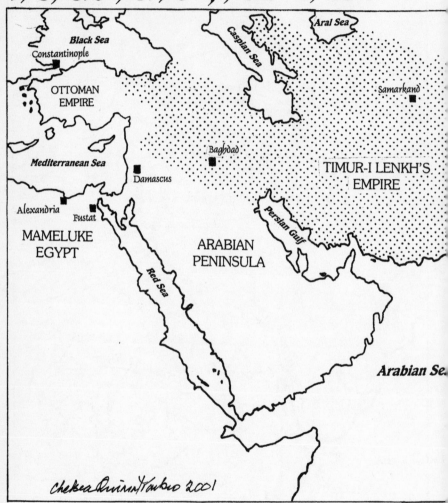

Aral Sea

Black Sea

Constantinople

Caspian Sea

Samarkand

OTTOMAN
EMPIRE

Baghdad

TIMUR-I LENKH'S
EMPIRE

Mediterranean Sea

Damascus

Alexandria

Fustat

Persian Gulf

MAMELUKE
EGYPT

ARABIAN
PENINSULA

Red Sea

Arabian Sea

Chelsea Quinn Yarbro 2001

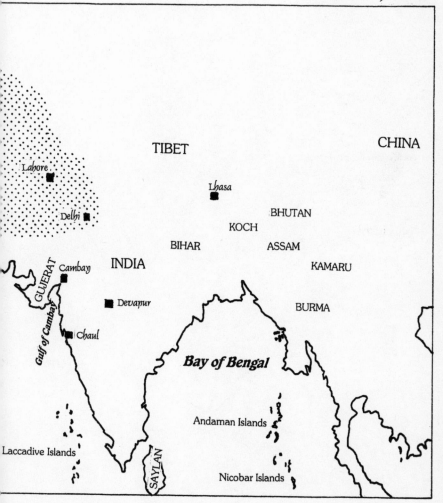

1400 AD

TIBET

CHINA

Lahore

Lhasa

Delhi

BHUTAN

KOCH

BIHAR

ASSAM

KAMARU

GUJERAT

Cambay

INDIA

Devapur

BURMA

Gulf of Cambay

Chaul

Bay of Bengal

Laccadive Islands

SAYLAN

Andaman Islands

Nicobar Islands

PART I

TIMUR-I LENKH

*T*ext of a civil proclamation given at the Mogul Sultanate of Delhi, on 21 January, 1398, by the calendar of the Roman Church.

People of Delhi, this is the law for marriage: it applies to all who live in this city, no matter what their customs may require or their religions may preach. In Delhi, this is the law.

Any man seeking to take a woman to wife must pay the bride-price asked by her father or brother, or, if she has no male relatives, to the Sultan. Failure to do this will invalidate the marriage and make any children of such an irregular union illegitimate and entitled to nothing from any member of the father's house.

Any man taking a slave as a concubine will be allowed to legitimize such issue as may come from the union until the child is two years of age. If the child is not legitimized by that time, it will be considered to be illegitimate and without family and may be kept as a slave or sold, on the wish of the father.

Any man taking a woman not a slave as a concubine will pay the bride-price to her male relatives that is commensurate with their station in life. Any children of such a union may be legitimized in the first two years of life; if they are not, they may be adopted by the woman's male relatives or enrolled in the service of the Sultan.

Any man taking a bride who is not of his faith may stipulate that the children of such a union are illegitimate in order to preserve the family in the faith of the husband and his father; the brothers of the wife may adopt the children if the husband of the mother is paid an agreed-upon price for the child or children.

Any man marrying a slave must first pay the price of her freedom to the Sultan and have the sale recorded before the union can be considered legitimate. Any man failing to pay such a price may not legitimize any children from the union.

Any man whose religion does not prohibit it may take as many as four wives without paying additional bride-prices to the Sultan, for the Prophet—may he be praised—has said that a man may take four wives. If a man seeks to marry more than four, the bride-price must be paid to the Sultan or any child of the additional unions will be held to be illegitimate and not entitled to any portion of his father's estate or name.

Any man may keep as many concubines as he may support without causing any of his legitimate wives to suffer on this account. Suffering includes starvation, privation, lack of shelter, denial of the rights of legitimate children, and compromise of obligations to the wives' fathers and brothers. The man keeping the concubines may not reduce them to a station less than that occupied by the male relatives of the concubine in question.

Any man whose religion prohibits him from having more than one wife may acquire such concubines as he can afford to keep. The children of such concubines shall be accounted his slaves unless he makes them legitimate before such children are two years of age.

Any man who puts away his wife for religious reasons will pay a bride-price to her male relatives, or to the Sultan if she has none. She will be considered a widow and may be put in the care of a guardian appointed by her husband for as long a term as the husband shall stipulate. The wife of such a man may be permitted to marry again if her husband does not oppose such an arrangement, and if it is not such a reduction in station or caste that would render the union ineligible either to his male relatives or hers. Should her husband wish her to remain unmarried, he will have to provide support for her commensurate with the support he provided her when he lived with her as her husband. Should he fail to do so, her male relatives would be entitled to demand such a sum from his family and to administer it on her behalf.

Any man who deserts a wife for any reason that is not of her instigation, and not the result of religion or leprosy, will be required to provide her bride-price to her male relatives and to release her unconditionally to marry again, should her male relatives secure another offer for her. If a man deserts one wife but not another for a reason that is not of her instigation and is not the result of religion or leprosy, the male relatives may appeal to the male relatives of the entitled wife for recompense for the deserted wife. If her male relatives do not find her another husband, the family of the deserting husband must make a place for her in one of their households at a rank not below that of concubine.

Any man who takes a wife who has been a widow will have full authority over her, her belongings, and any children from her previous husband who have not been provided for by the male relatives of the deceased husband. It shall be within his power to order the lives of such children as if they were his own offspring. He is not required to make them legitimate as of his blood, but he may do so if the male relatives of the deceased husband offer no objection.

Any man who dies while married to a fertile woman may leave a baby in her womb to comfort her; if that baby is delivered within three years of its father's death, it will be acknowledged as the child of the father and solace of the mother. If the child is born after three years, it is proof of the widow's vice, and may be stoned to death to preserve its father's name, and the widow will be cast out from the city or sold to a brothel to expiate her husband's honor.

Any foreign man, no matter what his customs and laws may be, must abide by Delhi's laws while in the Sultan's lands. Should he fail to abide by the laws, his wives and sisters will become the wards of the Sultan and given the rights and protections of the laws of Delhi.

Any woman without male relatives is to be considered the niece of the Sultan. All negotiations for marriage, all bride-prices, all compensations, are to be paid to the Sultan in lieu of paying her male relatives.

Women married in this way may not be married below the station or caste of their male relative, if they had such, nor are they to be given to husbands not of their male relatives' religion.

Any man is entitled to choose one of his daughters to provide for his care and the care of his wife or wives in old age. This daughter may not be married until her father has been dead for two years, and then she may marry only at the will of her brothers, or by order of the Sultan, if she has no living male relatives. She may occupy her father's house until her brothers find a suitable husband for her, or the brothers may pay her bride-price to the Sultan and let her remain unmarried and in her father's house for as long as the brothers are willing she should remain.

Look that all men of Delhi know the law and abide by it.

Sawan bin Tughluq
Deputy to the Sultan for Marriages and Inheritances

1

Along the backs of the bazaar stalls people gathered in knots to exchange the rumors they had heard during the day's buying and selling; it was late on an overcast, sultry afternoon that had been filled with distant thunder, a sign many took as ominous, since it was known that Timur-i and his army were on the move, although no one knew where they would turn next. The still air was heavy with the odors of the bazaar—spices, food, animals, dung, incense, perfume, sweat, and dust—and the lingering oppression of the weather.

"Timur-i will attack us. The Armenian who brings black wool to market says it is assured," said a seller of brasses. "He will not be satisfied until he has brought us under his control, and leaves Delhi in ruins, as he has so many other cities."

"How does he know this?" asked the spice merchant. "Has he ear of Timur-i, that he is privy to his plans?"

"Hardly that. It is because the Armenians are afraid of what he will do to *them*, so they wish it upon us," scoffed a dealer in muslin. "They would rather he try to fight us than set his sights on them. They don't have an army to match the Sultan's."

"That's very true," said the spice merchant, a bit too eagerly. "The Sultan's army is the envy of the world."

"But we no longer have Mohammed bin Tughluq as Sultan," the vendor of incense reminded them all: that capable Sultan had died almost fifty years ago and had all but vanished from living memory, leaving a growing legend in place of remembrance.

"That may be, that the Armenians would prefer Timur-i come this way, away from their homeland," said the one-eyed man who made and sold fried pastries. "If it is true that he is bound for Delhi, who is to blame the Armenians for their desires? Wouldn't we prefer that he attack Armenia?"

"They should not spread tales," said the spice merchant, and added with hardly a pause, "I was told that Timur-i is going to turn toward Sind, to seize the ports and raid the ships as they arrive."

"The Jagatai are all crazy," said the pastry-vendor. "All of them, from Jenghiz to Timur-i, they are madmen."

"Timur-i is a part of the Balas clan," said the spice merchant, smug in his knowledge.

"He is a Jagatai, for all that," the pastry-vendor insisted. "The rest of the Jagatai would not hate him so much were he not one of them."

The four men nodded, seeing the sense of this, and turned their talk to less worrisome things.

Not far away, a group of muleteers were standing with their animals, at the opposite end of the bazaar from the camel-drivers. "Well, I tell you," said the one with two fingers gone from his right hand, "I would not want to be in Timur-i's place if he tries to attack the Sultan—Allah favor him! They say he has only horsemen at his command, and not many thousands of them. The Sultan has foot-soldiers, cavalry, and war elephants. Timur-i would be very foolish to try to battle such a mighty army."

"So he might," said the oldest of them—a lean, raw-boned man with a cast in one eye; he was an incredible forty-one years of age— as he spat to show his opinion of Timur-i. "That is not to say he won't do it. If he does, I would want to be far away. For no matter who wins, it will be hard-going for the likes of us."

The others nodded and made gestures to keep away evil.

"Why should he want Delhi in any case? Has he not cities enough at his command? Why must he strive for more? Let him stay in the West, and bedevil the cities there. What need has he of Delhi?" asked a man in the yellow robe of a Buddhist mendicant. "Everyone knows there are other, richer cities nearer to the places he has already conquered. There are the riches of the Inner Sea to plunder, and the cities beyond Aleppo. Why should he not choose one of them rather than cross the mountains to come here?"

"Allah preserve us!" exclaimed the first. "Does he need a reason?"

"Shaitan advises him, and he obeys," said the oldest muleteer with conviction. "He may say he listens to that so-called saint he keeps by him, but if you ask me, Nur Sayyid Barak is nothing more than a sycophant, currying favor with Timur-i by finding passages in the *Qran* that support what Timur-i wishes to believe, and ignoring any word of the Prophet that does not approve Timur-i's actions."

"Or Nur Sayyid Barak may be the servant of Shaitan as well," said the mendicant, who knew of Shaitan from his Muslim traveling companions.

"If he is, he hides it well; he lives a worthy life," said the first, and began to move toward his animals to check them before preparing them to be readied for the short journey outward from the city to the merchants' hostels that housed those not of Delhi.

"Some say that Nur Sayyid Barak is dead, and buried in a tomb fit for Sultans," said the incense-maker.

"Except that he is at Timur-i's side," said the mendicant. "Many have seen him."

"He may well be trying to keep Timur-i from greater excesses," said the oldest muleteer. "He should preach peace if he is a true saint, as they claim."

"Allah preserve us if that is so!" said the muleteer with luxuriant moustaches.

The oldest muleteer did not respond to this interjection. "Tomorrow is the final day of this bazaar," he said to his mules.

"We come again in a month," said the oldest. "We have four other cities to visit between now and then. My master has brasses to pick up, and silk."

"Do you think it will be enough time to cover that distance?" the mendicant inquired. "You said you go as far as Bayana, Samdhar, and Hansi."

"And Bijnor. We have done it many times before," said the old muleteer. "My master and I know the way."

"Well, may Allah watch over you in your travels," said the muleteer who had extravagant moustaches. "And the Buddha."

"And Ganesh," said the man missing two fingers. "It never hurts to burn a little incense to Ganesh when one is involved in trading."

The others nodded at the wisdom of this, and one of the men put his hand on the hilt of his Afghani dagger. "Just as well to have a weapon or two, in case Ganesh and Allah and the Buddha are looking the other way when trouble comes."

There was a burst of laughter; the muleteers continued to saddle and load their animals, making desultory remarks as they did until the call to prayer was heard, when three of the men stopped their labors and went to the small well to wash, bowed toward the setting sun, then dropped to their knees to pray; the others paused in their activities out of respect and habit.

"We will have to be out of the gates soon," said the oldest muleteer. "The merchants' hostelries outside the city will be full in an hour. Tomorrow they will all be empty by this time."

"That they will," said the muleteer with the lavish moustaches. "And I do not want to spend the night at a campfire unless I have to."

The others agreed and put their attention to loading their animals.

"May your travels be safe, and may you profit from your labors; may your spirit be guided on its path as surely as your caravans find their way across the world," said the mendicant as he turned away, going away from the great red-granite main gate of Delhi. He, too, had a long road ahead of him and wanted to be outside the city tonight. He was bound north and east, to the majestic mountains and Nepal, Tirhut, and Bhutan, so he made his way through the city toward the North Gate, which, while less grand than the Great Gate that faced west, toward Mecca, was less crowded with merchants and had a small Buddhist shrine among the shrines to Ganesh and various Bodhisattvas of the region, just beyond the walls.

He had another reason for passing through this part of Delhi, one that had troubled him since his arrival three days ago; he could postpone his visit no longer. With a sigh and a half-muttered prayer, he took the side-street he had once known so well and went along to the house he remembered. Reluctantly he sounded the clapper that brought a household slave running to admit him, bowing in startled recognition.

"You do not have to do that," the mendicant complained, chagrined at this reception. "I am not deserving of it."

"But you are most welcome, Lord," said the slave, continuing to bow as he ushered the mendicant into the garden around which the building rose.

"Will you tell Avasa Dani that I am here?" the mendicant asked.

"At once, Lord," said the slave, and hurried away, leaving the mendicant alone in the shadowed garden. The mendicant stood for some time, taking in the beauty of the fast-approaching night; he heard the

Muslim call to evening prayers, and bent his head in respect.

Light from an oil-lamp glistened as someone came into the garden. "Nararavi?" said the familiar voice. "Is it you?"

"It is a mendicant," he answered.

She came nearer, holding the lamp raised so she could see his face. "It *is* you," she said. She stood very still. "Have you come home?" She was past her first youth, but handsome and dignified of manner, of moderate height and carrying herself with elegance; her face was well-proportioned, with large eyes, a straight nose, and a generous mouth that just now curved in a tenuous smile. She was dressed in the modified sari that women of Hindu lineage wore; its color was hard to distinguish, being a soft blue-grey that blended with the dusk. Her glossy black hair was combed back from her face and secured in a bun; she wore very little jewelry and did not paint her face except for the caste-mark on her forehead.

"No," he told her. "I have only come to do as I agreed I would do—to inform you that I still live and therefore you are still in the guardianship of the foreigner appointed to that post. Are you in the care of Sanat Ji Mani, if he yet resides in Delhi?"

"He does, and I am," said Avasa Dani. "And will remain so for several years more, or so Sanat Ji Mani has told the Sultan's aides, and paid the taxes they have levied for the privilege." She studied his face. "You look tired."

"I have traveled far and still have far to go," he said, unwilling to discuss himself with her.

She nodded. "Will you sign the register, to show you have been here?"

"Of course," he said.

A silence fell between them, one that was at once awkward and resigned. Both knew they were being watched, that every word they spoke was overheard and would be reported, but even without that, they would have had little to say.

"Nothing has changed," Avasa Dani remarked a short while later.

"No," said the mendicant.

Avasa Dani did not sigh, but some of the animation went out of her. "Do you know when you will return?"

"As to that, who can say? The Wheel turns and we are bound to it," he answered. "I am leaving for the mountains and east, to the shrines to the Buddha, where I will learn from the monks and worship at their temples, and then, if I live, I will go as far as Kamaru, and from there come along all the coast of the land—east coast, south tip, and west coast—until I reach the Indus River, and I will follow it inland, then cross the plateau to Delhi. I will pray every step of the way, and I will depend on the alms of those who follow the way of the Buddha." He spoke as if this were a minor undertaking instead of a harrowing journey.

Avasa Dani listened, appalled. "But that will take *years.*"

"It may," said the mendicant. "You will be provided for in any case, until ten years have passed and I have not signed the register."

"Certainly," said Avasa Dani, who, unlike many women, had been party to drafting the terms. "I know what is contained in the register."

"You do not wish to have another husband, do you?" the mendicant asked. "Shall I release you? The Sultan would not forbid it."

"No, I do not want another husband," said Avasa Dani, sounding very tired. "I am content to remain as I am."

"That is virtuous of you," said the mendicant.

Avasa Dani could think of nothing more to say to this man who had been her husband until he renounced the world four years ago; she lowered the lamp. The study seemed to close in around them, as if the shadows were palpable. "Are you keeping well?" It was an automatic inquiry, made almost without thought.

"I have alms and my wants are simple," said the mendicant. "When even those wants are gone, I will be worthy to serve the Buddha."

She held up her hand. "No. Do not tell me more. It will only distress me."

"Because you have not yet understood the way of the Buddha, nor why I follow Him," said the mendicant gently.

"You were once Nararavi, and you were dear to me. I do not know you now." She kept any trace of blame out of her voice, but she could not shut it out of her heart. "Perhaps if we had children, I would feel otherwise."

"That is what I have tried to tell you; the world is no longer holding me. I am grateful that we are childless, for children would bind me to the world as nothing else could," he said, making his words simple. "In time you may understand."

"Your god is not my gods," she said, recalling their occasional arguments about which gods were true gods and which were not.

"No. You do not comprehend religion—as what woman can?—and thus you fail to understand what I have done." His face was sad.

"You may believe that," said Avasa Dani with deep weariness.

"You are clever for one of your sex," the mendicant allowed. "Few women have your skills with numbers."

"Few women have my education," Avasa Dani reminded him.

"Because they have no gift for it," said the mendicant, ending the matter.

After another silence, Avasa Dani said, "Will you stay here tonight? This is still your house and you have a place here. I will order the servants to prepare a bed for you, and a suitable welcome for your return. You would have a good meal and a bath, and leave in the morning with coins and bread in your bowl."

The mendicant shook his head. "You see how easily the world tempts us? You do not think that you are bringing my faith into danger, for you suppose you must receive me if not as your husband as your guest. It is your lack of understanding that makes you do this, for I comprehend you mean well. Yet you do not know what peril you bring me. I will take alms if you will give them, and bread. I will sign the register and I will leave. This place is a snare, and I am in danger for every heartbeat I remain here."

Avasa Dani bit back the retort she longed to make. "You must do as you think wisest," she said, trying not to feel hurt by his condemnation.

"That is the beginning of wisdom in you, Avasa Dani, to know that you are not able to bend me to your will," said the mendicant. "You may yet gain understanding, as far as you may understand." In response to this she nodded, not trusting herself to speak. "The register is where I put it?"

"Yes. In your chest. It is still in your study." She heard the flatness in her voice and sighed a little.

"Then I will attend to that duty. When I am next at Delhi, I will sign again, and continue your life as you wish it. Be sure you show this to the Deputy to the Sultan for Marriage and Inheritance," he told her as he went into the house, making his way toward his study as if it had been only a day since he had been there and not three years. "I signed when I left, and when I returned the first time. I will sign now, and it will be ten years before your situation will change— should I fail to return in that time."

"Yes. I understand," she said.

"It is as well that you do," he pointed out as he stepped into the study; it was dark, for no lamps had been lit in the chamber for many months. "I will need light."

Avasa Dani clapped her hands, and very quickly—too quickly: he had been listening—a slave answered the summons, a lamp in hand, and a bowl of water for making ink. "Put them down next to the chest," she said, and waited until the slave withdrew to speak again. "Shall I remain?"

"Yes," said the mendicant as he opened the chest and took out his writing-box with its ink-cake and brushes. "You should see me do this."

"Adri, the steward, can witness your signing; he's not a slave and he is almost a Muslim." She was not entirely pleased with his calm assumption that she was unmoved by his return, or the implications of his signing the register, indicating his imminent departure. The sound of the grinding-stone on the ink-cake irritated her as much as a drone of insects might.

"You are a prudent woman," said the mendicant as he continued to grind the ink. "I am grateful for that."

"Then what can I be but proud?" she asked, hoping the sarcasm she felt was not in her voice.

"Pride is a blindness in the soul. Rid yourself of it, if you wish to achieve the Buddha's promise." The mendicant was satisfied with the ink. He unrolled the register and put a small brass figurine on it to hold it open. Then he dipped his brush into the ink and wrote his name and title, standing back so Avasa Dani could read it. "There. It is done. The Sultan's officials will accept this, and you will be able to continue as you are for another ten years." He blew on the ink gently to hurry its drying.

"Then you will go tonight," said Avasa Dani, wanting to learn all she could before he left.

"Yes. It is fitting." He swung around and looked at her. "You have no reason to want me to linger, Avasa Dani."

"I have concern for anyone embarking on such travels as you are doing," she countered, letting her annoyance show a little.

Her barb struck wide of the mark. "Then think of Sanat Ji Mani. He has come from much farther away than any destination of mine. When he returns to his homeland, he will go a far greater distance than I will." He turned back to the register, tested his signature with his thumb, and, satisfied it was dry, he rolled it up again. "I will not put it into the chest. You may do that after you have shown this to the Sultan's Deputy."

"Of course," she said. "Since you will not remain to do it yourself."

"No; I will not," he said, adding, "The register is sufficient."

"Yes." Avasa Dani waited for him to speak; when he did not, she said, "I have four brass coins and two silver ones."

"Give me no more than half," said the mendicant.

She reached down for the small purse of embroidered leather that hung from her low-slung belt. The coins clinked in her hand as she counted out three of them and held them out to the mendicant. "Here. Take them. I will order the cook to—"

He interrupted her. "Let me have the old bread when I go. Do not give me better; it would shame me to take new bread when there is old to be had."

"If that is what you want," she told him without inflection of any kind.

He did not face her as he went on, "You may not comprehend what I am doing, or why I have done it, but you have respected it, Avasa Dani, and that is a worthy thing. Not many men have wives who would be content to remain as you are. I will think of you when I pray." It was as generous an offer as he dared to make.

"If that is what you want," she repeated.

"I want to want nothing," he reminded her.

"Yes," she said. "Of course."

"I will go get bread from the kitchen, and water from the fountain." He still did not look directly at her. "I have found my true way, Avasa Dani; if only you could believe it."

"I do believe it, Nararavi," she told him with hushed intensity. "If I did not, I would oppose what you have done."

He gave a single chuckle. "A wife oppose a husband?"

"There are ways," she said.

"Then it is as well I left," he said. "And it is as well that I go now." He looked up at the sky. "I will sleep beyond the shrine to Lord Buddha tonight, and tomorrow, at first light, I will begin my journey."

Avasa Dani held herself in check, for as much as she wanted to challenge him, to convince him that his enterprise was reckless and dangerous, she was certain he would not listen to her, and they would part on harsh words. "If you are satisfied that you will find what you seek in this way, then may your path be easy and your steps protected."

"I do not ask for an easy path," he said. "But I thank you for your kind wish." He put his hands together in front of his face and bowed slightly. "Until I see you again, Avasa Dani."

She did not bother to plead with him. "Until I see you again, Nararavi."

He turned away and left her alone in the study, her oil-lamp providing only a very little, flickering illumination of the space around her, so that the shadows seemed vast and alive. She touched the register, thinking of what she would have to do in the morning, and realizing how little she wanted to do it. There was such finality in presenting the register, and all that it entailed. The deputies of the Sultan would insist on a formal review, and an assessment of her household. She did not mind having so many duties to perform, but she dreaded the questions she would have to answer, and the way she would feel when it was done. At least, she thought, Sanat Ji Mani would be with her—that was some consolation.

A while later the steward came to the study. "He is gone, Lady."

"Yes," she said, nodding.

"He took two lentil-cakes and a round of onion-nan made yesterday; nothing but bread, and none of it fresh-made. He would not have any meat or cheese." The steward was at a loss to know what more information he should provide. "I offered him raisins and cucumbers, but he refused."

"Yes," she said quietly.

"He took water from the fountain; he would accept nothing more." The steward rubbed his hands in distress, as if he thought he should have done more.

"Yes," she said, as if to soothe him. "I know."

"Shall we ever see him again?" the steward implored.

"If his Lord Buddha wills," she replied, and thought she had better burn incense to Ganesh tonight, and—in case Ganesh was too worldly a god—to Varuna and Vishnu in the morning, in case Lord Buddha should fail Nararavi on his travels.

"What will the Sultan's Deputy say?" the steward exclaimed, plainly with some idea in mind what that might be.

"What can he say? The terms were set out and agreed to four years ago and nothing has changed." She was becoming impatient with the man, and did not want to share his apprehension. "Adri, we will do all that we must, and trust to the gods that my husband will remain safe as he goes about the world."

"But Timur-i—" Adri said, and broke off.

"Timur-i will not bother himself with a lone mendicant Buddhist," said Avasa Dani, hoping it was so.

"He may not," said Adri as if he was certain of catastrophe. "But where Timur-i has been, devastation remains, and there are no alms to be had."

Avasa Devi held up her hand. "Adri: no more. It is beyond any help of mine but prayer. My husband has chosen his path, and we are bound to honor it. You have nothing to fear, for you, and the rest of the household, are provided for. Whether he returns or not, you will not be put out into the streets to beg and you will not have to give up your religion in order to be employed." She pointed to the door. "I am sure everyone is in an uproar. You are to reassure them. And see that is what you do, not raise new fears in their breasts."

"But it is very dreadful—" Adri began.

"You're not to say that. You may think that, but you will keep it to yourself." She stared at him until he looked away from her. "If the household wishes to keep a fast on Nararavi's behalf, they may do so tomorrow. Tell Chol he need not prepare a meal until sundown."

Adri scowled. "Not all will be satisfied, Lady."

"Perhaps not," said Avasa Dani, "but it is enough for now." She started to leave the room, then said, "Sanat Ji Mani has given the Sultan's Deputy enough money to pay all of you your living for more than ten years, in accordance with his agreement with my husband. He has done that for all the household, beyond the monies my husband set aside for all of you; none of you will starve, whether or not my husband returns. Tell them that, and they will be less worried."

"You do not think they are worried because of money, do you?" Adri said with feeling.

"I think it is a good part of your fears, yes," said Avasa Dani calmly. "You would not be provident if you did not think of such things. The world is more filled with beggars, who yearn for the gifts of the world than with mendicants, who have turned away from them."

"It may be so," Adri said, not willing to make a concession on this point. "And some will find it reassuring to know that they have been provided for."

"Very good," said Avasa Dani, feeling suddenly very tired although the night was young. "Now leave me. You have what you came for."

Adri bristled. "I was not merely seeking—"

"I know," she said, cutting him short. "Were my husband here, you would not have to speak to me at all. I have no father or brother or uncle to stand in his place, and Sanat Ji Mani is a foreigner. You had reason to be concerned." She had a sudden, baffling impulse to weep, but she kept her emotions in check; she would not behave so poorly before a servant, not even one she had known as long as Adri.

"The household is . . . irregular," said Adri, willing to grant that much.

"Yes. And my husband is aware of it. If he is not troubled by that, you should not be." She motioned him away from her and stood still while the steward obeyed her, leaving her alone with her lamp in the dark corridor.

Text of a letter from the manservant Rojire to the spice-merchant Tas Sarnga.

To the most excellent merchant Tas Sarnga who has long sold spices and other rare plants, woods, and medicinal substances in the city of

Delhi, this order given on behalf of my master, the distinguished foreigner Sanat Ji Mani, who lives in the Foreigners' Quarter near the North-Eastern Gate. This brings with it six measures of gold and two of silver, in fulfillment of our agreement.

Ten vials of lotus-oil
Ten vials of quicksilver
Ten measures of myrrh, powdered
Twelve measures of camphor-gum
Twelve measures of musk-flowers, powdered
Fifteen measures of longevity root, dried
Sixteen measures of bellweed, dried
Sixteen measures of thirst berries, dried
Sixteen measures of black-flower, dried
Eighteen measures of cured century-dung, powdered
Eighteen measures of flax-seed oil
Eighteen measures of saffron
Eighteen haws
Twenty measures of hemlock
Twenty measures of pheasants' eggs, dried and powdered
Twenty measures of milkweed thistle, dried
Twenty measures of cardamom seed
Twenty measures of rose-hips, dried
Twenty measures of willow-bark
Twenty measures of royal-face, stems and flowers, dried
Twenty-one tamarind pods
Twenty-two measures of beggars-cowl, dried
Twenty-five measures of poppy syrup
Twenty-five measures of grain-pod, powdered
Twenty-five measures of juniper berries
Twenty-five measures of spider-breath preserved in honey
Thirty large hands of ginger
Thirty measures of ease-root, preserved
Thirty measures of tiger-spike, dried and powdered
Thirty measures of syrup of aloe
Thirty measures of spirits of grape wine
Thirty measures of olive oil

Have these delivered to my master's house at the end of the Street of the Brass Lanterns, and you will receive another token for your service

Rojire

2

Prostrated before his sacred lamp, Rustam Iniattir prayed to Ormazd to keep him safe through the night that had just fallen. A Parsi, and a follower of Zarathustra, he was keenly aware of being alone in a strange country, one of a small community of Parsi living among those who did not share his language or his faith, his ties to Persia stretched to the breaking-point, in a place that was increasingly dangerous. He tried to think of his family, of his wife and four children, but when he did, panic began to rise in him and he was unable to keep his mind on his rite. "*What is it that comes out of darkness, but Ahriman, and all that is given to evil?*" he asked ritualistically, and made reverence to the lamp again. "*O you Soul of Light, guard me from the perils of darkness, lest I am lost.*" He looked up, hoping to see the little flame brighten as a sign his prayers had been heard, but instead he saw it waver as a door was opened somewhere in the cave-like shrine. Iniattir rose to his knees, shivering from what he told himself was cold.

"Rustam Iniattir," said a pleasant voice behind him; he had to be inside the shrine, for his words echoed hollowly and made it difficult for Rustam Iniattir to locate this intruder who was beyond the reach of the half-dozen lamps hung around the disk of the altar.

Terrified, the Parsi turned, almost stumbling as he rose to his feet. "*O Ormazd, give me your beams of light for swords, and your brilliance to put the manifestation of Ahriman to flight. Guard me with your luminous presence.*"

"*And bear me to your realm where darkness is banished forever,*" said the voice, finishing the prayer and surprising Iniattir almost into silence; he went on in the old Persian tongue, "I mean you no harm;

you have nothing to fear from me." The voice was mellifluous, reassuring, in an accent that Rustam Iniattir could not quiet identify; his pledges were accompanied by the purposeful sound of his boots on the stone floor, augmented by echoes, as he approached Rustam Iniattir.

"So we are told evil always promises us," Rustam Iniattir muttered, his hand going to the hilt of his dagger.

"As do those with beneficent intentions as well." The stranger spoke calmly, as if to quiet a startled child.

"If that is your purpose, why do you come at night? This is a time of Ahriman." Stating his apprehension so plainly made Rustam Iniattir clench his teeth.

"Do you think evil would dare to enter this shrine, even at night?" the voice inquired lightly. "You have said this is your sanctuary. You have made this a place of Light."

"And so it is," said Rustam Iniattir, trying to convince himself that the shrine was strong enough to protect him.

"Not everything abroad at night is of Ahriman's nature," said the voice, and finally its man of origin came into the circle of light.

Rustam Iniattir stared at the man. "Who are you?" he demanded. "I do not know you. You are not one of us."

"No, I am not," said the stranger, then added cordially, "I am called Sanat Ji Mani, at present."

"Is it your name?" Rustam Iniattir demanded, relieved that the face, illuminated by the lamps, was human—the features were Western: having the look of middle years, with dark hair, slightly curling, a wide brow, nose not quite straight, and eyes that were deep as the sea and dark as a starless night—and his manner respectful.

"It is close enough," said Sanat Ji Mani. He took a step closer and revealed himself; he was somewhat taller than Rustam Iniattir, dressed in a loose kandys of heavy black silk, with neat boots of red-tooled leather rising to his calves. He carried no weapons, and his only ornament was a small fibula of a silver-winged black disk worn at the neck of his garment. Simple though his clothing was, it was clearly of the highest quality.

"What are you doing here?" Rustam Iniattir made himself ask.

"I came to find you," said Sanat Ji Mani, as if the answer were obvious.

"For what reason?" Rustam Iniattir felt suddenly bold.

"Because I hope you and I might work together," said Sanat Ji Mani. He made a deep, reverential bow to the circular altar. "This may not be the place to talk of such matters, but I hope you will not refuse to deal with me because I sought you out in this shrine."

Reassured, Rustam Iniattir regarded Sanat Ji Mani with interest. "Why do you say this? You came here; it was your decision to come here."

"Yes, so you would know I am seeking you out in good faith. In another place, you might dismiss me, but here, you may be willing to hear me out." He had a quick smile that was gone before Rustam Iniattir was certain he had seen it.

"You have shown you understand my ways, at least a little. As to the rest, we shall see," said Rustam Iniattir, his manner more forceful than before. "Tell me what you want me to hear and then leave me to finish my devotions."

"Of course; I did not intend to disturb you, but I could think of no other means of meeting with you that would not put one of us at a disadvantage," said Sanat Ji Mani, and took a moment to be silent before saying anything more to Rustam Iniattir. "I have no desire to offend you, but I must tell you I have learned something of your business dealings."

Rustam Iniattir blinked at the effrontery. "How could you have done this? And why?"

"Your associates were willing to part with information in exchange for gold and silver," said Sanat Ji Mani without apology. "I am sorry I had to resort to such methods, for it may distress you and your business partners, but I am concerned that there may not be enough time to approach you through more usual channels, you and I being foreigners in Delhi, and our opportunities restricted on that account."

"There is much in what you say," Rustam Iniattir allowed neutrally, reserving judgment.

"Also, I have in the past dealt with one of your people, and he has disposed me kindly to you," Sanat Ji Mani said, remembering Kozrozd and his True Death in the Roman arena, more than thirteen centuries ago.

"Then I am grateful to my countryman," said Rustam Iniattir.

"I thank you for taking my meaning," said Sanat Ji Mani, then went on more briskly. "You are known to have contacts from here to Shiraz, to Trebizond, to Antioch."

"Not that that is anything to boast of," said Rustam Iniattir, not wanting to appear proud in this place where his God was worshiped.

Sanat Ji Mani nodded his comprehension. "Perhaps not, but there are many who are not so fortunate, or far-sighted. Nor do many merchants use the good sense you have shown in your dealings with these cities, which has led me to suppose you might be inclined to join in the venture I seek to propose. In these uncertain times, I would like to offer you the means to expand those contacts, to broaden your trading, and your position. I am sure you would find such opportunity advantageous, as would I." He paused. "I have jewels and gold. I have horses and mules and camels. And I have ships at Cambay, Surat, and Chaul. You need not fear I would not offer to undertake my portion of the cost of such an enterprise. I can afford to sponsor the enlargement I propose without imposing upon you for a single sequin of yours. You may come to my house and see for yourself that this is true. I am in the Foreigners' Quarter of the city, as you are, in the Street of Brass Lanterns. Mine is the last house before the wall, and it bears my sigil above the door." He indicated the fibula at his neck.

"If you have so much, why do you come to me?" Rustam Iniattir asked, his suspicions aroused.

"Because I do not think the Sultan—or more precisely, the Sultan's deputies—would grant me the license to broaden my business on my own, being that I am a foreigner from the West and the only one of my . . . blood here in Delhi. They fear I would undertake to cheat them of the taxes and duties they impose, having nothing to lose but my own liberty. Firuz Ihbal has said that I cannot be trusted to follow the law since I have no one of my own kind who could be held as hostage. Of course, he did not put it quite so bluntly. He said I would have to ally myself with those whose families live here with them." He saw Rustam Iniattir nod knowingly and went on, "You are part of a community, and the Sultan's men believe that will keep you compliant with the law." Sanat Ji Mani paused. "I would rather spend my wealth on business than on bribes. Surely you understand?"

"I will consider this," said Rustam Iniattir, admitting to himself that Sanat Ji Mani had made a very good point.

"How long will you want to make up your mind?" Sanat Ji Mani asked politely. "I will accommodate your request."

"I . . . I am not sure," said Rustam Iniattir, thinking this was much too abrupt. "I shall consider what you have told me, and then, if I have any questions, I will visit you in your house on the Street of Brass Lanterns, where you may expand on what you have said here. After such a conversation—if we have one—I will reach my decision."

"Of course. You will be welcome at any time," said Sanat Ji Mani. "I trust you will make inquiries about my dealings with others. I encourage you to do this, for I have done the same about you, and you should have as much information on me as you can acquire before you commit yourself and your fortune to any new proposition. There are merchants who can provide a report of me that is without undue bias. They will tell you what you want to know." He achieved another of his fleeting smiles. "I have a servant—Rojire he is called—who will admit you to my house at any hour you call."

"Then I will ask for him when I come. He will know that I am to see you?" Now that the worst of his fright had gone, Rustam Iniattir was beginning to be curious about this Sanat Ji Mani, who seemed so much more a foreigner than he, a Parsi, was.

"Yes. He is a prince among servants, and always knows what is wanted." Sanat Ji Mani shook his head. "If I do not hear from you in some fashion in six weeks, I will take it as a sign that you are not interested in any proposal I may have to make, and I will look elsewhere for a partner—reluctantly, I assure you."

"Six weeks is not very long," said Rustam Iniattir, somewhat alarmed at so stringent a limit.

"No, it is not," Sanat Ji Mani agreed. "But I know that Timur-i moves quickly and trade-routes that are safe today may be useless tomorrow."

"Of course," said Rustam Iniattir, shaken by the mention of Timur-i. "He is the very soul of darkness, that one."

"So he is," Sanat Ji Mani agreed. "But you would not deny that he is a danger to everyone who trades beyond the walls of Delhi."

"Yes. The more so now the Sultan is away, shoring up his fortresses, and leaving Delhi to his many deputies, most of whom are as rapacious as bandits, Firuz Ihbal being the first among many." There was a note of anger in his voice now, and a petulance that revealed the frustration the Persian merchant felt. "We Parsi must look to hired fighters to protect our caravans, and more often than not, those very fighters are also robbers, and steal what they were hired to protect."

"True enough," said Sanat Ji Mani, who had experience of such predation.

"So you will propose a way to protect a caravan from its guards?" He was being sarcastic now, but he made no apology for it.

"I will propose many things, if you are interested in what I might offer to you. And I will listen to any suggestions you may put to me," Sanat Ji Mani said this with a composure far more persuasive than enthusiasm would have been.

Rustam Iniattir stared at the foreigner. "I believe you will," he said at last, his reluctance to bargain with someone unknown to him finally giving way to a hope of opportunity. "Yes. I will give this proposition my first consideration, and I will send you word if I decide to pursue the matter. Six weeks is a short time, but it should be sufficient for me to make inquiries and to have answers." He looked up into the echoing dark. "You have what you have come for."

"That I do, and I will not tarry; you have been kindness itself to listen to me. May your God of Light show you favor for that." His face vanished as he stepped back into the gloom of the shrine, and turned away; there was the sharp report of his steps, which reverberated through the shrine and faded to the slough of the wind.

Rustam Iniattir stood still, trying to assess what had just happened to him; he was more baffled than alarmed, and that alone eased his concerns. He tried to resume his devotions, but he discovered more questions burgeoning in his mind, and they became a clamor beyond the reach of prayer. Annoyed, Rustam Iniattir finished his ritual abruptly and went out of the shrine into the blue of dusk, his thoughts buzzing with possibilities. As he made his way back to the Persian part of the Foreigners' Quarter of the city, he looked about him for any sign of Sanat Ji Mani, for he could not rid himself of the notion that the stranger might be following him, his dark garments blending with the night. Although he reached his house without incident, the sensation of being watched remained with him for some time.

It was not Sanat Ji Mani who had followed Rustam Iniattir from the shrine, but Josha Dar, a creature of the Sultan's cousin Balban Ihbal, whose task it was to watch foreign merchants and to report anything they did that might have consequences for the Sultan and his many deputies. Josha Dar had been shadowing Rustam Iniattir for six days, as diligent and ruthless as a rat, and was hoping his vigilance had finally been rewarded. When he was satisfied that Rustam Iniattir was in for the night, he went along to the gorgeous sprawl of the Sultan's palace, made his way past those petitioners who waited in their patient lines night and day for the chance to address the deputies. He found the path through the maze of corridors to the inner court of the west wing, and sought out Balban Ihbal in his apartments.

"It's you," said Balban Ihbal as Josha Dar saluted him with a fine, subservient air.

"Yes, Great Lord, it is I," said Josha Dar. He tried to present himself well; his small, bony body was held straight as a soldier's, and his weathered face was set in proper lines.

"Do you have anything for me?" He put aside a cup of aromatic tea and regarded Josha Dar with the expression of one severely tested. In the glow of a hundred lamps, Balban Ihbal, and all his surroundings, were touched with gilded light that enhanced the opulence of the room and its occupant: he was wearing brocaded silk the color of persimmons, and the ornamental braid on the front of the kaftan was shining gold. His turban was white but ornamented with a spray of Chinese pheasant feathers, each as costly as pearls. There were rings on his fingers and a golden cuff on his wrist, all gleaming in the luster of the lamps.

"I have been following the Parsi merchant Rustam Iniattir—" Josha Dar began, only to be interrupted.

"For six days now," Balban Ihbal finished for him. "What have you learned?"

"That he had a secret meeting tonight," said Josha Dar as if revealing a monumental crime. He raised his scrawny arms as if to demonstrate the enormity of his discovery.

"Where?" asked Balban Ihbal, not quite interested.

"At the Parsi shrine. You know, the cave in the old walls?" Josha Dar took a deep breath. "You cannot know what this place is like. The sons of Islam do not bow to flames."

"No; we bow to Mecca," said Balban Ihbal; he was not eager to hear about the false religion of the Parsi. "Yes, I know the shrine you speak of."

"Well," said Josha Dar, trying to recover his dramatic thrust, "I did not enter the place, but I saw another who did."

"And who was that?" Balban Ihbal was rapidly becoming annoyed with his spy, and told him, "If you have nothing significant to report to me, say so and go."

"But I do," said Josha Dar, and hurried on, "The foreigner, Sanat Ji Mani, entered the shrine shortly after Rustam Iniattir did."

"Perhaps he, too, is a follower of Zarathustra," said Balban Ihbal, taking another sip of tea. "There are a number of such men in Delhi, and they are all foreigners."

"I think not." Josha Dar held up his hand. "Followers of Zarathustra wear white when they go into their shrine. Sanat Ji Mani was wearing black."

"Such is his custom," said Balban Ihbal, dismissing the revelation. "My cousin, Firuz Ihbal, has said that Sanat Ji Mani always dresses in black garments."

"Perhaps he does," said Josha Dar. "But he is not one of the Parsi. You and I know that he comes from mountains to the north and west of Persia, beyond Constantinople."

"So I am told," said Balban Ihbal. "Yet it is possible that he is one who worships with them. Many of those who follow the Prophet—may he receive joy forever—are unlike those of our family. The Tughluq clan is not the only clan to embrace the True Religion. There are many, from China to Spain, who praise Allah. It may be that Sanat Ji Mani is one of other followers of Zarathustra."

"I do not think so," said Josha Dar, seeing his opportunity evaporating as he spoke.

"Well, you may be right," Balban Ihbal allowed. "In which case, what was the reason that Sanat Ji Mani went to the shrine?"

"To talk with Rustam Iniattir," said Josha Dar, his exasperation revealed in the blunt tone he used.

"About what?" asked Balban Ihbal. "If you did not hear them, say so."

"I heard . . . part of it," Josha Dar said, not wanting to be contradicted. "It was a strange discussion, and the shrine echoes so."

Balban Ihbal pulled at his lower lip. "What did they say?"

"They spoke of trade-routes," said Josha Dar. "Sanat Ji Mani suggested they could share their work." He coughed. "At least, that is what it seemed he did."

"And you do not know what more was offered, or if anything else was offered." He scowled. "Josha Dar, you have not yet done as I hoped you would do."

"I have persisted," said Josha Dar, turning pale beneath his walnut-colored skin.

"Not sufficiently," said Balban Ihbal. "I begin to wonder if I was wise in entrusting so much to you."

"You will be satisfied with my efforts," said Josha Dar as belligerently as he dared. "I will strive to do all you have asked of me, and more. I have not yet finished with Rustam Iniattir, and I will not rest while you have work for me."

"Yes, yes," said Balban Ihbal, sounding slightly bored. "You have told me this on many occasions. Thus far you have done well enough, I suppose. I see no harm in your continuing your observations." He sighed. "Follow the Parsi for a while yet, to find out what he is undertaking, and with whom. We cannot have the foreigners of this city sending messages to Timur-i Lenkh, in the hope of reward for their treachery."

"Do you think that Rustam Iniattir would do such a thing?" Josha Dar asked, shocked at the suggestion.

"He is a Parsi. He follows Zarathustra. Who knows what he might do?" Balban Ihbal shook his head. "I cannot sit by and let foreigners bring disaster on this city."

"No, of course not," said Josha Dar, his voice dropping to a strangled whisper. "What do you require of me?"

"What you have been doing," said Balban Ihbal. "You have been useful to me." It was a grudging concession, but it brought a smile to Josha Dar's face. "If you continue to be, then I will reward you. If you do not, then I will dismiss you."

Josha Dar knew that dismissal meant exile as well, for he did not follow the Prophet, and was considered outside his caste because his father had sired him on an Untouchable woman. He lowered his eyes, trying to express his gratitude and dedication to Balban Ihbal. "Tell me what you want, Great Lord, and I will hasten to do it."

"I have told you what I want. If you can prove that the Parsi are aiding the agents of Timur-i, then bring it to me at once. If you cannot prove it, then let me know it so that I may look elsewhere for enemies of the Sultan." Balban Ihbal took another sip of tea.

"And Sanat Ji Mani? Should I watch him, too? He may be part of any scheme the Parsi is fomenting." Josha Dar did his best not to sound eager, but he envisioned more success in finding hidden enemies if he pursued more than Rustam Iniattir.

"If he and the Parsi meet again, perhaps. Until then, confine your work to Rustam Iniattir." Balban Ihbal finished his tea and made a flicking gesture with his right hand. "You need not linger."

"But, Great Lord," said Josha Dar, not quite whining, "I have not eaten today. Surely you will spare a handful of chickpeas or a cup of lentils for your servant?"

Balban Ihbal sighed again. "Very well. Stop at the kitchen and say that you may have two measures of lentils and a round of flat-bread." He cocked his head as he reached into the tooled leather wallet that hung from his sash. "Here is money. Make it last four days. I will not receive you again until then."

Josha Dar took the coins so hastily that they seemed to vanish by magic. "You are all magnanimity, Great Lord."

"I am a practical man," said Balban Ihbal, as if the two were the same thing. "I will do what I must to protect Delhi and the Sultan."

"And I will be pleased to serve you in that," said Josha Dar, bending over at the waist as he backed out of the presence of the Sultan's cousin. Once in the corridor, he raised his arm to send the slaves who had gathered near the door scattering; he had no intention of providing any of them with fuel for their fires of gossip. He went along to the kitchens and sought out a slave he knew named Maras. He relayed Balban Ihbal's orders, adding an onion and a cup of soup to the menu. "I will drink the soup here and take the rest with me."

"Balban Ihbal is a generous man," said Maras in a tone that made it impossible to guess if he were sincere or sarcastic. He had been a slave all his life, and for most of those twenty-nine years confined to the kitchen, which had earned him a sizable girth and the belief he would not be sold as long as his skills were good.

"That he is, that he is," Josha Dar exclaimed, as if he might be overheard. "He is a most worthy deputy to the Sultan."

"As are they all," said Maras as he ladled out some cold soup; it was redolent of turmeric and cumin.

"Delicious," said Josha Dar, drinking eagerly and chewing the bits of lamb in the soup with gusto. "The Sultan keeps an excellent kitchen."

"He is Sultan," said Maras. "And whether he is here or elsewhere, he must maintain his household to his standard." Maras went to take a round of flat-bread from the shelf where breads were stored. He came back to Josha Dar with the bread in his hands. "Shall I put the lentils in this?"

"No; put them in this." He offered his drinking cup.

"As you wish," said Maras. "You will be able to carry it when you leave?"

"I will manage," said Josha Dar, anticipating his feast. "I will not take them far."

"Since it is night, I should think not," said Maras as he filled the drinking cup with stewed lentils. "This is no time to be abroad."

"I have a place of my own," said Josha Dar, volunteering no more than that.

"Then you are a fortunate man," said Maras in his usual flat tone.

"May the gods witness my gratitude." It was difficult not to feel satisfied with himself after such an evening as this.

Maras shook his head in warning. "In this palace there is only Al-lah."

"Then I will thank Allah," said Josha Dar. "Whatever is most suit-able, and whichever god has favored me, I am thankful."

Maras smiled with lupine ferocity. "Do not let Balban Ihbal hear you say that, or you will not have so much as a grain of salt from him again."

"But he will not hear me, unless you tell him what I have said. If you do, I will deny it, and in the end, Balban Ihbal will have to choose which of us to believe." He took his drinking cup and reached for the bread with his left hand.

Maras drew back in disgust. "You should not use that hand to touch food."

"I wash six times a day. I have no reason not to use both hands," Josha Dar countered, and kept his left hand extended.

Muttering something about casteless fools, Maras gave him the bread. "What of the onion?"

"Put it in my mouth. I will hold it with my teeth," said Josha Dar, and grinned.

Shrugging, Maras selected a large yellow onion, pulled the dry skins off it, and held it out for Josha Dar to bite. "There you are," he said as Josha Dar's teeth sank into the pungent bulb.

Josha Dar nodded and said something incoherent around the onion, then turned and left the kitchens, bound for the warren of streets around the rear of the palace. He went at a steady pace to his own niche in the old walls of the city, and slipped into the rocky alcove. He had a make-shift bed in the farthest corner of the place, and a single rush-lamp set on a ledge away from the entrance. It was a relatively safe place, one he had occupied for almost a year, and he regarded it as much his home as any place he had been in all his life. He sat down on his bed and began to eat, relishing his meal as a triumph over Balban Ihbal more than the savor of the food itself. As he ate, he decided he would watch Sanat Ji Mani as well as Rustam Iniattir, in the hope that one of them would do something that would bring him rewards and riches beyond his imagination.

Text of a letter from Firuz Ihbal bin Tughluq to Mahmud bin Ghurid.

In the name of Allah, the All-Merciful and All-Seeing, the peace be on you, Mahmud bin Ghurid, and upon your House from generation to generation.

As Deputy Procurer to the Army, I send you word to ask what is needed to reinforce our troops against any attack that may be made against the city of Delhi. In the absence of the Sultan—may Allah show him favor forever—I must ask for your assessment of needs so that we may prepare to keep this city safe from all invaders.

It will be necessary for you to stipulate all requirements, from the greatest to the least, so that no part of the army will falter or fail due to lack of supplies or other essentials. Do not stint for fear of cost, as that may prove a false economy at best. Do not think to gain favor by claiming greater readiness than is actually the case, for such assurances will be hollow in the face of a prepared enemy.

You must also submit a count of soldiers, their arms and their skills, for my scrutiny. We have men who are past their best years of service, and we must now replace them or suffer the consequences. Again, do not hesitate to stipulate what you know to be accurate. Such prevarication in this context would be commensurate to speaking a lie with your hand on the Qran. *No follower of the Prophet with hope of Paradise would do such a disgraceful thing; it would avail the Sultan nothing of worth to heed such deception.*

I will expect your accounting in a month's time. Surely that is sufficient for the task I have set you. If you fail to do as I have ordered, you will be blinded and left to beg, and a more worthy successor shall complete what you failed to do. Acquit this labor well, and the Sultan shall hear praise of you from my lips. To this I set my hand and swear to uphold,

> *Firuz Ihbal bin Tughluq*
> *Deputy Procurer for the Sultan's Army at Delhi*

3

A glowing pink flush suffused the room on the top floor of the fine house of red granite in the Street of the Brass Lanterns. It was a splendid building, handsomely proportioned; its twenty-three rooms and two gardens were built to the highest standards and as lavishly appointed as the law allowed foreigners to adorn their homes; the smallest windows were of costly glass, the larger ones of thin-sliced

alabaster, slightly milky and diffusing the shine of first light; the fur-
nishings were of fine woods and silks, the lamps were of brass, and
the fragrant odor of incense perfumed the air. Now that dawn had
arrived at Delhi again, the Muslims were at morning prayers, and the
followers of Zarathustra hailed the returning light with song. A breeze
came up, adding to the activity; the first odor of cooking fires blended
with the aroma of flowers rising into the sky where birds greeted the
rising sun, calling and fluttering. In the streets sudden industry
erupted, people of all ranks and stations bustling to make the most of
the morning before the heat became oppressive.

"In my homeland, the mountain passes are filled with snow," Sanat
Ji Mani remarked in the Greek of Byzantium to Rojire as he put away
the glass vessels with which he had worked all through the night; he
was dressed in a black Egyptian kalasiris of fluted linen, his head
uncovered, revealing short, wavy hair that was almost black but shot
with auburn high-lights that were emphasized by the angular, brilliant
luminance. "Yet here is an almost perpetual summer."

"True enough," said Rojire in the same language, his thoughts distracted by the task of separating the myriad small jewels spilled into
the tray before him, like so much colored sand. He frowned with
concentration, his faded-blue eyes narrowing in support of his effort.

"Not that I am complaining," Sanat Ji Mani went on, shutting the
cabinet doors and putting a bar-lock in place to keep them closed.

". . . sixteen, seventeen, eighteen—eighteen small rubies," Rojire
said, maintaining his concentration. He put these stones into a carved
wood box with others of similar size, then started in on the topazes.

"A pity I did not have time to grow them larger," said Sanat Ji
Mani, then lifted one shoulder philosophically. "Well, next time."

"These are not paltry," said Rojire as he made a pile of the topazes
and began to count.

"No, but they are not lavish, and the Sultan prefers large stones to
small." He stretched his linked hands upward. "Sometimes my back
is stiff after such a demanding night."

"Small wonder," said Rojire, then held up one finger as he began
to count.

Sanat Ji Mani went to inspect the athanor, the bee-hive-shaped
alchemical oven that stood in the center of the large chamber which

occupied most of the top of his grand house; the tile-like bricks were no longer glowing, but they were warm to the touch. Sanat Ji Mani walked around the chamber making sure all the windows remained closed, for an errant draft at this time could cause the athanor to crack, and it would take him several months to build another one. "I will open the windows before noon," he said to Rojire.

"Please," said Rojire. "The heat will be stifling if you do not." He swept the topazes into another small wooden box. "Twenty-nine."

"It will be stifling in any case." Sanat Ji Mani waved his arm as if to try to banish the increasing warmth. "Not too bad for a night's work," said Sanat Ji Mani.

"Yes." Rojire began to pick out emeralds, separating them from amethysts with great care. "Twenty-three peridots, thirty-one amethysts," he said as he prepared to sweep each group into its own box.

"Take out ten peridots for the Sultan; the largest ones," said Sanat Ji Mani, adding thoughtfully, "Or, more precisely, his deputies."

"Ten," Rojire agreed, and selected the best of the little jewels. "Where do you want them kept?"

"In the cedar box, with the dragon on the top; there are beryls and emeralds in it already," said Sanat Ji Mani. "I must see his kinsman tomorrow, and I will need to bring them both a suitable gift if he is to listen to me, and send my petition on to his nephew, along with a smattering of jewels to demonstrate my sincerity. A shame the Sultan has abandoned Delhi."

"It is," said Rojire. "But he must improve his fortifications throughout his territory."

"Um," said Sanat Ji Mani, skepticism giving his utterance a rising inflection. "And I must hope that he will see my petition in good time."

"You will need gifts for his ministers and secretaries as well as his deputies, if you want his attention," said Rojire, making no excuse for his cynicism as he retrieved the box Sanat Ji Mani had described.

"How many emeralds?" Sanat Ji Mani asked; the sun was intense, and he was beginning to feels its effects in spite of his native earth lining the soles of his shoes.

"Sixteen, I think," said Rojire. He placed the emeralds in one of the empty cubicles of the box.

"Give the Sultan seven of them; he likes emeralds."

Rojire nodded. "He likes anything costly and beautiful," he remarked. He straightened up. "Do you want something more in the box?"

"How many of the cubicles are empty?" Sanat Ji Mani inquired as if he did not know.

"Two," said Rojire. "What shall I put in them?"

Sanat Ji Mani paused thoughtfully, considering the gems he had stored in his simple wooden chest. "Perhaps the chalcedony egg and the pale-blue sapphire, the one with the elongated star; it is impressive and the color is unusual," he said at last. "Yes, that should complete the offering well enough."

"The sapphire is a fine gift on its own," said Rojire.

"Yes. And the Sultan will know that, when the box is finally presented to him." Sanat Ji Mani ran his hands through his hair, this action acknowledging the increasing heat.

"You may rouse the jealousy in many of the Sultan's relatives, and your generosity may cost you dearly," Rojire warned.

"It is a risk I am prepared to take," said Sanat Ji Mani, nodding to show he understood. "I will bathe when I have rested, and then I suppose I must prepare for my meeting with the Sultan's kinsman. I will need to decide how best to present myself. Firuz Ihbal is not a man to stint on ceremony."

"Particularly when the ceremony adds to his wealth," said Rojire sharply.

"True enough," Sanat Ji Mani agreed.

"And you are willing to make concessions to him," Rojire accused.

"As long as we are foreigners here, of course I am willing," said Sanat Ji Mani. "I am grateful to you for bearing my indignation, old friend. Otherwise, I might not be able to speak to that rogue Firuz Ihbal without being galled."

"I am pleased to be of service," said Rojire sarcastically. "I would prefer to waken you to the hazard of your circumstances."

"Oh, do not fear: I know them well enough. Yet I am grateful for your concern on my behalf." Sanat Ji Mani looked around the chamber. "It would be unfortunate if the Sultan should receive an unfavorable report of me. He may be a weak man, but that makes him dangerous, for he is more likely to strike out than a stronger man; he would need to see proof of his power as another, confident of having it, would not. I, being a foreigner, am weaker than he by definition, and therefore I am apt to be a target of his spite." He glanced toward the door. "Avasa Dani is supposed to come this afternoon."

Rojire nodded, aware that Sanat Ji Mani would not discuss the Sultan any longer. "I will have her taken to the library."

"Yes; if you will." He sighed once. "If only all this were easier," he said quietly.

"How do you mean easier?" Rojire asked, trying to keep any criticism out of his question.

"I mean that we are hemmed about with sets of laws and customs on all sides, and often they contradict one another; what the Hindu accepts, the Moslem will not; what the Buddhist venerates appalls the Zarathustran. We, being foreigners, and no part of any of their causes, are caught between them all." He turned toward Rojire. "Oh, I know, I know. We could return to the West, or go east, into China. It might be safer to leave while we can, or it might be changing one set of difficulties for another. But the very things I chafe against also interest me. There is a vitality here that commands my interest, and a satisfaction that makes me endure the difficulties. Difficulties are everywhere."

"True enough," said Rojire. "But you are willing to accept more of them than most."

"Because one of my nature must," Sanat Ji Mani reminded him. "I have not the luxury of the living, to be at home among humanity."

Rojire shook his head. "No one knows."

"I should hope not," Sanat Ji Mani said with feeling. "Avasa Dani may guess, but even she is not certain." He stared at the windows. "I will retire now. If I am not awake by noon, rouse me."

"Noon. I will," said Rojire, continuing to prepare the box with its gifts.

As he went to the door, Sanat Ji Mani said, "You are very patient with me, old friend. I am most grateful, but occasionally I wonder why."

"Whomelse should I serve in this world, my master?" Rojire asked mildly.

"You might not need to serve at all," Sanat Ji Mani pointed out.

"Possibly," said Rojire. "But it is my habit, and a task I know how to perform, and it pleases me to think myself useful. You ask none of the questions any other master would: you know why I never age, and why I eat only raw meat." He took a step back from the table. "I don't know what to make of these fits of humility you sometimes indulge in."

Sanat Ji Mani laughed once. "Yes, they are fits, are they not, my friend?" He managed a rueful smile.

"There is no other way to describe them," said Rojire. "Go. Rest. You will be more yourself when you waken."

"That I will," said Sanat Ji Mani, and went down the narrow stairs into the cool, dim recesses of his great house. His private quarters were at the rear of the building, shaded by the upper floor, and somewhat apart from the rest of the house. A sitting room made for receiving guests, elegantly furnished with fine woods and glowing silks, was the first of a suite of three rooms; the second contained a small Roman bath, ten hand-spans deep, ornamented with mosaic tiles and elaborate brass fittings as well as a marble couch beside the pool piled with pillows and cushions for resting after bathing; the third was his bedroom, and it was as austere as the other rooms were lavish: a narrow bed atop a long chest of his native earth and an old red-lacquer chest were the only objects in the room, which was significantly smaller than the other two. No paintings adorned the walls, no carpet lay on the floor. The small window over the bed was screened with woven reeds, reducing the illumination to twilight. Three clothes-hooks on the back of the door were simple, utilitarian objects, where Sanat Ji Mani hung his kalasiris before he climbed onto his bed and pulled the single cotton sheet up to his chin. In a moment he had fallen into a profound slumber that was more like dying than rest.

By noon all Delhi sweltered; in the markets the vendors pulled down the curtains of their stalls and began the mid-day rest after the followers of Islam had completed their prayers. Near the river half a dozen gangs of older children left off their rough-housing to seek the shade of the trees along the bank, where asses drowsed, their long ears drooping in the stultifying heat. A humming stillness enveloped the city under the remorseless glare of the sun.

In his chamber, Sanat Ji Mani wakened easily and suddenly, alert without being alarmed. He rose, went into the outer room, and took a loose Roman dalmatica of black cotton from his clothes-chest, tugging it on over his head as he made his way to his bath, a mosaic-lined room with high, shaded windows and a large polished-granite bathing-pool sunk into a foundation of his native earth. He stood on the edge of the pool for a short while, his dark eyes fixed on the middle-distance. Then he removed the dalmatica and let himself into the pool, welcoming the still waters as they rose half-way up his chest. He extended his arms and leaned back, floating on the tepid water in the pleasant gloom of the bath-chamber; as he rested in the stillness, he thought about his present situation and considered the possibilities open to him: he could leave Delhi and go any number of places; he could remain in Delhi and continue to accommodate the increasingly greedy demands of the Sultan's deputies; he could join the caravan he and Rustam Iniattir were assembling, leave the city, and return to it; he could venture deeper into India, toward the south where the Sultans had not conquered and where he might find a more congenial place to settle for a time. He sighed, and let his feet drop to the floor of the bath. He did not want to return to Europe, still devastated by Black Plague; China was intriguing but offered too immediate a reminder of T'en Chih-Yu, dead less than two centuries; to the west and north-west was the turmoil of Timur-i's campaigns; in Africa, his alienness would be too pronounced to provide him any measure of safety—his years in Tunis had shown him that; the Land of Snows was remote enough to offer him some protection, but the routes there lay through disputed territory, and he had no wish to become embroiled in local wars; the south was filled with rivalries and machinations that exhausted the peoples and led the lords to see enemies at every turn. "So Delhi it is, for now," he said to the empty air.

A moment later a servant appeared in the outer doorway. "Did you summon me, my master?"

Sanat Ji Mani looked up from his place in the pool. "No, Hirsuma, I did not. But thank you for being so alert."

Hirsuma bowed and closed the door.

This time Sanat Ji Mani kept his thoughts to himself; when he rose from the tub a short while later, he had made up his mind on several points and was preparing to put these decisions into action. He used a drying-cloth, pulled on his dalmatica once more, then went to his own rooms to get his sandals with the earth-filled soles and to drop a silver chain studded with rubies around his neck before going to the library to meet with Avasa Dani.

She was seated on a low rosewood chair piled with silken cushions; in her hands she held an open scroll, and she studied it with singular intensity, her concentration so intent that she did not hear him enter the library. When he spoke her name, she looked up sharply, her face darkening slightly. "I'm sorry, Sanat Ji Mani. I did not know you—"

"You have nothing to apologize for, Avasa Dani," he replied as he went to her side. "I did not mean to interrupt you."

She smiled up at him. "Still, I must thank you for your kindness to me, and not just for allowing me to study with you. You are a most generous man. So many would chastise me for failing to do them honor at once." Today she was dressed in gauzy silks the color of Egyptian lapis lazuli, and she wore silver rings on her fingers and had three of them hanging from both of her earlobes.

"So you have told me," he said, returning her smile fleetingly. "Yet you are the more generous of the two of us, I think."

Closing the scroll, she regarded him in bemused satisfaction. "We are not going to argue about this, are we?"

"If it would please you," he replied, and sank down on his knees at her side.

"Oh, my foreign friend, you are much too good to me," she said, a bit of regret in her voice.

"And how can that be?" he asked gently.

"My father would say you have indulged me beyond all reason, if he still lived. I have heard my half-sisters say it." She ran her finger along the edge of the scroll. "You have let me learn anything I wanted to learn."

He rested his hand on her arm. "Why should I not?"

"Because most men would not; it is not seemly for a woman to learn too much," she said, more abruptly than she had intended. "My husband was not entirely pleased when he discovered I was literate and had a gift for numbers. His family is very traditional, and they did not bargain on such a bride for him. But my connections were such that they could not refuse the match, and so, we were married." She shrugged. "When he decided to become a monk, a few of his relatives said I had driven him to it."

"Do you think you did?" Sanat Ji Mani could see the trouble in her eyes; he waited for her answer with no sign of impatience.

"Sometimes I do," she admitted. "But mostly I believe it is his Path to be a monk, his karma, and I do not challenge his inclinations, though I do not entirely understand them." She put the scroll aside, onto a table ornamented with lavish inlays of wood making a pattern of flying birds. "He would have liked me to withdraw from the world, but I am no Buddhist, and such an act would have been unacceptable to the Buddhists."

"You say he is amenable to our arrangement," Sanat Ji Mani prompted her.

"Yes. You do not compromise his family or mine. You do not offend those who worship the traditional gods, nor do you offend the Buddhists." She turned her arm so that she could take his hand in hers. "I know I am very much in your debt, Sanat Ji Mani."

"No, Avasa Dani," he countered. "It is I who am in your debt."

She regarded him skeptically. "Why do you say that?"

His dark eyes met hers. "You know why," he told her, his voice low, melodic.

"No," she said, shaking her head so that her earrings rang softly against one another. "If you used me as men use women, that might be different, for you would be doing a wrong, but what is between us is not of that nature."

He held her hand more protectively. "Does it satisfy you? that which is between us?"

"Oh, *yes*," she said with suppressed passion. "How can you ask?" She felt her face flush, for she had not yet been permitted to rouse him as he had her.

"I know you are fulfilled at the time, but later, you may have doubts, or regrets." He did not like to speak these words aloud, but they expressed the apprehension he had been sensing in the nine weeks since her husband had come and gone from her life.

"Not I," she said emphatically, then added with less certainty, "What of you? Do you have doubts?"

"No," he said, and knew it was not quite the truth, for they had lain together four times, and she would soon be in danger of becoming one of his blood when she died; one more encounter and he would have to explain this before they embraced each other again, or expose her to a risk she might not want to accept.

"But you are troubled," she said, aware that he was not wholly at ease.

"Yes," he said.

"Because your servants may spy on us and report to my relatives that I am not maintaining my chastity?" She touched his cheek with her slender fingers. "You need not worry on that account. I have spoken to my half-sisters and have said you are affectionate—and being a foreigner, your ways are unlike ours—but you do nothing that would give my husband a moment's qualms. They need not fear I will bring an incorrect child into the world on your account, and unless I do, what is said of me by servants is nothing more than envious rumor. No one will find us together in your house. Everyone knows that servants gossip, and that they often exaggerate. My relatives will not bring you before the Sultan's deputies for debauching a married woman."

"Have your half-sisters granted you so much?" He found it difficult to believe, although he did not want to contradict her.

She smiled, a roguish glint in her eyes. "Let us say they will believe me until I am with child, and then they will be happy to denounce me and seize my husband's goods for the sake of the family honor." Her smiled broadened. "Since that will never happen, they will have to continue to believe what I have told them."

He uttered a single chuckle. "You are a very clever woman, Avasa Dani."

Her suddenly demure manner was belied by her laughter. "I would not be here otherwise, and my life would be the poorer for it," she reminded him, and leaned over so that she could kiss him. Their lips met softly as a whisper, but ardor flared in them both; she slid from the chair, pulling three cushions with her, to kneel in front of him, their bodies pressed together, their arms circled around each other, each supported by the other. A sound between laughter and a sob rose in her throat and she loosened her silken garments in order to give him access to her body, then reached for his hand and slid it under the shining fabric. "Do not deny me," she murmured before resuming their kiss once more.

For an answer, he slipped his other hand underneath her clothing and began to caress her shoulders, her back, her flanks, her breasts. He felt her desire mounting with every nuance of touch he offered her. His fingers sought out the curve of her side, where she was especially sensitive, and awakened greater voluptuousness in her with his coaxing touch that heightened her yearning for more of his tantalizing fondling. As she leaned against him, moving her body to ignite his carnality still more, he stroked her arms, sliding the silk from her shoulders. "Slowly, my dove. There is no need to hurry."

She surged her flesh the length of his body. "Do not wait." She took his ruby-studded silver necklace and lifted it over his head, dropping it onto the table beside the scroll.

"There is time," he said, more gently still, and bent his head to kiss her shoulders, the declivity at the base of her throat, the swell of her breasts. "Enjoy all that you can."

"But you—" She broke off. As was true of most women of her caste and station, she had been instructed since childhood in the art of pleasing a man; she was still surprised that Sanat Ji Mani put her pleasure before his own, and showed little respect for the teachings of the scriptures.

"I will be better satisfied if you are more completely fulfilled," he said before he touched her nipple with his tongue; she hissed in breath in intense pleasure. "There is so much more you can know of your exultation; let yourself achieve it. You will give me the greatest gift if you will do this."

She shivered as he continued his ministrations, her eyes half-closed so that she might feel his every contact with her body; it was as if she were being riven with light, as if her whole being was burning as the hands of holy men were said to burn. From her head to her thighs, she quivered with growing frenzy as Sanat Ji Mani evoked responses from every part of her; she wondered if this wonderful frenzy could melt her bones, for they seemed to be softened within her. As much as she had been pleasured by him before, it had been nothing so splendidly consuming as this. She had not suspected there was so much rapture in her. When his lips touched the cleft at the top of her thighs, her trembling became a shudder, and she felt a little spasm shake her. She caught her hand in his hair. "That was—"

"There is more," he said, and continued his exploration, using his hands to summon greater sensation from her body than she had ever known.

"Ah." There was something gathering within her, centered at where his mouth and hand were most tantalizing. She could feel a delicious tightening in her loins. "Ah." It was almost impossible to breathe, for she might send herself over the brink; she swayed as if she were about to fall, and felt his arm come up to support her even as he rose and his other hand performed some unimaginable magic between her legs. "Ah. Ah. Ah." The cries were soft, but they came from the very root of her being. For a long, dizzying moment, she was caught up in the enormity of the release that went through her in deep pulsations, like a superb instrument played flawlessly. Then, as she came back to herself, she felt Sanat Ji Mani's lips on her neck, and she smiled. It was difficult to speak, but she knew she had to tell him. "There was more."

He kissed her again, his lips soft on hers, completing their joining as he had begun it. "You have been most kind, Avasa Dani."

She sank down onto the cushions, a marvelous lassitude coming over her. She was vaguely aware that she should dress herself again, but she could not bring herself to close her body away from all that had just transpired. "Will anyone come?"

"Rojire is the only one, and he will not until I call him." Sanat Ji Mani put his silver necklace back on, adjusting it to hang properly, then stretched out beside her.

"How did you know?" she asked, looking over at him. "I did not know."

"I have lain with you before, and I have learned much from you," he said, stroking her shoulder and arm.

She thought about his answer and decided she would have to be content with it for now. With a sigh she rolled onto her side. "I had better dress."

"Not on my account," he said, and took her hand in his so that he could kiss each of her fingers in order.

"No; on mine," she said with a hint of sadness in her voice.

He nodded and moved aside so that she could rise and pull her silken clothes about her, as if she were wrapping herself in a gorgeous cloud. Watching her, he knew it was now imperative to tell her the whole of his nature before they had another such encounter; he wondered if his revelation would blight the passion between them—it had happened before with others, and he told himself he would endure it happening again, but he could not pretend such a response would not cause him anguish. Long ago he might have tried to convince himself that her reaction was not important to him, but those times were long in his past. He decided he would have to talk to her in the next few days; not now, while her gratification made her movements liquid as dance—in a few days, before her need rose again. With a wry smile on his lips, he got to his feet and went to the door to call Rojire.

Text of a letter from Rustam Iniattir to Sanat Ji Mani, written in Parsi and delivered by an escorted slave.

My greetings and good wishes to the foreigner, Sanat Ji Mani, who abides in the Street of Brass Lanterns in the city of Delhi: may light shine upon him and all his endeavors.

I have today received word that the caravan we have sponsored has arrived in Shiraz and been received by your factor there with the cordiality and upon terms that you guaranteed would be the case. This is a most welcome confirmation of the agreement into which we have entered. I am pleased to tell you that it is most likely that the caravan will move on in a month, having traded in Shiraz such goods as we have agreed are to be traded there, and other goods procured for the next phase of the journey.

There are reports of activity on the part of Timur-i Lenkh that trouble me, for they are saying he is taking his men and striking off toward more wealthy cities than he has previously done. That may bode ill for Shiraz, or for Delhi. Delhi is far away, but it is said he and his men travel on the winds and can advance faster than anything but a storm. I am worried that this might lead to problems for our caravan, and I wish to consult you in case you are of the opinion that it would be wiser to permit the caravan to choose other routes in its travel to the west. You have knowledge of that part of the world, and

I would like to draw upon what you have learned, in case it becomes necessary for the caravan to alter the route it follows.

I have also been informed that there is illness in the cities of Ormuz and Damascus, and that is bound to have impact on all trading along those routes. Sickness is oftentimes unavoidable in this dark world, but it does not mean that it is prudent to put oneself in its path. I would favor turning the caravan toward the Mameluke Empire and the ancient land of Egypt, for surely our goods will find willing buyers in that place as they would in Aleppo or Trebizond. The Western traders come to Egypt as well as to the Black Sea, and they will deal with our men in either place, to our advantage.

In that two of my cousins are the leaders of the caravan, you may be certain they will do as I instruct them. As they rest at Shiraz, a message, carried by sea, and then ridden inland by courier, would reach them before they are intending to set out again. So that we may have a better understanding of our business in this difficult time, I propose to visit you in two days, when you have had an opportunity to reflect on all I have told you, so that we might have a frank exchange of our thoughts in these matters.

You have far more money invested in this caravan than I have, and you have supplied camels, asses, and horses for the trek. You will not want to endanger so much of value without having time to reflect on these various matters and deciding where your interests lie. As you have discerned from my remarks, I am inclined to send the caravan toward the Mameluke Empire, but you may have other preferences, and it is fitting, given your high investment, that your thoughts be included in our deliberations.

It is most distressing to me that this first venture of ours should have such a hindrance imposed upon it, particularly at this time, when we agreed there was much promise. I would not be offended if you reconsidered the caravan we discussed for China, as it is possible that travel eastward may be no safer than travel westward. You spoke of Tirhut, Kamaru, and Assam as being the most protected route: I do not disagree with you, but I question how much protection is possible at this time.

I am not averse to modifying the terms of our agreement, so that our current problems need not be added to by a reckless adherence to conditions that do not actually apply to circumstances at large. Do not doubt that I am as inclined as ever to undertake these journeys, but we may wish to shift our plans for departures to a time when our success is more assured than appears to be the case now. You tell me that you are not wholly dependent on the profits of our trade to keep you and your household, which may be just as well if our present enterprise encounters any more thwarting.

Let us consider the winter as a better time to commence our next venture, when the world is less active. If our eastern-bound caravan does not go high into the mountains, but keeps to the roads of the foothills, it should not be delayed by snows, and by the time the passes into China are reached, it will be late enough in the spring that the way will be open, and there will be a swift passage possible.

Until we have agreed on these points, I propose that we do not consider any new caravans, not even one to Russia, which we discussed as a possible speculative trek for the year to come. If we cannot resolve any disagreements we may have with our current plans, it would be sensible to wait before adding anything more to our shared obligations, for that would only result in disputes that would be unsatisfactory to us both, and to our traders as well. I ask you to consider all these things before we meet to evaluate our projects.

Rustam Iniattir
Parsi merchant of Delhi

4

Firuz Ihbal stared at the black-clad foreigner and scowled, his moustaches bracketing his mouth as if to emphasize his displeasure. "You have not yet explained why you are sponsoring a second caravan. Your first venture was questionable enough, but now you say a second one is in order." He sat back on his elaborately carved ivory chair that was not quite a throne and rested the tips of his fingers together, his eyes half-closed as he contemplated Sanat Ji Mani. At thirty-six, he was at the height of his power, and he knew it; he also knew he would not have many more years to enjoy his prestige and position as he did now, and was determined to make the most of it.

"If I did not believe that a caravan to China would be worthwhile, I would not ask to be allowed to sponsor one," Sanat Ji Mani said patiently, not the least intimidated by Firuz Ihbal's off-putting manner.

"But *why* do you believe it will be worthwhile? You yourself admit that it is unlikely that your first caravan will be able to reach the cities you intended it should." Firuz Ihbal sat forward a bit, as if he saw something suspicious about Sanat Ji Mani. Here in the audience chamber of the Sultan's palace, he was used to maintaining his authority with nothing more than a nod of his head, but there was something about the foreigner that perplexed him and made him wonder if he was truly as much master here as he believed he was. "You have proved you are a man of means, but you cannot continue to give away gems and gold forever. When you can no longer sponsor caravans and companies of soldiers for the Sultan, you will have to turn to our enemies in order to make your way in the world."

"When I cannot meet my obligations, I will sell my house and depart for whatever destination you may deem proper," said Sanat Ji Mani. "Until that time, you will have to admit that I have much to offer a merchant like Rustam Iniattir."

"Who is a Parsi and a Zarathustran," said Firuz Ihbal condemningly. "And has many caravans on the roads of the world."

"Who is willing to undertake the ventures as no Muslim would do," Sanat Ji Mani pointed out. "I mean no disrespect, Firuz Ihbal: you and I both know that there are sites where the followers of the Prophet are not encouraged to go. The first caravan Rustam Iniattir sponsored with me is bound for no such places, and half the men on the trek are of your faith. But going to the east, the faithful of Islam are not as welcome as they are to the west, and it is suitable for Zarathustrans and Buddhists to lead and man the journey. The chance of trading advantageously and returning with profits and goods is far greater for the enterprise Rustam Iniattir and I are proposing than would be the case for many of your—"

Firuz Ihbal waved him to silence. He sat still, disapproval in every line of his body. Finally, he made a fussy gesture. "Your point is taken, foreigner."

"Then you will consider it?" Sanat Ji Mani asked.

"I may," said Firuz Ihbal, one brow lifting as if in invitation.

"If I were to make a show of my gratitude for your permission?" Sanat Ji Mani suggested.

"Then I will probably consent. But I will not give you an answer for a month at the least; there is much I must consider in regard to your request. When my answer is ready, I will expect you to provide funds to arm another hundred soldiers as a sign of your earnest devotion to this city and the Sultan. Then you will have my answer." He clapped his hands and three slaves appeared and abased themselves. "Escort this man out of the palace."

The three slaves answered in chorus, "We serve you, Firuz Ihbal."

Sanat Ji Mani turned away without saying anything more, for nothing was expected or wanted from him now that Firuz Ihbal had laid down his terms. He was almost to the door when a word from the dais stopped him. "Yes, Deputy of the Sultan?"

"The jewels you brought me last time were nice, but the garnets and tourmalines you provided me today are the best yet. I was not as pleased with the diamonds." Firuz Ihbal paused, continuing in an insinuating tone, "I do not know how you come by these treasures, but I am pleased to receive them—in the Sultan's name."

"Of course, in the Sultan's name. And if you are satisfied, what can I be but honored," said Sanat Ji Mani, ducking his head in a show of submission to the Sultan's will.

"I will expect word from you soon concerning the arming of soldiers," Firuz Ihbal added as if it had slipped his mind until now.

"It will be my pleasure to do so. What manner of soldiers did you want armed? Guards? Horsemen? Foot-soldiers? Archers?"

Firuz Ihbal gave the question due consideration. "Archers, I believe. Bows, arrows, and armor. Two bows and fifty arrows per man, I should think."

"As you command, Firuz Ihbal, so it must be," said Sanat Ji Mani, knowing the request was outrageous and aware that protest was foolish; he prepared to leave the room. "I take my leave, and thank you for your time."

But Firuz Ihbal was not finished quite yet. "Remember, Sanat Ji Mani, that I particularly admire garnets. And pearls—big, freshwater pearls."

"I shall do so," said Sanat Ji Mani, bowing as the slaves surrounded him and removed him from the audience chamber. He allowed the slaves to escort him to the Foreigners' Gate, where soldiers let him out into the street where his manservant was waiting, holding Sanat Ji Mani's grey horse's reins from the saddle of his own bay.

"You were not very long," said Rojire in the Latin of Imperial Rome, aware that the direct glare of afternoon sunlight was causing Sanat Ji Mani some discomfort.

"No. Firuz Ihbal made his wants known most succinctly, and made sure I left the palace under ward." He swung into the saddle, squinting against the light.

"There is shelter in the street," Rojire said, pointing to a narrow lane shaded with high awnings stretched between the tops of the buildings lining it. "I should have refilled the earth in your soles, my master. I am sorry I did not."

"You need not apologize," said Sanat Ji Mani as he started his horse walking toward the shadowed lane; there were a fair number of people about for this time of day, but most of them were not hurried, and they willingly moved aside for the two mounted foreigners. "The full moon is just past, and there should still be some potency in the earth. The sun is so overwhelming here that this discomfort does not surprise me." He glanced back, his dark eyes fixed on the Foreigners' Gate, then he looked ahead once more. "I think we are being followed."

Rojire knew better than to look for himself. "Why do you say so?"

A train of mules clattering past made it difficult for any answer to be heard. "There is a skinny fellow who was loitering by the gate as I left—he was inside the walls of the palace and now he is outside." Sanat Ji Mani remarked in a tone that suggested he was making minor observations. He lowered his voice as the mules went their way and the noise dropped to a more bearable level. "It may be coincidence, but—"

"But you have reason to doubt it," said Rojire, and laughed as if this remark was amusing.

"I am reminded of Sorra Celinde, who went everywhere because she was a nun and unsuspect because of her vocation, and what mischief she caused." He smiled at this dire memory, now almost six centuries old. "She could account for her presence readily enough, and everyone accepted the coincidences, because what harm could a nun do?"

"Very well: I will be attentive to anyone paying over-much attention to us," said Rojire, and pulled his horse behind Sanat Ji Mani's as they entered the covered street. "Will you be allowed to send out the second caravan, do you think?"

"When Firuz Ihbal has settled on a large enough bribe, I should think so," said Sanat Ji Mani, raising his voice to be heard in the echoing street; it was as well they were speaking Latin, he decided as he saw faces lean over them from above.

"Will the Sultan ask for a bribe as well?" Rojire inquired.

"If he is in Delhi, no doubt he will. But if he is away, his relatives will ask it in his name," Sanat Ji Mani replied, ironically amused by his own observation.

"No doubt you are right," said Rojire with a tight smile. "How do you propose to deal with their demands?"

"I suppose I should make more jewels, and gold." Sanat Ji Mani was silent for a moment. "I do not know what they may demand, but I want to give them no excuse to express their discontent; some of the deputies would be delighted to imprison me and then ask for a ransom that would take everything I own, and still not be sufficient to their needs. Better to deal with their rapacity as I have done before than create opportunities for them that would end in being catastrophic for all of us."

"You and I, and Avasa Dani?" Rojire suggested.

"And Rustam Iniattir," added Sanat Ji Mani. "Where wealth is concerned, the Sultan casts a wide net." They were nearing the end of the narrow street and were about to cross one of the small market-squares that were set up throughout the city. "When we cross, you take the Street of the Lions, and I will take the Street of the Old

Temple. That way we may be able to cause our follower to betray himself."

"As you wish, my master," said Rojire, a note of doubt in his voice.

"You may stop and purchase something for the kitchen," said Sanat Ji Mani. "Some lentils and cheese for the staff and meat for yourself. If anything else strikes your fancy, add it to your selections. If the spy comes after me, you will have a fine opportunity to observe him."

"Very well," Rojire agreed. "But why will you take the Street of the Old Temple?"

"Why, to offer incense to the gods," said Sanat Ji Mani, as if this were obvious. "Since I do not bow to Allah, I must show some regard for an established religion."

"Probably," said Rojire, unwilling to concede the necessity. "But why to those gods? Why not to the Buddha?"

"Because most of the people of Delhi worship those old gods," said Sanat Ji Mani. "No one will question me for making such an offering; many foreigners do it. The Sultan's deputies would be displeased to know that I honor the Buddha, or the Parsi's God of Light, for they see those single gods as rivals to Allah. So I must respect all the gods, but I cannot make my preferences known without bringing disfavor upon me, and upon my household."

They had reached the market-square; Rojire drew rein and called out in the language of the people, "I will not be long, my master."

"Tend to your duties," Sanat Ji Mani responded. "I will see you at my house." He let his horse pick his way through the crowd; he was careful not to look for the scrawny man he had noticed earlier, but contented himself with going toward the Street of the Old Temple, diagonally across the square. He entered this street without incident, making his way through the moderate press of people, and went along to the Old Temple that gave the street its name: it was a large, pillared building of great age, with elaborate friezes showing the exploits of Shiva, to whom the temple was primarily dedicated. Sanat Ji Mani dismounted and looked about for someone to hold his horse.

"I will do it, exalted sir," said a boy of about nine. He held out his hand for the reins and a coin for his service.

Sanat Ji Mani gave him both. "I will not be long. See that nothing happens to him."

The boy looked at the small, gold coin shining in his hand. "I shall protect him with my life," he promised.

"I trust that will not be necessary," said Sanat Ji Mani, and went up the few, worn, broad steps and into the temple. Entering its shadow, he had an uneasy memory of Tamasrajasi in her temple, almost two centuries ago, and all that had happened there, the blood and the river that swept through; he shook off the recollection and gave his attention to the three large statues of Shiva that dominated the interior of the temple, flanked by Durga and Sarasvati, with niches dedicated to dozens of other gods.

He paused before the figure of Shiva, caught in the act of dancing, haloed by flames, his serene smile remote from the world. "Lord of the Dance," said Sanat Ji Mani in the language of Ashoka's time. He took two wedges of frankincense from the wallet hung on his belt and put them in the large pot of blackened brass where such offerings were made. Using one of the rushlights that hung before the statue, he lit the incense and bowed to Shiva as the first tendrils of smoke rose from his offering; he was aware that a few of the priests in the temple were watching him, their curiosity roused by his presence. As he rose, he glanced toward one of the priests, saying, "Shiva has great meaning for me, even though I am a stranger." He did not elaborate what that meaning was.

"So have all the gods," said the priest. "In life, a man will encounter all of them in one manifestation or another."

"Yes, he will," said Sanat Ji Mani with a smile as enigmatic as the one carved on the face of the God of Death and Transcendence.

The priest nodded toward the rising smoke. "A fine gift."

"To show my respect," said Sanat Ji Mani, touching his palms together and bowing to the priest. "Another time I will leave an offering to other gods."

"You will be welcome, foreigner," said the priest, managing to infuse a degree of cordiality into his voice that he rarely extended to such visitors as this one, a stranger alone.

"Thank you." Sanat Ji Mani dropped a half-dozen gold coins into the plate set out for donations; he knew this was generous beyond what most worshipers could afford; he made no attempt to draw the priest's attention to it, but bowed again, turned, and left the temple, squinting into the sunlight as it struck him full in the face.

The boy holding his grey grinned at him. "No one has touched him, exalted sir," the lad exclaimed.

"You have done well," said Sanat Ji Mani, giving him another coin before he vaulted into the saddle; crowing with delight, the boy ran off into an alley, shouting to a companion that they would feast that night.

By the time Sanat Ji Mani reached his house, he was stunned by the torpid heat; he left his horse with one of the grooms, and, contrary to his habit, he did not groom and feed the animal himself, but sought out his shadowy bath, where he spent the greater part of the afternoon in the cool water, attempting to relieve himself of the weight of the sun. By the time he emerged, the sun was low in the western sky and preparations for night occupied the residents of Delhi.

"You were followed," Rojire said without any mitigating remarks when Sanat Ji Mani found him at the top of the house. "That stringy fellow was behind you."

"I thought so," said Sanat Ji Mani. "I wonder to whom he reports?"

"Someone in the Sultan's palace, no doubt," said Rojire bluntly.

"No doubt," Sanat Ji Mani agreed. "But which of so many uses him?"

"Does it matter?" Rojire asked. "You warned me not so long ago that it might become difficult to accommodate the Sultan for much longer. I think the time may have come to consider finding—"

"—another place to live?" Sanat Ji Mani finished for him. "What place would that be, do you think? Here, at least, we know what we face, but elsewhere?"

"You say that readily enough," said Rojire, "but you have often put yourself at risk in the name of familiarity." He coughed. "I would not like to see you endure what you did outside of Baghdad again."

Sanat Ji Mani made a gesture of dismissal. "This is different, and well you know it."

"It is enough the same to make me worried," countered Rojire, then deliberately changed the subject. "I have gathered moldy bread for your sovereign remedy."

"Excellent," said Sanat Ji Mani. "Is the anodyne paste finished yet?"

"Yes. I have put it into jars, as you ordered," said Rojire. "I have also refilled the bottles of tincture for coughs and wheezing." He pointed to the shelves where these items stood, all neatly labeled in Latin. "The skin-paste with wool-fat and spider's-breath is in the alabaster jars at the end of the shelf."

"You have been busy," Sanat Ji Mani approved. "Is there syrup of poppies, as well?"

"The first mixture is done, and the second will be done tomorrow," said Rojire.

"That is good to hear. I will devote a few days to making other medicaments before I give orders to the armorers to make breast-plates for archers, and instructions to the boyers and fletchers for the bows and arrows that Firuz Ihbal requires in the Sultan's name." His tone was lightly ironic, but there was a sadness in his dark eyes that was more than annoyance at the avarice of the Sultan's deputy.

"You are worried," said Rojire, taking no satisfaction in being right.

"The Sultanate is weak. Many know it, and seek to hide that fact with displays of arms that mean nothing." Sanat Ji Mani sat down on the tall, Roman stool that stood in front of his longest table. "These deputies are more concerned about jealousies among themselves than they are about any enemies that might rise against the Sultanate. They do not understand how fragile their hold has become."

"And you think that they may be tested?" Rojire asked.

"I fear they may," he answered as gently as he could. "And they have no T'en Chih-Yü to hold their borders." He took a long, unsteady breath.

"Timur-i Lenkh?" Rojire suggested.

"He would have to come a long way, if all the rumors about his location are true, which is unlikely, knowing how rumors become distorted and magnified. But the Jagatai are known for their swift movement of troops, so it is not impossible," said Sanat Ji Mani, casting his mind back to his own experience of the troops of Jenghiz Khan, whose uncanny speed had broken the superior Chinese army and made Jenghiz's grandson Kublai the Emperor of China. "It could happen here."

"Yet you will not leave," said Rojire.

"No. Not now," said Sanat Ji Mani, a remoteness coming over him that Rojire knew could not be lifted by anything he might say.

"But you will not rule out the possibility?" Rojire persisted, not at all certain that he would receive an answer.

"I will not," said Sanat Ji Mani as a faint vertical line formed between his fine brows.

Rojire accepted this, unwilling to press for a greater response. He put his mind on preparing the lamps for Sanat Ji Mani's long night of work ahead of him. When he had finished pouring oil into all of them, he said, "It is time for the evening meal."

"Yes," said Sanat Ji Mani remotely. "See that the staff—"

With a sense of relief, Rojire said, "I will. I have issued instructions to the cook already on their behalf. They will all be fed: lentils, lamb, onions, rice, tamarind paste, two kinds of bread, and cheese." It was one of a dozen standard meals Sanat Ji Mani provided his household, but the recitation of this eminently pragmatic concern restored his equilibrium. "Fruit and honey for a finish."

"Very good," said Sanat Ji Mani, the severity of his expression softening. "I did not mean to push you out, Rojire," he went on. "I am apprehensive and I have visited my unease on you. If you will pardon my brusqueness?"

"Certainly," said Rojire promptly. "I should not have pressed you."

"Of course you should," said Sanat Ji Mani. "I have not behaved well toward you, for which I apologize." His quick smile was rueful. "I cannot give you my Word that I will never do so again."

Rojire chuckled. "Wise of you, my master." He put down flint-and-steel. "There. I will see to supper and then visit you again."

"Thank you," said Sanat Ji Mani. "And tomorrow we must go to the House of Service, to care for the injured there."

"Will Avasa Dani come with you?" Rojire asked as he went to the door.

"No; I doubt it. Her husband's family would not like it, and that would bring her trouble. I have authority from her husband, and I can allow her freedom in my own home, but her uncles would not like me to extend the same liberties to her beyond these walls. Nor would her husband, if he ever learned of it." He looked down at his

hands. "They are uneasy enough about the way he has arranged matters in his absence; I do not want to give them any reason to challenge
her situation. Her brothers-in-law could go before the magistrate and
insist that she be sequestered in her house and receive only female
visitors."

Rojire nodded. "She would like to assist you," he said quietly. "She
has told me several times she wishes to see how you treat the injured
and ill with your medicaments."

"I am aware of that; but it would be folly to put her so much at
risk. She is not foolish; she knows this." He went to the wall filled
with pigeon-hole drawers and opened one of them. "Go on. I will set
to work now."

"Do you want anything from the library?" Rojire was almost out
the door.

"Not tonight," Sanat Ji Mani replied with a gesture of obligation.

Rojire closed the door and descended the stairs to the ground floor,
where he sounded the clapper to bring the household to their dining
room. He then went to speak to the cook, and to carry the first of the
large, steaming bowls in to the servants.

Hirsuma was the last to arrive; he took his place hurriedly, as if he
hoped not to be seen. When the platter of flat-bread reached him, he
tore off half a round and shoved the platter along, his eyes moving
furtively as if he had been caught in a crime.

"What is the matter, Hirsuma?" Rojire asked. "Are you ill?"

"Ill?" Hirsuma echoed. "No. I am well." He plucked a morsel of
flat-bread with shaking fingers and bit into it eagerly.

"Then is anything else amiss?" Rojire pursued, aware that Hirsuma
was not himself.

Hirsuma coughed and spat out the bread. "You cannot speak to me
in that way. You are only a servant, and a foreigner. You are nothing
in Delhi."

"Our master is a foreigner," Rojire reminded him. "He is a good
and generous man, is he not?"

"He is," Hirsuma allowed. "But he is a foreigner. *You* are a foreigner. I was born in Delhi, as my father and his father were. I do
not have to bow to foreigners."

"But you will take the money and the food provided by foreigners," Rojire pointed out. "As a native of this city, should you not uphold its honor and respect the man who employs you?"

"You cannot speak to me so," Hirsuma insisted. "I may do as I think best. You cannot tell me how I am to behave."

"I saw you speaking to a scrawny fellow this afternoon," said Garuda, the under-steward. "You stayed with him for some time."

"He was seeking alms. I said I would need permission to give him any," Hirsuma said, a bit too quickly.

"You spoke to him longer than that," Garuda said, and looked to Rojire. "He is not to be trusted if he will not tell you what transpired."

Hirsuma shoved himself away from the table and got to his feet. "I do not have to listen to this. It is all falsehoods."

Rojire held up his hand. "You are accused of nothing but talking with an alms-seeker. Where is the harm in that?"

Mollified, Hirsuma stood still, his hands bunched at his sides. "You do not know anything. None of you know anything."

"Very true," Rojire agreed at once. "And for that reason, we ask. In our situation you would do the same." He indicated the thick cushion on which Hirsuma had been sitting. "I am only looking out for the household; I would expect the same of all of you."

Garuda swept his arm out, indicating all fourteen men seated around the table. "What our master-steward says is true. It is for the good of the household that we know these things." He grinned encouragement. "What has caused you agitation?"

"It is nothing," said Hirsuma, a note of resentment in his voice now. "They are all being foolish."

Before more challenges could be issued, Rojire said, "If Hirsuma says it is nothing, then we must accept that it is nothing." He got to his feet. "Dine well, and retire content."

The men at the table acknowledged this usual salutation with exclamations of good-will as Rojire departed; alone in the kitchen, Rojire began to cut up a raw chicken, all the while listening closely to the low murmur of conversation from the dining room, hoping to glean some more information than what little he had learned. He was familiar with the complaints of servants, but wondered if this was dif-

ferent: he was worried about Hirsuma, for it was obvious that the
servant was trying to conceal something—but what? and why? The
description of a scrawny fellow alerted him, reminding him of the man
who had followed him and Sanat Ji Mani earlier that day. Of course,
Rojire reminded himself, there was more than one scrawny fellow in
Delhi, and that most alms-seekers were far from robust, but he could
not rid himself of the conviction that this was the same man.

A burst of raised voices cut into Rojire's musing, and he set his
partially eaten chicken aside to return to the dining room, where he
found Hirsuma on his feet again, and Garuda and Bohdil, the head
groom, facing him angrily. "What is the meaning of this?" Rojire inquired, taking a calming tone with the belligerent servants.

"He has been telling secrets to enemies of our household," said
Garuda.

"I heard him," added Bohdil. "The rascal he spoke to tried to pry
opinions from me, but I would not give them." He put his hand to
his chest. "I know what my duties are, unlike some others."

"Very good of you," said Rojire. "But what of Hirsuma?" He looked
toward the houseman. "Did you do this thing? Were you careless with
the truth when you said you only spoke of alms with—"

"He lied," said Bohdil. "He told the man many things."

Most of the servants listened in rapt attention: this was more excitement than they had had in many months, and they were determined to get full value from the confrontation.

"I did not!" Hirsuma insisted, his face darkening with indignation.
"The man said he had heard that our master was greedy and lazy,
taking advantage of the hard-working people of Delhi; I told him that
it was far from the case." He shook his head once, like a lion worrying
prey. "I said that our master gives alms at the temples and mosques
of the city, and that he goes to the House of Service every fortnight
to treat the injured and ill as an act of charity. I said that many others
born in Delhi would be the better for doing as our foreign master
does."

Bohdil nodded. "That is what I heard."

Garuda pointed at Hirsuma. "You did well to defend our master,
but you should not have told that man so much. You should not have
lied when you were asked about what you have done. You have made

it worse for yourself." He glanced at Rojire. "How many strokes?"

Rojire held up his hand. "No. He is not to be beaten."

"Then how long will you confine him?" Garuda demanded. "We will keep guard, so that he will not be fed."

"Nor will he be confined and starved," said Rojire.

There was a shocked silence at the table; Garuda muttered something under his breath, and then said, "You must ask our master how many strokes."

"I have no need to ask," Rojire said. "Sanat Ji Mani does not beat his servants, just as he does not keep slaves. He does not confine them to starve them, either." He paused to let the men consider what he had said. "You believe that this man has done wrong to the household, and has slighted our master, and that may be true, but I tell you that he is not to be punished for what he has done, or not punished by beating or starving. It is not our master's way."

"If he is not beaten or starved, why will he not betray our master again, or why would not others among us?" Garuda asked, his words sharp.

"Because if there are any more lapses, on Hirsuma's part or any other's, he will be turned out of the household and another servant hired in his place," said Rojire. "Our master will allow an error in judgment, but not a pattern of untrustworthiness."

"How can he be so lax?" Garuda was stunned by what he had heard. "His household will soon be in disorder if he takes no pains to keep the servants from—" He swung his hands through the air as if the words were too offensive to utter aloud.

"You have heard what will happen, to Hirsuma and anyone else," Rojire said calmly. "If this has been an honest mistake, Hirsuma will not suffer for it. If he is duplicitous, he will be so again, and he will be turned out of this house forever. That is our master's way, and he will not change it." He did not add that Sanat Ji Mani had been a slave and a servant many times in his long past and had reached a point where he no longer wanted to punish those who worked for him with anything other than dismissal.

Garuda mumbled something about the foolishness of foreigners, but stopped when he saw Rojire stare at him. "If it is his wish, it shall be done," he said, catching himself.

"Very good." Rojire stood in the servants' dining room a little longer, letting the silence sink in, then said, "I will inform our master of what has happened here before I retire tonight. If he has anything to tell you, I will announce it in the morning." With that, he withdrew and went back to his meal; he ate in a preoccupied manner, for he was distracted by worries as to what Hirsuma's business with the stranger might mean. When he was finished, he reluctantly prepared to climb to the top of the house again, this time to inform Sanat Ji Mani that it appeared their misgivings had been well-founded and that they were being spied upon.

Text of a letter from Atta Olivia Clemens to Sanat Ji Mani, written in the Latin of Imperial Rome and carried by caravan from Aleppo to Delhi by way of Tabriz, Herat, and Ghanzi. Delivered fourteen months after it was dispatched.

To my most enduring, most esteemed friend, Sanct' Germain Francis-
cus, in whatever fabled city he now finds himself, the most affectionate
and eremitic greetings of Olivia, who is presently on the island of
Rhodes, and heartily tired of it.

There has not been an outbreak of Black Plague for more than a
decade now, and people are beginning to hope that the worst is over.
There has been enough time that travel is returning to acceptable levels
and trade is beginning to resume. I have seen an increase in merchants
venturing out from Venetia and Genova in large numbers in the last
year, and I trust this is an indication that the world is going to restore
itself at last, although some are saying that God will bring about the
Apocalypse at the dawning of the year 1400, when the Pale Horse
shall come again, and none will survive his visit; it is a view some
clergy are eager to embrace and encourage. I cannot share this pious
dread, having seen more than enough of slaughter and pestilence to
know that no matter how devastating it is, it is never so total that
nothing and no one survives it. If the Crusades were not sufficient for
that task, the Black Plague is not.

I plan return to Rome in a year or so if these favorable signs con-
tinue, and that butcher, Timur-i does not make another skirmish into

the lands just over the water to the east of here. I thank all your forgotten gods that Timur-i is a horseman and not a sailor, or half these islands would be empty already. What stories they tell about him! I am often astonished to hear otherwise sensible men say that he cannot be killed because he is the get of a whore and a demon, or that he can summon the desert winds to drive his enemies from the field. I do believe he makes towers of dead bodies as a warning to others, but that he rides his horse to the top of the piles seems like a risk of a good horse to me, and therefore I am skeptical that he would do it. I would ask you, but I would prefer you have no experience of him and his cavalry.

Niklos has built a number of boats and offers them to fishermen for a share of their catch; this has made him well-esteemed here, and the usual doubts that might be held in regard to our isolated lives have been diminished through his good sense and good business. Of course, we can always use the largest of these boats to leave Rhodes if that becomes necessary, as I think one day it must. I do not like to rely on our neighbors to welcome us as passengers aboard their boats, and this spares us that eventuality. When we depart, Niklos will leave his other boats to the monastery near the old Crusaders' fort, and that will satisfy everyone. So you see, I am prepared to go when the time is right.

What of you, my old friend? Are you prepared to leave that distant city—and are you still in Delhi, or will this letter wander all over those distant lands following your elusive trail? I know you have said that Delhi is as safe a place as any in this world just now, and that may be true, but I cannot help but wonder how long that safety will last. Timur-i is not the only man with dreams of conquest and ready followers, and many of them are waiting to strike in those places where the Plague left many vacancies in the ranks of the powerful. The Plague began in the East, and it killed many there as well as in the West. Do you have no concerns, or are you indifferent to your fate again? When you left Europe, you said you were tired of finding death everywhere, and of the suspicions that made travel prudent. Yet those of our blood must do so in times of such travail, or die the True Death. You taught me that, back when Traianus was Caesar, and I have striven to accept that verity, harsh though it often is; I ask you to remember your own lesson and maintain yourself prudently, as you would advise me to do, were our circumstances reversed.

Living here, in this isolated place, I have had to resort to visiting likely men in their sleeps instead of taking a lover, as I should prefer to do. But I fear that there are too many persons watching all foreigners here, and most of them are willing to see devils everywhere, and to rise against them to be rid of them. It is the result of the Plague, of course, and not limited to Rhodes alone. I find the circumspection this imposes upon me to be as vexing as it is necessary. I long for knowing and a touch that is for me, not the dream I provide. Still, it has been safer here, though I live like a nun, than it would have been in many other places, so, although I may dislike the accommodations I must make, I am nonetheless grateful for the opportunity such accommodations provide. It is one of the many ironies I have come to appreciate since I came to your life, all those centuries ago, when you pulled me from my tomb.

If you receive this, I would be grateful for an answer, no matter how long it may take to reach me; I can be patient when I must. I know the blood-bond between us is unbroken, and will be so until one or the other of us is wholly gone from this world, but a few words on a sheet of vellum are always welcome, for I cannot help but recall those times when your silence was the result of difficulties beyond the usual for our kind, and how nearly I came to losing you at those times. Delhi may not be Saxony, or Spain, or Tunis, or the Land of Snows, but the remoteness of the place troubles me; indeed, you may have already left that city for places still more remote, and where this will not find you for a number of years. I cannot help but be worried that you will go to a place I cannot discover you, as you have done before, and that I will have to wait decades to know what has become of you. Or worse: you may die the True Death far from me, and I will not be able to mourn you except through the breaking of the blood-bond. I am still Roman enough to want to make a monument for you, if I must lose you, as an outward sign of my inward grief. You may chide me for needless anxiety if you like, but I cannot be entirely sanguine with you so far away, and Timur-i on the rampage, and the Turks up in arms against him. If you tell me all is well, I will try not to fret too much.

When next I write to you—assuming I learn in the next few years where to find you—it will probably be from Rome. Greece is all very well as a place of escape, but I grow homesick for my native earth, and, as I have said, it will be soon that Niklos and I will depart, and not solely because I miss my homeland; we have been here long enough to engender questions I would prefer not to answer. Rome may be half a ruin, but it is my ruin, and I long to see the broken walls of the Flavian Circus again, and to walk the roads the Legions trod so long ago. And before I grow maudlin, I will send this on its long journey, telling you it brings my

Everlasting love,
Olivia

on Rhodes on the 17th day of March in the Christian year 1397

5

Although his hair was rust-colored and his eyes grey-green, the pilgrim was from the vast grasslands and desert in the far west of China; his staff and begging-bowl were his only belongings, his one tattered robe his only clothing; his feet were misshapen from his arduous walking. Sunburn had made his skin a ruddy-brown and toughened it to the texture of leather. He held out his bowl to Rustam Iniattir and asked—in a fairly good version of the local dialect—for water and a handful of rice or lentils. "For the Buddha. I ask for the Buddha."

Rustam Iniattir shook his head. "I am not a follower of the Buddha," he said, preparing to leave his house and enter the busy, mid-morning bustle of the streets; he tried to shrug past the pilgrim only to have the man sink down at his feet.

"No. You are Parsi. You follow Zarathustra," said the pilgrim in a thread of a voice. "I have met your caravan in my travels." He ducked his head. "I was told you are a worthy man, that you would not turn a pilgrim from your door."

"My slaves will give you lentils, and water, if you knock on the side-gate," said Rustam Iniattir, still attempting to leave.

The pilgrim pulled himself a short way, then moaned as he scraped his left foot on the dusty step; a trail of blood appeared through the thick calluses of his bare sole. He huddled in shame, not looking at Rustam Iniattir. "In the Buddha's name, I thank you for your charity." It was the usual acknowledgment of alms, and ordinarily Rustam Iniattir would have heard it and gone on his way, but the pain in the pilgrim's every lineament held his attention.

"What happened to your foot?" he asked, pausing to look down at the pilgrim.

"In the mountains between Khotan and Lahore, I . . . was injured. Occasionally it distracts me from my purpose." He stared at Rustam Iniattir. "It has taught me the truth of *Followers of the Buddha should learn to endure all discomforts: heat, cold, hunger, thirst, and pain.*" He brought his features back under control. "I am all right. I must atone for my lapse."

"It might be better to have that foot examined and treated," said Rustam Iniattir. "You could easily be made ill by it."

"That is dharma," said the pilgrim, getting onto his knees and pulling himself up his walking staff.

"You are prepared to let it kill you?" Rustam Iniattir asked, incredulity making his voice rise. "I did not know the Buddha expected such immolation from his followers." He did not want this pilgrim to come to harm in front of his house, for that could result in questions being asked by those in authority that would not redound to his advantage; the Sultan's deputies would exact a high price for such a misfortune.

The pilgrim shrugged. "I take what the world sends me, that I may become indifferent to it, as the Buddha was in His Compassion."

"And do you not accept compassion from anyone?" His voice sharpened as the possibilities of the situation became more obvious to him. "You are suffering, little as you want to admit it. You deny others the chance to show their compassion so that you may perfect yourself? Would you reserve Enlightenment for yourself alone? You will take alms but nothing more?" Rustam Iniattir reached out to the pilgrim and helped him to stand, noticing as he did that the man's skin was very hot; he was glad now that he had listened to his aunt's husband discourse on the precepts of the Buddha. "You are suffering, and there can be an end to it. You need not deny your hurt because it is from the world. The Buddha does not require that you embrace infection to show you are not moved by the needs of the flesh; I know that much of his teaching." He paused, and continued in a resigned tone, not quite knowing why he bothered, but unable to leave the pilgrim to his begging and his fever, "I am acquainted with a man who is most capable with medicaments. Let me take you to him so he can treat you, that you may continue your pilgrimage. He will give you ease for your hurts." He felt puzzled with himself, but he remembered that Zarathustra had taught it was a sign of belief to aid those in need; it would be a worthy act, and it would get this strange pilgrim away from his house. "I will take you to him."

The pilgrim shook his head. "I should master this."

"And so you shall, once it has been treated. You are not an old man, pilgrim, and you should not throw your life away. To die tranquilly in old age is a high achievement, but to surrender your life to stubbornness is not. If you have too much pride to be healed . . ." He left the rest unspoken, for he knew enough of Buddhist teaching to suppose the pilgrim would be shocked by such an accusation.

The pilgrim nodded, his face unable to conceal the chagrin he felt. "I will go with you." He steadied himself with his staff. "But I seek nothing but the end of desire."

"Certainly," said Rustam Iniattir. "I will walk slowly." He stepped into the stream of people on the street, his attention on the pilgrim; he did not see Josha Dar emerge from behind a stack of cotton bales to go after them.

"Your caravan was bound for Herat. The leader said he is your cousin," said the pilgrim, as if he needed to explain more thoroughly why he came to Rustam Iniattir.

"That he is—the son of my father's sister," said Rustam Iniattir. Most of the leaders of his caravans were his relatives, either by blood or by marriage; it was one of the few ways he could ensure honesty in his distant transactions.

"A good man," said the pilgrim, "as far as the world goes."

"That he is," said Rustam Iniattir, not wanting to debate with this stranger the merits of worldly ambitions and success, for he knew from experience with his aunt's husband that such discussions led nowhere, serving only to frustrate all who participated in them. As he reached the corner of a broad central street, he asked the pilgrim, "Do you have a name, pilgrim? What shall I call you?"

"I am from Kua-chou in Shensi, and I am called Lum." He spoke flatly, as if he did not like imparting so much.

"Lum is your family name, or your personal name?" asked Rustam Iniattir, who had had dealings with the Chinese before and took pride in knowing some of their traditions.

"Lum is my personal name. I no longer have a family name," said the pilgrim, and did not elaborate.

"Lum from Kua-chou in Shensi it is, then," said Rustam Iniattir as he stood aside for three vile-smelling camels to pass; he made sure Lum was right behind him. "Why should you come into Delhi, Lum?"

"To see the shrines to the Buddha; I have vowed to visit all the places holy to the Buddha that I can before I cast off this body, for the sake of my soul and the protection of my family. Delhi has a shrine I wish to see. I had learned that the Mui were here," he went on, using the Chinese word for Muslims, "but I know them from before. We see many of them, as we see the Black-Haired, in Kua-chou. We have been there longer than any of them, though we are few and they are vast in their numbers." He held his staff more tightly.

"Good enough," said Rustam Iniattir, resuming his slow pace now the camels were by them, their bells tinkling as they stalked through the market-square at the other end of the street. "It isn't far to the house we seek, and the man who will help you; you will soon see for yourself how much skill he has in treating injuries," he went on. "He, too, is a foreigner, and must live in this quarter of the city."

Lum nodded. "It is the way." He was managing to walk fairly easily now, his pace steady for all its sluggishness; behind them Josha Dar slipped along from door to door, never taking his eyes from the two. He grinned in anticipation of what he would report that evening, for surely he would deserve a reward for his diligence.

At the entrance to the Street of the Brass Lanterns, Rustam Iniattir paused once again so that Lum could rest. "Almost there," he said, still perplexed with himself for the help he was extending to this unlikely pilgrim from China. Perhaps, he told himself, Sanat Ji Mani would understand his actions and explain them to him.

"Your acquaintance is wealthy," said Lum with suspicion as he peered down the street, his eyes narrowed to slits at the finery he saw around him. "These are very fine houses."

"It seems he is," Rustam Iniattir agreed carefully.

"Yet he will tend to a pilgrim?" Lum was dubious and reluctant to go on.

"That you will learn when you speak to him," said Rustam Iniattir, making this a challenge. "He has tended to others before you."

"If he receives me at all, he may send me away," said Lum. "But I will go with you to his house."

Rustam Iniattir did not know what to say in response to this. He folded his arms and very nearly left Lum where he stood. Then he mastered his annoyance and led the pilgrim forward again.

Garuda opened the door to the urgent summons of the clapper; he peered out at the Parsi and sighed. "My master is in his library. He is busy today." Little as he wanted to admit Rustam Iniattir and his companion, Garuda did not have the authority to refuse them entry; he opened the door with an air of condescension that would have earned him a rebuke had Sanat Ji Mani or Rojire seen him; he was a native of Delhi, he reminded himself, and this was his city where foreigners had to be tolerated.

"Then go tell him Rustam Iniattir is come with a pilgrim in need of his help," was the crisp response.

"If you insist," said Garuda. "But he may not wish to be disturbed."

"He will decide that for himself when you inform him," said Rustam Iniattir patiently, used to the attitude of Indian servants with foreign masters.

"You will wait here," said Garuda, and vanished into the interior of the splendid house.

"This is not the abode of a humble man," said Lum.

"It is the home of a wealthy one, in any case," said Rustam Iniattir. The small courtyard where Rustam Iniattir and Lum waited was decorated with potted plants and a number of small statues, some of familiar gods, some of unknown ones. Lum noticed a Teaching Buddha set in the shade of a flowering bush, and touched his hands together as he bowed to it; Rustam Iniattir turned away, knowing it was rude to watch a man at worship.

"My master," said Garuda as he returned, "will see you in his study. If you will follow me?"

Knowing it was useless to remind Garuda that he knew the way, Rustam Iniattir touched Lum on the shoulder. "We will go with this servant."

Lum only nodded and moved along behind Garuda. He kept his gaze steadily ahead, so that he would not be caught up in the elegance around him, a sign of worldliness that would compromise his dedication to asceticism and the Buddha. He almost stumbled going down a shallow flight of stairs; he gave a little cry of pain and dismay, saying immediately, "It is nothing."

"I think perhaps you have come here just in time," said Rustam Iniattir, who, aware now of how feverish Lum was, made no attempt at concealing his alarm. He stopped at the door where Garuda paused; Rustam Iniattir scratched on the wood and was relieved when he heard the foreigner call, "Enter," from within.

"When you are leaving, summon me," said Garuda as he withdrew farther along the hall.

"That I will," said Rustam Iniattir as he opened the door and stood aside for Lum to precede him.

Sanat Ji Mani, in a Persian kandys of fine black linen and loose Persian trousers of heavy dark-red cotton, was seated at a rosewood table, four antique scrolls lying open before him. A shaded window let in the perfume of blossoms, and the subdued light was pleasant for the eyes. He rose as he took stock of the pilgrim, then turned to Rustam Iniattir. "You have brought someone to me?"

"I have. He was begging in front of my house. He is injured. I thought it would be best to put him in your care," said Rustam Iniattir, his tone uncertain as he stayed in the doorway. "I could not ignore him. It is not our way." He said this last pointedly, for the custom of the worshipers of Shiva and the rest of the pantheon of Brahmin gods were disinclined to take an active part in the lives of any strangers.

"You have done well, Rustam Iniattir, and I thank you," said Sanat Ji Mani with a sincerity that took the Parsi aback.

"How can you be grateful?" Rustam Iniattir inquired, more baffled than ever.

"Do you wish to treat me?" Lum asked at the same moment, incredulously.

Nodding, Sanat Ji Mani approached Lum. "You will need treatment if you are to continue your journey. You are a pilgrim, I see from your staff and gourd, and by the look of you, you come from the western reaches of China."

Lum blinked in surprise. "I am from Shensi, the fortress-town of Kua-chou."

"Near the end of the Great Wall, is it not," Sanat Ji Mani said, looking intently at the newcomer. "I was there once, many years ago." He did not mention that those years were reckoned in centuries, or that, when he was there, the world was in disarray and Kua-chou was under siege and in the grip of famine.

"Yes," said Lum, making an effort not to be astonished.

"Not many there are dedicated to the Buddha," said Sanat Ji Mani conversationally. "You must have come by your faith in an unusual way."

Lum went silent at once; he turned away from Sanat Ji Mani, dismay and rebuke in his weathered visage. "How can you treat my foot?" His blank face made it plain he would say nothing more about himself.

"It depends on what is wrong with it," said Sanat Ji Mani as if unaware of the state of the pilgrim's mind.

"Is there any reason I should remain?" Rustam Iniattir asked abruptly.

"Not on my account," said Sanat Ji Mani. "If there is something more you would like to discuss with Lum, it might be best to come back before sundown. He should be feeling better by then."

"Well?" Rustam Iniattir said to Lum. "Shall I return?"

"If you want to know more of your kinsman who told me to seek you out," said Lum, the tone of his voice revealing much more than the words he spoke. "Otherwise, you need not concern yourself with me."

"I think it would be a solace to you and to Lum if you see him improved," said Sanat Ji Mani, aware of how much curiosity the Parsi possessed, and how alone the Chinese pilgrim felt.

"Solace. Yes," said Rustam Iniattir, seizing on this acceptable excuse and looking over at Lum. "I will come again, when I go to pray."

"It is as you wish," said Lum with studied indifference.

Rustam Iniattir made a formal gesture of departure and stepped out of the study, to find Garuda waiting for him. "Well, I might have anticipated this: you are named for a mighty bird, and you perch everywhere, and you seek to see everything," he said to the under-steward, careful not to make his observation too comminatory.

"My father was devoted to Vishnu," said Garuda. "He named me to honor the god's mount." He pointed his finger at Rustam Iniattir, something he would not do had the Parsi been of his own people. "You do not honor the gods."

"We honor Zarathustra's teachings," said Rustam Iniattir, and began to stride down the corridor. "You have your gods, I have mine. And your master has his." This last reminder was intended to remind Garuda of his position in the household, and it succeeded.

"I meant nothing against you, O Guest of My Master," Garuda said, lowering his eyes and assuming a self-effacing manner. As they reached the garden-courtyard, Garuda went directly to the outer door and held it open for Rustam Iniattir. "May you go in safety."

"May your gods show you favor," said Rustam Iniattir, giving more attention to this servant than he would have done any member of his own household. With a slight inclination of his head, he departed, stepping out into the street with a frown of displeasure marring his features; he still wondered if his concern for the pilgrim Lum had sprung from the altruism of Zarathustra's teaching, or from some less worthy impulse. He would have to return to his shrine to appeal to Ormazd to reveal to him what had caused him to extend his help to so unlikely a man as Lum. He was so preoccupied that he was unaware of Josha Dar as he joined the people in the street.

In the house of Sanat Ji Mani, Lum was not yet at his ease. He clung to his staff and listened skeptically to what the black-clad foreigner was saying. "It is not right that I should rid myself of suffering while the world suffers so much," he declared, interrupting Sanat Ji Mani's explanation of what might be done for him.

Sanat Ji Mani shook his head once. "You do not think that the Buddha expects you to embrace your ailments; that would be inappropriate, and self-indulgent. Did not the Buddha teach that to refuse the antidote to poison is an embracing of ignorance and suffering? You have been poisoned by your wound and now you have the opportunity to recover. The Buddha would not encourage you to forgo it."

"You cannnot know the Holy Texts." Lum was apprehensive now, as if he had to prevent Sanat Ji Mani from examining him; better not to know what injury he had sustained than to be helped by this foreign man.

"I know more Holy Texts than you can imagine," said Sanat Ji Mani with a note of weariness in his voice that caught Lum's attention. "So, yes: I know the Buddha did not encourage his followers to seek suffering, or to—"

"Do not preach my faith to me," said Lum sharply.

Sanat Ji Mani shook his head. "You are afraid, and fear is born of illusion, according to your Holy Texts. I believe the Buddha taught that a man's inner mind is more his enemy than any external foe; you have allied yourself against your body's health, and that is not a sign of virtue, but of irresponsibility."

Lum stared down at his foot as if he wanted to be able to disown it. "It should not impose so much."

"Bodies are like that; they impose," said Sanat Ji Mani as gently as he could. "Come with me, and we will deal with this as quickly as possible."

"Are you certain you can heal me?" Lum wanted to know before he moved.

"I am certain I can treat you. Your healing is as much up to you as to my medicaments," Sanat Ji Mani replied. "It may be that you can improve on your own, but I doubt it."

"Why do you say that?" Lum asked, remaining where he stood.

"Because your flesh smells of inner decay; it is not strong yet, so you may still be able to recover from it," said Sanat Ji Mani in a level voice. "Those of my blood are sensitive to such odors. Many another might not recognize it, but I have known that scent of old." As he said it, a nimiety of memories came back to him of the sick, the wounded, the dying: disease, war, famine, flood, fire, devastation—he had seen them for over three millennia and had never grown used to any of them. "If you have no treatment, you will surely die of that inner decay. It will get into your blood and that will be the end of you."

For a long moment Lum said nothing, and then he started toward the door. "I believe you. You may treat my foot, but you will do nothing beyond that. I do not wish to lose my simplicity."

"If your simplicity is genuine, you have nothing to fear; health will not imperil you," said Sanat Ji Mani, his words a bit brisker than they had been. He held the door and pointed toward the flight of stairs at the end of the hall. "Go to the next level. I will follow you."

Shrugging awkwardly as he steadied himself on his staff, Lum did as he was told; climbing the stairs proved more difficult than he had anticipated, for his balance was precarious, and pain slowed him down. Little as he wanted to admit it, the opportunity for treatment allowed him to admit how much discomfort he was in, and it troubled him. As he reached the top of the stairs, he stopped again. "Where should I go?"

"Fourth door on the right, the one with the brass latch," said Sanat Ji Mani. "You need not announce yourself; the room is empty."

"Very well." Lum stumped his way along to the door and pressed the latch. As the door swung open, he nearly fell.

Sanat Ji Mani was at his side at once, steadying him and supporting him across the floor to the bed set against an elaborate screen. "Lie down here," said Sanat Ji Mani, and then he called out "Rojire!"

Lum was just settling down on the bed, his staff set against the wall and his begging bowl on a shelf beside it, when a middle-aged servant in a short blue-grey kaftan came into the room. "My master?" If the sight of Lum surprised him, he made no sign of it.

"I need a vial of my sovereign remedy, clean bandages, a strong drawing poultice, a cleansing agent—the aloe-and-spikenard should do it—and a draught of syrup of poppies," said Sanat Ji Mani. "All that and a basin of hot water, along with my narrow knives, if you would, please." He looked down at Lum. "Perhaps later willow-bark tea, to bring down his fever and stop the worst of the swelling."

"As you wish," said Rojire, and withdrew.

"My manservant will not be long," said Sanat Ji Mani, going to examine Lum's feet. "Your injury to your left foot is damaging your right. You are pulling the sinews of your right foot in compensation for the injury to your left," he said as he looked them over. "How long ago did you injure the left, and how did you do it?"

"It was three or four weeks since it began to pain me. The hurt itself took place sometime before that," said Lum. "I was coming down the mountains to Lahore, and a long, thin spike went into my foot. I removed it easily enough, and washed out the dirt that built up on the drying blood. I supposed I needed to do little more than that; my soles are as tough as camels' feet." He caught his lower lip between his teeth, as if describing the event made his affliction worse. "In a few days, the hurt seemed gone, and I thought no more about it. Until I was on the road here, and it began to hurt once more, and the puncture opened."

"The ailment was inside your body, not outside," said Sanat Ji Mani as he laid his hand very softly on the infected foot. "It is hot."

"Yes," said Lum. "And my body has taken the heat." He said this reluctantly, a sense of shame going through him as intense as his fever. "It goes from my foot upward."

"Yes, it has," Sanat Ji Mani agreed grimly, wondering if the pilgrim's foot could be saved at all. "I hope it is not too deep in your body."

"I have allowed myself to be brought into the world, to be turned from my mission, and all for a spike in my foot." He licked his lips and said something in his own tongue, a dialect Sanat Ji Mani had heard but did not know.

"You have not erred, Lum," said Sanat Ji Mani as kindly as he could. "The world is full of spikes and thorns and stings."

"All the more reason not to be caught by them." He twisted in an effort to look at his feet, then lay back. "I strive to rid myself of all desire."

"Then do not desire to do yourself harm," Sanat Ji Mani recommended. He took a step back and studied Lum: the man was very ill, that much was obvious. There were faint, reddish lines leading from his foot up his ankle, a sure sign that the decay had taken hold. "I will clean out your wound and treat the flesh. You will have to remain here, off your feet, until the decay is stopped." He lowered his head. "I trust you will be willing to do what is best for your recuperation, though it is not how you have lived of late."

"If I improve I will decide," said Lum. "May I have some water? I am thirsty."

"Of course," said Sanat Ji Mani. "But just a very little bit now. I will give you a sleeping draught shortly, and when you waken, I will have a great flask of cold tea for you."

Lum was immediately suspicious. "Why should I have a sleeping draught?"

Sanat Ji Mani regarded him patiently. "I will have to draw the decay from your flesh. It will be painful, and you are likely to thrash around if you are not asleep. I will have enough to do to get the decay out of you without having to fight you in the process." He gave Lum a little time to consider this, then added, "You will have less done to you if you are asleep."

It was a while before Lum nodded. "All right. If it is what you must do, then I will consent." He closed his eyes as if experimenting with sleep. "How long will I sleep?"

"As long as necessary, I trust," said Sanat Ji Mani, and looked up as Rojire came into the room with a box in his arms.

"The basin of hot water is coming. Bohdil is bringing it." He put down the box and opened the top. "The servants are talking," he said in Roman vernacular.

"Yes," said Sanat Ji Mani so indifferently that Rojire was not sure he had understood.

"They are saying you have allowed a dying man into this house— a dying foreigner." Rojire saw that Lum was listening. "You know they dislike the omen."

"Let them say what they want," said Sanat Ji Mani, looking through the items in the box.

"I could forbid them," Rojire suggested.

"They would only talk the more, and outside these walls," Sanat Ji Mani told him as he took out the large vial of syrup of poppies. "Make a draught of this for Lum; I will need it in a short while," he went on in the local dialect. "He will need to sleep deeply."

"How deeply?" Rojire asked.

"Deeply enough to permit me to complete what I must do, and then to have a restorative time, so he may regain his strength." Sanat Ji Mani took out the bandages, setting them on a low table near the bed Lum occupied. "And boil my knives with stringent herbs after they are sharpened." It was a trick he had learned from the physicians with the Roman Legions, and he had never found reason to abandon the practice. "When they are ready, bring them to me on a fresh drying cloth."

"Do you want anything more from the kitchen?" Rojire asked.

"Yes. Tell them to make a combination of green and willow-bark teas, and cool it, for Lum to drink when he wakens." Sanat Ji Mani had his drawing poultice out, and he spoke to Lum. "I am going to apply this to your foot. It is very strong and you may find it uncomfortable, but, if you are able, remain lying on your back. If it becomes too unpleasant, tell me."

"You are going to use the poultice now?" Rojire stopped in the door.

"Yes. As soon as the basin of hot water is here so I can wash his foot and see how much of it the injury has corrupted." Sanat Ji Mani maintained his calm demeanor, though he was keenly aware of the difficulty ahead of him.

"And after you apply the poultice?" Rojire promted.

"When it has had time to work, I will see if the infection will drain; if it does not, I will open the wound so that it can be cleaned. Then I will dress his foot with my sovereign remedy and bandage it so that it has a chance to heal." He was aware that these questions were being asked for Lum's benefit, for Rojire had helped Sanat Ji Mani tend the sick and injured since Vespasianus ruled in Rome. "We will see how he goes for the night and in the morning we will decide how to proceed." He looked down at Lum. "You may have to rest for a day or two, but you may use that time for meditation." He knew any recovery would take much longer than a few days, but he did not want to add to Lum's distress.

Lum could not entirely conceal his alarm. "The Parsi is returning tonight," he reminded Sanat Ji Mani. "He will expect me to depart with him."

"I will explain matters to him," said Sanat Ji Mani, and turned as Bohdil scratched on the door. "The hot water comes." He went to open the door, astonishing Lum in doing such a humble task while Rojire was in the room to serve him. "Put it down on the floor at the foot of the bed."

Bohdil did as he was told, watching Lum out of the tail of his eye. "Is there anything more?" he asked hopefully.

"Rojire will go with you to the kitchen, and give you instructions," Sanat Ji Mani said as he took a soft cloth in his hand and sat on the floor at the foot of the bed where Lum lay. "I am sorry that this will be painful."

Lum could not keep from tightening his fists in anticipation. "I am ready. Do as you must."

Taking Bohdil by the elbow, Rojire guided him out of the room into the hallway and toward the back-stairs, leaving Sanat Ji Mani to begin his ministrations to the red-haired Chinese pilgrim.

Text of a report submitted to Murmar bin Tughluq, the Sultan's Minister of Taxes, Rents, and Revenues, by his cousin, Balban Ihbal bin Tughluq.

In the glorious Name of the One God Allah, the acknowledgment of the one True Faith, which is Islam, and in highest respect and devotion to our kinsman the Sultan, this brings the greetings and protestations of devotion to you, Murmar bin Tughluq, and to our family, on this, the shortest night of the year.

I have been compiling reports from various informants throughout the city, and in consultation with others of our family serving the Will of the Sultan, the substance of which I present to you now, as I will present the same to the Sultan—may Allah give him long life and many sons—at the first opportunity. I ask you to make note of the contents and to correct any error you may find in the material, so that all the information I provide to the Sultan—may his splendor increase from year to year—will be as useful as it may be, and garner us distinction among our kinsmen.

I have listened to the trader Mahannad of Meerut, who arrived not three days ago, and who has reported that there is fear that Timur-i Lenkh is moving again, and perhaps will come in this direction. If he does this, we will need to improve the number and quality of arms we have for the defense of this city. It is said that the speed of Timur-i's cavalry is swifter than demons can cross the sands, that his horses trot from dawn until sunset without slowing or tiring, so that his men go five or six times as far in a day as most cavalry does. This may be a lie, but we cannot afford to think it is, or to ignore the implication. I recommend we prepare for sudden attack, and to that end, you should increase customs taxes for all traders entering and leaving the city. You should also be alert to the presence of spies among those who enter and leave the city, for it is not unlikely that our enemies will seek to discover the extent of our preparedness as well as determine who among our population might be counted on to support their ambitions. The world is not so friendly a place that you can ignore the possibility that Timur-i, or some of his men, will not do their utmost to enter Delhi and seize its riches to their own ends. While I pray that this will never happen, I believe it is wisest to be prepared for such an eventuality.

I have a number of other informants among the population, and now I am being told by them that many of the foreigners living here fear for their safety, should there be an attack on Delhi. Many of the foreigners suppose that we will use them to buy the safety of our own people. I have instructed my informants to make note of which foreigners among us complain of this the most vociferously, so that we may be alert to their fright-mongering and so do our utmost to silence all of those who would lead the people to panic. One of my informants has said he has heard camel-drivers say they do not wish to come here for a while, for they have heard rumors from Trebizond to Shiraz that Timur-i is going to come here. Another informant has said that pilgrims coming here are afraid to linger, not wanting to become hostages in a war that could break out at any time. A third informant I have tells me that foreigners who have lived here for some time are begin-

ning to worry that they may be made to bear the brunt of the cost of any war, and many are seeking to hoard or hide their wealth so they will not suffer too many losses at the hands of your officers.

I am posting more men in the markets, so that they may monitor all that is being said, as well as make note of the strangers who venture among us. I have the services of many good men, and the reports of others set to watch specific foreigners. I have made these various men loyal to me by my assurance of money for reliable information, and protection from any actions taken against them by the foreigners in question. I have detailed accounts for all these men, and if you are interested in what they contain, you have only to ask and I will provide you with faithful copies of their accounts, as I have already indicated. You will find, if you decide to review these accounts, that we will do well to be vigilant in our efforts to keep a close watch on the people of the city who speak against us, particularly those who are foreigners, and therefore more willing to sell their loyalty to other foreigners.

There is a party of pilgrims bound for Mecca who will leave at the next full moon, six days from now. I have decided to ask five of the men making this holy journey to become our eyes and ears in their travels, so that upon their return, we may have the advantage of their observations, the better to be ready against any attack that may come. It is altogether fitting that pilgrims do this for us, for they have the opportunity to travel without any fear that Timur-i would keep them from completing their pilgrimage; he does not interfere with pious men, for which we may thank Allah, the All-Merciful.

We will have to persuade the Sultan to consider coming here to make himself seen if we are going to be able to quiet the apprehension among the people of our city. My informants are convinced that one of the reasons there is so much unease is that the Sultan is busy tending to reinforcing his fortresses and is not paying heed to the protection of Delhi. While you and I understand that the fortresses are in more need of repair and reinforcement than Delhi is, our people do not know this, and they see his continuing absence as an indication of his own fear, and not a demonstration of his circumspection. I do not know if they will continue to accept the Sultan's deputies as carrying his authority while he is gone. If we cannot maintain our authority, it may be that a single rumor will be enough to throw the people into panic and leave us exposed to ruin as surely as if Timur-i and his cavalry were at our gates. You may believe that we are protected, but my informants convince me that this is not necessarily the case; I feel it incumbent upon me to inform you of this on behalf of our kinsman, the Sultan—may Allah favor and protect him and his people—so that we may continue to do his will.

Balban Ihbal bin Tughluq

carried by mute and deaf messenger for mutual protection

6

"I have been thinking about what you told me," said Avasa Dani as she leaned over Sanat Ji Mani, her arms going around his neck from behind; it was a still evening, with the lingering heat of the day drawing the aroma of flowers and greenery into the air, so that the library of his house smelled of jasmine and ginger.

"And what was that?" Sanat Ji Mani countered, turning his head to kiss her before rolling up the scroll open before him.

"About what would happen to me if you and I were to fulfill our needs together again; I have had many weeks to consider what you said." She rested her head on his shoulder, her arms remaining around him. "You said that if we lie together one more time, I would partake of your nature, and become like you upon my death if my body was not beheaded or burned."

"Or your spine severed in any other way," Sanat Ji Mani said somberly; he put the scroll aside and swung around to face her. "It is not something to consider lightly."

"So you informed me," she said, and kissed his brow. "I would have to live on the passion of the living, and their blood. I would have to avoid full sunlight unless I was guarded by my native earth. I would not be able to cross running water. It is all very troubling," she admitted. "The more I consider it, the more reservations I feel."

"Good; give full attention to those reservations. I do not want you to change to my life if you have any doubts about it: it is a momentous step to take, and it is not an easy way to live," he agreed. "There are necessary precautions I mentioned to you, and which you must include in your lucubrations: I keep chests of my native earth with me in my travels whenever I can, and I line my soles with that earth once a month. Direct sunlight is still uncomfortable for me, as it is for all who come to my life. I have my native earth in my saddles and the floors of my carriages, but it is sometimes not sufficient to keep me from real pain; without such protection, open sunlight can be agony for me. It would be the same for you."

Avasa Dani sighed. "If my children had lived, I would not consider any of this," she said slowly. "But they died shortly after they were born, poor, shriveled creatures not many weeks old, and looking ancient as men of fifty."

Sanat Ji Mani stared at her. "You did not mention your children."

"No." She looked toward the window. "There is little to mention. There were two of them, three years apart, both girls, which embarrassed my husband, who was sure he was at fault for taking pleasure in the body, and so he stopped. Then he gave himself to the Buddha, and put his dead children behind him forever."

"I am very sorry," said Sanat Ji Mani. "I should have realized it was more than hurt about your husband leaving that was in you. If there is anything—"

"You can make me like you," she responded at once. "I will have no grandchildren, and so I must have longevity, or perish completely."

"Longevity at a price," Sanat Ji Mani reminded her. "And one has already been exacted from you." He was puzzled by her state of mind, and sought to find a way to understand. "You will not be able to reclaim a family."

"I understand that." She smiled wistfully. "But I will have something that is mine—a life that I have shaped, not that has been shaped for me."

"You cannot entirely escape the demands of those around you; none of us can," Sanat Ji Mani warned her. "If you make the attempt, you will draw unwanted attention to yourself, and you will be thought a monster."

"Even over time?" Avasa Dani asked. "Will it always be thus?"

"It has been so far," he answered somberly.

"Yet you say that you have lived long," said Avasa Dani, "for all you must do to keep living."

"Longer than you can imagine. More than three thousand years." He knew she did not truly believe him, but he went on. "My father's kingdom was overrun by his enemies, his children slain or made slaves; I was one of the latter; they did not know that I could not be killed by the method they tried, for I had been initiated into the priesthood of our people, and was proof against most deaths. I could also have no children from the time I was initiated, as is true of all who come to my life." His hand went to the center of his torso; he could feel the old, white scars left over from his disemboweling that had put an end to his breathing life, so long ago.

"You are not dead," said Avasa Dani; her silver earrings rang their high notes.

"Not in the usual sense, no," Sanat Ji Mani replied. "But I do not live as you do, nor any of those around you."

"Did you have children, when you lived?" Avasa Dani held her breath as she waited for an answer, her hand brushing his arm as if to gain strength from that minor contact.

"I was given to our god, who made me like him when I was still a boy. Those born at the dark of the year did not have heirs. I had nephews and nieces, but it is not the same thing," he said steadily.

"No, it is not." She tried to laugh and failed. "Why do you tell me this? You make yourself more a stranger than you are."

"Because I do not want to expose you to an existence you may not desire for yourself. It is difficult to maintain this kind of life. Once you become of my blood, you will be a stranger wherever you are, and however you live, because you will not be one of the truly living. Those of my blood live in constant exile, and nothing can change that, Avasa Dani, not fortune, not honors, not the fulfillment of your heart's desire. Do not discount the price of being always a stranger: it is exacted in many, many ways." He took her face in his hands. "You do not have the opportunities I do; women in this part of the world are not often given much liberty." Nor did they have it in other parts of the world, he added to himself, but there were places where the limitations placed on women were not quite so severe. "Here most women lead sequestered lives, and the few who do not are scrutinized constantly. You cannot readily travel on your own, or establish yourself in many cities beyond the Sultanate without putting yourself at risk."

"I might find a way to accommodate your life, and mine," she ventured. "If I decide to be like you, I may not need to relinquish everything from my life."

Sanat Ji Mani shook his head. "You cannot change by halves: I want you to understand that once you are one of my blood, you cannot turn from it unless you die the True Death."

"The True Death," she mused aloud. "It sounds dreadful."

"I cannot say; I have not yet experienced it," he told her, recalling the torment he felt whenever one of his blood came to the end of life. "I do know that once one of mine has died the True Death, the blood-bond is broken, but not until then." He kissed her mouth gently. "You will not dishearten me if you prefer to stay as you are."

She kissed him with fervor. "You say the bond endures until the True Death?" she asked when she could speak again.

"Yes. Once you have changed, once you have died the first death and come to my life, the bond is constant, one of the few consolations of our state." He touched her cheek, so lightly that the breeze through the room seemed more palpable. "Do not think that living as one of my blood must live is easily done for male or female. I fear it is nothing of the sort."

"You are going to warn me once more that I may have difficulties if I become like you, are you not? that I will have to change how I live. You want to protect me, I assume, and I am grateful that you do." She moved back a step, out of his immediate reach. "I know I should listen to you, and consider all you say; I have thought of little else for the last six weeks, and meditated on all you told me, and written down my thoughts as they became clear to me, so that I might contemplate them further. Among other things, I have pondered the adversities of travel, and the daunting prospects of being among strangers in faraway places. Then I have compared those risks to those

I would encounter remaining here in Delhi, as I am, and I know I should be prudent, circumspect—but I am not so willing to set aside the advantage you offer as you want me to be."

"How do you mean?" he asked, his dark eyes on her, his demeanor serene, his voice mellifluous and level.

"You have told me the disadvantages, but there must be advantages, other than living longer than most do. You have not elected to live as you have for as long as you have because it is an abhorrent obligation." She let the observation hang between them. "For all the difficulties you encounter, they are not sufficient to—You are not so overcome by the demands of your circumstances that you find it more a burden than a benefit."

"That does not mean it is not a burden," Sanat Ji Mani said seriously. "On occasion I feel it most heavily. All of us do."

"Life as the living know it can be that way as well, for some without surcease," said Avasa Dani. "You do not suppose that all of us never have much to bear."

"No; I do not suppose that. Life demands much of the living," said Sanat Ji Mani, his memories roused by her remark.

"Then you should also realize that many of us would not reject out of hand what you offer," she said somberly.

Sanat Ji Mani said nothing for a short while, then told her, "Many have, and for excellent reasons. There are stringent demands on women who choose this existence."

"There are demands on a woman in *this* existence, and well you know it," Avasa Dani countered. "To be hemmed in and constrained on every side by law and tradition from the day of birth to the end of our lives, to—"

"And that will not change simply because you do," Sanat Ji Mani warned her. "You will not escape the strictures of the place in which you live. You will always be isolated once those who were your living companions have died and you remain alive. In fifty years all your contemporaries will be gone, in a century, most of their grandchildren will be. If you remain here, you will quickly become an object of fear, so you will need to leave Delhi. You must go to where you are not known." He thought of Olivia, her annoyance at her self-imposed banishment on Rhodes, and wondered if she had returned to Rome yet, to her native earth and the sanctuary it provided. "Hazardous as travel is for men, it is more so for women, and those of my blood need to travel."

"You are discouraging me," Avasa Dani accused him. "You may tell me as many times as you like, you will not frighten me."

"I am not trying to: I am trying to tell you what you will have to face," he replied quietly, a lonely tenderness in his dark eyes. "To be of my blood is irrevocable. There is no retreat from it, no modification of our true nature, no means to avoid our need. You cannot be half a vampire and half a living woman. So I repeat: you may not want to do all that you must to live the life those of my blood must live. Once you change, you cannot return to what you were." A sharp image of Heugenet fixed in his thoughts, and he realized one of the most pressing reasons for his reservations regarding Avasa Dani was linked to Heugenet, who had knowingly come to his life only to relinquish it a decade ago when she no longer needed to protect her son and his position.

"But you will help me," she said, kissing his ear. "To live your life."

"When I can," he assured her. "But we will not often be together, and you will need to fend for yourself."

She rested her hands on either side of his neck. "Then you will not take me with you when you go?"

"You may be living still then," he reminded her. "Your uncles would do their utmost to keep me from taking you from this city, no matter what rights your husband granted me."

"I do not care. If you go, you must take me with you, living, and put me where I may wait for death without fear," she told him.

"Your husband's family would be—"

"I would be gone, so it hardly matters what they would be. My family might have to pay back my dowry, but otherwise they would not mind, since I can provide them money enough that no cost will come to them. I am something of an embarrassment to them now, and they would not be upset if I were no longer here." She sounded more saddened than angry, but her hands tightened. "If I am in a place where you are, I will be safe enough. You will not discourage me, Sanat Ji Mani. You have offered me a gift, and I accept it with full understanding."

"Perhaps," he said enigmatically, then went on, "since you have decided to be one of my blood, when you die I will aid you if I can. But I may not be able to, and if you are alone, you will have to be prepared to manage for yourself." He turned and looked at her, concern for her making his ariose voice a bit rougher than usual; his penetrating dark eyes held her as surely as his arms could. "Avasa Dani, be certain: to be one of my blood is not a decision to be made on a whim, or assuming you will have no risks. I cannot emphasize that enough. That is why I have repeated the dangers to you, so that you will encompass the whole of what you will become. You will not free yourself from the exigencies of life, for that would remove you from humanity. We do not dance on the burning ground, with Shiva, nor do we revel in the mortality of the living, knowing it will not easily touch us." As he said this, other memories, this time of Csimenae filled his mind, unbidden: she was still alive and in her remote self-styled adytum, far away in the fastness of the Pyrenees. "You will not be able to shape the world to your liking simply because you have come to my life."

"I had not supposed I could," said Avasa Dani, frowning slightly.

"Coming to my life is no guarantee of centuries for living," he added. "The world can impose upon you in ways you cannot escape."

"You made that clear before. I comprehend your reservations, or as much as I can do, living as I am." She reached out and took his hand, kissing his fingers one at a time. "Yet you tell me that what we do we do in love."

"If that is what we seek, yes," he said carefully. "There is fulfillment in love that cannot equal anything that dread and fear can offer."

"If what you have given me is any example of what those of your blood can do, then I must suppose that I can also achieve the same when I am like you." She smiled at him. "I do not wish to change to your life to remain your mistress; I am wholly cognizant that is impossible. You made it very clear that once I am like you, we can no longer be lovers, but that until the moment of my death, we can."

"That is so," said Sanat Ji Mani, watching her intently, and pulling his hand back from her.

"I have been missing you, these last months, and I am alive. I long to be embraced again, to know passion as you waken it in me." She came up to him and sank onto his lap. "You do not know how much I treasure your love."

"You are willing to accept my life when you die?" he asked as he smoothed a few wisps of loose hair back from her face before enfolding her in his arms.

"I am willing to enter into your life when I die, to live as you live, to seek the living as you do, to keep myself in all the ways you have described; I know you will not always devote yourself to me, and that I must find others to nurture me once I die. I know that many I find I will have to approach subtly, unperceived but as a dream. I grasp it all. You have shown me what I will have to do in order to flourish, and I am certain I am capable of the life you describe. I am not a desperate woman wanting only to be rid of an inaccessible husband, I am looking beyond that, to what my life could be, were I like you," she said, her tone of voice gently musical. "I will be one with you through the blood-bond, and I will find love to sustain me."

"You do realize that those of my blood are hated and feared?" He kissed the arch of her brow. "Most of the living despise us, and seek to destroy us. Very few among them are capable of giving their love knowingly, and fewer still are willing to risk becoming—"

"Night demons?" she suggested. "Creatures of Shiva?"

"If you will," he granted her.

"You have found me, and others before me, and will find others after me," Avasa Dani said tranquilly. "I will find others, as well. I am content with that."

Sanat Ji Mani drew her close against him, "It will be necessary, if you are to survive. And there is solitariness even when there is love."

"Yes. I understand that," she said. "I may have lived my life thus far within the walls of my father's and my husband's house—and yours. But I have read widely, I have studied much, and lately, since you have allowed it, I have listened to the pilgrim Lum, and heard him tell of all he has seen, and I have wished—oh, I have wished— to see those things for myself, to know all the marvels that fill the world. I know it is unsafe in the world beyond these walls, but I am not afraid. What terrifies me more than anything you have described is that I might remain sequestered until the day I die, and know nothing more than the house of my father, my husband, and you. It is not enough, Sanat Ji Mani. It is not enough." She kissed him slowly, her mouth soft on his. "I know what I want, no matter what may come," she said before she kissed him again, her acquiescence in the intensity of her embrace.

His hands moved over the silk of her garments, molding the fabric to the curves of her body, the urgency of his touch echoing her own. "Since you will have me, Avasa Dani . . ." He rose, lifting her in his arms as he did, and carried her to the window-niche on the far side of the room; it was wide and deep, with a dozen silk-covered cushions piled in it, opulent and inviting. He sank onto his knees and laid Avasa Dani on the cushions as the scents of the garden grew stronger. Slowly, luxuriously, he loosened her clothing. "You are magnificent," he whispered as he bent to kiss the rise of her breasts.

She trembled, feeling heat and chill at once. "You are *everything*," she murmured as his tongue flicked her nipple. Nothing in all her instruction for erotic pleasure had revealed what Sanat Ji Mani had imparted to her and which she welcomed now as the deliverance she sought; her skin tingled in excitation, her body softened, her mind floated. Gradually she surrendered to the rapturous sensations that had wakened with her desire. A delicious languor came over her as Sanat Ji Mani slid her garments back from her torso, to lavish kisses where the silk had been. "Yes. There," she breathed, as Sanat Ji Mani lifted her clothes from the top of her thighs and began lightly to stroke her hips and abdomen; her flesh trembled under his caress.

He was astonished and gratified by the frenzy of passion that welled in her; he responded to her every movement, every sigh, every nuance of reception she offered him. He felt her gather, gather, gather, and release in deep, blissful waves; he continued to fondle the sea-scented folds at the top of her thighs, seeing her amazement as she stared at him in disbelief. "There is more, Avasa Dani. I want you to know it."

"How . . . ?" She closed her eyes as the vividness of her rapture took possession of her, more prolonged and profound than any she had known before; she gave herself over to ecstasy and Sanat Ji Mani. When Avasa Dani could trust herself to move again, she began by opening her eyes and turning her head; Sanat Ji Mani still lay beside her. "You knew it was . . ." She could not find the words to finish.

"Let us say, I sensed," he said, so gently that she wanted to weep.

"It is done?" she asked, though she had no doubt.

"It is done," he assured her.

She curled into a ball amid the cushions. "Good," she whispered.

He remained where he was until she began to drift into sleep; then he moved away from her, her fading elation still within him. He walked toward the door so silently that as he opened it, he found Hirsuma hovering near-by with no apparent reason to be there.

"My master," said Hirsuma, putting his hands together and bowing. "I did not know . . . that you were in your library."

Sanat Ji Mani regarded Hirsuma wearily. "If you must lie, then please lie well," he said. "You wanted to know what was happening in the library, did you not." He knew the answer, but waited to hear what Hirsuma might say.

"I was curious, my master. Nothing more. Just curious. All men are curious. I am no different: you are foreign, and—" He stopped as he saw the expression in Sanat Ji Mani's compelling eyes.

"Were you paid to spy on me, or was this simply an opportunity of the moment?" Sanat Ji Mani did not sound angry, but Hirsuma took a step back from him. "You may as well tell me now, for I will find out eventually."

"You will beat me," said Hirsuma, who expected nothing less. "Or you will order Garuda to beat me."

"No. I have said I do not beat my servants, and I will not make an exception for you, no matter what you have done." Sanat Ji Mani moved a short distance away from Hirsuma. "But you were warned what would happen if you continued on your disloyal course, so be all this on your head. You have persisted in your betrayal, and now you will answer for it. You will be dismissed, of course, and I will tell anyone who asks that you served me poorly."

Hirsuma smiled weakly. "An empty threat. You are a foreigner and my fathers have lived here for generation upon generation."

"You do them no honor," said Sanat Ji Mani with an inflection that struck Hirsuma as much as a sudden cold wind would.

"You are not the one to say so," Hirsuma blustered, his fear making him want to run from Sanat Ji Mani, now much more imposing than Hirsuma had ever thought he was.

"Perhaps," said Sanat Ji Mani. "Still, you know what will become of you now. You may collect your belongings, then come to the servants' hall; you will leave from there, where all the others may see you go."

Hirsuma shook his head. "I will go, but not with the household watching."

"There, I am afraid, you are wrong," Sanat Ji Mani said smoothly. "You will do as I say, or I will find you and take you before a magistrate, and I will have all the household to support my complaint of you. That will be far more unpleasant than leaving from the servants' hall; suborned servants are branded, are they not."

"Yes," Hirsuma said, turning pale.

"If you think you can leave this house secretly and I will not find you, you are mistaken," Sanat Ji Mani said; Hirsuma believed him. "Do not take too long. Garuda will have the servants waiting to see you go."

Hirsuma nodded in capitulation. "I will come there as soon as I have my belongings together."

"Good. Do not dawdle about it," Sanat Ji Mani told him before he slipped back into the library to light a few more of the oil-lamps that hung there.

A little while later there was a scratch on the door; Rojire said, "Hirsuma is gathering his things."

Sanat Ji Mani opened the door. "Thank you, old friend. Did you happen to notice how long he was trying to listen?"

"Not very long. Garuda has been observing him, as has Bohdil, and they are quick to tell me of anything suspicious." Rojire paused, glancing over his shoulder to be sure they were not under surveillance. "He has not conducted himself properly, and that offends the others. Had you not caught him, they would have, and they would have turned him out far more angrily than you will."

"Then it is just as well I discovered him." Sanat Ji Mani glanced at Avasa Dani, who was sleeping soundly. "If you will remain near-by until it is time for Hirsuma to leave?"

"Of course. It will not do to have another take up where Hirsuma has left off," Rojire said.

"And the next one might be more subtle than Hirsuma has been." Sanat Ji Mani frowned slightly. "Do you know to whom he has spoken? Is it that same scrawny rascal who has been following me and Rustam Iniattir?"

"I believe so. I gather he reports to one of the Sultan's deputies," said Rojire. "I have seen Hirsuma meet the fellow twice since he was told not to."

"Just as well to have him gone," said Sanat Ji Mani, his tone distant. "The other servants will be reassured."

"Yes," said Rojire. "I will do what I can to see how they respond when he is gone."

"Thank you," Sanat Ji Mani told him. "I must suppose that Hirsuma is not beyond causing mischief, and may go to Avasa Dani's family to speak against her, in the hope that accusations will be brought against me. I will have to avert that."

"Avasa Dani should be able to thwart any efforts they may make," Rojire pointed out. "She is a resourceful woman."

"Yes, she is," Sanat Ji Mani agreed. "I am often struck by it. But she is still a woman, and that may yet work against her in this city."

"Do you think she may be at risk?" Rojire asked.

"I do. And so do you, or we would not be having this discussion." Sanat Ji Mani paused, sunk in thought. "Something must be arranged, and soon. I will have to speak with her uncles."

"They will want gold, whatever you do."

"That they will," said Sanat Ji Mani. "Unlike her husband."

"As pious as Lum and as ready to leave the world," said Rojire. "She has asked Lum to explain it."

"And has he?" Sanat Ji Mani wondered aloud, expecting no answer. "She must be protected. It will be arranged."

Rojire inclined his head. "Then I will leave you, my master."

"For now. Summon me when Hirsuma is ready to depart." He went toward the door with Rojire and let him out. "You have done well."

"I might have done better, had I realized what Hirsuma was doing when he began; I put his actions to spite, not to malice," said Rojire. With that, he was gone, leaving Sanat Ji Mani to restore order to Avasa Dani's garments and to place a scroll near her, so that it would appear she had fallen asleep over her studies. That done, he returned to his own quarters to dress for seeing Hirsuma off the premises.

By the time Rojire came to escort him from his apartments, Sanat Ji Mani presented his usual self-contained appearance, but in a grander presentation than was his habit: his black brocade Persian kandys was perfectly draped, his wide, dark-red-leather belt neatly in place, his black-silk Hungarian gatya tucked into low Persian boots. The silver collar around his neck was studded with rubies and held his eclipse sigil displayed in silver and black sapphire, as did the ring on the Saturn finger of his left hand. His foreignness added to his dignity, as he intended.

Bohdil was clearly distressed, wringing his hands and saying, "How will I explain? How will I explain?" over and over again.

"Hirsuma is a kinsman of Bohdil's," said Garuda, to account for this uncharacteristic behavior. "It is a disgrace for all his family." The oil-lamps in the servants' dining hall were lit, casting a brassy light over everything, and making the night beyond the windows seem darker by contrast.

"Why?" Sanat Ji Mani asked, although he knew the answer. "Only Hirsuma spied on me. The rest are blameless."

"That is not our way, my master," said Garuda, clapping his hands to silence the servants. "Where is Hirsuma?"

Rojire moved away from the main table to avoid being an interloper among the others.

"He is still in his quarters," said Javas, who tended the horses. "He must be summoned."

"I'll do it," said Sipati, the inventory-master. "Since he is to be dismissed, he must be brought from his quarters so that no one can say he did any roguery on his way out of the house."

Sanat Ji Mani shook his head once. "Very well. Garuda, if you will? Go fetch Hirsuma from his quarters."

Garuda did not quite smile, but he squared his shoulders at this granting of authority and left the dining hall at once for other parts of the house. An awkward silence descended at his departure, which was broken only when Daltil, the under-cook, brought a pot of mint tea from the kitchen.

"Very good," Sanat Ji Mani approved, and stood back so that the servants could fill their cups without fear of insulting their master.

No one spoke as they drank their tea, but some began to fidget when the time passed that Garuda should have returned with Hirsuma. The time dragged on, and Bohdil began once more to wring his hands.

"Rojire," Sanat Ji Mani said softly, "if you please, see what has become of Garuda?"

Rojire did as he was asked, slipping out of the room almost soundlessly. He returned quickly, his ususal calm demeanor disturbed; all those in the servants' dining hall turned toward him. "My master, you must come. Garuda has been struck unconscious, and Hirsuma is gone."

Text of a report from Azizi Iniattir at Sirpur to his uncle, Rustam Iniattir, carried by Askari Daitya, caravan leader, to Delhi.

To my most esteemed uncle, the leader of our family, the respected Rustam Iniattir, your nephew and factor in the city of Sirpur sends his most dedicated regards, and takes this opportunity to report on our business in this place.

Your caravan from Rajmundri and Hanamkonda will bring this account to you. I will entrust it to your caravan leader Askari Daitya, who has much to present to you of his own industry. His caravan has done very well, and, barring trouble on the road, should arrive in good time to add to the fortunes of our family. He secured some fine silks from China, which were traded for the Turkish goat-hair yarns he took to Rajmundri. He has also bought rare woods, which he traded spices to get, and pearls, which he received in exchange for the carded wool bales from Trebizond. He has been astute in his dealings, and I have complied with his request for two more mules to carry these goods to Delhi.

I have also spoken with the leaders of caravans from Assam and Malabar. There is concern among them all that prices in the northern ports and cities may increase sharply as Timur-i's forces continue to harry about the world, destroying all in their path. I have also heard that many believe that Timur-i has been overthrown and cast out, and a younger man now leads his murderous horde. I have seen no proof of this, nor have I discovered a convincing denial. Whatever may be the case, from the Black Sea to Kashmir, all merchants go in fear of what Timur-i's horsemen will bring. It matters little if Timur-i is in the van or no.

For that reason I would recommend that for the next several years, you concentrate your efforts to the south and east and leave the north and west to Timur-i. I do not say this for my advantage alone, although I do acknowledge that what may be misfortune for many others would be advantageous for me. Situated as I am, I can bend my efforts to the family's benefit, so that while others are forced to risk much for an increasingly unsatisfactory return, we may profit from these unsettled times and make the most of this opportunity. I am not indifferent to the suffering of those in the path of Timur-i's fury, but I would be foolish not to see how it could work to our family's advantage. If you will send your next two caravans in my direction, I will see to it that they go to places where they may trade safely, and where they will have full value for their goods.

The caravan of Manah Spentas has not yet returned from Jajpur, but I am not yet alarmed, for the weather has been severe, and that may cause delays as much as more dire events. I will send out scouts to look for them if I do not see them in a month. Manah Spentas told me, on his way out to Jajpur, that he anticipated doing good business this time, for the merchants in Jajpur have come to trust him and are eager to see what he brings. I would recommend you marry one of your daughters to him, so that he will continue to work for our family and not be lured away by promises others might make to him. I have only two daughters and both are promised already, or I would venture to make such a marriage myself. You, as I recall, have three daughters who will need husbands. Manah Spentas is Parsi, and he comes from a family in good standing. Consider it, I ask you, for the sake of the family and of the business we do in the eastern cities. One day, you might install him as factor in Jajpur, which would be a most advantageous arrangement for us all.

The caravan of Ismalli Heitan, our rival, arrived yesterday from the south; it was well-laden and Ismalli Heitan was boasting of his achievements. I paid him little notice, but I did glean one bit of information which may prove useful to you: there has been a ruction among the brass-workers in the south, and as a result, the quality of the brasses has suffered. It may take some time before order, and *quality, has been restored. I mention this as a caution to you, for it was the one disappointment Ismalli Heitan mentioned in his otherwise fulsome chronicle of his journey.*

In the fervent hope that more Light than Darkness fills your life, and that our family prospers as a result, I apologize if I have written anything that gains your displeasure, and I beg you will consider it is the plight of any man charged with the task of providing accurate information.

Azizi Iniattir

At Sirpur, seven weeks past the Summer Solstice

7

Lum tested his foot and nodded. "Yes. This is very good," he said. "The pain is completely gone and the wound is healed cleanly. Who would have thought it would take so long? Nearly nine weeks." He walked around the garden courtyard of Sanat Ji Mani's house, practicing for his return to the road. Over their heads rain pattered on the broad parchment screens that had been put in place against the weather; weak afternoon light lent a milky glow to the garden.

"Feet are slow to mend, and your infection went deep. There is a small scar," said Sanat Ji Mani, reminding the pilgrim that the incision which drained the infection would mark the place all his life.

"Better than a lost foot; or worse than that. I have realized that my injury could have killed me, and most painfully. For all that the suffering of life should not dismay those of us who follow the Buddha, I am grateful I was spared such an end," said Lum. "You have been most kind to me, although I have no claim upon you and cannot repay all you have done, in this life. Perhaps Lord Buddha will show me how to succor you in another reincarnation."

"Perhaps," said Sanat Ji Mani.

"You may rest assured that the Wheel will turn for all of us," said Lum. "I know I should not intrude upon you for another day, but—"

"I understand your concerns for the weather," said Sanat Ji Mani. "You may leave when it suits you."

"It is inappropriate for me to accept aid I do not require," said Lum a bit stiffly.

"But you will travel more safely once the rains have slacked off," Sanat Ji Mani pointed out. "They will begin to decrease in a month."

"That is too long," said Lum, a bit unhappily. "I cannot justify remaining here another month when I am capable of walking without pain."

Sanat Ji Mani said nothing for a short while, then remarked, "You are bound to the south, are you not? where the rains linger longer than they do here in Delhi. If you wait even three weeks, the worst of the weather should be over, and you will not have to fear flooding, or mired roads."

"I fear nothing of the hazards of the world," Lum said piously.

"You believed that with your foot, and you see how well it served you," Sanat Ji Mani responded, smiling to take the sting out of his words.

Lum bit back a sharp rejoinder. "I have no right to question you, after all you have done for me. Yet I hope you do not think poorly of my devotion to the Buddha."

"Quite the contrary," said Sanat Ji Mani. "You have shown a devotion that is most unusual in religious men: few of them would have walked so far with an infection raging in them to show how little the world could touch them." He looked about the courtyard at the lush plants. "You say you do not wish to remain because you are capable of leaving. I have no doubt there is work you can do here—you could help tend the garden, if you would like something to justify remaining until the summer rains are over."

"It is not suitable that I should," said Lum with a hint of regret in his voice. "I should take my begging-bowl and my staff, and be on my way."

"Whatever you wish," said Sanat Ji Mani. "You are healed and you have your wits about you. No doubt you will know what suits you best."

"It would be an easy thing to become accustomed to luxury," said Lum. "The Buddha warned against it, specifically. I did not comprehend the reason for His strictures until I came to your house, and learned for myself how insidious ease can be, and how readily one can be seduced by it, even while enduring pain." He sat down on the small stone bench in the corner of the courtyard. "As there can be a too-great attachment to the body, so there can be a too-great attachment to comfort, and that will pollute the spirit of the most devout."

"Lord Buddha was a Prince," Sanat Ji Mani said.

"So He was. He knew the snares He taught." Lum took a deep breath. "I will pray for you, but I cannot remain here. Rain or clear, I will depart in the morning at dawn, bound southward."

"Then I will wish you safe travel and pleasant companions on the road," said Sanat Ji Mani, putting his hands together and inclining his head.

Lum returned the courtesy automatically, but said, "I cannot make up my mind: you are either the most generous of worldly men, or you are the most accomplished seducer."

Sanat Ji Mani's smile was fleeting. "Perhaps I am both," he said.

"I doubt it," said Lum, and turned to leave the courtyard.

"Lum," Sanat Ji Mani said, stopping the red-haired Chinese in his tracks. "I am going to prepare a packet for you, containing medicinal supplies for you to take with you. You may need it."

"I must not accept such things for myself," said Lum.

"Then use it for the relief of others," Sanat Ji Mani said gently before turning away and giving his attention to the boxes of aloes that stood at the end of his courtyard garden. He was still tending his plants when Rojire came upon him toward day's end.

"Lum has announced he is leaving," said Rojire in the Latin of his youth as he came up to his master and bowed, Roman-style.

"Yes. He told me earlier he would," Sanat Ji Mani agreed in the same language.

"While the rains are in full pelter," Rojire went on.

"He is determined to go," Sanat Ji Mani said. "He does not want to be seduced from his religious vocation."

"He never said so," Rojire exclaimed in disbelief.

"Not precisely, no; but something very like," Sanat Ji Mani responded.

Rojire shook his head. "And you—you had nothing to say about this absurd scheme?"

"My old friend, what could I say?" Sanat Ji Mani paused for an answer; when none was forthcoming, he went on, "Lum is a grown man, and he has chosen a purpose in his life to which he adheres with tenacity. That you or I might not agree with his decision has nothing to do with what he is committed to doing. If you are certain you have the right to do so, you may try to dissuade him if you wish. For my part, I will make up a box with ointments and tinctures for him to take with him; I will instruct him in their use, and I will hope, for his own sake, that he has no occasion to use them on himself."

"You are not going to try to change his mind, are you," said Rojire.

"No," Sanat Ji Mani said. "I am not."

There was a silence between them as the rain beat its tattoo on the parchment screens. Then Rojire shrugged. "I will have a water-skin made ready for him, and have lentil-bread prepared."

"He may not accept it," Sanat Ji Mani warned.

"He may not," said Rojire. "But it will be offered in any case. He may share it with beggars or feed it to goats."

"He may," Sanat Ji Mani said, a trace of amusement in his dark eyes.

"You could insist," Rojire went on. "You've saved his life: he would have to listen to you."

At this Sanat Ji Mani chuckled. "Given his opinion of me, I doubt it." He took a pot of fox-glove and moved it to another part of the courtyard. "Let him do as he must, Rojire."

"He could die. He is not as strong as he thinks he is," Rojire declared.

"Then he will discover it for himself, and he will decide what to do." Sanat Ji Mani paused in his activities. "What is it about Lum that makes you so protective of him? You have seen many others who have endured as much, or worse, than he, and you did not try to keep them from harm as you have Lum."

"I cannot say what it is," Rojire admitted. "He rouses my sympathy. It may be that he has undertaken so thankless a pilgrimage, or that he has given up his family."

"You have not been impressed by other pilgrims we have known," Sanat Ji Mani reminded him.

"Not generally, no," said Rojire. "But most of them were Muslim or Christian."

"Do you feel sympathy for Avasa Dani's husband?" Sanat Ji Mani asked.

"Hardly," Rojire said with a single snort of laughter. "I think he has behaved . . . shabbily."

"Yet you admire Lum, who has done the same thing," Sanat Ji Mani pointed out.

"He has not left a wife behind in precarious circumstances," Rojire said.

"Are you certain of that? He has said nothing of the conditions of his life before he became a pilgrim: in fact, he has conspicuously avoided giving any information about himself. Perhaps even now there is a family in Kua-chou that is begging or sold into slavery because of Lum." Sanat Ji Mani watched while Rojire considered this. "He could be using his pilgrimage as an excuse for desertion."

"He may, but I will not believe it: he is no Frater Paulinus," said Rojire at last. "I will grant you that there is some secret in his past that weighs on him, but I will not account him a coward because of it."

"You are always a staunch ally," Sanat Ji Mani said with genuine feeling.

At last Rojire shrugged. "Well, no matter what accounts for it, I am concerned for Lum's welfare, and I cannot be at ease with his departure."

Sanat Ji Mani nodded. "Tell him, if you think it will make a difference."

Rojire shook his head. "No. It would seem a slight to his faith, wouldn't it?"

"Very likely," said Sanat Ji Mani. Picking up without effort a tub containing a young willow, he added, "You will do as you think best."

"If I can determine what that is," said Rojire; he glanced up at the screens. "It will be dark soon. Do you want lamps brought out to you?"

"It would probably be wiser than not," Sanat Ji Mani decided aloud. "Have Garuda do it. He has been trying to show his reliability since

Hirsuma left, to make up for his lapse in dealing with Hirsuma."

"All right." Rojire paused. "Have you learned anything about him?"

"Hirsuma? only that his family refused to take him in when he came to them. I have been told he applied to the Sultan's household for work, but was not given any."

"He is not a reliable man," said Rojire, as if that settled the matter.

"On the contrary: he is most reliable. He will always strive to do that which will bring him influence over others." Sanat Ji Mani left off his labor and motioned to Rojire to come nearer. "I have noticed that the scrawny man Hirsuma spoke to is still watching this house from time to time."

"As have I," said Rojire. "And I have once sent him about his business."

"That might not be entirely advisable," Sanat Ji Mani said. "But it's done."

"Why is it not advisable?" Rojire asked.

Before Sanat Ji Mani could answer the clapper sounded outside the courtyard door. "I am not expecting anyone."

"Shall I admit him?" Rojire knew that only men would present themselves at the door in this fashion.

"Yes, if you would," said Sanat Ji Mani in the Delhi dialect. "Then ask Garuda to bring lamps out here."

"As you wish, my master," said Rojire in the same tongue; the call to sunset prayers came from the mosques of Delhi. He opened the gate, bowed a welcome, and went to issue the order for lamps.

Standing in the doorway was Rustam Iniattir, his garments wet, his boots muddy, his stance dejected. "I have been visited by the Sultan's Minister for Taxes, Rents, and Revenues," he said miserably, not bothering with a greeting.

"Murmar bin Tughluq," said Sanat Ji Mani. "What did that camel-thief want?" He did not hesitate in using such an epithet for Murmar bin Tughluq, who, in his youth, had been branded a thief for stealing asses and camels.

"Money, of course. The excuse is Timur-i. They say he could well attack this place, and that they must improve the fortifications and improve the army. As a foreigner, I am expected to contribute more than the Muslims or the followers of the Brahmin gods. If I do not give what he asks for, he will call me a spy and confiscate everything my family has." He stepped inside and closed the gate behind him, but not before Sanat Ji Mani caught sight of the furtive, gaunt figure he had seen so often before.

"Then I would reckon he will pay me a visit for the same purpose," Sanat Ji Mani said with unruffled calm.

"Does it not outrage you?" Rustam Iniattir asked, more downcast than indignant.

"If I dwell upon it, it probably will," said Sanat Ji Mani. "But I have long ago accepted that the world is full of injustice, and there is little I do to change it."

"We will have to pay most of our profits from our caravan in taxes," said Rustam Iniattir. "It had such promise, and now this."

"The caravan will not return until next spring," Sanat Ji Mani reminded him. "By then, the tax may have been suspended."

"I have never known a tax, once levied against foreigners, to be lifted," Rustam Iniattir said wearily. "If the Sultan is going to take so much of my money, I will have no choice but to go elsewhere, so that I might profit from my efforts and keep enough of the profit to live in reasonable comfort." He stared at the screens in the last gloom of day. "Ingenious. Where did you learn such a trick?"

"In a place called Gaul," said Sanat Ji Mani. "Many years ago." It had been when he had accompanied Gaius Julius Caesar on campaign and seen the Roman troops use such screens to shelter in their earthworks; he smiled a little. "There the rain was cold."

"As it is in the mountains to the west of here," said Rustam Iniattir. He paced the courtyard, his countenance drawn with worry. "Ever since the Sultan's officers came, my thoughts have been in turmoil and I cannot decide what is best to do. I have no wish to leave, but if I remain, I must pay the Sultan's taxes, by which I will be ruined and my family will suffer greatly."

"You have factors in other cities, do you not? You do not have to remain here, do you?" Sanat Ji Mani asked, although he knew the answer.

"I have factors in six cities, and all of them are my relatives." Under happier conditions this would have been a boast; now it was only a forlorn admission.

Sanat Ji Mani spoke slowly but with increasing persuasion, "Then consider changing your abode to a place less demanding upon you. Why not appoint one of your nephews to be your factor here and take your family to another place until the danger of Timur-i is past and there is another Sultan in Delhi? You will still have to pay taxes, but you will only have to support your nephew and his family, not your wife and her children, and your concubines and their children."

"But travel just now is not safe," Rustam Iniattir said with uncharacteristic timorousness.

"It is rarely safe," Sanat Ji Mani reminded him. "You are a merchant, and you know that better than most."

Rustam Iniattir sat down on the little bench. "I do not want my family to suffer. If we travel and find worse than what we have left, I will have failed them."

"It is an honorable concern you have," Sanat Ji Mani assured him. "But if you find a safer haven, will you not rejoice that you had the foresight to leave when you could? I am not advising you lightly, nor do I want you to go for my own welfare; you are no longer secure here, and that will impinge on all you do, to your detriment." He approached his Parsi friend. "Delhi has been your home, and the home of your father, and his father, for generations. It is hard to leave a place when it has become as much home to you as your own country was."

"You may say so," said Rustam Iniattir with a slight shake of his head. "But your situation is not like mine. You came here only a few years ago, you have no wife or concubine or children to protect, so you may gad about the world without care, and have no worry beyond the soundness of your horses."

"It may seem so," Sanat Ji Mani allowed. "And yet, do you know, I would not recommend this course of action to you if I believe it would not benefit you, no matter how inconvenient it may be. Live in another city until you are sure you may return here without losing all you have labored so long to acquire." He stood still. "Rojire," he called out. "Where is Garuda with the lamps? It is getting quite dark." This very ordinary request broke the tension building between the Parsi and the foreigner.

"You are being sensible," Rustam Iniattir said. "I know it; I almost agree with it."

"Ah," said Sanat Ji Mani. "Almost."

"I have seventeen people dependent upon me. What am I to do? Even if I put my nephew Zal in charge of our affairs here, where are we to go?" He began to wring the water from his sleeves. "There are members of our family scattered throughout the world, but none are beyond the reach of Timur-i, if his sights are set upon them. Where may we be protected against him?"

Sanat Ji Mani considered briefly. "You have a factor in the Mameluke Empire, have you not? At the end of the Red Sea?"

"Yes. My cousin Rozdin is there, with his family." Rustam Iniattir coughed as if trying to loosen his chest. "I have thought of them. But how can I reach them? To get there we would have to cross through Timur-i's lands, and who knows what misfortune would befall us?"

"You would not have such trouble if you went by sea," said Sanat Ji Mani gently. "You could travel away from the Jagatai clan. I have ships that ply the waters of the Arabian Sea. If you are willing to travel south to Cambay in Gujerat at the mouth of the Sabarmati River, I could arrange for a ship to be at your disposal." As he spoke, he became more certain that this was the most provident thing to do. "You have little to fear once you are aboard my ship. Timur-i cannot ride his cavalry after you."

Rustam Iniattir gave another short, tight cough and began to knead his left shoulder with his right hand. "There are pirates." He looked up at Sanat Ji Mani, who noticed that the color had drained from his face. "There are storms. This is the season of rain and wind."

"Yes," Sanat Ji Mani allowed, a slight frown forming between his fine brows. "And so you must go on one of my largest and strongest ships."

"Why have you said nothing of your ships before?" Rustam Iniattir demanded suddenly, and interrupted himself with a series of sharp, barking coughs.

"Rojire!" Sanat Ji Mani called out as he went to examine Rustam Iniattir. "Go to my room in the top of the house and bring me the chalcedony flask. Quickly." He laid his hand on Rustam Iniattir's forehead. "You are clammy."

"I am in wet clothing," said Rustam Iniattir. "You have no reason to fuss over me."

"On the contrary; I am not fussing, I am guarding my respected associate," said Sanat Ji Mani, now touching the Parsi's neck and feeling his racing pulse. He concealed the distress he felt with a calm, steady manner. "You have worried yourself into a dangerous state. I have a tincture that will help you."

"You need not bother," said Rustam Iniattir, a bit testily.

"Well, that may be," said Sanat Ji Mani, "but your family would not thank me if you were to collapse here, so I ask you to permit me to avoid that possibility; the Sultan's deputies might find it questionable and decide I am holding you prisoner. If you would recline on the bench?"

"This is foolishness," said Rustam Iniattir as he did what Sanat Ji Mani asked; he stifled a moan as he lay back.

Belatedly Garuda arrived with the lamps, stood shocked for a long moment, then asked tentatively, "Do you want these hung, my master?"

"Of course I do," said Sanat Ji Mani as he loosened Rustam Iniattir's belt. "Most of them need to be here, where they can illuminate what I am doing." He did not need the lamps to see, but was aware that his lack of them would cause comment in his household.

"Shall I fetch the pilgrim?" Garuda inquired, reluctantly going about his task.

"Why?" Sanat Ji Mani countered; he could see that Rustam Iniattir was having trouble breathing.

"To pray for him," Garuda said. "Each of them has linked his karma with the other. The pilgrim's prayers will help him."

"Do not bother Lum for the time being. Rustam Iniattir is not in mortal danger," said Sanat Ji Mani with a confidence he did not possess. "I will need some tea made of turmeric and ginger. Go to the kitchen and order it, then bring it to me as soon as it is ready." This was as much to give Garuda something to do as to get the tea. He snapped off one of the young willow's branches, pulled back a length of bark and held it out to Rustam Iniattir. "Chew this. It will help you."

Rustam Iniattir, still doing his best to control his coughing, did as he was told. He tried to speak but could not keep from coughing his dry, hacking coughs. He chewed more vigorously to show he was making an effort.

Garuda finished hanging the lamps and hurried off toward the kitchen, going at a more rapid pace than was his wont; Rojire passed him in the corridor as he returned with the chalcedony flask.

"There you are," Sanat Ji Mani approved. "In good time." He took the flask, opened it, and, raising Rustam Iniattir's head with one hand, held the flask to his lips with the other. "Drink this. You need not spit out the willow-bark."

"How much?" Rustam Iniattir asked, wheezing a little with the question.

"Not too much. I will stop you if you take too much." Sanat Ji Mani watched carefully as the opalescent liquid trickled into his mouth.

Rustam Iniattir sputtered as he strove to drink the tincture, straining it through the chewed willow-bark in his mouth. At last he licked his lips as Sanat Ji Mani removed the flask. "The taste is . . . strange."

"So it is," Sanat Ji Mani agreed. "But it will do you good, in spite of that." He eased Rustam Iniattir's head back onto the bench. "If you will lie there and chew on the willow-bark until Garuda brings the tea?"

"If that is what is required," said Rustam Iniattir in a tone of great concession; his little coughs had lessened and his skin was no longer whey-pale.

Rojire tugged Sanat Ji Mani's sleeve. "What is wrong? What happened?" he asked in Latin.

"His pulse was too rapid and he could not breathe fully. The tincture will slow his pulse and he will recover. The willow-bark is useful, too." Sanat Ji Mani answered, still in the Delhi dialect. "He has become over-anxious and as a result, he has reached a point where his sinews are too tight to work properly."

"I recall you have dealt with this condition before," Rojire said, keeping his tone neutral.

"And not always successfully," Sanat Ji Mani agreed, this time in Latin. "Still, I think he will be himself again if he does not continue to fret."

Rojire glanced over toward the place where Rustam Iniattir lay. "What has troubled him so much?"

"He is being subjected to ruinous taxes. I suppose I will also soon have higher demands made on me as well. The Sultan wants to increase his army." Sanat Ji Mani sighed. "I am glad of the warning: I will spend the next few days making more jewels. You, old friend, must prepare to leave."

"Are we going away?" Rojire asked without any sign of surprise.

"You are going to escort Avasa Dani away from here while I can still arrange passage for you both. I will pay her uncles enough to keep them from protesting. You will go with Rustam Iniattir and his family to Cambay, and there go aboard either the *Silken Wind* or the *Eye of Night*, whichever is departing for the Red Sea, and you will go to Alexandria and wait for me there."

"You are telling me to leave you here?" Rojire asked with some heat.

"I depend upon you to deliver Rustam Iniattir, his family, and Avasa Dani to such safety as can be found away from this city. You will have to depart quickly, and I cannot do that, for a number of reasons, the first being that if all of us should leave at once, the Minister of Taxes, Rents, and Revenues would probably seize everything we have; I would prefer to keep title to this place if I can, and I know Rustam Iniattir does not want to sacrifice all his family has striven to achieve for the last two centuries. I will tend to the business of settling our affairs, and as soon as I have put all in order, I will come after you." Sanat Ji Mani sighed. "I can pay the higher taxes for a while, but Rustam Iniattir cannot. And his nephew may need some help before he is ready to manage his work as factor."

"When you say quickly, what do you mean?" Rojire was still suspicious. "I know you of old, and I know your ways. I remember Leosan Fortress, as you should, as well."

"This is nothing like Leosan Fortress, or Karmona." Sanat Ji Mani looked up at the screens above the courtyard, noticing the shine of the lamps on the parchment. "Ten days, I should think, would be time enough for Rustam Iniattir to make ready, and you as well. Then go south."

"You can instruct me on the route later," Rojire said irritably, then relented. "I will make the arrangements."

"Thank you," said Sanat Ji Mani with such simplicity that Rojire was moved in spite of himself.

"Should I ask Lum to delay his departure so he can travel with us?" Rojire proposed, his demeanor unchanged, although he once again spoke the Delhi dialect.

"I doubt he will accept such an offer, but make it, if you wish to," Sanat Ji Mani said, also in that language, handing the chalcedony flask back to Rojire. "Now, if you will, go and fill a vial with this tincture and bring it to me. Garuda will be here with tea in a moment, and I will have to tend to Rustam Iniattir as soon as he returns."

"As you wish, my master," said Rojire, going toward the door.

"And Rojire," Sanat Ji Mani said after him.

"Yes?" He waited to hear what Sanat Ji Mani might say.

"To answer your question before Rustam Iniattir arrives, about the scrawny man: I must assume he is a spy, and anything that can be turned to my disadvantage will surely fuel his purpose." Sanat Ji Mani made a philosophical gesture, then walked across the courtyard to continue his ministrations to Rustam Iniattir, accompanied by the steady murmur of the rain.

Text of a letter from Kanwar Gotanipi, military commander of the north-western quadrant of Delhi to the Sultan's Leader-Commander of the Army.

To the most potent, honorable, and just Leader-Commander Ahdin bin Daulat, your most loyal and sincerely devoted lieutenant Kanwar Gotanipi submits his report at the Autumnal Equinox, with the heartfelt prayer that it will find favor in your esteemed eyes.

I have, in accordance with your orders, conducted an inspection of the walls of my quarter of the city, and I submit to you now my estimations of what I have seen. First, the repairs ordered by the late Sultan Firuz—may your Allah show him favor in your Paradise—and may I be pardoned for writing his illustrious name—are substantial enough, although the material used was not of the highest quality nor the workmanship of the strictest standards. Still, I must tell you that

I am satisfied that all but the most ruinous attack might be withstood behind the walls here. There are undoubtedly other parts of the city that are in more urgent need of shoring up than this quarter.

The gates in the walls are generally in good repair, although one, made of thick planking and iron staples, has a few rotten places in the wood, which may cause you to decide to replace the planking. The frame is also not as strong as it might be—if it were reinforced, it would be more able to withstand any attack. I do not say this is required, but it may be advisable. The archers' walk high on the wall is in reasonable condition, although the stones are loose in three places: I have marked those places on the enclosed chart.

You made specific reference to the foreigners who live in this part of the city, and to that end, I will tell you that Shighriz of Bukhara has brought more sheep- and goat-skins into his warehouse. He has paid the tax on them grudgingly, but he has paid it in full, and so cannot be denied the right to sell his wares. He has informed me that he will have another caravan arriving, bringing skins and wool, and some tanned leather as well, in the next month or so, all of which should be acceptable to the Sultan's deputies. Also he reports that one of his wives has died and her ashes have been sent back to her father in Bukhara.

Maliq Keral, the merchant of Sind, has reduced the size of his household. He claims it is because his taxes are too high, and that he is being singled out for unjust claims because he is not a Muslim or a devotee of traditional native gods. That he has taken up the teaching of the Satvas has brought him under scrutiny from Muslim and Brahmin alike, for the Satva sect is looked upon with suspicion by many. His complaints have been passed on to the Minister for Taxes, Rents, and Revenues for his review. Also, I have noted that he was so disrespectful of the Sultan that he actually called the Sultan by his name, showing how far he has strayed from the conduct expected of a resident of Delhi. He might as well be living among the Turks, or the Chinese if he has so little regard for our great Sultan.

The family of Taray Sroashar is in arrears with payment of their taxes, and he claims that he cannot put his hands on the amount required before his grace period has expired. I have perused his house, and I am persuaded that he has funds he has not admitted to pos-

sessing. He claims his holy books teach that the End of the World is near, and that paying taxes now is useless, for himself and for the Sultan. Such an unorthodox teaching is open to question, and I believe that this may be nothing more than a ruse to avoid the taxes he owes. I have informed him he will not be allowed to leave Delhi until at least three-quarters of his tax obligations are discharged. He may try to be forgiven this debt, but it is my belief that if he leaves the city, none of the money will ever be paid.

The Parsi, Rustam Iniattir, has departed the city, as you know, leaving behind his nephew Zal to tend to the family's affairs. Rustam Iniattir paid the departure tax without argument and so was allowed to go on his way. He was accompanied by the manservant of the foreigner Sanat Ji Mani, Rojire, who is escorting Avasa Dani to a safer place, in accordance with the terms for guardianship left by her husband when he took up the life of a mendicant.

As to Sanat Ji Mani, he has declared his intention to depart from Delhi after the Winter Solstice to return to his homeland. He has paid an advance on his departure taxes and has signed a pledge to deed his property to the Sultan for his use. He continues to offer his medical skills to those in need, and for that reason he has been excused from the secondary foreign-residents' tax. He has not asked for any greater reduction of his taxes, and I am certain he will not renege on his commitments now.

The family of Raghavan Chayn has lost three children in as many weeks, and they have honored the dead in accordance with their traditions. The observances he has requested to make are incomplete, and it is his obligation to continue the ceremonies for the dead; any lack of diligence on his part will meet with dishonor to his family and disgrace to the memory of his children. Raghavan Chayn has also asked that he might have his taxes reduced until the dark of the year so that he may abide by the period of mourning his faith requires. In this instance, since two of the dead children were boys, the request is not unreasonable, and it is my recommendation that you grant him the relief he seeks. Not to mourn within the dictates of his beliefs would be a most reprehensible act, and one that would not redound to the Sultan's credit.

I have included my evaluation of holdings of all the foreigners keep-

ing household in this quarter, some one hundred sixteen of them, not just the ones singled out above; most of them have made no changes in the conduct of their lives over the last six months, and for that reason, I have not included any specific reference to them. If you would prefer a more comprehensive, individual itemization of particulars for each, you have only to ask me, and I will undertake the inquiry at once. You will want to review those amounts before I pass them on to the Minister of Taxes, Rents, and Revenues, in case you wish to assess a higher amount for the cost of your defenses. Whatever that amount may be, append it to my report, and I will see that it is brought to the Minister's attention at once.

The Travelers' Camp, inside the North-West Gate, is not very full just now. Not many want to be abroad in the rains. I do anticipate that more travelers will come as soon as the weather changes, and then we shall have the revenues from them as well as from the other foreigners who live here to bolster your depleted coffers. I shall be certain that some of my men mix with the travelers to learn their news and to apprehend any spies that may be sent among us. In two to four weeks, we will be busy again at the Travelers' Camp.

Submitted to you in the hope that it will fulfill your mandate, and with every assurance of my continued dedication to the Sultan,

Kanwar Gotanipi

In the Foreigners' Quarter, sent by messenger

8

"The rains arrived late, and they are leaving late," said Firuz Ihbal; he was as worried by the continuing downpour and thrashing winds as he had been apprehensive about their late appearance. He paced the gallery of his lavish house, occasionally turning to glare out at the wet.

"If it halts our work, it also halts Timur-i," said Iksander Mawan, his most trusted eunuch. "Allah is Great."

"*If* Timur-i is where we suppose he is, and *if* the rains are falling farther west as they are here, then perhaps you are right," said Firuz Ihbal at his most grudging. "I cannot say."

"And that is what most distresses you, Estimable Lord," said Iksander Mawan, his voice high and strong; there was nothing the least effeminate about him—not even his lack of a beard made him seem less a man for what had been done to him. "The men you have dispatched to scout for him have not returned and they are feared lost. This troubles you, as well it should. You fret because you do not know if they have fallen into the hands of Timur-i, and he has wrested information from them that may cause him to come here rather than attack another place, or if they have met with some other danger."

"Yes, yes, yes," Firuz Ihbal admitted impatiently. "I still hope that one of the scouts will come back, and shortly, to tell us what we are to face. We cannot prepare to meet a foe we do not know but that they are ferocious and cruel. Since the Sultan remains away from Delhi and it falls to me to act in his interests, I am willing to build up the army as much as possible, but I would prefer to know what we will have to fight with it before I empty the treasury."

"You have nothing to worry about," Iksander Mawan assured him. "You need only display all the might of Delhi, and Timur-i, demon though he may be, and servant of Shaitan, will hesitate to attack such fortifications as we have here."

"May Allah grant it," said Firuz Ihbal more devoutly than usual. "This city is strong, and our soldiers are prepared."

"Are you going to let your worries undermine your determination, Estimable Lord? or are you going to embrace your strength and show the people they have nothing to fear?" Iksander Mawan spread his large hand on his mail breastplate. "We stand by you, and by the Sultan. There can be no doubt that we have the might to prevail in any battle."

"Yes. Of course," said Firuz Ihbal. He clapped his hands, and at once a slave came and bent double before him. "I wish to see all the army commanders this evening, to hear their reports. Tell them they must attend or lose their commission." With a gesture he sent the slave running off.

"A prudent move," said Iksander Mawan. "Any dismay brewing in the army will surely end if it can be shown that the leaders are prepared and confident."

"Which I must find out if they are," said Firuz Ihbal with less satisfaction than Iksander Mawan expressed. "If we must deal with Timur-i, then we cannot be laggard." He began to pace again. "If only I knew what was happening in the west. Our scouts do not return, and that is ominous. I have spoken to leaders of caravans, and all they tell me is that Timur-i can move his troops at four-days' march in a single day."

"That is idle talk," said Iksander Mawan. "They cannot travel at such speeds."

"They say each man has six horses. Six. Every man leads five and rides one. When his mount tires, the soldier saddles another, and so forth, and the horse he has been riding becomes one of the led. The horses all rest at the end of the day, and then continue on the next morning. Doing that, they can move at a trot from dawn until sunset for four days. Then they must rest a day, or they lose horses." He pulled at the ends of his mustaches. "If it is so, and he does move his army in that way, he is as dangerous as they claim. We cannot hope to keep ahead of such a force."

"But six horses for each man! and moving at a trot all day? Even if it were possible, the cost of it is prohibitive. Think of the expense of keeping six horses per man. They would need an army just to maintain the animals. How are such horses to be fed and watered?" Iksander Mawan was shocked. "What leader can keep so many?"

"Apparently Timur-i can," said Firuz Ihbal unpleasantly.

"That is the kind of fear that will undermine us all," said Iksander Mawan, shaking his head. "You must shut such thoughts from your heart and put your faith in Allah—"

"Whom Timur-i also worships," Firuz Ihbal reminded him as he continued to move restlessly about the room. "This is not some unconverted fool, but another Muslim. Would that he had the ancient faith of the Jagatai, so that Allah could show His Greatness by overcoming Timur-i on our behalf. But Timur-i prays five times a day as we do, and to Allah. How can the All-Compassionate favor one of us over the other?"

"Surely Timur-i's devotion is not so whole-hearted as yours," said Iksander Mawan. "The man is in the saddle from sunrise until sunset—you have said it yourself. He cannot be as pious as you and all the Tughluq clan is."

"You are hoping to ease my apprehension, and it is kindly of you, but at this time, I reckon that apprehension serves me well, and it is Allah Himself Who inspires it in my breast, not some trivial worry sprung from a lack of faith." Firuz Ihbal paused at the window. "The markets have been poor. Many merchants will not pay our customs and take their goods elsewhere, yet this is the time we need their goods, and their news, the most."

"Lower the customs," Iksander Mawan recommended. "Say it is because the rains have lasted so long, but give the merchants some concession so they will enter the city again."

"If the Sultan will approve such a reduction, then that may be the solution," said Firuz Ihbal, a bit sadly. "It would be better to have the money and the information, but you are probably right, and information is needed as much as goods."

"So it seems to me," said Iksander Mawan. "You may want to consult with your kinsmen, particularly Murmar bin Tughluq."

"Yes. He is still Minister of Taxes, Rents, and Revenues. He has been lining his pockets since the customs increased, but he might consent to take less for himself if he can be made to understand the urgency of the situation." He tugged at his moustaches again. "I will have to speak with him carefully. I do not want it said that I am working against the Sultan's interests."

"No, indeed," said Iksander Mawan, recalling the prolonged and hideous execution of the last official accused of such chicanery. "Better to show your devotion first and question the motives of others after your own are established."

"You are a wise fellow, Iksander Mawan," said Firuz Ihbal. "I will keep all you have said in mind. Now I will see my informers." It was an abrupt decision, but not an unexpected one. "Show them to the ante-chamber of the Yellow Room. I will see them individually. You will listen behind the ivory screen and give me your opinion when they have gone."

Iksander Mawan put his hands together and bowed. "As you wish, Estimable Lord, I will do."

"I am grateful," said Firuz Ihbal without much thought. "I will begin shortly."

"It shall be as you desire," said Iksander Mawan, and withdrew from Firuz Ihbal's presence. Once out of the private apartment, he strode along the palace corridor with purpose, inwardly pleased that other household slaves made way for him. As he reached the reception area, he found five undistinguished men waiting, all of them silent, and most unwilling to look at the others; one glanced about nervously from time to time. "Workers for Firuz Ihbal, come with me."

The five rose in response to Iksander Mawan's order, moving awkwardly, as if trying not be associated with one another. They formed an irregular cluster beside the handsome eunuch and allowed him to lead them back along the course he had come.

"Whom will he see first?" asked the man with a patch over one eye and a jagged scar on his jaw; he was known as Mirza and was known as Firuz Ihbal's assassin among the criminals of Delhi. "And how long will we have to wait to give our report?"

"That will be the pleasure of Firuz Ihbal to decide," said Iksander Mawan. "I will see to it that you have food and drink if you must long remain here for your audience."

"Just as well," said Josha Dar, who had already waited longer than he wanted to.

"You will be thankful for the attention of Firuz Ihbal," said Iksander Mawan bluntly.

"Why? He isn't Nasiruddin Mohammed bin Tughluq, is he?" The man who spoke the Sultan's name aloud was a thick-set, arrogant fellow who had the look of a bully.

The others stopped still and stared at him. Finally Iksander Mawan moved to confront the man. "You have done an importunate thing, Itimad, to speak the Sultan's name. You shall be punished for it." He clapped his hands, summoning a fair number of slaves. "Take him."

Itimad shouted his protests. "The Sultan is a coward! He has left us to face Timur-i alone! He should be driven from all Delhi!"

Iksander Mawan raised his hand and struck Itimad a blow that sent him reeling. "Enough!" he bellowed. "This man disgraces the Sultan in his palace. Have him flogged and his arms broken so he can do no more mischief, and turn him out of the city. Do it now!"

Watching this, Josha Dar felt himself go cold. He did not hold the Sultan in high regard, but he knew better than to proclaim this to the world—and in the halls of the Sultan's palace. He licked his lips as he saw Itimad dragged away, still shouting, and struggling in the grip of the four slaves who held him.

"Come along," Iksander Mawan said to the remaining four.

"What if Itimad has useful information?" asked the one-eyed man.

"We will discover it," Iksander Mawan said, so coldly that the four men with him moved a little farther away from him, and followed him in silence back to Firuz Ihbal's apartments.

Firuz Ihbal saw the oldest of his informers first: an aged man, bent, and walking with a stick, but with sharp eyes and keen ears. "You have something to tell me, Bahbu. I am listening."

Bahbu began at once. "In the markets I have heard that many men traveling from the west have been taken captive and sold into slavery among the Afghani people. They do this so that their men may continue to fight their invaders. They also seize goods bound for our city, and they demand high prices for it in their markets."

"That is nothing new," said Firuz Ihbal critically. "You must have something to say that is more important."

"I have heard that there are followers of the Brahmin gods who are conspiring to mount opposition to the Sultan and to bring him down before Timur-i can arrive and destroy the city. They are afraid that the Sultan will desert them in time of need, and leave them to Timur-i's army. They plan to offer him the rights of plunder if he will spare Delhi." Bahbu shivered as he clung to his walking-stick, knowing that Firuz Ihbal might lash out at him for such an accusation.

"And do you believe that?" Firuz Ihbal asked smoothly. "Do you think they will do such a thing?"

"I think they will try," said Bahbu. "Or at least, I think they intend to try. They are certain that Delhi will be sacked and razed and all its people slaughtered if any attempt is made to defend it."

"Do you agree with them? that Timur-i will destroy this place?" Firuz Ihbal was pulling on his moustaches as he gave his full attention to the old man.

"I think it may come to that," Bahbu said quietly, cringing.

"And so you agree with the traitors?" Firuz Ihbal asked smoothly.

"Not with what they plan to do, no," said Bahbu at his most ingratiating. "But I think if Timur-i comes here, he will want to ruin the city."

"And do you think he can be bribed?" Firuz Ihbal pursued.

"I have no idea; Timur-i is not reputed to be influenced by bribes, but he may accept one if it is grand enough. I do know that Timur-i is said to enjoy carnage and to take satisfaction in devastation." He stood very still, half-expecting to be struck for his temerity.

"Anything else?" Firuz Ihbal asked after a short, nerve-wracking silence.

"No," said Bahbu, who wanted only to escape from the palace and return to his begging-place in the Camel-Drivers' Market.

Firuz Ihbal tossed him two silver coins. "Go with the thanks of the Sultan," he said, and called for Iksander Mawan. "See him out and bring me Mirza."

"That I will," said Iksander Mawan, all but picking Bahbu up and carrying him out of the room. "Mirza," he said to the waiting men as he shoved Bahbu along.

Mirza rose from the bench where he sat and went to make his report.

"Never mind what you have to tell me," Firuz Ihbal said abruptly as soon as Iksander Mawan had withdrawn from the room. "The others will give me reports enough. I need you to tend to a private matter for me. And as soon as possible."

"What might that be?" said Mirza, smiling a little.

"I have a cousin who is proving a nuisance," said Firuz Ihbal in a measured way. "I have done my best to reason with him, but without success. He must not be allowed to interfere in these dangerous times. In fact, he must be prevented from continuing his reckless policies. I rely on you to find a time and place to rectify the situation—away from the palace—"

"Of course," said Mirza quickly, not wanting to hear the order aloud.

"Of course; you understand," Firuz Ihbal agreed. "It must appear that robbers did it; all his slaves with him must be killed, and his escort."

Mirza nodded, doing his best to maintain his calm demeanor. "I will need to have help to do as you require," he pointed out. "It will be costly."

"I would expect so," said Firuz Ihbal.

"My men will need to be paid for their silence," Mirza added.

"If they will not accept a single payment, you must see that your men do not live to speak of it," said Firuz Ihbal.

Mirza bristled at this. "I will not kill my own men."

"You will if you wish to continue to live to serve me," said Firuz Ihbal in a tone of such utter certainty that Mirza was shaken. "You will tend to the matter before the next full moon, and you will do all that you can to be sure that nothing is attributed to you, or to me."

"If you tell me so," said Mirza. "But your cousin may be as well-guarded as you are. I cannot assume otherwise."

"Perhaps not," said Firuz Ihbal. "But you are a subtle man, and you have been able to get around guards before now."

"And I may again, if your cousin is not suspicious." He faltered, not knowing if he should ask. "Which cousin do you wish to have . . . moved out of your way?"

"Murmar bin Tughluq," said Firuz Ihbal very softly.

Mirza paled. "The Minister of Taxes, Rents, and Revenues!" He shook his head. "The man has an army about him."

"Which he pays with misgotten gold," said Firuz Ihbal. "He is draining the treasury while he raises the taxes to equip the army, or so he claims. More of the money goes into his coffers than into soldiers' pay." He coughed. "If we are to be ready to face Timur-i, we must spend money now, on those things that will make us safe."

"But it is so great a chance," said Mirza. "If we do not succeed"—he dared not say *fail*—"we will be executed after torture, and—"

"If you do not succeed, you must spare yourself suffering and kill yourself, as must all your men." Firuz Ihbal scowled. "We must also slow down the departure of foreigners from the city. We need their taxes and we can use them to bargain with Timur-i if it comes to that."

Mirza nodded slowly. "Your cousin is not doing that."

"My cousin is making money from them, taxing them as they depart at a rate that rises steadily. I have supported this in the past but now I am less certain that this is as wise as I thought at first, for I assumed many would remain to avoid the taxation. It seems now that this is not the case, for many of the foreigners are accepting the terms of departure, leaving us with only a few rich merchants to depend upon."

"But killing your cousin," Mirza whispered. "How could that make a difference?"

"It could because I will then be appointed to his post, and I will institute better policies." There was no doubt that Firuz Ihbal was satisfied with this arrangement. "I have put my plans before my cousin and he has ignored them, no matter how beneficial they are."

"And you are certain you would be the new Minister?" Mirza asked, his voice still low; he glanced uneasily about, fearing they were observed.

"I am," said Firuz Ihbal. "I have been assured I would be." He paused. "You have to do this. There will be a handsome reward for your work, and advancement as well. You will be my immediate personal protector, and that will mean privilege and favor beyond anything you have known before."

Mirza shook his head. "It will not be easy."

"No, it will not," Firuz Ihbal agreed. "Yet I am sure you can accomplish the deed in a way that will satisfy us all."

"Some will suspect you," Mirza warned him. "If you are advanced by his death, you will be under suspicion."

"There is nothing new in such suspicions," said Firuz Ihbal. "My great-grandfather, the Sultan Mohammed bin Tughluq was rumored to have killed his father to gain the throne, and he regularly ordered rebellious subjects murdered. Yet he is considered a fine Sultan, and our House still rules Delhi."

"True," Mirza conceded.

"You do not need to worry about tongues wagging. It will mean little to me once I am Minister. It should not mean anything to you, either." Firuz Ihbal motioned to Mirza to come nearer. "You should not fear this plan. It opens your future."

"Very well," said Mirza, his capitulation indicated by a slow nod.

"Excellent." Firuz Ihbal beamed at him. "I want you to begin your efforts quickly, and make them worthy of me. I will await word of your success." He motioned to Mirza. "You may depart. I will see Josha Dar next. Tell Iksander Mawan to admit him."

Mirza pressed his hands together and bowed before leaving the chamber. He found the eunuch waiting near the door. "He wants Josha Dar next."

"I will attend to it," said Iksander Mawan, waiting while Mirza started toward the side-door through which he had been admitted. "Take care not to be observed."

"I know what is expected of me," said Mirza as he prepared to slip out of the palace and into the narrow alley-way.

"Then go, and Allah show you His Compassion," said Iksander Mawan before he went to fetch Josha Dar.

A sudden, high shriek rent the palace air—Itimad was being punished. A second one followed, with a curse hidden in it.

Iksander Mawan looked steadily at Josha Dar, who was trying to walk on as if he had heard nothing. "Thus to all who would harm the Sultan," he said righteously.

"Allah is Great," said Josha Dar, his thoughts in disorder. He strove to restore his composure, and had very nearly succeeded by the time Iksander Mawan opened the door to the private audience chamber.

"There you are," said Firuz Ihbal, nodding once to Josha Dar. "Have you something to tell me?"

For an instant, Josha Dar trembled, then he touched his fingers together and bowed. "Yes, Estimable Lord, I do have information for you."

"Well, and what is it?" Firuz Ihbal asked, his tone level and his eyes hard.

"I have spoken to a pilgrim returning from Mecca, and he has imparted to me the most recent activity of Timur-i and his army." He hoped that no one else had such current news as he, for Firuz Ihbal would not look favorably upon old or inaccurate information. "He is said to be bound for Kabul."

"Kabul?" Firuz Ihbal scoffed. "No one has ever defeated those wild men. This time Timur-i will be stopped and we will be spared."

"From there, he is bound for Lahore," Josha Dar added, wincing as he spoke. "He could reach us after the dark of the year."

"If he can make his way from Kabul," said Firuz Ihbal. "You say this report is reliable?"

"A pilgrim returning from Mecca would have no reason to lie about such a thing." Josha Dar shrugged. "I can find the pilgrim and bring him to you, if you want." He hoped Firuz Ihbal would not make such a request, for he feared the pilgrim had already left the city.

"No, no," said Firuz Ihbal. "A man on a pilgrimage is not to be interfered with." He cocked his head. "What of the tales of Timur-i being killed or overthrown?"

"I have heard them, of course," said Josha Dar. "And they may be true, but that doesn't change the danger his army represents. If Timur-i is gone, he has a successor, you may be sure of that."

"So you have nothing to report that makes it clear what has become of him?" Firuz Ihbal pulled at his moustaches. "It would be better if we know."

"I will do my best to find out," Josha Dar promised. "I have also heard that your kinsman, Balban Ihbal, may be working against the Sultan, in the hope of putting Asaf bin Tughluq in his place."

Firuz Ihbal went still. "Balban Ihbal? Supports our second cousin? The man is a capable soldier, but he cannot lead Delhi, not in the face of Timur-i," he said at last, horrified at the magnitude of this treachery. "I am in charge of the army. I know which of the officers have the support of the men."

Josha Dar realized he had hit upon something valuable. "But Balban Ihbal knows the mood of Delhi. Without the Sultan here, there is a sense in the people that they are no longer protected. I believe it is the intention of Balban Ihbal to find someone who can keep the city safe." He had to go carefully, aware that Firuz Ihbal, like all the Tughluqs, had a volatile temper. "He is trying to stem the tide of people leaving the city. He wants to preserve—"

"He hasn't the least notion how that is to be done," Firuz Ihbal interrupted. "My cousin has his abilities, but he is also greedy, willing to accept bribes and to hold himself ready to serve those with the most wealth."

"It is possible that he might be pleased to help you, had you a candidate to offer," Josha Dar suggested. "You should discuss this with him."

"I think not," said Firuz Ihbal in a thoughtful tone; he changed abruptly, waving Josha Dar away. "I have a great deal to do. You have given me much to think about."

"It is my pleasure to serve you," said Josha Dar, bowing deeply.

"You also want gold from me," Firuz Ihbal growled. "Still, I will buy your diligence and your silence. If one syllable of this is heard beyond these walls, I will know who has uttered them and I will know you for my enemy." He tossed four gold coins to Josha Dar.

Josha Dar caught them adroitly. "You are most kind," he said as he slipped the money into a pouch hidden in his clothing.

"I know what is worth the price," said Firuz Ihbal. "I will need your report again in two days."

"I may not learn anything in two days," Josha Dar protested, paling.

"You had better," Firuz Ihbal recommended. "If you do not, you will have little reason to rejoice."

"Yes, Splendid One," Josha Dar said, retreating from the threat he had just received. "In two days."

"Before mid-day prayers," Firuz Ihbal added. "Iksander Mawan will admit you."

"Yes, Splendid One," Josha Dar repeated as he backed toward the door; the gold in his pouch seemed to be made of fire, for it felt as if it burned his skin. He was grateful when the door between them closed and Iksander Mawan appeared to show him out of the palace.

Text of a letter from Rojire to Sanat Ji Mani, written in Imperial Latin at Yemen and carried by Sanat Ji Mani's ship *Wave Racer* to Cambay in Gujerat, and from there by messenger to Delhi; never delivered.

To my master, called Sanat Ji Mani, living at Delhi, from the servant known as Rojire, greetings from Yemen.

We have reached this port without trouble or difficulty, and the prospect for a swift journey up the Red Sea is very good. The rains are behind us, so the seas have been fairly calm, and we anticipate more of the same. All your goods and belongings have come through the voyage without serious damage, and should continue to do well for the rest of our travels.

The place we did find trouble was Gujerat—there is great unrest there, and the belief that Delhi has become so weak that it cannot defend itself, let alone them. I would not be astonished to learn that the region has separated itself from its ties with Delhi, especially if

Timur-i comes into the region. If the Sultan is relying on Gujerat to support him, he may be disappointed, nor do I think Gujerat is the only part of the Delhi Empire that will fail to support the city. You may have to find another way to the sea than through Gujerat to Cambay. I would not think it is a safe place for a foreigner to be.

Avasa Dani has been ill for most of the voyage—the sea does not agree with her: it may be that your blood is working in her already, though she has not yet come to your life. Whatever the case, she has passed several wretched days in her bed. I have tended her as I said I would, and she has not fallen into any lethargy or taken a fever yet. Now we are on land again, she swears she will not board a ship again, but she also knows that she must.

Yemen now is not the Yemen of a thousand years ago. It is no longer powerful and rich as it was; the old fortifications are gone, and they no longer control all the traffic into the Red Sea as they once did. What they now call the Years of Dark Storms, and the Chinese call the Year of Yellow Snow, took a toll from which they have not recovered. Many cities suffered in that time, but few of them retain the scars quite as visibly as Yemen does.

Rustam Iniattir and his family have been much troubled by second thoughts, and one of his children cries every day, wanting to return to Delhi. I cannot blame him for his doubts, but I believe what he saw in Gujerat unnerved him enough to convince him that he has made the right decision in leaving Delhi; until he saw that unrest, I believe he was afraid he had made a mistake in leaving Delhi, after all. Now he is saying that if Timur-i does not attack the city, there may still be rebellion in the streets, and should that happen, foreigners will suffer the most, especially if the Sultan does nothing to protect them, and he is preparing a letter to his nephew even as I write this to you. You, of course, need no such warning for your protection, do you?

I have decided that we will journey to your house in Alexandria, and there Avasa Dani may devote herself to the study she so enjoys. There are not many of her countrymen there, and she will have to abide by the laws of Islam, but still, I believe it will be safer in Alexandria than in Tyre or other cities in the eastern arm of the Mameluke Empire: Timur-i has sacked Baghdad and could still strike toward Egypt. If we reside at Alexandria, we will be more protected and,

*should Timur-i come this way, we will have the sea by which to escape.
If it comes to that, we will go to your old villa outside Roma. It may
be a ruin, but we can manage there for a while, and you can find us
without difficulty. I have been offered the opportunity to stay with the
ship when it leaves the Red Sea and continues down the east coast of
Africa, but I have turned down the kind offer—a man with light skin,
sandy hair, and blue eyes may not stand out over-much in Alexandria,
but in the south of Africa, I would be set apart at once, and no one
would consider me anything but foreign; under such circumstances, I
could do little to guard Avasa Dani, or to hide myself if it were necessary.*

*All of your goods that we carry with us have survived the voyage,
including your red-lacquer Roman chest, although there is a new
scrape on its side. The four chests of your native earth are in fine
condition, and the container of jewels is still intact. You have no reason
to fret about any of these things, for I can think of no reason why
they should not reach Alexandria as intact as they are now—the pirates who have prowled these coasts like wolves are raiding farther
south along the coast of Africa, for they do not want to be captured
by those dispensing Timur-i's justice; the sailors all assure me that we
can continue the voyage without fear of attack, although they carry
weapons against such a possibility.*

*We will leave in two days, but I wished to send this to you while
I have the opportunity to give this to one of your ships' captains. I
hope he will be diligent in having this placed in your hands before
spring.*

*As I am writing in Latin, I will sign myself by my name as it was
when I lived*

Rogerian

*On October 24th, 1398, according to the Coptic priest who keeps an
old chapel here*

9

Garuda held up his head defiantly. "I am sorry it has come to this," he said. "But it would be unwise for me to remain here. I have spoken with my brothers and they agree that I must go."

Sanat Ji Mani inclined his head slightly. "I have no wish to compel you to serve me if you desire to leave my employ," he said in a neutral tone. "I will pay you your full wages and prepare a letter for your next employer." It was a courtesy expected of foreigners, as Sanat Ji Mani knew.

Looking abashed, Garuda shook his head. "No. I want no such letter. There are too many who would take it amiss."

"As you like," said Sanat Ji Mani. His study was filled with morning light, sufficient to be enervating to him; he longed for his austere bedchamber and the restoration of his native earth. That would not be possible today, he knew, and he put it out of his thoughts.

"I am grateful that you . . . accommodate me thus," said Garuda, staring around the room. "I will depart after sundown, taking my things with me."

"As you wish," said Sanat Ji Mani. "You need not hurry on my account."

Garuda missed the ironic note in Sanat Ji Mani's tone. "You have been good to me, my master, and I am sorry to have to deal you such a blow as this. I would have stayed had there not been so much trouble. The Sultan's return, and his swift departure has put everything into disarray. Everyone knows the omens are dire."

"Yes: they did not need the Sultan to tell them that," said Sanat Ji Mani with an edge of impatience in his tone. "It were better he did not come here if he did not intend to remain. Ten days at the palace, throwing everything into confusion, and now he has gone again. Thanks to the Sultan, there is panic throughout the city." He looked toward the window, saying distantly, "I am a foreigner, and just now foreigners are not welcome in Delhi: and yes, I understand your burden. In your place I might well do the same thing." He went to his chest beneath the shuttered window and used his key to unlock it. "I will give you full wages until the next full moon, and then I will add a month's wages for good service, for you have given me excellent service." He began to count out the coins, taking his time so that Garuda could see he was giving the full amount.

"Thank you, my master," said Garuda awkwardly.

"You have no reason to thank me; it is I who ought to thank you. You have done the work you were hired to do, and I am obliged to recompense your service, which I am glad to do," said Sanat Ji Mani. "I would prefer both of us to be satisfied with the conclusion of our work together than either of us harbor suspicions and resentments."

"But many another would dismiss me without paying the balance of my wages, and not even the magistrates would reprimand him," said Garuda.

"Perhaps not, if they were natives of this city," Sanat Ji Mani said. "It matters little, in any case, for I would not want to deny you what you have earned."

"Well, you do not need so many servants now, in any case," said Garuda, feeling vaguely as if he owed a more comprehensive explanation to Sanat Ji Mani. "You can manage well enough with a smaller staff. You have not entertained, nor brought the injured into the house, nor taken on the guardianship of another man's wife for many days, and will probably not do so again, so you will not lack for service with a smaller staff."

Sanat Ji Mani gave a quick, ironic smile. "Very true. My household can be reduced without compromise of duties." He handed the money to Garuda. "There you are. Count it now, and satisfy yourself it is the whole amount."

Garuda began to be embarrassed. "I have no reason to question you, my master. You have never been ungenerous."

"But you might decide, at some later time, that I had not given as much as I assured you I would," Sanat Ji Mani said firmly. "This way we will both be certain you are adequately paid."

With a shrug, Garuda began to count, and finally said, "It is more than sufficient, my master. You did not need to pay me so much."

"You may not think so in a month," said Sanat Ji Mani. "This way, we understand one another, which avoids later unpleasantness." He locked his chest again. "How many other servants are considering leaving?"

"I . . . I do not know . . ." Garuda stared down at his feet, afraid to go on.

"Does that mean they have said nothing to you, or that you do not know the specific number who wish to go?" He asked the question kindly, but Garuda still winced.

"It means that some have said one thing one day and something else the next," said Garuda. "It is a most troubling situation."

"I agree," said Sanat Ji Mani. He stood still for a long moment, then said, "You will do me a service, Garuda, if you will tell the others that I will not hold it against them if they, too, wish to leave. Let them have a day to decide. I will speak to them at the evening meal, and they may tell me what they wish to do."

"I do not think I—" He stopped, his face darkening a couple of shades.

"I will hold it as a favor if you would do this; they will accept the offer more readily if it comes from you instead of me, and it would be easier to deal with a single departure of many servants rather than a straggling trickle of the same number over weeks," Sanat Ji Mani said, feeling a fatalistic certainty that he would not keep most of his staff once this opportunity was presented to them; too many of his servants were demoralized by the worsening crisis in the city and were eager to follow the Sultan's example and flee. "If you would add to the good care already given, do this for me, and with my thanks."

"If you like," said Garuda, sounding miserable. "You may lose a considerable number of your servants if you make such an offer."

"Then I lose them," said Sanat Ji Mani. "It does me no good to have men around me who do not wish to be there." He thought back to the years of his life he had been a slave, and how the subservience of his position had worked on him: even the centuries in Egypt had taken their toll. "I would make no such imposition on anyone."

"Is that why you have no concubines?" Garuda dared to ask.

"In part," said Sanat Ji Mani, surprised that Garuda would speak of such things. "That, and foreigners are under scrutiny that might bring misfortune to a concubine." He did not elaborate, but memories of Cyprus came back with a sudden intensity.

"Females are not to be trusted," said Garuda. "You are a wise man."

It was useless to protest this was not what he meant—it was also reckless: Sanat Ji Mani lowered his eyes. "You may go to the others, Garuda."

Knowing this dismissal for an order, Garuda bowed his head. "I hear and obey," he said, his hands pressed together as he bowed over them before withdrawing from Sanat Ji Mani's presence.

Left alone, Sanat Ji Mani began to calculate what he owed his servants in wages and to prepare to pay them. He had no worry about the amounts that would be required, for he had more than enough to cover any sum—in his laboratory he had prepared over three measures of gold, and would now augment the gold with a quantity of silver—enough to buy ten war elephants, if only Firuz Ihbal knew of it—which, fortunately, he did not. He took a sheet of vellum from his writing-table drawer and, choosing a trimmed pen, he began to write down the sums he owed his staff. It did not take long, and when he was done, he felt strangely at loose ends, not knowing to what he should next give his attention. He paced around the room, then went out of it abruptly, stifling the urge to call for Rojire. The stairs to his laboratory were lit with hanging lamps, still burning from their night-time use, though they did little to increase the brightness; the sunlight was strong enough to penetrate into the stairwell, its intensity giving Sanat Ji Mani a mild degree of discomfort.

The athanor stood open, ready for the next crucible, and the equipment set out on the two trestle-tables was clean in preparation for the new wonders Sanat Ji Mani would perform. He walked quickly to the cabinet that contained his supplies and took out four earthenware jars sealed with wax. He stripped the wax from the jars with a practiced pass with a little knife, then began to measure out the various elements into a retort of Egyptian glass; he had done this often in the last two thousand years and could almost judge the amounts by weight as by measure. Satisfied, he added acid from a special glass vial, and sealed it again at once, using a glass stopper and wax before continuing on with his task. He placed the retort in the athanor, then gathered up the special fuel that gave the little oven its uncanny power, set it to heat, and busied himself adjusting the shutters to mute the impact of the sun.

By the time the sun was directly overhead, Sanat Ji Mani was removing silver nuggets from the retort, preparing to melt them and pour them into coin-molds of Byzantine design. He did his best to ignore the fatigue that slowed his body and his thoughts; that would be gone when the sun was past its zenith, and it no longer vitiated him; even with the year winding down to its close, the sun in this region was enough to be a burden while he worked at his self-appointed task. These coins would be used to pay the servants who wished to leave his employ: he was convinced there would be a good number of them, for now that Garuda was leaving, the others would take it as a sign that this household was no longer safe.

Mid-afternoon saw the first of the coins ready, the silversmithing equipment and coin-molds set out on the longer table for easy reach. It was demanding work, but not arduous, and Sanat Ji Mani was grateful to have something to occupy his attention as the day passed. The wealth these coins represented would have shocked many of the servants, who knew their master had money, but no notion of how much. Sanat Ji Mani continued to work, making more coins as quickly as he could until he had enough to fill a lentil-basket twice over. Satisfied, he put the rest of the nuggets away, cleaned and stored his equipment, then went down to the servants' dining room just as the Muslim call to sunset prayers faded from the air.

Garuda was at the head of the table, waiting for the cook to bring out their evening fare; he had clearly told all the servants about their master's offer, for all of them had an apprehensive expression on their eyes as they turned toward him. "My master," said Garuda, starting to rise.

"No longer," Sanat Ji Mani said with a hospitable smile. "I am pleased that you have stayed until now before leaving. I will miss your presence in my house."

This was gracious enough to reassure the others that this was not going to be a trial, nor was it to be as unpleasant as Hirsuma's departure had been. Many of the men visibly relaxed, and sat back, anticipating an interesting evening.

"I will not leave," Bohdil, the head groom, announced, breaking the anticipatory silence.

"Thank you for that," said Sanat Ji Mani. "I would not like to have to tend to all the horses and the goat by myself." His smile flashed again, and eased the men's minds further.

"I should like to leave," said the kitchen supervisor, who bought all the food and kept track of its use. "My family wishes to depart for Baran; my mother is from there, and we believe it may be safer there."

"I will see you have your pay at first light tomorrow. You may leave before the end of the day," said Sanat Ji Mani, adding carefully, "As your final task, I would like to have your kitchen inventory before you go, so the work may be taken up by another. I am certain you have kept excellent records, and that bringing them up-to-date will not be an onerous duty."

"Certainly," said the kitchen supervisor, relieved that this went so well. "I will present a catalogue of all supplies and foodstuffs in the kitchen before I leave. Is this to include the crock of moldy bread?"

"Yes, it is," said Sanat Ji Mani, who used the moldy bread to make his sovereign remedy for fevers and infections. "You need not do it this instant. So long as I have it before you go, I will be satisfied."

"I will stay," said the bedroom steward, a slim young man named Dapas. "I am glad to stay."

"Thank you," said Sanat Ji Mani, looking up in time to see the cook arrive with the evening meal.

"I will go," said the cook. "But my assistant, Shudra, will remain." He indicated this youth, coming behind him with a large basket filled with a variety of fried breads. "You will not need to find another to make your meals. He will do well enough." With that, he sat down and prepared to eat.

"As you wish," said Sanat Ji Mani, then looked at Mukhi, the carpenter.

"I will stay, at least until the dark of the year passes," he said. "I may go then, but not now."

"I appreciate your dedication to my house," Sanat Ji Mani told him carefully, and waited to hear what was said next.

In the end, Sanat Ji Mani was left with five servants to staff his house: a steward, a cook, a groom, a carpenter, and a messenger. He paid the rest, and provided each a bonus for his service, and allowed three days for those leaving to pack their belongings and depart.

Dapas, who at sixteen now found himself steward of the household, took Sanat Ji Mani aside the following morning after wages had been paid, saying, "I am told that this house is watched."

"I am not surprised," said Sanat Ji Mani. "I became aware of it some months ago, and given the current state of affairs in Delhi, I suppose it is to be expected."

Somewhat nonplussed by this response, Dapas did what he could to recover his dignity. "I thought you should know that I am aware of it, too."

"Yes," said Sanat Ji Mani. "Very good. I am pleased that you are attentive."

Relieved to hear this, Dapas went on, "What would you like me to do about it?"

"Why, nothing," said Sanat Ji Mani. "That would only lead to more surveillance and increased suspicion, and in these times, such attention is dangerous. If you want to keep an eye on the man who watches this house, I would not object, providing it does not interfere with your other duties."

Dapas nodded a bit stiffly. "I will do. I will report what I see to you before the evening meal."

"Thank you," said Sanat Ji Mani, wondering how many of his departing servants would talk to the emaciated man who had been observing the house for many months.

"I will tell the other four to have nothing to do with him," Dapas said, as if sensing Sanat Ji Mani's concerns.

"That would be appreciated," said Sanat Ji Mani, deliberately obliquely. "I know you are prepared to do more, but in this case, it is not necessary."

"As you say," Dapas murmured, touching his hands together and bowing.

"I am going to my quarters to rest," Sanat Ji Mani said. "I will rise in the afternoon and bathe. Have the bath ready for mid-afternoon. I will call you when I am ready."

"Very good, my master," said Dapas, bowing again.

"And, if you will, send Nayakar to me," Sanat Ji Mani added. "I have a message for him to carry to the nephew of Rustam Iniattir."

"At once, my master," Dapas assured him as he left the study.

Nayakar appeared so promptly that Sanat Ji Mani supposed he must have been listening at the door. "What do you want me to do, my master?" he asked, bowing over his hands. He was aware of his advancement within the household and clearly intended to make the most of it; his self-satisfaction colored his whole demeanor.

"I am going to write a note. I would like you to carry it to the house of Rustam Iniattir and give it into the hands of his nephew—no one else." He took a sheet of vellum and a trimmed quill pen, pulled the ink-cake from its drawer, poured water on it, ground it until there was a pool of black in the shallow well, dipped the quill into it, and began to write.

"Am I to bring a reply?" Nayakar asked.

"No. Only see Zal and put the letter into his hands," said Sanat Ji Mani, sounding a bit remote as he continued to write.

"Shall I deliver any other message? Is there some additional news you wish me to impart?" Nayakar's eagerness reminded Sanat Ji Mani of an unridden colt.

"No; delivering the letter to him will be sufficient, thank you," said Sanat Ji Mani, hoping to curb some of Nayakar's enthusiasm. "It is a simple task."

"As you wish; I will take the message to Zal Iniattir, and no other," said Nayakar. "Am I to return directly, or are there other errands you wish me to perform for you?"

"Come back as soon as you are done," said Sanat Ji Mani, reading over the page, then sanding it before he rolled it and secured it with a band of silk.

"As you wish, my master," said Nayakar, taking the vellum into his hands.

"Nayakar," Sanat Ji Mani asked in an off-handed way, "Can you read?"

"A few words, my master, no more," he said. "Rice. Street. Cost. Delhi. Father. Truth. Caste." He ticked off his list with pride.

"Still, better than most," said Sanat Ji Mani. "Thank you for telling me."

"I know the banners of most of the shop-keepers," Nayakar added. "You may send me to any of them if you need goods purchased."

"Excellent," Sanat Ji Mani approved. "I will keep that in mind." He motioned Nayakar away. "You may leave now. I believe you will find Zal Iniattir at his uncle's home; he has moved his wives and children there since Rustam Iniattir departed. If he is not there, ask his steward where he has gone, seek him out wherever he may be, and give this to him."

"As you wish, my master," said Nayakar, and withdrew from the study. He went through the house holding the rolled vellum as conspicuously as possible, wishing that more of the few remaining servants could see him in his newly exalted role. At the side-door, he said to Dapas, "I am bidden to take this to Zal Iniattir, and to return at once."

"Then be off with you; use the clapper when you return," said Dapas, not willing to be impressed by Nayakar's boasting. He held the door open, and closed it as soon as the young man stepped out. "Do not be laggard in your work; do as you have been instructed— nothing more and nothing less." He peered out the slit in the door to see if Nayakar went the right direction on the Street of Brass Lanterns and was relieved as he watched the young messenger turn and go toward the shortest route to Rustam Iniattir's house. Satisfied, he stepped back from the door and went to report to Sanat Ji Mani that Nayakar was on his way. Had he continued to watch he might not have been so pleased, for as Nayakar reached the corner, a scrawny man in a loincloth and shawl stepped out of the shadows.

"So you are leaving, too," Josha Dar said in what he hoped was an encouraging tone.

"For a short while. I have this message to carry to the house of Iniattir," Nayakar declared, not quite bragging, but showing off nonetheless.

"You are not leaving the household?" Josha Dar asked in a tone of astonishment.

"Of course not. I am not afraid of Timur-i, or his ghost." Nayakar smoothed the front of his clothing, doing his best to present a good appearance.

"Very commendable," said Josha Dar. "Would more persons in Delhi were as brave as you."

"Only a fool would be frightened. Look at the Sultan's army. How can a pack of wild horsemen stand against archers and war elephants?" He grinned. "We shall see the end of Timur-i if he should be foolish enough to come here. Then the ones who have left the city will be chagrined, for they will see their cowardice for what it is. Even the Sultan will know he should have remained here. Those of us who are loyal to Delhi must stand by the city now, or be disgraced."

"Fine sentiments," said Josha Dar, falling into step beside Nayakar. "I do not mean to keep you from your duties, but you impress me with your convictions."

"You are good to say so," Nayakar told him, accepting this praise with an inner sense of vindication that made him smile a little.

"Most of your comrades in the foreigner's house did not have the same faith you do," Josha Dar prompted, hoping to learn more.

Nayakar did not need much encouragement. "I am ashamed of many of them. It is one thing when a family decides they all must go, but only a few had that excuse—most of them were just frightened, and they let themselves be ruled by their fright. It is not as if they were driven off by abuse, or want. They have been treated well by Sanat Ji Mani, who is a most generous and worthy man, for all he is a foreigner, and they still left without hesitation." He spat. "Cowards and unbelievers, all of them."

"But you have remained," Josha Dar said approvingly.

"And four others." Nayakar smiled. "Sanat Ji Mani has given each of us two pieces of gold for staying with him. That is something the others have forfeited." He reached the next corner and turned right. "Iniattir lives in this street."

"The Parsi?" said Josha Dar as if unfamiliar with the name.

"Yes. My master has done business with the uncle and now sends word to the nephew." He held up the vellum once again. "The Parsi are strange folk, but my foreign master is not troubled by them."

"Perhaps their foreign ways are similar," said Josha Dar, who knew this was not so. "They may find understanding, one with the other."

"I do not know," said Nayakar. "Sanat Ji Mani is not of the Parsi: he comes from a much more distant place, called the Land Across the Forest."

"An odd name," said Josha Dar, shrugging even as he rejoiced inwardly at this tidbit of information that should please Firuz Ihbal bin Tughluq.

"It is of the West," said Nayakar, as if that explained everything. "In their tongue, it is Transylvania."

"Transylvania," Josha Dar repeated, tasting the word.

"He is known as a great healer there," Nayakar went on as he approached the side-door of Rustam Iniattir's house.

"He has healed the sick here, I have heard," Josha Dar said, and realized he had gone too far, for Nayakar turned toward him, his eyes alive with misgiving. Hoping to repair the damage his remark had done, he added, "It was gossip in the market for many days when he healed the foreign pilgrim's foot." Looking at the young messenger, Josha Dar saw he had made matters worse, not better.

"You have been spying on my master," said Nayakar firmly. "You are one of those who seek to harm him."

"No," said Josha Dar. "Nothing of the sort. He is interesting. All foreigners are interesting." He could hear the desperation in his voice but was powerless to stop it.

"Tell me, how long have you been watching my master, and for whom?" Nayakar demanded, his skin darkening as indignation mounted in him.

"I have not watched him," Josha Dar protested, holding up his hands to show his innocence. "I have done nothing that deserves your scorn."

"Hah!" Nayakar exclaimed. "You may have fooled me at first, but I comprehend now what you are doing, and I am ready to hold you accountable. I will tell my master what I have seen, and what you asked, and then we will find out what will happen next." He tried to make this sound as threatening as possible, for he was beginning to be frightened.

"You misunderstand me, young man," said Josha Dar. "I mean nothing to your master's discredit. If you would only believe that."

"How can I, when you have—" He stopped talking, made a gesture of disgust, and approached the side-door of the Parsi's house. "Be off with you," he shouted over his shoulder, and could not help but look to see if Josha Dar obeyed him.

The steward who opened the door looked harried; he heard Nay-akar's errand and informed him that Zal Iniattir was at the storehouse on the Street of Foreign Merchants. "You will know it by the white crane on the banner. My master will receive you there."

"I will attend to this at once," Nayakar said, and vowed inwardly to speak to no one but Zal Iniattir and his servants until he was once again inside Sanat Ji Mani's house. He went off through the crowded streets, looking about as he went, searching for Josha Dar and any of the other spies he was certain were following him.

Zal Iniattir came promptly to receive the message, gave Nayakar a silver coin and sent him away, saying he would call upon Sanat Ji Mani himself after evening prayers.

"I will tell him," said Nayakar, bowing over his joined hands. "He will receive you whenever it suits you." He was not quite certain this was so, but good manners encouraged such an assurance. He left the storehouse and made his way back toward the Street of Brass Lan-terns, sure his progress was observed by myriad eyes. And as he walked, he became increasingly convinced that he had made a terrible mistake in not leaving Sanat Ji Mani's service while he had the chance.

Military report from Lahore, carried by special couriers, delivered in Delhi to Firuz Ihbal bin Tughluq on 2nd November, 1398 by the Roman calendar.

In the Name of Allah, the All-Compassionate, may my eyes be blinded and my tongue cut from my mouth if I report inaccurately or fabricate any events or details with the intention of misleading the officers and deputies of the Sultan—may Allah give him worthy sons and many victories—in regard to the dangers present in Lahore.

We did not take the brunt of his army, but we have been badly damaged by the efforts of his men, which I am bound to report to you, as the Sultan's men; for Timur-i is bound to the south-east, di-rectly toward you, and it is not unlikely that you will have to fight him soon. For all the rumors that Timur-i has been cast out by his own army, or he has died, we at Lahore have no reason to think this is true. The soldiers we fought called themselves the men of Timur-i, and those few we were able to capture screamed his name before they died.

Timur-i may say he is the follower of the Prophet, and keeps true to the Laws of Islam, but he does not conduct himself as if this is true. For one thing, when he or his men fight, they take almost no slaves: they kill all they capture unless there is some very persuasive and immediately useful reason to keep a captive alive. Many rich men of Lahore paid high sums to keep Timur-i from our city, and to the extent that the whole of his forces did not attack us, I would have to say that their efforts were successful.

Four companies of mounted men came to Lahore, each company arrayed in its own color: we could look out and see ranks of yellow, white, red, and green. So great was their discipline that the companies did not scatter in battle, but remained intact, as if they were invisibly yoked together for the assault. Were it not for the fact that these troops are our deadliest enemies, I could find it in my heart to admire their skills as soldiers. As it is, I can only condemn their dedication to war.

Their camps were impressive to see—hundreds of tents, many of them large and splendid, and a number of carts and wagons carrying such things as a farrier's smithy, a saddler's shop, and a bath-house. I have been told that the full army has much more of the same, and that it becomes a city in itself every time it stops. Yet, cumbersome as it is, this army is said to travel as far in a day as a merchant-train does, except when rough terrain slows it down.

We were able to watch their work from our walls, and hideous it was to see: they began with the people living beyond the city walls: they rounded up the farmers and camp-keepers and their families and slaves, brought them near to our Northern Gate and hacked them all to bloody scraps, which they left near the Gate, while they rode around the walls firing their arrows up at our defenses, occasionally wounding or killing one of our men. Some of the arrows dropped into the streets, and a few struck persons unlucky enough to be abroad at that time. The soldiers of Timur-i have a cry they give when fighting, and it is more terrible than the baying of wolves in the winter.

Eventually the Western Gate was set on fire with flaming arrows fired by Timur-i's soldiers, and when the fire was put out, a great many of the mounted men poured through the opening, killing as they went. The people of the city were appalled, and many tried to flee, only to be cut down and their dismembered bodies flung onto the pile of slaughtered farmers, which was now beginning to putrefy.

The soldiers of Timur-i attacked the Southern Gate next, and very nearly had the same success as they had had on the Northern Gate, when they were summoned to their thrice-damned master's side, and abandoned their assault on the city. They took all the livestock from the farms around the city, most of it butchered before they left, and they set fire to the largest buildings.

If this was only a small part of Timur-i's army, I pray to Allah— may He Will favor to all who serve Him—that I never have to face the whole of it. May he fall in battle and be in Shaitan's talons before he can do more harm to the Sultanate. You must prepare to face the demons of perdition, for Timur-i's army is no less than that. Your army must be ready to fight off these soldiers without hope of mercy from them. Timur-i knows nothing of clemency, and cannot be bribed. Do not think that money will ransom your city: it will not. It may persuade Timur-i that you have more treasure than you have admitted, and he will sack Delhi, and pillage it, to be sure he has got the most from it before he kills your people.

This scourge is worse than any plague, for plague only kills men and animals—Timur-i Lenkh destroys all in his path, and rejoices in the ruin. If you are going to stand against him, you must use all the might of your army at its full strength, or be prepared to die under Timur-i's arrows and shimtares. Do not underestimate his ferocity, or assume that because he is an old man, he has lost his cunning or his ruthlessness.

May Allah bear witness to what I say, for on my life it is a faithful account of what I saw.

Jahsi Madur
Chief scribe to the Army of Lahore

10

"They will be here in a day or two," Zal Iniattir said to Sanat Ji Mani as they walked in the confines of the courtyard garden at the rear of the Iniattir house. "The caravan-leader who arrived today saw the dust of their travel."

"Is he sure that is what he saw?" Sanat Ji Mani asked, and went on, "I do not doubt you, or him, but dust in the air is not so remarkable—"

Zal Iniattir laughed angrily once. "This dust was; it covered half the sky, and he could hear the soldiers shouting. Roshin is not one to make fanciful tales on such matters. He knows Darkness is abroad in the land."

"Perhaps he knows it too well, and sees it where it is not," Sanat Ji Mani suggested, all the while keenly aware that if Timur-i did not come this month, he would arrive the next; he knew also that he had waited too long to leave.

"Not he. Perhaps another might, but not Roshin. He is a steady man, pragmatic." Zal Iniattir looked over his shoulder. "I think it is time I took my family out of here, at least until the rains come again. I will be ready to leave in two days."

"It is probably a wise thing to do," said Sanat Ji Mani, chiding himself silently for his own laxness. "Have you decided where you will go yet?"

"I have spoken with Askari Daitya, who is prepared to lead another caravan to Sirpur, if he can accommodate me and my family in the doing of it. I have said I will pay him twice his usual fee for escorting us to Sirpur. My cousin Azizi Iniattir is there and he will receive us, I am sure of it." Zal Iniattir shook his head vehemently, as if in response to a challenge. "I am not betraying my vow to my uncle. He did not ask that we remain as sacrifices."

"No, he did not," Sanat Ji Mani agreed. "And Sirpur is a long way from Delhi."

"Yes. It is," Zal Iniattir admitted. "I would like to believe that Rustam Iniattir would approve of my decision. Askari Daitya does."

"That is something worthwhile," Sanat Ji Mani agreed.

"I mention this because you may want to come with us," Zal Iniattir went on. "I have spoken to Askari Daitya about including you, and one or two servants, and he has said, so long as you provide your own animals and provisions, he would accept your company for the same price as I am paying him."

Sanat Ji Mani touched his hands together and bowed. "I am touched by your kindness, Zal Iniattir, and I will consider your offer. I have already made a petition to the magistrates to leave Delhi after the Winter Solstice, but I may be able to persuade them to allow me to go before that, if I provide incentive enough."

"In gold?" Zal Iniattir asked.

"Or jewels," said Sanat Ji Mani.

"Yes, they might make such an allowance," said Zal Iniattir, "if you paid them enough."

"So I think," Sanat Ji Mani agreed. "They will expect a good sum for granting my request." He had already paid a hefty amount to file the petition, but he was willing to double it if he could secure the necessary permissions to leave in order to keep title on his property in Delhi and to protect the two servants still under his roof: Bohdil and Shudra. He was well-aware that if he departed without permission of the authorities, his lands, house, goods, stock, and servants would be seized by the Sultan's ministers in lieu of the taxes—some invented on the spot—he would have levied against him.

"It is a bargain, whatever they may ask," said Zal Iniattir with feeling. "My uncle would advise you to make all arrangements as quickly as possible, I know. You have protected him: now let him protect you."

"You are very generous," said Sanat Ji Mani. "And I am grateful to you. I will see what can be done with the magistrates."

"So many are leaving every day that I cannot think of any reason they should require you to remain," said Zal Iniattir, doing his best to be encouraging. "You have never argued with them on any point they made before now. Why should you begin?"

"They may not see it that way," said Sanat Ji Mani, a touch of irony in his voice.

"Why should they not?" Zal Iniattir asked, and then answered his own question. "Of course. You have paid them much money, and they would like more of it. You have given gold and supplies to the army, as well, and Firuz Ihbal bin Tughluq wants as much as he can demand of you."

"It is something that touches you as well," said Sanat Ji Mani.

"So it does," Zal Iniattir said. "That is why I am going day after tomorrow. Send me word by sunset tomorrow and I will make whatever arrangements you like." He bowed slightly. "You have been most kind to us, and whatever your decision, the House of Iniattir is in your debt."

"Not by my reckoning," said Sanat Ji Mani, who was suspicious of gratitude, knowing how quickly it could turn to resentment.

"You say so, but my uncle has commanded me otherwise," said Zal Iniattir. "I will not linger, for I have much to do. But tell me that you will be ready to leave and I will send my slaves to bring your chests and cases to the caravan."

"You are most kind," Sanat Ji Mani said, making a formal European bow. "I will send you word as soon as possible."

"I will await it eagerly," Zal Iniattir said, and prepared to show his guest to the door.

Sanat Ji Mani paused to look about the garden one last time. "It is very pleasant here."

"That it is," Zal Iniattir said. "I will miss it."

"I can see why," said Sanat Ji Mani. He had reached the gate. "Whether or not I go with you, I wish you a safe journey and a prosperous return."

"I will hope there is something to return *to*," said Zal Iniattir. "May your gods protect you." The two bowed again, and Zal Iniattir let Sanat Ji Mani out of the gate.

There were many people in the streets, most of them in a hurry, all of them evincing the kind of restlessness that was not far from panic. Even a few women were about, none of them Islamic, all trying to find a haven from dread and Timur-i.

At his house, Sanat Ji Mani was met by Bohdil, who gave the most cursory of greetings before saying, "The Sultan's deputies have taken all but two of your horses. They say it is for the army, and they may take one more." He was clearly upset by this development, but did his best not to make a greater issue than necessary of the event. "They are taking horses from everyone, and asses. They want mounts for as many of their soldiers as possible."

"If they are facing Timur-i, I can see why they might," said Sanat Ji Mani. "Did they take tack as well?"

"Yes. Bridles and saddles and pads and halters," said Bohdil. "one of the men wanted to take your forge, but could not find a way to lift it. They may send others to claim it."

"They must be more desperate than I thought," said Sanat Ji Mani quietly. He pondered briefly, then looked up. "Have you somewhere to go beyond Delhi—to the east, not the west?"

Bohdil looked at his master uneasily. "Yes. I have cousins in Kol."

"Good," said Sanat Ji Mani. "I want you and Shudra to take the two remaining horses and leave at once. Go to Kol and wait there until I send word for you to return."

"You cannot want this," said Bohdil, aghast.

"In general, no, I do not. But Timur-i has made what I want impossible, so I must do what I can to minimize his damage." Sanat Ji Mani saw the dismay in Bohdil's eyes, and went on, "I will provide you with money, and one or two jewels, so you need not be beggars. But hurry. I want you away from here as soon as you can make yourself ready. Gather your belongings. I will saddle the horses for you, and then fetch your coins." He gestured, sending Bohdil off before he started toward the stable. Once there, he lit four of the oil-lamps and began to groom the two horses left in the stalls. He worked quickly, not bothering with combing the manes or tails of the two mares. He saddled and bridled the horses and led them into the stable yard to the trough so they could drink. He patted the neck of the nearer mare, saying, "You will do better away from here, my girl."

Bohdil was the first to return, an improvised pack slung over his shoulder. "I have told Shudra, but he is afraid—he does not know how to ride a horse."

"He will learn," said Sanat Ji Mani, a determined note in his light reply. "Leave by the southern River Gate. No one will stop you there if you give them a bit of silver."

"Must it be now?" Bohdil asked as he prepared to mount the taller mare.

"I fear it should have been yesterday." Sanat Ji Mani sighed once. "I should have been more circumspect."

"Do you think Timur-i is really going to attack Delhi? How can he hope to succeed?" Bohdil leaned down to set his stirrups.

"He has not failed before," Sanat Ji Mani pointed out, then glanced up as Shudra came out of the house, an untidy bundle clasped in his arms, his clothing in disarray; he muttered what seemed to be an apology to Sanat Ji Mani, who went on, "I am sorry to have to require this of you. I do not want to have to answer to your families for your lives."

Shudra stared at the grey mare waiting for him, and blanched. "I cannot," he whispered.

"Bohdil will help you," Sanat Ji Mani said as if he had not heard.

"But I have never ridden anything but a donkey," he protested.

"This mare is well-trained. Let Bodhil take the lead and she will follow after. You have nothing to fear from the horse," Sanat Ji Mani said pointedly. "Remaining here can be dangerous." He held out his joined hands to assist the assistant cook to mount. "Go as fast as you can, as far as you can tonight. It is almost the dark of the year, and you have many hours of night to hide your escape."

Bohdil made an impatient sound with his tongue. "Come, Shudra. Hurry. They may shut the gates at any time, and we will be stuck here." He nodded to Sanat Ji Mani. "You said you would provide us money . . . ?"

"Yes. I will be back in a moment," Sanat Ji Mani said, going into the house and directly to his study. There he removed a dozen gold and half-a-dozen silver coins from his chest, then took them out to the two servants in the courtyard. "Here. This is your wages to this day, and some extra. It will pay for food and lodging and allow you some left over when you reach Kol."

"Burn incense to Ganesh, my master," said Bohdil. "And to Vishnu." He swung his horse around to face the gate. "You have been kind to us. May it ease your karma."

"Thank you," said Sanat Ji Mani, opening the gates for them. "Leave quickly."

Bohdil clapped his heels to the mare's side and she moved forward, the second mare followed after, Shudra clinging to the saddle. "Until fate brings us together again," he called back over his shoulder.

As soon as the two were outside, Sanat Ji Mani closed the gate and barred it, then went back into his empty house, climbing to the laboratory on the top floor, where he busied himself making several vials of his sovereign remedy from the two large jars of moldy bread. He was still keeping watch over the athanor when the sun rose, made glarey by thin, high clouds. He told himself that when his final batch of sovereign remedy was finished, he would break up the athanor and make his way to the house of Zal Iniattir, to join his family in their departure to the south-south-east. It was the most sensible thing to do, given that Timur-i was approaching. He estimated he would complete his work by mid-day; he would forgo the pleasure of a long nap: he would sleep when he was well beyond the walls of Delhi. He was preparing a saddle-bag for his jars and vials when a sharp pounding on the door caught his attention; having no one to answer the summons but himself, he made his way down to the front door, where he found six armed men from the palace waiting.

"You are Sanat Ji Mani?" asked the leader of the man without the courtesy of a greeting.

"I am," said Sanat Ji Mani, wondering what new tax was about to be imposed upon him.

"You are the wealthy foreigner who heals?" the leader persisted.

"I suppose I am," said Sanat Ji Mani, sounding wary and tired at once. "I am foreign, I do possess some wealth, and I have some skill with medicinal materials, but I am not a physician in the sense of those men trained in this city." He did not add that he had received his initial instruction in treating the injured and ill at the Temple of Imhotep in the Egypt of the Pharaohs.

"You have healed the sick and wounded," said the leader. "You have treated those with fever and they have recovered."

"Upon occasion," Sanat Ji Mani answered steadily, which was enough for the leader of the soldiers.

"We serve Firuz Ihbal bin Tughluq: he wishes you to attend him at once." This was an order with only the faintest pretext of being an invitation. "You are to bring your medicaments and tools, and whatever other supplies you may need."

"I have work on-going. I will put myself at his disposal shortly after noon," said Sanat Ji Mani as politely as he could.

"You are to come with us—now." The leader laid his hand on the hilt of his shimtare. "We are told to bring you, and your things."

Sanat Ji Mani took a long breath. "May I have a few moments to keep my work from spoiling? I will need to go into my house to fetch my supplies, in any case. It will not take me very long to do the things that will let me salvage my work."

The leader considered this. "I will come with you. If you try to escape or to barricade yourself inside your house, I will hack off your hands in punishment."

"I will try to do as you wish," said Sanat Ji Mani, feeling the desperation of these men. "You have my Word on it. You do not have to compel me with threats." The thought of having to live so horribly maimed was enough to make him proceed warily; he wanted to provide the soldiers with no excuse to harm him.

"Your word may satisfy some, but I will watch you," said the leader, signaling the others to remain where they were. "This is a most important errand, and we may not fail."

Sanat Ji Mani went up the flights of stairs with a swiftness that had the leader panting with effort; he reached his top floor several steps ahead of the soldier, and used that minuscule time to conceal most of his apparatus. Then he grabbed the saddle-bags and thrust the waiting vials and jars into them just as the leader of the soldiers heaved himself into the room. "I am almost ready," he said, regretting now that he had not dismantled the athanor earlier that morning.

"Well, make haste," said the soldier gruffly, having to say something to maintain his authority.

"I am doing my utmost," said Sanat Ji Mani, and pointed to a small case of medical instruments. "If you will carry that for me, I would be grateful." He could have carried it himself, but that would draw attention to his strength and could lead to speculation that would not be welcome.

"As you wish," said the soldier, taking the case into his hands and holding it gingerly. "Is it fragile?"

"Not particularly, but carry it charily; the instruments are valuable."
And virtually irreplacable, he added to himself. He took a last look
around the top room of his house, wondering vaguely if he would ever
see it again. Over the centuries he had left so many houses behind,
he reminded himself, he should be used to such loss by now.

"What is it?" the soldier asked.

Sanat Ji Mani gave a single shake of his head. "Nothing." He went
to the stairs. "Come. It is time to be off."

"Very well," said the soldier, descending the stairs behind Sanat Ji
Mani, the small chest held out ahead of him like an offering. "I am
told to bring you to Firuz Ihbal bin Tughluq, who is on the walls of
the city."

"For what purpose?" Sanat Ji Mani asked, wanting to know why he
had been summoned in this abrupt way.

The leader of the soldiers interpreted the inquiry another way: "Firuz Ihbal bin Tughluq is watching the approach of Timur-i's army.
They are to the west-north-west of the city, and coming quickly."

"Ah," said Sanat Ji Mani, understanding at last. "Yes. He had to
come, did he not."

"He is here," said the leader as they reached the ground floor again.
"You will put yourself at the disposal of Firuz Ihbal bin Tughluq. He
will decide what you are to do."

"He is going to fight?" Sanat Ji Mani went to the gate where the
other soldiers waited.

"As Allah Wills," said the leader of the soldiers.

"Of course," Sanat Ji Mani agreed, stepping outside and pulling his
gate closed. "Very well. Tell me where I am to go."

"We will escort you," said the leader, and motioned his men to
form an escort around Sanat Ji Mani, marching him out of the Foreigners' Quarter and off toward the north-western battlements of
Delhi. The soldiers cleared a way through the streets where restless
excitement had reached a dangerous pitch, for there were now hundreds trying to escape from the city, all of them trying to reach the
eastern gates, away from Timur-i's advancing hosts.

"Come this way," the leader shouted to Sanat Ji Mani as they
reached the entrance to the marshaling yard where men, horses, and
elephants were crowded together in an attempt to face the brunt of

the attack. The leader guided Sanat Ji Mani along the edge of the marshaling yard, and pointed to the base of a tower that gave access to the battlements. "The archers are forming their companies at the next gate," the leader said, as he and his men urged Sanat Ji Mani up the stairs and into the tower.

"You cannot come any farther," said Kanwar Gotanipi, resplendent in his silks and mail. He blocked the way to the battlements.

"Firuz Ihbal bin Tughluq sent for this man," said the leader of soldiers. "We were ordered to present him."

"I command this quadrant of the city," said Kanwar Gotanipi. "I say you must turn back."

The leader of the soldiers signaled to his men. "You may command this quadrant, but we serve the Sultan and his deputies. You must permit us to pass or answer to Firuz Ihbal bin Tughluq for our failure to comply with the orders we have been given."

Kanwar Gotanipi stood very straight. "You have no authority to do this."

"I have more than you do," said the leader of the soldiers. "Stand aside, you Brahman fool, and let us get on with our work."

There was a long moment of stillness, then Kanwar Gotanipi stepped aside with an elaborate shrug. "If you wish to be reprimanded, what is it to me?"

The leader of the soldiers did not dignify this petulant remark with any comment; he nodded to his men and Sanat Ji Mani as they went out onto the battlements and into the brisk wind, where Firuz Ihbal bin Tughluq waited, surrounded by men in various kinds of armor, all of whom were peering out into the middle distance where a vast cloud of dust rolled into the shining sky.

"How long do you think it will take them to reach the city?" Firuz Ihbal asked without turning.

"The mounted troops will be here soon, I should think," said Sanat Ji Mani. "The rest of the army will take a little longer—perhaps until tomorrow."

"So fast," said Firuz Ihbal. "But I suppose you are right." He sighed and gave his attention to Sanat Ji Mani. "We must be ready to meet them, to show them the futility of attacking us."

"I doubt you can persuade them of that," said Sanat Ji Mani drily. "They must think you have something worthwhile, or they would not be here."

"So you say," Firuz Ihbal declared. "But they also worship Allah, and they will honor our faith."

"They have not done so for other followers of Islam," Sanat Ji Mani said quietly. "Why should they make an exception for you?"

"We are a great city, and we have done nothing to deserve slaughter." Firuz Ihbal stared at Sanat Ji Mani for some time. "In any case, there will be casualties, and I will require your help in treating wounded men." He clapped his hands. "I will order the slaves to make a place for you to do your work. When the men have all been tended to, you may take your treasure and go without any hindrance. I swear it as if my hand were on the *Qran*."

Sanat Ji Mani was keenly aware that such vows meant nothing unless the man's hand actually was on the *Qran*, but knew this was not the time to challenge Firuz Ihbal. "I would not want to see men suffer if I could do anything to prevent it, no matter what cause they fought for," he said, his manner self-effacing enough to satisfy Firuz Ihbal. "You need not offer me a bribe to do what must be done."

"Very well," said Firuz Ihbal. "I will make you no promises then."

"Very good," Sanat Ji Mani said, not entirely sincerely. "You may select a place for me to work without fear that I will do anything to harm you or your men."

Firuz Ihbal looked about curiously. "I do not think we will lose many men. The men of Timur-i are fierce, but they are not as many as we are." He pulled at his moustaches. "You are aware, are you not, that this is a battle that we must win, for the Sultan."

"A pity that he is not here," said Sanat Ji Mani. "The people would not be leaving in such great numbers if the Sultan had remained here."

"It must seem so to a foreigner. You are planning to leave, are you not?" Firuz Ihbal spoke sharply, not quite accusing Sanat Ji Mani.

"You have my petition," said Sanat Ji Mani. "You were considering what tax I would have to pay to leave sooner than I requested."

"The tax will be forgiven you, foreigner, when you have done your service here." Firuz Ihbal spat copiously. "There is grit in the wind."

"Yes. And there will be more than grit, bye and bye," said Sanat Ji Mani, more to himself than to anyone else.

"You will do the Sultan this service," Firuz Ihbal commanded, and pointed toward Kanwar Gotanipi. "See that he is given the facilities we spoke of. And find that worm Josha Dar: I have work for him."

Kanwar Gotanipi took a step back, his face gone blank with fear. "Josha Dar left this morning, Exalted Lord," he said. "He told me he was acting under your orders."

Firuz Ihbal glowered at Kanwar Gotanipi. "And you believed him—Josha Dar?"

Sanat Ji Mani looked from one man to the other, trying to read the extent of the shock each had sustained; he could see that the two men were disturbed by this news but for different reasons.

"He has done many things for you, Exalted Lord," said Kanwar Gotanipi.

"He has been useful," Firuz Ihbal conceded, his manner less imposing. "You have committed a minor fault. You have nothing to fear from me."

"I will not fear you, Exalted Lord," Kanwar Gotanipi said staunchly, but with hands clenched at his side.

"The Sultan will praise your service when this is done," Firuz Ihbal added in a tone suffused with weariness. "You will not be held accountable for what that spy has done."

Kanwar Gotanipi put his hands together and bowed. "The Exalted Lord is gracious," he said. "I will attend to this foreigner at once."

"Very good," said Firuz Ihbal, waving them both away. "Send Iksander Mawan to me. I have work for him."

"I will," said Kanwar Gotanipi as he nodded Sanat Ji Mani in the direction of the stairs. "You will descend ahead of me. You cannot run."

"I had not intended to try," said Sanat Ji Mani, entering the tower and making his way to the steps. "I suppose you have much to do, readying for Timur-i."

"All Delhi does," said Kanwar Gotanipi. "You are only one of many who must be prepared for what is coming."

"I saw the army marshaling," Sanat Ji Mani remarked as he started down the stairs. "It is going to be a hard-fought engagement."

"As to that, I believe the Sultan's men have found a way to preserve the city, to keep the walls from being breached. It is a plan most carefully conceived. We have spent many hours in deep thought and long discussion, and I am sure the Sultan will have reason to rejoice." Kanwar Gotanipi kept Sanat Ji Mani moving as he spoke, using the handle of his short whip to urge the foreigner along.

"If that is the case, it is a shame that the Sultan will not be here to see it," Sanat Ji Mani said, his irony lost on Kanwar Gotanipi.

"We will meet them outside the walls, with all our archers and elephants and mounted men. Our numbers alone will drive them back, for although they are strong fighters, they are not as numerous or as well-armed as we. They will see this, and it will give them reason to consider, for they will know they will lose many men, coming against us. That is when we will sue for a reasonable peace, while we may preserve our city and our fortunes from all Timur-i's forces might do." Kanwar Gotanipi could not conceal his pride in this scheme. "They may try to fight, but in the end, they will have to flee before our greater power."

Sanat Ji Mani strove to conceal his dismay. "Why not fight from behind the walls, letting them protect you? Surely you know that Timur-i's greatest strength is in the open, where his mounted men can maneuver?" He asked calmly enough but it was an effort to maintain his composure.

"Because Timur-i will not be discouraged except in the open. He has always attacked fortifications, and is not frightened by them. But he can be met by superior force in the open. He will try to drive our forces back inside the walls. We will not permit him to do that. We know how he uses his men, and what we must do to prevent his assault on our walls. If Delhi were not so well-armed and had such a huge army, your fears would be well-founded, but it is not right that so powerful an army as ours remain hidden behind the walls when a single act would show Timur-i that assault is futile. We have one hundred twenty war elephants as well as ten thousand cavalry and twenty thousand infantry and more than ten thousand archers on the walls— at least four times the men Timur-i is said to have. Our leaders know this from all the reports they have had." Kanwar Gotanipi made a victory salute. "It would be better if the Sultan were here, yet we will prevail. It is essential that we prevail."

"Certainly," said Sanat Ji Mani. They were at the base of the tower and he did not know where to go next so he waited for Kanwar Gotanipi to come to him. "The wounded I am to treat—how are they to get to me? If you want me outside the walls, I might be overwhelmed by the battle and be of use to no one. If you keep me inside the walls, with your soldiers outside, how am I to treat them?"

"We have slaves to carry them to you," said Kanwar Gotanipi as if it were an obvious solution. "You will be inside the wall. Look across the marshaling yard and you will see an embrasure in the wall?" He pointed. "You will have tents put up for your use, and slaves assigned to assist you."

Certain that he was facing disaster, Sanat Ji Mani said, "I would prefer the help of old soldiers, not slaves. The work you want is bloody, and many slaves cannot accept the blood—old soldiers can. They know battle and will not shrink at what they see."

Kanwar Gotanipi considered this request. "You may have hit upon something important," he allowed. "I will speak to Firuz Ihbal on your behalf, and perhaps he will agree with you."

"If you like, I will address him myself," said Sanat Ji Mani, thinking a bribe might secure the support he sought more quickly than a simple request.

"No. You must make your tents ready. They must be prepared before the army marches out of the gates. I will attend to it later; I will tell you what Firuz Ihbal has decided." Kanwar Gotanipi motioned Sanat Ji Mani to follow him, and began to make his way across the confusion on the marshaling ground.

Sanat Ji Mani threaded his way behind Kanwar Gotanipi, his eyes shaded as the mid-day heat ate at him, presaging the catastrophe he was convinced would come.

Text of a declaration posted and announced everywhere in Delhi by the deputies of the Sultan.

To the people of Delhi, this is the law in this time of occupation, for it has pleased Allah to give the victory over us to Timur-i Lenkh and his men; Timur-i Lenkh, who is a faithful follower of the Prophet, has set his hand upon the sacred Qran and sworn that there will be no more killing here so long as his orders are obeyed in every particular, without question or resistance, and that should the people of Delhi traduce the vows of the Sultan's ministers and deputies, the soldiers of Timur-i Lenkh will at once begin both sacking and pillaging of Delhi: we enjoin you all to adhere to these conditions and to uphold the honor of the Sultan in sparing this city from the ruin Timur-i Lenkh has wrought elsewhere:

All soldiers of Timur-i Lenkh are to be given access to every house and other buildings within the city without let or hindrance. They are to be allowed to seize anything that they wish, and no one is to deny them anything they may demand. Failure to comply with this order will result in everyone within the city not of immediate use to Timur-i Lenkh being put to the sword and the city destroyed.

All soldiers of Timur-i Lenkh are to be fed and clothed to the limit of the household, without question and without any let or hindrance. Failure to comply with this order will result in the total destruction of the household refusing food and clothing to the soldiers.

All soldiers of Timur-i Lenkh are to be allowed such access as they may wish to women and boys, and no complaint is to be made at any choice they may make, either by the head of the household or by the women or boys in question. Failure to provide that access will result in the immediate killing of all the household where the soldiers have been denied such access.

All soldiers of Timur-i Lenkh are to be provided slaves to aid them in their plundering, to act as bearers and to serve the soldiers in any way they see fit. All households are to make their slaves available to the soldiers of Timur-i Lenkh. No slaves are to be held back or de-nied the soldiers, who are to be given full and total rights to all slaves within Delhi, of any nature whatsoever. Failure to comply with this order will result in the destruction of the household refusing its slaves to the soldiers.

All soldiers of Timur-i Lenkh are to be allowed to enter any and all temples of Delhi and remove any and all objects that they may choose to remove. No one is to protest their selections, nor are any priests to attempt to keep them from entering the temples. Failure to comply with this order will result in the slaughter of the people and the destruction of the city of Delhi.

All persons of Delhi harboring the sick, the mad, the ancient, or the deformed must bring those persons to the magistrates and present them to the judgment of the officers of Timur-i Lenkh. No persons are to be held back for any reason, nor are the infirm to be exempted from this order. Failure to bring such persons will result in the slaughter of the entire household where the person was harbored.

All persons of Delhi shall prepare a record of all household members to present to the magistrates for their review and evaluation. All women living in Delhi are to be listed separately from their husbands, sons, brothers, fathers, and other male relatives. Those women lacking suitable husbands shall be given to those soldiers of Timur-i Lenkh who seek wives, the rest are to be subject to the will of Timur-i Lenkh, and his disposal is to be regarded as being one with the Will of Allah.

All persons of Delhi possessing horses, asses, donkeys, or camels, are to bring them, their tack, and suitable food for the animals, to the magistrates for the consideration of the captains of Timur-i Lenkh. Failure to bring such animals, tack, and suitable food, as stipulated here will result in the slaughter of the entire household withholding such animals.

All persons of Delhi employed in defending the city will present themselves to the magistrates for the review of Timur-i Lenkh's officers. Failure to comply with this order will result in the slaughter of all the household and relatives' households of such persons.

All persons of Delhi engaged in supporting the defense of Delhi will present themselves to the magistrates, along with any instruments, weapons, tools, supplies, shelter, foodstuffs, clothing, or other materials used in such support, prepared to give a full account of their activities to the officers of Timur-i Lenkh, along with a full and accurate report on how such instruments, weapons, tools, supplies, shelter, foodstuffs, clothing, or other materials were actually employed in the defense of the city. Failure to comply with this order in every particular will result in the slaughter of all those engaged in supporting the defense of Delhi, along with their households.

All persons of Delhi with oxen and buffalo are to bring their animals, suitably yoked, to the plain before the Western Gate of Delhi, *for the purpose of piling up the carcasses of men and animals. Failure to appear with the oxen by mid-day tomorrow will result in the slaughter of the persons and their oxen and buffalo, and the destruction of their households.*

For the honor of the Sultan and the Will of Allah, let everyone in Delhi comply with these orders and do all that he can to preserve our city. This is the Word of the Sultan, on whose behalf it is signed by

Firuz Ihbal bin Tughluq,
Acting Minister of Taxes, Rents, and Revenues
Balban Ihbal bin Tughluq,
Acting Leader of the Army of Delhi
for Sultan Nasiruddin Mohammed bin Tughluq

11

By the third day of Timur-i's occupation of Delhi, the air was sodden with the stench of rotting flesh: from the dead elephants, horses, and men beyond the city gates to the growing heaps of severed limbs and mangled torsos within, the city had become an abattoir, its streets slick with blood, and the sounds of shrieks and moans as constant as the sighing, stinking wind. The inhabitants all wore the dazed expression of the conquered while the soldiers of Timur-i bullied their way through the streets, making the most of their subjugation of the place.

The broad square in front of the Magistrates' Building at the rear of the palace was filled with more than a thousand people, each striving to comply with the orders issued to Delhi two days ago; most of them had been waiting for more than a day to be heard. Few of them spoke amongst one another, although occasionally someone would weep or pray. From time to time, Iksander Mawan and Josha Dar would make their way through the confusion in the square, searching for those the officers of Timur-i, or Timur-i himself, wished to see.

Sanat Ji Mani sat on the far side of the square in the protective shadow of the old Temple of Yama, which had been looted the day before and now stood empty of everything but insects and crows. He had seen Firuz Ihbal killed earlier that day: his crime, according to the executioner, was holding back wealth from Timur-i Lenkh; Firuz Ihbal's body had been hacked to bits and thrown onto the mound of mangled dead growing near the steps to the Magistrates' Building, the largest of five scattered about the city. Now he occupied his thoughts with various plans for escape, not yet satisfied that he could get out of the city without being summarily beheaded: that would be True Death for him as much as for any living man. He felt sickened by what he witnessed; he was no stranger to carnage, but this was more appalling than anything he had seen since the Plague-stricken cities of France, fifty years ago. Not even the butchery of Jenghiz Khan was as grisly as this massacre in its guise of legality. He found the memory of T'en Chih-Yü, dead at the hands of Jenghiz Khan's forces, haunted him as he waited for whatever experience was coming: he had learned to be patient over his long life, and now he was inclined to sit and give his attention to the sad, frightened mass before him; he was tempted to offer his assistance to a few of the most afflicted but knew this would only lead to demands from many others and would create more trouble than it eased.

It was mid-afternoon when Iksander Mawan approached the place where Sanat Ji Mani waited, and singled him out. "You. Foreigner. In black."

Sanat Ji Mani rose. "Yes?" He bowed slightly, feeling suddenly conspicuous in his fluted-linen Egyptian kalasiris.

"Come with me. Bring your supplies—those you carry in that bag, those you used to treat the Sultan's soldiers. There are questions you must answer. Do not try to avoid this. You will have to justify yourself, and failure to respond promptly will not help you." He snapped his fingers and indicated a spot in the air half a step behind him. "Keep close or you will be lost in the crowd and I will have to dispatch soldiers to find you."

"I will keep close," said Sanat Ji Mani, who had seen half-a-dozen men in the square die under the shimtares of Timur-i's soldiers since dawn came over the afflicted city.

"Very good," said Iksander Mawan, and set off through the thick of the waiting men, his flail held high as a sign of authority and an implied threat; Sanat Ji Mani ignored the weight of the sun as best he could and kept half a pace behind Iksander Mawan. He was certain that exposure to sunlight was the least of his trouble now.

The interior of the Magistrates' Building was worse than the square, the rotunda busy as an ants' nest, with men packed into it so tightly that there was hardly room to stand, let alone move through the crush. Although all doors were open, the air was stagnant, the sickening, sweetish odor of decomposition mixing with the more alliaceous smell of frightened men. Various slaves of the Magistrates' Building scurried about in an effort to complete their tasks in spite of the overwhelming number of waiting men.

"Come with me," Iksander Mawan shouted to Sanat Ji Mani, cocking his head toward the largest interior door.

"Yes," Sanat Ji Mani called back, so that Iksander Mawan could be sure he heard.

The door was flanked by eight of Timur-i's officers, each in the armor and color of his cadre, all armed with bows, lances, and shimtares, silent and ferocious. With them stood a magistrate, his demeanor as cowed as the officers' was grand. Iksander Mawan was motioned to go in; Sanat Ji Mani was searched for weapons, then allowed to enter the high-vaulted chamber beyond.

An ivory chair had been placed at the back of the room and on it sat an old man in gleaming armor; his features showed the heritage of his Turkish father and Mongol mother as well as the effects of a life lived on campaign. Sanat Ji Mani saw that the man's hair had been darkened with walnut-stain, and that around his face was a faint line of white; Timur-i Lenkh wanted to keep the illusion of youth as long as possible. His mouth was sensual and hard at once, and his eyes were flat as stones. His right foot turned inward; even through his elaborate boot Sanat Ji Mani could see that the foot was misshapen from an improperly healed injury. He carried a small ceremonial whip in his hand, which he twitched from time to time, much as a cat might lash its tail.

Two high-ranking soldiers stood behind him, shimtares drawn and ready, and next to them were two men from Delhi: Sanat Ji Mani recognized one of them as the scrawny spy who had watched Rustam Iniattir and him for several months. The other man was a magistrate;

his eyes stared out of dark hollows and there was a bruise on the side of his forehead the size of a mango.

"On your face, foreigner," ordered the magistrate, his voice strident with fatigue. He did not bother to look at Sanat Ji Mani.

Sanat Ji Mani prostrated himself, his bag of medicaments and tools laid down ahead of him so that he would not be accused of concealing anything. The red-granite paving was cool under him, far less unpleasant than standing in the sun had been; he lay still while one of the two officers came and walked around him, nudging him once with his foot before returning to his place behind the throne.

"This is Sanat Ji Mani, a foreigner from the West. He has done business with the Parsi and contributed to the Sultan's coffers. He has no slighting report against him beyond his dealings with foreigners. As he is a foreigner himself, and has paid his taxes, this is not held to be a fault in him," said the magistrate in a flat delivery that gave no hint of approval or disapproval.

"You may rise," said the old man in the tongue of Persia.

Sanat Ji Mani got to his knees, lifting his bag as he did. "You are Timur-i Lenkh," he said in the same language.

"I am. And you are Sanat Ji Mani." He pointed to the sack. "Those are your medicines? And your tools?"

"Some of them," Sanat Ji Mani said carefully. "I have more at my house in the Street of Brass Lanterns."

Timur-i turned to Josha Dar. "You say he has cured the ill and saved those taken in fever? He has preserved the wounded?"

Josha Dar looked uncomfortable. "I have seen men he has treated live where they should have died."

"Does he speak true?" Timur-i demanded of Sanat Ji Mani. "I despise all liars—remember that as you answer."

"I have a degree of skill and can sometimes help men recover from sickness and injuries." Sanat Ji Mani looked directly at Timur-i. "Sometimes I cannot."

"It is as Allah Wills," said Timur-i, and glared at Sanat Ji Mani as if he expected to be contradicted.

"Yes; as Allah Wills," said Sanat Ji Mani.

"Then you are faithful to Islam?" said Timur-i, surprised.

"No, but I respect it," Sanat Ji Mani responded.

"You follow your foreign gods, because you are foreign. Yet Islam is for all men, and you must, in time, come to embrace it, as will all mankind," Timur-i declared, and accepted Sanat Ji Mani's nod as acknowledgment enough. "I am told you cared for the soldiers of Delhi, treating their hurts. Did you?"

"Yes; the deputies of the Sultan commanded my services: I would have offered them in any case." He wondered how long he would have to remain before this fierce old man; he dared not move.

"He spent days with the city's sick before you came to Delhi, Puissant Lord," Josha Dar volunteered. "I followed him more than once, and I saw him tend them, even the poorest. He did this without apparent coercion."

"A fine example," said Timur-i as if he meant it. "More men should do such good to others." He stared musingly at the far wall. "So the Sultan's deputies—treasonous dogs that they are—knew his skills and used them for their own ends."

"That was not all. They taxed him more than most," Josha Dar added smugly. "I saw them take bags of gold from his house."

"Wealth *and* compassion," marveled Timur-i sarcastically. "You must be a clever man, foreigner."

"I have striven to make my way in the world," Sanat Ji Mani said, "as an exile must."

"Ah," said Timur-i. "An exile. You came here of necessity."

"Delhi was a haven to me," said Sanat Ji Mani, making a gesture to show his gratitude. "I accepted the terms of the safety I found here, and I was glad to have it so." This was true as far as it went, he thought. "My native land is far away and in the hands of powerful men. What could I be but grateful to the Sultan and the city for what I have found here."

"Nasiruddin Mohammed bin Tughluq is Sultan no more. He forfeited Delhi when he left it. I will choose one worthy to hold this empire for me," said Timur-i bluntly.

"As Allah Wills," Josha Dar exclaimed, and saw Iksander Mawan wince.

Timur-i took this remark in good part. "I attune myself to Allah—the Glorious, All-Merciful—and I do His Will. He shows His Will in my victories." There were murmurs of agreement and adulation from those gathered around the ivory chair, and two of his officers shouted a terse salutation. "You see—my men know that I will uphold their faith; they are devoted to me in this world as they seek Paradise." This observation needed no more explication; Timur-i glared down at Sanat Ji Mani. "If you were to tend to my wounded, would you help them, or would you poison them and give them fevers?"

"It is my sworn duty to treat those I can without regard for who or what they are, and has been since I was taught by masters, many years ago," said Sanat Ji Mani, recalling his centuries in the Temple of Imhotep. "I cannot save all of them—no one can. But I can help most, if only to ease their passage from this life."

"How can you know that such ease is needed?" Timur-i fixed Sanat Ji Mani with an accusing stare. "Allah alone knows the hours of a man's life."

Sanat Ji Mani was not intimidated. "You have been in battle and seen men hurt past all cure," he said calmly. "Yet you know their injuries will bring hours or days of agony before the body finally surrenders the soul. Think of those with broken backs, or men with wounds to their bowels, or lungs. You cannot save them. I cannot save them. Not Allah Himself can save them for very long. All those with such injuries suffer hideous pain before they die. Many of them go mad with it. Those who have such hurts, I help lessen their pain for as long as my supplies and my skills permit me. If there is fever or infection, I have a sovereign remedy which can sometimes bring a cure. I can stitch up open wounds and set broken limbs. I can treat pulled tendons in man and beast, I can reseat bones in their rightful sockets, I can offer anodyne to anyone with pain." His voice remained low and steady.

"Then Josha Dar has spoken aright," said Timur-i, and glanced at the man with a look that said he had been spared again.

"I do not know what Josha Dar said to you," Sanat Ji Mani told Timur-i. "I know what I can do. I know also that there is a limit to all medicaments, and that the virtue of a cure for one is not always sufficient for another."

"Josha Dar has said many things. I have listened," said Timur-i, his tone ominous.

"I have spoken truth," Josha Dar insisted. "And you, Sanat Ji Mani, be glad I did, for otherwise you would be hacked to death like so many others."

"Then I must thank you," Sanat Ji Mani said ironically.

Timur-i nodded. "On your face," he ordered: Sanat Ji Mani obeyed, still holding on to his sack of supplies; he was under intense scrutiny by the Turkish-Mongol warlord, but his enigmatic gaze revealed nothing of his thoughts. Finally, Timur-i made a gesture. "He will do. Prepare him to travel. Have the smiths do it now, so he will have time to recover." He motioned to two of his officers. "He looks strong. Use a new sword, not an old one."

The two officers bowed deeply, then went and pulled Sanat Ji Mani to his feet. One of the men took hold of his bag. "We will keep this for you: you will have need of it."

"There may be more supplies at his house," Josha Dar said.

"Have them brought," Timur-i ordered. "Take them to the infirmary against his coming."

Sanat Ji Mani felt no sense of relief at this remark, for he could not convince himself that he had been spared anything by this unexpected decision of Timur-i's. He stood still for a long moment, then said, "Very well," he said in the old-fashioned Mongol language learned almost two centuries earlier at Karakhorum. "Take me where you must."

One of the men was willing to look surprised, and he said, "Do not make a fuss and this will be easier for all of us."

This assurance did not give Sanat Ji Mani any relief—if anything, he was more troubled—but he knew it would be betise to attempt to escape in this crowded place with Timur-i Lenkh himself watching; he strode off with the two men escorting him, hoping that his long life had not finally come to such an ignominious end.

"Into the courtyard," said the officer holding his bag. "Toward the smithy."

Sanat Ji Mani was somewhat surprised, for he had not seen many of Timur-i's captives wearing collars or manacles, or chains—he understood that all of them were impractical for Timur-i's style of travel, which required speed uppermost. Still, he supposed, since Timur-i had decided to make use of his medicinal skills, he would not want to give Sanat Ji Mani the opportunity for escape. Sanat Ji Mani winced at the memories of other times he had been a slave as he continued across the stable courtyard toward the smithy.

"We will have to bind you," said the officer with his bag. "If we do not, the procedure could go awry and you would not want that."

"I suppose not," said Sanat Ji Mani as they approached the smithy.

The other officer called out, "This one is to be stapled. You are to use a new sword."

From inside the smithy there was an oath of complaint, and two muscular men in leather aprons came out, one of them holding heavy tongs. "For this fellow?" he asked. His skin was hard from the constant heat of his work, and his hands were thick as paws.

The officer called back "Yes. And make it quick. We do not want to waste the day here."

"Bring him in," said the older smith and gestured toward a grooming stall. "Secure him there."

The officers did as they were told, the one carrying the bag saying, "It is better if you do not fight. I will leave your supplies with you, so you will be able to tend to the staple when you are ready."

Sanat Ji Mani still could not think how a staple might be used, but he nodded. "Thank you."

The officers confined him efficiently with heavy ropes while the smiths busied themselves on their anvils, their hammers making a penetrating clang that jarred Sanat Ji Mani; he could not see what the smiths were working on the forge, but he smelled hot metal, and supposed this could be the new sword. He could envision a number of uses for that sword, none of which were pleasant. He wanted to tell them that all attempts to brand him had left no marks, but he knew they would not listen.

"Remove his right boot," said the smith.

The officers did as they were ordered while Sanat Ji Mani wondered why they should do such a thing; he said nothing, waiting uneasily.

"Small foot," one of the officers reported. "You can use a small sole."

"Very good," said the smith, and went on working with his hammer. "Confine his leg. Most of them kick when being fitted." He laughed and struck another blow.

The two officers seized Sanat Ji Mani's right leg. "It will be done quickly," one of them said as if to quiet his anxiety, but only serving to increase it.

"Don't let him squirm. If the blade doesn't go between the bones, he'll be of no use to us," said the smith, approaching with something hot in his tongs.

The second smith carried a piece of wood roughly the shape of a foot, but broader; it was about as thick as a thumb is long, and he laid it against Sanat Ji Mani's bare sole, the wider side to the outside of the foot, then bent Sanat Ji Mani's leg so that the wood was on the floor. The soldiers gripped more tightly as the smith with the wood took hold of his toes.

Just before he bent over, Sanat Ji Mani saw what was in the tongs— a sword-blade, still glowing from the forge, bent in a U shape, both ends sharpened. He tensed futilely against what was coming. The first sizzling touch of the hot metal on his foot sent pain rioting up his leg, and when the smith adroitly hammered the staple into place in three swift blows—one end through Sanat Ji Mani's foot, the blade slipping between the bones and into the wood, the other into the wood on the outside of his foot—the odor of burning meat mixed with the acrid scent of heated metal. It was swift and the hurt was so enormous it stifled the scream in his throat.

"Water," one of the smiths ordered, and a moment later it sloshed over the newly placed staple.

"That will stop the festering," the other smith declared; Sanat Ji Mani hardly noticed: he was consumed with agony that leached all thought from his mind and drove him into a stupor.

"He's fainted," said the officer with the bag.

"Just as well," said the older smith. "Let him sleep it off." He gestured to a stall near the rear of the smithy. "Put him there. No one will bother him."

The two officers slung Sanat Ji Mani between them and carried him off to the rear stall.

"Better leave his bag with him. He'll want it when he wakes," said one of the officers.

The other dropped the bag beside Sanat Ji Mani's supine body. "See no one touches this," he called out to the smith.

"That I will," the smith said with a nonchalant wave.

"We must report to Timur-i," said one of the officers.

"Tell him it was successful—clean through the foot and no bones broken. That man will not run anywhere so long as that staple is in his foot." The smith chuckled.

"Send word if he becomes feverish," said the other officer.

The smith waved him away, and signaled to the other smith to bring more work to the forge.

Report on the sack and pillage of Delhi prepared by the surviving priests of Shiva, carried by messenger to Sultan Nasiruddin Mohammed bin Tughlaq.

By Allah the All-Seeing, the All-Compassionate, your god, O Sultan, this is a full and accurate account of what transpired in your city of Delhi during the time it was occupied by Timur-i Lenkh and his army. It was the dark of the year in many ways, and we of Delhi paid the price. All of us, no matter what station or caste or loyalty or devotion, have had to endure that which must please only Kali, for a bloodier time has not come to Delhi from the foundation of the world.

When the army went out of the gates, it fell into the hands of the army of Timur-i Lenkh, and suffered a decisive defeat. Timur-i Lenkh brought his army into the city and issued edicts that promised looting only provided certain strictures were adhered to; failure to abide by these requirements would bring swift destruction.

For a few days the people kept to the terms of the surrender, and only valuables were taken. But it was inevitable that a few would protest losing all their goods and their slaves. At first the army of Timur-i executed those who tried to keep their treasure hidden, punishing the transgressor and his family but not calling others to account for the greed of a few. The city's magistrates sat in judgment on those who transgressed and meted out the justice Timur-i Lenkh required, and many were brought into the service of his occupying army.

It went as well as could be hoped, with less than two hundred killed for their refusal to give up what Timur-i Lenkh required; but then a merchant—a man of your faith, Ismalli Heitan—refused to hand over the gold and jewels he had stored in the cellar of his house, and the killing began in earnest. For the next two days there was nothing but extermination in Delhi. Thousands upon thousands fell under the shimtares of Timur-i Lenkh's army, and their bodies were piled up in the market-squares where the paving-stones were so covered in blood that goats and cattle would not enter them, and dogs sated themselves on the decaying flesh of those who had been their masters.

Timur-i Lenkh has vowed to make another man Sultan of Delhi, to rule the empire—shrunken as it is—for him. You, he has declared, have lost Delhi for failing to defend it. He, unlike you, has promised death to those who remain in Delhi and will not embrace Islam. Those of us who are of the old faith are to be put to death in the morning. I have been ordered to prepare this account for you as a last act of devotion to you as the ruler of Delhi, which Timur-i has claimed for himself and his adherent.

Many hundreds of those who are not to be killed are now slaves of Timur-i Lenkh. He has made native-born men of Delhi and foreigners his property if he has reason to want their capabilities or other attributes to augment his might or the strength of his army. He has taken one priest from this ruined temple to serve him as translator. Others have been ordered to care for his animals and his troops. Most of them have been branded and a metal staple put through their feet so that they cannot run. I myself have seen more than fifty men so constrained, Delhi-born and foreign together.

As to women, most of them have been killed, but a few have been handed over to Timur-i Lenkh's soldiers for their pleasure. Also young, comely boys have been put into whoredom. A few have managed to kill themselves before they had to succumb to Timur-i Lenkh's men, but most have accepted their fate with resignation; they know that they might be killed at once if they do not let their bodies be used by the soldiers, and they would prefer to live than to die.

Delhi is a slaughterhouse today. It will be worse tomorrow when all we priests join the dead. The city should be burned to ashes and the ashes scattered to the winds, but Timur-i Lenkh is not so kind as to do this: he gloats over the carcasses piled up, and seeks to increase their number as a sign of his potent might. We accept the turning of the Wheel with the followers of the Buddha, who will be our brothers in dying.

Surely now that the days are beginning to lengthen again Timur-i Lenkh will abandon Delhi and seek new conquests. When he leaves there will be nothing but bones to give witness to what has happened here, and their testimony will be mute. In that day, my soul will be glad, for the destruction will finally be at an end.

May your Allah protect you from the army of Timur-i Lenkh. May he restore you to your throne, if there is a throne to claim when all of this is over. I sign myself your subject and the faithful priest of Shiva, Who will bring me to the Burning Ground.

Rishi Harata Medha

PART II

TULSI KIL

*T*ext of a letter from Zal Iniattir to his uncle Rustam Iniattir, carried on the merchant ship *Dolphin's Eye* to Fustat in the Mameluke Empire.

To my most respected uncle, the leader of our family, my greetings from this place in the Vindhya Mountains where we have found sanctuary at last. Asirgarh is not as fine a city as Delhi, but we have been received here with hospitality, and we are safe for the time being. Here they will tell us the law and we will abide by it for the good of our House.

We were able to leave Delhi before the army of the Sultan was humiliated by Timur-i and therefore we have kept most of our treasure, although certain sums had to be paid to bring us safely here. I will try to establish our House here and once again begin trading on the merchants' roads of the broad world where Timur-i has not brought destruction.

I have not yet met with the camel-drivers and muleteers who carried our goods from Delhi; I fear some of them may have seen this as an opportunity and claimed our crates and chests as theirs, and struck out to other markets on their own. I am resigned to losing some of our goods in this fashion, but most should arrive in due course.

Our House owes a debt of gratitude to Sanat Ji Mani: truly he is named, for he is a treasure of an ancient soul. He made it possible for me to escape without sacrificing all our goods and our holdings, which I despaired of doing. Without his help, we would not have won free of Delhi before it fell and all would be lost. I do not know if he himself escaped, but I have heard that few did once Timur-i entered the gates of the city.

There is a rumor that Timur-i was overthrown at Delhi and his nephew put up in his place. They say that Timur-i now wanders the roads, lame and blind, afraid and without friends. I do not know if I believe this, for I have heard something of the kind before, but everyone is saying it, and it may be true. I have it on good authority that the soldiers of Timur-i are preparing to leave Delhi and to continue their rampage across the land.

It is assumed that Timur-i will remain in the north, which is why I have chosen this city to the south. This place is not as fine as Delhi, but it has many things to recommend it. We have mountains and two rivers between us and Delhi, so that even if Timur-i's army should strike out in this direction, we will have time enough to leave, if we must.

In this new city, we have purchased a house and I have gone to the Camel-Drivers' Market to learn as much as I can about the state of trade in this place. I have not been successful at all I have sought to accomplish, for these people do not know Parsi and they fear us as strangers; I am engaged now in reassuring the people, for I know we will not prosper until we are welcome.

To that end, I am planning an entertainment for the merchants of the city. It will be costly, but I cannot doubt it will prove to be beneficial to our House. It is allowed for foreigners to prepare such entertainments if they do not compromise any merchant native to this city. It will be my intention to bring no criticism upon our House in this or any venture.

I have asked the magistrates in this place how I might best go about this, and I am told that sponsoring a festival for an occasion they call Danja would be a useful means to accomplish our ends. Danja occurs on the second full moon after the dark of the year, which does not give me much time for preparation, but I shall contrive somehow.

You will need to find ships that come to Suret, Daman, and Chaul in order to reach Asirgarh without passing through lands caught up in fighting, such as is still the case in Gujerat. It will be some while until Cambay is a safe harbor for ships carrying our goods, for although the primary battles are over, thousands of those trying to escape Timur-i have flooded into Gujerat in the hope that they will be beyond Timur-i's reach there. We would be likely to lose all our cargo to thieves and taxes if we attempted to sail into or from that port.

Believe me when I tell you that as much as we have lost, we have not lost as much as we might have. We will be able to reestablish our House in its position of achievement once again, no matter what Timur-i's soldiers do in the world. It is heartening to me to see the opportunities around us, for I had not thought we would be so fortunate for many years to come.

I am already forging agreements for caravans, and although we have had to give up much of our wealth and our goods for trade, we are not without means. The merchants here are eager to find new markets and I can assure them of such. We can outfit a new caravan in a month or two. We still have three caravans traveling; they will reach Sirpur before the rains come, and with what they bring we can continue our trading. You, too, are now able to enter into trading, and that will benefit our House.

We have taken a house in the Foreigners' Quarter, in the Street of the Weavers. I have paid handsomely for it, and it should suffice for several years. The magistrates have approved our ownership and I have made a gift to the local ruler, who is inclined to be well-disposed on our behalf. I will purchase slaves and engage servants within the next two months, as I make arrangements with the city government for such enlargements.

I have asked for permission to dedicate a cave to our faith and the wisdom of Zarathustra. I have not been given an answer from the magistrates in this city, but I am hopeful of an answer soon. When they decide if we are to be allowed to worship, I will notify you at once, so that you may include prayers for us as we will pray for you.

I trust you will receive this quickly and will have an answer to me before the rains begin; I would not ask you to try to get us word in such bad weather. If I must wait a year instead of half of one to hear from you, so be it. Our work continues and our House endures.

With utmost respect and dedication,
Zal Iniattir

at Asirgirh, by messenger

1

At the middle of the afternoon of the second day on the road away from Delhi, Timur-i ordered Sanat Ji Mani into a covered wagon. "You are like the white-skinned ones, whose eyes are red; you burn," he announced. "You shall not have to ride in the sun. I need you able to work, foreigner, or my men will kill you and leave your body for the carrion birds to feast upon. Let him be put out of the light." He motioned to his nearest lieutenants. "Give him to the jugglers and tumblers and fools. They will look after him. He will be no danger to them." With that he set his sturdy pony cantering away.

Sanat Ji Mani looked up through pain-clouded eyes at the hard-faced officers who tugged him off his mount and slung him over the rump of one of their small, tough horses, then took his saddlebags of medicaments and rode without speaking to the rear of the line of troops and wagons, dust swirling around them as thick as smoke; it was a long way to the last of the wagons, and the officers kept their horses to a brisk trot. The block of wood attached to his foot bounced heavily with each step the horses took, sending a dull, gnawing pain up Sanat Ji Mani's leg; the small supply of native earth in the sole of his left boot provided little anodyne against his hurts. It was almost sunset and the army would make camp soon; he welcomed the coming dark with an eagerness that was almost passion.

"Djerat!" one of the officers shouted. "Djerat, come!" He drew his horse alongside a large wagon surmounted by a fully rigged tent; the wagon was pulled by six mules and was driven by a woman covered in dark-red, curling hair.

"What do you want?" the driver demanded in a high, sweet voice.

"Timur-i wishes you to carry this foreigner with you. He is reputed to be a healer, so look after him well. He is to come to no harm. And keep his supplies with him." The second officer laughed. "I will catch his horse and bring him to your wagon to be tied to the rear. You may have a use for him."

"Can this foreigner not ride?" the woman asked.

"He can, but the sun has left him blackened and blistered," said the first. "Look for yourself." He reached out and caught his hand in Sanat Ji Mani's hair, lifting his head to show the driver the extent of the burns on his face.

"Is it Timur-i's wish that he ride with us? With us? Why us? You say it is Timur-i who orders us to—" The woman sounded surprised and a bit anxious, and as she pulled her wagon out of the immediate line of horses and vehicles, she added, "Are we to be paid for this?" as she pulled her team to a stop.

"In favor," said the second officer. "Come. Help us get him into your tent." He pulled up his horse and swung out of the saddle.

Djerat sighed. "I am with child," she reminded the two officers. "I will call Tulsi to help you—she is strong and capable." Before they could approve this, Djerat raised her voice. "Tulsi! *Tulsi!* Come here! These men need your help."

Sanat Ji Mani was lowered to the ground, protesting weakly that he could stand on his own. "I will get into the wagon, officers, and I will recover."

The taller of the two men shook his head. "You are burned badly, foreigner. Let the woman aid you."

The shorter officer handed down Sanat Ji Mani's sack of medicaments and tools. "Here. You must keep this with you."

Before Sanat Ji Mani could take it in hand, a muscular young woman of diverse heritage, with short-cut brown hair and grey-green, almond-shaped eyes, appeared in the opening of the tent. She wore leggings and a short caftan, all in red-orange silk. "I will take that," she said, jumping down from the driver's seat and landing with a forward somersault that left her standing almost directly in front of the dismounted officer. "He looks frightful," she said.

"I will heal," Sanat Ji Mani muttered through cracked lips as he reminded himself that the road to Baghdad had been much worse.

"Perhaps," said Tulsi, making a face. "The backs of your hands are black and oozing."

"I will heal," Sanat Ji Mani repeated, raising his voice as much as possible. He could not see Tulsi very clearly, but he found himself reminded of Tishtry, thirteen hundred years gone in the Roman Arena.

Tulsi regarded Sanat Ji Mani with distaste. "I do not want to touch him," she admitted, batting the air with her hand as a particularly dense wave of dust surged over them. "But I suppose I must."

"I can stand," Sanat Ji Mani said.

"And you can fall over, too, no doubt," said Tulsi. She looked at the two officers. "How long has he worn Timur-i's stirrup?" she asked, indicating the staple.

"Six weeks," said the taller officer. "He has mended well. There was no festering."

"Then maybe he *is* a healer," said Tulsi, sighing before she stepped forward and wedged her shoulder under Sanat Ji Mani's left arm. "We will look after him. He will ride in the tent and his burns will fade. You may report to Timur-i that we have him in hand." She turned carefully, making sure Sanat Ji Mani did not drag his stapled foot. "We are going to the rear of the wagon, stranger. There is a way into the tent there." She steadied him, holding out her free hand. "Give me his things."

The taller officer reached down and picked up Sanat Ji Mani's bag and handed it to her. "There. See he improves." He vaulted back into the saddle, gathered up his reins, then, with his comrade, set their horses cantering toward the head of the line once again.

"Come, stranger," Djerat called out. "We must join the march again."

"I am bringing him, Djerat," said Tulsi, carefully making her way toward the rear of the wagon, balancing Sanat Ji Mani against her side. "The stirrup hurts?"

"The sunburn is worse," Sanat Ji Mani told her, trying to smile without success. As terrible as he felt, in some remote part of himself, he was alert to Avasa Dani, far away, and undergoing a change of her own; this provided him a little distraction from his present affliction, and he concentrated on it for the relief it brought.

"No doubt," she said as they reached the end of the wagon. "I am going to fetch steps for you. Lean on the wheel," she said, and slid out from under his arm.

Sanat Ji Mani staggered two steps to the large rear wheel and sagged against it, glad of the wedge of shadow the tent above him provided; once inside, he promised himself to rest and let his body work its cure. The passing wagons and horses of Timur-i's army sounded like constant thunder in his ears, and he longed for silence.

Tulsi appeared in an opening in the back of the tent, a two-step stool in her hand; she dropped out of the wagon and set this in place. "I will help you climb. Start on the stirrup first. It will lift you a little higher."

"Very well," said Sanat Ji Mani, and stumbled into the sunlight. It took him longer to get up the steps than he had anticipated, and he had been glad of Tulsi's assistance. As he half-stepped, half-fell into the tent, he whispered his thanks as he stretched out on a pile of folded carpets, his bag under his shoulder.

"Plenty of time for that when you are well," said Tulsi as she pulled the steps into the wagon and called out, "Djerat! Go!"

The wagon lurched forward as the mules were put into motion again and the wagon was guided back into the river of vehicles moving along the Sultan's Road toward Lahore.

It was well into the night when Sanat Ji Mani awoke, his body aching and his hunger intense. He sat up, trying to remember where he was. As he tried to move his legs the events of the afternoon came back to him, and he put his hands to his eyes as if to shut out the knowledge; he was in a wagon inside a tent, and all around him Timur-i's army was camped. On the other side of the wagon two figures slept, one on a narrow, footed bed, the other on a pallet of thick-woven pads of yak-hair; Sanat Ji Mani recognized the hair-covered driver on the bed and Tulsi on the pallet. These two women, he realized, were part of the entertainers who traveled with Timur-i's army, and as such, never saw combat. He shifted his posture to be more comfortable and stared down at his hands, the darkness offering only slight impediment to his vision; the skin was still cracked but it was beginning to heal, and the blackened crust would fall off in a day or two if he stayed out of the sun.

"Stranger?" Tulsi's sleepy voice startled Sanat Ji Mani, and he looked up abruptly.

"I am awake," he said softly.

"You slept long," she said, keeping her voice low.

"For which I thank you," he said. He looked up at the night sky through the opening in the tent's rear flap. "We are half-way to morning. Do not let me rob you of your sleep."

She scrubbed her hand through her hair. "That is a nice thing to say, that you thank me."

"Why; you have done me a service and I am grateful," he said.

"Most people do not . . ." She let her words trail off into a yawn. "Do you want anything out of your sack, to put on your skin?"

"No," he said. "My skin will recover now I am out of the sun." He paused. "Will you permit me to ride inside this tent tomorrow?"

"While your skin is burned and cracked? Most certainly. Timur-i expects that of us, to keep you with us until you recover." She yawned again.

"Timur-i may expect it, but you are the one providing the shelter," Sanat Ji Mani pointed out, and fell silent for a short while. Then, "You have helped me," he said.

"You talk funny," she told him as she rubbed the sleep from her eyes. "Old-fashioned, like my grandmother."

Sanat Ji Mani did his best to soothe her. "I learned your language long ago."

"It sounds like it," she said. "Your teacher must have been old, too." She giggled.

On her narrow bed, Djerat began to snore.

"Old enough," said Sanat Ji Mani, recalling the blind musician in Karakhorum who had taught him, almost two centuries before.

Tulsi stretched, lithe as a cat, and sat up. "Some of the men speak the language of the Turks," she said as if she disapproved.

"Timur-i Lenkh's father is a Turk," Sanat Ji Mani pointed out.

"His mother is Mongol, and he rules from the power of the Jagatai, not the Balas." Her lips pursed in disapproval.

"I would guess that Timur-i rules from his own power," said Sanat Ji Mani, his voice gentle.

Tulsi looked at him. "Perhaps," she allowed after a long moment's thought. She got onto her knees. "Why do you help him?"

"I have no wish to be hacked into pieces," Sanat Ji Mani said as honestly as he could.

"But you are a foreigner and a captive," she said.

"As long as I am, it would be wise to be useful, would it not." He let her consider her answer; when she did not speak, he went on, "I will do what he requires of me to the full extent of my capabilities, not entirely because I want his favor, but in part because I have pride in my skills. I do not want to fail Timur-i because I do not want to fail myself."

She stifled a laugh. "You are as bad as I am."

He smiled, and this time it worked. "You take pride in your skills, too."

"Of course. I earn my living through them," she said, and considered him. "I suppose you do, too."

"Upon occasion," he agreed.

"Yes; you have not always treated the sick—you seem too prosperous, and your manner is too elevated." She moved a little closer to him. "Are you a grand prince, cast out of your kingdom, or a leader of men who has been betrayed? Or were you the betrayer?" She considered the last and added, almost to herself, "No, I do not think so. Perhaps another of your family was a betrayer and you have paid the price."

"Nothing quite so exciting, I fear," he said, glancing at Djerat to be sure the hirsute woman was still asleep.

"But there must be some mystery. You are from the West, yet you were found in Delhi." She stared at him eagerly. "How is that possible?"

"Men from the West travel," said Sanat Ji Mani. "Not as far as Delhi, most of them, but some have gone all the way to China." He thought back to his days in Lo-Yang and wondered how this curious young woman would respond to knowing he had taught in China in the years before Jenghiz Khan invaded from the north. "You, too, have a tale to tell, by the look of you."

"Nothing remarkable," she said quietly.

"Still, I would like to hear it. You are inquisitive; so am I." His eyes held hers, compelling an answer.

Tulsi lowered her voice to just above a whisper. "My father came from Kiev in Lithuania—or so he said. He trained bears. My mother was a contortionist, from Shang-tu. They met in Samarkand. I was born there. I was given my name by a fortune-teller from Budaun: Tulsi Kil. All those in our troupe were named by him, for luck."

"Samarkand is Timur-i's city," Sanat Ji Mani said.

"Yes." She waited, a frown growing between her brows. "Well?"

He studied her face. "What do you wish to know?"

"Where you come from, of course, and how you happen to be here." She made an impatient gesture.

"Oh." He leaned back, wondering how much he should tell her. "I am not from Delhi, as you have said. I am from the West."

"That is obvious," she said. "I knew that before you told me anything. You have heard what I think of you. How have I erred?"

"I am from mountains far to the west of here, called the Carpathians. Just at present, Hungary and Wallachia rule the region where I was born. I am an exile." Nothing that Timur-i had heard from Josha Dar would contradict that, Sanat Ji Mani knew.

"You are a captive of Timur-i Lenkh," she corrected him, sounding weary. "We are all his captives, one way or another."

"True enough," Sanat Ji Mani said. "But captive or not, I am still an exile."

Tulsi smiled a little. "You are more than that. I can see it in your face."

Sanat Ji Mani touched the peeling skin of his forehead. "If you can see anything but this burn, you astonish me."

"You know what I mean," she said with a chuckle. "You are not so hidden as you think."

There was something in her remark that struck him deeply. "Why do you think I am trying to hide?"

"I have not discerned that yet," she admitted. "In time I will." She stretched again. "You may want to remain awake, but I do not. We must be moving again at first light or Timur-i will kill us for being stragglers." She lay back on her pallet and pulled the two rough-woven blankets up to her throat. "Keep guard, stranger."

"I will," Sanat Ji Mani assured her.

She raised her head to look at him. "I believe you," she said, and turned away to rest, her head on her outstretched arm.

He went to where the mules were tied and had the first sustenance he had had in days; it was little enough, but it gave him some strength, and he began his restoration, patting the mule on the neck, saying to the animal, "It was not enough to harm you, and it has revived me." He limped back to the wagon, moving faster than he had before.

Morning saw them on the road again, the army moving at a steady pace toward the River Indus. Mounted soldiers rode back and forth along the line, keeping all the carts and wagons together, allowing none of them to fall behind.

Djerat sat on the driver's seat and managed the reins with the easy competence of long practice; she paid no attention to Sanat Ji Mani and Tulsi, who remained under cover of the tent. As the day wore on, the wind picked up and soon, both Tulsi and Sanat Ji Mani were busy keeping the tent tied to its wooden frame; it proved a difficult task and made the two of them work increasingly harder as the afternoon brought stronger gusts of hot, dry air from the south-west.

"The stay is torn!" Tulsi shouted as a flap of cloth pulled away from its moorings; the tent sang like the sail of a ship as the wind took gleeful hold of it.

Sanat Ji Mani went to her side, a length of braided silk cord in his hand. "Here. This will hold," he said as he caught the tattered stay and pulled the flap against the frame, knotting the cord to the end of the tent fabric. "This will tighten the more it is pulled." He had learned it from Roman sailors when he had crossed the Oceanus Britannicus the first time in the company of the troops of Julius Caesar.

Tulsi examined the knot skeptically. "I will check it later," she said, and went to secure the rear opening once more. Fine, silky grit filled the air and scoured everything in its path. "The mules will have harness sores tonight."

"I have a medicament that may help them," Sanat Ji Mani volunteered. "When we have stopped at the end of the day, I will tend to them." And, he added to himself, he would have the chance to take a little blood from the mules again—not enough to weaken them, but sufficient to sustain him for a time; the lack of a supply of his native earth, and having just one boot to keep it in was beginning to take a toll on him. Without blood or his native earth he would soon fall into a stupor and waken from it only for ravenous appetite.

"Will you treat animals as well as men?" Tulsi asked in some surprise.

"If it is necessary, of course I will." He took hold of one of the stays holding the ceiling of the tent and refastened it to the frame. "When this storm is past, the stays will all need to be resewn. Otherwise, they will snap in the next hard blow." Half-standing in the moving wagon with a thick wooden block under his right foot was no easy trick, but Sanat Ji Mani was still strong enough to manage.

"I suppose you will help me?" Tulsi said, making no excuse for her sarcasm.

"Yes, if my hands are no longer too burned. I know how to use a needle." He was pleased to see her surprise. "I am not an incompetent, Tulsi Kil. I have learned a few things in my travels."

"So you may have," she conceded, and tucked in a portion of the lining of the tent that wind was attempting to tease out of the rear flap.

It was an enervating afternoon, and by the time the order came to stop for the night, everyone was worn-out; the horses and mules all drooped with fatigue, and many of the men and animals were irritable with fatigue. Only the wind capered on, lively as ever.

"I hate dust," said Djerat as she attempted to remove it from her hair using a small ivory comb; her thick, curly hair was standing up and sparking, and every effort to tend it brought another crackle.

"Use one of the mules' brushes," Sanat Ji Mani recommended, his manner kindly and his tone polite. "You will have less trouble."

Djerat stared at him. "I may have hair all over me," she said slowly and with immense dignity, "but I am not yet an animal."

"I never thought so," Sanat Ji Mani said at once, trying to undo any slight she may have assumed, "but I think the brushes for the mules might get the dust out with less discomfort than a comb: it is what they are designed to do."

Tulsi was laying a campfire in anticipation of the evening meal; this suggestion claimed her attention. "He may have an idea, Djerat."

"Do you take his part?" Djerat countered sharply. "He is a stranger. I am your travel companion. And this is my wagon."

"He also has offered something useful. Try the brushes. If they do not get rid of the dust, you can always go back to combing." Tulsi went to the wagon and pulled out a box of rough planking, containing the brushes, picks, and salves used on the mules. She took out the smallest of the brushes and tossed it to Djerat. "There. See if it works."

Grudgingly Djerat took the brush and, beginning on her forearm, began to ply its stiff bristles along the grain of her hair. "It is quicker," she conceded.

"I will help you as soon as the fire is going," Tulsi said, and glanced at Sanat Ji Mani.

He took her meaning. "I will start the fire. You may help Djerat, if you like."

Tulsi smiled. "Yes. Another good idea."

Sanat Ji Mani went to the stack of wood and dried dung that Tulsi had piled up. He took flint-and-steel from the small wallet hanging from his belt and gathered up a small mound of wood scraps and dried bark. Cupping his hands to keep out the worst of the wind, he struck the flint with the steel and saw a spark leap; the third one caught, and a tiny spot of flame poked out of the kindling. Using a small stone, Sanat Ji Mani shoved the kindling inside the stack of fuel, and watched as it began to burn in earnest. "There," he said as he rose awkwardly to his feet, trying to balance on his uneven footing.

"There will be supper shortly," said Djerat, her tone a bit more cordial. "You can have a share."

"Thank you, but I will fend for myself," Sanat Ji Mani said. "Among my people, it is considered improper to . . . to feed with more than one person."

"An odd tradition," said Djerat, shrugging. "If you do not want to eat with us, so be it. Feed or starve as you like." She signaled to Tulsi. "Bring the pot. There are goats being slaughtered tonight and I will go get our share."

Tulsi did as she was ordered, returning with a good-sized metal cauldron in her arms. "Here," she said as she handed it to Djerat.

"Good. You tend the fire and I will go get our meat. Bring the rice and the onions and a good measure of water so we may get to cooking as soon as I return." Djerat swung away and was about to go off to the center of camp for their rations of goat when Sanat Ji Mani claimed her attention once more.

"If you do not mind, I will examine your mules and see they have no injuries from the dust. I can treat them if they do; I will check their hooves, too, in case of any trouble—"

Before he could go on, she gave him a curt response. "Do as you like." Saying that, she toddled off, the pot held clasped to her front like an enormous, metallic pregnancy.

"You must not mind her," Tulsi said from her place beside the fire, which she was building up by adding small, cut branches to it. "Djerat has not often been shown anything but mockery, and that makes her doubt courtesy. She is not accustomed to accommodating strangers, and she is—she wants to guard me from harm."

"Ah," said Sanat Ji Mani as he went to take grooming brushes from the box Tulsi had opened. "Have you need of guarding?"

"Sometimes. Not very often. The soldiers get drunk now and then, and they do not—" She broke off.

"They are allowed to drink?" Sanat Ji Mani asked. "I have been told followers of the Prophet do not drink." Brushes in hand, he walked back to the line to which the mules were tethered.

"Not wine. But mare's milk that has fermented is another matter, or so Timur-i has been told by his teachers." If Tulsi thought this was an odd interpretation of Islamic law, nothing in her voice or manner revealed it.

Sanat Ji Mani reached the mules and stood still while they took stock of him. Then he moved toward the first one and began to brush his neck, working down and back. Dust flew from his coat in plumes and the mule dropped his head, ears flopping in satisfaction. Brushing the close-cropped mane proved a bit more difficult, but the mule did not protest the care. Sanat Ji Mani continued back and down until he had brushed off the rear legs and the scruffy tail; he had found four abrasions from where the harness and dust had worn away hair and skin, leaving a small scab on the pale coat. "I'll treat that later," he promised the animal before moving to the next in line. By the time Djerat came back with her allocation of goat, Sanat Ji Mani was working on the fifth mule. He was prepared to bring his medicaments to tend the hurts as soon as the grooming was done, and he reported as much to Djerat.

"Do as you must," she said, setting down the pot next to the fire. "Tulsi, bring the onions. Why haven't you fetched them before now? Quickly. I want to eat before the night is half-gone."

"I will," said Tulsi, and went to get the strings of onions from the wagon.

"So," said Djerat, glowering in Sanat Ji Mani's direction. "You fancy her."

"I admire her, certainly; I admire you," he said as he completed his work on the fifth mule and moved on to the sixth.

"Because you like this pelt?" she scoffed. "No; I can see you are taken with her. I warn you she will not have congress with you. She is a tumbler and her living depends on her abilities. She will not risk starvation or death for a length of hot flesh in her woman's portal."

"I would not ask it of her," said Sanat Ji Mani, brushing the chest of the sixth mule.

Djerat laughed unpleasantly. "All men pledge that, and all of them lie."

"Tulsi is coming," Sanat Ji Mani warned, and fell silent as Djerat busied herself putting rice and water into the pot.

"Here are the onions," said Tulsi, glancing from Djerat to Sanat Ji Mani and back again as if sensing something in the air between them; she said nothing but as she handed the onions to Djerat, the older woman seized her arm. "What is it?"

"You trust too readily. You must remember what happened to your parents, child," Djerat implored her.

Tulsi went pale and took a step back, pulling herself free of Djerat's grip. "I never forget that. Never."

Sanat Ji Mani watched this exchange with curiosity mixed with concern as he busied himself grooming the sixth mule: whatever message Djerat sought to give, he doubted it was to his benefit; he would have to proceed with care in all he did, for he was certain he would be under intense scrutiny from now until he left Timur-i Lenkh's army.

Text of a letter from Rogerian to Sanat Ji Mani, written in the Latin of Imperial Rome, sent from Alexandria to the Red Sea and carried on the *Sea Maiden* to Chaul; never delivered.

To my master, known as Sanat Ji Mani, residing at Delhi in the Delhi Sultanate in the Street of Brass Lanterns, the greetings of Rogerian from Alexandria in the Mameluke Empire of Egypt.

I have claimed your house in this city, and have paid such fees as have been assessed against it to the authorities of the Mamelukes. I will remain in this place for five years, and if you have not reached here by the end of that time, I will go on to Rome, to the estate of Atta Olivia Clemens where I shall remain for another five years. Do not ask me to wait longer than that: if Saxony and Spain taught me nothing else, they showed me the folly of delaying a search for you too many years.

The house is in need of repairs which I have authorized, and which should be completed within the year. In the meantime, I have paid the laborers as you would want them to be paid, and I will provide bonuses for early completion of their work. When you arrive here, the house will be to your liking. I have also commissioned masons to build an athanor for your use—the old one has fallen to ruin and would not be safe to use. I have taken the three jars of gold from the hiding place in the garden well, and if I must, I will take another three to continue to support this household and pay the authorities the various taxes they impose. I have taken care to conceal my explorations of the well, going into it only late at night; I am sure I have not roused the curiosity of anyone in this part of the city in doing this, just as you would require were you here to make such decisions yourself.

Rustam Iniattir has made a place for himself and his household in the city of Fustat, a place convenient for merchants and where his faith is not as condemned as it might be in other cities. He is working at setting up more caravans, and I am providing him with funds in your name, with the assurance that you will continue your ventures with him when you arrive here. He is considering sending one of his sons here to Alexandria, but that will require more money than he can spare, and he will not permit me to pay for such an establishment, for he fears becoming too indebted to you. He may change his mind in a year or so, and I have informed him that the offer for such support will not be withdrawn.

As regards Avasa Dani, I have much to report: shortly after we arrived here in Alexandria she was taken with a fever that, in a matter of ten days, killed her. As you must be aware, she woke to your life two nights later, and I have endeavored to help her to meet the demands of what has happened to her. She has informed me that she

will not remain in this house now that she is a vampire, and she is
seeking some means of making her way in the world that will not
endanger her or you. I have tried to persuade her that you would
prefer she stay here until you come, but she will have none of it. She
is a married woman and her first loyalty must always be to her husband, although she will never see him again in this life, even though
he may again come to Delhi. For that reason alone she is unwilling to
accept your hospitality now that she has changed. She is aware of
your blood-bond, and has said that she seeks no stronger connection
than what you have already. I have not been able to find a convincing
argument to put before her in this regard, and therefore I have offered
her such money as she may need to establish herself as she wishes.
You would want her to have what she seeks, I know, and to that end,
I will strive to accommodate whatever demands she may have in days
to come.

I have not yet informed Rustam Iniattir of Avasa Dani's death, in
case he should visit here and find her apparently living. I do not know
when I will tell him, or what, precisely, I shall say, but for the time
being, it is just as well that he continue to believe that she is alive. It
will be less awkward to maintain the fiction than to explain her presence if he has been informed of her death.

There is fear in the Mameluke Empire that Timur-i will once again
come westward and strike at the city of Damascus and perhaps make
another attempt on Jerusalem. If he should succeed in these places,
everyone is afraid that all the Nile will be open to his army. According
to what we hear in Alexandria, Timur-i turned westward after sacking
Lahore; I hope that is true, and that he did not, in the end, try to
reach Delhi, or, that if he did, you have found some way to leave the
city before he arrived. If that is the case, this letter may never reach
you, but it may be just as well, for it would mean you are safe.

Do not worry for your holdings here: I will look after them, and
after Villa Ragoczy outside of Rome as well if I must journey there. I
will prepare a copy of this letter and place it in the secured niche
behind the ovens in the kitchen where you will know to look for it,
and copies of any others I may write to you from time to time. I trust

you will look to your safety while you are still in Delhi, and will travel here as swiftly as ship and caravan will bring you.

Rogerian

On the 29th day of January in the Christian year 1399 at Alexandria

2

"At Kabul we will turn north through the mountains toward Samarkand; after the long journey through the mountains, we will once again see the city of blue and gold that Timur-i has built," Djerat said over her shoulder to Sanat Ji Mani as they waited in the line of wagons to be ferried across the River Sutlej, a fast-running tributary of the Indus. It was a blustery day, and although the sun was warm, the wind, coming from the north, was cold from its passage over distant mountain snows. "There we will have rewards for our work, and we will join in the feasting."

The soldiers had rigged a pair of huge pulleys from two enormous tree-trunks set into the banks opposite one another; the pulleys were strung with ropes as thick as a man's forearm which the soldiers used to tug the wide barge across the swift-running river. The ferry-line ran through the barge and kept it rigorously on course in the treacherous current; fully loaded, the barge could carry three wagons and up to a dozen horsemen at a time, and it had been in continual use for more than two days.

"It is a long way to Samarkand," said Tulsi, sitting on the edge of the driving-seat next to Djerat, her expression more thoughtful than the older woman's.

"We have made the journey before, and will again—without the foreigner for company, I hope." She intended that Sanat Ji Mani hear this; she raised her voice enough for it to carry into the tent on the wagon. "You cannot want to be with the jugglers and tumblers and fools, can you, foreigner?"

"No doubt Timur-i will arrange something before you travel again," said Sanat Ji Mani with every appearance of good humor.

"Once we are there, in Samarkand, we will see what becomes of you; Timur-i will have had time to test your value and your abilities," Djerat continued. "If you have not proved your worth, Timur-i will be done with you: you will be killed and your bones given to kites."

Sanat Ji Mani thought of those birds with an inward shudder, but he maintained his aplomb. "We cannot know what Timur-i will do."

Djerart laughed. "He will make short work of you—of that I have no doubt. Unless you fulfill your promise, he will be rid of you."

"And that would make you happy," said Sanat Ji Mani, rising to the challenge at last.

Djerat sloughed around on the driving-seat and looked directly at him through the tent-lap, her eyes like shards of obsidian in her hairy face. "Yes. It would make me happy." Then she turned back to face her team, showing no interest in anything he might say in response.

It was Tulsi who was shocked. "You cannot mean that," she protested.

"Yes, I can," said Djerat.

At the same instant, Sanat Ji Mani said, "Yes, she does."

Tulsi held up her hands, appalled at this. "You are both disgusting," she said in a low voice, as if her quiet would lessen their reaction.

"He is the one who is disgusting," said Djerat. "You are blinded to his faults because you think he is smitten with you. He is no different than any other man, who seeks only to have his pleasure and has no thought beyond the end of his member."

Sanat Ji Mani said nothing, sitting back in the wagon in the shelter of the tent; he looked down at his small, well-shaped hands, noticing that they were almost free of burns now, but that the skin still had that stretched, tender look about it. Another two weeks and he should be fully recovered. He did not want to argue with Djerat, not because of her accusations, but because of the dismay they caused Tulsi; Djerat was right: he was attracted to the young tumbler.

A sudden cry erupted from the front of the line, and immediately shouts and howls went up as consternation spread through those waiting to cross the river.

Djerat stood up, her hand shading her eyes as she squinted down at the excitement below. "A man is caught in the pulley-cable," she said at last. "The ropes are cutting him in half. They may have to kill him to get him free."

This brought Sanat Ji Mani to full attention. "How badly is he hurt? Can you see?" He reached for his bag of supplies and went to the rear of the tent, climbing out of it with difficulty as his stapled foot compelled him to limp. As he reached the ground he called out, "Stop the cable. Stop the cable!"

Watching him try to hurry, Djerat laughed. "Save him if you can, foreigner. See if they will let you."

The people in other wagons made way for him as he stumbled down the bank to the tree-trunk supporting the pulley and cable. A few of them jeered as he passed, but most stared at him with the horrified fascination of developing tragedy.

An officer stood at the foot of the tree-trunk, staring up at the huge pulley overhead; the ropes were taut and quivering, and other soldiers milled on the bank, staring toward the barge now halted at mid-stream, with the injured man flailing against the side of the craft; below him the river carried a smear of red.

"He is dead anyway," said the officer when Sanat Ji Mani asked him to stop the cable. "We will kill him quickly, and that will be the end of it."

"Can no one swim out to him?" Sanat Ji Mani asked. "He needn't be made to suffer any more hurt if someone will swim out to him."

"He is caught in the rope. It will have his arm off, and then he will be cut through the chest. Why risk another man to save one who is already dead?" The officer shook his head.

"He may be, but not yet," said Sanat Ji Mani. "So he may also be saved."

The officer stared at Sanat Ji Mani, then recognition came into his face. "You are the foreign healer, are you not?"

"I am," said Sanat Ji Mani; the sun was already leaching the strength from him; he could feel his face redden and his body begin to shiver.

"If you wish to try to save him, I will stop the cable, but the rest is up to you." He favored Sanat Ji Mani with an ironic nod, then bawled out orders to stop the cable. "There. Do as you must."

Sanat Ji Mani glanced at the swirling waters of the river, feeling already the first twinges of vertigo running water always evoked in him. He steeled himself against the ordeal that was to come; he handed his bag to the officer. "Keep this for me, if you would."

The officer took it. "If you like. I would rather give it back to the tumbler." There was an amused glint in his eyes as he watched Sanat Ji Mani start toward the river. "That stirrup makes for poor swimming," he remarked.

People fell silent as Sanat Ji Mani reached the edge of the river and bent down to take hold of the ferry-line where it entered the water; more than a thousand eyes were fixed on him as he entered the water, his arm wrapped around the ferry-line. Almost at once nausea hit him as the water surged around him. Grimly he began to pull himself forward on the ferry-line, his hands straining, his body aching; the barge seemed leagues away. He concentrated on reaching the barge, focusing on the man whose blood flamed in the river.

"Watch out!" someone on the barge called out as a large branch came sweeping down on him.

Sanat Ji Mani wrapped both arms around the ferry-line and held on with all his waning strength; the branch brushed against him, trying to snag his clothing: he felt the fabric at his shoulder give way, leaving a rent in his short, black kandalys that reached all the way down his back. Gasping, he continued along the ferry-line, the stirrup as heavy as a boulder on his right foot. For a moment he vividly recalled his afternoon in the Flavian Circus, fighting crocodiles in an aquatic venation; he used the memory to drive himself forward. After what seemed an eternity, he touched the rough-sawn logs of the barge; he took a firmer grip and began to pull himself around toward the trapped and bleeding man while those on the barge shouted to him.

The man was still half-conscious and trying to shout. Immense, bleeding welts scored his arms and shoulder. At least, thought Sanat Ji Mani as he made his way toward the man, the cable had not cut him across the abdomen, for then nothing would save him from an agonized death; the kindest thing would be to kill him quickly, had that been the case. But as the rope lay against the man's shoulder and back, he had a chance to survive. Sanat Ji Mani felt a renewal of purpose as he thrashed along the length of the barge, the river pulling at him as he strove to reach the injured man. He struggled nearer, reaching out to take the man's nearest arm.

"Get away!" the man shouted, trying to kick out at Sanat Ji Mani.

"I can help you," Sanat Ji Mani called back.

"They'll chop me to bits in a moment. Get back!" He coughed as he swallowed more of the river.

"Not yet. I have a little time to try to get you free," Sanat Ji Mani said loudly; he was an arm's-length away from the man, and could see the panic and agony in his eyes. "If you will let me help you—"

The man howled, anger and anguish giving the sound an undeniable urgency. "Let them kill me and be done with it!"

"Not quite yet," Sanat Ji Mani said, as much to himself as the trapped man. "I am going to try to hold the cable out from your body. I will not be able to do it for very long. Do you think you can slip out from under it?"

The man shook his head violently but said, "I can try." He watched Sanat Ji Mani with disbelief as the foreigner closed the gap between them. "You'll be caught," he warned.

"I doubt it," said Sanat Ji Mani. "I think we can slip away together."

"They will kill us both if you do not succeed," the man told him over the noise of the river and the shouts of those watching from the barge above.

"Then we had best not fail," Sanat Ji Mani sputtered as the barge swung, sloshing water over him.

"The river is very fast," the man said, panic in his voice.

"Then keep hold of me," Sanat Ji Mani recommended. "I will hold on to the ferry-line." There was grim determination in this promise, for he knew that once in the grip of the current, he was too weak to fight the river, and would be swept away.

"I will," said the man, desperation turning his vow to a shriek.

Sanat Ji Mani nodded. "Be ready," he ordered, angling his body away from the barge and slipping under the cable so that his shoulder took the tension; the hemp cut his clothing and chafed his shoulder, and the stresses thrummed in the fibers of the cable but there was room enough for the trapped man to break away. "Now!"

The man let go of the barge and wrapped his bloody arm around Sanat Ji Mani's waist, holding on with such purpose that he nearly dragged them both underwater. As the barge bobbed and rocked with the release of the cable, the man clawed his way up Sanat Ji Mani's torn garments to thrust his head out of the water, breathing emphatically and shouting he was alive, all the while forcing Sanat Ji Mani underwater, where his strength was sapped by the running water. Slowly the barge began to move again. Sanat Ji Mani kept hold of the ferry-line, letting the cable pull him and his charge to the far bank.

As they reached the shallows, the man let go, staggering to his feet, blood running down his body lending his bronze clothing an encarmined glow; Sanat Ji Mani swallowed hard and forced his thought to other matters. The man kept moving, leaving a bright trail behind him, raising his arms with an effort, shouting he was alive, and only then gave his attention to Sanat Ji Mani, who was on his knees in the rough-pebbled sand. "You did it!" he exclaimed, waving his hands as if to restore feeling in them. "You did it!"

Sanat Ji Mani got slowly to his feet, the stirrup feeling as if it were made of lead instead of steel and wood. "Your wounds must be treated," he said. "You are still not beyond danger."

"Why say that?" the man demanded. "I am alive. You are alive. What more can happen? The rest is nothing."

"You will not think so if the abrasions become putrid," Sanat Ji Mani warned him. "Better to treat the hurts now. You will have bruises and other pain as well. As soon as the wagon in which I ride is over the river . . ." He glanced at the barge which was almost unloaded. "Will you bring the wagon of Djerat, the hairy woman, over in your next load? They have my medicaments, and I can tend to this man's hurts."

The man commanding the barge nodded. "I will do it."

"Thank you," Sanat Ji Mani said; he could feel his skin burning, and he looked about for shade. He did not want to use any of the wagons, for he did not think he would be safe lying in their shadows. Finally, he saw a small overhang where a rocky promontory made a bit of shade over the River Sutlej, and he pointed toward it. "I will rest there until Djerat is across."

"As you wish," said the barge commander; he pointed to the man Sanat Ji Mani had pulled from the river. "What about him?"

"He should lie down and be given tea to drink," said Sanat Ji Mani. "If one of the wagons that have come across will let him rest in the interior, I will tend to him when my supplies arrive." He felt tired to the bone; that shadow was tantalizing and he longed to lie in it. "I will be over there. Under the rock."

The barge commander shrugged. "Do you want tea?"

"No, thank you; nothing," he said, knowing it was not the truth: his esurience was burning within him as furiously as the sun burned without. Limping heavily on account of the stirrup, he trudged away into the shade and lay back against the jumbled boulders, finding them as restful as any soft bed he had ever known. He settled himself and closed his eyes, grateful for even a short respite from the sun.

He woke a short while later, alerted by the chittering of river otters gathered farther down the bank that something was amiss. He stretched and discovered that sunburn had stiffened his skin once again. Slowly he sat up and looked about.

On the river the barge was once again in trouble: the ferry-line had apparently been frayed by the stresses of being caught in mid-stream while Sanat Ji Mani helped the trapped man. Now the barge swung about in the river, no longer held on course by anything more than the cable. The drivers of the wagons aboard had to wrestle with their teams to keep their mules and horses from panicking. Men began to shout as the barge started to break away from the heavy cable, tipping dangerously, flinging two men and their horses into the water.

Sanat Ji Mani scrambled to his feet and limped to the edge of the river, watching the men and horses carried away downstream, the screams of animals and men shredding the afternoon. He stared back at the barge and saw it pitching as the commander strove to steady it using only the cable; for a short while, it seemed he would do it, but then the barge teetered, and the right rear jutted suddenly upward, dumping all but a few men into the river. Djerat's wagon came down amid a tangle of harness and tent; the mules brayed their terror and Djerat cursed as they were caught by the current. Sanat Ji Mani moved thigh-deep into the water, hoping for a chance to help guide the wagon to safety. As he watched, Tulsi climbed out of the rear of the toppled tent, his bag of supplies over her arm; she saw him, and waved to him, shouting something he could not hear. On impulse, he went another step into the river and was in water above his waist. Memories of another river, nearly three centuries ago, in Spain, were powerful, but not enough to keep him from going deeper: Tulsi and Djerat were struggling with the wagon and might soon be pulled underwater. He had no strength left to fight the water; with the curious otters observing from the bank, he slid away after the wagon.

The Sutlej carried them some distance into ever more desolate territory as the hills gave way to the first spread of arid flatlands where the wind lost its chill. Finally, when the first streamers of approaching sundown were beginning to color the western sky, the wagon was snagged on a sandbar; two of the mules were dead, the other four were battered and spent by their ordeal, and could only be got out of the river by cutting them out of their harnesses and being led to the shore where they remained on shaky legs, their heads down and long ears drooping.

Djerat had not fared much better: her thick hair was heavy and her shoulder gave her pain from striving to keep her team alive in the river. She cursed long and thoroughly, blaming Sanat Ji Mani for every misfortune that had been visited upon her since her family sold her to the man who offered them enough gold to buy a bigger mill until the present. She then turned on Tulsi. "You. You are an ungrateful wretch. Your mother was a scorpion and your father was a viper. You are nothing but pain and trouble." She slapped Tulsi across the face. "Everything is ruined because of *him* and *you*."

Sanat Ji Mani stepped up to her. "All that may be true, but it does not get us through the night, which is coming soon. If we move away from the river—"

"And why should we do that?" Djerat rounded on him, prepared to belabor him with her fists.

"Because animals come to the river to drink at night. All kinds of animals." He said it gently. "Those two dead mules will be fought over. It is wiser to move ourselves than be rid of the mules."

"And you believe we can get far enough to be safe?" Her question was incredulous. "How are we to do that?"

"We can lead the mules still alive and pull the wagon ourselves. There is still time before sunset. We need not go very far: perhaps half a league." He pointed to a single tree some distance away. "That far."

"And you think we will not be in danger there?" Djerat jeered.

"No, but I think our danger will be less, especially if we build a fire," he said pointedly.

"But you will not pull the wagon, not with your foot in Timur-i's stirrup," said Djerat.

"I will pull, and I will lead a mule," he said, and started away to right the wagon.

"You think he is right," Djerat accused Tulsi. "You want to do this thing."

"I think he may be right," Tulsi replied cautiously. "And right or not, I think we would be safer away from the river."

"Do you suppose a campfire will keep hungry lions at bay?" Djerat asked. "We have four living mules that are weak from the river. Look at them. How can they fight off anything larger than a mongoose?"

"They will stand a better chance away from the riverbank than at it," Tulsi said. "I am going to help him pull the wagon. You can lead the mules. They know you."

Djerat flung up her hands in disgust. "Very well. But if either of you slacks, I will not take up your burdens."

Tulsi smiled bleakly. "I would not expect you to." She paused. "I will fill a bucket with water so the mules will not be thirsty during the night."

There was a groaning and a crash as the wagon was set on all four wheels again; its tent sagged, dripping, clearly revealing that one of the support rods for it had broken, giving the wagon a raffish, lopsided look. "You can pull and I will push," said Sanat Ji Mani, going to the rear of the wagon and leaning against it; the vehicle rolled forward over the uneven ground. "You can guide it." He looked around at the mules. "There are halters in the wagon, I hope?"

"Under the driver's seat," said Djerat, frowning as she spoke. "I will give you one. You will have to deal with the mule yourself." She trudged up to the wagon and reached under the seat to pull out a handful of rope halters. "Here."

He caught the halter she tossed in his direction. "Very good." Sorting out the halter, he started toward the worn-out mules, trying to decide which to lead.

"Take the jenny with the notched ear," Tulsi recommended from behind him. "She is the most sensible."

He nodded. "Very well," and was relieved when the mule proved tractable, resisting only a bit when Sanat Ji Mani led her toward the wagon. "We are ready to begin," he said as he took his place at the back of the wagon once more.

"Oh, all right," said Djerat, and handed a halter to Tulsi, holding two for herself. "We'll bring the mules, and head for that tree."

Tulsi said nothing more as she caught one of the jack-mules and led him back to the front of the wagon. "There is nothing for them to eat," she called out to Sanat Ji Mani.

"I will find something before morning, when the land is most still. In the meantime, you are right to bring water." He gave the wagon another gentle push, and this time it rolled more easily, being away from the uneven ground carved by the river. He was keenly aware that he would have to find food for the mules and for himself before dawn, for once the sun rose, his strength would be gone.

"Where will we go? Timur-i is bound for Lahore and Kabul, and we cannot catch up with him," Djerat complained as she haltered the two remaining mules. "We cannot stay here on the edge of this dry plain. We will die of thirst or starve."

"Do you want to stay with Timur-i?" Sanat Ji Mani asked, doing his best to keep the incredulity from his voice.

"Why not?" Djerat countered; she led the mules up to the wagon and took her place on the other side of the wagon-tongue from Tulsi and prepared to pull. The slanting rays of sunset cast long shadows across the hard-packed earth, showing they were moving north by north-west.

"He is a capricious ruler, and he has had men executed for laughing," Tulsi said. "You know he is not safe." She grabbed the hitch-ring on the wagon-tongue and began to pull as well; the wagon trundled along at a steady pace. "This works," she said in some astonishment.

"So long as the ground is flat," said Djerat. "And there is not too much scrub."

"By the time we reach hills or mountains, the mules will be ready to pull again," Tulsi said, trying to be encouraging; they were a third of the way to the tree.

From some distance away a first roar sounded the end of day; the mules danced on their leads, suddenly alert and nervous. Other animals set up howls and cries as if in answer to the lion.

"Save your breath for work," Sanat Ji Mani recommended as he shoved harder on the rear panel of the wagon; he was growing light-headed as he pushed, and he knew he would not be able to keep up his efforts for much longer. The mule he led minced along, ears moving to catch every sound, aware that creatures were gathering, anticipating dusk.

Both women were willing to abide by his order, husbanding their strength and making for the tree. By the time they reached it, the sky was much darker in the east, and the brilliance in the west was giving way; a few night-flying birds were headed into the sky, and occasionally a bat fluttered by.

"What do we do now?" Djerat asked as she dropped the wagon-tongue. "We are at the tree and it is almost dark."

Sanat Ji Mani led the mule forward and set down an armload of dried scrub and dung he had picked up as they went from the river-bank to the tree. "First I build a fire. Once we have that, we will be protected." He had felt in his wallet for flint-and-steel and had been glad to find them still in place. "Then we can consider what is next to be done." He did not wait for any response, but began to lay a fire not far from the wagon. "You will want to tie the mules where they will be in the light."

"I suppose you think this solves everything," said Djerat. "You have only to light the fire and we will have nothing to fear."

"No," said Sanat Ji Mani. "I believe we all have good reason to fear."

As if to punctuate his words, a second roar blared in the night as the afterglow continued to fade from the sky. Tulsi pulled the mules nearer to the wagon while Sanat Ji Mani made a pile of twigs and strove for a spark from flint-and-steel.

"Then you are planning to use our gratitude to compel us to obey your wishes." Djerat cocked her head. "You do not assume I am unaware of your intentions."

Sanat Ji Mani continued his work. "No, I do not think that, as well you would know if you took a moment to reflect." He heard her shocked intake of air; he went on, "You and Tulsi may decide on a course I cannot agree to, and if that is the case, I will not try to persuade you against your will to accept what I plan." A bit of flame had started; he fed it with kindling and blew on it gently to set it burning.

"You are a dangerous man," said Djerat.

"But I have made us a fire, so, for the night, accept that I have my uses," he said with an ironic smile as he stood up, shuffling a little to accommodate the stirrup. "I will keep watch while you sleep," he went on. "In the morning, I will rest." He would need to get out of the sun, for his new burn was already painful and a second day of exposure would be excruciating.

"Indeed you shall," said Tulsi before Djerat could speak. "I, for one, will be happy to have a night to rest."

"And in the morning, when he is gone and the mules with him, what will you say then?" Djerat asked spitefully.

"I will say it is a poor sport who does not leave two mules to pull the wagon for us," Tulsi answered sharply.

Sanat Ji Mani stared into the fire, his ears attuned to the sounds in the night; back at the riverbank a fight had begun, possibly for the dead mules, and on the broad plains many creatures were moving. One of them, he was certain, would feed him before sunrise, and provide a meal for the two women; it would get them all through the following night and for the moment, he hoped that would be enough to maintain their antipathetic alliance long enough for them to find a haven.

Transcription of an oral report made by Ariq Sati, company commander, to Timur-i Lenkh.

Most Esteemed Lord, favored by Allah and beloved of the Prophet, I come to you to fulfill my duty as your company commander of mounted archers called the Bronzes, to report on an incident that occurred during the crossing of the Sutlej two days since.

While the various wagons were being ferried—most of the troops having already crossed—a man of my company, attempting to keep a crate of food from overbalancing into the river, was instead himself thrown off the barge. He was wedged between the barge and the pull-cable, which was giving him severe injuries—later inspection showed he had been cut to the bone on his shoulder and upper arm—and causing the barge to be stalled at mid-stream.

The order was given to cut the man out of the pull-cable so that the barge could continue to move when the foreigner Sanat Ji Mani volunteered to release the man—one Jahan Baidu, a distant member of your clan, most exalted Lord—and attempt to save his life. He was allowed to do this only because the trapped man was a relative of yours and therefore deserved the chance to live. It seemed an impossible task for anyone, but it was best to try to save Jahan Baidu, and so the foreigner went into the river in spite of your stirrup on his right foot. The current was strong and swift, which hampered the rescue, but in spite of everything, Sanat Ji Mani was able to free your relative, who made it to the shore, Sanat Ji Mani behind him. I, myself saw both men on the northern shore immediately after the rescue, so I have no doubt that it was entirely successful.

The ferry continued its work, but the stay-line had been damaged, and at the next laden crossing, it broke, leaving the barge at the mercy of the river. All three wagons on it washed away, as did the eleven men and four women making the crossing; most watching were afraid of the swiftness of the river and would do nothing but go to the bank and thrust poles out for the unfortunates to grab. As you are aware, there is a bend through rocks just below the ferry-crossing, so the opportunity to pull those flung into it out of the river was brief. Only two were brought safely to shore; the rest were swept downstream and I dispatched two riders to search for any survivors. The barge itself suffered damage when it careened into the rocks a short distance downstream. It took most of the afternoon and evening to repair the barge and replace the ferry-line before we could continue with the crossing. The riders I had sent out returned with two bodies and a third man who was badly injured but still alive; he was put in the care of the farriers to set his bones and then into the hands of the herbalist. I do not know if he will live, but there is some hope for him.

The crossing of the remainder of the wagons and men was almost complete when I came away to make this report, and it has proceeded without any other disruption. All but five wagons had been taken over the river by the time I rode out, and by now all must be across.

All in all, we lost very few persons, animals, wagons, and supplies as a result of this mishap. I can state that no significant amount of food was washed away, and that only two horses were. There were upward of twelve asses and mules lost, and three wagons swept away, which is unfortunate, but at least it was only jugglers, fools, and tumblers who died. The jugglers who toss flaming arrows were in one of the missing wagons, and the woman covered in hair and the tumbler with grey eyes were in the other; they are not so great a loss as would be the men from the Inland Sea with the four trained tigers, or the jugglers who perform while standing on galloping horses. I will not go so far as to say we were lucky, but I am convinced it could have been much worse. In a situation such as this, I must point out that we might have endured much less tolerable expirations.

Most puzzling of all is that the foreigner, Sanat Ji Mani, cannot be found. I have done my best to discover what has become of him. Two men report that he went into the river a second time, when the barge overturned, in an attempt to save those who were on it. It may be that he did. I did not see this myself, so I cannot say for sure he did it, but given what he did before, I cannot think it would be unlike him to make such an attempt. If he did go into the river, it carried him away, and it is likely he has drowned or been killed against the rocks. I know he did not try to escape, for we searched the country for some distance around, and a man with a stirrup on his foot could not go far, or fast. I must conclude that my two men have given a good account of the foreigner, and that he did indeed do his utmost to pull the unfortunates from the river. It is likely his body may wash up far downstream where it cannot be recovered. I am satisfied that he is gone, and unless you order a search made for him, I am going to count him among the casualties of the ferry-crossing.

As regards your relative, Jahan Baidu, I wish I could report that all that was done to save him was sufficient, but I fear it was not:

Jahan Baidu had bled a great deal, which took the heat from his body. He soon became cold, and his skin went pale. By nightfall, he was shaking as if lying in mountain snows. My own physician did his best to treat him, but it was in vain. The rope had sawn too far into his flesh and his bleeding could not be stopped. Any movement brought about a welling of blood, and eventually, he fell into a swoon, and passed from that into death before the night was half-spent. Prayers for him were offered with sunrise prayers, and he was put into a grave with a marker showing his lineage.

That is as much as I can tell you. You may question me further or question my men and you will be told the same thing. I regret that any misfortune should come to one of your family while under my command and I beseech you not to hold this against me when you decide what is to be done, for the sake of my father and brothers, who serve you with devotion as I do; no one knows better than you, Exalted Lord, the hazards of campaigning, and as regrettable as these losses are, they must be counted among the misfortunes of marching an army, and not the lapse of anyone under your banner and command.

Copied by the scribe Yesun Toq and signed by

> *Ariq Sati*
> *Commander*
> *Bronze Company*

3

Djerat stood at the ford, arms akimbo, her expression clearly visible through the curling hair on her face. "I will not turn away from La-hore. If you believe you must go back across the river, you will go without my wagon, or me." It was early in the day and the sky was brassy with high, thin clouds that gave the expanse around them a henna-like color promising stifling heat by mid-morning.

Tulsi shook her head. "I have no wish to leave you," she said, her head lowered and her voice deliberately soft. "I do not think—"

"No. You do not. You listen to that foreigner, and you take leave of everything you have learned. Do you suppose I cannot see it? You are infatuated with him. You have invested him with all your wishes and dreams, so that if he says 'turn east and south' you say 'yes; we must do that' all the while forgetting that you have been kept by the army of Timur-i, which is the most powerful army in the world." Djerat pointed to her wagon, standing a short distance away from the riverbank; Sanat Ji Mani was occupied trimming the mules' hooves. "He is useful, I grant you that, but he is foolish."

"Because he does not wish to follow Timur-i?" Tulsi asked. "Why is this a foolish thing? You have seen what his army has done to cities from Damascus to Delhi: why should you want to view more destruction?"

"Because Timur-i is rich, and powerful beyond reckoning. All the kings of the world bow down to him, except the Emperor of China, who is his kinsman," said Djerat flatly. "He is generous with those who please him. He gave me a pearl once for taking off my clothes to show I am hairy all over; I brushed myself from head to toe for him. Where else could I hope for such largesse? You may be able to perform in any market-square and eke out a living, but I cannot share your gamble: too many are inclined to call me a wolf-woman or bear-woman and hunt me as if I were a beast. I will put myself in such danger for no one—no one." She strolled a few steps farther away from the wagon, putting them well out of hearing.

"You might find safety in other cities—cities Timur-i has not touched," Tulsi ventured.

"That is *his* opinion, is it not?" Djerat said, and spat. "You have no thought about what is to come, do you? You listen to his tales and declare that you are in agreement with all that he says. But you do not consider that a man who cannot stand to walk in the sun may have a hard time in the world. You would be his servant, and he could offer you little for your devotion. He says he is an exile, that his country is in the hands of those who are not his people, and you do not question this."

"Why should I?" Tulsi countered with some heat. "All he has said has been true, when I have tested it."

"And what can you test, you stupid girl?" Djerat demanded. "He knows medicaments, I will give you that. But how can you show any of his other claims are true? He may be nothing more than a charlatan who has assumed a role for himself; you cannot put him to the test to find out. He cannot swear on the *Qran*, and it might not mean anything if he did, for he is not a Muslim. You are willing to believe him, but there is no good reason you should. He is from far enough away that he might claim anything with impunity. You say he has jewels and gold in his pack, along with medicaments and other supplies. How do you know that he does not have bits of colored glass and base metal painted in saffron to look like gold? Many another has been fooled by such ruses." Her derisive chuckle was high and shrill.

"Why would he say they are jewels when they are not? And the gold is gold," Tulsi protested. In their two long days of travel she had been worn down by Djerat's constant belittling of Sanat Ji Mani. Now that they were at a ford, she realized matters had reached a head. "He has done much for us. Have you no gratitude?"

"No; why should I? I did not ask for his help. I never wanted it." Djerat sighed. "He is an intruder who chose to follow us into the river. Neither you nor I summoned him. He is nothing to either of us but a man riding in the wagon. All that has come after is on his head. I cannot say anything to his credit because of what he did." She pursed her lips. "If he makes us his responsibility, what is it to me?"

"Your mules have survived, thanks to him," Tulsi pointed out. "You lost only two, but without him you might not have any left."

"They have benefitted him as much as they have me. And, yes, two of them drowned, in spite of him." Djerat shrugged.

"But he has done all he can to be useful. Surely that is worthy of regard." Color mounted in her face. "He is a—"

"He is another set of hands, yes. He is strong enough, and has some abilities that are useful, and many problems that are not: he cannot endure the sun. He is a foreigner from a place that will provide him no ransom, or so he claims. He has habits that are not the habits of our people. He is also a man with a staple through his foot. He might as well proclaim himself a criminal and be done with it," Djerat jeered.

"Is that what you believe? It is almost as if you think he has imposed upon us," Tulsi said, astonished at what Djerat told her.

"Well, has he not?" Djerat inquired softly. "From the first, he has made us beholden to him, and expressed demands because of it."

"What demands are these—beyond sheltering him from the sun?" Tulsi challenged, her anger coming to the fore.

"He has expected us to comply with his wishes," said Djerat, frowning her resentment as she spoke.

"Why should he not?" Tulsi pursued. "His wishes have been to our benefit as well as his."

"Perhaps," said Djerat. "But we would not have been on the barge when it overturned had he not ordered us out of our place in line. We would still be with the army and safe, not out here in these wild places—"

"There is a village across the ford," Tulsi said, pointing toward the walled cluster of mud-brick houses. Sounds of activity within the walls sounded across the river-ford—shouts and the shrieks of children a reminder of how close they were.

"And who knows what manner of men live there," Djerat said as if in agreement. "You suppose they are there to aid us, but if they are not? What if they prey on those who must cross here? Think of what they might do."

"I cannot imagine what they might do," Tulsi said roundly. "Neither can you. If they are by a ford, they must deal with travelers often."

"Exactly what I mean," Djerat responded. "How they deal with travelers is what we do not know: none of us knows. They might be robbers or slavers or cannibals."

"They might be farmers and builders, too," Tulsi said. "I am willing to take the chance."

"If you do, you will do it without me, or my mules and my wagon." She lifted her head, sensing triumph. "If you follow him, you do so with nothing from me."

"But how are we to manage, if he has no protection from the sun? You see how readily he burns . . ." Her words trailed off as she encountered the sardonic light in Djerat's eyes. "It means nothing to you, does it."

"No—nothing. I am going to find Timur-i's army and hope that I might be welcome there still. What you do is for you to decide. If you come with me, I will be content with your company; if you go with him, I will be content with my own." Djerat folded her arms. "He has been good to the mules, I will give him that."

Tulsi scowled. "You do not suppose that he has only that to recommend him."

"It is all I have seen of his worth," said Djerat. "Everything else has brought me trouble." She began to walk back toward the wagons, her face so set that the uncompromising lines were apparent in spite of her hair. "You will have to decide, Tulsi Kil, which of us you intend to travel with, for I cannot and I will not go out of my way for him or you."

There were many questions burgeoning in Tulsi's thoughts, but she could not bring herself to continue wrangling with Djerat, who had taken her in and provided her a place in her wagon for the three years since her parents had been abandoned at the side of the road, each with an eye gouged from its socket, both with brands on their arms and foreheads. "He may not want my company," she muttered.

"Then the matter is easily settled," said Djerat, clapping her hands once in satisfaction. "You will remain with me and he may go wherever he pleases. We will be rid of him and think no more of him."

"But I will have to ask him if he wants to travel alone," Tulsi appended, her tone once more assertive. "If he would prefer that I remain with you, then I will. Otherwise I will go with him."

Djerat stopped and turned her disapproving stare on Tulsi. "You are determined to work against me." She stared off at the horizon. "Very well. Let us put him to the test. You will abide by his decision, as will I."

Tulsi swallowed hard. "I will." She began to walk more quickly, her stride lithe and clean, giving no hint of her inner dismay. "Whatever the result, it will be settled."

"That it will," said Djerat, keeping up in steady, emphatic steps that came down heavily on her heels.

From his place in the shade of the wagon, Sanat Ji Mani paused in rasping the hoof of the third mule; the rising sun was beginning to sap his strength and he relied increasingly on the slight protection of the wagon's shadow. He straightened up slowly, releasing the animal's on-side rear foot as he did, and stepped back to avoid the quick kick the mule gave. He slipped the rasp into his belt where the other farrier's tools hung, clanging softly together as he moved. Although he had given no indication of it, he had heard most of what the two women said, his hearing being keener than most. "I am nearly finished," he called out. "One mule to go."

"I will not keep you from your work long," Djerat exclaimed with a predatory eagerness that caused Tulsi to blush.

"Very well," said Sanat Ji Mani, inclining his head out of courtesy.

Djerat and Tulsi were a few steps from the wagon, both of them intent on arriving first as if they had agreed to race. Tulsi was half a step ahead of Djerat, and she allowed herself the ghost of a grin as she touched the side of the vehicle; behind her Djerat looked glum as she said, "It is time we come to a decision."

Sanat Ji Mani listened attentively, hardly moving; Tulsi glanced at Djerat and began, "You have said you want to cross the river at this ford and go south into the heart of the land." She saw him nod and went on, "Djerat wishes to rejoin Timur-i's army."

"I have said so from the first," Djerat pointed out, not looking at Sanat Ji Mani. "And I will do it."

"Yes," Tulsi said. "That is true; you have said so. We all know your wishes. This is the place where a decision must be made, or so Djerat has decided. She will not cross the river. You intended to cross."

"Where is the difficulty in that?" Sanat Ji Mani asked without any sign of discomfiture.

Djerat took over. "If it were only your leaving, there would be no difficulty, but you wish Tulsi to go with you. I wish her to come with me."

"Then it is Tulsi's decision to make," Sanat Ji Mani said. "I will not tell her what to do, but I would be glad of her company."

"Hah!" Djerat pounced. "You seek to awaken her sympathy for you. You, with the staple through your foot and skin that burns after the touch of the sun. She is a woman who is easily gulled. You are working on her to turn her away from me."

"Not that, surely," Sanat Ji Mani said in a conciliating manner. "I would appreciate her company—and yours, if you were willing to provide it: nothing more."

"What man who is not a eunuch means that?" Djerat asked of the air, then confronted Sanat Ji Mani. "You have sought Tulsi from the moment you saw her. You have planned to take her from my care. You will use her and discard her when she no longer amuses you, and then she will be alone and homeless in the world, and prey to the whims of any man with shelter and a meal to offer her. She will become pregnant and her child will die by the roadside. You will be gone. It will mean nothing to you."

Sanat Ji Mani contemplated Djerat, an unnerving compassion in his enigmatic gaze. "Because such happened to you, it does not follow it must happen to Tulsi. Not all men use women so callously."

Djerat stood as if frozen. "How *dare* you!" she burst out at last.

"It *is* what happened to you, is it not," Sanat Ji Mani said. "You have such concern for Tulsi Kil because of your experience, which is commendable of you."

"You are ridiculous—absurd!" Djerat insisted. "Do not listen to him, Tulsi. He seeks to confuse you."

"Why would I do that?" Sanat Ji Mani asked. "I hope she would have her mind clear to weigh her decision—a decision you require her to make, not I."

"That is another sophistry," Djerat accused. "You want her company you say, which means you, too, must have her decision."

"Hers or yours," Sanat Ji Mani replied. He nodded toward the village across the ford. "There must be a meal to be had there. You have said you are hungry."

"We must all be hungry; I know I am, and that we must be fed, all of us," said Tulsi to forestall further bickering. "As must the mules. If we cross the river, we can eat while a final decision is made."

This recommendation was so eminently practical that Djerat made a brusque gesture of consent. "The mules need fodder. Very well. We will cross. After we have eaten, I will tell you now that I will come back to this side of the river and go toward Lahore. Nothing will change that."

"I will finish trimming the mules' feet while you have a meal," Sanat Ji Mani said. "You will want that done."

"Not that I cannot do it myself," Djerat reminded him. "Tie them to the wagon-tongue, and let us get over the water."

Sanat Ji Mani took the improvised rope harness and hitched up the mules to the wagon. At last he handed the hempen reins to Djerat, who had climbed onto the driving-seat, and swung up into the tent on the wagon. The shadow engulfed him, providing a needed surcease from the sun. He lay back on the floor, prepared for a short period of intense vertigo and discomfort he would receive from the running water.

"Do you want anything to drink?" Tulsi asked from her place in the rear of the wagon. "We have a little water left."

Sanat Ji Mani resisted the urge to laugh. "No; thank you, no water."

The wagon began to roll into the river, the mules splashing as they made their way through the wide, shallow stretch of water; the wagon swaggered after them as the river rose more than halfway up the wheels. Finally the wagon emerged from the water a short distance from the village walls, to be greeted by a group of children, who ran out from the gate shouting and beckoning to Djerat, a few of them staring in disbelief at her hairy visage.

"Get back, you urchins!" Djerat shouted. "Get back. You will frighten the mules."

The children answered in an unfamiliar tongue; a few of the older ones ran back into the village, summoning their elders by the sound of it.

Eventually a man with greying hair appeared at the gate; he stood still, his full attention on Djerat, and finally asked, "Are you alone?" He spoke a variation of the Delhi dialect in a low and deliberate manner as if that would make him more comprehensible.

Djerat understood him well enough to answer, "There are two more in the wagon."

"Not so many." He motioned the children away from the wagon. "It is well you have come to our village. We have feed for your mules and a meal for you and your companions. We will not demand much money."

"Good; we have traveled far and we are weary," said Djerat, her skeptical tone of voice belying her. "Where shall I put my wagon?"

"Over there," the man said, pointing to a frond-covered arbor just inside the gate. "There are seats for you and a barn for your team; there are stalls beyond the goats' pen."

Djerat drove her mules up to the barn and got down from the driving-seat. "We are arrived," she called out to her passengers; at once Tulsi came out of the rear of the tent and did a series of cartwheels and somersaults for the children watching. "Have the foreigner get to work on the hooves before we do anything else," Djerat ordered, cutting Tulsi's demonstration short.

"That I will," said Tulsi, and opened the rear flap for Sanat Ji Mani. "She wants the hooves done. There's just one more mule to do, is there not?"

"I heard her; there is just the one mule remaining," Sanat Ji Mani said as he climbed out of the wagon, still feeling somewhat queasy from their passage through the river. He did his best to walk evenly, but could not. "I wish I did not draw attention in this way," he remarked to Tulsi, nodding at his right foot.

"It is a dreadful thing," she said sympathetically.

"More importantly, it is easily noticed and recalled. If Timur-i sends soldiers after us, they need only say a foreigner with a stirrup on his foot and they will learn where we have been." He put his hands on his farrier's tools. "These are not very useful as weapons." This was not entirely true: he had seen nippers and rasps used as instruments of torture, but that did not recommend them to him.

"No. We have no bows and arrows, no shimtares." Tulsi shook her head. "I can fight with a staff if I must."

"Hardly enough against Timur-i's soldiers, if it comes to that," said Sanat Ji Mani, thinking back to the beautiful sword Saito Masashige had given him at Chui-Cho fortress almost two hundred years ago. How relieved he would be to have that weapon with him now; it would be as welcome as a chest of his native earth, but the sword was in his homeland, at the remote stronghold he maintained there for his occasional use. He consoled himself with the realization that Timur-i would surely have confiscated the katana had he had the opportunity, and so it would not be available to him now in any case. He would have to improvise a weapon, if the need for one arose. "We will have to think of something."

"Do you suppose Timur-i is searching for us?" Tulsi asked uneasily, lowering her voice still more so they could not be overheard.

"I am not sure," Sanat Ji Mani admitted. "He may wish to make an example of us, or he may not consider us worth the effort."

"Then you think we are safe?" Tulsi stared at him, her grey-green eyes wide.

"No. I do not think that," he answered drily. "Neither do you."

She ducked her head. "No." They had reached the front of the wagon, and Tulsi patted the rump of the nearest mule. "Are you going to unhitch them?"

"It would make my work easier, but I may not, just in case we may wish to depart quickly," Sanat Ji Mani said, smiling at the children who stood around them. "Given Djerat's apprehension, I am not sure I want to have the team separated from the wagon. I can take care of the mule without unhitching him."

"I understand," said Tulsi with a nod. "I will entertain these folk, and you can finish your work here in the shade. You do not want that burn to worsen."

Sanat Ji Mani gave her a thoughtful look before going to the one mule still needing his hooves tended to; the sunlight was enervating, but with the mat of fronds to provide shade, he was not so exhausted as he feared he would be; at mid-day it would be another matter, for the sun's intensity would make the shade less a protection than it was now. He laid his arm along the last mule's back and scratched the animal high on the withers; the mule craned his neck, his upper lip pushed forward in ecstasy as Sanat Ji Mani's fingers worked their magic. When the mule was at ease, Sanat Ji Mani bent and lifted the on-side front foot. "This will not take long," he said, using the nippers to trim away the edge of the hoof; the mule swung around and nudged Sanat Ji Mani in the hip, as if urging him to get on with it. "I will, I will," Sanat Ji Mani said to the mule as he continued to ply the nippers.

"You say you will not be long: not too long, I trust?" Djerat asked as she came up to him. "You must be hungry."

"Do not wait for me," Sanat Ji Mani said. "I will take nourishment later, when we are truly safe."

"Then you fear we may be in danger," she said, not quite accusing him.

"I think it is possible," he said, trading the nippers for his rasp.

"Do you suppose they mean us harm?" Djerat asked, glancing at the children.

"I do not know what they mean us," Sanat Ji Mani replied. "That is why I am careful."

The old man who had offered them village hospitality came up to Djerat. "Who are you? Where are you going?"

Before Sanat Ji Mani could speak, Djerat said, "I am Djerat. I am going to Lahore and Kabul." She gave Sanat Ji Mani a challenging look.

Tulsi was walking on her hands to the delight of the children; one or two of them tried to do the same and toppled, laughing, into the dirt. Tulsi dropped her feet down so that they almost touched her head.

"Is she a holy woman?" the old man asked as he watched Tulsi perform.

"What? She holy?" Djerat laughed. "No. She is a . . . an acrobat, a tumbler. She does these things for amusement, not for religion."

The old man frowned, the good-will going out of his face. "So," he said measuringly.

Sanat Ji Mani moved on to the on-side rear hoof, all the while keeping a covert watch on Tulsi Kil. The mule fussed at having his hoof lifted, but finally brought it up, muscles tight, while Sanat Ji Mani went to work with the nippers again.

"What about water?" Djerat said to the old man. "We are thirsty."

"There is water, in those skins hanging in the door. They are filled from our well, not the river." The old man smiled proudly. "Our well is sweet."

"I am sure it is," said Djerat, adding, "How much to buy a skin of water?"

The old man frowned. "A goat-skin contains a lot of water. I would want a gold coin." This price was outrageous and both the old man and Djerat knew it.

"A silver coin—nothing more," said Djerat. "The river might not be so sweet as your well, but its water is abundant and we may drink from it for nothing more than a prayer."

"Then do so. We will keep our skins." He contemplated Djerat. "Your food will cost you silver coins."

Djerat was about to give him a sharp answer when Sanat Ji Mani spoke up. "I have gold," he said, reaching into the wallet that hung from his belt. He took out a small coin with the Sultan's seal upon it; he tossed it to the old man. "That should buy food for us and for our animals and leave enough for a skin of well-water."

The old man snatched the coin out of the air and bit it. Satisfied, he thrust it into the top of his leather waist-band. "This will do." He clapped his hands. "Food for our visitors. Now!"

"Why did you do that?" Djerat asked Sanat Ji Mani in an under-voice. "Now he knows we have gold."

"He knows I have gold," Sanat Ji Mani corrected her and went on trimming the mule's hooves.

"You have put us in danger, for they will assume if you are willing to give up so much, you have much more to give," Djerat hissed, glancing at Tulsi who was busy performing feats of contortion for the villagers who had gathered to watch her. "They will want to rob us, perhaps imprison us for ransom."

"Perhaps," Sanat Ji Mani said, not wanting to argue with her. "But as it turns out, there are more coins in my medicinal supply bag; I took a few out last night for just such a circumstance as this—oh, not a fortune, but enough to provide for our needs for some time if we are not reckless with spending; these people will probably not want anything more but another coin, which I shall give them. They will treat us well in the hope of getting more, and you may eat without worry. When you are done, we must decide if we are traveling north or east."

"I am traveling north. Do not think to alter that. I am taking my wagon and my mules back across the river and I am going to find Timur-i's army. You may come with me, or you may leave, but I will not change my mind about where I am bound, whether or not I have any of your coins to aid me. I will not be bought off by you." She folded her arms. "Also: I will not let you take Tulsi with you. She will not be safe, traveling with the likes of you."

There was a note in her tone that caught Sanat Ji Mani's attention. "How do you mean—the likes of me?"

"I know you have done more to my mules than groom them and tend to their feet. You have gone to them in the dark of night and leaned against their necks. I have found marks there, and a little blood, in the morning. Tulsi Kil is no mule. You will not have her to yourself. I will see to it." There was an expression of irate triumph in her bright little eyes.

Sanat Ji Mani met her furious gaze steadily. "Your animals have taken no harm from me and neither will Tulsi Kil if she is willing to travel with me."

"So you say!" Djerat swung away as two men emerged from the house behind the arbor with trays of fruit, spiced lentils, and lamb with onions in yoghurt. "You finish your work."

"I will," said Sanat Ji Mani, and bent over the mule's off-side rear hoof.

"Tulsi! Come! There is food!" Djerat went to sit on one of the low benches under the frond-mat, leaving room for the trays to be placed before her; she patted the stool beside her. "Come, girl. You must eat!"

Tulsi left off her performing and came over to the arbor; she was panting a little from her exertions and there was a sheen of sweat on her face. "This looks most satisfactory," she said, looking over at Sanat Ji Mani. "Are you not joining us?"

"I am not yet finished with trimming this mule's hooves," he said, aware it was not quite an answer. "Have what you want. I will fend for myself."

"Yes," said the old man, sitting down near them. "Have what you want. If it is not enough, you can always buy more." His smile showed missing teeth and happy avarice.

"You've had all the money you will get from us," said Djerat as Tulsi sat down on another low stool. "What about something to drink?"

"We have mango pulp with fermented goats' milk," said the old man proudly, aware that this was a luxury in such a village as his.

"I'll have some," Djerat declared, thumping her hand on her thigh. "For this woman, too. Bring each of us a large cup of it."

The old man clapped his hands together and issued more commands. "You will have it. What of the foreign man?"

"Nothing for him until his work is done," said Djerat with a satisfied smirk. "He will let you know what he wants." Her glance in Sanat Ji Mani's direction was sly, insinuating many things.

"It is strange for a woman to have charge of a man not her slave," said the old man. "How does it come about?"

"Timur-i put him in my care," Djerat said, very nearly boasting.

The old man drew back, shocked. "He is a slave of Timur-i Lenkh?" Fear raised the pitch of his voice almost five notes. "You brought Timur-i Lenkh's slave here?"

"He is not a slave," Tulsi said. "He was captured at Delhi when the city fell. Sanat Ji Mani is a healer, and Timur-i wanted his skills."

Djerat glowered at her. "Because, as you see, he cannot endure the sun, he has traveled in my wagon for protection." She realized the old man was still unconvinced. "Timur-i had a white-skinned brother, who died because of the sun. He has shown this foreigner favor because of his brother, I think."

The old man nodded, somewhat mollified. "I had heard that about the brother; they say his eyes were red. I have also heard that Timur-i has been supplanted by his rival and is now left to wander the roads a beggar."

"I have heard that, too," said Djerat, sensing that they were once again on easy footing. "But I saw Timur-i for myself, six days ago, riding his mouse-colored horse and leading his army. No one had usurped his place."

"Indeed," said the old man. "Here are your cups. Enjoy your drink." He moved away from the arbor, saying as he went. "It is not fitting that I stay with women alone. You are not my wives."

Djerat called out her thanks and took her cup from the man who proffered it. "Very good," she told him by way of dismissal.

From his place with the mules, Sanat Ji Mani watched the two women eat; he realized this might be his last morning in their company, that from this place their journeys would lead them in different directions. For just an instant, he felt despair and a loneliness so intense that it made the ache from the sunlight seem diminished by comparison. Then he went to the mule's off-side front foot and bent to trim it.

Text of a letter from Rustam Iniattir in Fustat to Rojire in Alexandria, carried by hired courier.

To the servant of the most worthy foreigner, Sanat Ji Mani, the greetings of Rustam Iniattir from his new home in Fustat, which now, I fear, must become my home for generations to come. Our house fronts a road that they say the Romans made more than a thousand years ago. It is a worthy place for so old a House as that of Iniattir.

Alas, that it should fall to me to send you such dreadful news, but I must tell you that I have just received a letter from my nephew, Zal Iniattir, who tells me that Delhi is no more, that for those who were not fortunate enough to escape, the soldiers of Timur-i delivered death to most of them, and slavery to the rest. I regret that I can provide no news of your master, which I fear we must receive as indicating misfortune, if not tragedy. My nephew has said that it was because of Sanat Ji Mani's aid that he was able to leave Delhi before it fell, and for that alone I would be enduringly grateful to him; well I know that the House of Iniattir would be a shambles were it not for Sanat Ji Mani. To that end, I pledge a third of my fortune to pay his ransom if it should ever be demanded, and I will ask my kinsmen to prepare like amounts to be used on his behalf and none other.

My nephew is now in the central-south of the land, and has made a place for himself there. He believes we can restore our House to its position of high regard within a few years. While I am not so optimistic, I think it is not impossible for us to maintain ourselves well enough, so that should you need our funds for ransom, you need not fret that it will be unavailable to you. I wish you to know that no matter how difficult our situation may be, we will not shirk our duty to Sanat Ji Mani. Those who follow the way of Zarathustra may not turn aside from their obligations simply because they are inconvenient.

I received your letter informing me that Avasa Dani has died of a fever. What a sad ending for such a fine woman. I have asked my family to remember her name with honor in our prayers. It must be a blow to you, entrusted, as you were, with her safety and protection. I cannot imagine what dismay you must feel at this most lamentable occurrence. It is nothing when compared to the loss of your master, but it is still a shock. She had come so far. With her husband on his extended pilgrimage there is no way to inform him of her death, for even should he survive his journey, he will find a ruin when he comes again to Delhi. What a terrible predicament for you: she has no male relatives left to receive your report, and you cannot find your master to tell him of her demise, either. For a meritorious servant such as you are, this is an unenviable predicament. I cannot advise you, for I have never before encountered such a conundrum as this one with which you are presented.

You indicated that if you receive no word of your master in a few years, you will travel to Rome, to await him there. If you decide to leave Alexandria, I ask you to inform me, so that I may know when and where you are to be found in case I hear anything deserving of your attention. You say that your master has holdings near Rome, and that you wish to be in that city if he does not send you word to meet him in another place. I see the wisdom of this plan, but I urge you to leave staff at the house in Alexandria. If you cannot keep servants there, I will send those of mine that I can spare to maintain the house until such time as his death is confirmed. I trust this arrangement will be satisfactory to you. I do not intend to intrude upon you, but I wish to do my part in making it possible to discover what has become of your master. My son has been told to continue this arrangement should anything happen to me before your master's fate is known.

In your letter, you were kind enough to provide the name of a merchant at Tana on the Byzantine Sea. I will avail myself of the introduction you have provided, for, as you have said, Immuk Suza has markets as far away as Kiev in Lithuania and Gran in Hungary, which I am certain can be turned to our mutual advantage. For many years I have longed to find new markets and new trading-goods, and now, you provide me an opportunity that I had not thought to encounter in this life, and for which I most sincerely thank you. You may be certain I will not make light of this opportunity you have made possible, and I will pledge a third of my success to the use of your master, who may yet have need of it, if he has survived. It is the least I can do; you may repose your confidence in my Word, as your master must have told you.

I await your response most eagerly, and I pray that we may both soon have the joy of welcoming your master into the land of Egypt in the Mameluke Empire. In the meantime, I hope you will be spared any greater grief than what you have already suffered.

Rustam Iniattir
Parsi merchant of Fustat

At the Vernal Equinox, from the house of Iniattir in the Street of the Old Highway

4

Night had fallen; the village of mud huts was silent under the wheeling stars and the sound of the river was muted as if it, too, slept. In the community barn, Sanat Ji Mani awoke gradually, hunger making him groggy, the scent of animals filling his nostrils. He sat up and brushed the straw from his hair as a nanny-goat turned to look at him in mild curiosity. His wallet was still on his belt and his sack of medicaments and supplies lay at his feet, the strap slightly frayed where the goats had nibbled on it. He got to his feet, trying to piece together the events of the day after their arrival in the village: Djerat had departed in the early afternoon in a state of outrage; he had retired to this stall in the barn while Tulsi busied herself making a pack she could carry on her back. This recollection brought him fully awake. "Tulsi?" he called out softly, half-anticipating silence for an answer.

In the stall opposite, something moved in the straw, and then she sat up and yawned. "Is it late?"

"Not particularly," he replied. "We have most of the night left to us." He looked around the barn, taking stock of their situation. "The gate is barred, I suppose."

"It is," she answered. "But there is a litch-gate on the far side of the village, away from the river. It is not barred. I checked it this afternoon, while you were resting."

"Did the villagers know you found it?" Sanat Ji Mani asked, attempting to assess the use of her discovery.

"No; I made a tour of all the streets, tumbling for them," she said, a hint of pride about her.

Sanat Ji Mani regarded her steadily, the dark no hindrance to his sight. "You are tired. You were busy for a long time today."

"Not so much as you might think. I lay down with the villagers for the heat of the day, and I retired at sunset. I will be able to go some distance before I am exhausted." She stretched and stood up. "I made the pack."

"Very good," he approved.

"I also bargained for two tanned hides and a knife. I thought we would need them, for clothing and shoes." She paused, as if uncertain how to go on. "I took another gold coin from your wallet."

"Very good," he repeated.

Tulsi sighed her relief. "With Djerat gone, I thought you would not mind."

"I would not mind had she been here," Sanat Ji Mani said gently.

"But she is gone," said Tulsi, a forlorn note in her words.

"As she said she would do," Sanat Ji Mani added.

"I know." Tulsi swallowed audibly.

"Do you miss her: of course you do," Sanat Ji Mani said. "How could you not."

"I suppose I do," she said reluctantly. "But I do not want to go back to Timur-i's army. Had you not asked me to stay with you, I would still not have gone back."

Sanat Ji Mani took a halting step toward her. "I hope one day you will tell me why."

"One day I will," she said, glancing toward the door of the barn. "We can get out without trouble. I checked that, too."

"Very good," Sanat Ji Mani said again.

One of the goats bleated; the others in the barn raised their heads from their low-set mangers, ears moving, alert to anything.

"Someone is coming," said Sanat Ji Mani, his keen hearing having caught the approaching tread. "One man, I think."

"Then we should be going," said Tulsi, leaving her stall and going toward the door. "I put the hides in the pack, and a small skin of water. You have your sack of medicaments, and your wallet. We need not linger."

"I regret I cannot run," said Sanat Ji Mani, doing his best to follow after her without making too much noise.

"So do I," said Tulsi, no hint of distress in her voice. "If Djerat had left the farrier's tools, you might have something to fight with."

"She has mules to care for," Sanat Ji Mani reminded her.

"Still, it would have been useful to have one of them." She was at the door, prepared to open it; she waited. "I will take him off-guard," she whispered.

"Good idea," Sanat Ji Mani approved as he limped toward the door, his sack slung over his shoulder.

She made a gesture of determination, and prepared to shove the door hard as soon as it was touched from the other side; she rested her pack against her leg so she would not be hampered in her movements by its weight, and readied herself to throw the man off-guard. The man on the other side of the door stood still, something jingling as he prepared to enter the barn; Tulsi took a deep breath and shoved the door outward with all of her strength. The man fell back, groaning a little as he landed.

Sanat Ji Mani moved as quickly as he could, going to the supine villager, prepared to knock him unconscious. "He is carrying chains," he whispered to Tulsi.

"So they are slavers or keep travelers for ransom," she said in an undervoice. "See that he cannot follow us."

"I will," said Sanat Ji Mani, and dragged the man a short way around the end of the barn, then secured him with his own chains. "Your friends will find you in the morning," he said softly to the man, who had begun to struggle against the chains. "It will be easier if you lie still." Then he reached down and pressed his fingers against the man's neck, holding them in place until the man fainted. Straightening up, Sanat Ji Mani returned to Tulsi. "Where is the litch-gate?"

"At the far end of the village. Follow me." She started off between two of the houses.

Sanat Ji Mani did his best to keep up with her, moving along as quickly as he could, trying not to drag his stapled foot. Neither of them spoke until they reached the narrow wooden gate. "What lies beyond?" he said in an undervoice.

"Fields and a narrow path. At the edge of the fields there is a road, leading to the south." She paused. "I do not know where it leads."

"Then we will find out," said Sanat Ji Mani, standing aside so Tulsi could pull the gate open. He waited while she slipped through, then went after her, tugging the gate closed behind him. "Clever. No one can get through there with any animal larger than a goat."

"No doubt they knew that," Tulsi said, still keeping her voice low. "They force their visitors to abandon their goods and teams to leave, or be taken prisoner." She set out at a moderate pace so that Sanat Ji Mani could keep pace with her. "Do you think they will follow us?"

"It is possible but unlikely. I doubt the fellow we caught at the barn will come to his senses until midnight, and by then we will have gone some distance: two leagues at least." This guess was optimistic and he knew it.

"However far a league is," said Tulsi.

"A bit more than a Chinese li over flat ground," said Sanat Ji Mani. "Two Roman leagues are about six thousand paces." He hitched the strap of his sack to a better-balanced place on his shoulder, then did his best to even out his walking; he was acutely aware that by morning his legs and back would ache from the effort he was making, but he kept up his genial demeanor. "Once we turn to the south we will quickly be well beyond Timur-i's reach: he is bound northward."

"So he is," Tulsi said, holding the front straps of her pack with both hands. "And why should he bother about either one of us?"

"Why indeed," Sanat Ji Mani said, staring off into the night; he could hear the cries of animals in the brush beyond the fields and he paid close attention to them.

"Is anything hunting us?" Tulsi asked, aware of what he was doing. "Are there animals tracking us?"

"I do not think so; not yet. We are too close to the village for any of the wild beasts to come after us." He wanted to pick up the pace but knew it would only serve to exhaust him sooner. "If there is anything to fear, I will tell you."

"I am grateful," she said, and fell silent as they continued along the narrow track toward the road, which proved to be dry and deeply rutted. "I think farmers use this road," she said. "Cart wheels and many kinds of hooves." She pointed to the uneven surface.

"So it seems," Sanat Ji Mani agreed, worried what trying to drag Timur-i's stirrup over this puckered road would demand of him.

"You might do better keeping to the verge," Tulsi suggested. "I will walk there as well."

Sanat Ji Mani made a gesture of concession. "You are right; trying to walk on the road would be grueling."

Tulsi made her way to the far side of the road and onto the dusty shoulder. "This is wide enough."

"Yes," he said, and stumbled over the furrows to join her. "Do you want to lead, or shall I?"

"I am faster, but you see better," she said. "You can lead for a while."

Sanat Ji Mani stepped around her. "If I lag, tell me."

"If it bothers me I will," Tusli said, and worked the stopper from the water-skin. "Do you want any?"

"I will drink later," he told her, peering ahead. "The road curves around to the east some distance ahead, at the base of that line of hills."

"Do you think we will reach it by dawn?" She wiped her mouth with the back of her hand.

"It is possible," he said, trying to estimate the distance. "Ask me again at midnight and I will have a better estimate to give you."

"All right; I will," said Tulsi, prepared to wait until they had covered more distance. "We do not want to be caught in the open when the sun rises."

"No, we do not," he agreed, wondering what else she might have noticed about him.

"Would you be willing to hunt before you sleep? I can cook a fowl over a fire as well as anyone; I lack a knife, but I will make do." She kept her full concentration on the narrow shoulder of the road, staying four paces behind him.

"I have medicinal tools in my sack that will serve as knives; I will give you one," he said. "I will hunt before dawn."

"Good." She fell silent again, until they had gone half a league farther along the road; her breath was steady and her pace did not flag. "Timur-i had my parents killed. He made his army watch, and all his jugglers and tumblers as well. He thought my father was training a bear to attack him."

"And was he?" Sanat Ji Mani asked in a neutral voice, aware she was lying.

"No. It is no easy thing to make a bear attack a certain person. Oh, my father could have done it, given enough time and access to Timur-i's clothing, but he had neither. He would not have done such a thing, in any case, for Timur-i gave him a good living. But Timur-i sees enemies everywhere." Tulsi took a deep breath. "He had my mother killed with my father because she was his wife. He had no other reason. They did not die quickly. Timur-i watched it all, smiling. I will never forget how he smiled."

Sanat Ji Mani wanted to offer Tulsi comfort but was aware she wanted none, that she had chosen this time to tell him so that he would not console her. He considered his next remark carefully. "How old were you?"

"Nine or ten," she answered. "I was kept on because I am a good tumbler and acrobat; I had no brothers, and a girl is no threat at all."

Visions of Tishtry and Olivia, of Nicoris, of Csimenae, of Gynethe Mehaut, of Ranegonda, of Heugenet went through Sanat Ji Mani's memories; all of them were capable, accomplished women, brave and determined, yet Timur-i would consider them insignificant because they lacked brothers, if not while living, in his life. He tried to find the right words to encourage her. "Then Timur-i is blind."

Tulsi stopped walking for a moment; then a spurt of laugher erupted from her. "Yes. He is blind." She began moving again, lengthening her stride to catch up with Sanat Ji Mani.

By midnight they had gone farther than Sanat Ji Mani had supposed they could; he knew he was tiring rapidly in spite of the strength the night lent him. He looked toward the hills and estimated they were four leagues away—too far to reach in one night. "We will need to look for shelter before dawn. I will hunt and you can have what I snare. If there is shelter from the sun, I will do well enough," he said, meaning the discomfort would be tolerable.

"A solid roof would be best, would it not?" Tulsi asked. "You would rest better completely out of the sun?"

"Yes, but that may not be possible," he told her, looking ahead along the road for anything that might provide them protection from the sun.

"You read the stars, I think," she said carefully. "You will know when we must stop walking and prepare for the daylight."

"I know something of the night-sky," he agreed. "I will not let us be caught in the open at sunrise." He heard the distant bray of an ass, and for an instant he missed Caesar, the shaggy donkey who had accompanied him through Plague-stricken France and in his travels for the next twenty years. How useful Caesar would be just now! He chuckled sadly and put the memory from his mind.

Tulsi cocked her head. "You find the coming of dawn amusing?"

"No," he said quietly. "I heard the donkey and wished we had one."

"Do you want to steal one?" Tulsi asked without any hint of condemnation.

"No. I do not want to draw any more attention to us than we must." Sanat Ji Mani peered off to the left. "There is another village that way."

"Shall we go near it?" Tulsi asked.

"No; I want you to step off the road and wait a bit." He was aware of her concern and went on, "I hope I can find a chicken or some other bird you can roast in the morning. Birds should be easier to catch near a village than in the fields."

"Do you think so?" Tulsi was still uncertain.

Sanat Ji Mani took his sack from his shoulder and turned toward her. "Keep this by you; it will hamper my hunting, and the stirrup is trouble enough."

This reassured her. She took the sack and held it tightly. "I will wait for you."

"Listen closely. If you hear anything that tells you I am in trouble, continue down the road, and remain on it. I will find you as soon as I can." He did not want to add to her apprehension, but he did not want to put her in danger on his account. "If the road divides, take the branch leading south. That way you can travel on, and I will not lose you."

"All right," she said nervously.

Sanat Ji Mani looked down into her face. "I will not leave you to wander these roads alone, Tulsi Kil: believe this."

"I am trying," she responded with an unsteady attempt at a smile.

"Very good," he approved, and stepped off the road into the scrub that lined its path; the growth was not too dense and he could make his way through it without much difficulty, although he twice caught his stirrup on a tangle of roots and had to struggle to keep from falling. He reached the edge of the village a short while later and stayed in the cover of the brush as he tried to get the lay of the land around the rough wooden stockade that surrounded the small houses. Such a small and isolated place would probably not have a night-watchman: the villagers would rely on their animals to warn them of approaching danger. He saw a small pond; it smelled of ducks and other water-birds. These would be his targets if only he could keep from alarming them; they would quack and honk and screech if disturbed. From inside the walls of the village came a sudden barking of three dogs; the birds sleeping around the pond responded with the uneasy sounds of disrupted rest. Goats and sheep bleated, and from the undergrowth beyond the village, rustling branches and a high, guttural cough announced the presence of a leopard cat, or a fishing cat; both these animals were fierce fighters but generally shy of people, and both were smaller than leopards or tigers. Sanat Ji Mani remained where he was, watching to see if a striped feline head would emerge from the brush. The cat coughed again and the dogs renewed their barking.

Taking advantage of this ruckus, Sanat Ji Mani went to the edge of the pond, and was met by a flurry of wings as ducks, egrets, geese, and cranes strove to take flight. He made a determined snatch at the nearest large bird and succeeded in catching a Siberian goose. The bird honked and battered its wings, trying to snake its head around to peck at its captor's eyes; Sanat Ji Mani held on until he could take what he needed from the irate bird. When he was done, he spat feathers out of his mouth and broke the bird's neck; the loss of the goose would be attributed to the hunting cat and would not cause anyone in the village to suspect his theft. At least, he told himself, the goose would provide Tulsi two good meals: that was a relief.

"I heard noises," she said as he came up to her beside the road and handed her the goose.

"I was not the only cause," he said.

"A goose," she approved. "Good-sized, too."

"I will help you pluck it when we find a place to remain for the day," he said.

"I will flay it; then there is no need to waste time plucking, if you have a knife I might use. I know there is one in your medicinal supplies," said Tulsi, then lowered her eyes, abashed at her temerity. "I will look for herbs to rub on the flesh."

"As will I," said Sanat Ji Mani. He hoped to find shelter soon, for carrying this newly dead bird would attract cats and jackals; he did not want to have to fight off such animals. "You may have one of my knives," he told her as he took his sack from her. "I will give it to you now."

"Do you think we will find shelter before first light?" she asked as she took the little knife he proffered.

"If we are not too particular about it," he answered, watching her begin to cut the skin away from the bird's neck. "A hut, a cave, a place we will be protected."

"Yes," Tulsi agreed. "You see better in the dark than I do. You will know the place before I do. If you will tell me where to look, I can—" She stopped, her whole body attuned to listening. "I thought I heard—"

Sanat Ji Mani's keen hearing picked up a flurry of activity from the pond. "It's not after us. I think it is leopard cat: something about that size was stalking the birds when I caught the goose. It must have found a meal."

"I will drop the skin and the guts as soon as I am done," she said.

"Throw them as far as you can. You do not want the scent leading a hunter to us." His voice was low, as if he did not want to be overheard.

Tulsi relaxed and resumed walking. "Do you know where we are going?"

"Away from Timur-i; eventually I would like to reach Chaul on the west coast and cross the Arabian Sea." The prospect of ending the discomfort of this journey with many miserable days in the hold of a ship was daunting, but he did not flinch at the anticipated wretchedness; he would be leaving danger behind, and that more than compensated for what he would have to endure.

"Then you are going to leave?" Tulsi asked in a small voice.

"Yes. You may come with me, if you like," said Sanat Ji Mani.

"I may; I will think about it," said Tulsi.

"Pick up kindling as we go. We will have need of it," he added. "I will find fuel for us."

Toward the end of the night as they reached a rolling series of hillocks, Sanat Ji Mani found the ruins of what had once been some manner of fortress or guard-post. Most of its stones were broken and worn, but there was a cellar beneath the scattered flagging of the inner courtyard, and they levered a few of the paving-stones aside so they could go down into it, careful in where they walked, for snakes and spiders often occupied such abandoned places.

"I do not smell anything larger, not even bats," said Sanat Ji Mani as he went unsteadily down the narrow steps.

"Is that good?" Tulsi remained in the opening they had made; she had a fair amount of dry twigs and leaves in the skirt of the short gauze caftan she wore, more than enough to get a fire going once they chose the place. The goose lay beneath the kindling, its skin, feathers, and innards neatly removed while they walked; it was a skill she had learned long ago, traveling with Timur-i's army, for no one stopped the march for so minor a thing as food preparation. Tulsi kept the slender little knife Sanat Ji Mani had provided her for the task.

"It may be. Leave a little hole in the stones when you come down; otherwise you and I will be choked on the smoke from your cooking fire." Sanat Ji Mani looked around the cellar and saw a crude wall-carving of Yama, the Lord of the Dead. Dust had drifted into the cellar and eddied against the walls; there was no sign that the cellar had been used to hold bodies—not so much as a knuckle-bone protruded from the dust, no footprint marred it.

"What is it?" Tulsi hesitated, aware he had seen something.

"A carving, nothing more." He put down the small dry branches he had been carrying. "I think we will be safe here."

"Good," she said. "I am worn out. How did you keep walking?"

"I had no wish to remain in the sun another day." He thought of the road outside of Baghdad, and did his best not to shudder. "This is large enough to be comfortable and small enough to be safe. Bring me your kindling and we'll have a fire soon enough."

"Will the smoke attract attention?" Tulsi asked as she came down into the cellar, her free hand extended in front of her so she could feel her way in the dark; her hand touched him.

"It may, and it may not." Sanat Ji Mani dropped down onto his knees. "Give me the kindling." He took his flint-and-steel from his wallet and prepared to start their fire. "I am going to pile up the dust; it will absorb the grease from cooking."

"There is a lot of fat on a goose," Tulsi agreed, bending over to watch; the spark caught and brightened, giving a wavering illumination to their confines. "Yama," she said as she recognized the god on the wall. "Is this his temple, do you think?"

"No. There are no signs of it," Sanat Ji Mani said distantly as he nursed the fire into life. "It may be this was a last retreat position, where death was all that was left." He added the first branch to the fire and was pleased to see it catch quickly. "Come. You need to prepare a skewer for your goose."

Tulsi squatted down beside him. "I already have." She held up a straight stick about the length of her forearm. "I will manage from here."

"Very good." He glanced up at the narrow opening where the smoke was drifting; beyond the stones the sky was beginning to pale. "Just in time," he said, more to himself than to Tulsi.

"Can we rest here for a day?" she asked as she pushed the stick through the goose.

"The day after would be a better day to rest," he said. "We will be farther away from the ford, and therefore harder to find if Timur-i should decide to look for us." He paused. "And there is something I must do: I will have to rest at least two days after I do it."

She heard the tentative note in his voice; she looked around. "What is it?"

"I must remove this staple from my foot," he said as calmly as he could. "I cannot continue with it in place."

"Can you do that?" She was so startled she almost dropped the goose into the fire.

"Yes," he said flatly. "I can remove the staple. But once I do, I will have to rest—"

"Are you sure you can do it? It will take strength, and there will be pain." Her expression grew more apprehensive.

"I am aware of that," Sanat Ji Mani said as gently as he could.

Tulsi collected herself. "There will be blood, and festering. You will need a long time before you can walk."

"Those of my blood do not fester," said Sanat Ji Mani, "but we heal very, very slowly. I will be able to travel, but I will limp for some time, probably as badly as Timur-i limps." He attempted a smile to hearten her.

"But for two days you will need rest," she said, her attention more on the goose than on him, for the first, fragrant sizzle fired her hunger.

"Yes, two days at least; and darkness," he said.

After a long moment during which the tips of the goose's wings began to char, she said, "And blood."

Text of a letter from Rishi Harata Medha, priest of Shiva at Delhi, to Sultan Nasiruddin Mohammed bin Tughluq; carried by mendicants.

To the Sultan of Delhi, Nasiruddin Mohammed bin Tughluq, for whom the favor of his god Allah is given in misfortune, the greetings of Rishi Harata Medha, priest of Shiva in your city of Delhi.

The puppet of Timur-i Lenkh who is said to rule here has continued to impose the rule of plunder that brought this mighty city low three months since. The people of this city suffer many cruelties and deprivations on account of this man. You would not believe the devastation wrought here, or the afflictions of your people, for they are almost beyond the capacity of words to describe.

Of the many people who lived here, only one in five remains, and in such abject misery that many wish for death to end their woe. The wells have been contaminated by the men of Timur-i, who threw severed limbs and heads into the wells during their destruction, so that now all the water is foul, but for the river water, and it is suspect, for the soldiers who remain here—and there are about a thousand of them—have made their latrines upstream so that we cannot rely on the river for wholesome water, either. When half the garrison leaves, which it is said they will do when the rains come, the river may be kinder to us. As it is, the few of us remaining here have had to send our two surviving slaves out of the city to the wells in the east, which requires crossing the river and carrying barrels a long distance. This is an onerous burden now, but when the rains come and the river rises, it will be impossible.

The soldiers regularly make fires of the wrecked buildings in the city, and often the fires spread. In the last month, over a hundred sacked houses have been burned to the ground, and more will be burned before the next full moon. Which they shall be we do not know, but eventually all will be claimed by fire. When there is nothing more to burn, I cannot imagine what these fell men will do. Timur-i's sycophant who claims to rule here has ordered that stone buildings are to be demolished in order to build up the walls and other fortifications of the city, and so what fire does not consume, the soldiers will bring to ruin another way. Soon Delhi will be nothing but rubble and ashes, unwanted by any ruler, and inhabited only by rats and vultures.

Let no one say the people remaining here lack courage: everywhere those who have survived try to go about their lives as best they can, knowing that at any instant, the soldiers of Timur-i might ride them down in the streets, steal all of what little they have left, or any number of other hideous things. Those who can take what they can salvage and slip away in the night, hoping they are not caught escaping, for then their fate is appalling: they are tied by arms and legs between trees and the archers use them for target practice; what becomes of their women—for there are still a few women in Delhi—is so loathsome that only Kali would welcome such offerings.

I do not know how much longer I will be able to report to you; my temple is of stone and may soon be taken down for repairing the breaches in the walls. When that happens, I, too, will join those streaming out from Delhi to wander the roads, begging for bread and water. Perhaps your Allah has routed our Gods in this place and is exacting a high price for our obduracy; Gods may be cruel but they cannot be unjust, or so your religion has taught. Since I can see no probity in the rulings meted out to us, I must believe that Shiva has allowed this to happen, and that if we lose this temple, we will find another away from this city. Until that time, I will do my utmost to report to you as often as I am able, so that you will know what has become of your once-glorious city now that its enemies have brought it low.

Rishi Harata Medha
priest of Shiva at Delhi

5

Djerat reached the edge of Kabul on a windy afternoon; from the rise south of the city she could see the banners of Timur-i's army skidding on the wind, and she sighed her relief; it had been a long journey, she had lost another mule since striking out on her own, but finally she was back where she knew she was welcome. She drove around the edge of the city to the encampment on the north-west side of the walls, knowing she was a strange sight, with the tent on her wagon half-gone, the stays holding it upright broken, and her harness made of ropes instead of leather; she began looking for the tents of entertainers, trusting she would not be stopped before she reached them. The odor of cooking lamb made her stomach growl, for she had not eaten more than a handful of boiled lentils for the last three days.

"It's Djerat!" shouted the stilt-walker as he saw her approach down an avenue of wagons and tents. "Look! She's alive!"

There was a bit of excitement as this news spread, and it grew, accompanying her along the avenue between the wagons and tents; half-a-dozen tumblers came out of their tents to welcome her back, and one of them did a back-flip in appreciation, then a few jugglers hurried toward her, one of them throwing axes in celebration. A few women came out of the entertainers' tents, one or two of them smiling. More shouts of greeting came, and finally Keiglu, the Master of Jugglers, came from his tent—the largest of those in the entertainers' sector—and motioned to Djerat to stop her wagon. "Djerat: what a happy surprise; we counted you among the lost," he said to her without any of the usual formalities of welcome.

"And so I thought I was, many times, since the moment we were overset into the river," she said, tugging her worn hempen reins before climbing down from the driving-seat. "On the road here I often feared I would never see Timur-i's army again." She matched his brusque manner with her own. "It has been a difficult task to get here."

"I should think it was," said Keiglu, awaiting an explanation.

"I am famished. My mules are, too. Let us have something to eat and then I shall tell you everything," she said. "And something to drink. We are all thirsty, my mules and I."

"No doubt," said Keiglu, and clapped his hands. "She is hungry. See she is given some food." Two of Keiglu's slaves went scurrying off to do his bidding while he approached her wagon. "You have much to account for," he said, turning from her wagon to her.

"I will need a new wagon; I will do what work I must to get it—I expect no favor," she conceded under his narrow scrutiny. "I was afraid I would lose a wheel before I reached this place. If you look at them, you will see why. One is not straight on the axle. The roads are rocky and without help, alone and unguarded, some of the places through which I passed . . ." Her words straggled off. She stopped herself from an unseemly display of weakness. "You traveled here. I need not tell you how the roads are."

"Some are very hard," Keiglu declared as if to accept an apology. He came up to her. "Yet you came back to us."

"Yes. I came." Djerat could not conceal her pride in her accomplishment; she stood a bit straighter. "It took many, many days, as any who can count will know, but I was not discouraged."

"That is to your credit," said Keiglu. "Yours is a feat worthy of praise."

A few of those in the crowd gathered around shouted agreement, and someone hooted a cheer. There was a murmur of comments that moved through the crowd with the wind.

"Why did you come back?" Keiglu asked, so casually that Djerat sensed a trap.

"Where else should I come? this is my home. You are my family." She looked around, trying to smile. "I belong here: with you."

"Yet you return alone," said Keiglu. "What of Tulsi Kil? What of
the foreigner with the burned skin?"

"They are . . . gone," she said, and was about to go on when a skinny
man in ill-fitting clothes came through the crowd gathered around her
and her wagon; Djerat gazed at him a moment, her thoughts uneasy,
then she went on, "They left my wagon days ago, when I turned north
to find you."

"Then they are still alive?" Keiglu asked.

"I cannot say. I would doubt it," Djerat replied. "They had little
food, few supplies, and his foot is in Timur-i's stirrup. They cannot
travel fast or far. They cannot fight. There are only two of them. No,
I do not think they would live long in such conditions."

"How many days ago was that?" Keiglu held up both hands, fingers
spread. "More than this?"

"Yes," said Djerat. "I recall it was sixteen days ago." It was nineteen,
but Djerat was wary of the skinny stranger, who was known to be
Timur-i's spy.

"Tell me the whole of it," said Josha Dar. "I will give my report to
Timur-i himself, for he will want to know what became of Sanat Ji
Mani."

Djerat spat. "Him! He was worse than anything! Useless foreigner!"
She pointed at Josha Dar. "You will tell Timur-i that his high regard
was wasted on that foreigner; he is well-rid of that feckless creature."

A buzz of conversation went through the gathered throng: this
smacked of intrigue, and all of them wanted to hear more.

"Why do you say that?" Josha Dar inquired, so politely that Djerat
felt sullied by him.

"What good is he—was he? He has some skill with herbs, but so
do half the women in this camp. He could set limbs, but any farrier
can do that." Djerat looked directly at Josha Dar. "You may say what
you like, I know this man is a leech, living on the good opinion of
those gullible enough to believe his claims."

"But he served Timur-i," said Keiglu, upset by Djerat's animosity.

"He did nothing to deserve your praise?" Josha Dar asked, almost
servile in his manner, which distressed Djerat far more than Keiglu's
distress. "Well?"

"He did care for my mules. He is good with mules," she said reluctantly. "In his way he is clever, but he did not show more than competence in other matters. And because of his skin, he had to ride under the tent by day, as indolent as a dancing girl. What kind of man does this?" Too late she remembered that Timur-i had had a white-skinned brother. "His eyes are dark, remember, not red."

"Still," Josha Dar said quietly, "it might be best not to say that too frequently." He leaned forward. "How did he and the tumbler come to leave you?"

Now the crowd was fully engaged, and a few of them tried to move closer to hear her answer; Keiglu frowned, and a few moved back, but most paid him no heed, watching Djerat, their expressions intent, most of them holding their breath. In spite of her dawning apprehension, Djerat was secretly delighted to be the center of so much attention. She wished she had had a little time to neaten herself before talking to Keiglu and the rest, but she determined to make the most of this opportunity; she had been preparing her account for days, rehearsing it mentally as she followed Timur-i's army along the hard mountain roads.

"When the ferry overturned, we were swept away with the others. Apparently Sanat Ji Mani jumped into the river with the intention of saving us, but he is not a strong swimmer and so was more hindrance than help to us. We rode the current a considerable distance. Two of my mules drowned, and the rest were battered about by rocks; they were tangled in the harness and eventually the harness had to be cut away, or all of us would have been pulled under. As it was, we clung to the wagon and hoped to find a place to come ashore. From time to time, we saw bodies of those from the ferry who were less fortunate than we; they fell away, trapped by eddies and the boulders, and eventually, only we were left in the swift river, and we were at the mercy of the river's caprice. We came out of the hills to the opening of a vast, dry plain, and it was there we were finally able to reach the banks without coming to harm." She looked at Keiglu. "I do not know how far we went, but it was a great distance. We spent our first night under a single tree, a fire our only protection against lions and jackals. Half the night we made new harness out of ropes, and then Tulsi Kil and

I slept while Sanat Ji Mani tended the fire and cared for the four mules left to me. When we rose in the morning, we saw that the land before us was parched, and empty of villages we could see. So we began to retrace the river and eventually we reached a cattle-ford that led to a small farming village. By then there was a rise in the land, and the village had farms; we were going away from the arid wastes, which we all knew was wise."

"You were planning to come back to Timur-i's army?" Josha Dar asked when she faltered.

"Yes. From the first I had no other intention." She pursed her lips indignantly. "But Sanat Ji Mani had other plans. He quickly used his wiles to inveigle Tulsi Kil to take his part and to plan to go another way; he spent time with her, poisoning her thoughts against me and against life with Timur-i's army: there was nothing I could do to convince her of his perfidy. You know how young women are when a personable man shows them a little notice—they lose all sense and bend their will to the man's whim, and so it was with Tulsi Kil. Everything Sanat Ji Mani said she drank as if it were the waters of life itself, and to me—her friend from the death of her parents to that very hour—she paid no heed, preferring the foreigner and his ridiculous promises to her duty and the love of a comrade."

Keiglu shook his head. "What despicable behavior. She is a girl without honor."

"Oh, no," said Djerat quickly. "She is only caught in the clouds by a man with persuasive ways; you must not blame her for what he did. She has never met anyone like him; he fascinated her, and she fell under his spell as surely as if he were a magician and not a healer." She did her best to sound disappointed rather than angry. "It is not her fault that Sanat Ji Mani is the kind of man who uses women to his own ends. Let no one here think that she lost all her character; say, rather, that her qualities were subverted by a villain."

Josha Dar studied Djerat for a short while, then said, "I would not have thought Sanat Ji Mani would so abuse anyone. He did nothing of the sort in Delhi; there he behaved with utmost propriety."

"Perhaps in Delhi he was not tested, or he was able to hide his activities . . ." She realized that last had been a mistake.

"He could not hide from me," said Josha Dar caustically.

"No. No, of course not." Djerat stared at Keiglu, hoping he would help her out of the morass she had made for herself.

He did. "How did it all come to a head? You said you had crossed the river to a village?"

Almost giddy with relief, Djerat resumed her story, gathering confidence as she went along. "At the village where, I told you, we wanted to get food, he demanded that Tulsi Kil remain with him, and cursed me for wanting to return to you. He did not listen to anything I said, nor did he let Tulsi Kil question him in regard to his decision; using bluster and menace to coerce her into taking his part, then offering her flattery and blandishments for acquiescence. You would have been troubled, had you seen him: he was most immoderate in his demeanor—he bullied the poor girl, threatening her and plying her with sweet words by turn. He ignored me, saying I had no part in her decision, and dismissing my protests as those without merit." She folded her arms. "He compelled her to perform for the villagers to pay for our food, and then he disdained what she had provided."

"You mean he would not permit her to eat?" Keiglu asked irascibly; he was dissatisfied with what he heard and would have said more, but Josha Dar motioned him to silence.

"No. He would not touch it himself," said Djerat. "It was not fine enough for him: she had done all she could to get it, and yet it was beneath him to take any of it. He did not care if she had any of it."

"And did you eat it?" Josha Dar inquired with a smile.

"Yes. I was hungry and I would never look down on food got by honest endeavor, no matter how simple it might be." She tossed her head. "You may think this is making too much of a minor thing, but it is not. I traveled with this man in my wagon, and I know more of him than any of you." She looked away from Josha Dar. "This man expressed contempt for everything Tulsi Kil did for him; he made no apology for his behavior and he would not allow for her feelings except those that added to his own high opinion of himself."

Josha Dar coughed delicately. "That may be your opinion: I observed the foreigner for the greater part of a year and I never saw him evince such things as you describe." He shrugged. "But as you say, the conditions on the road were not the conditions at Delhi."

"True enough," said Djerat, uneasiness making her sullen. "I cannot assume that he wanted anything more than to be served and gratified. While I was coming back to this army, I decided that he was pleased by being able to bend Tulsi to his will as much as he wanted her subservience. It was a sport to him, a way to show his prowess." She swung around to face Keiglu. "You have seen such men before, as have I."

"That I have," said Keiglu. "There are many who keep entertainers around them to add to their consequence, not to provide them amusement, but to show others that they can keep men and women for nothing more than their diversion. So long as we can regale them with our feats to their order, they treat us well." He coughed and added hastily. "Of course, Timur-i is not such a man: he keeps us for the delight of his soldiers, for the relief of the tedium of campaigning, and for those who come to him to negotiate their capitulations."

"It is as well that you know this," said Josha Dar, and stared at Djerat again. "You say you left Sanat Ji Mani and the tumbler Tulsi Kil at the village at the cattle-ford?"

She realized Josha Dar was not about to let the matter go. "Because he insisted, yes. He declared they would be able to walk far enough away that they could not be found. He called the wrath of his gods down on Timur-i's head—"

"As do so many who have tested his will," Josha Dar interjected.

Djerat scowled. "Timur-i showed Sanat Ji Mani mercy, and the foreigner has rewarded him with treachery."

"So you say," Josha Dar responded.

"What else would you call it?" Djerat exclaimed. "You cannot tell me that refusing to come back to the army is an act of loyalty."

"It may be, but not loyalty to Timur-i," said Josha Dar. "Did he say nothing of where he intended to go, or why?"

"He spoke of going east," Djerat said, a sour note in her voice.

"Which means south or west," said Josha Dar, certain that Sanat Ji Mani would not be so reckless as to reveal his plans to Djerat. "Probably south. Had he wished to go north, he would have crossed the river with you. He would have to cross the river again to go west, as

well. So it is south." He paused, considering the possibilities. "Or he
and Tulsi Kil may have gone along the Sutlej and crossed at another
point. That would be the most useful thing to do, for he would know
that if ever we received report of him, we would look for him in the
wrong places." He pointed at Djerat. "You tell us he is persuasive, but
you were not caught up in his devices; Tulsi Kil was. How did that
come about?"

Djerat was getting angry but struggled to disguise it. "He chose to
work on her; I drove the wagon—she rode with him, providing him
an opportunity to engage her. If you have heard him speak, you know
how interesting his discourse can be. Tulsi Kil listened to his tales as
if they were the adventures of heros." Under the thick hair on her
face she could feel her skin darkening with emotion. "Had he ridden
beside me on the driving-seat, he might have used his wiles on me."

"Possibly," said Josha Dar. "And yet I am uncertain." He pulled at
his lower lip. "I think you should tell all this to Timur-i, for he wishes
to know what has become of Sanat Ji Mani; he has said so."

Had going before Timur-i been her idea, Djerat would have been
delighted by the prospect; as it was, she balked. "You cannot do this;
I have not eaten, my team is weary, I am unprepared. Why should
Timur-i want to know the fates of a foreigner and a tumbler?"

"That is not for you to know, or for me." Josha Dar reached out
and took her by the elbow. "Keiglu will attend to your wagon and see
your mules are fed and watered. You must come with me."

Djerat struggled against him, even though it was unwise. "Let me
go. I will walk beside you. I am no thief, to be hauled along by the
likes of you."

Josha Dar chuckled but released his hold. "It is all one to me how
you come, so long as you do come."

"You behave as if I have offended Timur-i in some way," she went
on, trying to regain the advantage.

"If you lie—Timur-i hates liars beyond all things—you will offend
Timur-i, and you will pay for it," Josha Dar said.

"You do not think I am lying," Djerat protested. "You cannot think
I would lie after all I have done to return here. I was alone on the
roads for many days, and I could think of nothing more than the joy

of coming once again to the army. If I intended to lie, I might have found a number of more convincing tales to tell than that Sanat Ji Mani and Tulsi refused to accompany me."

"I do not think you are lying," said Josha Dar as they passed beyond the ranks of wagons and tents to the massed companies of fighting men, all in their company colors with their weapons in place as they made ready for Timur-i's inspection.

"Then why do you accuse me?" Djerat asked, almost too confused to be angry.

"I do not think you are telling the truth," said Josha Dar.

"But—" Djerat began, and floundered.

"Lying and not telling the truth are not the same things," Josha Dar said. "As a spy, I know that better than anyone." He stopped walking as a mounted company of archers in green clattered past in double-file. "Those who do not tell the truth without lying are the most dangerous of all deceivers, for they often deceive themselves."

"I do not have to endure this," said Djerat.

"If you wish to remain with the army, you do," said Josha Dar. "Do not think that because I am from Delhi I do not have Timur-i's ear, for I do. I proved my worth to him when he conquered my city. I knew then that I must serve him or lose my life, and so I have pledged my devotion to him. I know the penalty if I traduce him."

"Which you hope to avert by calumny against others," she finished for him; they were approaching the front line of the inspection and Djerat was becoming agitated.

"No; I will do what I pledged to do, as I am doing now," he said, and stepped up to the edge of the lines of mounted soldiers. "There he is." He pointed down the front of the Red Company; at the far end, the company leader had dismounted and was leading Timur-i's mouse-colored horse by the bridle along the front of his soldiers. "As soon as he reaches us, I will present you to him, to give your account."

"In front of all these?" She flung her hand out, indicating the army.

"It will suit Timur-i very well," said Josha Dar.

"And you as well, I think," said Djerat, watching as Timur-i came nearer.

Josha Dar said nothing; he dropped to his knees and bowed his face to the ground, and after a moment, Djerat did the same.

It was a while before Timur-i came abreast of them; he signaled to the Red Company leader to halt. "The Delhi spy is here," he said, with no hint of emotion. "And the hairy woman. She was gone for a time. Why do you stop me here?"

"I hasten to obey your commands, Exalted Lord: you asked to be told if any report was made concerning those lost in the capsizing ferry," said Josha Dar, daring to speak. "She has just returned to the camp and has information to impart to you."

"Ah." Timur-i motioned to the Red Company leader to leave him. "You brought her to me for that?"

"It was your wish to learn what became of her, and the foreign healer who rode in her wagon," Josha Dar reminded Timur-i.

"So it was. I could have used the foreigner's skills after the skirmish yesterday; we had many wounded. But my Arab physicians managed well enough." He made a gesture with his horse-hair fly-whisk. "You have done well to bring her to me, Delhi spy. I will reward you later. Tell me what happened, hairy woman."

Djerat started to rise, only to be pulled down again by Josha Dar. "I cannot talk hunched over like a hunting mongoose."

"Then stay on your knees and tell me what transpired," said Timur-i.

Feeling both slighted and favored, Djerat did her best to order her thoughts. "It was a terrible thing, to be tossed into the river as we were." She went on to repeat what she had told Keiglu, emphasizing her determination to rejoin the army, and her distrust of all Sanat Ji Mani had done. "So I left them at the cattle-ford village, his imprecations still in my ears, and I came along the old road to Kabul, in the wake of your great army, Exalted Lord."

"At the cost of another of your mules," said Timur-i.

"Yes. My animals are tired and hungry, and so am I," said Djerat, thinking of the food she had been promised but had not yet received.

"Those following armies must expect hardships." Timur-i directed his attention to Josha Dar. "Well, spy? What do you think? Has she reported truly?"

"Perhaps she has, as she sees it," said Josha Dar. "But I suspect her jealousy has colored her account."

"Jealousy?" Djerat repeated incredulously, not allowing Timur-i to speak first. "What makes you say I am jealous?"

"You speak enviously, and you describe a man I have observed in terms intended to add to your consequence at his cost." Josha Dar lifted his head enough to be able to look up at Timur-i. "I do not like Sanat Ji Mani; he is a foreigner and therefore suspect. But I know his qualities, and I will not listen to him being maligned and not speak against such misrepresentations." He pointed to Djerat. "You have tried to make him seem untrustworthy—"

"He *is* untrustworthy!" Djerat shouted. "He is a seducer! He has set the heart of Tulsi Kil against me! He disdains the rule of Timur-i!"

Timur-i gestured her to silence; he sat staring off between his horse's ears, tapping his fly-whisk against his shoulder. The only sound was the jingle of tack and the slapping of banners on the wind. "I will make a decision before nightfall. Feed her and bring her to my tent when the sun is its own width above the mountains." He gestured dismissal, tapped the Red Company leader on his head with his fly-whisk and prepared to move on to the next company drawn up for inspection.

"You cannot listen to him!" Djerat called out, pointing her accusing finger at Josha Dar. "He is serving his own ends!"

"Be silent, hairy woman," Josha Dar ordered her. "He will kill you if you speak again."

Djerat realized this was not an empty threat; she swung around and faced Josha Dar. "You are trying to disgrace me. Why are you doing this, when I have done nothing to deserve it?"

"It is not my decision. You spoke against a man I defended." He rushed on, "If I did not refute what you said, I would be answerable to Timur-i, and I do not wish to be executed over this, so I have done as I must, and challenged your report before him and I have done all that I can to ensure he will not order me killed for telling him untruths, but will decide how your account is to be received in balance against mine." He stopped, and then continued more calmly, "You may not like my doubting you, but you must understand my purpose: you and I cannot both be right, and it is Timur-i who will judge which of us he believes and the one he finds lacking truth will pay the price of falsehood." Josha Dar shuddered and turned away from the front of the ranked soldiers; the aroma of cooking lamb mixed with the odor of horses' sweat and leather. "Go back to your wagon. Have your meal. I will come to fetch you when it is time to go to Timur-i's tent."

"Keiglu may not allow me to go," said Djerat, holding her head up.

Josha Dar laughed. "If you think the Master of Jugglers is going to defy Timur-i, you have been in the sun too long."

"I have told the truth," Djerat insisted.

"And so have I. So one of us must be mistaken in our truth," said Josha Dar.

Djerat rounded on him. "You defend a scoundrel."

"I would defend Shaitan himself, or Yama, if it would save my skin," said Josha Dar. "I do not like Sanat Ji Mani—I have said so. But I have not seen any of the reprehensible things you describe in all the time I have watched him, and if I do not vindicate my report, I am useless to Timur-i, which means also that I am dead." He laughed. "You have value to him as an oddity. Even if he does not believe you, he may spare you for that."

"You . . . you *turd*! You *offal*! You are worse than the excrement of pigs and turtles!" She lurched away from him, almost physically ill from his presence.

Josha Dar did not approach her. "Have your meal. Take care of your mules and your wagon. I will come for you later in the day." He offered her an ironic salaam.

She wanted to rail at him, accuse him of every loathsome thing she could think of, but suddenly she was afraid, and for the first time since she had left Sanat Ji Mani and Tulsi Kil in the village at the cattle-ford, she wondered if she had made the right decision to return to Timur-i's army.

Text of a list of decisions given by Timur-i Lenkh at Kabul.

Be it known that I, Timur-i Lenkh, Exalted Lord of Samarkand and Ruler of the Middle of the World, favored of Allah and victorious in battle, do give out these decisions before the city of Kabul near the beginning of the 63rd year of my age:

For the crime of horse theft, the archer Sibbu Ali is to be tied between two trees and shot to death with arrows by the archers of his Company, the Azure Company; his own horses will be given to Eshmut Tusi, from whom Sibbu Ali stole. His body is to be left to rot as a warning to others.

For valor on the field, the soldiers of the Green Company are to be given each two pieces of gold and be excused from taxes for a full year, and for the next year, required to pay only half the amount usually required.

For the crime of adultery, the woman of Huf Fasal is to be opened at the belly and her womb removed so that she can never again disgrace what was made sacred by marriage; this to be done in the public eye of all the camp, so that no woman will think her crimes are safe. She is to be given no succor during her death-throes and any attempting to end her suffering shall share her fate. As to her lover, he is to be made a eunuch and sent to the slave-market in Mecca, where he will wear a placard telling how he came to lose his male parts. The monies paid for him are to be donated to the pilgrims at Mecca to ensure their safe return to their families.

For rescuing the armorers stranded on the road, Abaq Rukh shall be given a pearl the size of a pigeon's egg to be set in the hilt of his shimtare as a sign of his service to the armorers and to my cause against the Faithless Ones. His sons may call themselves Abaq's Pearls in commemoration of this laudable act, and to encourage others to be equally scrupulous in their duties.

For the crime of counterfeiting coins, the metal-smith Ankra of Tabriz is to have his hands lopped off, the which he will wear around his neck until they rot away, to show that no one may coat base metal with gold or silver and profit from such deception. His eldest son is to be castrated and sold into slavery, the money from which sale shall go to remunerate those Ankra cheated. His daughters are to be given to my soldiers to be used for their pleasure.

For providing shelter for 20 head of pregnant mares during the severe windstorm of four nights ago, Zhalil Karli shall receive three emeralds from my treasury and his pick of the foals of these mares, limited to one filly and one colt, when the mares shall deliver their young.

For the crime of subversion, the cook Wan Shao-Hsia will be boiled in his own cooking pot; those who have followed his seditious teaching will eat the stew his flesh makes and they will pay two strings of copper cash to my treasury for their lapse. These followers are to witness Wan's execution so that they will not be able to deceive themselves concerning their meal. Should any of them attempt to refuse this punishment, their eyelids shall be cut away and they will be left by the trail to live or die as Allah wills.

For hunting game and providing 33 wild sheep for the army to feast upon, the men of Bronze Company are to share my table tonight, and are to be given each one silver coin from my treasury, in appreciation of their perseverance and purpose. Each man is to receive an extra measure of grain for his horses, and the Bronze Company shall march immediately behind me when the army sets out again in two days.

For the crime of cowardice in battle, Mangu Miran shall be given to the captured women of our Jagatai foes who have brought so much pleasure to my men. These women shall be provided small knives to use in punishing Mangu Miran, which knives are to be confiscated and accounted for when they have done with disposing of this unworthy soldier.

For tending the delivery of 20 foals without the loss of a single animal, Ayjal the farrier is to be given his choice of the foals and the reward of one piece of gold for every foal, that is, 20 pieces of gold from my own treasury. In addition, he is to be allowed to attend the mares of my herd, to supervise their foaling and to tend the dams and foals through the weaning; in recognition of his abilities he may call himself Timur-i's Foaler.

For the crime of lying, the hairy woman, Djerat, is to be flayed and her skin preserved with its hair as a reminder to all, and to entertain the curious.

For the service of leading the Yellow Company away from an ambush, Latif Umar is to be given an emerald from my treasury and two horses from my herd, along with a permanent exemption from all taxation for as long as he shall live.

For the crime of stealing, Ghotar Illish is to have his right hand struck off and his right eye plucked out, so that he will no longer be able to steal, nor will he be tempted by what he sees.

For the service of exposing falsehood, the Delhi spy, Josha Dar, is to receive five gold pieces from my treasury and be allowed to ride in the wagons accompanying my own wagon.

For the crime of selling spoiled grain, the Kabuli merchant Yusef is to be prepared a double portion of gruel made from the grain, which he shall then eat in total, or be beheaded on the spot.

For providing the horses of Black Company with new saddle-pads, Tuma the saddler is to receive 4 silver pieces from my treasury and the skins of all the sheep killed by Bronze Company.

For winning at chess against me, the foreigner of the Land of Snows, Rje Chilonhgpa, shall be hacked to pieces and his bones made into chessmen for my board.

For bringing me nine bales of fine silk from China, the merchant Sing Tso-Mao, is to be given three asses and a camel to aid him in his travels and to promote his business; also he is to be accorded safe passage to Trebizond so that he might continue his endeavors on my behalf.

This is my judgment. It is balanced, just, in accord with our traditions and our holy religion. I am even-handed in meting out rewards and punishment, as our Qran teaches. Let no man question what has been decided. Let all be carried out at once.

Timur-i Lenkh
at Kabul
by the hand of the scribe Yesun Toq

6

"Your foot has not healed yet," Tulsi said to Sanat Ji Mani as they sat by a small lake in the luxuriant light of the full moon. They were far from the Sutlej now, south and east of the city of Samdhar; the arid plain was behind them, and they were in wooded uplands. Traveling by night, they had avoided towns and cities, wanting to leave no record of their journey; when they encountered villages, they waited until daylight, found a shaded place where they performed for the people—Tulsi doing her acrobatic tumbling, Sanat Ji Mani offering conjuring tricks or medical treatment—in exchange for shelter and a meal for Tulsi. "It is forty-one days since you . . . pulled out the stirrup." Her voice caught in her throat as she remembered the harrowing event; even the recollection made her feel slightly ill. "There is still an open wound through your foot. It has not knit so far." She glanced down at the boot he had fashioned for himself, and saw the shine of blood on the rough leather.

He shook his head once. "I am not badly hampered." It was not entirely the truth, for he had none of his native earth to restore him which left him vitiated and made his recovery more difficult.

"You say that, but you are exhausted by the sun and your injury continues." She wanted him to see her concern. "I worry for you."

"Thank you; I will recover in time." He realized this was not enough, that she wanted more from him. "I do not mean to cause you apprehension, I apologize for that. I am highly complimented by your concern, though it is unnecessary."

"But you bleed, and the sun burns you," she said. "Say what you will, I am troubled on your behalf. I wish you would mend, and your skin not . . . char the way it does when you are long in the sun. How can you improve if you continue to be hurt?"

"I told you those of my blood heal very slowly. The cut will close eventually but I will limp for some time." He smiled to solace her; his sack lay on the ground beside him, next to her pack. "And I *will* heal; you have my Word on it. You must not worry."

"But I do. I saw how weak you became after the staple was out, how exhausted and pale you were, and how dreadful your burns . . . I fetched . . . sustenance for you. I know how much you have endured." She looked across the lake. "You will want to catch more birds tonight, I would guess."

"Not just at this moment," he told her. "You had eggs and cheese today. If I catch ducks tomorrow, that should suffice. Tonight I would like to find heartier fare."

"Will your foot allow it?" She was anxious for him. "You may not want to take on furred game yet."

"Would it trouble you if I did?" he asked, thinking she might have an aversion to his hunting hooved animals, although she had not mentioned it before.

She nodded, her thoughts clearly on something else. "You have taken care of me. In spite of all this, you have taken care of me."

He did not speak for a short while, then he laid his small hand on hers and said, "Not as well as I should like."

"Oh." Tulsi started to pull her hand away, then stopped as her expression changed slightly, as if she had thought of something new.

"You deserve better than I have been able to provide," he said. "If things were otherwise, I would see that you did not have to suffer on my account."

"How would you want to care for me?" Her question was nervous and playful at once; she stared down at his hand on hers. "If you could?"

"First, I would not remain here. I would want to take you to one of my houses, in some part of the world where you could live your life as you liked, a place where war could not reach you and you would be beholden to no one for your livelihood." He heard how forlorn he sounded, and deliberately made his tone more hortatory. "You have great skills. You are clever. You have much to offer. It would be an honor to be able to give you the opportunity to achieve all that you seek for yourself: do you know what that might be?"

For a long moment she considered her answer. "I think I would seek to have my own troupe of tumblers and acrobats and to travel the world freely. I think I would want to be well-fed and safe, and dressed in silks that are not old and torn." She was wistful and revealing so much of her dreams did not come readily to her. "I would like to find the most able practitioners of my art to be in my troupe, so that we would awe all those who saw us perform."

"Then I wish I could help you to have that troupe," he said, so simply that she believed him utterly.

"How could you do that? If you have wealth, as you say you do, you cannot use it now, and we are alone in a part of the country neither of us knows. How can that change? No one can find us, and we cannot reveal ourselves." She was optimistic and discouraged at the same time. "If I could have my troupe, where would it be?"

"You said yourself you would travel the world," he reminded her, watching her as she thought about this.

"Yes," she said at last, "but that was my aspiration, not anything I can have, not in this world. I have been through enough of it to know that." She turned toward the sound of a night-bird's cry. "If it could be, that is what I would want, that's all."

Little as he wanted to admit it, Sanat Ji Mani knew her reservations were well-founded. Twelve or thirteen centuries ago, it would have been different, for then the Roman Circus would have provided a venue for her that included fortune and travel, as she wished to have; now there were very few places that would welcome her alone or with a troupe. "You should be able to have some of what you seek," he told her, hoping to provide a little solace.

"How is that possible in this life?" She pulled her hand away at last. "You are kind to me, and I know that is as much as I can hope for in this world."

Sanat Ji Mani shook his head. "Tulsi, listen to me: you are a re-markable woman, and not because you can do somersaults in the air, or walk on your hands with your feet touching your head." He sat very still. "I will hunt in a while. There are mousedeer in the forest. I should be able to catch one."

"I have heard of them," Tulsi said, her manner becoming politely distant. "Are they really as small as mice?"

"No," he said. "But they are very small, for all that. I will not be at risk trying to catch one." He got to his feet, picking up his sack and slinging its strap over his shoulder. "Let us find you a place to rest while I go hunting." He stared around him, his night-seeing eyes find-ing much activity in the undergrowth. Finally he spotted a half-fallen tree with a hollow beneath it. "Come," he said, offering her his hand to pull her up. "I will make sure you are not exposed to animals or snakes."

Tulsi followed after him, adjusting her pack on her shoulders as she went. "There are more animals in the forest now."

"And there will be more as we go south: animals are plentiful there, all sorts of animals," he said, casting his mind back almost nine hun-dred years to the Year of Yellow Snow, and the catastrophe it had been. He had seen reports of thousands of animals dying in the forests and on the plains throughout Asia, and recalled some of the greatest devastation had been in the south, near the site of the cataclysm that brought the hard years. In the intervening centuries, most of the animals had multiplied again, but there were a few that had vanished forever in that appalling year and the decade that followed.

"What are you thinking?" she asked him, aware that his thoughts were elsewhere.

"I was thinking that life is fragile," he replied, banishing his memories for now.

She could not speak for a bit; an emotion she could not name overwhelmed her. Finally she told him, "Is this what you realized when you lay in a stupor for three days?"

"No; I have known it a longer time than that," he said softly. He motioned her to stop, pointing to show where there were deep impressions in the bank. "Elephants have come here to drink," he said.

"Wild, do you think?" She knew that wild elephants could be dangerous.

"It might be wisest to assume so," said Sanat Ji Mani, continuing on cautiously. "We will hear them moving if they come our way."

"And tigers?" Tulsi glanced over her shoulder.

"We should also assume they are about," he said.

"There are tigers around the Inland Sea," she said. "And in China."

"There are tigers in the snows of Russia and T'u-Bo-T'e," said Sanat Ji Mani. "And many kinds of leopards."

"So you are not the only one hunting tonight," said Tulsi, trying to make light of her sudden fear.

"I am never the only one hunting, night or day," he said evenly. He was half-way to the hollow and paused to look at it again, trying to discover anything that might be dangerous to them.

Tulsi hugged herself as if taken with a sudden chill. "How long will you take to find this mousedeer you speak of?"

"I cannot say; not one instant longer than necessary. I hope I can snare one quickly, so that you do not have to wait long into the night for your supper. If you build up a fire, you should have a meal by midnight." He could not keep from a pang of regret; the mousedeer would provide them both nourishment, but he wished he and Tulsi shared something more than their companionship. He set that notion aside; she had not sought anything more from him than what he had provided from the first and it was not in his nature to demand.

"If you are not back by sun-up, what then?" It was a question she had asked every night he hunted; he answered her as if he had not done so before.

"Wait for a day and a night. If I do not return by the next dawn, go south and east to the city of Sirpur and find the Parsi merchant known as Azizi Iniattir. I have told you about the Parsi merchants, have I not? Tell him Sanat Ji Mani has sent you and that I will join you there when I am able. Tell him you are under my protection, and that in the name of Rustam Iniattir you are to be his guest." He had no doubt that she was capable of making the long journey on her own, but he was uncertain about her willingness to claim hospitality on his account.

"Who is this Rustam Iniattir?" she asked, as she had wished to do for the last ten nights.

"He was a merchant from Delhi; now he is at Fustat in Egypt, safe from Timur-i. He and I have had business dealings together." Sanat Ji Mani motioned her to halt again. "There is something in the brush up ahead. If you will wait here, I will see what it is." He moved away into the forest, graceful in spite of his limp. The underbrush parted around him; he found his way to a near-by clearing and saw half-a-dozen blackbuck grazing; these large antelopes were opulently horned, and their distinctive black-over-white markings made them easily recognized. They were too large for Sanat Ji Mani to try to hunt them in his weakened condition; he slipped back into the cover of the underbrush and was soon emerging from the screen of leaves not far from where Tulsi stood, her hand on the medical knife he had given her. "You will not need that."

She tried to laugh and ended up making a nervous whinny. "You surprised me," she said by way of excuse.

"That was not my intention," he said, and bent down to pick up a thick section of root that was almost as long as he was tall. "This will let us know if there is anything in the hollow you would not want." He hefted it, letting her see how substantial it was. "You may keep this by you while I go hunting, providing you do not use it against me when I return."

"I would never do that," she said, her face flushing.

"Perhaps not," he agreed. "But it would not benefit either of us if you did."

She nodded, saying, "No. It would not." Impulsively she laid her hand on his arm. "The blood you take when you hunt, is it enough? You have lost flesh, and I do not suppose it is entirely from your foot." There, she told herself, she had done it.

"It is . . . adequate." He laid his hand over hers once more. "I am grateful that you notice."

"Adequate," she repeated. "As lentils and peas are adequate? It will keep you from starving but you will not thrive."

His dark eyes met her grey-green ones. "Yes."

In the clearing beyond the undergrowth something startled the blackbucks: they rushed away in a burst of noise that set birds shrieking and sent other creatures pelting off through the forest; Sanat Ji Mani hefted the length of root he carried, prepared to use it to fend off any animals that might run toward them.

Tulsi gave a little cry of alarm, looking about as if expecting to see a large, ferocious beast bearing down on them. "Do you have to hunt tonight?" she asked in a small voice.

"No, I do not: if you do not mind going hungry," he answered gently.

"I would rather be hungry than turn into some creature's meal," she said with feeling. "Stay with me. If you need blood, well, I have enough to give some to you." She tried not to be frightened as she made this offer, and very nearly managed it; she was so close to answers she had longed for since the first time she had seen Sanat Ji Mani that she had to contain her excitement or be overcome by it. "I will give you blood, if you want." She tried to discern his thoughts as they stood in the scintillescent moonlight, the dark forest pressing in on them.

Sanat Ji Mani released her hand but only to brush her cheek with the back of his fingers. "You need not sacrifice yourself, Tulsi Kil. I am not such a ravening monster that I must require so much of you."

She looked about in confusion. "I . . . that was not . . . I meant . . ."

"You meant that you will give me blood," said Sanat Ji Mani calmly. "But that is not what I would want from you, were you to give it, or not all I want."

"But . . . you drink blood. I know you do." She pointed at him, her eyes narrowed. "I have seen you do it."

"Yes. I drink blood." He began to move again, going toward the hollow. "It is my nature."

"Well, if you need it and I have it, why not take it?" she asked. "Is mine less satisfying than that of birds? or mousedeer?"

"No; it is not." He kept walking, his limp more pronounced, as if the weight of his emotions were too great a burden.

"Then why do you refuse?" she persisted. "Why should you not take my blood? Would you kill me?"

"Of course not," he snapped.

"Are you like a snake, and your bite is poisonous?" She slipped on the mud at the edge of a pond and involuntarily reached out to steady herself by grabbing his arm.

"No." He helped her to regain her footing. "It is not like that, Tulsi."

"Then what *is* it?" she implored him. "I do not understand you."

He waited until he had her full attention. "It is that I want too much of you—blood is the least of it."

"Do you eat flesh as well?" Her voice quivered slightly. "I have not seen you do it."

"No, I do not eat flesh," he said testily. "What I would want of you is nothing like that."

"Then what is it?" She had summoned up her courage again. "Sanat Ji Mani, tell me. We have been through too much for you to keep such secrets from me."

He could not disagree with her. "All right." He turned to face her directly, his compelling gaze fixed on her. "What I would want of you is touching, the closeness and fulfillment that brings you joy."

"What kind of joy?" Suspicion made her abrupt with him.

"The kind that comes from the release of the body, the gratification of flesh and spirit." He was very still.

"You mean you want to become my lover?" She took a step back.

"In my fashion, yes, if you desire I be that." He watched her intently, sensing her ambivalence. "If you do not desire it, then I will not pursue it."

"I . . . I do not know what I desire," she said, her hands shaking.

"Then I will wait until you do." He pointed to the hollow. "Come. Let us get you settled."

"And you will stay with me?" she asked, hating the fear she heard in her voice. "Just tonight? There is something about this place that makes me . . . edgy."

"If you want me to stay with you, I will." He would miss the requisite blood he sought, but a single night without it would not be too enervating; if he had his native earth with him, the lack would be little more than an inconvenience, without it, his needs would be keener but not truly unendurable.

"Yes: I want you to stay. If you leave, I fear something dreadful will happen." She lowered her eyes, abashed.

"Very well," he said, thrusting the length of root ahead of him to make enough of a disturbance to chase away any creatures lurking in the hollow. "If you have such misgiving, there is no more to be said. I will remain with you all night."

"Thank you," she said, a bit embarrassed now that he had agreed.

"It is not so cold that we would need a fire for warmth, at least not until much later," he went on; they were almost to the hollow and he proceeded with care. "We may light one for protection, but it would also alert others to our presence, which you may not want to do. Shall I make a fire or not?"

"You ask me?" She was startled by his question.

"Yes. You have an intuition of peril: you will know better than I whether or not a fire will benefit us." He thumped the root on the ground; a small flock of startled birds took to the air, the flapping of their wings as loud as loosed arrows. Then a large snake wriggled away through the underbrush. "There. The place is empty."

Tulsi smiled nervously. "I did not mean to make such a fuss."

"A sensible precaution is hardly a fuss," Sanat Ji Mani told her as he took the last half-dozen steps up to the hollow and ducked inside it. "We should be safe enough now."

She came after him, thinking herself in a leafy cave; she stretched out her arms and turned around slowly. "It is larger than I thought."

He swatted cobwebs out of the way and motioned to her to come farther into the hollow. "If you keep toward the back, no one can see you unless he is standing in the opening."

"That is comforting," she said, and wondered why. What was it that niggled at her so? She picked her way to his side. "You could put a horse in here."

"Close quarters for a horse," he said.

"You know what I mean," she reprimanded him playfully. "It is sheltered and a good hiding place."

"By the smell of it, there have been nilgai sleeping here." He pictured two or three of these large, big-shouldered antelope lying close together in the hollow.

"Will they return?" Tulsi asked, glad to have a question that was safe.

"Not while we are here; for all their size nilgai are timorous creatures," he answered. "I should think most of the animals will give us a wide berth, if they can." He crouched down and patted the mat of leaves. "I'll get a few leaved branches from outside to make this a bit softer for you." He handed her the length of root. "Keep this, in case you need it."

Before he could step outside, she touched his arm again. "Do not go far."

"I am only walking around the thicket," he assured her. "I will not need much time. You can decide about the fire while I am working."

She sighed. "I will try."

"That is all I ask." He went out into the night, going a dozen steps away from the hollow so as not to make any broken branches too obvious an indication of their presence. He pulled down four branches, good-sized ones with large leaves, and dragged them back to the hollow; his foot was aching and he suspected he should change the wrapping again, to remove the grit that had worked its way into the wound.

"Is that you?" Tulsi whispered as he came back to the hollow with his branches dragging behind him.

"Yes. If you will stand aside, I will put these down for you."

She moved quickly, wanting the protection of the hollow as much as his presence. "I have heard nothing distressing," she said, her nervousness flaring once more.

"Neither have I," he said, putting down the branches to form a springy pallet. "And the branches have obliterated our tracks, in case anyone should attempt to follow us."

Her smile was quick but genuine. "That was clever."

He sat down on the edge of the branches. "More pragmatic than clever," he told her. "We will contrive to protect ourselves."

This time her smile lasted longer. "You have been very good to me, accommodating me as you have. No one has done so much for me before."

"No one has led you into such jeopardy as I have, either," he said, a note of self-condemnation in his voice.

"I have traveled with Timur-i's army. I have long known danger." She sank down behind him. "I prefer this to battle."

"You should not have to deal with either," he said. "By all the forgotten gods, I hope I can bring you at last to the life you want for yourself."

"That you would like to do it is enough," she said, lying back on the branches and looking past him into the limpid night.

"No, it is not," he said. "For now it is all I can do." He swung around to look at her, an apology forming on his lips.

Tulsi put her arms around his waist and hung on as if she were afraid of falling. "Do not talk about it," she said. "Please."

"Very well," he said, stroking her fine brown hair.

"It is too hard, hearing these things from you," she said, her forehead pressed against his side. "I know you would change the world if you could. Let that suffice."

"If you like," he said, so kindly that she began to weep; he continued to stroke her hair, saying nothing while she cried herself out. Gradually she stopped. "You have been through too much, Tulsi Kil."

"I was born to it, you were not. You have suffered more than I, and you did not shed a single tear," she said, pulling away from him.

"Because I cannot; those of my blood have no tears to shed." He looked at her in the darkness, seeing her face more clearly than she knew. "It is our nature."

"You never cry? Never?" She stared at him incredulously.

"Alas, no." He took a deep breath. "You are more fortunate than you realize."

She considered him while she wiped the last of the wetness from her face with her fingers. "Why do you say this?"

He did not answer her directly. "Without tears to release it, grief lasts a very long time. Those of us who live long have much to grieve." For an instant, Csimenae's angry features rose in his mind, and then vanished as Heugenet took her place; he shook his head to banish both memories.

"Why do you have so much to weep for?" Tulsi asked, truly curious.

Sanat Ji Mani regarded her steadily. "Most of the men and women I have known are dead—that is the price of longevity."

"And exile," she added, and moved closer to him once more; he said nothing for a short while, then he lifted her hands and kissed them. "Why did you do that?"

"It is a sign of respect in the West," he said. "Men kiss the hands of Kings, of high-ranking priests, and the women they love, to show devotion."

She pulled her hands away. "No. You do not mean that."

"Why do you say that? Why would I not?" He made no move to touch her.

"Because I want it too much," she whispered.

"Ah," said Sanat Ji Mani.

"I have not wanted anything so much, not even my troupe of ac-robats and tumblers." She could not bring herself to look at him. "I do not know what to say. I should not have spoken."

"Then shall we share our chagrin, or shall we seek other remedies?" Sanat Ji Mani asked, his desolation of spirit beginning to lift. "You may choose whatever course you wish."

"But it might be ruined," Tulsi exclaimed in an undervoice.

"Because you spoke, or because of how you feel?" Her answer was crucial; he waited for it attentively.

"Because now you know," she answered.

Text of a report sent to Azizi Iniattir in Sirpur from Zal Iniattir in Asirgarh.

To my most esteemed and dedicated kinsman, Azizi Iniattir, the greet-ing of Zal Iniattir from the city of Asirgarh where our House is now established and ready to continue our business as before, and where we may hope to flourish as we have done in the past.

Askari Daitya has arrived here with almost half his caravan, which is better than we had hoped, for we all feared he had perished in the fighting that broke out after Timur-i sacked Delhi. He himself is well and most of his men who were not killed or taken to be slaves are healthy, a blessing that is doubly sweet to our House, for it means we have salvaged some of what we believed we had lost, and we have kept our most accomplished caravan leader. I have informed him that you are still in place in Sirpur, which was welcome news to him.

To add to our happiness, Manah Spentas has come here from Gujerat, his goods in fine condition. He says that the conditions in Gujerat are improving and that it will soon have a Sultan of its own, free from the battles and bickering among the Tughluqs and Timur-i's puppet.

This news encourages me to hope that in a few years we might be able once again to use the port of Cambay for shipping, for once the turmoil is over in Gujerat, the Sultan will want all the revenues he can garner, and payment of customs duties is a fine source of gold and favors. Manah Spentas intends to return to Gujerat after the rains. They will not begin for some weeks yet, but Manah Spentas has made enough money to be able to afford time to himself, to arrange for another wife and to establish a house for her here.

I have twice sponsored a banquet for the high-ranking officials of the city, and have gained favor through this demonstration of goodwill. It is most promising to be received as a person of respect in Asirgarh, and it bodes well for our future. It is my plan to hold another banquet in a month to ensure our place in the city, after which I shall write to you again to inform you of any benefits that may accrue to us.

We have once again heard rumors that Timur-i has been deposed by his own men, and has been abandoned to wander the roads of the world, lame and half-blind. This has been suggested before, and so I am disinclined to believe it. Still, it is persistently told and many believe it is true. Who knows—this time it may be the truth. If you learn anything that confirms or contradicts this report, I ask you to send me word at once. If the trade routes are free of his soldiers, it will be good news for us and all merchants.

The news from Delhi, such as it is, is more discouraging. I have been informed that the men supporting the Sultan Nasiruddin Mohammed bin Tughluq have been fighting with those advancing the claims of Timur-i's man, and as a result, the ruins have become a battleground for those who seek to establish power in the city; it is not unlike vultures fighting over the bones of a water buffalo. So long as the dispute continues, Delhi will continue to be a place of death and want.

You have informed me that you have heard from Rustam Iniattir in Fustat, and that he has secured permission for sending out caravans and trading in the goods they bring, which is welcome news to all of us. To have access to the Mameluke Empire and all that lies beyond is as useful in its way as being able to reach the principalities of Russia or the rich markets of Lithuania. I am planning to avail myself of his market-places, and I advise you to do the same. Let us pray that this arrangement will continue for many generations, and expand the success our House has worked so hard to achieve.

My second wife has given birth to twin boys, which I take to be a propitious omen. I have named the older Rustam and the younger Zal, to remind us all how we are joined together in our endeavors. If they live through childhood, I will know myself to be a most fortunate man. I am sorry my second wife did not survive their birth, but my first wife has taken them to her bosom as if she had borne them herself, and so I have no fear for their well-being.

Write to me soon with as much news as you can. I will pay for a messenger if you are not yet able to afford such an expenditure. You and your family are in my prayers, as are all of the House of Iniattir; I trust I am in yours as well.

Zal Iniattir
Parsi merchant of Asirgarh

7

There were huge stone statues of elongated heads flanking the gates of the town, most of them quite old, judging by the weathered features. Beyond the gates was a market-square with a well and a pair of temples facing each other across the stalls where vendors were just setting up for business. The sky was an opalescent pink, the morning breeze fresh, and the heat of the day had not yet taken hold.

"Will you need shelter?" Tulsi asked as they approached the gates.

"Yes, but not just at once." He was only marginally uncomfortable, and he knew how much of the sun he could tolerate before his burns returned.

"Then I will find a place for you," she said, "and then I will perform."

"There may be a fee to pay first," he reminded her. "I have a few coins left—not very many, but they should suffice to cover any tax."

"And I will get coins for what I do," said Tulsi proudly. "You need not worry about that. I will buy my own food, too. You need not steal any lambs or kids for me."

"As you wish," he said as they approached the gates. "May your gods show you favor," he called out in the dialect of Delhi to the three stalwarts standing guard behind the gigantic heads. The answer they gave was incomprehensible but for two words: *traveler* and *entry*. Sanat Ji Mani tried again, this time in the language of the Malwa region which this town, lying between Lawah and Chitor, might know.

One of the guards nodded. "May your gods be equally gracious."

Sanat Ji Mani limped forward. "My companion and I have traveled far," he began, only to be interrupted by the guard, who pointed to his ragged appearance and laughed.

"And not well, by the look of you." He spat. "You have no caste-marks. Are you Untouchables, or outcasts?"

"Neither," said Sanat Ji Mani. "We are foreigners, as you can see."

The guard tossed his head once in acknowledgment of this. "What do you want?"

"An opportunity to ply our skills. My companion is a tumbler; she has performed in many places, including before the great Timur-i Lenkh. She is renowned in the north," Sanat Ji Mani said, putting his palms together and bowing to her.

"What are you telling them?" Tulsi asked.

"How accomplished you are," Sanat Ji Mani said, and continued to the guard. "She is willing to perform in your market-place."

"How will she perform?" The guard shook his head. "No, no. We have no need for traveling whores here."

"She is not that," Sanat Ji Mani said sharply. "Let her demonstrate her skills and you will see she is not what you think." He turned to Tulsi, holding out his hand for her pack. "They need to see what you can do; one of those somersault jumps of yours should convince them of your gifts. He does not believe you have the ability I have described."

"Given the state of my clothes, I would not believe me, either," she said before taking a few steps back, running half-a-dozen paces and then launching herself into the air, doing a full forward rotation of her body before landing on her feet. As she rose, she reclaimed her pack once again.

The guards all stared, and the one with whom Sanat Ji Mani had spoken made a gesture of compliance. "Very well. She may perform. But if she does anything beyond that, she will be whipped, and so will you. What is your skill, stranger? Do you do more than live off her?"

Sanat Ji Mani stifled a sigh. "If your priests are willing that I exercise my art, I have with me a few medicaments; I can treat the injured. I have done so for many years." It was no more than the truth: he had begun his healing work three thousand years earlier in the Temple of Imhotep.

"You may have a place near the temple." The guard pointed to the nearer one. "If you do anything false, you will be beaten and your woman taken away from you."

"She is not mine to have her taken from me," said Sanat Ji Mani. "She is my companion, nothing more."

"Yet you let her earn for you." The guard laughed. "No doubt that is only out of her kindness that she does." He glared at the two of them. "I have told you what is permitted, and our terms. If you enter the gates, you accept the terms."

"I understand," said Sanat Ji Mani, and summed up the gist of what the guard had said to Tulsi, adding, "I will pay the fees now; that should make him more inclined to give us the benefit of the doubt." He held out two small gold coins to the guards. "This is for her, and for me. I have my materials in my sack and will administer them for a few coppers."

"A seller of potions, are you?" The guard chuckled. "If any of your medicines do not work, you will be whipped."

"I am willing to take that risk," said Sanat Ji Mani.

"You should use them on yourself," the guard added. "You halt along like a spavined horse."

"What is he saying to you?" Tulsi asked, not liking the guard's tone.

"Nothing very important," Sanat Ji Mani replied. "Ignore him." He added to the guard, "If I had not used my skills, I could not walk at all. As it is, I depend upon her to help me."

"If you think it best, I will, but men of this sort do not like being ignored," she said in response to the part she understood, with an uneasy glance toward the guards.

"I think they may find a reason to separate us, and that would be difficult." Sanat Ji Mani held out his hand to her. "Hold on a moment, to show them we are together."

She laid her hand in his. "Will this make any difference?"

"It may." He turned to the guards. "She is willing to entertain until the mid-day rest, and from late afternoon until sundown. She will not do more than that. The gold should be enough for permission to perform."

"It is ample," said the leader of the guards.

"Then we are satisfied if you are," said Sanat Ji Mani, releasing Tulsi's hand.

"This money will do for today. If you want to continue tomorrow, you will have to pay more." The guard smiled. "You treat her well."

"I treat her as she deserves," said Sanat Ji Mani.

"Do you not command her?" the guard asked.

"No, I do not. I have no right to command her, nor does any man." He took a step forward, favoring his right foot as he did.

"It is a good thing she is the acrobat." The guards laughed among themselves.

"Oh, beyond question. Even if my foot were healed, I could never do the things she can," Sanat Ji Mani said with a genial smile.

"You say you do not command her," the leader remarked.

"I say it because it is true," Sanat Ji Mani declared. "She has been given her liberty because of her talents. No man is to deprive her of what she has been given."

"And who was it who gave it to her?" the guard asked.

"It was Timur-i himself, who conferred her full liberty upon her." It was a daring lie, but one that could not be gainsaid.

The mention of Timur-i caught the attention of the guards. "He has not come here."

"But he might," Sanat Ji Mani pointed out. "And if he does, you do not want it said that you failed to honor his decrees."

"Perhaps not," said the guards, and whispered among themselves. Finally the leader spoke again. "Neither of you will be kept from your performing, but neither of you will be given any unusual favor. You will stay in the market-square like everyone else." He stepped aside and gave his attention to a man leading three heavily laden asses.

"What did you say about Timur-i?" Tulsi asked as they went through the gates.

"That he freed you," said Sanat Ji Mani. "I thought it would allow us the chance to work here without having all our money taken."

"How much did you pay?" she asked.

"Two gold pieces," he said. They stared about the market-square where stalls were being erected. "I think there will be a place for you at the end of that row."

She followed where he pointed. "Yes. There is room enough." She turned back. "What about you?"

"I will sit in the shadow of one temple for the morning and ask if I might move to the other for the afternoon." He touched her hand. "During the mid-day rest, stay by me."

She nodded. "I have no desire to try to find a safe place on my own." Her voice dropped. "I may be ready by then."

He shook his head. "Not yet, Tulsi, and not here. You need not be concerned for me; I have weathered worse than this."

"On the road to Baghdad. Yes; you told me." She looked away, toward the market-square.

"And the Roman arena. It was tolerable only for its brevity." He rubbed his chin, recalling other places that had tested the limits of his strength. "At least I can do something to earn a little money, something useful; I still have enough medicaments left to treat most minor conditions. If someone is seriously ill, I doubt I can do them much good."

"Then select your patients with care, and stay where I can see you," she recommended; she handed him her pack and started away along the aisle between the market-stalls.

"That I will," he said, resigning himself to a day of lancing boils and treating rashes. He stayed in the shadows as much as he could as he went along to the temple on the eastern side of the market-square: it was a wide building, fronted with shallow stairs leading up to an elaborate colonnade that served as the formal entrance to the holy building. Statues of gods, some of whom Sanat Ji Mani did not recognize, stared down at the market-square from large niches, their feet covered in offerings of fruit and flowers. He chose a place at the end of the colonnade and sank down on the steps, setting out a row of vials at his feet. From here he could watch Tulsi perform while he dealt with anyone wanting his help.

At the open space, Tulsi began to tumble, working out how much room she would have and how she would use it. Her first cartwheels— two on the ground and one in the air—attracted the attention of a spice merchant who had just finished setting out his wares in his stall. She did a back-flip and grinned automatically as he tossed a copper coin to her. She picked it up and slipped it into the pouch sewn into her sash, then sank into the splits as a kind of bow. It was a promising beginning, she told herself as she glanced at Sanat Ji Mani.

The morning passed quickly enough; the market-square was busy, and the day was hot. Tulsi performed frequently and ended up with a good amount of coins for her trouble; Sanat Ji Mani was less busy, but by mid-day he had a handful of copper coins to show for his work. As the sun glowed like a forge overhead, the market shut down; vendors and buyers alike went to rest out of the stultifying heat.

"I am going to buy something to eat," Tulsi called out to Sanat Ji Mani as the vendors lowered their awnings for the heat of the day. "Do you want anything?"

"I leave that to you," said Sanat Ji Mani, putting his vials back in his sack, slinging it over his shoulder, grabbing Tulsi's pack, and standing up slowly; his foot was aching and the sun had sapped his stamina to a point where he only wanted shelter and rest. He leaned against the nearest column and watched Tulsi purchase two skewers of goat-meat cooked with cumin and ginger, and a large round of flat-bread filled with onions, nuts, and raisins.

She came up to him with her meal in her hands, making her fingers shine with oil. "I had a good morning," she announced.

"I saw you were watched eagerly." He smiled at her. "Even the guards came to watch you."

"They did," she said, taking a bite of the bread. "This is very good," she said through her chewing.

"It has a wonderful aroma," he agreed, and added, as he saw her startled expression. "Just because I do not eat does not mean I do not know the value of good food."

"You will always surprise me," she said, and squinted up at the sky. "Where shall we rest?"

"There is an alley-way just on the side of this temple. I think it will remain in shadow all day." He held out his hand to indicate the way, and was pleased when she took hold of it. "Come, Tulsi. We both need time to rest."

"That we do," she agreed, her greasy fingers slipping through his.

"Then let us find a place," he said, and bowed to her Roman fashion.

"You have some very strange ways, Sanat Ji Mani," she told him as she followed him into the deepest shadows beside the temple, nibbling at her meal as she went. "I did not like the manner in which the guard looked at me," she said quietly; the stones took up her whisper and repeated it.

"How do you mean?" he asked, looking about for a place they would be hidden and comfortable at once.

"He raked me with his eyes. Some men look at women that way, as if to take off all their clothes and their skin, too." She paused at the edge of an old niche, now standing empty. "This might do."

"It might," he agreed, and stepped into it to look around. "I do not think it will be too unpleasant."

"No spiders, no snakes," she reminded him.

"I see none," he assured her.

"Then I will come in," she said, climbing the steps to join him. "You are pale."

"I am tired," he admitted, dropping down onto the stone floor, his sack beside him. "I am sorry about the guard. If you would rather not perform this afternoon, then tell me and we will leave as soon as the market begins again."

"Do we not need the money I could earn?" she asked.

"How pragmatic you are," he said. "Yes, it would be useful, but it would not be necessary."

"Then I will perform and you will stay a little nearer, so the guard will not forget that you and I are together and he may not do what he wishes to do." She took a bite of the flavorful goat-meat, chewing heartily. "This is very good. A pity you cannot taste for yourself."

He paid no heed to her last remarks. "There is enough room for you to lie down," said Sanat Ji Mani. "The stones are hard, but you can rest on them."

"And you?" She sank down, her legs crossed. "This is very pleasant. There are not many places in the town that are cooler, I would guess."

He wondered how she intended her observation. "It should be a proper bed, and with curtains to draw around it."

"Is that what you want for yourself?" She continued to eat, licking her fingers from time to time.

"My bed is narrow and it lies atop a chest filled with my native earth. Most would find it hard, but to me, it is better than cushions of silk." He thought, as he said that, of his houses in various parts of the world, each still containing beds for his use. It would be wonderful, he told himself, to be able to reach any one of them.

"Why do you like such a bed? You could have any you wanted; why choose something so austere?" She was half-finished with the first skewer and almost a third done with the bread; she concentrated on the meat.

"I like it because it restores me," he said, leaning back against the stone wall. "All those of my blood are restored by our native earth."

"Um," she said through a full mouth. When she had swallowed, she said, "You have told me you need your native earth to restore you, yet you and I have managed without it, and with only the blood of animals to nurture you."

"And I am less than I could be," he said, once again choosing his words carefully. "Not just because of weakness and burning."

She stared down at the steps. "I will soon be ready and you need not—"

He held up his hand. "No. This is not meant to persuade you."

She sighed and took another bite of goat. "You cannot tell me you do not think of it," she said between chews.

"Of course I think of it, but not for hunger alone. There is that in you that draws me to you, your courage, your—"

"I know," she said, waving him to silence. "You have told me before and I believe you mean what you say." She ate more, not looking up from her food. "You do not suppose I would refuse you, do you?"

"If that is what you want, then it is right you refuse me," he said, bending forward to look at his right foot.

"As I will do, but not forever," she said.

"It may be forever, if that is what you decide to do." He opened his shoe and poked at the cloth wrapped around his foot; it was a bit bloody, but the stain was fairly dry.

"I will be ready in a while, perhaps a few days, perhaps a month," she said. "I am almost prepared." She pulled off a strip of the bread and wrapped it around two chunks of goat-meat.

"That does not trouble me, Tulsi," he said, closing his shoe again.

"Does it not?" She stuffed a large bite into her cheek.

"No." He gazed at her, saying nothing for a time. "We will be able to travel a fair distance tonight, and still have time to rest."

"Are we still going south?" The question was a neutral one; she already knew the answer.

"Yes. We will go south for many leagues, until we may safely turn west." He stretched. "We will know to turn west when we find merchants coming from that direction; we have not done that yet."

"And we will continue south until we do?" she asked, trying to imagine how long they might wander.

"Or until we learn that it is safe to go westward," he said, and did not explain how that would happen, uncertain of it himself.

Tulsi pondered their situation. "How much longer will we have money for traveling?"

"That will depend to some degree on what we have to pay for, and how much we have to pay," he answered.

"But you do not have much left—money, that is?" She thought of the coins she had earned and smiled a bit.

"I have a few gold coins, a few silver ones, and a handful of copper ones. I am running low on medicaments—you know that." He shook his head.

"Then we will become beggars," she said steadily.

"Not quite that," he responded. "Nothing so dire."

She cocked her head. "But we will have to earn our food, or steal it."

"As we have been doing," he pointed out gently.

"Yes; but now it is prudent, not necessary. Soon it will be essential." She licked her fingers clean and lay back. "I will finish the rest of it when I waken."

Sanat Ji Mani laid his hand on her cheek. "Do not fear. We are not destitute yet."

"No, not yet," she said, turning onto her side and closing her eyes, her head resting on her extended arm.

Watching her drift into sleep, Sanat Ji Mani felt fatigue possess him as immediate as a fever. He leaned back again and longed for slumber, but knew it would elude him. He would have to make the most of the rest he could achieve by half-measures; the lack of his native earth was wearing on him. Not since he had washed ashore in Saxony, more than four centuries ago, had he felt so depleted as he did now. He did his best to clear his mind of intruding recollections but could not shut them out completely: Tishtry guided her quadriga around the Circus Maximus, Nicoris built up fires along the low battlements, Gynethe Mehaut lay before the altar in Karl-lo-Magne's city, Ranegonda on the beach at Leosan Fortress . . . He lapsed into a dazed languor that only ended when he heard a loud cry from the market-square.

Tulsi woke abruptly, a bit disoriented. "What was that?"

"Someone yelled," Sanat Ji Mani said, getting to his feet.

"Why?" Tulsi wondered aloud.

"I do not know," said Sanat Ji Mani, and listened intently as the shout was repeated. "A person of rank is coming, it appears."

"What person is that?" Tulsi was more aware of her surroundings now, and she peered out of the niche with curiosity.

"I have no idea. They are saying *the lord*," he explained, and listened to the sudden bustle. "The guards are demanding the vendors to return to their stalls."

"Because the lord is coming?" Tulsi lifted her hands impatiently. "What should we do, you and I?"

"Do you want to perform for this lord?" he asked her.

"No. No, I do not," she said, shivering in spite of the heat. "I . . . I do not want to do anything for this lord."

Sanat Ji Mani nodded. "Then perhaps we should slip away while everyone is preparing to receive the lord," he suggested. "There should be a gate in the wall behind the temple; there usually is." He took up his sack and pointed to the last of her food. "You may want to take this with you."

"I do," she agreed as she shouldered her pack. "These lords are always hard to please. I have the sense that he might be more arbitrary than most."

Sanat Ji Mani was already moving down the alley, away from the market-square. "You do not need to justify your wishes to me, Tulsi," he said, his voice filled with kindness. "You do not want to remain: we shall not."

She flashed him an uncertain smile. "You are good to me."

They continued down the alley to the rear of the temple and found a number of rough huts clustered near the wall, ragged children and thin women watching them silently from the doors and windows of the ramshackle buildings. One of the women pointed away from the temple, then held out her hand; Sanat Ji Mani gave her a copper coin and motioned to Tulsi to stay close to him.

"Who are these people?" she whispered as she closed the gap between them.

"Prostitutes, either for the priests or for the temple," said Sanat Ji Mani.

"How can you be sure?" She shuddered as a naked little boy threw a pebble at her.

"There are no men here," Sanat Ji Mani observed. "And no sign of men."

Tulsi reached for his hand. "Poor creatures."

"That they are," Sanat Ji Mani said, and continued in the direction the woman had pointed.

Sanat Ji Mani and Tulsi were almost to the wall when there was a commotion behind them, and two of the guards appeared at the other end of the clump of huts; a shout went up, and the men started forward only to be set upon by half-a-dozen women. The guards tried to shove them away only to find others in their place; Tulsi glanced back once, then kept her face turned toward the wall and the tumble of stones where a section of it had fallen in.

"They are after us," she said to Sanat Ji Mani.

"That they are," said Sanat Ji Mani again, steeling himself for the ordeal of climbing the broken wall; the sun was overhead and his foot was starting to ooze blood.

"Why are the women doing this?" She tested the first stone and climbed onto it, holding her hand down to him. "Come."

He took her hand, grateful for her help. "I do not know," he said. "Perhaps the guards seek them out, perhaps the women want to help us do what they cannot do."

"Climb this wall?" Tulsi asked in amazement as she continued upward.

"Leave this place," Sanat Ji Mani replied, feeling his skin begin to tighten with burning.

Tulsi clambered upward, saying, "Hold on to my leg. We'll go faster if I do not have to turn back every few steps."

Sanat Ji Mani did as she ordered, his jaw set with determination. He could hear the shouts behind them getting louder; the sound spurred him on. As they reached the top of the toppled stones, he paused long enough to look back for an instant: he saw four guards coming toward them with grim expressions on their faces; one of the men was yelling something about Timur-i.

"Hurry," said Tulsi, already half-way down the other side. "We can run for the trees."

"Perhaps you can; I will do my best," he said, trying to make light of their situation.

"You will run if I have to carry you," said Tulsi, now on the ground and waiting for him to reach her; he said nothing more as he put his whole concentration on getting off the wall. As his foot touched the ground, Tulsi came up to him and wedged her shoulder under his arm. "Come on. I will support you." Before he could say anything she had her arm around his back and was half-dragging him away from the heap of stones they had just crossed. She headed directly for the line of trees and ducked into them, the leaves whipping across them as they hurried on. Only when they could not see the walls of the town did Tulsi slow down to a walk. "There," she said, letting go of Sanat Ji Mani.

He struggled to say upright; pain sizzled up his leg and through his body, his skin had already cracked on his face and hands, and he felt weak as a newborn calf. "I will be all right," he said.

"If we get clear of this town, you will," she said. "We must keep moving. They will search for us."

"And they must not find us," he agreed, preparing himself to continue on through the sun-spangled trees.

"What did they want? Why were they chasing us?" Tulsi asked, setting her pace to his.

"I have no idea," he admitted. "But I do not want to find out."

"Why did they yell about Timur-i?" she persisted. "Is he searching for us?"

Sanat Ji Mani shook his head and put his mind on walking.

Text of a report to the Emperor of China from his personal intelligence gatherer, written in code and carried by special courier.

In the Fortnight of the Dragon Boat Races, this most insignificant person takes it upon himself to fulfill his duty to the August Wielder of the Vermillion Brush with this, his second report since the Emperor of the Middle of the World was gracious enough to bestow so important a mission on this unworthy person.

This unimportant person begs to tell you that he is continuing his travels through the lands of the Hindu and Buddha. In that regard, this person is pleased to report that his foot has completely healed and that he has only a little limp from the injury. This humble person is most deeply grateful to the foreigner Sanat Ji Mani for all he did to aid me during the time this person was in Delhi pursuing your most revered purpose. It is the hope of this insignificant person that the Buddha will spare him suffering in this life for his goodness to me, and his most excellent care. It is also this person's sincere hope that this foreigner was not among the thousands killed by Timur-i at Delhi.

This unimportant person wishes to inform the most Celestial Emperor that the many refugees from Delhi are growing fewer in number, for which reason this unworthy person has come to believe that most of those who could escape have done so and all that remains now are the few who have become servants to the soldiers of Timur-i left behind to guard the city for his pleasure. Those who have left Delhi tell tales of rapine and continued destruction, both of which have already been visited on that city far beyond its deserts. This person is afraid that anyone left in Delhi must be considered lost to the world.

This dutiful person has seen upheaval in the regions that were not so very long ago firmly allied to Delhi and are now establishing themselves apart from that city and either man claiming to be Sultan there. It is a most upsetting thing, to see how quickly the hold of the Sultans has been lost. Nasiruddin Mohammed bin Tughluq may say it is his right to rule, but there is so little left, this person wonders why he should bother himself over so minor a holding. It makes no sense that Timur-i would waste his troops holding the city for him, when it is clear there is no advantage to be gained from it. This person believes it would be prudent to wait for a year before attempting to establish any contact with Delhi, for it may be that in a year there will be no reason to do so.

This unworthy person wishes to report that there have been accounts of travelers having seen Timur-i wandering the roads, a beggar. There have been rumors before now of his displacement from his leadership, but it is always a tale heard from another, and as such, subject to doubt. This person has not yet heard any story that is convincing enough to gain credence among those who are not awed by the marvelous. Should this person come upon any information that would present creditable evidence that Timur-i is indeed no longer the leader of his army, this person will speedily inform the Wielder of the Vermillion Brush all he has learned.

Rains will soon come to this part of the land; for the time being, the heat is ferocious. The heat of the great Northern Desert is nothing to it. This heat is like being stifled by a hot, wet blanket. It is impossible to breathe without discomfort; men and women collapse under its impact, which is worse than a beating with bamboo rods. This humble person is glad, just now, that he has no animal to care for, since this weather is sufficiently draining to exhaust even the hardiest pony. Walking may be agonizing, but it can only take a toll on this person, not on any other. Once the rains come, there will be mud, and that, too, will slow the progress possible to anyone on the road; this person begs the most August Emperor to forgive him for needing more time to cover the distance agreed upon, but nothing this person can do will make the roads more passable once the wet comes, or more endurable now that the height of the summer is soon to be upon us. No one could do better than this person has done, and few could do as well, given what this person has had to survive. This most insignificant person does not ask for pity; no, he has no need of it, nor desire for it. He seeks only to help the August Emperor to understand the scope of the demands that are placed upon him as he struggles to fulfill the mission entrusted to him.

This person will send his observations by courier in another three months. May the Celestial Emperor continue to enjoy the favor of Heaven, and may the August Dynasty never cease to rule.

Lum

8

A man with a cracking tenor voice was singing a Greek love-song in the street below; from her window in Sanat Ji Mani's study, Avasa Dani listened, the louvers on the shutters open only enough to admit the spanking breeze off the sea. She was longing for dusk and for the familiar sounds of Delhi, not this discordant Greek barking. She attempted a smile, telling herself she was being foolish, that had she remained in the city of her birth she would be dead by now. Her laughter was rich: she *was* dead.

From his place on the far side of the reception room, Rogerian looked up, startled by the sound. "Gracious lady?" he asked in her native tongue.

"No," she said in the Greco-Arabic dialect of Alexandria, "You indulge me, and you must not. As much as I want to speak my old language, I must learn this new one, and to do that I must . . ." She faltered, looking for a word. "I must practice."

"Then," he said in the Alexandrian idiom, "I will do as you ask."

"And you must correct me if I make mistakes, or I will not improve." She ducked her head. "I rely on you to help me learn."

"My master would applaud your decision," said Rogerian, putting aside his household records and approaching her. "It is very difficult, to be so far from home."

"What is difficult is the knowledge that I can never return," she said, the merriment fading from her face.

"You can return, in time," Rogerian said gently.

"No, I cannot," Avasa Dani countered. "There is nothing to return to. Timur-i Lenkh destroyed it."

Rogerian could not disagree. "In time Delhi will be rebuilt."

"Perhaps. But it will then be less my home than it is now." She rose from her seat. "I have no reason to complain. I live comfortably and my needs are met; I have more that is mine than ever I had in Delhi, and yet I miss it."

"That is not uncommon, to miss the place of your native earth." Rogerian frowned, his mind on the problem Avasa Dani's death had produced. He had been enough beforehand to have brought a chest of Delhi earth with them but he knew it would not last much more than a year, when more would be needed.

Again she laughed, but this time the sound was sad. "I never realized how vulnerable Sanat Ji Mani is; now that I am like him, I cannot forget. Soon I must find a way to have the love that will give me life, and I must do it without exposing what I am." She looked up at the ceiling. "There are not many opportunities for any woman to do that."

"Yes, it is difficult, and not only for women—although the limitations you face are more obvious," said Rogerian. "Those of his blood must come to terms with these things or they will not last long." As he spoke, he thought of the one glaring exception to this: Csimenae, who had fled to the remote peaks of the Pyrenees with the full intention of creating another clan around her when it seemed safe.

"I have not yet decided if I wish to last long," said Avasa Dani. "I can tell that, too, is not an easy decision to make, for I do not yet know what I am to do with the years ahead of me. I cannot batten on Sanat Ji Mani for decades and decades, so I must find a way to live on my own, and to keep away from the scrutiny of the world: I have the chance to live many hundreds of years, but it may be that I will not want to, and how am I to know?"

"You need not make up your mind at once," Rogerian pointed out, his manner appreciative and grave. "No one requires a quick—"

She held up her hand, and went on in her native tongue, her speech coming readily and with an eloquence she did not yet possess in the Alexandrian dialect. "I know; but for myself, I must determine how I am to live before I become accustomed to this life you have provided me, so that I do not expect comfort and protection at every turn, for that is not how my life must be now that I am undead." Her stern demeanor softened. "You have been generous beyond anything I could have hoped for."

"My master is your host," Rogerian said. "I do his bidding."

"You could do his bidding without making my stay as pleasant as it has been; my servants in Delhi did their work well, but it was not given in the spirit of good comradeship you have shown me from the first," she said in a tone that brooked no opposition. "That is why I know I cannot remain much longer, and risk becoming habituated to your cordiality. Once I take this life you have shown me as my own, changing will be increasingly difficult. If Sanat Ji Mani returns, then matters may be different, but if he does not . . ."

"You say he is alive," said Rogerian. "Your blood-bond is unbroken."

"Yes. He is alive. That knowledge has kept me in this house as nothing else has, not even my lack of understanding of the language."

She turned to the window once more. "But it will not suffice, not for long, and you are as much aware of it as I am: I must find a place in this world where I can live as I must without obligation to anyone, not even Sanat Ji Mani."

"He would want you to remain here as long as you like," Rogerian said, aware that his assurance would have little bearing on her.

"Perhaps. But I would not benefit from it. I would become as I was before, waiting at the pleasure and will of the men around me. All my life, I have been taught that my first worth is how I please my male relatives, from my father to my brother to my husband. My mother schooled me well, teaching me to put men's needs before my own, to be compliant, to make men's satisfaction the goal of all I did. I was an apt student." She rose to her feet. "While I was in Delhi, it was all I could do. But now? here? I need not embrace those limits."

"This place is ruled by Islam," Rogerian reminded her. "Women live much the same way you did in Delhi."

"But some do not. I have watched what happens in the streets and in the market-places, and I know that there are women who do not live restricted lives; I have seen them and I know that they are not compelled to live apart from the city. Alexandria is a port, and all the world comes here." Her smile was automatic but there was a glitter in her eyes that hinted at ferocity. "I have not been here long, but I know Alexandria has its own place in Egypt, unlike any other city." She cocked her head. "That man singing so badly is singing in Greek, and last night I heard an argument in two languages, neither of which I had heard before."

"Many port cities are thus," said Rogerian, trying to discern her intent, and worrying that he already had.

"Yes. This part of the world is like Delhi, in that there are many different peoples here, but it is unlike Delhi in that most of them come by sea from places remote to the port. Venetian and Genoese galleys are at the wharves, as are hulks from the far north with their furs and amber, and the ships of Byzantium, with all the wealth from the Old Silk Road in their holds. I have heard that they come throughout the year: on any day there are forty or more ships in port." She came away from the window. "These men are seeking adventure."

"Many of them are," Rogerian conceded carefully.

"And they want adventure in many forms." She lowered her eyes. "Some of that adventure comes from women."

Rogerian tried not to look dismayed. "Such women live hard lives. You think you will be unobserved in that life? It is not the case. Women providing entertainment for men have to deal with the judgment and strictures of men."

"As do all women," said Avasa Dani, her expression filled with determination. "I am not set upon that life, yet, but I have been thinking of this, and I am considering making an establishment of my own, where I will not have to take on the desires of men, but where I can arrange matters to suit the men but where the women will be guarded and safe, and where the money they earn is not all given to the men who rule them." She folded her arms. "I have not yet worked it out to my satisfaction, but I am well-enough aware that this is one of the few things I can do where my life will not be remarked upon. It is also a life I understand."

"It is a dangerous life," Rogerian warned her.

"And being a vampire is not?" she asked, going on tentatively, "The more I think of it, the more I see that I must not remain a guest here, but must have the means of meeting many strangers, strangers who will not ask questions or hold my desires against me. How else may I have the chance to gratify my needs without exposure? I am a woman, alone in a foreign country—what other course is open to me? If I become mistress of a house of assignation, I will see many men, and I will have the opportunity to select those who interest me, and I could then decide if I desire them enough to pursue them. A man may intrigue me, and because of that, I may lie with him, or visit him in a dream, as Sanat Ji Mani described, while he lies in my house, after which he will be gone, without harm from me, and at most, only the memory of an unusual encounter."

"But such women can be cast into prison," Rogerian exclaimed.

"What is that to me? Do you think a hareem is not prison? There may be fountains and birds and sweetmeats, but there are also guards, so there is no liberty—do you not see that? I have a husband. I cannot be wife to another—how could I bring such disgrace upon myself?"

Avasa Dani asked, her indignation sharpening her tone. "And if I married again, I would be unable to look farther than my husband's door for what I must have."

"But you would be ranked just above a slave, living the life you plan," Rogerian said to her.

Avasa Dani made an impatient gesture. "Do you think married women are not slaves to their husbands?"

Rogerian had heard many of the same complaints from Olivia over the centuries and he knew Avasa Dani was right. "I cannot argue."

She was startled. "Well," she said when she had recovered herself. "Then why should you, or any man, protest if a woman makes what is required of her a means of her living instead of her servitude? Why should I be kept from making my necessity an employment?" She took a turn about the room, and resumed the Alexandrian dialect. "I have not yet decided how I am to do it, but I know what must be done."

"If that is what you truly want, then you have only to tell me, and it will be arranged," said Rogerian, doing his best not to be downcast. "But before you enter on such a course, speak to the women whose trade it is—so you will not trade one prison for another."

"I will, and I will heed what I am told," she promised him. "But I will also ask you to find me a house, a good one, not far from the waterfront, where sailing men might be willing to go. I must find a place to begin."

"Talk to the women first, I beg you," Rogerian said again. "You may have hit upon the means to have the life you want, but you have not had to endure that life." If only Olivia were here in Alexandria, he thought, he could take Avasa Dani to her. "You say you know how these women live; be certain you do."

"If you deem it necessary, then bring a few of them to me, and I will speak with them." She lifted her head. "If you will not, then I must seek them out for myself."

"I will bring a few such women to you," said Rogerian, capitulating. "All I ask is that you listen closely to what they tell you."

"I will do," she said, and pointed to the window. "Will you give that fellow some money so he will go away? His singing is *terrible.*"

"It is," Rogerian agreed. "All right." He started out of the reception room, then paused. "It may take me a night or two to find women who will speak to you."

"That is acceptable," said Avasa Dani.

"Do you want them separately or severally?" Rogerian asked; he wondered how he was going to convince pleasure-women to speak with Avasa Dani.

"Perhaps two or three together, and four groups or more," she said, so quickly that Rogerian knew she had made up her mind about it already.

"Not tonight, but tomorrow night I will find the first for you: tonight I must inquire about houses," he said, and went to bribe the tenor. He did not see her again until toward the end of the night, when he found her in the gallery over the garden.

Avasa Dani made a gesture of greeting. "You have something to tell me?"

"I have," he said. "I have been about the city, as you requested, and I have information to impart to you." He had taken his tone from hers and was rewarded with a crisp nod. "There are three parts of the city where houses of assignation may be found. There are a number near the waterfront and they cater to sailing men; these houses are rough and they are often closed by the magistrates of the city, and the women branded and their noses cut off."

"You are not saying this to discourage me, are you?" Avasa Dani asked, unable to keep from wincing.

"No. I am telling you what I have found out." He let her think this over. "There is a second area where such houses flourish, near the customs houses, between the Greek and Italian quarters. Most of the men who go there are merchants and other travelers. Those houses offer more than the ones at the wharves—they have singers and dancers and they provide meals and other pleasures than the use of women." He paused again. "Most of the keepers of those houses pay regular bribes and so are left alone by the magistrates most of the time."

"They pay bribes, you say?" Avasa Dani tapped her fingers on the gallery rail. "How much?"

"I did not find out. I suspect it changes from time to time, depending on the success of the house and the demand for such houses." He waited a long moment again, then said, "The third sort of house is found in quiet parts of the city, in gracious houses with all the appearance of wealth that are appropriate to the streets where they are located. These houses are the most discreet because they are the most luxurious and perverse. Some entertain only men desiring men, some are established for those who want children, some for those who want pain, some for those who want several lovers at once, some for those who wish to watch performances of all manner of lewdness." He shrugged. "Most of these houses have been established for a very long time. They demand high prices, but they also pay enormous bribes, and they do not tolerate competition."

"So you are saying—and none too subtly—that I might do best looking for a house of the second order: one for merchants, where there are bribes paid but not ruinous ones, and the men who frequent them may be relied upon to have unexceptional tastes." She waited for his answer.

"It would seem that you would have the opportunity you seek with the least risks in such an establishment, yes," said Rogerian. "Many of those houses thrive for years and years."

She nodded. "I see."

"If you want to look at the streets, I will have you carried there in a palanquin, to view them for yourself." He coughed delicately. "I will also take you to the other sorts of houses, so you may compare them, if you like."

"Let us go early in the day, at first light," she said, looking up at the sky. "Not tonight, tomorrow, when I have had time to think." She made a gesture, dismissing him.

"You will see that I have reported accurately," he said.

"I do not doubt it, but I want to see for myself," she replied.

"Tomorrow night, then, I will bring two or three women to you, and when they are gone you can see the houses," he said as he withdrew.

Avasa Dani wished him a good night, then rose and went to her quarters where she sat down before the carved chest she had brought with her from Delhi. She opened the drawer which contained the records of her husband's visits during his pilgrimage, wondering where he might be now: had he escaped Timur-i? Was he still alive? Was any part of him Nararavi still, or had he become completely a pilgrim with only enlightenment in his thoughts? Would he ever return to Delhi? Sighing, she put the register back without unrolling it. By to-morrow night, her first steps would be taken into a life she could only imagine. Would he be angry with her decision to become the owner of a house of assignation, or would he simply consider her caught in the toils of the world, and deserving pity? Would he ever know what she was doing, or would he consider her lost? She frowned. If she was caught up in the world, was it not Nararavi's fault? Had he re-mained at Delhi, had he continued to be a husband to her, she would never have left. "And I would still be in Dehli, and I would be truly dead, not undead as I am, in Alexandria." It was a strangely comforting thought to hold in her mind as she sought out her bed that was set atop a chest of her native earth.

Rogerian was as good as his Word: shortly after sundown the next evening, he met Avasa Dani in the reception room. "I have three women with me, one from each of the houses we discussed."

Avasa Dani was nervous. "Will I need you to translate for me?"

"You may," said Rogerian. "You may not."

"Then stay when you bring them in." She took a seat on a low divan. "You may present them."

Rogerian went out into the broad hall and signaled to the three women sitting there. "The foreign lady will see you now," he said, and stood aside for the three to enter the reception room, bowing to them European style to show his respect. Following after them, he closed the door against any prying eyes the household servants might have; they were disapproving enough without knowing what Avasa Dani wanted from the women. "This is Nitsa, Gelya, and Vardis. They are your guests." He turned. "This lady is Avasa Dani." He stepped back, leaving the four women to study one another.

Nitsa was dark-haired and pale-skinned with hazel eyes, perhaps twenty-five, slender to the point of skinniness; she moved provoca-tively in her Greek clothing. Gelya was the oldest of the three—at least thirty—with hard lines in her heart-shaped face and white in her light-brown hair, and there was a brand on her shoulder; she was in

Alexandrian dress but wore no veil. Vardis looked to be little more
than thirteen or fourteen, with a cloud of curly dark hair, deep-olive
skin, and kohl-lined eyes the color of soot; she wore silks the color of
persimmons and the coins dangling from her belt were gold. The three
women chose not to sit together, preferring to occupy piles of cushions
apart from each other; they faced Avasa Dani expectantly and with
varying degrees of wariness.

"Welcome to this house," said Avasa Dani. "If you would like food
or drink, I shall have it brought to you."

The women exchanged uneasy glances, and Gelya said, "We are
hungry and thirsty. If you have wine, we would welcome it." She
stared at Avasa Dani, then directed her gaze to Rogerian. "Which of
you will see to our wants?"

"We have wine," said Rogerian. "I will order a meal brought to you
at once." With that, he went to the door and clapped for Kardal, the
steward. "Wine and food for our guests, if you please."

Kardal took a deep breath. "It is not well to have such women in
this house, Friend-of-my-Master."

"They are our guests. Do not dishonor our master by refusing hospitality," said Rogerian.

"But women like that—" Kardal broke off. "Very well. I will bring
the food myself. None of the others will."

"And for that you will be thanked and given a token of appreciation," said Rogerian. "You may tell the rest that I will remember how
they have behaved."

Kardal lowered his eyes. "You must not blame them, Friend-of-my-
Master."

"But I do. And Saint-Germanius will do so as well, when he returns." He remained in the doorway while Kardal withdrew, then went
back to a carved rosewood chair behind Avasa Dani. "Wine and food
will be brought shortly."

"Thank you," said Avasa Dani. "My guests will be grateful for it."
She leaned forward, resting one arm on the rolled bolster at one end
of the divan. "You have been paid for your time here, have you not?"

"We have," said Gelya for them all, a jaded smile on her lips. "I
have pleasured women before, but I do not know if—"

"I have not," said Nitsa. "I have spent most of my life learning to pleasure men."

"Surely you have occasionally done other things?" Vardis said. "You may have had to pleasure more than one man, or a man and a woman?" Her smile was beatific but it did not reach her eyes.

"I have not had to," said Nitsa.

"Then this will be your chance to learn something new," said Gelya, smiling at Avasa Dani.

Avasa Dani held up her hand. "I did not ask you to come here for my pleasure but to find out about your work and your lives."

Gelya laughed outright. "Saints bless us, why? Why should you want to know about us? You have a good life and you want for nothing; you live well here, and you are not accustomed to doing what we do, little as you think you are."

"You are partially right: I want to know because you have experience of a way of life unfamiliar to me," said Avasa Dani, unperturbed by the derision she sensed in the women before her. "I am eager to know about the way in which you conduct your business."

"Why?" Gelya demanded. "So you can keep your husband from coming to us instead of staying at home?"

"No," said Avasa Dani. "Because if I am to establish a house of assignation there is much I must know; I rely on you to teach me."

The three women exchanged glances and laughed, Gelya the most openly, Vardis behind her hand. "You must be joking," Gelya said. "Why would you do this? What makes you believe you can manage such an establishment?"

There was a tap on the door; Rogerian went to answer it, and came back with a tray holding three cups and two jars of Italian wine. He set this down on a brass-topped table and poured out measures for the three women, carrying the tray to each of them.

"I will not know how to answer until you tell me what you know," said Avasa Dani.

"This smells very good," said Vardis, and took a deep sip; the others followed her example.

"You do not join us?" Gelya asked sharply as she put her cup down.

"No; I do not drink wine." Avasa Dani met her direct gaze. "I paid you to inform me. I would like value for my money. Surely you understand that."

"None better," said Gelya. She had more wine.

"Why would you want to establish a house of assignation?" Vardis asked, tasting her wine with practiced delicacy.

Avasa Dani smiled again. "I do not know that I do want to: I am hoping you will give me enough information that I may make up my mind."

"Keeping a house of assignation—any house of assignation—is a costly business," said Nitsa. "This is very good wine."

"I supposed it might be," said Avasa Dani. "But how is it costly? How much must be paid? And for what?"

"Well, any house needs women," said Gelya, "or boys, or both. They must be kept, and fed, and housed, and clothed. Then there is the house. It must be staffed and kept up. There are greedy officials who demand a portion of your earnings, and they must be paid promptly and in full or the house is closed and everyone suffers."

"I see," said Avasa Dani. "In fact, it is much like any other business. Except that it is not, is it? You, Gelya: tell me about how you practice your trade."

Gelya spat. "On my back."

The other two laughed, and Nitsa remarked, "The men you serve must not be very imaginative if you are only on your back."

"Most are off ships and so randy they would fuck a knothole." Gelya took another drink of wine. "Some want sucking, but most are tired of that and want a woman's parts."

"It must be disappointing," said Vardis, carefully wiping her mouth.

"Oh, you think you will never have to lie down for sailors, girl?" Gelya challenged. "I thought that once, too, but I have learned otherwise." She picked up her wine-cup and drank.

"Why do you say that?" Avasa Dani asked.

Wine had loosened Gelya's tongue and she answered readily enough. "When I was sold to a brothel-keeper I was six; my family was poor and I was their youngest daughter. The brothel-keeper paid well for me and took me from Smolensk to Constantinople and put me to work in a very grand, very discreet house where I served high officials and wealthy men. I was a beautiful child, and I was much in demand. But when I was thirteen, I became pregnant and so they sold me to a brothel in Antioch, along with my son, who was taken away from me as soon as he could walk. It was a good house, but not so fine as the first." She stopped abruptly.

"Is that the tale you tell the sailors?" Nitsa asked snidely.

"No," said Gelya. "I tell them—when they ask, which they rarely do—that I preferred sailors to my husband, who was old and feeble. They favor that story over another." She drank the rest of the wine and looked at Rogerian. "Is there more?"

He went and refilled her cup, saying to Avasa Dani in the language of Delhi, "The wine hits her fast—she must be very hungry."

"Possibly," said Avasa Dani. "How did you come here from Antioch?"

"I came by way of Tyre, where I was branded, so by the time I got to Alexandria, I could only find work in the stews." She drank again, recklessly, eagerly. "Once you are branded, the better places will not touch you. If I had stayed in Smolensk, I would have ended up a drudge in a household, or a servant at an inn, since I would never have enough dowry to marry, so this life is no worse than any I might have expected, and better than some."

Rogerian had gone to the door to get the tray of food; he lingered there, unmoving, waiting for the women to finish speaking.

Vardis shook her head. "I was born to this life. My mother, and her mother before her, were whores. I was born in a brothel and no doubt I will die in one." She drank again. "If I am lucky, I will die young, and not have to end up begging or taking on ten sailors in a night."

Gelya bristled and drank more wine. "It is better than starving."

Avasa Dani glanced at Nitsa. "And you? How did you come to this work?"

"I was foolish," she answered. "I was the daughter of a farmer, and my family wanted me to marry well, so they made sure I was seen in the neighborhood—in the company of my brother, of course—and were selecting likely suitors for me. But one day, my brother was busy and I went to the market alone. The local landholder waylaid me and forced himself on me in spite of my coming betrothal. He impregnated me, and my family was disgraced. To recover their good name, and to be rid of me, they made arrangements to have me brought here to Alexandria and put into a house of assignation—it is more than a brothel, no matter what anyone says. I have been here for eight years, and I have come to accept that I will not return to Macedonia."

"Because you will disgrace your family if you do?" Avasa Dani asked.

"Because I have a fever; it is slight, but it burns in me day and night, and one day it will consume me," said Nitsa without any display of emotion. "Already it has eaten away some of my flesh. I have been given medicaments, but they do little but lessen its pains. My daughter already died of it, not quite two years ago."

There was a moment of silence; it was enough for Rogerian to open the door and claim the tray of food brought by Kardal. He carried it to the table in the center of the room and set it down. "Enjoy this fare; I am told the doves in honey are especially good—so is the chicken with almonds and cinnamon, and the bread is just out of the oven," he said. "I will pour more wine if you should want it." He busied himself opening the second jar.

"Have what you like," Avasa Dani encouraged them. "And while you eat, you will tell me how you would prefer that houses of assignation be run, and I will learn from you."

The three women were still suspicious, but the aroma of the food was tempting and the wine had suffused their spirits with camaraderie; they moved closer to the table, prepared to eat.

"I would like to have more guards, to keep out the bullies and the brawlers," said Gelya as she reached for one of the doves.

"I would like it if all our money was not lost to clothing and other minor things," said Vardis.

"How do you mean?" Avasa Dani asked, listening closely.

"Well, a portion of the fees paid are supposed to be kept by us, but one needs a new scarf, or a garment gets torn and must be replaced, and soon there is nothing left of one's earnings and, in fact, one is in debt to the master of the house." She broke off a piece of bread and reached for a heap of chopped eggplant with lemon and olive oil. "I would be glad to be able to keep a portion of my earnings."

"That happens everywhere," said Gelya, eating with determination. "No one will give us what is ours."

"Would you work in a place that promised you could keep your earnings?" Avasa Dani asked evenly.

"Of course I would," said Gelya.

"They all promise that," said Nitsa.

Gelya laughed to show her scorn. "Perhaps where you are, they do. Where I am they do not bother with such pretense."

"But if you could have your money, would you come to the place that provided you with the money?" Avasa Dani persisted.

"Yes," was the answer from all three women, in varying degrees of eagerness.

"And you, Nitsa, what would you like?" Avasa Dani addressed her calmly.

"I should like to be sure I will not be thrown out to starve when I am too ill to work," she said, her voice dropping; the other two women stopped eating to look at her.

Avasa Dani met her eyes. "If that happens, you will come here, and you will be cared for until the end. You will not be left to die in the streets." She pointed to Rogerian. "He has heard me say it; he will honor my Word."

The three women turned their eyes on Rogerian.

"I will," Rogerian said, and bowed to Avasa Dani for emphasis. "None of you will be turned away from this door."

"Very well," said Avasa Dani. "What else would you like changed in your houses of assignation?" She steepled her fingers and leaned back to listen as the women continued to talk over their meal and their wine.

Text of a letter from Vayu Ede to the Rajput Hasin Dahele, presented in person at Dahele's principal city of Devapur.

To the most illustrious, most puissant, most revered of Rajputs, the great Hasin Dahele, the greetings from Vayu Ede, Alvar, the humble possessor of poetic gifts and singular vision, all of which he seeks to place in the service of the mighty Hasin Dahele.

Too long have your deeds gone unsung, and your virtues unheralded. In a world beset with suffering and harshness which is the plight of the living, you are a shining example of moral excellence and magnanimity that is a glorious example to leaders and rulers everywhere. By my visionary senses, I see you are to be given an oppor-

tunity far beyond any known in this world so far: it is to be you, most awe-inspiring Rajput, who lifts up the mighty Timur-i, who has become an outcast and a beggar. Timur-i will come to you, and you will raise him again to power, and will serve as his right hand, and inherit all his empire when Timur-i leaves this world for the next. You will impose justice and grandeur where there has only been destruction and rapine. It is the will of the Gods that you will rise to undo the many wrongs, and through your prudence, bring happiness to your people who deserve it. I see this as clearly as I see your fine new palace rising behind the new walls of Devapur, and as clearly as I hear your name spoken of with respect and veneration by those fortunate to live under your wise and beneficent rule.

My visions tell me that you deserve the favor that fate has ordained for you, and you are ready to receive this endowment as your due. I have come to you to record these splendid events as they unfold, and to make them known to everyone. Any man so favored as you are deserves the adulation of all, and I will devote all my skills to ensuring that you are credited for what you have done and what you are yet to accomplish. Anyone in your Principality of Beragar, which lies in the border region to the west of the frontiers of Berar and Bidar, and might be dismissed as too small to be important, will want to be prepared for the change you will soon bring upon them, and then upon all of the country from China to the Land of Snows, from the Bay of Bengal to the Arabian Sea. I hail you now as the Conqueror of the World, as all shall hail you in time to come, when you succeed Timur-i and enlarge his Empire beyond anything dreamed of by his followers who have so callously cast him out, and who shall pay more dearly for their betrayal than even a poet of my abilities can describe. Let me dedicate my poetry and my vision to your cause, and let me spread your glory far beyond Beragar to the ends of the earth.

I dedicate myself to your cause, and to the finding of Timur-i, so that you may begin your advancement at once. I will watch the people who come into your city, and I will find Timur-i and present him to you. I will make it known that you are to lift him up from the calamity that has befallen him, and through this most generous act, come to rule the world.

I have no desire other than that of serving you in your time of

*loftiness. I ask that you consider my plea and receive me into your
presence to tell you more of what has been revealed to me. To demonstrate my vision, and so you may know it to be true, I tell you now
that you will find a man in your city, a foreigner, of middle years,
with dark hair, who favors one foot, and who is wary of sunlight. He
will be accompanied by one who serves him, also a foreigner. They will
be in ragged clothes but those who see them will be drawn to them.
When this man comes—and he will come as the year runs on to its
close—I will have him brought to you. He will deny that he is Timur-i,
but others will recognize him. Do not doubt that you will be advanced
by him once you restore him to his most potent place at the head of his
armies, and therefore do not fail to observe every courtesy and favor
to the man who will seem nothing more than a beggar. You must take
him in and show him honor, for then you will always enjoy his gratitude and will be the most powerful Emperor in the world that has
been or the world that is coming.*

*I prostrate myself before you, Omnipotent Ruler,
whom I esteem as highly as the gods,
Vayu Ede*

9

Outside the rain drummed down, hissing on the leaves and the flimsy
roof of the shed where Sanat Ji Mani and Tulsi waited for the storm
to pass; it had blown in during the night and had not abated all day.
The air whipped about them and several leaks let in steady trickles
that turned the earthen floor to damp mud that smelled faintly of
sheep-dung.

"Do you think this will continue through the night?" Tulsi asked as
she stood in the doorway, staring out into the weather.

"It is likely," said Sanat Ji Mani. He could feel a sense of vertigo
developing as the water ran from everything; he clenched his jaw
against it.

"And tomorrow—what then?" She did her best to close the door that hung on a single leather hinge, and succeeded only in pulling it off the side of the building altogether; she struggled to put it in place across the opening.

"Tomorrow we must hope there is a little clearing. You and I will both need sustenance by then." He wanted to get away from this abandoned building before it fell in around them.

"Will we travel if the rain is still coming down?" she asked.

"We may have to," he said with a wry smile as he pointed at another leak from the roof. "I do not think this place will hold together much longer."

Tulsi made an abrupt gesture to show her frustration. "We could have reached that village last night if we had kept on walking."

"The bridge is out, or so the man on the donkey told us," he reminded her.

"Perhaps he lied," she said. "Or the crossing might have been shallow enough . . ." She did not go on. "You were right to insist we come here, but it is still not a very good place."

"No, it is not," he agreed, lying back on the bed of a wheelless wagon. "But it is better than trying to find shelter in the forest. You saw the chital deer—they were leaving the trees behind."

"Are you so certain it is because of flooding?" Tulsi shook her head. "Why just the deer and no other animals?"

"I do not know," Sanat Ji Mani said quietly. "I have told you what my guess is—that their resting-place has been flooded out—and I can do no better than that."

"Have you no interest in the reason?" she asked, snapping her fingers in disapproval.

"Yes. But I do not want to try to move about in all this running water until night has fallen," he said, adding, "Perhaps not even then."

She heard the weariness in his voice and came back to his side. "You are worn out."

"So are you," he said, running his hand over his slow-growing beard, thinking it needed trimming.

"The light does not work upon me as it works on you," she said. "And running water is no barrier to me."

He reached out and took her hand. "You have my gratitude for remaining with me; you could do better on your own, I suspect."

"If I were lucky, I might. If I were unlucky, I could be taken as a slave, or raped, or killed. No one pays any attention to entertainers on the road, the more so if they are female." She took a deep breath. "You are protection for me, and I am thankful that you have not tried to sell me before now."

Sanat Ji Mani was deeply offended; he kept his temper with an effort. "Do you truly suppose I would do such a thing? What kind of wretch do you think me, Tulsi Kil, to suggest I could use you so traitorously?" He sat up, his features set in stern lines. "You are not mine to sell, nor would I if you were."

She laughed. "You could say I was and no one would doubt you," she told him. "You would not have to scratch for coppers, but have gold in your hands again."

"I would not do anything so reprehensible," he said.

"My father bought my mother from her uncle," she said. "You might change your mind, if we have to contend with many more difficulties."

"I will not change my mind," he said brusquely.

She decided it was best to abandon this fruitless argument. "Well, you will or you will not: time will show which."

He rubbed his eyes. "Thank you." He put his sack under his head—it was nearly empty now but he could not make himself give it up, as if that would be the final reduction to beggary—and leaned back once more.

She sat down at the end of the wagon-bed, huddled up, for although the day was warm, the damp was becoming unpleasant. "Tell me some more of your life, Sanat Ji Mani."

"Why?" he asked. "You do not believe me."

"No, not entirely; but I like to hear your tales. They are exciting, and they make me think that life will always change." She put her elbows on her knees and her hands under her chin. "I like the stories about the Romans. They sound wonderful, having such grand entertainments, and letting their women make lives for themselves."

Sanat Ji Mani sighed. "Not all women were so fortunate, and not all Romans were wonderful. The entertainments could be bloody." He stared up at the rickety roof. "You would have done very well there, particularly in the time between Julius and Traianus. Not everyone flourished, although it was a better time than many others. There was law that was intended to put all the citizens and subjects at the same level. But some could not use the law for protection, and some turned the law to their own ends."

"This was a long time ago, you say?" Tulsi prompted, her eyes shining like a child's for a loved story.

"More than thirteen hundred years," said Sanat Ji Mani. "I was there for more than a decade while power went from one man, to another, to another, and so on. It began with a youth called Nero and settled down again when Vespasianus and his grown sons came to rule: Titus and Domitianus. I was gone from the city before Titus wore the purple." He paused. "Emperors wore purple," he explained.

"Were they as grand as Timur-i Lenkh?" she asked as if the question were a ritual.

"Much grander. They had fine cities and good roads, and aqueducts that brought water long distances; their Empire stretched from Britain to Egypt, from the Atlantic Ocean to the Black Sea." He shook his head. "It lasted longer than many others, but not so long as some."

"Timur-i's Empire will last longer," said Tulsi. "Longer than the Emperors' of China will."

"No," said Sanat Ji Mani. "It will not."

She looked at him, her face masking her anger. "Why not?"

"Because Timur-i likes war more than he likes peace, and he does not trust his own deputies to serve him," he said flatly. "He appoints few men to supervise what he has conquered, and those he does appoint, he will not have faith in, and so he provides them inadequate support, for fear they will use that support to stand against him. He cannot have a legacy if he will not provide his lieutenants with the authority to do the work he demands of them."

"He is careful for the sake of his clan," said Tulsi.

"Do you really think so," he said. "Timur-i does not want to relinquish one jot of power and is convinced that anyone seeking it—other than himself—is a usurper." He closed his eyes. "Even the Emperor of China—who has reason to fear usurpers—appoints lieutenants and grants them the authority they must have to act in his stead. Timur-i has made himself master of an Empire and rules it as if it were still only a clan. He calls himself an Emperor and conducts himself like a chieftan."

"What do you know of such things?" Tulsi asked, too sweetly.

"Enough to know Timur-i's Empire will be gone before he has been dead a century," said Sanat Ji Mani.

She had no immediate answer. "You must not speak against him," she said at last. "He will find out."

Sanat Ji Mani laughed. "How could he, and what would it matter if he did?" He reached out and touched her arm. "You are not in his camp and you will not be in his camp again unless you decide to go there, as Djerat did."

"You would stop me if I tried," she said, not quite sulking.

"No, I would not," Sanat Ji Mani said. "I might ask you to consider your decision, and I might point out the risks, but if it is what you want to do, I will not stand against you." He felt grief pluck at him, grief for the many times he had not been able to spare his companions from pain.

"It would be hard for you to manage without me, would it not?" she pursued, exacting revenge for his words against Timur-i.

"Yes, it would," he said bluntly. "As being alone would be difficult for you."

Whatever she had been about to say, she held back, and finally, reluctantly, smiled. "You have the right of it. I do not want to travel alone; I have said as much. So we remain together for now." She sat back. "Later I may change my mind."

"Later you may find a patron who suits you," said Sanat Ji Mani.

"I hope I might," she said, wistfully dubious. "How am I to find this patron in all this rain and away from cities?" She put her pack aside and stretched out beside him. "If you had the wealth you say you have elsewhere, you could be my patron."

"It would please me very much," he said, putting his arm around her shoulder. "If we reach Chaul and you cross the sea with me, I may yet be."

She chuckled. "It would be a fine thing."

"It would," he agreed, thinking he missed the comforts he had enjoyed not so long ago; it would be most gratifying, he told himself, to return to a comfortable house with a library for reading, instruments for music, and a laboratory for alchemy.

"Do you truly believe we will reach Chaul?" she asked, resting her head on his shoulder.

"Yes. It is proving more difficult than I had expected, but I do not doubt we will get there." He stroked her hair. "The land is full of little princelings who squabble over territory like cocks over dunghills."

She remained quiet for some little time, then said, as if continuing with a conversation already begun, "The women you have known— are there many of them?"

"I suppose some would think so," said Sanat Ji Mani. "I have lived a long time."

"And do you forget them, over the years?" How forlorn she sounded, as if all her hopes had been dashed.

"Those who have known me, no, I do not forget them; they are part of me and I am part of them. I could more easily forget my hand than a woman I have touched, who knows that I have touched her." He turned his head toward her.

"You never forget anyone?" she asked in disbelief.

"Those I visit in sleep, as a dream, they are a dream for me as well, sweet and ephemeral, not intended to last. I often forget those women, in time. But those who receive me knowingly, every one is clear in my memory, and will remain so until I die the True Death." He kissed her forehead; it was a chaste kiss, a gentle benediction. "I will not forget you, whether or not I taste your blood."

"Have you visited me in sleep? as a dream?" She shivered as she asked.

"No, Tulsi Kil; I have not," he said.

"Why not?" She was genuinely puzzled. "You could have done."

"No, I could not; I told you I would want more from you than a fleeting impression of satisfaction." He touched her face with his free hand. "I would not abuse your trust of me so egregiously."

"Um," she said, reserving judgment.

He could not let it rest. "I value your friendship and your good opinion, Tulsi; I would do nothing to jeopardize either. If that means there can be nothing more between us than what there is now, I accept it. But I cannot help but wish for intimacy, so that you and I would experience each other more fully."

"And you would be nourished," she said in a small voice.

"It comes back to that, does it not? You think that because I am a vampire, I must be without honor, that I am ruled by my esurience. If you so distrust me, why do you remain with me?" He kept his voice level even as emotion roiled within him.

"I do not distrust you," she said. "But you are right; I fear what you are."

"And the only way I could convince you otherwise would be to compel you to do what you do not wish to do." His enigmatic gaze rested on her face. "So we are at a stand-still."

"You will not leave me," she said, one arm across his chest as if to weight him down. "Say you will not."

"No, I will not," he said with kindness.

She stared into his dark, dark eyes and finally said, "If you do, I will kill myself."

"Why would you do that?" he asked, trying to fathom her intent. "What would you gain? If you do not desire congress with me because you fear death, what is the advantage of killing yourself?"

"I will not be at the mercy of the world." She tightened her hold on him. "I will not have it all be for nothing."

He drew her closer to him. "How can it be for nothing: you have not turned away from what life has offered you."

"I have turned away from what *you* offer me," she said.

"That is hardly the same thing," he said, managing to smile at her. "I wish you were not afraid, Tulsi, of me, of the world, of anything."

"How could I not be afraid?" She clung to him. "I have been dreaming about how my mother and father died. There has been so much killing."

"Yes," he said. "There has."

"All will end in death, no matter what we do," she whispered.

"Soon or late, it will," he agreed.

"Does that not trouble you, that all will end in death?" Beneath her indignation there was yearning.

"It did, a long time ago. I have come to terms with it: I have had to." He held her gaze with his. "That does not mean I find it easy to say good-bye, for I do not."

She held him tightly. "How long will you live?"

"I have no idea," he answered. "In that I am the same as any breathing human."

This time her silence lasted longer than before. "You say you do not take much blood, not from . . . from women." She tried to sound disinterested. "Not as much as from birds and beasts."

"You mean," he said as gently as he could, "you want to know if I take enough blood from a knowing partner, or a dreaming one, to be dangerous: no, I do not. With animals, it is different, for most of them are small, and do not have much to spare, and are needed as food for the living. Also, I get only blood from birds and beasts; from living humans I have the nourishment of touching, and that is better sustenance than anything." He was keenly aware of the places where their bodies met, even through clothes, but he strove to give no sign of this.

"Then your women who die do not die on your account," she said.

"I have told you that before. No, Tulsi, they do not die from what passes between us, or they have not for more than three thousand years." He looked up as another leak brought a ribbon of water through the roof, splattering onto the earthen floor an arm's-length away from where they lay in the wagon-bed. "When I first came to this life, I was what you fear, but I learned the folly of it, and I changed."

"You could have become more cautious, better at persuading women to forget their safety and embrace you." Her arm across his chest tightened. "Once they succumb to you, you would be free to do whatever satisfies you, and they could not stop you—could you not?"

"No doubt," he said drily. "But I do not."

"I want so much to believe you," she cried. "But I dare not."

He gave a quick, one-sided smile. "If that is the case, I can say nothing, do nothing that will end your apprehension." He laid his hand lightly on her arm. "Yet I want you to believe me."

She sighed. "If I knew someone who could tell me you had treated her well, that would be different."

"There are such women, but none of them are here." He laughed sadly. "When we reach Alexandria, you can meet one."

"If we reach Alexandria," she said. "That is a long way across the ocean, you have said."

"Beyond Damascus," Sanat Ji Mani agreed, choosing a city Timur-i had sacked.

"Do you think we will reach it?" She snuggled closer.

"Yes, I do. It is a direct journey across the sea when we are aboard a ship. That is not a difficult matter to arrange: once we reach Chaul, I will be able to get passage aboard one of my ships, or one of Rustam Iniattir's ships, and once the Mameluke Empire is reached, it will be an easy thing to cross to Alexandria." He did his best to minimize the dangers they might encounter; Tulsi was frightened enough without being told of storms and pirates on the ocean, and the desert and thieves in Egypt.

"I know it is never an easy thing to travel—I have been with Timur-i's army most of my life." She tried to break away from him, and although he released her arm, she could not bring herself to move. "It is just that I am lonely."

"Ah, Tulsi Kil," he said tenderly, "so am I."

"Are you? You have said as much, but I wonder how you can be." She sighed and relaxed.

"Why do you say that?" He looked directly at her.

"Because I cannot see how you could endure your loneliness, if you are truly lonely. How can you stand to live?" She waited a moment. "I am so lonely I feel as if the flesh has been stripped from my bones. If you care for those you say you love, and they are lost to you, how can you bear the anguish of it?"

He answered indirectly, recalling his time in the Land of Snows, not quite two centuries ago. "Do you know what it is to be in the high mountain passes, when the wind whips the snow so that it stings and your face is numb—when you know you must continue to move, no matter how arduous movement may be, or die of the cold?" He saw her nod. "My loneliness is like that, when I admit it to my life. Most of the time, I concentrate on the immediacy of things—staying dry, or keeping my life in order—but the isolation is never gone."

"But that is *terrible*," she exclaimed. "To have so many losses, that only increase: how can you continue on?"

"If I value those I love, I do them no honor by turning my back on the life they shared with me." He shifted the arm she was lying on so he could touch her shoulder. "When you perform, you honor your mother and father, do you not? Well, living is how I value those I have loved and still love, though they are lost to me."

She looked past him, staring at a point beyond the walls of the abandoned building. "What if I want to be with you only because I am lonely, and I am afraid only that I will be lonely still?"

"I have known less . . . reasonable explanations for seeking love," he told her thoughtfully, Csimenae and Heugenet both coming to mind. "Do you want me to persuade you to change your mind so that you can be angry if I disappoint you? I will not. Do you want me to tell you I can end your loneliness? I cannot."

Tulsi made a sound of distress. "Yes, I want you to change my mind, and in part so I can blame you for doing it." She moved suddenly, moving her hand from his chest to his head and pulling him down to kiss him directly on the mouth. "There."

"It is a beginning, if you want to begin," he said to her.

"And you: do you want to begin?" She still held her hand tangled in his slightly waving hair, keeping his head a finger's width from hers.

"Yes, but not against your will to begin," he answered, studying her demeanor; he perceived her doubts and attraction together.

"Here, in this place, I do want to," she said, growing breathless. "I may not want anything other than your company at another time."

"That does not bother me," he said, compassion suffusing his features. "I want what you want, no more and no less."

She was about to challenge him again when she sighed abruptly and tugged his hair so she could kiss him again; this time it lasted longer, and became sweeter as it went on. When she moved back, her face was flushed and her eyes were huge. "That was . . . not what I expected." She let go of his hair.

"And what did you expect?" he asked, his compelling eyes fixed on hers.

"I . . . am not sure. Nothing like . . . what you did." She laid her hand on the side of his face. "I felt . . . awakened."

Sanat Ji Mani smiled slowly, with deep delight. "If that is what you felt, what can I be but beguiled." He lay still, sensing her need for consideration.

"You are not going to press your advantage?" She sounded confused again.

"I was not aware that I had an advantage," he responded. "It seems to me that I am being tested."

"Are you angry?" she asked urgently.

"No," he said, and knew it was entirely the truth. "I want you to be certain of your decision, whatever it may be, and whenever you may make it."

She levered herself upward so that she could stare down into his face. "I would be furious, to be tested in this way."

He chose to give her an honest answer. "There was a time when I would have been vexed, but that was more than fifteen hundred years ago."

"Are you really so old?" She was studying his face. "You do not look much more than thirty-five or forty."

"I was thirty-three when I came to this life, a mature age then. My family was known for being long-lived." He fingered her hair.

"Were they vampires, too?" She had trouble speaking the word.

"No. They were not." He paused, startled at how keenly he could still feel their loss. "It would not have mattered if they had been."

Without warning, she lowered herself to kiss him again, this time letting the kiss evolve from easy contact to something much more profound, more sensual and complex, filled with promises and hesitation. When she pulled back this time, she was trembling. "What do you want of me?"

"What you seek for yourself," he answered, the incipient joy in his face mirroring her own.

She bit her lower lip. "I do not know what that is."

"Then I will help you to define it, if you want to," he said, warmth in his voice and his eyes.

Tulsi sank down on his chest. "If I become pregnant, I cannot perform, and then we will truly be beggars." She paused. "I was pregnant once; Djerat gave me herbs and it was over. She cannot give me herbs now."

"You will not become pregnant," said Sanat Ji Mani, enfolding her in his arms, wanting to shield her from her experience.

"All men say that. Djerat warned me many times how men lie, and how women must bear the consequences. She was right." She touched his face where the beard began. "Men will do or say anything when lust is on them."

"Many will do," he agreed. "But I do not. Do not fear me for that, Tulsi; there is no reason to, I give you my Word: I will not make you pregnant because I cannot make you pregnant. Those who are undead cannot create life." He brushed her hair out of her face, still holding her close to him.

Tulsi contemplated this for a short while. "That may be true," she allowed at last, realizing as she spoke that she wanted to believe him, to be convinced of his good intentions and her own safety. "But how can you achieve what you need if you do not—"

He laughed once. "There are many ways to find release, not just the one," he answered her. "Those of my blood take the pleasure they give, nothing more and nothing less. What you have, I have. If you want to try, and dislike it, that will be the end of it."

It was her turn to laugh, with an edge in the sound. "You will not demand again what I have given once?"

"No, if it is not what you want," he told her somberly. "There would be no reason to do it."

She scrutinized his features as best she could. "If I tell you that you must not go on, will you stop?" Before he could answer, she went on, "You will say yes in any case, will you not?"

"I will say yes because it is true," he replied.

"Which is either the truth or a lie, and I cannot know which unless I—" She moved atop him again. "How long will it take?"

"That depends on you," he answered. "It will be as long or as brief as you wish."

"Truly?" She waited for him to speak; when he said nothing, she went on. "All right. You may begin, but if I tell you to stop—"

"Then I will stop," he promised her, and drew her down into another kiss, one that opened her lips and evoked sensations she had not known before. As he kissed her, he caressed her shoulders, then her back, and finally her breasts, his small hands gentle and knowing, unhurried in their elicitation of pleasure.

"Oh!" Tulsi cried softly as she broke from their kiss; Sanat Ji Mani at once stopped what he was doing. "No. Go on," she whispered. "I will tell you to stop when I want you to stop."

He resumed his fondling, then, as his hands moved lower, his lips took up what his fingers had left off, teasing at her nipples until they were hard as buttons. He took his time, searching out the hidden passions of her flesh until she was trembling.

"You can do what you want now," she said, catching her breath in her throat.

"No, not yet," he said.

"Why not?" She pushed back from him on quivering arms.

"Because you are not ready yet," he said, continuing his summoning of her responses; gradually her tension gave way to a rapturous languor. He opened the sea-scented folds at the apex of her thighs and a jolt of satisfaction went through her.

"You can—" She was about to say *finish* when his fingers drew a second and more intense response that plucked the word from her thoughts and left her gasping in ecstasy as her body found its first astounding spasm of fulfillment.

"Now you are ready," he murmured as he moved to nuzzle her throat, and they lay with amplectant limbs, and blended gratification, through the last of the wet afternoon; they neither noticed nor cared when the ceiling sprang another leak.

Text of a letter from Atta Olivia Clemens at Rome to Rogerian in Alexandria; written in the Latin of Imperial Rome.

To my most highly regarded friend and the loyal companion of my treasured Sanct' Germain, the hasty greetings of Atta Olivia Clemens, from Sanza Pari, three thousand paces beyond the walls of Rome.

I have only just returned here from Rhodes, or I would have answered you sooner; I hope the delay has not inconvenienced you. I must tell you that I am leaving tomorrow for France; I have learned that an ambitious Baron is attempting to take over my horse-farm near

Orleans, claiming the exigencies of war make it necessary. I intend to stop him.

Yes, I agree with Avasa Dani, Sanct' Germain is as alive as he has been for thirty-four centuries, and although he may be in danger, he has not suffered the True Death. I also agree it is infuriating of him to go off on these journeys on his own, with never a word to anyone. I have never liked his determination to be so far from his native earth without companions or protection. It is most thoughtless of him to put his friends through so much worry on his behalf, going to outlandish places and not informing us of his location or condition. He is a most exasperating man, to be sure. When he returns, you must inform me so that I can give him my thoughts on the matter. To be forever fretting about my oldest and most cherished ally is not something that delights me, and so he should be aware.

There is more disapproval of Wenceslas of Bohemia, and a movement to depose him. The Holy Roman Emperor, it seems, ought not to be a spendthrift sot who passes his time in drunken revels instead of managing the Empire. I cannot suppose that Wenceslas will meekly submit if he is challenged. This may yet lead to internal wars in the German States, which would be most unfortunate, coming at a time when the world is finally beginning to recover from the three Plagues. I mention this in case you should decide to travel into Italy or north, into German territories. This may turn out to be a difficult time in that part of the world.

If you come to Rome, you may, of course, stay at Sanza Pari, whether I am here or not. I will inform Niklos Aulirios to make arrangements for you, in case you have enough of Alexandria and want to wait for Sanct' Germain here rather than there. I confess it would be reassuring to see you again—a reminder that we are all capable of surviving no matter what the world throws at us. You may even bring Avasa Dani if you like. She will be welcome here, if she decides to come with you.

I will have this carried to Ostia today and sent aboard the first reliable ship bound for Alexandria. You should receive it within twenty days, perhaps sooner if the weather is favorable. Send word to me in Orleans if you have anything to impart, as I will send word to Alexandria until I am notified you are not there anymore.

Enough of this. I must go to supervise the packing for my journey. May you travel safely, and may I, as well.

Atta Olivia Clemens

At Sanza Pari, outside Rome, 13th August, 1399 of the Church's measure.

10

Outside the Great Gate of Devapur there was a line of merchants and farmers waiting to be admitted; it was almost dawn and the sky was showing the first rosy glow of dawn. The forest beyond the walls of the city rustled and rang with the emergence of day-dwelling animals while the small farms between the trees and the walls bustled with activity. Rajput Hasin Dahele's Guards were making their way along the waiting line, spears in their hands, supervising the crowd. A babble of Hindi, Gond, and Kola made it plain that this market was an important one, drawing merchants from far away as well as more local growers and craftsmen. Toward the back of the line, Sanat Ji Mani and Tulsi waited to be let into the city with the rest.

"How many coppers do we have left?" Tulsi asked as she watched the Guards approaching in their gaudy uniforms. She had taken her pack off her shoulders and held it leaning against her leg.

"Six," said Sanat Ji Mani. "Enough to pay our gate-fee and to buy you something to eat. Beyond that, we will have to earn more."

"Will you be doing conjuring?" She sounded uneasy. "They may not want you to do such tricks."

"I may, and I may not. Let us see what the Guards tell us." He did his best to reassure her with a quick smile, but he was aware that she was not solaced.

"I will do as many performances as they allow," she told him fervently. "So you and I will not lose everything."

"Let us hope that will not be necessary," he said, and paused to listen to the people gathered around the Great Gate. Although he recognized a few of the languages and dialects, he knew none of them well enough to converse readily, which he knew could be a problem.

"What do we do if the Guards want a bribe?" she asked.

"Let us wait until they ask for one," he recommended, shifting his weight to ease his right foot.

"All right," she said nervously, and tried to contain her apprehension.

"They have not reached us yet, in any case," he pointed out. "They may not go to the end of the line, for the sun is almost up, and the Gate is opened at sunrise."

"That would be reason enough for them to deny entrance to any they have not questioned." She was about to make another, more caustic, observation when the first brilliant rays sliced along the sky, cutting through the trees and casting shadows as long and sharp as lances. "The Gate will be opened now."

"Move with the others in line and we will attract little attention," he said, turning away from the sun.

"I shall hope we pass unnoticed—and untaxed," Tulsi said.

"Indeed," he said, holding his empty sack before him as if it still contained something more than a few coins.

Ahead of them the line began to move as the Gate swung inward, groaning loudly on its massive brass hinges; an answering shout arose from the crowd and those at the head of the line surged forward. The Guards went back to the city walls, forming a line next to the Gate. A good number of merchants were waved through.

"There—you see?" Tulsi said, pointing. "Men of means are allowed in."

"We are not to the Gate yet," Sanat Ji Mani said.

"No; but when we get there, we will be denied entry, I know it." She looked about nervously. "Look. They have pulled that man with the load of charcoal out of the line. They will do the same to us."

"Perhaps," Sanat Ji Mani said. "If we are refused admission, we can set up out here, so that those coming and going from the city will see us, and we can earn some money that way."

"If the Guards will let us," said Tulsi bleakly.

"We will manage somehow. Chafing at what may not happen serves no one." He laid his hand on her shoulder. "I know you are anxious—I do not blame you—but you cannot improve our chances by fussing."

"Do you tell me you are not apprehensive?" she asked as they moved closer to the gate with the rest of the line.

"I am disquieted by our circumstances," he told her, wanting to ally her fears.

She rounded on him. "If we have nothing to eat tonight, what then?"

"Then I shall hunt," he said. "I hope it will not be necessary, but if it is—" He made a philosophical gesture.

"It does not bother you, this necessity?" She noticed they were nearing the Gate, and stopped speaking.

"Yes, but not so much that I cannot do it," he said in a low voice, moving forward carefully to conceal his limp as much as possible.

They were almost through now; a customs man sat at a table just inside the Gate collecting fees and issuing writs for the market. There were three men standing behind him, all officials of the city, by the look of them; one was white-haired and had a deeply lined face and wore a heavy gold chain indicating his importance. The others deferred to him, which he obviously expected them to do, listening for his opinions before voicing their own.

"Who are you and what is your purpose here?" the customs officer asked in Hindi, and repeated his question in Gond.

Sanat Ji Mani answered in accented-but-passable Hindi, "We are entertainers. The woman is a tumbler and acrobat. I conjure. We have come a long way."

"By the look of you, you must have," said the customs officer. "A tumbler and a conjurer. How long do you plan to perform here?"

"Today, possibly tomorrow," said Sanat Ji Mani. "If things go well."

"And where have you come from?" the customs officer demanded.

"I come from far away; so does my companion," Sanat Ji Mani said, and felt Tulsi grow nervous with all these questions.

"That is obvious," said the customs officer and turned to the old man with the chain. "What do you think?"

"I think the Rajput Hasin Dahele will want to see them." He nodded twice, his whole demeanor reeking of sagacity.

The customs officer addressed Sanat Ji Mani. "Our Rajput would like to speak with you, if you would be good enough to go with these Guards?"

Although Tulsi could not understand what was being said, she was aware something had happened. "What did they say?" she asked edgily.

"They want us to go with the Guards. Apparently they think the local Rajput wants to see us." Sanat Ji Mani was able to preserve his outward calm as he spoke to the customs officer once more. "Why would your Rajput be interested in the likes of us? Does he enjoy tumbling, or conjuring?"

"Not quite," said the old man, and bowed slightly to Sanat Ji Mani. "Come with us, if you would. You will suffer no harm from anyone, I assure you."

"And just who are you, that you can give such assurances?" Sanat Ji Mani asked, his tone growing sharper.

"I am the Alvar poet, Vayu Ede; I am advisor to the Rajput Hasin Dahele." This time his bow was deeper and more respectful.

Tulsi looked about in dismay. "Why do they want us?"

"I have not been informed; I will translate anything I am told," Sanat Ji Mani said, hoping to lessen her misgiving. "Perhaps if we go along, we may discover what the Rajput wants."

"But I need to perform. We will not earn any money if we must wait upon the Rajput, and that would be—" She stopped as two Guards came to flank her and Sanat Ji Mani. "Are they taking us to prison?"

"Perhaps," said Sanat Ji Mani. "But I doubt it. The Guards have not drawn their weapons."

"Small comfort," said Tulsi, reluctantly walking as Sanat Ji Mani kept pace with the Guards. "Why do you not run?"

"Because I cannot, not with my foot as it is, and the sun in the sky. I would be caught quickly, and that might make our situation far worse than it appears to be right now." He tried to soothe her. "If nothing else, we should get some food out of this."

"Do you think so?" She tossed her head. "Timur-i would be as likely to order us whipped as to feed us."

"We do not know that this Prince is as despotic as Timur-i," said Sanat Ji Mani, and noticed that the Guards were listening; he wondered if they could understand the language he and Tulsi shared, and decided to be more circumspect. "It might be best to wait until we find out what this Rajput wants of us."

She caught his intention at once. "Yes. You are right," she said, and fell silent.

They made their way through the streets, passing a number of temples and open squares, some of which were readied for markets, some of which apparently served other purposes. The city itself was good-sized—about half as large as Delhi—with an array of buildings that went from squalid to grand, spreading over a cluster of rising hills toward a palace that crowned the highest point of the land, a gorgeous citadel built more to impress than to defend. As they approached the magnificent entrance to this enormous building, the road grew steeper and Sanat Ji Mani limped more with the effort of the climb; he was glad that they had not much farther to go, for between the sunlight and his half-healed foot, he was becoming exhausted.

"Tell me if you need my shoulder," said Tulsi, her voice low.

"I think I can manage, but thank you," he said. "We have only a short way to go."

Tulsi kept silent, her eyes on the palace ahead of them; it shimmered in the morning light, its white-granite walls brilliant, its ornamental stone-work in jasper and malachite, its domes glistening with rosy marble, its watch-towers topped with large brass finials that shone like gold where the sun struck them. A cadre of Guards lined the way from the first door to the interior of the palace, their weapons sheathed, but their presence carrying an explicit message. The servants of the Prince wore dark-green livery, an unusual requirement in this part of the world; it revealed, more than the palace, the wealth of the Prince who reigned, for it meant he could afford to spend a great deal on his household. "So many of them," she whispered to Sanat Ji Mani as they passed the first door into the palace and faced three more, all standing open.

"It is intended to impress us," said Sanat Ji Mani in an undervoice.

"And it *is* impressive," said Tulsi, glancing at the groups of servants gathered to watch them. "I have not seen the like since Samarkand."

"Oh, yes, it is impressive," said Sanat Ji Mani, grateful that they had nearly reached their destination.

A last pair of doors swung open revealing the main reception hall. Windows stood open along the eastern wall, admitting the glowing morning light so that the whole room was luminous; a contingent of Guards lined the approach to the carved-ivory throne that stood at the top of a tall dais, just at this moment empty; as Vayu Ede motioned Sanat Ji Mani and Tulsi forward, a sudden twangling of hidden instruments filled the air, and the Guards bent almost double at the waist. A door at the rear of the dais swung open and a man in gorgeous silks, golden ornaments, and many jewels came to sit on the throne; he was still fairly young—no more than thirty—with handsome features and an impressive moustache beneath a strong nose and deep-set eyes. He was full of energy, and he had the air of a man used to being obeyed.

From a hidden alcove, a strong-voiced herald called out, "This is Hasin Dahele, Rajput of Beragar, Grandson of Raja Hasin Napadas, Lord of many elephants, Protector of the Gods, Master of the city of Devapur, the Most Fortunate, Most Exalted ruler. All bow low before him."

"We are supposed to bow," Sanat Ji Mani told Tulsi, and did it himself, copying the manner of the Guards.

"Do I bow?" Tulsi asked. "Or are women expected to show more deference?"

"Try bowing," Sanat Ji Mani recommended, and sighed with relief when she did.

"Who are these people?" Hasin Dahele asked, addressing Vayu Ede.

"They are strangers, Greatness, come from far away; they have not come here before—no one at the Gate recognized them," the self-proclaimed poet announced. "He says he is a conjurer, she calls herself a tumbler."

"And is this true?" Hasin Dahele addressed the new-comers.

"As far as it goes, Greatness," said Sanat Ji Mani. "It is what we do to earn our living now."

Vayu Ede inclined his head and shot a penetrating look at Hasin Dahele. "They have not always done this."

"The woman always has," said Sanat Ji Mani at once, not wanting to speak anything but the pristine truth. "I have not."

"It is as I said, Greatness, is it not?" Vayu Ede inquired in a manner laden with implication.

Rajput Hasin Dahele folded his hands. "It may be; it may be." He leaned forward on his throne. "What are your names and where do you come from?"

"What is he asking?" Tulsi asked softly.

"He wants to know who we are," said Sanat Ji Mani, and went on in Hindi to Hasin Dahele. "The woman is Tulsi Kil. She has been part of a troupe of entertainers all her life until she became separated from them a few months ago. She has been traveling with me since then." He paused. "I am called Sanat Ji Mani. I come from far away."

"That is apparent from your speech to your garments to your features; no one in this region resembles you," said Hasin Dahele. "Tulsi Kil and Sanat Ji Mani, you say?" He leaned back and clapped his hands. "You will be my guests, and welcome in my palace. You are to be fed and clothed and treated as I would be treated."

"Greatness," said Sanat Ji Mani, "we are most grateful, and we mean you no disrespect, but, if I may ask: what have we done to deserve such distinction, for we are unaware of anything we have done that would entitle us to your hospitality?" He knew from long experience that the favor of Princes, especially unearned favor, could carry with it a heavy burden. "We are strangers in your land, and we have come here with nothing."

"All the more reason I should receive you well," said Hasin Dahele curtly. "Go. Enjoy your meal, put on new clothes, and we shall speak again."

"Greatness," Sanat Ji Mani persisted, bowing to show respect, "I most humbly request that you tell us more: you must understand that we have been on the road for some time and have not often encountered kindness, let alone such generosity."

"I will explain more once you are rested and comfortable," said Hasin Dahele in a tone that closed the matter. "Vayu Ede, go with them and see they are attended to properly." He clapped his hands again, then rose from his throne. "We meet again in the late afternoon."

"Come," said Vayu Ede to Sanat Ji Mani. "A bath is being readied, one for you and one for the woman, and then there will be a meal, and you will be allowed to rest through the heat of the day." He waited until Rajput Hasin Dahele was out of the room to turn toward the other end of the reception hall. "This way. Both of you."

"Do you think we should?" Tulsi asked when Sanat Ji Mani had summarized the agenda laid out for them.

"I think it would be sensible, at least until we have learned more. At the very least, you will be fed, and we will have better clothing." He indicated his thread-bare, travel-smirched garments. "Do not tell me you would prefer what we have."

"No," she said hesitantly. "But I do not want to be made a captive for the sake of a few rags, either."

Sanat Ji Mani, doing his best to keep pace with Vayu Ede, said, "We cannot bolt now. We could not get out of this palace without being stopped. Oh, yes, the windows are open, but this room is toward the rear of the palace—that long approach went through the center of the building—and we would still have to get out of the grounds if we are to escape; there is a wall to climb, as well. Perhaps you could do it, but I cannot; I cannot move quickly enough." They had passed the door through which they had been admitted, and were continuing on toward the end of the vast chamber.

"But could we not hide, and . . ." She shook her head. "No, of course not. You are right. We will take stock of our situation when we can better understand it."

"You make it sound so galling," he told her.

"Because it is," she responded. "I do not like not knowing why we have been singled out."

"Neither do I," said Sanat Ji Mani, "but so long as we are not in immediate danger—"

"Are you certain we are not?" she asked.

"No; but I am willing to reserve judgment for the time being." They were almost to the end of the reception hall.

Vayu Ede paused in front of another door, this one somewhat smaller than the main one, but decorated with an inlaid pattern of leaves worked in ivory and precious stones. "This leads to the domestic part of the palace. The Prince's family have their quarters here, and they are not to be approached in any way. You need not worry that you will stumble upon them by accident; Guards are posted outside their wing, and you are not to go beyond them. I think you will find the guests' accommodations to your liking." He opened the door, motioning to Tulsi and Sanat Ji Mani to come through.

Sanat Ji Mani told Tulsi what Vayu Ede had said, adding, "We should keep to the restrictions they place on us for now, and proceed carefully so that we do not do anything to create suspicions about us."

"I should think not," said Tulsi with feeling. "Oh, Sanat Ji Mani, I wish you could hold me for just a moment. I feel so . . . alone here."

"You are not alone," Sanat Ji Mani promised her.

She did not answer, giving her attention to the luxurious western wing of the palace: there was a magnificent series of apartments off the corridor down which they walked, each one furnished opulently, with aromatic woods, lovely silks, and carpets woven by masters. All the rooms were good-sized, with shuttered windows to keep out the mid-day heat without blocking air. She was mildly startled when Vayu Ede stopped in front of one of these rooms and bowed her into it. "For me?"

"He indicates so," said Sanat Ji Mani, and then said to their guide, "I want to be near her, as near as your custom permits."

"You will be across the hall," said Vayu Ede. "And you shall have the chamber at the end of the corridor for your bath." He smiled benignly.

"Are we permitted to bathe together?" Sanat Ji Mani asked.

Vayu Ede looked a bit startled, but said, "There is nothing to say you may not."

"Then, if you would, arrange it," said Sanat Ji Mani, and relayed what had been said to Tulsi.

"Do you think they are trying to keep us apart?" she asked, frowning at the thought.

"They may be, but I doubt it. If they had wanted to do that, there are many ways they could have accomplished it by now." Sanat Ji Mani kept his voice low, but there was power in it, holding her attention. "We will try to discover what their purpose is, and as soon as we do, we will know how to act."

"If you say so," she said dubiously.

Sanat Ji Mani nodded to her, but spoke to Vayu Ede. "What shall we do now?"

"The bath will be readied for you. While you bathe, your clothes will be taken, washed, and mended; you may have them back if you wish, but it is the honor of the Prince to clothe you, and there will be garments waiting for you when you return from bathing. I will tell the slaves that you and your woman are to bathe together, so they will not be shocked to see you both." He bowed, his fingers pressed together.

"They are going to examine our things," Sanat Ji Mani to Tulsi. "While we bathe."

"And attack us while we have nothing with us," she said, a combination of disgust and fright in her stance. "If we refuse, they will only make it worse."

"Very likely," said Sanat Ji Mani.

"Should we request other arrangements? I have your knife still. I can keep it with me, in case we have need of it." She was careful not to touch the knife hidden under her sash.

"That is an excellent idea," said Sanat Ji Mani, and went on to Vayu Ede. "How are we to manage this? You say these are our chambers, and that the bath is at the end of this hall. How do we do this?"

"There are robes in your rooms; leave your clothes, don the robes, and go along to the bath," said Vayu Ede. "When you return, new garments will be set out for you; I will come for you and take you to the Prince's morning dining room."

Tulsi listened to Sanat Ji Mani's version of this with growing unease. "I do not like it," she said sternly, "but I doubt there is much I can do about it."

"Very little," Sanat Ji Mani agreed. "Keep alert as we go; we can discuss this further while we bathe."

"They will be listening," said Tulsi, unwilling to go into her appointed chamber alone. "Wherever we are."

"Very likely," Sanat Ji Mani said, and, aware of her wariness, said to Vayu Ede, "Would it be permitted for the two of us to occupy the same room: we have done so for many weeks and we are used to it."

Vayu Ede considered the matter, then said, "If she has served you, then it is fitting that she remain with you. You had better share the room appointed for your use; it is larger and the bed is more generous. I will inform the Illustrious Prince of your request and its disposition."

With that he bowed. "I will return when you have bathed." Then he leaned toward Sanat Ji Mani and whispered something to him, stepping back at once. "It is true." With that, he turned away and went back the way he came.

"What did he say?" Tulsi asked.

"You may stay in my chamber with me," said Sanat Ji Mani, too startled to repeat the second message. "I think they will be glad of having us both in one place."

Tulsi put her hands to her face in horror. "You mean we could be more easily attacked together than apart? Yes, I see," she went on, giving him no chance to answer. "How foolish of me, to play into their hands."

"The two of us are stronger together than apart," he said, hoping to lessen her growing dread. "It is better that we are together, I think."

She nodded several times. "Yes; yes, you are probably right. Neither of us can vanish if we are together."

"You cannot vanish from me, no matter what others may do," he said gently. "The blood-bond holds me to you. In time, it may hold you to me."

"If I lie with you six times," she said impatiently. "Yes, I know; you told me, more than once." Impulsively she left his side to gather up the robe left out for her. "Let us do as they ask. Whatever is coming, let it come quickly."

"Very well," he said, following her into the chamber that had been allocated for his use. "When we bathe, I will not lie in the water; you may, but for me it would be most . . . unpleasant."

She paused as she started to strip off her clothing. "As you were in the river?"

"Nothing that extreme," he said, and turned away to undress; he had to admit his clothing needed to be patched or destroyed; were he in his own house, he would consign it to the rag-bin. "Running water or tide-driven water makes me ill; standing water only makes me queasy."

"That sounds unsettling," she said, skinning out of her trousers and leaving only her loin-cloth in place. "I will not surrender this."

"There is no need; you can remove it in the bath," he said, casting away the short kandys he had been wearing for so many days; beneath was a sleeveless shift in frayed black cotton, with a tear on the shoulder and pulled seams on the sides. He pulled this over his head with some trepidation, reaching for the robe laid out for him, intending to cover the swath of scars that ran across the whole of the front of his body from the base of his ribs to be covered by his leggings secured at his waist. He very nearly succeeded when Tulsi took hold of his arm.

"What are those?" she asked in a hushed voice.

"They are how I was killed, and why I could walk again," he said as he slipped his robe around him; the soft saffron color seemed odd to him, who habitually wore black.

"What did they do?" Her voice was hushed, her eyes very wide. "I can see why you kept them covered all this time."

Working the bands of his leggings, he peeled them off and dropped them with his other garments; he pulled his robe more completely closed and secured it with the sash he had been provided. "I was disemboweled, but they did not sever my spine or burn me, so—"

She held up her hand. "Of course. You returned."

He tugged off his hand-made shoes and put them near the bed, hoping they might not be taken away. "As soon as you are ready."

"I am taking this," said Tulsi, holding up the little knife. She was wearing a robe of pale blue-green now, and it brought out the color of her eyes.

"A very good precaution," Sanat Ji Mani approved. "Who knows if we will need it."

"Do you expect trouble?" she asked, looking directly at him.

"No, but that does not mean we can avoid it." He stepped into the hall and looked around. "I see no one."

"But we are being watched, are we not?" She went past him, starting down the corridor with a determined stride that turned into a flying cartwheel. "There," she said as she landed. "Look all you want," she added to the walls.

Sanat Ji Mani followed after her, his thought distracted by what he had heard Vayu Ede say so quietly and what they might portend: *I know who you are.*

❖   ❖   ❖

Text of a letter from Rishi Harata Medha to Sultan Nasiruddin Mohammed bin Tughluq.

To the most Excellent Naisuddin Mohammed bin Tughluq, favored of your god, Allah, and devotee of the Prophet Mohammed, the High Priest of Shiva sends his greetings for the last time.

We who have struggled to remain in Delhi are now faced with the necessity of leaving or starving, and while death is not feared by us, we do not wish to succumb through the agency of men, but the Will of the Gods, Whose work the world is. For months we have attempted to maintain our temple and our place in what remains of the city, but it is becoming impossible.

Conflicts among the followers of Timur-i's man and your supporters have destroyed most of the farms and orchards in our vicinity, and therefore no one has any food to bring to market. The warriors seize any they come upon and confiscate livestock for their use, so that the few people within the walls are left to scavenge like pi-dogs or like vultures. No one worships now, not any god. The call to your prayers is not often heard, for those making such calls become targets of archers.

There is disease everywhere and the wells stink from the carrion rotting in their waters. The river is nothing but a sewer and even though the rains have begun, they cannot alleviate all the pestilence that is abroad in these streets. Those who do not starve still sicken and then die, their agony unattended and no record made of their death. Vermin are the only creatures flourishing in this charnel house—they and the vultures are sating themselves on the dead.

The children of the city—those remaining here—are gaunt and their bellies are swollen. Every day we find their bodies where they have gone to sleep the night before and never wakened. Women, too, are dying rapidly, sacrificing their food to their husbands and children. A few get by prostituting themselves, but some of them are killed for dishonoring their families and others are beaten by the soldiers because they are women of the streets and no laws protect them.

In fact, there is no law here any more. I and my three remaining priests have become a haven for those seeking to find security in the city, and we can no longer offer that. We have tried to do as you requested and tend to those still living in the city, but it is no longer possible and there is no reason for us to remain, not when there are temples in other places where we could be welcome and safe. It is lamentable that we must abandon our temple, but we have remained here longer than we had intended to fulfill your purposes. Since that has become an unendurable task, we are leaving the city in two days time—when your messenger puts this into your hands, we will be gone.

May your god Allah and our Gods spare this city any greater grief than it has already suffered.

Rishi Harata Medha
High Priest of Shiva at Delhi

PART III

SANAT JI MANI

T ext of an edict from Hasin Dahele, Rajput of Beragar, to the people of Devapur, his principal city.

It is my Will that all those living in Beragar, especially those in and around the glorious city of Devapur, shall give heed to this and obey:

First: it is my intention that this city and all of Beragar should prepare for war.

To that end, new taxes must be levied. Any transaction beyond that of purchasing food and foodstuffs shall give five percent of the transactions into my treasury. Failure to do this will result in confiscation of the goods of the transaction, or equal service being rendered to my household. Those who transgress twice shall have their eyebrows cut off, and those who transgress a third time shall have lips cut off and the miscreant be turned over to my army to serve as a laborer for a year.

All merchants entering the city shall pay an additional five percent on the value of their merchandise as well as the transactional levy as described already, and failure to adhere to these conditions will result in the confiscation of all goods brought for sale, as well as any beasts

of burden owned by the merchant, which beasts are to be given to the
army for the use of the soldiers.

Second: I require that all those traveling away from the city shall
leave a report of where they are bound and the duration of their stay.

Anyone going beyond the frontiers of Beragar shall pledge to act
in accordance with my interests; it shall be the traveler's duty to make
note of anything he sees on his travels that might have bearing in any
way upon the war I will wage. Thus the traveler will make a record
of all roads and their condition; all bridges the same, including their
width, height, composition, and capacity; the number and type of
boats, ferries, barges, and the like; the fortifications of any towns and
cities; modifications or enlargements of existing fortification; the size,
composition, and character of any armies found; the level of readiness
in these armies; the types of weapons and their number; what animals
they have for battle; the general wealth of the rulers commanding the
armies; any unrest among the populace, and its cause; any signs of
previous battles or uprisings; any apparent stockpiling of supplies,
foodstuffs, matériel; or any other information germane to achieving
my victory. Those not intending to return are to leave a pledge of gold
or property behind to ensure their loyalty to Beragar and me. Any
duplicity shall result in the forfeit of gold or property.

Any returning traveler unable to provide a modicum of intelligence
will suffer the loss of three fingers. A second such failure will enlist
his oldest son in the army for the duration of the war that we are
going to wage.

Third: I command that all houses with stone walls are required to
reinforce the walls and roofs of the houses to secure them against any
attack, and that all owners of stone houses shall donate twenty new-
cut stones to the shoring up of the city's walls. Those who have stone
houses adjacent to the walls shall contribute double amounts of stones,
for their own protection as well as the city's.

All those attempting to avoid this duty will be fined double the cost
of labor of making the reinforcements, and shall be required to donate
thirty new-cut stones for the city walls. Those who have barns or other
housing for animals inside the city shall reinforce these buildings as
well. Those with wooden roofs shall replace or overlay the wood with
stone or tile so that any attack will not result in fire or collapse of

roofs. Failure to comply in these particulars will result in the confiscation of housed animals for the use of the army, and the eviction of the household from houses with wooden roofs.

For those in wooden or wattle houses, there will be a ten percent reduction in taxes for those who fortify their houses with stone and replace their roofs with bricks. Those who make no effort to fortify their wooden or wattle houses with stone shall be taxed at an additional ten percent, and if the houses are not fortified, they will be subject to demolition should the city face a battle or a siege.

Fourth: I decree that all marriages, births, and deaths shall be taxed at a rate to be determined by my customs officials, to add to the equipping of the army.

Those seeking to delay paying this tax shall find it doubled for every fortnight that passes. The sole exception to the doubling tax shall be in the case of the death of priests, whose living brothers will be asked to address the Gods on behalf of Beragar and Devapur, which shall serve in lieu of the doubling tax.

Fifth: I require that all those who work with wood or metal shall donate two days' labor a week to assist in the preparation and stockpiling of weapons.

Those who will not comply are to be confined in my prison until they are willing to do what must be done. During such confinement, no one is to help or shelter the families of the incarcerated; doing so will result in similar imprisonment.

Sixth: I decree that all those having stores of wood and metals are to bring half of them to my palace for the use of the army as weapons. With the single exception of furniture, all wood and all metals are subject to evaluation and inclusion in this seizure.

Anyone attempting to hold back woods and metals will be branded on the arm, the entirety of his woods and metals taken for use of the armorers; a fine of half the value of his belongings shall be imposed on any such man as well. Anyone willing to donate more than is stipulated will receive a ten percent reduction in regular taxes as well as preferred defense of his property and household should the war reach the city walls.

Seventh: I compel all those having beasts of burden or beasts of slaughter to donate ten percent of their animals to the army for their use. For those having fewer than ten animals, I require the following substitutions: one lamb, one chicken, or one goose for every five sheep, chickens, or geese owned by the man in question, to be given to the army procurers within three days of notice by them.

Failure to provide the required animals to the army procurers will result in the seizure of all but one of each creature stipulated. In the case of donkeys, asses, and horses, all such animals will be taken. For those possessing an elephant, the use of the animal by the army for a period of a year is demanded, and the use of the elephant does not exempt its owner from any other assessments made against him, his household, his animals, or his property.

This is the sum of my Will at this time, and to it I have set my hand: by the dark of the year we shall be prepared for war.

Hasin Dahele
Rajput of Beragar

1

They lay tangled in their sheets, her leg across his, her head on his arm, his hand in her hair. From the open window the night wind bore in the scents of blooming and rotting flowers mixed with the more distant tang of smelted ore from the foundry located a short walk from the palace; this single reminder kept it apparent that the appearance of peace was illusory, for otherwise the whole of the city of Devapur presented the semblance of prosperity and the outward display of invulnerability.

In the fortnight since they had arrived at Devapur, Sanat Ji Mani and Tulsi had settled into a kind of routine, visiting Hasin Dahele every few days, having polite discussions that seemed to be cordial enough but without much substance; occasionally the poet Vayu Ede joined them, but most of the time he did not, preferring what seemed to be chance encounters in the corridors, or after sunset in the gardens. The servants of the palace treated Sanat Ji Mani and Tulsi with respect, presenting them with more fine new clothes and offering them savory meals: generally they were left to their own devices so long as they remained inside the palace grounds; Sanat Ji Mani had not yet been able to discover what Vayu Ede had meant: *I know who you are.*

Tulsi stirred, blinked at Sanat Ji Mani, and settled down on his shoulder. "You were not asleep, were you?"

He gave a single, small shake to his head. "I sleep very little."

She laughed softly. "And during the day."

"Whenever possible," he said.

She considered him seriously, contemplating his attractive, irregular features in the spill of moonlight. "Tonight would make four times," she said after a long silence.

"Yes; it would," he agreed. The silken sheets rippled on his silk-wrapped shoulder like water; he did his best to smile at her, curious to discover what she intended.

"I would still be safe from you, would I not?" She laid one hand on his cheek where he had shaven off his beard.

"Yes, for this time and the next. After that, you would become one of my blood upon your death," he reminded her. He shifted a little so that his night-robe would not bind against his arm.

"I understand that," she said. "Does that mean we can only make love six times, and then must stop?"

"No. There is no limit on how often while you live if you are willing to come to my life later. If you are not, then five times is all you can be sure is safe. Six times generally ensures you will come to my life when you die." He said nothing more, waiting for her to decide.

"Well, tonight at least, let us make love. I have now and another time before I must make a final decision, do I not?" She stretched to kiss him, all the hesitation that had worked upon her now gone; her mouth was eager on his, her lips open, her tongue busy. Her hand slid into the top of his robe, moving over his deep chest and down to the top of his scars. Breaking off the kiss, she said, "I cannot imagine how dreadful this must have been."

"It was: dreadful." He did not stop her touching the white band of skin, although he found it unnerving.

"You must have suffered a lot," she went on, still keeping her hand on the hard, white skin. "They took so much."

"I do not remember it well," he lied; the event remained vivid in his memory through all the centuries since it happened. "I know I howled with the pain of it."

"So did my father—he howled," said Tulsi, and moved to kiss him again.

Evading her kiss, Sanat Ji Mani said, "I hope it did not last long, for both your sakes," with a depth of feeling that surprised Tulsi; little as he liked to admit it, he was troubled by combining such memories with their awakening passion.

"It seemed ages and ages, but it was just an afternoon," she answered, staring at the bright wedge of moonlight that lit the foot of their bed. "I can still remember the smell."

"You should not have had to see it," said Sanat Ji Mani. "You should not have been there."

"Timur-i commanded that everyone see," said Tulsi. "I hid some of the time, but I heard it all." She put her hand on his chest. "Do you not want me to become one of your blood, Sanat Ji Mani—is that it?"

"No, it is not," said Sanat Ji Mani. "If I wanted that, I would never have touched you, no matter how famished I became."

She stared at him for a while. "You are a very strange creature, Sanat Ji Mani," she said finally, and resumed the seductive movements of her hand, but this time staying above the line of scar tissue, along his chest and shoulder, softly insistent. "I still want to know why— why would you not take what you needed from me? We were all alone on the road. No one would have stopped you."

"Because," he said as patiently as he could, growing tired of repetition, "I wanted more than your blood. If you doubt that now—"

"No," she said, stifling a giggle. "I just like to hear you say it: you want more."

He touched her face tenderly. "Never doubt it." At the back of his compelling eyes was an ancient pain, one that took her unaware.

"Have I upset you?" She moved closer to him, seeking consolation as much as wanting to bestow it. "I did not mean to."

"It is not you, Tulsi; it is something from long before I knew you," he said, remembering Nicoris, and how she died the True Death.

"It is another woman," said Tulsi with an irritated tinge to her words. "It *is*, Sanat Ji Mani. Do not lie to me."

"No; I will not lie." He fingered the opening of her silken robe. "I was recalling another woman, yes, but not in comparison." It was far more complicated than that, but he did not know how to explain it without causing Tulsi distress.

"I cannot believe that. Why else would you think of her now?" She pushed herself up so that she was half-sitting beside him, both hands joined and holding her raised knee.

"I would think of her because she, too, did not want to believe my love." He said it simply, making no excuses, offering no larger explanation.

"Was she like me?" Tulsi demanded.

"No: no one is like you, or like her," said Sanat Ji Mani, his eyes on hers until she looked away. "Tulsi?"

Tulsi considered this for several moments, her expression distant. Then she looked down at him. "I have a favor to ask of you, Sanat Ji Mani."

"I will do it if I am able. What is it?" The steady assurance in his response gave her the courage to go on.

"For tonight, and the next night, can we pretend I am the only woman? The only one you have ever had, or ever will have? That there have been no others?" The plaintiveness of her request moved him.

"You do not want me to lie," he pointed out, "and that would be lying."

Outside the window a night-bird began to sing, its liquid melody pouring out through the garden, as sweet as a serenade; Sanat Ji Mani had an instant's recollection of being a troubador in France, fifty years before, and wishing he had been able to improvise just such a wonderful song then.

"No," she protested. "It would be *pretending*. I know there have been others and will be others, but just for now, let me pretend that I am the only one. Please."

Sanat Ji Mani was uncertain how to answer her. "I cannot deny the love I have had, as I cannot deny loving you."

"I do not ask you to *deny* it," she said, exasperation making her curt.

"You want me to pretend," he said before she could repeat it. "You would like me to have my love be for you and no one else."

"Yes. Tonight, and the next time we lie together. Say you love me and only me. Or, if you cannot do that, say nothing of anyone else. If there is a time after that, I know it will have to be different. But I want you to see: I have never had someone who was mine alone. I would like to know what it is like." She leaned toward him a bit, laying her hand along his face. "You can do this; I know you can."

"But almost no one has had someone who was theirs and theirs alone, even the women in the hareems have children, if they are fortunate, as well as their husbands, and devoted as they are to the man they have married, they defend their children most constantly," Sanat Ji Mani said. "To suppose otherwise is an illusion; and those who do have one and only one person to complement their lives are not always pleased with the arrangement."

"I do not care," she said petulantly.

"It would lessen what we are to each other," he said as kindly as he could. "Why do you ask it of me?"

She tossed her head, letting her hair fall about her shoulders in soft disarray. "It is what I want: is it so impossible?"

Sanat Ji Mani rolled onto his side and laid his hand on her joined ones. "No, Tulsi. It is not impossible," he said, his voice low. "All right. If you like, tonight there is just you and me, no one else, ever. I will love you and only you."

She sighed. "Thank you." Beneath his hand, her fingers loosened.

"Do you know what else you want?" He carried her nearer hand to his lips, kissing each finger and then the palm.

"Yes, and I know I cannot have it," she said, glancing at him and away, pulling her hand out of his.

"Ah. You would prefer me not to be impotent," he said with understanding sympathy. "That I cannot change." He was surprised that she would be willing to set aside her dread of pregnancy for him, but also suspected that one of the reasons she wished for it was its safe impossibility.

In the garden, the serenade had become a duet, two birds twining melodies together in an endless string of variations. They rhapsodized leggiadrously, expanding their song as they went, as if to enchant the whole palace with their spell.

"It is unfortunate," said Tulsi, and added nothing more.

Sanat Ji Mani let himself be charmed by the birds, eventually reaching out to Tulsi, running his hand along the silk covering her arm. "This is lovely cloth, but your skin is far more exquisite."

Tulsi began to smile. "Do you like it, really? My hands are rough from my work." She looked down at her short, blunt nails and her worn palms with their calluses and healed cuts.

"Not so rough that they are incapable of caresses," he said, seeking to give her the sense of satisfaction she longed for.

"Perhaps, if you have not had softer," she murmured.

"I will not make comparisons," said Sanat Ji Mani.

"Then I will: I have seen the Rajput's women once or twice; they are like wonderful flowers. I am a weed." Tulsi pointed to the well-defined muscles in her leg. "I am not soft and pliant as they are."

"Oh, you are pliant," said Sanat Ji Mani with a hint of laughter. "I have seen you bend backward, balance on your forearms, and rest your feet on your head. As beautiful as the Rajput's women may be, they are incapable of half your feats."

"That is not what I meant," said Tulsi, trying to look haughty and instead appearing vainglorious. She quickly changed her demeanor. "I sometimes wish I could be more like them."

"From what I know of you, you would enjoy it for a day or two, and then the restrictions would chafe at you and you would long for the market-place and a crowd to watch your tumbling," said Sanat Ji Mani. "You are too free-spirited for the life those women live. Think how confined they are."

"They are confined," she agreed, "but they are cared for."

He studied her face, trying to find the source of her distress. "That they are, because they must be," he said, tracing the line of her brow, her cheek, her jaw with one delicate finger. "They cannot manage for themselves."

"They are freer than the women of a hareem," said Tulsi, following the movement of his finger as if it left a trail of scented oil. She arched into the caress as a cat would, doing her utmost to feel the whole of his touch.

"While that is true, it is also an admission of limitation," said Sanat Ji Mani, continuing down her neck to her collar-bone, tracing its elegant bend from neck to shoulder and back again, unhurried and sensuous.

"I could not live in a hareem," Tulsi admitted, and took a sharp breath as his finger began to descend through the loose opening of her robe.

"No, I do not think you could," said Sanat Ji Mani, opening his small hand so all his fingers were touching her, moving between her breasts; Sanat Ji Mani rose enough to be able to face her, both hands now working on her flesh without haste, luxurious as the feel of silk, but more persuasive; her robe was open from top to bottom, giving him access to her body and concealing her flesh at the same time. All the while he watched her face, seeing every nuance of expression and using it as a guide to her gratification.

"Why is it?" Tulsi asked suddenly, "That women must be wholly subjected to men? I know the priests say it is what their gods all command, but they are men themselves."

"That they are," said Sanat Ji Mani, still stroking her. "You are not so very subjected to men, are you."

"Not as much as many women; they do not even think about it, do they?" she conceded. "But I am still— It is unfair."

"Yes. It is unfair," he agreed.

"And there is no way to avoid it," she said. "If I am to be with you, it must be as your woman."

"That is not what I want, Tulsi." Sanat Ji Mani regarded her steadily. "I do not think it will satisfy you."

"I want all this with you, and more, but I do not want to capitulate to my desires." She stopped his hands and half-closed her robe.

"I wish you were more able to trust me," said Sanat Ji Mani, watching her with dawning ruefulness in his eyes. "I cannot undo what has been done, but I am sorry I cannot bridge the gap. You deserve better."

"It is not a lack of trust, exactly," she said.

"What is it, then?" he asked.

She took a little time to gather her courage. "If I come to your life, I will not have to devote myself to you, will I?"

Sanat Ji Mani shook his head. "No; you will have to make your own life. All those of my blood must do so. Those who do not," he added, wincing inwardly at the image of Csimenae, "put themselves and all of our kind in danger."

She nodded. "I see." For a short while she sat unmoving, then she took his hands in hers. "Go on. I want you to go on."

He recommenced his ministrations, still moving slowly, all the while contemplating her face. "I will not demand anything of you that you do not wish to give, now or ever; I do not love that way," he promised her. "It would appall me if you suffered on my account any more than you have already." Gradually he eased her robe open again.

Tulsi's eyes were half-closed. "Better wandering the roads with you than riding in a wagon with Timur-i's army," she murmured.

For a response, he moved a little closer to her, using his lips to accentuate what his hands were doing, to enhance the pleasure he gave; her shivers and sighs marked his progress and led him to more discoveries as the silken robe brushed against his face. He did not speak, concentrating instead on unspoken things, and their touching, where sensation blurred and ran between them, anticipating the moment of fusion when their contact would reach to the depths of their souls.

"How do you . . ." She paused as new feelings awakened in her, some of them in her body, some in a more remote quarter, "um . . . do you . . . you . . ." She was silent but for her deepened breathing.

He did not shift his position, but he broadened his search; his hands moved leisurely, deliciously, from her breasts to her hips and back again, never demanding, never intrusive; he felt her begin to move with his hands, and ardor glowed in his dark eyes. His mouth grazed her taut belly and moved lower, gradually working his way to her opening legs. He found the nubbin that awakened to his touch, thrumming as wonderfully as the birds' song. Lingeringly he began to draw out the first trembling prelude to fulfillment; he would not rush her, and so, when her release came, he did not cease his coaxing, but continued to evoke pleasure from her until a second, more intense culmination shook her the length of her body and to the limits of her passion. He cradled her in his arms, their bodies touching from neck to knee, while her elation reached its greatest peak of intimacy, then began to fade; he lifted his head from her neck.

Her head was thrown back, her eyes closed with the enormity of her abandon, and the joy that suffused her face was like sunlight. Gradually she returned to herself, opening her eyes slowly, as if reluctant to give up the rapture she had achieved. "I did not know," she said at last.

"I hoped," said Sanat Ji Mani, still holding her close to him.

"Nothing ever—" She moved enough to be able to lean forward and kiss him; in the garden the birds' song seemed suddenly very loud. "You never told me—"

"There are things that cannot be told, only felt," Sanat Ji Mani said, kissing her gently on the arch of her brow.

"But how did you know?" She put her hands on the back of his neck and held their faces less than a thumb's-length apart. "You *knew*."

"I hoped," he repeated, meeting her luminous gaze with his own.

She took a deep breath. "The other times this did not happen, not this way. It was pleasant before, very pleasant, and I was satisfied. But this—"

"I had not yet made myself trustworthy to you," Sanat Ji Mani told her. "I am honored that you are willing to trust me."

"How can this be a question of trust? Why should trust matter?" she asked, and brought one hand around to stop him from speaking. "Do not tell me anything. I do not want to be told. I will think about it, and then you and I will discuss what I have learned, when I understand more than I do now."

He nodded. "If this is what you want," he said around her fingers.

"It is," she said, letting go of him and lying back, her happiness already diminished by what she knew was around her. "I feel as if I could fly off into the night, that I could fly across the world."

"A wonderful feeling," he said, stretching out beside her.

She stared up at the ceiling. "I wonder if I am dreaming, if all this is nothing more than a sleep-vision, and that I will wake in the morning and it will fade; I will forget it all, and you will have no notion what I mean when I say that you lifted me out of the world." She smiled her contentment. "Even if it is only a dream, it is a splendid one."

Sanat Ji Mani touched her nearer hand. "It is no dream. In the morning you may be sure of it."

Suddenly her eyes opened and she turned to him in alarm. "When we do this, it does not hurt your foot, does it?"

He chuckled. "No, Tulsi, it does not hurt my foot." In fact, he added to himself, the nourishment she provided would help to heal the lag-mending wound.

"Oh. Good." She closed her eyes once more, and sprawled back on the cushions at the head of the bed. "This had better not be a dream."

"My Word on it; it is not," he said, his voice deep and sweet. "If you doubt it, touch your neck and you will know better."

She murmured a few fragments of words as she succumbed to slumber; her breathing grew regular, her body relaxed, and her face softened. After a little while, she said, "Loving," and a bit later, she added, "Keep safe."

Sanat Ji Mani lay beside her hardly moving, his body still feeling the last thrill of their intimacy; he kept watching her and listening to the birds with their limitless improvisation; the moonlight slid across the bed and started up the far wall before the sky paled and the night-birds gave way to the dawn chorus of day-thriving creatures. All the while he could not rid himself of the conviction that he and Tulsi were under observation, a thought that made him uneasy. As dawn broke in the east, Sanat Ji Mani rose long enough to shutter the window, and to return to the bed for a morning of slumber.

When he awoke, Tulsi was busy practicing her tumbling and ac-robatics in the limited space of their room. Sitting up in bed, Sanat Ji Mani watched her, admiring the limberness and strength of her body, and the expert control she had achieved.

Although she did not stop her work, she said to him, "You had better ask the servants for food. They will wonder if you do not."

"What would you like to eat?" Sanat Ji Mani asked as he rose from the bed.

"A little fruit and some fowl. I have had breakfast already, some time ago." She did a back-flip, then sank into the splits. "I need to practice in a larger space."

"I will see what can be arranged." He shed his robe and reached for the loose pyjamas of embroidered dark-red silk the Rajput had provided him. Dressing quickly, he was just buttoning the front of the long, skirted tunic when a palace servant presented himself to ask for his orders. "I would like some fruit and a leg of fowl, if you would."

The servant pressed his palms together and bowed double, saying, "At once, Honored Guest."

As soon as the servant was gone, Tulsi sighed. "I wish I knew the language they speak. I recognize a few words, but for the most part, I might as well be deaf and mute." She brought one leg up along her body and guided her foot behind her head. "In this place they are not so impressed with these postures," she said as she did the same with the other leg. "Their mystics tie themselves in all manner of knots. I would not bother to practice them, but I must keep working to retain my flexibility."

"A sensible precaution," said Sanat Ji Mani. "It may not impress the people of Devapur, but it impresses me."

"Then I shall continue," she announced, and got herself out of her tangle of limbs. "Could you teach me to speak their tongue?"

"I do not speak it expertly," he reminded her. "But I can help you to learn a few phrases that can be useful." He sat down on the hassock farthest away from the window. "If you decide to come to my life, you will need to learn how to acquire a language, so you can travel more easily." He contemplated the air. "First, listen to the habitual words: greetings, affirmations, negations, names. This will give you a feel for the forms of the language. Then learn the words for specific things, such as the foods you like, landmarks, clothing, and all manner of things. With that much you can make yourself understood at a rudimentary level. Then you need the words of action: give, take, move, put down, and all the rest."

"I know a few words; I have figured them out. I can recognize a number of names, or perhaps titles. But I do not know enough to use them." She was walking on her hands, approaching and retreating.

"Listen carefully, and you will learn more," said Sanat Ji Mani. "When the servant brings the food, pay attention to what he says, and we will discuss it when he has gone."

"Very well," she agreed, hopping along on her hands. "You should have seen me perform for Timur-i—I would go through six hoops of fire, each one in a different way, and end up on a pole, holding myself out to the side, like a banner in a stiff wind. He gave me silver coins for doing it. I mistimed once, and set my hair on fire."

"What did Timur-i do?" Sanat Ji Mani asked, looking at her askance.

"He laughed," she said. "Timur-i finds the misfortunes of others amusing." There was no condemnation in her tone, no self-pity in her demeanor. "He gave me extra coins because I finished the performance."

"As well he might," said Sanat Ji Mani. "You were in grave danger."

"Not so much as those who work with bears, or tigers." She sat down not far from him. "I have seen a tiger swipe a man's head off with a playful pat. The worst that has ever happened to me was a broken arm, years ago; my parents were still alive. One of the farriers set it, and it healed straight and true."

"You were lucky," he said.

"Not so very much: if the farrier had bungled the work, Timur-i would have had him stoned to death." Tulsi shrugged. "He does not accept failure."

"That is apparent," Sanat Ji Mani agreed, looking up as there came a knock at the door. "Yes? Who is it?"

"I have brought your food, Honored Guest," said the servant, his voice raised only enough to carry through the door.

"How much of that did you understand?" Sanat Ji Mani asked Tulsi quietly, calling out, "I will come shortly."

"I think he said food and called you what all the servants call you," she replied.

"Very good." He got up and went to the door where the servant was waiting with a brass tray. "I will take that."

"Let me, Honored Guest," the servant protested.

"You are kind, but among those of my blood, eating is a private thing. I thank you for bringing this. I will return it when I am done," Sanat Ji Mani said as he took the tray from the servant's hands. He was about to step back into his room when something occurred to him. "Why is the foundry so busy?"

"The foundry?" The servant seemed mildly surprised by the question. "They are making weapons. I thought you knew."

Sanat Ji Mani shook his head. "Why are they doing that?"

"In your honor." The servant bowed deeply. "We are preparing for war."

Text of a report from Azizi Iniattir at Sirpur to Rustam Iniattir in Fustat.

To my most excellent kinsman and worthy uncle, the greetings of your obedient nephew at Sirpur, and the prayers of my family for the welfare and happiness of your own.

The goods you shipped to me have arrived and I am eager to get them to the markets around me and on to those our caravans can reach, particularly the textiles and the fine vessels. These are unlike most seen in this region, as you know, and for that reason alone should fetch a good price. I shall set my older sons to making arrangements for the sale of these items. As to the jewelry from Venice—wherever that may be—I do not know what market we may discover for them. They are unlike what is worn here, but their novelty may be enough to create interest in the pieces. As you say, they are small and can bring a good price for each piece—providing someone wants them.

I am waiting for the arrival of our caravan to Assam, for there should be goods in those chests that will be most useful to you. I would like to think that you will be able to sell jade where you are, and the brass bells that so many caravan-drivers like. I have also been told that there will be some fine knives and daggers in that load, and those most surely will be good items for you to offer to the merchants of Fustat.

I anticipate sending a new shipment to you after the dark of the year, which is coming more rapidly than I would like to admit. Soon it will be a full year since Timur-i sacked Delhi and all our of family was thrown into confusion. I cannot yet grasp the enormity of that event, although I have seen for myself its impact upon the land and on the people. I will include in the shipment as much information as I have been able to piece together about what has befallen those who were residents of Delhi and have been scattered to the winds as if they were seeds in a field. I have asked the caravan-leaders to make inquiry wherever they go, and I am gradually assembling enough information that it could be useful, and that I will gladly pass on to you.

The rains are heavy this year; since they began in midsummer, we have had to deal with flooding. Already we have been taxed to help pay for a replacement bridge and to clear a landslide from the road. I do not often want to lay our money, but in these instances, the results will benefit me and our family, and so I have sent double the amount to the Rajput here, with the request that half of it be held in reserve against other emergencies. I am certain this degree of participation in the welfare of this region will stand us in good stead at other times.

We are beginning to hope that our fortunes will be restored in part before another two years pass—that is, if there are no new battles or plagues to impinge on our business and to rob us of our caravans. I have made offerings to gain us the favor of Light, as I know you must *have done. I do not want to see us in such straits as we have been, and I am prepared to devote myself to bringing about our complete restoration of wealth and reputation. I ask you to join me in this venture, for without you, I cannot do any of this without placing myself beyond the family, which it is not my intention to do. When you have decided, send me word, and I will abide by your edict; I also pray that your thoughts are in accord with mine, so that all our family may prosper and flourish once again.*

With all respect and devotion, I dispatch this to you with the ardent hope that you will have it in hand before the dark of the year is sixty days gone.

Azizi Iniattir
Merchant of Sirpur

2

On the west side, the garden was deep in shadow, and it was there that Sanat Ji Mani found Vayu Ede sitting through the slow afternoon; the poet held a writing-board on his lap and was putting verses down on a scroll.

"Oh," he said, looking up as Sanat Ji Mani approached him in his garments of mulberry-colored silk that blended with the flowers on the shrubs; he rolled the scroll closed at once.

"The ink will smear if you do not let it dry," said Sanat Ji Mani.

"If it is fitting that the words be lost, then so much the better," said Vayu Ede. "Verse is always struggling to escape its words in any case." He set the writing-board aside and put a lid on his ink-well.

"Very true," said Sanat Ji Mani, preparing to take a seat on the opposite bench. "You told the servants you wanted to see me? Here?"

"Yes; yes, I did," said Vayu Ede. "I believe it is time we spoke of— oh, any number of things."

"What might those things be?" Sanat Ji Mani said, finding himself on guard and concealing it. "What do you want to tell me?"

Vayu Ede shrugged. "What might *you* want to tell *me*? You are a man with a secret, that much is established."

"Everyone has secrets," Sanat Ji Mani countered with a cordial smile. "Who among us reaches the end of childhood without a host of his own?"

"You prefer the shadows, I see," Vayu Ede observed, as if he had not changed the subject. "Is there anything that bothers you about the light?"

"I burn readily," said Sanat Ji Mani. "For that reason and many others I find the sun can be exhausting."

"Yes; it can." Vayu Ede gestured an invitation to sit. "I have not seen you outside the palace during the day, or at least not since you arrived."

Sanat Ji Mani sank onto the marble bench, choosing the end where the shadows were deepest. "I have preferred to remain indoors, and since Rajput Hasin Dahele has been kind enough to allow me this favor, I have been able to keep from exposing myself to the sun, for which I am very much grateful. Is that why you asked me to come to the garden during the day: to see how I would fare in sunlight?"

"I did not have any presuppositions, but it does appear you are hiding," Vayu Ede observed.

"Does it seem so to you? Then why did you require my presence here—to establish that I fear discovery?" Sanat Ji Mani spoke lightly enough, but his eyes were intent, the blue that flickered in their black depths like a flame.

"I invited you; you make it sound as if I commanded you," said Vayu Ede.

"Given the way in which I and my companion have been received, I would not think a command would be so unexpected." Sanat Ji Mani's features were world-weary now, reflecting his long experience with the high price of favor.

"There is some truth in your expectation," said Vayu Ede.

"And what truth is that?" Sanat Ji Mani inquired. "How am I expected to express my gratitude?"

"It is a good thing that you know when to be grateful. But you have no doubt learned such things in your travels," said Vayu Ede.

"Yes," said Sanat Ji Mani, somewhat puzzled by this remark.

Vayu Ede said nothing for a short while, then remarked as if resuming a conversation, "You have some experience of war, have you not?"

"More than I want," said Sanat Ji Mani.

"Ah, yes; many brave men say this as they get older. No doubt you have had time to think about all war has done for you." Vayu Ede tried to appear nonchalant, and failed. "You said your father's land was usurped by your enemies."

"That was a long time ago," said Sanat Ji Mani, thinking back through the intervening centuries to the Carpathians, and the kingdom his father had maintained there.

"Your father and his father and his father before him ruled there: do I understand that correctly?" Vayu Ede put his scroll into the pouch on his belt.

"I told you that some days ago," Sanat Ji Mani said.

"Bear with me for a while, if you would," said Vayu Ede. "Your enemies came from the East, or so you said. Have I got that right?"

"The east and the south," said Sanat Ji Mani, remembering the clients of the Hittites who had over-run his father's kingdom.

"You had allies in the West?" Vayu Ede asked, his tone of voice unchanged.

"I do not know if you would call them allies: those of my people who could escape went westward. It is not quite the same thing. Eventually they settled in a new land; they became a new people, and forgot the old kingdom in the mountains, or most of them did." Sanat Ji Mani had seen where his people had gone, more than a century after they had been defeated by the Romans, when their new kingdom was old.

"A kingdom in the West," said Vayu Ede.

"Yes," said Sanat Ji Mani. "West of where the people began." He was careful not to name the people or the lands they had occupied; he was sure that Vayu Ede wanted to know those things, and by holding them back, Sanat Ji Mani felt he had not given up more than he should to this odd old man.

"I see," said Vayu Ede, thoughtfully pulling at his lower lip.

Sanat Ji Mani waited for what was to come next; he did not move, nor did he do anything to suggest he was uneasy. When Vayu Ede stared at him, he endured it without staring back. He finally said, "If you have no reason to keep me here, I would prefer to return to the palace."

Vayu Ede behaved as if he had not heard this. "You have said you saw Delhi in ruins, did you not?"

"I did," said Sanat Ji Mani. "It was a direful sight, one I should not want to see again, or its like." He tried to read Vayu Ede's expression and failed.

"You also said you were bound for Lahore when you and your companion were accidentally separated from Timur-i's army—do I have that right?" Vayu Ede offered Sanat Ji Mani an encouraging smile.

"Yes. That is what happened," Sanat Ji Mani answered.

Vayu Ede put his hands together in a gesture of contemplation. "A most interesting account. We hear many things in this part of the world but we rarely have the opportunity to have a first-hand report given to us. It is most helpful to our plans. I thank you for this."

"I cannot imagine how any of this will serve you, but if something I have said is useful, I am glad of it." Sanat Ji Mani squinted up through the leaves, trying to calculate how much longer he could remain exposed and not burn again.

Vayu Ede noticed this. "You are uncomfortable." He looked up toward the sun. "I do not want to cause you any more discomfort. Return to the palace, if you like."

Sanat Ji Mani rose. "You are kind; I thank you."

"Your thanks are appreciated," said Vayu Ede. "I will remember them in times to come." He leaned back as if he intended to rest a while.

It was a curious remark to make, Sanat Ji Mani thought, but said, "Your gods favor and care for you." He began to move away.

"Sanat Ji Mani," Vayu Ede called after him, as if a last detail had just occurred to him, "it is a pity about your limp."

"It is inconvenient," Sanat Ji Mani responded, not quite agreeing.

"And you came such a long way on foot, in spite of it," said Vayu Ede.

"With Tulsi Kil's help," Sanat Ji Mani said, puzzled by these remarks.

Chelsea Quinn Yarbro

"Ah, yes. The tumbler. A most interesting companion, I should think; capable in so many ways," he said, and waved Sanat Ji Mani away.

Sanat Ji Mani returned to the palace, trying to decide what Vayu Ede had wanted of him, that he had summoned him to the garden for a conversation that might have taken place anywhere and at any time. He made his way along the now-familiar corridors, his thoughts preoccupied and somewhat troubled. By the time he reached the room assigned to him and Tulsi, he was more concerned than he had been when he left the garden; he stepped through the door and was mildly worried that he did not find Tulsi waiting for him. He recalled she had spoken of her plans to bathe, and, deciding she must have gone to the bath at the end of the hallway, he left his room and went to seek her out. At the door of the bath, he called out her name. "Tulsi. May I come in?"

The answer was a moan.

"Tulsi!" Sanat Ji Mani cried out. "What is it?"

"Can . . . not . . . ." Her voice was weak and thready, and there was the sound of feeble thrashing in the water.

Sanat Ji Mani waited no longer; his strength was not as great as it would have been had his native earth been in the soles of his shoes, but concern fueled his body and he was able to shove the door inward, off its hinges, the noise as loud as an explosion. He stood for an instant, taking stock of the room with its three deep marble bathing pools set in the polished granite floor, and one lavish fountain; satisfied she was alone, he moved to the deepest of the three where Tulsi was holding onto the rim of the large marble basin, her face the color of milk-curds, a mess of metal-scented vomit on the stones. "Tulsi! What has happened?" He did not wait for her answer, pulling her from the water and into his arms with all the urgency he could summon.

"Poison. I think." She looked up at him with glazed eyes. "It was . . . the fowl . . . or the sweet rice-gruel." Her voice was hoarse and each word emerged as if with spikes attached; even breathing seemed painful for her.

"How?" Sanat Ji Mani demanded, then went on, "Tell me later." He wished he still had his vials of medicaments to treat her, but he had run out of them more than two months ago, and could not avail himself of them now. Very gently he laid her down on one of the sheet-covered couches that lined the wall. "Lie still. I am going to bring you water; I want you to drink as much of it as you can, to flush out any lingering poison." He brought one end of the sheet up across her body to dry her.

She blinked. "I . . . was sick."

"A good thing, when you are poisoned," said Sanat Ji Mani as he searched for the ladle to bring her water from the fountain. When he could not find it, he filled his cupped hands and brought her water that way.

Tulsi sputtered as she attempted to swallow, her eyes apologetic all the while. "I did not . . . think . . ."

"That anyone would do this?" Sanat Ji Mani said, his ire concealed under attentiveness. "I would not have thought so, either." He blamed himself that he had not expected something of this sort: anyone enjoying the favor of a ruler—even so minor a one as Hasin Dahele— would acquire enemies as a matter of course: a foreigner like Sanat Ji Mani would be likely to attract more rancor than the usual courtier. "I should have been more on guard, Tulsi; I am sorry you have been hurt on my account."

"No . . . oh, no," she said, and tried to hold on to him as he went to bring another handful of water.

"You have paid a price that was mine, not yours, to pay," he said as he filled his hands again, wishing that they were not so small. He came back to her side and trickled more water into her mouth. "This is not your battle."

"If it . . . is yours," she said, coughing once, "it is mine." She coughed again, and retched, her face turning dark red.

Sanat Ji Mani rolled her onto her side and braced her while she cast up the last of what had been in her stomach. As she began to sob, he held her, ashamed that he had exposed her to such danger; he wrapped the sheet more securely around her. "It is my fault you are hurt," he said, angry with himself for allowing this to happen. "You have only tried to care for me. There is no reason you should have to suffer on my account."

"No," she said. "You have . . . nothing to . . . apologize for." Her lids were getting heavy, and there were tears on her face.

"We will settle that later," he said finally, gently wiping her cheeks. "Let me bring you more water. I do not want any of the poison remaining in you to do more damage." He went to fetch some more, all the while mastering his temper: there was a time, perhaps fifteen hundred years ago, when he would have confronted Hasin Dahele to demand answers for how this had happened, but the intervening centuries had taught him discretion; now he realized he would have to approach this more circumspectly, or leave them both exposed to other assaults. As he carried his handsful of water back to Tulsi, he steadied himself as he prepared to nurse her, for he would not entrust her care to anyone else.

"I . . .'m sleepy," Tulsi muttered as Sanat Ji Mani put more water into her mouth. "Let me . . . sleep."

"You will rest shortly," said Sanat Ji Mani. "For now, I am going to clean the floor and then take you back to our room."

She blinked, chagrined. "You should not . . . it is . . . wrong."

"Tulsi, I have done far worse than clean floors in my time," he said, and went to get a floor-brush and a rag from the basket containing all manner of cleaning gear.

"You must not . . ." Tulsi protested again.

Sanat Ji Mani ignored her as he scrubbed the vomit from the floor and concealed it in the rag. "There. No one will know what happened here," he said as he stood up. He took the rag to the servants' door and dropped it in the basket where other rags were collected. "When they come upon this, they will not be able to tell what happened, or who took care of it."

"I never meant . . . that you . . ." She tried to sit up and groaned with the effort.

"No, Tulsi. Stay where you are. I will carry you." He took stock of the room, his swift perusal catching all the details of the baths. "It is all right."

She held out her hand to him. "I . . . am so . . . sorry," she whispered and began to weep in earnest.

"You have nothing to be sorry for. You did not poison yourself," he said grimly as he went to pick her up. "Your arms around my neck, if you please, and your head on my shoulder," he told her as he carried her toward the door he had ruined. He paused on the threshold for a moment, wondering why the sound of his breaking in had not brought servants running; the reasons that occurred to him were all sinister, and left him feeling more worried than before. He had had enemies before who had moved against him by stealth: Cyprus was still a vivid memory, as was Frater Ignazius.

"I can walk . . . if you . . . put me down," Tulsi offered, not quite struggling to get out of his arms.

"It would be best if I carry you, so no one will know you have been hurt," said Sanat Ji Mani, making his way along the corridor to the room they shared. "Let those who are watching us think we are having a tryst."

"How can they?" she asked, smiling weakly.

"They will see what we want them to see," Sanat Ji Mani told her. "For now, it is useful that they not know of your ordeal."

"Why not?" she asked as he carefully lowered her down onto the bed.

"Because we do not know who poisoned you, or why, and it is important that we not let the poisoner know he succeeded," Sanat Ji Mani said, touching her face tenderly. "Let him believe he has failed in his efforts, and he may reveal himself."

"But . . . might he not . . . strike again?" She put her hand to her throat. "It burns."

"It will improve," said Sanat Ji Mani. "You have my Word."

She nodded, and pinched her nose to try to stop her tears. "I . . . This is . . . foolish."

"Never mind," Sanat Ji Mani said, and straightened up to look for a serving tray that might contain the remnants of her meal; the servants had removed it. "That is inconvenient," he said to himself.

"What is?" Tulsi stared up at him.

"I was hoping to find out what poison was used," he said. "I would like to have known."

"Why?" She used the corner of the drying-sheet to wipe her eyes.

"Because it might give me some notion of who was doing it," said Sanat Ji Mani, a thoughtful frown deepening in a vertical line between his brows.

She lay back, trying not to cough. "Hurts," she said.

"The hurt will stop," said Sanat Ji Mani, wishing he still had syrup of poppies to give her to ease her.

"I know," she whispered. From her place on the bed she studied him, aware that he was shielding her from the worst of his suspicions; it both pleased and aggravated her that he was so protective of her. "What will you do . . . if you find . . . who did this?"

"I do not know; yet," he answered, coming back to her side and bending over her. "At least you are not hot, that is something."

"Would heat be bad?" She took hold of his hand and tightened her grip.

"Yes," he said. "It would."

"It might mean . . . I would die?" She asked this calmly, though her fingers held his like a vice. "Tell me."

"It is possible," he said.

She nodded, accepting this. "Will it matter . . . that I am still . . . alive?"

"To me, most certainly," he said. "But for the poisoner, who knows? It may be that you were not supposed to die, only to be frightened." Or, he added to himself, that I was the one the poisoner wanted to kill.

"Or the poison . . . might have been . . . for you." She seemed to know his thoughts. "They do not know . . . you do not eat."

"The thought had crossed my mind," he said drily. "But whether the intended victim was you or me, it still means that we have at least one enemy in this place, and very likely more." He glanced around the room. "What bothers me is that I cannot tell why."

"It may be . . . jealousy," Tulsi suggested.

"It may. Or there may be another reason entirely."

"What reason?" She coughed a little, averting her face as if embarrassed.

"I think we are being held for ransom," he said, more bluntly than he had intended. "I think the Rajput is planning to barter with Timur-i, trading influence for us."

"But why should he . . . do that? Timur-i has no . . . use for us," she whispered.

"I have not yet learned enough to know," said Sanat Ji Mani gently. "But it seems that Vayu Ede believes I avoid daylight because I am afraid of being seen. What else would cause him to think that, than that you and I have someone to fear? And I have admitted being with Timur-i's army." He was annoyed with himself for revealing so much to the poet.

"I know," said Tulsi.

"Vayu Ede and Hasin Dahele must have plans for us. They are keeping us isolated, and the Rajput is arming his country for war." Sanat Ji Mani frowned. "I should have seen it before now."

"Why?" she asked.

"I have been about the world enough to know that ambition leaves its mark on men." Sanat Ji Mani stroked her hand. "I should have seen it in the Rajput, but—"

"Timur-i is . . . in Samarkand," said Tulsi, and cleared her throat.

"I doubt the Rajput knows that." He paused thoughtfully. "Considering what happened at Delhi, I cannot blame him for his apprehension."

"Is that . . . all of it?" She stared up at him, her grey-green eyes pleading with him for reassurance.

"I cannot tell. Not yet." He looked toward the window. "I fear I have been foolish. I must do what I can to remedy that."

Tulsi lifted her hand to touch his face. "You found us protection . . . and safety. That . . . is not foolish."

"It may prove not," he said. "If I can find out what is happening. If we are hostages, we will have to be especially careful."

"How will you know . . . if we are?" Her voice was growing more hushed, but she persevered. "What will you do . . . to find out?"

"I have not decided." There was a keenness in his eyes that held her attention.

"When you do . . . will you . . . tell me?"

"Yes, Tulsi, I will tell you," he said in a tone that brooked no doubts. She pulled his hand to her. "And I . . . will help you."

"We shall see," he said, aware that she would need time to recover and that during that time she would be vulnerable.

"I . . . will help you," she repeated, determination lending sound to her words.

"You have done more than anyone could ask already. If you would please me, help me by recovering." He wanted to remove her from all danger, but knew that was impossible.

"I will . . . help you . . . to help myself," she said.

He could not argue with her. "Very well; but do not tax yourself. The poison was powerful and you will need time to regain your strength," he said. "You cannot hurry healing."

"As your . . . foot shows," she said, doing her best to sound relieved.

"It is not the same thing," he told her, his voice sharper. "I know I will heal in time; you do not yet know how badly you have been injured; I implore you to let your body restore itself at its own rate."

"If I were like you . . . if you made me . . . like you . . . would I die?" She stared at him, her eyes unreadable.

"Yes, but you would not remain dead." He tried not to remember his hasty decision to save Csimenae by bringing her to his life, and what had followed that well-meaning but reckless decision. "It is for you to decide."

"With so . . . many enemies, I confess . . . I would be . . . less worried if . . . I knew I . . . was safe from harm," she whispered.

He made a gesture of frustration. "We are fighting shadows."

"Worse than shadows," said Tulsi.

Sanat Ji Mani nodded. "Yes; worse than shadows."

"Is there . . . nothing we can do? Now?" She twisted his hand with the force of her emotion.

He bore it, knowing she had to release her feelings somehow. "Perhaps. We must be careful and clever. And we must not be frightened: frightened people make terrible mistakes and we can afford none."

"I am not . . . frightened; I . . . am angry," she said, and ended in a cough as the full strength of her rage shook her; it shocked her to be so taken by wrath.

"Yes," said Sanat Ji Mani, taking her hand and bending to kiss her palm. "But anger can make you rash, and that may lead to more trouble than you are prepared to endure. You have had too much to deal with already."

"But I . . . am angry," she said, almost choking.

"Well and good," he said, "Let the anger work for you, not against you."

She regarded him skeptically. "Against me?"

He nodded. "You could be spurred by it to take chances in the hope of returning hurt for hurt and only make it easier to be hurt again. Fury, like grief, can suspend your good sense, which you need, especially now, for our enemy has shown his hand, and that means he is becoming desperate. Desperate men are as foolish as frightened ones." He had seen that demonstrated so many times in his centuries of life that he had come to expect it. "School your mind as you school your body and you will prevail."

Tulsi contemplated his face. "Will you . . . be angry for me?"

"I am," he said with purpose. "I will."

She managed to smile. "Then I will . . . be content."

Text of a letter from Atta Olivia Clemens in Rome to Rogerian in Alexandria; written in the Latin of Imperial Rome.

To that most excellent and long-suffering manservant Rogerian, the respectful greetings of Atta Olivia Clemens from within the city of Rome.

It truly is vexing to have Sanct' Germain gone for so long—it reminds me unpleasantly of Spain and all the efforts you made to find him after he escaped the Emir's son. It is possible, of course, that he has sent you messages that have not reached you: it has happened often enough before. Still, since neither you nor I have had anything from him, I cannot help but believe that he is at some disadvantage and must be unable to get a letter out to us. However, I do not yet think it advisable for you to go looking for him; one of the two of you missing is sufficient, and as I know he has not died the True Death, it is probably wisest to remain where he can find you than to go chasing back to that foreign place in the hope of locating him.

In your letter you tell me that Avasa Dani has found a house that will suit her enterprise and you ask me if you should make the arrangements she requests. Consider her situation: she is a woman, alone, in a country that has little use for women beyond their bodies. What else is she to do? I cannot see how you can deny her, for although it is not what I would choose, it is what she wishes to do, and Sanct' Germain has said he will provide her a living. He has, has he not? And you are honor-bound to see that his pledge is carried out. You may not see the advantage in her plans, but, given what you have told me about her, I am certain that there is merit in her scheme. She is not a woman who knows how to live apart from men, nor does she want to learn to. Her plan to establish a house of assignation is a reasonable one, at least in Alexandria, where such houses are customary and have been for two thousand years. There would have been a time when you would not have hesitated, when the Romans ruled there and the laws of Rome prevailed everywhere. That was the Rome of my living youth. This is not the Rome I knew when I was a child, when the women of the lupanar had their own fortunes and the high regard of the city, but even today, a woman, well-placed and discreet, can make a life for herself. And since this Avasa Dani does not intend to whore herself, but to manage the house, she will undoubtedly become as powerful as women may who have not married powerful men. Be sure she has someone to guard her, and let her take care of the rest. I do not mean to chide you, but I think that Avasa Dani has made a sensible decision, and one that will allow her to protect her true nature most effectively.

You may wonder why I am living within Rome's walls again: I must tell you that I returned to discover my villa was missing most of its roof, which has been temporarily replaced to keep out the winter rains, and then, when the weather improves, there will be new tiles put in place. A few of the walls may have to be rebuilt, and I may decide to expand the north wing while I am about it. This will take time, so I have engaged a house on the Palatine Hill, where I can keep a garden and a small stable. It is suitable for a widow, and although the cost of maintaining it is ridiculous, I have laid out the necessary gold and will remain here until my villa is habitable again. I have reprimanded my steward for neglecting the place so shamefully. Niklos Aulirios is dividing his time between tending to me and supervising the necessary repairs. The only worthwhile outcome has been that I have had an opportunity to renew my acquaintance with the Papal Court—and what a viper's nest it is.

You cannot imagine how the factions have been sniping at one another while His Holiness Boniface IX of the Roman Obedience does his best to be rid of Benedict XIII in Avignon. I thought there was trouble before, but now, I might as well be at the Sultan's Court, with all the intrigue for which the Turks are famous, for they have nothing on this quagmire. Two Popes allied with two countries is madness, and you may see it in all they do. If these men suppose they are serving any purpose but their own, they must have lost their wits. Surely they cannot believe that they are benefitting their religion with such skull-duggery: I cannot imagine how they could conduct themselves more reprehensibly than they are doing now. However, they may yet find actions more appalling than what I have seen to heap more shame on themselves and their Church. They would undoubtedly burn me at the stake for what I have just written, so I ask that you destroy this letter when you have done with it. I have no desire to die the True Death just now, or at such messy hands as theirs.

They say the King of England is in prison and his cousin, Henry, son of John of Gaunt, rules in his stead. If that is so, it will, I fear, incite more hatred within the Plantagenets and may lead to feuding. They are a pugnacious lot, and no one seems to be able to talk peace to them. So, if Henry Bolingbroke has his way, Richard will abdicate in his favor, and then that will be the end of Richard II. Henry is not so foolish as to leave a deposed King alive while he is trying to establish his claim. If the Popes were not locked in their own battles, they might have the power to intercede before England gets bloody, but that is too much to hope for, given the climate in Rome and Avignon, and England will pay the price, I fear.

I have visited Villa Ragoczy, and have discovered that it is in rather better repair than mine; I will have the builders inspect it and tend to its upkeep as it is needed. The steward there has been attentive to the property, and his family is providing most of the labor the estate demands. The land is in good heart, the orchards have been bearing well, and the vineyard is flourishing. Sanct' Germain will be satisfied with what he finds when next he visits the place. There is to be a feast for the local farmers at Villa Ragoczy at the Nativity, which the Church approves, and which the steward has provided in Sanct' Germain's name for the last ten years, or so I am told.

So if you will take my advice, Rogerian, remain where Sanct' Germain expects to find you, in Alexandria, and see Avasa Dani established in the house she wants. For now, this is the best service you

*can render Sanct' Germain. And never fear: when he finally returns I
will scold him enough for the both of us.*

With the assurance of my friendship,
Olivia

*by my own hand at Rome on the 29th day of November in the
Church's year 1399.*

3

Near midnight Sanat Ji Mani went out of his room into the garden;
it was cool, with a lazy wind stirring the leaves and carrying the scent
of jasmine, for even at the dark of the year, blossoms flourished in
this warm, fecund climate. Overhead the constellations of winter hung,
some familiar, others less so; Sanat Ji Mani studied the stars. He found
the Hunter with his distinctive belt of three stars, Betelgeuse at the
shoulder, Rigel at the knee; then the horns of the Bull, with the Ple-
iades and Aldebaran behind and below them, all directly overhead;
Sirius, cold and bright, Pollux, and Procyon shone down from their
ancient places. To the south there was the constellation the astrono-
mers at Delhi had called the Djinn, marked by the brilliant Achenar,
and another they had named The Emperor's Crown with Canopus at
its apex. To the west, Deneb hung just above the shoulder of the wall,
and in the east Regulus was rising.

He stood for a while, reacquainting himself with the winter sky,
assembling and reassembling the patterns of stars according to the
Egyptian, the Greeks, the Romans, the Arabs, and the Chinese, thinking that in the many, many years he had studied them while he walked
the night, he had seen them change and move—very slowly, but over
the centuries they brightened and dimmed, slid, and occasionally vanished in a flash or snuffed out as if a candle had been extinguished.
His ruminations began to pall upon him, so he strolled beside the high
wall, still glancing up from time to time; he was no longer interested

in the stars and their courses along the night, but in the men who kept watch down the wall, lances in their hands. As he approached the rear gate, one of the Guards confronted him.

"This way is locked," he said, his stance making it clear that the door would not be opened for him, locked or not.

"When will it be opened?" Sanat Ji Mani asked politely. "Your Great Gate opens at dawn. I must suppose this gate is opened then as well."

"It is opened when Rajput Hasin Dahele orders it to be open." The Guard lifted his lance, not aiming it, but suggesting that would be his next move.

"Then it is usually closed and locked," Sanat Ji Mani said.

"Yes. All the garden gates are locked. It is to protect the Rajput's family—and his guests." The Guard cocked his head. "You need not linger."

"Of course not," said Sanat Ji Mani. "I was hoping to find a higher vantage-point to look at the stars, but if the gate is locked, I will not bother." Saying that, he turned and ambled back along the fence, unobviously taking stock of the other Guards stationed along the wall. There was no point where he could approach the wall unobserved; he nodded once, grimly, before going into the palace and seeking out his room.

Tulsi was lying on the bed, deeply asleep, her pale-green silken robe closed tightly, the sash knotted in place. In the ten days since she had been poisoned, she had been deeply fatigued, her appetite poor, and her state of mind withdrawn. She stirred as he closed the door but she did not waken.

Sanat Ji Mani sat down on the pile of cushions on the far side of the room from the bed and gave himself over to thought: for all the courtesy they had been shown, Sanat Ji Mani was now convinced they were indeed prisoners. What he had not been able to discover was why, and what it was that Hasin Dahele wanted of him: and because he did not have those answers, he was increasingly eager to escape. He decided he would go out to the mustering court tomorrow night, to try to determine when the Guards were changed, and how that was set up, so that he might discover a break in their routine that would provide the chance for him and Tulsi to leave. Not, he reminded himself, that Tulsi was in any condition to leave; she would need another week at least to regain her strength and shake off the lethargy that had taken hold of her. Putting the tips of his fingers together, Sanat Ji Mani contemplated their situation, trying to decide what to do.

"You are awake," Tulsi said from her place on the bed. "How long have you been sitting there?" Her voice was still a bit rough, but it had improved noticeably in the last three days, a sure sign her body was finally beginning to heal.

"I did not want to disturb you," said Sanat Ji Mani.

"I like to have you beside me," she reminded him, holding out her arms to him. "Come. Lie here with me."

He rose and went to the bed, stretching out and extending an arm so she could rest her head on his shoulder. "I tried the garden."

"Is it like the others?" She sounded half-awake but she was trying to pay attention. "Are we surrounded by the Rajput's men?"

"Yes. There are Guards everywhere." He touched her hair.

"Then we are truly captives," she said.

"It appears so," Sanat Ji Mani agreed. "I would like to know why. So far I have been unable to find out."

"You have asked the Rajput—directly?" Tulsi laid her hand on his chest.

"I have tried. He has fobbed me off with protestations of courtesy and gratitude for my company." Sanat Ji Mani gave a single shake to his head. "I cannot get an explanation out of Vayu Ede, either."

"Is he the only one who speaks with you—still?" There was a note of panic in her question.

Sanat Ji Mani inclined his head once. "He may be the only one given permission."

"Because he knows so little," she said with a hard sigh.

"Or because he is charged with learning things about us; that would seem to be his purpose," said Sanat Ji Mani.

"I do not trust that one. He is too . . ." She cleared her throat and tried again. "He is too unworldly, and yet he is busy in the world."

"That is true," said Sanat Ji Mani quietly, absently stroking her arm.

"He knows something," she said, scowling.

"Or he thinks he does, which may be worse." Sanat Ji Mani studied the ceiling as carefully as he had studied the sky. "If I knew what he has decided about the two of us, I would know better how to learn from him."

"If he thinks he has such knowledge, he may tell the Rajput things we would not like." She waited a long moment for him to speak. "He could make up something dreadful."

"He could, but I doubt he will," said Sanat Ji Mani, giving her a reassuring cuddle. "If he tells too many tales, the Rajput will not trust him, and he wants that trust more than anything; it shows in everything he does."

Tulsi shook her head. "I do not understand him, and that makes me restive." She bit her lower lip. "If I had someone besides Vayu Ede to watch, I could learn much more. But isolated as we are—" She slapped the pillow to express her annoyance.

"Observe him; he will show himself to you if you do." He moved slightly so that she would be more comfortable. "No doubt he is part of the problem we have encountered here, but what part?"

"I cannot think," said Tulsi, disgusted. "They have put us in this silken prison, and will not say why. They attempted to kill me—or you—and for no reason." She flung up her hand and made a fist of it.

"Oh, there is a reason," said Sanat Ji Mani. "When we know what it is, we will have gone a long way to learning who made the attempt."

Tulsi shook her head. "And if you cannot find it out—what then?" She turned away from him. "What will become of us?"

"I do not know yet," said Sanat Ji Mani. "I hope we will be able to escape this place, and soon." He flexed his right foot, a rueful expression clouding his features. "If I did not have to deal with this—"

Tulsi sighed. "It is improving. I have seen you get better. But it is so slow."

"Those of my blood—" he began.

"—mend slowly. So you said; I had no idea you meant this slowly." Tulsi's frown deepened and she shoved herself up on her elbow. "You told me it would take more than a year, but I thought you were being cautious."

"Unfortunately, no," he said wryly. "I was run through with a lance once, many years ago. It did not touch my spine, so I lived, but it was four years before the wound in my side healed." Although the injury had occurred a thousand years before, it was still a distressing memory; a ghost of the pain seared through him.

"Then you could be limping for another two years at least," said Tulsi, dismayed at the prospect. "How are we to escape if you cannot walk quickly, or far?"

"I suppose we would have to steal horses," said Sanat Ji Mani, so coolly that Tulsi was uncertain if he was jesting or not.

"Steal horses," she repeated, as if saying it aloud would make it more comprehensible. "Do you think you could?"

"The Rajput has a large stable. With a little forethought, we should be able to get away with two horses without too much trouble." He still seemed remote.

"And how are we to do this?" Tulsi asked.

"I have not come up with a plan yet," he confessed. "But I must begin to work on one. I cannot believe we are to be kept as we have been kept for much longer."

"Do you mean we could be imprisoned—more than we are now? Could we be separated? Put in cells or chains?" Whatever annoyance she felt toward him vanished at the thought of it. "Would they do that to us?"

"I do not know what they would do," Sanat Ji Mani said brusquely. "That is what troubles me. I only know they must do something."

"Why?" Tulsi asked. "Why not go on as they have been for . . . for years?"

"Because the Rajput is preparing for war, and that means he cannot permit two strangers to have access to all his people and his palace. He has been courteous for a reason, and that we cannot forget. We must be more confined, or we must be used in some way." He paused thoughtfully. "He may want us to serve as spies for him, which would explain why he has treated us well and watched us closely."

"Then why the poison?" Tulsi gestured him to silence and answered her own question. "There may be other spies in the household who know the Rajput's plans. His enemies may be our enemies as well."

"That is possible," said Sanat Ji Mani.

"Or he may have run out of uses for us and now wants to be rid of us," Tulsi went on as various theories jumbled in her mind.

"Yes," Sanat Ji Mani agreed.

"That was why Hasin Dahele was so interested in finding out where we had been: he intends to go north and wants as much intelligence as he can gather," she went on, her animation increasing. "Yes. That must be his purpose."

"He may be wanting to extend his frontiers," Sanat Ji Mani speculated. "The old Delhi Empire is in disarray; I doubt Hasin Dahele is the only Rajput who wants to take advantage of its collapse. He could be planning to rout the minor forces Timur-i left behind and occupy the region as his own."

"That is a long way to go," said Tulsi. "We have walked most of the way, and it took many weeks." She sat up. "But that is what he wants from us, is it not? Someone who knows the way and has been over the roads recently. If he is going north, he will need scouts to guide him along the way, for he cannot rely on the people to do so. The rains have made a difference in the roads, but I begin to comprehend . . ." She let the rest of her thoughts go.

Sanat Ji Mani was half-convinced she was right. "It makes sense," he told her.

"If he is determined to go to war with us to conduct him, I do not know how we are to get away." She leaned toward him. "Could we escape once the campaign begins?"

"It would be more dangerous than going now," Sanat Ji Mani said slowly. "But it may be our only opportunity."

"What of the other Rajputs in this region?" Tulsi asked suddenly. "Do you think they are with Hasin Dahele, or against him?"

"I do not know," said Sanat Ji Mani. "If they are against him, he is going to have a hard time of it, for he will have to fight his way through their opposition. If they are with him, he may be able to carve out enough territory to make himself a Raja, and not the grandson of one." The possibility of battle sickened him: he had seen too much of it through the centuries to believe it was anything more than chaos and slaughter, and that most of its gains were not sufficient to justify the suffering it created.

"Would he not have messengers going out to secure the friendship of the other Rajputs?" Tulsi wondered aloud.

"He could certainly do so," said Sanat Ji Mani, going on musingly, "unless he is planning to surprise them with his campaign, to move before they can mount any resistance, in which case he would be wise to keep his plans to himself."

"And keep travelers like us where he can control them," she added.

"Yes." She got up from the bed. "Do you think this will happen soon?"

"I would suppose after the dark of the year: there is a time before the worst of the heat comes when he might safely wage war without having to battle the climate as well." Sanat Ji Mani watched her as she began to pace. "You realize this is all our surmise, that we cannot be certain of any of it."

"I realize that we may have guessed incorrectly, but we know the Rajput is planning something, and this makes as much sense as anything we might expect, given what we know. He must have a campaign in mind, that much is obvious." She stopped still and pointed at him. "You have suspected this from the first, have you not?"

"Not this specifically, no," said Sanat Ji Mani. "I am still not convinced of it." He could see she did not entirely believe him, so he went on, ticking off his points on his fingers. "We know he is preparing for war: he admits as much. We know he is interested in where we have been: we have been repeatedly questioned about our travels. We know he does not want us to leave: we are guarded at all times. We know someone in this palace wants one or both of us dead: there has been an attempt on your life. We know that the Rajput is eager to learn about Timur-i: his poet and he have asked many questions about him. Therefore we assume we are hostages, or that we have some other strategic role in the Rajput's plans. The rest is conjecture, and, tempting though it is to tell ourselves that we have hit upon the truth, we must not succumb to the mistake of confusing our suspicions with what we know."

Tulsi shook her head. "We must know more than that."

"What?" he asked, his manner mildly inquisitive. "We suspect we are watched, but have you ever caught anyone watching us?"

"No," she admitted.

"Then it is only a supposition." He let her deliberate his remark, then said, "We suspect that Hasin Dahele plans to go north when he begins his campaign, but has he ever said that is his intention?"

"No," she said.

"For all we know, he has detained travelers who have come from other places and given them the same hospitality he has shown us, and for a similar purpose, but we are supposing what that purpose is." Sanat Ji Mani rose. "No one has ever mentioned that, have they. No."

Tulsi thrust out her jaw. "Why should they?"

"Why, indeed," he countered. "You have worked out a very plausible explanation of what has been happening," he went on, only to be interrupted.

"But it may not be accurate," she said for him. "Very well; I will accept that. But I do not like the uncertainty that leaves."

"Nor do I, Tulsi; nor do I," said Sanat Ji Mani. "I wish we had someone—someone reliable—who could tell us more, but we do not."

"Do you think that is part of the plan?" Tulsi asked, coming back to him.

"It may be; it seems unlikely that it would be wholly accidental that we have been kept away from most of the people of the palace; and, of course, it is advantageous to Hasin Dahele to keep us guessing." He went to the window. "I am going to find out about the stables tomorrow night, when I look at the marshaling court."

"So you still think we should steal horses?" She sounded startled by this. "Should we not wait until we know more?"

Sanat Ji Mani answered her in a sardonic tone. "We know enough to realize it would be wisest to flee."

"I suppose we do," said Tulsi. "Is it possible, do you think? Can we escape?"

"At least I should explore; if it is too dangerous to attempt, I will find that out." He shook his head slowly. "In any case, we should be prepared to depart quickly if the opportunity is presented."

"All right. I will ready my pack." She grinned in anticipation.

"You might as well announce it to the world that we are planning to go," Sanat Ji Mani said as gently as he could. "Do nothing that is different from what you have been doing. Just lay by a few things— nothing obvious—and make sure you can gather all of them in a sack you can conceal under your clothes."

Tulsi tossed her head. "What about my pack?"

"Leave it where it is. And when we go, it must stay behind." He glanced around the room. "Have you picked up any more of the local tongue?"

"Yes," she said proudly, and was about to demonstrate when he held up his hand to silence her.

"Do not let them know. Right now, it is your only advantage, and it is a small one, at that. They know I can speak their language; let them continue to presume you do not. That may make them more unguarded in your presence, and they may let something slip that will be useful to us, later." The ploy had proved useful several times in the past and he did not underestimate its value.

Tulsi appeared to be disappointed by his stricture, but nodded her understanding. "No doubt you are right," she said reluctantly. "Timur-i sometimes used this trick, I know."

"Do not confuse Hasin Dahele with Timur-i," Sanat Ji Mani recommended. "They are very different men."

Tulsi was about to protest, then fell silent. At last she sighed. "I suppose Hasin Dahele will use war-elephants to fight."

"Very likely," said Sanat Ji Mani. "You have heard them trumpeting from the compound just outside the city walls. I cannot believe all of them are used for logging."

"They may be," said Tulsi, herself unconvinced. "There is a great deal of logging done around Devapur. Most of Rajput Hasin Dahele's wealth comes from wood."

"Yes; you are correct. The elephants could be part of the logging; they may be nothing more than that. But it does not seem likely. He has too many soldiers with the elephants." He stared out into the night. "If there are more horses than stalls in the stable, that will tell me something, too."

"Do you think they will let you into the stable? If the Rajput is planning war, he may want to keep all his preparations hidden." She came to stand beside him.

"I am sorry to have gotten you into all this," Sanat Ji Mani said when they had been quiet for a little while.

"I came of my own accord," she reminded him.

"You could have gone with Djerat and returned to Timur-i's army," he reminded her, laying his hand on her shoulder.

"And go back to following the soldiers? Thank you, no." She folded her arms as if against a sudden chill.

"You would not have been poisoned," he pointed out.

"That may be. But who knows what else might have happened to me?" She did not expect an answer and was offered none.

Sanat Ji Mani turned to her and kissed the arch of her brow. "That is very kind of you."

She shook her head. "I am not kind," she said, with the hint of a stammer in her words. A moment later she broke away from him. "I could practice in the marshaling yard in the morning. That way I can have a look at the stables from the outside without making it seem I am doing so. These soldiers will want to watch me, and they will not notice what I watch." She swung around toward him. "Thus far you have taken most of the risks, and I do not desire you to continue to be the only one."

Concealing his surprise, Sanat Ji Mani said, "After what you have been through, I would have thought that you have risked more than enough. You do not have to expose yourself in this way."

"I want to," she said more emphatically. "It is appropriate that I do as much as you have done. I know how to estimate an army's preparedness; I have seen it all my life. I may not know as much about the showy horses they have in the stables here, but I know the points to look for."

"There is no question you do," said Sanat Ji Mani.

"Then let me go to the marshaling yard. You will attract suspicion, going there without cause. But if I go, practice my tumbling and my acrobatics, and, while I am resting between movements, praise their horses, you may come later in the day and ask to see them. They may let you into the stables, especially if I can choose one horse to admire above all others, and you can then ask to see the horse I have spoken so well of. Seeing this one horse, you may be able to see much more, just by being in the stables. I know something of campaigning, but not as much as I reckon you do." She took hold of his arm suddenly, her fingers gripping; she looked directly into his dark eyes, pleading. "You have been taking all the risks, and I cannot accept that, not if I am to leave with you. I have been lying here for days, thinking there is nothing I can do. But there is, there is."

"It is a very clever idea," he conceded, still reluctant to let her undertake anything so hazardous.

"I think so, too," she said mischievously. "As to performing, it is time I did a proper display. I do need the practice; I have not had enough room to do a full routine anywhere but the garden." She leaned against him easily. "It will be good for me to entertain again, as well as look about me, too."

"What if you are not allowed to do it? You will be in full daylight, and I will not be able to help you." He was chagrined by this admission. "You will have to deal with the situation on your own."

"I have done so most of my life," she said, and was aware that her circumstances had been different, for with Timur-i's army, there was a whole community of entertainers, and they provided a kind of protection she could not have here.

"I am not pleased with you taking such chances," Sanat Ji Mani told her. "But I have to acknowledge the advantages of your plan, and however averse I am to this risk you want to take, I have nothing as likely to succeed to offer in its place."

"Then I shall do it," she said, finally sounding calm. "I will hold their attention while I study everything I see. Some of my tumbling may take me directly to the door of the stables." She smiled impishly. "I can pretend to slip, and perhaps get inside."

"Do not take on so much," Sanat Ji Mani warned. "If you try too much, they may become leery, and that could work against you. Find out as much as you can in as ordinary a way as you can, and from that, we can begin to make our plans."

Instead of bowing, Tulsi bent backwards and then slowly lifted her legs into a handstand. "Watch, Sanat Ji Mani," she said. "I will discover everything we need." She began to walk away from him, lowering her feet to rest on her head.

"I hope you may," said Sanat Ji Mani, frowning slightly.

Although she saw his face upside down and by moonlight, she knew enough about him to be aware that he was worried. She righted herself. "What is it?"

He shook his head as if to dismiss pesky quibbles. "We are assuming our guesses are correct. What if we have misread the whole situation? There may be some other explanation for the way we have been treated that we have not anticipated."

"And what might that be?" she asked, growing more sure of herself and her mission with every breath.

"I cannot tell." He rubbed his eyes. "That is what troubles me."

Tulsi chuckled. "You may be right, and there is something insidious that we do not know about," she said. "But given what we have learned, we must act upon it, or remain inert and vulnerable. I would rather be wrong in action than in passivity."

"And I," he said. "But to be precipitous would be folly."

She came up to him. "Tomorrow night we will both know more, and we can decide then if anything we have done has been too heedless. Until then, I want to rest; it is going to be a demanding day tomorrow."

Sanat Ji Mani embraced her and gave her shoulders a reassuring shake before sitting down beside her on the bed while she stretched out to resume her interrupted slumber; he felt great pride in her, and with it, great compassion. He hoped that their decision would not put her in greater danger than they were in now, yet, even as he was cognizant of it, he understood that his hope was in vain.

Text of a report compiled from merchants and presented to Rajput Hasin Dahele.

To the most excellent, the most exalted, the most esteemed, the Rajput Hasin Dahele, the greetings and protestations of loyalty and dedication to your cause from the merchants Chandra Chauris, Riti Natadasa, Kautilya Jati, and Ghangal Sunpavar, all respected men of good repute who seek to aid you in your expansions of your frontiers.

Know, O Rajput, that in our travels, we have seen that there is much disorder in the lands beyond those you rule, and that disorder cries out for rectification, so that dharma may be restored to all those who live in these abandoned places. For that reason, we are preparing to reveal to you all we have seen, in the hope that it will aid you in your quest to bring regularity out of disruption, as has been shown to please the Gods; for those who give themselves to destruction surely bring it upon themselves, and many pay the price for the actions of a few.

Thus Riti Natadasa reports that on his journey over the mountains to the west, he saw that there is upheaval still spreading from Gujerat, where there is still much upheaval and unsettledness among the people, so that some are forced to flee for fear of losing their lives. He says that most of these people are poor and now have less than before; he has seen many begging, and others dead of starvation and misery. So if it is the Rajput's desire to improve the lot of his people, he would do well to go elsewhere for them, as he cannot hope to improve the lives of so many unfortunates. Also, because of this increase in persons wandering the roads, many travelers are set upon by those made desperate, and they are robbed, some of them even killed. An army might not have much to fear from such creatures, but they might prove inconvenient for the army, not only as thieves, but as unreliable scouts or untrustworthy servants. Riti Natadasa has said he will not be going west for many more months, for he has no wish to encounter any more desperate men.

Kautilya Jati, who has recently returned from Sirpur, says that trade has been picking up there, and the merchants are anticipating an improvement in their businesses, as the depredations of Timur-i have ceased for the time being. He reports that many merchants who have been forced to leave Delhi have now begun to make a living once again, one that can flourish beyond the Delhi Sultanate. He has heard that it is acknowledged as the truth that Timur-i was deposed and abandoned alone on the roads, and that the reason for his army's retreat to Samarkand is to fix the new lords in place, and to seize the power Timur-i has held for so long. Many travelers, pilgrims as well as merchants, have said that there are many looking for Timur-i upon the roads, for it is known that his officers will follow him rather than his usurpers if they are given the chance. He says he himself has tried to find Timur-i, to avail himself of the power that man can command, as even a merchant knows the worth of an army.

Chandra Chauris, who has been in the north through the rains, says that there has been damage done to the roads by flooding, but that nothing is so wholly destroyed that it is impossible for anyone to travel upon the roads without coming to grief. He informs you that if you decide to go north, that you would be well-advised to send builders ahead to make the repairs you will require, for it will benefit no one if you are unable to make progress due to the impassability of the roads. They do not need full reconstruction, but there are ruts and holes and other impediments that would be better for the attention of builders, particularly if the Rajput should wish to move a considerable number of men and animals over them. Elephants, of course, can manage for themselves, but even they make more progress over well-repaired roads.

Ghangal Sunpavar has seen gold and jewels from China more than he has from the West, so it must be assumed that Timur-i's Empire is in disarray, for no trade is making its way through his territories. If this is the case in a year, it will be a very bad thing for all merchants, but for now, it can be made less destructive by improving the level of trade with Assam and other eastern regions, all the way into China. Gold and jewels are recognized everywhere as having value, and Ghangal Sunpavar believes that the more the merchants of Devapur have of each, the more powerful all Beragar will be in the world, for it will be known that gold flows to the coffers of Hasin Dahele, not out of them, and those who might consider opposing the Rajput will know that such a venture will lead to ruin, because that fight would be too costly in men and animals as well as in gold. To that end, Ghangal Sunpavar has decided to conduct all his business in gold and jewels, and to place at the disposal of the Rajput Hasin Dahele half of his fortune, as a show of faith in all the Rajput's endeavors.

This is the sum of the report of the merchants of Devapur whose wish it is to assist the Rajput in his efforts. They all proclaim their fealty to the Rajput, and will report to him regularly on any facet of their dealings that may have significance to the Rajput's expansion of territory.

Submitted by the scribe Shivaji Prata, with his avowal that this account is full and accurate, and in accord with the words of the merchants, on this, the first full moon after the dark of the year.

4

"You have honored the Rajput by visiting his stables again, I am told," Vayu Ede said to Sanat Ji Mani as the two encountered each other in the main corridor of the palace at dusk; the servants were busy lighting the oil-lamps and setting handfuls of aromatic wooden chips to burn on the braziers that stood in the junction of two corridors, just ahead of them.

"Last night, yes," said Sanat Ji Mani as disinterestedly as he could; it was his third such visit in ten days. He was wearing yet another set of pyjamas, this one in a rich bronze shade the color of lamplight; his boots were also new, of tooled, dark-red leather that reached to his calves; they were handsome but lacked the earth-filled soles he craved, and his right foot remained painful and tender.

"How good of you, to take the opportunity to view the horses the Rajput has made his own." If there was any sarcasm in Vayu Ede's observation, it did not make itself heard in his voice.

"The Rajput has many horses," said Sanat Ji Mani. "He has much to be proud of."

"And you are a fine judge of such animals," said Vayu Ede.

"I have some knowledge of horseflesh," Sanat Ji Mani answered carefully.

Vayu Ede laughed aloud as if this were a great witticism. "The Rajput has said he would like to inspect his stables with you."

This was so unexpected that Sanat Ji Mani could not at first decide what to answer. Finally he bowed his head. "I am at the Rajput's service, of course."

"And so I shall tell him. It might be as well to do it tomorrow night, before the Rajput takes his cavalry on maneuvers. He has planned to have an inspection in any case, and you will make it far more worthwhile; you have your experience and he has his. Between you there should be a most useful discussion."

"I welcome it," said Sanat Ji Mani with the odd sensation he and Vayu Ede meant very different things.

"Excellent," Vayu Ede said, pressing his hands together and bowing deeply. "Shall I tell him you will meet him—shall we say?—just before sunset in the marshaling yard? Your companion should have finished her performance for the day, and that way, the soldiers will be in good fettle."

"That would be satisfactory," Sanat Ji Mani said, wondering if it had been wise to allow Tulsi to continue her demonstrations; it had seemed useful when she suggested that since her first performance had been so enthusiastically received, offering more of them would be strategically useful, but now it seemed that this was less beneficial than it had appeared.

"Then I will wish you good sleep. In these long nights, who is safe beyond his bed?" With that, Vayu Ede was gone.

Sanat Ji Mani, who had endured winters in the far north, found these nights hardly worth recognizing, but he kept this to himself as he made his way to the room he shared with Tulsi. As he walked, still favoring his right foot, he was struck with the last thing Vayu Ede had said: *In these long nights, who is safe beyond his bed?* Was that only a remark of a man ready to sleep, or had there been a threat hidden within it? He considered all the possibilities and decided he could not be certain either way; Vayu Ede was given to flights of language that were the mark of his profession of poet, so it was difficult to discern his purpose. The isolation within the Rajput's palace made it difficult to establish any sense of proportion in such remarks, and it would be easy to overestimate their importance as to underestimate them. Sanat Ji Mani was still pondering the ramifications of those words when he entered the door of his room and found Tulsi in trousers and a tunic of light-weight cotton half-way up the wall in a corner, using the angle to climb higher. "More practicing, I see," he said.

She sighed and dropped lightly down. "The wood is oily, and that makes the climbing difficult. I could not do it at all in silk."

"I am agog, no matter what the condition of the wood, or your clothes," he told her.

She heard the coolness in his tone. "And you seem caught up in—in what?"

"Rumination," he answered, taking his place on the side of the bed. "I will venture out later. For now, it is fitting that you and I give the appearance of sleeping."

"Sleeping?" She came to stand beside him. "Why should we sleep?"

"It is expected of us, I gather," he said, stretching out without removing the tunic or trousers he wore. "I think we may be watched for part of the night."

"More spies," she said, sighing again. "This is most wearing."

"That it is." He held out his arm, making a place for her beside him. "But for the time being, we can do nothing more than keep their suspicions at bay."

She lay down next to him. "True enough," she said. "I have a handful of coins from the soldiers tonight. I have added it to what they have thrown to me already. If nothing else, we will not have to leave here wholly without means."

"That is a very good thing," Sanat Ji Mani said, then added, "I am supposed to inspect the stables with the Rajput tomorrow evening."

"What on earth for?" Tulsi exclaimed, sitting up abruptly.

"I hope to find out," said Sanat Ji Mani. "Vayu Ede has noticed that I have been looking at the stables, and made the offer just as I was coming back here."

"And what does it mean, do you think?" She got up and began to pace. "Have they learned our plans?"

"Not that I can tell," Sanat Ji Mani answered. "But I intend to find out as much as I may tonight, so that I will not be wholly unprepared tomorrow evening."

"Very well," she said automatically. "And what if you discover we have been trapped—what then?"

"Then we must try to leave before dawn. I hope it will not be necessary. Neither you nor I are quite ready to leave this place. But if we must perforce—" He gestured resignation. "I will return well before the sky lightens."

"If we have to flee." She sat down on the side of the bed once again. "I should have saved food from supper."

"We will manage food, for you and for the horses," he said confidently.

"I will rely upon you for that?" She jumped into a back-flip. "I cannot perform anywhere near Devapur. Word of it would get back to Hasin Dahele and we would be hunted down." She sank, cross-legged, onto the floor. "No, if we slip away from here, we must travel as we did before—we must go a long way, staying off the main roads, and bringing as little attention to ourselves as we can. We will have to hide often, and move by night." Then she looked directly at him. "It would be wisest if you rely upon me for nourishment."

Sanat Ji Mani sat up. "Does that mean you want to come to my life?"

"I have not yet decided. But I know you will not be able to travel quickly unless you have more than birds' blood to sustain you." She saw the dismay in his face. "It is the prudent thing to do."

"Becoming a vampire is not a matter of prudence," he said sharply. "Do not argue with me. I will not lie with you again unless my life is what you want. Anything else would be repugnant to me, and disastrous to you; believe this, for I am in deadly earnest." He steadied himself and went on, "If this is not what you seek for yourself, the intimacy that has grown will be lost, and there will be nothing more than necessity in our bond. You may be satisfied with that, but I would not."

"But it would make our escape—" she began.

"That is too high a price for getting away." He met her eyes.

"Is it so terrible, then? your life?" Her voice was angry. "Have you lied to me?"

"It is so terrible, and I have not lied," he replied in a quiet voice that did not permit any argument. "It is a rare thing, to come to this life, to the shared blood-bond that is the gift that comes with knowing. But for those reasons, and others, you must not make the change a sacrifice or an act of defiance, or anything that would taint it, turn it to something unwanted or cruel. And, Tulsi, it would be cruel to use you as a source of food." He said it bluntly and deliberately, and watched her take it in.

She stared at him a short time. "Well, I must take your word for it," she said at last. "I only thought it would be worthwhile . . ."

Sanat Ji Mani sensed her ambivalence. "You were more generous than you know to make such an offer," he said softly. "That is the crux of the matter: you do not know what you offered and it would be unkind of me to exploit your selflessness."

Tulsi quivered where she sat. "That sounds a bit daunting," she admitted.

"Good; I intended it should," he responded.

"All right; I will not ask to come to your life—*if* I ask to come to your life—for your advantage." She rose gracefully. "I will ask for mine."

His smile surprised and reassured her. "That would suit me entirely."

She came back to the bed. "We're supposed to sleep, you said?"

"Yes." He once again made a place for her at his side. "I will leave about midnight, before the Guards change, and the ones on duty are getting sleepy." He fingered the bronze silk he wore. "I shall change my clothes; I might as well carry a torch with this on."

"Is that its purpose?" Tulsi suggested.

"Possibly," he said. "More likely, it is our host displaying his opulence. This is much grander than that mulberry silk that has been taken for washing."

Tulsi peeled out of her cotton garments and reached for the robe of magenta silk, the most recent one the Rajput had provided her. "These are very nice," she said, meaning all the clothes she had received. "I never thought to have so much fine apparel as I have now." She knotted the sash loosely around her waist. "We look like a fire together, do we not?"

"I suppose so," Sanat Ji Mani said, thinking back to his years in the Court of Karl-lo-Magne, when royal favor was a costly privilege.

"Will you tell me what you see in the stables?" she asked, and yawned.

"When I return from the inspection tomorrow evening, I will," he promised her.

"And then we can plan our escape, if we do not have to go before dawn," she said.

"Yes," he said. "Sleep, Tulsi."

"Wake me if—"

"If I must, I will."

Tulsi snuggled a bit closer to him. "Good," she murmured.

Sanat Ji Mani waited until she was soundly asleep, then eased out of the bed and began to pay attention to the hall, listening for the soft footfalls of servants and the distant closing of doors. It was times like this that he missed reading, for it would have pleased him to spend his waiting time in study; but books were not available, and he had to content himself with his thoughts and his memories.

Shortly before midnight, he rose, went to the chest and took out a robe of sienna-colored silk, pulled it on over the bronze pyjamas, and slipped out of the room, going down the corridor to the stairs that led to the side-garden that gave on to the marshaling court. It was not difficult to deepen the slumber of the dozing sentry; Sanat Ji Mani waited until he heard the man snore, then slipped through the gate and made his way to the rear end of the stables, ducking between the enormous tack-room and the first aisle of stalls. Some of the nearer horses whickered at him, but none of them raised the alarm by neighing loudly. Moving quickly, Sanat Ji Mani determined that most of the stalls had two horses, indicating a build-up in numbers. He made a quick pass through the first aisle and went on to the next, checking on the horses there, and in the four aisles beyond. When he had finished, he glanced across the arm of the courtyard to the next stable, which fronted on the forward part of the marshaling court. This was the building Tulsi had seen a little of, and it was the place where Hasin Dahele kept his own mounts. Tempting though it was to cross the courtyard and continue his review, Sanat Ji Mani hesitated, aware that the Rajput's personal horses were apt to be guarded. Neither stable had easy access to any unguarded exit, not even to an exercise pen or a paddock outside the walls, which meant that any escape on horseback could only be done with confusion to mask it. Sanat Ji Mani checked the tack-room, looking for saddles and bridles, and found them set on wedges and pegs affixed to the wall, many of them newly installed, the wood still showing where the saws had gone; at least tack was accessible, that was something.

He had just stepped out of the tack-room when a gong sounded the change of watch; Sanat Ji Mani moved back into the shadows of the stable to observe the sentries coming off their posts, noticing how well-disciplined they were and how quickly they went about their duties; all the Guards were more heavily armed than they had been two nights ago. The prospect of war weighed heavily on Sanat Ji Mani as he made his way back to the room he shared with Tulsi, and kept him awake until the sky was glowing with the coming of day.

"What did you find out?" Tulsi asked once she had stretched and yawned herself awake.

"Not as much as I would like and too much to comfort me," he replied. "I think it is important that you and I be ready to move soon. Not this morning, because the Guards on the walls are carrying bows as well as spears, and that makes the chances for a successful escape much smaller than when all the Guards carried was spears."

She thought about this. "Bows do give an advantage," she said, trying to appear unconcerned. "We should probably not try to outrun arrows."

"Truly," said Sanat Ji Mani.

"Did you get into the stables?" she asked, trying to find something encouraging to talk about.

"The rear stable, yes; not the front stable. There has been a definite increase in horses, for they are stalled in pairs, not alone. It will not be easy to get out of the stables and through the gates—both are in full view of the Guards." Discouraging as this was, Sanat Ji Mani knew he had to tell her what he thought. "I was not impressed with most of the horses," he added. "Too much Mawari in the stock. They are sickle-hocked, most of them, and will probably not hold up under a long campaign, although I have heard they are tough and light-keepers." As he said this, he remembered the Spiti ponies that had brought him and Rogerian through the mountains of the Land of Snows; they were narrow-bodied and straight-necked, but they had managed the rigorous journey better than many other breeds might have. "The Rajput would do well to find some Caspian stallions, or a Turkmene line to add shoulder and heart-room to his stud." He did not realize that Tulsi was staring at him until he glanced toward her.

"I did not know you have had so much experience of horses," she said a bit faintly.

His smile was quick. "I have had a long time to learn," he told her. "I have come to put a great deal of value on stamina in horses, but even more on temperament."

She pursed her lips, giving his remarks some thought. "What did you think of Timur-i's ponies?"

"Oh, they are tough as leather, and can trot forever," said Sanat Ji Mani. "But most of them are straight-shouldered and have trouble with their backs after they are ten or so. You have seen how few older ponies are used for fighting, and when they cannot be used for war, they become food; those ponies, left to themselves, are long-lived." He looked past her, mentally watching the hardy ponies of Timur-i's army. "And most of them are intractable and mean. They are not trained to be willing, but that is not the whole of it; the breed is obstinate."

"And you think the same of the Rajput's horses?" she asked.

"I think they, too, are not raised for willingness." He stopped talking.

"What is it?" Tulsi could not fathom what commanded his attention.

"I must think of something to say that will please the Rajput that will not make it appear I have no understanding of horses," he said.

"You will think of the best approach; you are very skillful with words." There was no tinge of criticism in her voice, and no suggestion of blame in her manner, but he brought up his head as if stung.

"If you mean that I—" He stopped as he saw the shock in her eyes. "I apologize. I thought you meant that I have manipulated you with words. And, I own, I have."

"Not to my disadvantage," she said, and changed the subject. "You should rest while you can, and while the sun is most enervating. I will break my fast and return here before morning is half-over. Then you can prepare for your meeting with the Rajput this evening."

"Very sensible of you," said Sanat Ji Mani. "I will take your advice and sleep as much as I can."

Tulsi came to the side of the bed. "I shall say no one is to disturb you; the servants are not to enter this room."

"Thank you," he said, preparing to surrender to the torpor that among his kind passed for sleep.

She bent and kissed him lightly. "You have done much for me, Sanat Ji Mani. Even if you do not get us out of this, I am grateful to all you have given me."

He whispered a few words in a language she did not recognize, and lapsed into a stupefaction that quickly resembled near-death.

When he woke again, it was mid-morning and the sound of servants washing the floors in the corridor echoed along the stones and rose and fell like the sea. He rose and stripped off his robe, revealing his bronze pyjamas beneath. He brushed the lustrous silk and smoothed his hair, and stepped out into the hallway to go to the baths, wanting to present himself newly clean to the Rajput. The basins were empty and the fountain splashed rose-scented water. He chose the tepid pool and set his clothing aside before he got into the water; he did his best to ignore the queasiness the water imparted to him, and finished his washing quickly. His slow-growing beard was in need of shaving again, and he resolved to tend to it the following morning, aware he would miss Rojire more than ever while he was at the task. He was about to get out and dry himself when he heard voices in the hallway. He made himself very still and listened.

"Why do you encourage him to go to war?" asked a man Sanat Ji Mani could not recognize.

"Because it is his karma to be a conqueror," said Vaya Ede. "I have seen it in a vision."

"But how can you know he will win?" the first man pursued. "Ber-agar is prosperous now; where other Rajputs have been riddled with foreigners and intrigue, we have done well. Why risk this good fortune in the hope that war will—" A portion of what he was saying was lost—"that better can be had."

"Timur-i will make it possible," said Vayu Ede; whatever else he said faded, leaving Sanat Ji Mani to mull over the little he had heard: what had Timur-i to do with the Rajput's ambition, unless he was committed to claiming a piece of the Delhi Sultanate? That would account for his desire to keep Sanat Ji Mani and Tulsi with him, and for his build-up in horses and equipment. Who were the men he had overhead? And why were they having such a discussion at so late an hour? Was it to keep their remarks private, or had they intended to be overheard?

Tulsi was waiting in their room when he returned, dry and dressed, his dark hair still damp. "The women of the household are not talking to me," she announced. "Until now they have tried to speak to me, even though they knew I could not understand."

"Which is no longer entirely the case," Sanat Ji Mani pointed out.

"Very true," she agreed. "But they have tried to include me, to engage me in ways that did not need words. Today I might as well have been a statue in the garden."

"And what did you do?" Sanat Ji Mani asked.

"What *could* I do?" she countered. "I sat and ate and said nothing. I tried to understand as much of their conversation as I could."

"Did you learn anything of interest?" Sanat Ji Mani knew that she now had a rudimentary grasp of the local dialect and would understand most simple conversations.

"Only that the Rajput is planning to set out on a little campaign to press his frontiers back to the Godavari River, to establish a defined border on the north. At least, that seemed to be the sense of it." Tulsi paused, her eyes focused on a distant place. "There is a gap between the pass to the coast and the source of the Godavari River, isn't there?"

"Yes," said Sanat Ji Mani, recalling the maps he had seen in Delhi. "The pass is not an impossible one to use, and there are trade roads there." He frowned. "So Hasin Dahele is going west. Does he want to control the ports, or is he planning to seize the coast and work his way up to the Sabarmati River?"

"That is in Gujerat, and there is still fighting in Gujerat," said Tulsi.

"Then he might plan to swing inland, and take the mountain regions." Sanat Ji Mani frowned. "There is still something we do not know in all this."

"Do you think you will be able to find it out?" Tulsi goaded. "Because if this unknown thing concerns us, then it would be best if we could find out what it is." She took a deep, uneven breath. "Sanat Ji Mani, I am getting frightened, and I do not want to stay frightened."

"I can hardly blame you for that," said Sanat Ji Mani. He shook his head. "Neither you nor I have the look of the people of this region, or we might be able to hide among the populace and make our way out of Beragar at our own pace. But that is not possible. So we must use other means."

"Tonight? After you review the stables?" She sounded eager.

"Do you want to be back on the road again, Tulsi? Are you certain you would not prefer to remain here in this place, with comforts and pleasures around you?" He was not entirely serious, but he wanted to be satisfied that she had considered all that might happen to her once they left the palace.

"I would rather not have to worry about poison, Sanat Ji Mani, or the possibility of separation, or the problems of being among strangers who may mean me ill." She leaped up and grabbed hold of the main ceiling beam, and began to perform her contortions around it. "This can keep me well enough in other places. I only want to vanish."

"To vanish?" he repeated, wondering if he had heard her aright.

"Yes; we are too visible here, and that attracts us notice that is dangerous. If we could simply disappear, we would be safe." She stretched along the beam, sinuous as a snake.

"You astonish me," said Sanat Ji Mani, watching Tulsi extend and twist around the beam.

"I saw a python a few days ago, and he gave me this idea. I have not achieved as much as I would like, but I think this can be advantageous." She let go of the beam and landed on her feet. "Next I have to practice moving through small spaces, and then I will have something to rival the mystics who meditate in various postures. I do not wish to be made to look paltry by old men in meditation."

"However you use it, I am truly impressed." Sanat Ji Mani touched her face gently. "You have great courage, Tulsi, and you are resourceful. I cannot think how I could have come so far without you."

"I would not have gone anywhere but in the back of Djerat's wagon if you had not been with me." Her smile had a little weariness in it, a fatigue that was more than physical. "I will be glad to be gone from here."

"Particularly since the Rajput is bent on going to war," Sanat Ji Mani agreed. "So. When I return tonight, we will make our plans."

"Very good," said Tulsi, her voice dropping to a near whisper. "After tonight, I will tell you what I have decided."

"If you wish," said Sanat Ji Mani. "You need not hurry your decision on my account."

"I will not," she said a little louder.

"Then I will welcome your decision, even if it is to postpone it," he said. "I would rather you be sure of your answer than that you feel duty-bound to give me one at a specific time."

"More of your foreign gallantry," she complained with mock severity.

"Hardly that," said Sanat Ji Mani.

"Whatever it may be, I enjoy it." She took his hand in hers and guided it down the front of her body. "How soon can we be gone?"

"As soon as it appears we may get away without harm." He paused while something nudged in the back of his thoughts. "If Hasin Dahele is going on a preparatory campaign, then we should be able to slip away in the general confusion. I doubt anyone will notice we have gone until nightfall."

"Does that mean tomorrow?" She made no effort to conceal her excitement.

"I would think so; tomorrow," he said, "if the Rajput keeps on with his plans."

"Then I will continue my provisioning. I have some food already, but I will get more, and I will take as many of the garments we have been given as I can. We need not be beggars at once." She cocked her chin. "I have coins, too."

"Each very useful," said Sanat Ji Mani, fighting the niggling sensation that he was not aware of all he needed to be. "I wish I had more to bring to this venture."

"You have knowledge and your knives. For the time being, it will be enough," she said, then stared down at her feet. "I should tell you: I have never ridden a horse before." In response to his startled expression she said, "I have often watched the soldiers ride and train, so I know the way of it, but entertainers were not allowed on horses in Timur-i's army, for fear they would go to the enemy. So all I know is how to drive mules. I can handle the reins, I think, but the saddle will be strange to me."

Sanat Ji Mani chided himself inwardly for assuming that Tulsi would know how to ride; it was an inconvenience to them now, but he said, "You are a most capable woman, and you do not let yourself be ruled by ignorance. I will try to find a smooth-gaited horse for you"—no easy thing in the Rajput's stables, he added to himself—"and I will rely on your skills as an athlete to be able to maintain your balance. Balance is the heart of it."

"So I think—about balance." she said. "Timur-i's soldiers all clung to their horses like monkeys when they crossed hard ground."

"Yes," said Sanat Ji Mani, thinking of his fine Turkish saddles lost at Delhi, his flexible Persian saddles, still in Rojire's care, and the old Spanish saddle at Villa Ragoczy in Rome, all of which he wished he had with him now. He was unfamiliar with the saddles of this region and hoped they would not be difficult to ride. "But consider this, Tulsi: if we are to escape from men on horseback, we, too, must be on horseback, or we will not succeed; it does not matter who recalls our passage if we can stay ahead of our pursuers. If that means that you have to ride as best you can, then you must. Otherwise we will be caught."

"All right," said Tulsi. "I should have told you before now, but I did not think we would be able to escape on horseback; I thought we would go on foot."

"Well," said Sanat Ji Mani, the kindness of his tone reassuring her, "I am glad you did not wait until we were in the stalls to tell me."

"I would not do that," she said, still embarrassed by this lapse.

He gazed at her, his care for her lighting his dark eyes. "I am not angry with you, Tulsi. I would not be angry with you if you had done something much worse than omitting to mention that you cannot ride."

Slowly she raised her eyes to his. "All right." She turned away. "Does this make the escape more difficult?"

"It does not make it easier," said Sanat Ji Mani. "But I will keep this in mind."

"So long as you do not say we cannot go because of it." She sounded like a chastened child.

"No; I would not do that," he said, wondering why she was so upset.

"Because I would go if you had to tie me across the horse like a dead sheep," she declared. "I would not mind traveling that way."

"You say that because you have never had to do it," said Sanat Ji Mani, thinking back to the long trek from Rome to Ravenna traveling in just that manner.

"All right, I never have." She came and stood in front of him. "But if it would help us disappear, I would do it."

"I would not ask that of you," he said, hoping to ease her anxiety.

"If you must, you must," she insisted.

Sanat Ji Mani saw the worry in her eyes and said, "If it is necessary, I will do it, but only if all else fails."

She grinned at him, her mercurial shift in mood as troubling to him as her dejection. "Then we will get away for sure."

Text of a letter from Rustam Iniattir at Al Myah Suways to Zal Iniattir at Asirgarh; carried by sea-captain and caravan leader and delivered by hand.

To my most worthy nephew, the greetings of Rustam Iniattir from the port of Al Myah Suways where I have just purchased the Evening Star *and the* Glory of Medina, *both good merchant ships, to add to our House and our commerce; both are fitted for the crossing of the Arabian Sea and have size and weight enough to ride the storm winds if that is necessary. They are made of teak and bear three sails each and have been tested on two previous crossings from the southern port of Manjurur to Al Myah Suways and back.*

If you would consider sending one of your sons to me, I will establish him as my clerk here, provide him a house and enough to live on in reasonable comfort while the family's expansion is made secure. In addition to these ships, I have the agency for Sanat Ji Mani's ships as well, which means that there is opportunity for us to do more than gamble with wind, wave, and tide. We have already proven our worth in managing Sanat Ji Mani's business, and this gives us a reputation that goes before us. I am not asking you to risk a child on an enterprise that could bring the boy to grief, you see. I ask you to consider this offer carefully. If I do not hear from you by mid-summer, I will next approach Azizi about one of his sons.

The seasons here in Egypt have been uniformly hot. Even when the Nile floods, there is little cooling from its waters, for although the water brings life to the fields, it does not stop the might of the sun. I have made arrangements in Fustat to reinforce the cellars of my house there, so that it is not flooded when the Inundation comes again. There is not the season of heavy rains such as one had in Delhi, although there are squalls in winter.

It has been a most instructive time; I can hardly imagine that it is just a year since I arrived in Egypt, in the Mameluke Empire, with more hope than gold to sustain me. Yet so it is, and the House of Iniattir has much to be proud of, including the triumph we have achieved in spite of all Timur-i could do. I have thanked the Forces of Light many times for all that has been salvaged for us, and I am grateful that Darkness has not yet spread itself over our family. So many others have been devastated by Timur-i and his army, but we have not had to suffer the catastrophic losses visited upon so many. Is it a failure of gods, or is it something more encompassing, a rise of Light, as Zarathustra promised? I can only pray it is the latter, for then good fortune will be found throughout the world and ignorance be ended, along with the power of Darkness.

Through the good offices of Rojire, Sanat Ji Mani's manservant, I have been able to participate in several trading ventures that have extended our market-place well beyond the ones we have now. Our first ship has returned to Alexandria from England and the Low Countries, bringing woollens and honey and salted fish. This may not seem very impressive to you, but I am keenly aware that for a first round of trading we have done very well. In another year, we will expand our goods in these markets to include muslins from you and Azizi, which we will exchange for hemp and other textiles as well as preserved fruits. One day I may even take the journey to these distant, fabled lands to see where our trade stock has ended up. Rojire has said that there are merchant-houses in England that do business abroad often, and seek to trade with the Turks. If that is their wish, why should we not make the most of their desires? I shall inform you of my plans as I approach the time I have set aside for this venture. If your son is here, he will be able to handle the shipments from these distant places, and make a name for himself in what is already a distinguished family.

I have put forty pieces of gold aside toward the purchase of another ship, with the intention of adding to the amount with every success we achieve. As soon as I have enough, I will make the purchase and add another ship to what I intend will one day be a mighty fleet of merchant vessels plying all the waters of the world, from this port to

China, and from Fustat to England and the lands of the Danes. I am told that the Danes have yellow hair and blue eyes, but I doubt it is so. Blue eyes I have seen before, but yellow hair? I know there was a Chinese pilgrim who stayed with Sanat Ji Mani whose hair was the color of rust, but that is not what I have been told the Danes have— their hair is like brass or parched grain. I will believe it when I see it. For now, I am content to arrange to trade with them, whatever the color of their hair may be.

I will hand this letter to Jumma Shamahdi, who is Captain of the Evening Star with instructions that it be given into the care of our factor in Chaul. From there, it will reach you as soon as a caravan leaves for Asirgarh. It is my hope that this be in your hands no more than two full moons after the dark of the year.

Rustam Iniattir
Merchant of Fustat and Al Myah Suways

5

Rajput Hasin Dahele sat on a showy dark-bay with a long head and narrow chest, horse and rider gaudily arrayed in gold and jewels, both of them far more suited to ceremony than battle. Even the curved shimtare that hung from the Rajput's fringed belt was designed for display rather than use, having a dozen jewels in its quillons and a pearl in the hilt. Before him rode his mounted troops, all in fine clothes with a full complement of weapons: bows, quivers filled with arrows, lances, shimtares, spears, and rings of caltrops. The setting sun blazed on their shining brass and brilliant silks, adding its own gilding to their already flamboyant display. The smell of leather and horses was strong on the still, warm air.

"What do you think, Sanat Ji Mani?" asked the Rajput of the man standing beside his horse. "Are they not formidable."

"They are quite splendid," said Sanat Ji Mani, not quite answering the question. He had concealed his disappointment at this full review readily enough, for there were too many eyes on him for him to do otherwise.

"Tomorrow evening, we shall see the elephants in review, along with asses and wagons for provisions, and then I will announce my plans." Hasin Dahele smiled broadly, giving his attention to Vayu Ede, who sat on his mule on the side opposite Sanat Ji Mani. "You see? They are the finest army ever assembled."

"They are most remarkable," said Vayu Ede, his expression oddly hungry as he watched the troops clatter by.

"I know this is going to be a most worthwhile venture. Once we have secured the north as far as the Godavari, we will be able to establish fortresses to further the larger campaign; without the fortresses, we will not be capable of holding onto any territory we seize. I have already made plans to garrison the fortress with men skilled in using defensive weapons, so that I may keep my others ready to go forth on my orders." His smile widened. "What do you think of my planning, Sanat Ji Mani?"

"I think that if you must go to war, preparation is crucial." He paused. "But no matter how you plan, no campaign will go as you expect, and you will never achieve your goals in the manner you planned."

"Sensible words," said Hasin Dahele, his smile becoming a smirk. "I thank you for giving me the benefit of your experience."

"More observation than experience," said Sanat Ji Mani, his brows arched to show his degree of skepticism.

Hasin Dahele laughed. "You would say that, would you not?" He gestured to a company of spearmen. "I am going to be sure each of them has fifteen spears to carry. Do you think that is sufficient?"

Sanat Ji Mani shrugged. "It may be, but that will depend upon the battles, and they are unpredictable."

"But fifteen is a prudent number, is it not?" Hasin Dahele persisted.

"Better than ten, and less cumbersome than twenty," Sanat Ji Mani replied, trying to take his tone from the Rajput.

"My notion exactly," Hasin Dahele exclaimed. "I knew I would do well to ask you."

Vayu Ede regarded Sanat Ji Mani with an air of satisfaction. "You are prepared to say that this army is ready for war?"

Sanat Ji Mani shrugged. "I have no knowledge of your foes, their armies, their defenses, their preparedness, their strength, or any other aspect, and so I can only say that this army is well-equipped; if it is also well-supported, then, if there is to be war, they are as ready as any army is." He looked up at the Rajput. "Your land is in good heart, your people are not deprived of their holdings and their families. You have sought to be a wise leader. Why do you want to go to war?"

"A strange question for you to ask," said Hasin Dahele. "You, of all men, should know that war brings with it riches and land. We have not made our frontiers firm, and it is time we did. While we are about it, we should expand our frontiers and make borders of them."

"I know that many wars begin with such ambitions. I have rarely seen any of them prove to be worth the price they demand." Sanat Ji Mani thought back to stands against Hittites, against Babylonians, against Egyptians, against Ethiopians, against Boetians, against Persians, against Scythians, against Germans, against Britons, against Huns, against the marauders outside Baghdad, against the Turks, against the Mongols of Jenghiz Khan . . . there had been so many battles—more than he could easily remember—and all of them left misery for both sides in their wakes; it hardly mattered which had been the aggressors and which had been encroached upon, the results were always the same: broken bodies and ravaged land, slain or enslaved people, ruined cities, obliterated towns and villages, livestock slaughtered, devastated crops, men maimed, famine and disease everywhere.

"You know that frontiers do not become borders if they are not fought for," said Vayu Ede with such emphasis that Sanat Ji Mani was shaken out of his repellant reverie.

"I know that is what everyone believes until they go to war," said Sanat Ji Mani.

Hasin Dahele laughed aloud. "Very clever, Sanat Ji Mani. You have wit, and you have much knowledge." He looked about him, pride in every sinew of his body. "I know this is an enviable force, one that will do much to bring land and glory to Beragar."

"I hope you are not too much disappointed by your victories," said Sanat Ji Mani.

"How can a victory disappoint?" Vayu Ede asked, his expression darkening.

"A victory that loses friends and animals and matériel can be so costly that failure would have been preferable. The conquest you seek always takes a toll of the triumphant as well as the vanquished." He held up his hand. "I know you do not want to believe this, but I must tell you I have seen it before, many times, and I know in war you must be prepared for the high price of victory." He nodded toward the soldiers on review. "You, O Rajput, have made excellent preparations, but you are not prepared." His right foot was aching but he did not shift his stance.

"How can you say this to me?" Hasin Dahele demanded, his face darkening. "You see what my army is, how my men are—"

"You have asked me to advise you. I am doing my best to comply with your order," said Sanat Ji Mani, making no excuse for his tone or his interruption.

"You speak as if you have lost battles," said Vayu Ede, the observation critical. "You have not enjoyed the sapidity of victory."

"If I have not, it is only because I have found little to savor in victory," Sanat Ji Mani said bluntly. "I wish I could spare the Rajput the pain and defeat that comes with war, no matter how unvanquished he may be."

Hasin Dahele nodded. "You want me to understand that the Gods will not bestow Their favor without requiring sacrifice. I understand that." The sun was almost down and the sun came directly from the side, shining like molten brass, making long, spiked shadows on the marshaling yard, and throwing them against the far wall, so that an army of dark ghosts also seemed to be passing the Rajput on parade.

"Then content yourself with a show of force and do not undertake a campaign," Sanat Ji Mani urged him, knowing it was useless to argue with him.

"I will not let others claim what is mine to hold," said Hasin Dahele in a hard voice. "I am prepared to lose some of my men, some of my horses, some of my elephants, and some of all our supplies. I know that such losses are part of campaigning. I am aware that some of the people will suffer, and that many will be deprived of home and possessions due to necessity. It is what war demands. Any man fighting must be prepared for such contingencies. But I will have what is fated to be mine. You must comprehend why I must do this."

"I know you see a necessity now that may not exist," said Sanat Ji Mani, aware that he was not persuading the Rajput of anything.

"You do not know Beragar. You are thinking in terms that do not apply in this place." He gestured Sanat Ji Mani to silence and stared straight ahead at his companies of spearmen who were riding past him, their curved shields on their left arms, their spears in long sheaths slung on the right sides of their saddles. Next came lancers, with high-canteled saddles to help support the riders, so that a thrust with their weapons would not unseat them. Each of them was equipped with three lances and oblong shields that could be swung sideways to protect the flanks of their horses. Four companies of lancers went by, then came a small company of messengers with few weapons, their leather armor sewn with brass plates, and their horses protected by more brass-sewn leather. Finally, eight companies of light cavalry, with shimtares and mail armor, passed in review; their mail made a pleasant ringing to accompany the sounds of their horses hooves.

At last, Hasin Dahele spoke again. "So you see," he exclaimed as if continuing their conversation without interruption, "there are enough men, they have good weapons, they are ready to go forth— in fact, they are eager."

"Because they have not yet fought," said Sanat Ji Mani.

"After we make the Godavari our border, they will be ready to take on my campaign. You will come with me and advise me." He bent down and tapped Sanat Ji Mani on the head. "You are my counselor for war, Sanat Ji Mani." The sun dipped below the mountains and only the butter-colored glow remained in the western sky; all over the marshaling yard torches and braziers were lit, replacing the brilliance of sunset with pools of shifting brightness, giving the night a greater darkness by contrast.

Sanat Ji Mani turned to the Rajput, shocked. "I am a foreigner. I am not one of your people. How can you entrust this position to me?"

Again Hasin Dahele laughed. "It is fated to be so. Therefore it is so. You will advise me, and from your wise counsel I will achieve the world. Surely you know this must happen." He touched his mount with his heels and the horse moved forward, mincing toward the front stable. "Come with me, my counselor."

Sanat Ji Mani complied, staying even with the horse's shoulder. He had little to say until they reached the stable, and then he held the Rajput's horse's bridle while Hasin Dahele dismounted and handed his mount over to three stable-slaves; all around them soldiers were turning their animals over to the grooms and stable-hands who cared for the horses. "Are you taking any of your stable-slaves on campaign?"

Hasin Dahele chuckled. "They are slaves of the palace. Why should they go with us when they would only slow us down?"

"Then why do your soldiers not tend their own mounts?" Sanat Ji Mani asked, keeping his voice level. "On campaign, the horses will need as much care as your men, and without slaves to do it, you may find it is impossible to keep all your horses sound."

"An interesting point," Hasin Dahele conceded as he started out of the stable, walking toward Vayu Ede, who waited at the side entrance to the palace. "I will consider it."

"You will need farriers, too," Sanat Ji Mani went on. "One for every twenty horses at least, or you will not be able to keep your men mounted."

"One for every twenty horses is a great many farriers," said Hasin Dahele. "Why should I have so many? There are villages along our path of march who will tend to any of the horses that may need it."

Sanat Ji Mani shrugged. "If you wish to entrust your horses to farriers whose loyalty is untested and unknown, what is it to me?"

Hasin Dahele stopped still. "How do you mean?"

"Only that if I were your enemy, and I knew you were relying on farriers not of your own army, I would send in my men to harm your horses under the guise of caring for them." Sanat Ji Mani offered Hasin Dahele the blandest of smiles. "Think of all the harm I could do without risking a single soldier. A whole company might be disabled before anyone was aware of what was happening."

This took Hasin Dahele aback. "I take your point," he said as he resumed walking. "With your experience, you must have had many occasions to see this happen."

"I do not know why you should think I have any particular experience, but any sensible commander will always seek ways to damage the enemy without inflicting hurt on his own men. If you had been attacked, I would suppose you would do this to turn the advantage to your favor." Sanat Ji Mani could not rid himself of the uneasy sensation he had had for many days—that the Rajput had made up his mind about this proposed war, and that included Sanat Ji Mani's role in it, and that the Rajput had assumed Sanat Ji Mani's complicity in his plans.

"You are a most useful counselor, as I knew you would be," said Hasin Dahele. "Very well. I will consider more farriers. And perhaps a few stable-slaves, too, so the horses will not be exposed to our enemies except in battle."

"You would do well to carry as much of your feed as you can; your enemies will not be above supplying blighted hay to you, or grain with rot, or burning fields that would otherwise go to feed your animals. If your horses do not eat wholesome things, they will sicken, many will die, and you will not be able to put many men into the field." Sanat Ji Mani recalled how such misfortune had stopped the advance of the Avars, nine hundred years before. Then it had been a happenstance of hard weather, but their opponents quickly learned from what nature had done and enlarged upon it, with disastrous results to the Avars.

"You are loading my army with so many things," Hasin Dahele complained, continuing onward. He pointed to Vayu Ede as he came up to the poet. "This man's visions have guided me this far; now you will add your knowledge to his vision. It will bring glory to all of us; you will see it yourselves."

Vayu Ede's features all but glowed with satisfaction. "You will do what Timur-i could not accomplish. You will be the Ruler of the World." His use of the titulary form was sincere, much more than flattery.

Hasin Dahele grinned. "I long for that time," he said. "If the Gods have marked me for this, I will comply with Their mandate." He said this without a trace of humility, but in the manner of a man accepting a task to be done.

"And you will be remembered into long ages to come. Timur-i has shown the way to greatness," Vayu Ede went on, nodding in Sanat Ji Mani's direction. "You will achieve greatness beyond any known before. The Gods have shown me."

"The Gods are epic warriors; They know battles that make our most ambitious seem puny," said Hasin Dahele, and glanced at Sanat Ji Mani. "I have much to fulfill. You will assist me to do this great work, for so it is written."

Sanat Ji Mani listened with a cold sensation gathering in his chest; he knew he could say nothing that would deter Hasin Dahele from entering upon this catastrophic course: the Rajput believed the gods required it of him, and that he was therefore destined to conquer. This was troubling, and all the more so because Vayu Ede was feeding Hasin Dahele prophesies that encouraged war and subjugation. He tried to summon up a few sensible words to persuade the Rajput to reconsider his campaign; all he could say was, "You should be wary of too much favor from your gods: they often play cruel jokes on those they single out."

Vayu Ede chuckled. "As many others have learned." He folded his hands. "The Gods have shown me what is to come. I am only Their instrument, as is the Rajput. All is Their Will."

"Then it would be wise of you not to depend overmuch on their beneficence," said Sanat Ji Mani.

The Rajput quickened his pace as he entered the palace. "You will be given provisions for the campaign. You have only to tell Vayu Ede what you require and it will be yours. You may choose your mount from among my personal horses. You will ride with me in the morning; I will order an umbrella made to provide you shade on campaign so your skin will not blister and burn." He looked directly at Sanat Ji Mani. "I know the sun is harsh, and that you, more than many, suffer on its account."

A frown flickered over Sanat Ji Mani's face and was gone. "You are most kind, but I hardly deserve such favor. I am a foreigner, and an exile. I have nothing to offer you beyond a little prudence gleaned during my travels."

"You are my promised advisor. I will see that you are always able to advise me," said the Rajput in a manner that stopped all protest.

"If I fail you, what then?" Sanat Ji Mani spoke curtly.

"You will not fail me; the Gods have shown it." For punctuation, the Rajput slapped at the jeweled hilt of his sword. "Tend to it, Vayu Ede."

Vayu Ede motioned to Sanat Ji Mani. "I will come to your room directly and you may present me with all the things you will require."

"And my companion?" Sanat Ji Mani asked, fearing for Tulsi's safety.

"She will remain here, where she will be guarded for you," said Vayu Ede. "A slave will be assigned to care for her, and you may be certain she will be protected from harm."

"I have arranged it already," said Hasin Dahele, settling the matter. "She will continue to be my honored guest. You need not worry on her account."

"She does not know your language," Sanat Ji Mani persisted. "You make a mute of her if you will not allow her to travel with me."

"She will be cared for," said the Rajput with finality. "If you should die on campaign, she will be kept as part of my household until her death. Surely you cannot expect more?"

Sanat Ji Mani bowed over his hands. "I am grateful, but I ask you to reconsider. She and I have traveled far together."

"She is to stay here, Sanat Ji Mani. That is the end of it." The Rajput turned on his heel and strode away toward his private quarters.

"Be relieved, foreigner," said Vayu Ede. "If the Rajput did not hold you in high regard, your companion would not be treated so well."

Knowing that Tulsi would not see it this way, Sanat Ji Mani said, "I am sure the Rajput does her and me honor."

"As well he might," said Vayu Ede with another of his cryptic smiles. "You have not yet shown yourself, and that is to be expected; you do not know whether the Rajput is worthy of such revelation. I have told him that you will know when he is ready to be proclaimed. After you see the elephants and you accompany the army on their first enterprise, you will know that he is a righteous heir."

"No doubt his father thought so while he lived," said Sanat Ji Mani, hoping to discover what Vayu Ede meant.

"His father died eleven years ago, taken by the Blood Fever. Many died then." Vayu Ede bowed to Sanat Ji Mani.

"It is always hard to lose a father," said Sanat Ji Mani, preparing to leave the old man and go to his own quarters; already he was anticipating Tulsi's outrage when he informed her of the Rajput's plans.

"It would have been harder still for Hasin Dahele's father to lose a son," said Vayu Ede. "The Rajput's grandfather lived many years and ruled wisely; his son was not so fortunate."

"How old was the Rajput's grandfather when he died?" Sanat Ji Mani wondered what Vayu Ede intended in telling him these things.

"He was fifty-six, older than I am by almost a decade. So his son had only three years to reign before Hasin Dahele came to rule." Vayu Ede pulled at one strand of his long, white hair. "The grandfather is remembered, the grandson will be remembered, the father is forgotten."

Sanat Ji Mani nodded to show he had heard. "Let us hope Hasin Dahele will rule many years and be remembered with pride."

"May it be so," said Vayu Ede, apparently satisfied with Sanat Ji Mani's remark. "Go make ready. I will come to your quarters when I have finished my evening meditation."

Accepting this dismissal readily, Sanat Ji Mani made his way along the corridors to the room he shared with Tulsi; as he walked, he pondered, and arrived at the door to the room with nothing resolved. He scratched at the door. "Tulsi."

She admitted him at once, her smile fading as she caught sight of his face. "What has happened?"

"The Rajput has ordered me to go with him on campaign," Sanat Ji Mani began.

"When?" She slammed the door.

"In a matter of days," he answered. "It has all been arranged."

"Then we can use that for our escape," she said, but without certainty.

"It would be possible, if the Rajput would agree to allowing you to come." He spoke as gently as he could. "I do not want to leave you here alone."

Tulsi took a step back. "Allow me to come?" She glared at him. "You mean I am to remain here?"

"Unless I can persuade him to change his mind," said Sanat Ji Mani.

"I am to be a hostage; is that not the way of it," she said. "The Rajput has decided that I will be a hostage."

"That is what I think," said Sanat Ji Mani. "I will try to speak to him, to change his mind, but I doubt—"

"How soon do you have to go?" she interrupted.

"Tomorrow there is another review, and then he intends a beginning thrust to secure all the land from here north to the Nar—"

"—manda," she finished for him. "So soon."

"He believes his gods have chosen him to be the conqueror of the world," said Sanat Ji Mani. "I gather Vayu Ede has had visions to that effect, and so the Rajput is eager to fulfill this grandiose dream."

"You sound disgusted," said Tulsi.

"That is the least of it," said Sanat Ji Mani, going to sit on the edge of the bed. "For some reason, both of them are convinced that I must be part of the venture."

"Then they are fools, both of them," said Tulsi, her voice catching in her throat. "How can you go with the army, in daylight? What will become of you?"

"The Rajput is ordering an umbrella made for me, to keep the sun off me," said Sanat Ji Mani sardonically. "He is aware that I burn in the sun."

"Oh, very good," Tulsi approved with heavy sarcasm. "You are provided an umbrella, and this is to help you? He gives his foes something to shoot at; the umbrella is large. The bowmen will aim at it. A good diversion." She flung up her hands. "You will be in pain *and* a target. What other honors does he plan for you?"

Sanat Ji Mani rose and went to her, standing behind her, his hands on her shoulders. "I will manage, Tulsi. I have endured worse."

She shook him off. "Why are you not refusing? Why do you not tell him no?"

"Because I am afraid of what he might do," Sanat Ji Mani admitted.

"And so you let him do this?" She swung around to confront him. "You let him separate us to appease him?"

With a sigh Sanat Ji Mani dropped his hands. "I had not expected this. I did not know he planned that I should go on campaign with him. If I had thought he had such intentions, I would have approached the matter differently from the beginning. The whole plan is repugnant to me, in large part because I will not be with you. You say you are a hostage: I agree. I wish I did not. If I could spare you this, I would, but I cannot, not without chancing something far worse." He waited for her to speak; when she remained silent, her shoulders stiff, and her head held at a defiant angle, he went on. "I admit it has been pleasant to live in comfort, and because of that I may not have as-sessed our danger for what it was. I still do not know why Hasin Dahele thinks his gods have appointed me to advise him. But he has determined that this is the case, apparently since we arrived here. I do not know that we could have avoided this at the first. Tulsi, I apologize for bringing you into this, and I give you my Word I will do my utmost to get you out."

"Do you think you can?" Her challenge stung.

"I know I will do all that I can to bring it about," he said.

She stared into his eyes, her face set. "Then you will go with him."

"I think I must. Perhaps if I do not endure the rigors of the ma-neuvers he has planned, he will not insist I remain with him." Sanat Ji Mani looked away from her toward the window. "I can probably get you out of the palace before I go tomorrow, but I cannot guarantee that you will not be hunted if I do, nor can I be certain of what may happen to you if you are caught." He turned toward her again.

"I have been poisoned here," she reminded him. "How am I to feel safe?"

"I have no answer for you," he admitted. "But if you allow me to speak to the Rajput again, then something may—"

She waved him to silence. "No. It is probably best that we obey him for now. I know how Timur-i's soldiers behaved to run-away cap-tives and I would rather drown in urine than have that happen to me." Folding her arms, she said, "You will have to go tomorrow without sustenance. I will not lie with you tonight."

"I would not want you to, not with so much disruption around us," he told her. "You have enough to dwell upon without that."

She studied him intently. "Are you being compassionate or am I unacceptable in my current state of mind?"

"Do you want to open your soul to me just now?" Sanat Ji Mani asked kindly.

"No." She glared at him.

"Then you have answered your own question. Tulsi Kil, I do not go where I am unwelcome; you should know this by now." He touched her arm lightly.

"I know," she said, and began to weep. "And I am torn. I want two things and cannot have both. Will I curse myself for refusing what I may decide I want, or do I prefer to stay as I am, and never change to one of your blood? Which shall I do? What will be the right answer for me? Which will I regret the most if I do not do it?" She took a step back from him, dashing tears from her eyes with the flat of her hands. "You: say nothing." It was a command. "Do not speak to me. This is for me to decide, not you."

Sanat Ji Mani nodded, feeling her ambivalence as if it were a solid presence in the room. He stood still, knowing he could not comfort her, and chagrined that he could not.

Finally she composed herself, coming up to him, her demeanor cool. "Tomorrow night, I will know what I want of you," she said, and turned away before he responded.

Text of a letter from Lonpah ST'amlontohr, merchant of T'u-Bo-T'eh, to Azizi Iniattir of Sirpur, carried by caravan leader, written in Tibetean, Hindi, Gond, and Sanscrit.

To the most well-reputed Azizi Iniattir, the greetings of Lonpah ST'amlontohr, merchant of Lhasa; my clerk has sworn to write this in four tongues in the hope that you yourself will be able to read one of them, or will have a clerk, as I have, who can read one of the tongues here.

Now that the first caravans of spring are departing, I have ordered this be prepared for you, as the merchant most likely to have interest in this proposition, and the wherewithal to act upon what I am going to suggest to you.

I have recently purchased some textiles from a merchant who had them from one of your caravans. The textiles are of excellent quality and have provided me with quick profit, which is why I have taken it upon myself to write to you. I will give this to my caravan leader with instructions that he pass it to one of your caravan leaders to bring to you, in the hope that I might encourage you to consider sending a caravan to T'u-Bo-T'eh with the textiles so that both of us may enjoy a higher profit and the direct access to the markets each of us represents.

For my part, I can offer several sorts of goods, including religious scrolls that are much admired in the lowlands. Also, there are high-quality gems that I can secure for the right price, and these will be welcome in any market. I have access to skins, as well, particularly the mountain leopard, bears, and several kinds of goats. Many of these are highly sought. I have dealt with a number of hunters whose families make the skins ready for selling, and if I can assure them of wider markets, they will increase their hunting with the intention of sending the extra skins to you, in the lowlands. There are fine copper horns made here, and although some of the lamas do not approve of selling these sacred instruments, the makers are more than willing to provide them to me. I do not think you have had much like them to sell before. I am also able to supply gongs and bells, but these are heavy items and not readily transported down the mountains, and so I should not want to trade too many, for they would not allow for other loads on any beast carrying these gongs and bells, which would make them very costly to anyone who wished to purchase one.

I have fourteen Spiti ponies and nine yaks to bear my merchandise down to the markets your caravans have reached, and if you have need for more goods, I can acquire more animals to carry them. My brothers have herds of ponies and yaks, so my access to them is readily had, and I will not put myself at any disadvantage in paying more to carry the goods than I can hope to gain from trade. I tell you this to assure you that I am ready to undertake any amount of trade you require.

If such an arrangement is satisfactory to you, inform me of it and I will provide a guide to lead your caravan to Lhasa so that we may begin what I trust will be an association that is useful and profitable to us both. With the Sultans gone from Delhi, merchants like you and me can enjoy the trade that has so long been impossible.

Lonpah ST'amlontohr
merchant of Lhasa

6

From his vantage-place at the crest of the hill, Rajput Hasin Dahele stopped and pointed to the town below them; the streets were busy, the market crowded, and the fields beyond the walls were filled with activity. "There. You see?" The air around them smelled of green things and fertile fields as well as the richer, more pungent odor of the forest at their backs.

"I see," said Sanat Ji Mani, his head aching from the morning's exposure to the sun; the huge silken parasol provided some relief, but not enough to eliminate the discomfort of being in daylight without the protection of his native earth in the soles of his shoes. Beside him, the young officer assigned to hold the umbrella did his best to keep Sanat Ji Mani in shadow.

"How would you deploy your men to take the town with as few losses as possible?" Hasin Dahele was enjoying himself hugely, thrilling to his panoply and all the accouterments of battle.

"I would set up my companies on the hills around the town and then send in an envoy to ask for surrender," said Sanat Ji Mani as quietly as he could, for the army was tremendously noisy. "They know you are coming."

"All the more reason to attack," said Hasin Dahele. "We will lose the element of surprise if we wait much longer."

"You do not need an element of surprise, which you have lost, in any case; they know you are here," Sanat Ji Mani said. "It is a small town, the walls around it are wood, designed to keep animals out and livestock in, not to hold off armies. Your elephants would have it down in a single charge."

"Then let us charge," said the Rajput eagerly.

"Why bother? It is unnecessary," Sanat Ji Mani said, knowing his cautions were fruitless.

"Has exile taken all your spirit?" the Rajput asked. "Why should I hesitate to show my strength?"

"Because those people are weak. Do your gods require you to punish the weak in order to deserve your favor?" As he spoke, he wished he knew which of the myriad gods Hasin Dahele sought to honor, for there were many among them who were blood-thirsty.

"My men are avid for an opportunity to show their mettle," said Hasin Dahele with a hard look at Sanat Ji Mani. "And my Gods do not expect me to falter."

"Then let them prove themselves on something more worthwhile than that town; find a city that is armed that will be a suitable offering to your gods, not this gathering of farmers and workmen," said Sanat Ji Mani. "There is nothing to boast of in taking such a place. Fifty men on horseback with bows and lances could do it. You have five thousand soldiers at your back. That is many more than every man, woman, and child in that town."

"Just my point," said Hasin Dahele. "We will have an easy victory and everyone in the towns and villages in this region will know that we must be reckoned with. Others will be glad to surrender to avoid the fate of this town. We show our might here and we will not have to battle again."

Sanat Ji Mani stared at the Rajput, knowing it was an uncourteous thing to do. "You asked my advice and I have given it to you. It may not be to your liking; you may take it or not as you see fit. This is your campaign."

Hasin Dahele grinned. "So it is." He signaled for his nearest aide. "Tell my first two companies of archers to charge the fields and drive everyone back into the town; if they will not go, kill them. If there are any Untouchables, do not pollute yourselves with them. Capture what animals you can—except the cattle—and those you cannot, kill for our cooking pots." He turned to Sanat Ji Mani. "You see, I will make the most of this opportunity."

The pang that took hold of Sanat Ji Mani had little to do with the sun, or the lack of his native earth; he was sick at heart. "You are not being prudent, and that will cost you in time to come," he warned the Rajput. "This is not a crucial fight. You are risking your men unnecessarily and you are going to bring about needless destruction in a place that would serve you better as an ally than a foe."

"A town, so small—what kind of ally is a place like this? Better to subjugate the people, teach them to fear me, and let them serve as an example to the rest of the region." The Rajput lifted his hand and the first company of archers started down the hill, the men lifting their bows and notching arrows as they rode.

"The town holds the valley. You may have use of this valley, O Rajput," said Sanat Ji Mani, not wanting to watch what was happening.

"Why would I want so minor a place?" the Rajput asked. "It is a town of little worth or importance."

"If you ever have to retreat over this ground, the valley may be crucial to you and your army. It could be a haven." Sanat Ji Mani saw Hasin Dahele shake his head. "I know you do not intend to retreat, but that may not be your decision to make."

"There is no army strong enough to drive my army back," said Hasin Dahele with such arrogant confidence that Sanat Ji Mani winced. "The Gods are guiding me. No other Rajput has been favored by the Gods as I have."

"There is no army you know of, but that does not mean that another Rajput might not be planning exactly what you are attempting to do, and with a force stronger than the one you command, and believe that his gods favor him as yours favor you." It was a useless observation and Sanat Ji Mani knew it; he gestured to the valley. "Leave them in peace and they will shelter you in your hour of need. Attack them and you will never be safe here again."

"How can you, of all men, say such things to me?" The Rajput rose in his stirrups and gave a second signal that put his men into the charge. "They will have this settled by evening, and then you and I may see what we have."

"I would rather remain outside the walls," said Sanat Ji Mani. "There is more safety away from where the battle was fought than in its place." He pointedly turned away from the Rajput and the first skirmishes in the fields below.

"My spearmen," Hasin Dahele shouted. "Follow the archers! First and fourth companies!" He dropped his arm and gave a bellow of enthusiasm to send his men off. At once the spearmen set the horses plummeting down the hill; thundering down the slope, five horses missed their footing and fell in a thrashing tangle of legs that tripped another four before the spearmen could guide their mounts around the fallen.

"Are you going to send slaves to help them?" Sanat Ji Mani asked as the horses neighed and men screamed in pain.

"I may, when all the spearmen have passed," said Hasin Dahele. He was breathing fast and his color was heightened with excitement; one of the horses collapsed and lay still. "That one will have to be pulled off to the side."

"Have the tack removed. You cannot spare the saddle and bridle any more than you can spare the horse," said Sanat Ji Mani watching the rider stumble to his feet, clearly dazed; he took a step, screamed and fell. "I fear the soldier has broken his leg."

"How can you be sure from this distance?" Hasin Dahele demanded.

"I have seen men hurt in battle, and I know how they behave," Sanat Ji Mani answered, not quite daring to go down the hill himself to see how badly the man's leg was broken, not in the open sunlight with the Rajput watching him. "If his leg is not set quickly, he will take a fever and he may die. You cannot want that to happen."

"He will have to wait until the village is in my hands," said Hasin Dahele, dismissing the whole matter with an impatient wave of his arm.

"You could stop the attack now, and demand a surrender. It would spare your soldiers more hurt. You will lose only those men injured when their horses fell," Sanat Ji Mani said, doubting that Hasin Dahele would listen to him.

"Why would I do that, when victory is so readily had?" He was about to signal his other two companies of spearmen when he paused. "Why do you not want me to fight for this valley?"

"I have already told you: because it is unnecessary, and because it creates enemies. You will have enough of them without adding to their numbers." Sanat Ji Mani sighed. "Also, you have just begun your campaign and this kind of battle is profligate: you will need your spears and arrows and men and horses later. Wasting them now on a needless assault is squandering, not strategic campaigning." He indicated the town. "Those are not warriors, they are farmers and artisans. You have no reason to fight them."

"And yet you warned me against farriers, as subtle foes who could compromise an entire company of horsemen," the Rajput mused aloud. He signaled his spearmen. "They need to be tested," he said as he gestured them into motion.

The two companies pelted down the hill, taking care to dodge around the fallen men and horses, all of them raising their spears and shouting. They were an awesome sight, and the townspeople below were transfixed by the soldiers' terrifying onslaught. The first wave of archers were nearly to the town walls, the second line spreading out behind them to cross the fields to capture those working the crops. A wailing arose from the valley, the sound combining the cries of those attacked and the shouts of the soldiers.

"They are doing well," said the Rajput as he watched his soldiers' mounts turn the fields to mud and to chase down those farmers making for the town gates. "I will have slaves from this."

"And you will have enemies," said Sanat Ji Mani.

"So long as they fear me, I do not mind enemies," the Rajput countered. "You should understand how important fear is."

"No doubt," said Sanat Ji Mani, appalled by what he heard.

"My enemies will know not to expect mercy from me, and they will be wise." Hasin Dahele laid his hand on his sword. "This is the beginning of my conquest of the world."

Sanat Ji Mani stared down at the pandemonium of battle, and saw the first futile attempts at resistance; he glanced at the Rajput and read no horror in his handsome face, only glee and beneath that something more sinister—perhaps gloating—in the man's dark eyes; Hasin Dahele would not be stopped now, and Sanat Ji Mani recognized this with despair. His arm was aching and he saw that the shade from the umbrella had shifted. "I am being burned," he said.

"Tend to your duty," the Rajput snapped at the aide holding the umbrella. "This man is not to have sunlight fall on him. If you fail, you will be burned as you have allowed him to be. I will have your arm thrust in a fire."

"Do not do that," Sanat Ji Mani interceded. "It is bad enough one of us be hurt—hurting him will not make me better."

"Are you asking for mercy for him" Hasin Dahele laughed low in his throat. "For a man who has let you suffer?"

"Yes," said Sanat Ji Mani, "as I would hope he would do for me."

Hasin Dahele shrugged. "I will forgive him—this time. For your sake."

"I am grateful," said Sanat Ji Mani, managing to keep the irony out of his voice. "There will be agony enough for everyone before this campaign is done."

"Move back into the trees," Hasin Dahele ordered, without saying anything about Sanat Ji Mani's additional remark. "I will summon you when the battle is done." Saying that, he spurred his dark-bay and went cantering down the line of mounted men still waiting to enter the fray.

"We had better do as he says," the aide recommended.

Sanat Ji Mani gave a single nod. "There is nothing to see here."

The aide stared at Sanat Ji Mani, shocked. "There is the battle."

"And all battles are confusion and anguish. I do not need to watch another to know that." He swung his horse around. "I will sleep a while, for the night is going to be long, and the demands many."

"How can you be certain of that?" the aide asked, bustling to keep the umbrella in position as he and Sanat Ji Mani made for the trees.

"It is always so after a battle. The wounded and the dying will need succor and the dead will have to be given the rites of death. Why should this battle be any different." Sanat Ji Mani stopped to look toward the soldiers waiting in the cover of the trees. Most of them were edgy, anticipating their entry into the fighting. "What will become of them?" He was not aware he had spoken aloud until the aide said, "They will further the glory of the Rajput."

Ahead of them, two elephants rigged out for war loomed out of the shelter of the trees, their mahouts straddling their necks, and behind the mahouts, howdahs with three archers in each. The big animals were restless, swaying as they stood, their trunks moving as if to begin their battle now. Slowly they ambled forward, each ponderous step guided by the mahouts as they began making their way toward the village. A dozen more elephants fell into line behind them.

"The villagers will tremble," said the aide with great satisfaction.

Sanat Ji Mani shook his head. "There is no need for such measures. The town will fall without using the elephants."

"But they will destroy the walls, and it will be told everywhere that the Rajput cannot be resisted," said the aide. "That will serve Beragar well."

"It will also warn other rulers to increase their armies and strengthen their city walls, so the Rajput will not have a quick victory." Sanat Ji Mani almost smiled as he rode into the shadow of the trees; the shield they provided from the piercing rays of the sun was as welcome as nightfall. He drew in his horse, feeling a little strength returning to him. "I will go to rest for the afternoon."

"There is no camp for you to—" the aide began.

"I will find a sheltered place and that will suffice. If you will attend to my horse, I will thank you for your good service." He was already looking away from the reserve troops, trying to find a place where the leaves were the thickest and the shadows the most dense. "If the Rajput has need of me, wake me. If not, let me sleep until I rouse myself."

The aide bowed in the saddle. "I will do as you wish, Illustrious Foreigner."

Sanat Ji Mani found the title excessive but knew it would only trouble the aide if he did not accept it. "You are very good," he said as he spotted a mound of vines and trees a short distance away. "This will suit me very well."

"There may be snakes," warned the aide.

"I will be careful," Sanat Ji Mani assured him as he swung out of the saddle and handed the reins to the aide. "Come for me at day's end and I will be ready for you."

Reluctantly the aide took the reins and nudged his horse away from the thicket that Sanat Ji Mani was exploring. "I will summon you if there is need."

"Very good," said Sanat Ji Mani, glad to be in a place that would protect him as much as anything other than his native earth could. He dropped to his knees and ducked into the heart of the vines and leaves, going cautiously in order not to disturb anything that might have taken shelter there. Finally he matted down a few small branches and lay back on them, his whole body aching for rest, his soul longing for sleep. For a long moment the image of Tulsi hung in his mind, and he yearned to speak to her, to know she was safe. He questioned himself again on his decision to travel with the Rajput, for he still was not certain she was not in danger on his account, and that troubled him; how was he to protect her while he was not with her? How could he defend her now that they were separated? What could he do to guard her? He tried, as he had tried for the five days the army had been on the march, to think of some means of securing her freedom and safety, but nothing occurred to him and he was left to fret over what he could not change. Then his enervation caught up with him; he closed his eyes and succumbed to the stupor that was the slumber of his kind.

Shouts and drum-beats woke him as the sun dropped low in the west. Whoops and screams mixed on the air as the Rajput's army claimed the last remains of the town as their tattered prize; Sanat Ji Mani emerged, limping, from the thicket where he had rested to find the aide waiting for him, holding the reins of his horse and grinning eagerly. "What is it?" Sanat Ji Mani asked.

"They are branding the captives, so they will be known as slaves forever," said the aide. "Many men were captured, and many women. Also children, some too young for branding."

"I am certain the Rajput is pleased," said Sanat Ji Mani, his body refreshed but his spirits wearier than before.

"The Rajput will take the slaves back to Devapur and decide which he will keep and which will be taken to the coast and sold to the Arabs." The aide grinned. "This will be a most fortuitous expedition. The army has fought and there are slaves gained from it, and the rule of the land."

"A great achievement," said Sanat Ji Mani drily as he mounted the dun mare he had chosen from the Rajput's stables.

"You will see for yourself. The Rajput has ordered me to bring you to him." The aide nodded in the direction of the hill. "We must make haste or the light will be gone."

"I am sure there is fire enough in the town to guide us," said Sanat Ji Mani, making no effort to disguise his distaste. He pulled the mare's head around and started toward the slope leading down to the village.

"The Rajput has had a feast prepared for his men. All the goats and all the sheep in the town have been slaughtered and set to cook over fires." The aide was full of anticipation.

"Have they." Sanat Ji Mani knew that this boded ill for the night. "Have the soldiers been given anything other than water to drink?"

The aide laughed aloud. "You are a most perspicacious fellow, foreigner. Yes, there was honey-beer found—barrels of it. The Rajput said it was to be given out to his men, first to those who fought, and then to the rest of his army." He put one hand to his chest. "I am to have mine when I bring you to the town and present you to the Rajput."

"I am sure you are looking forward to it," said Sanat Ji Mani, his sincerity masking apprehension.

"Of course." The aide led Sanat Ji Mani to the broad swath of trampled vegetation when Hasin Dahele's army had descended the hill. "We have lost thirteen men and nine horses. There are fifty-three wounded and injured that I know of, but there are probably a few more. The man you said had broken his leg is one of the worst hurt, although there is another man who was struck in the eye and one who fell into a fire, but most have nothing more than cuts and bruises," he babbled excitedly. "There was a camp of Untouchables on the edge of the fields, and we drove them away."

"Untouchables," said Sanat Ji Mani, thinking of those unfortunate enough to be born into the under-caste, who were considered contaminated by the rest of the people; war would be hardest on them, who were already condemned.

"They will not be allowed to foul our victory," the aide boasted.

"How could they, indeed," Sanat Ji Mani said, drawing his horse in to look at the town: the order of the morning was gone and in its place was devastation, where the army was setting up a camp for the night as if to set the seal on what they had done; fields were uprooted and trampled, the walls of the town had been pushed down on the south-eastern side and the houses around that portion of wall were tumbled into heaps, two of them blackened where they had caught fire. At the center of the town, where the market had been, there was now a collection of tents, the Rajput's being the grandest. Huge cooking fires burned throughout the town, and soldiers were gathered around them. Outside the walls in a hastily improvised stockade the townspeople huddled together while a group of aides went among them, gathering information and recording what they learned on palm-leaves.

"Done in less than a day," said the aide proudly.

"The Rajput must be pleased," said Sanat Ji Mani, and put his mare in motion down the hill.

"The soldiers are saying that they will conquer all the way to the mountains at the Roof of the World," the aide went on. "They say that this has shown them how mighty they are."

"To defeat a town of less than half their number is an accomplish-ment," said Sanat Ji Mani flatly.

The aide mistook his intent. "Oh, yes. We did not need more than a third of the army to do it. In time to come, more will fight, but for now, it is proof that the Gods are with Hasin Dahele. By the time the rains come, his rule will extend far and wide and his army will be feared from mountains of the Afghani to China, and south to the ends of our lands."

Sanat Ji Mani cut into this rhapsodizing. "The Rajput wants to ex-ceed the conquests of Timur-i—he has said so. This is his beginning."

"Just so," said the aide, stopping his tongue at last.

The sounds of celebration were drifting upward, filling the night. Around one of the huge spits men were dancing, singing a song in praise of Ganesh, Shiva, and Kali, while cooks cut off slabs of sheep and goat for them. Other fires had musicians gathered near them to play while the men ate and drank. The odor of sizzling meat was almost strong enough to conceal the metallic scent of blood and the stench of fear that lingered from the battle.

The aide led the way to Hasin Dahele's tent, dismounted, and held the reins of Sanat Ji Mani's dun mare. "He is waiting for you, the Rajput, and his poet." This last was an afterthought, and one with which the aide was not wholly comfortable.

Sanat Ji Mani dismounted, alighting gingerly on his sore foot. "You have done your duty." He bowed slightly to the aide, startling him, and then went into the Rajput's tent.

"Ah! There you are! At last!" shouted Hasin Dahele as Sanat Ji Mani paused just inside the tent-flap; he was seated on a carved-and-inlaid chair of fine wood, flanked by braziers and protected by two Guards. His silken garments were torn and dirty and his hair was in disorder, but he beamed at Sanat Ji Mani. "Come in!"

"I hear you have sustained light losses," said Sanat Ji Mani without any formality.

"Light enough," said Hasin Dahele. He was drinking honey beer from a metal bowl. "This is very good. I will have them bring you some."

"Thank you, no." Sanat Ji Mani noticed Vayu Ede sitting on a stool off to the side. "How do you like the fruits of victory?"

"I like them very well," said the Rajput, as if the question had been directed to him.

"And you, Vayu Ede?" Sanat Ji Mani asked.

"It is the first step toward what the Gods have promised," he said, but in a subdued tone.

"Your gods offer strange gifts, do they not." Sanat Ji Mani came a few steps farther into the tent. "This one was easy, O Rajput. Be content with it."

"I will, I will," said Hasin Dahele. "For now. We will camp here tomorrow and the next day we will return to Devapur to show my people how we have succeeded. I will then prepare for a true campaign, and you will see that your woman has come to no harm." He wagged a finger at Sanat Ji Mani. "I know you think of her. I want you to be satisfied that she will come to no harm in my palace." He chuckled. "Then you can concentrate on advising me. And no more of this notion of accepting a surrender instead of showing force of arms."

"Why do you want my advice? you do not take it," said Sanat Ji Mani, hoping to be able to reach the Rajput while he was inclined to listen. "Why not leave me in Devapur when you go on campaign again?"

Hasin Dahele laughed merrily. "As if you do not know why." He sat back on his chair and grinned. "You must see what I do to know I am worthy." He stopped smiling and shouted, "Slave! Bring me meat and bread! I am hungry."

Vayu Ede got up from his stool. "You will be able to tell us how we have done," he said to Sanat Ji Mani. "The Gods demand it."

So it comes back to the gods, Sanat Ji Mani thought, and only said, "I am a liability on campaign. I need to stay out of the sun, which is inconvenient."

"But you know war," said Hasin Dahele. "You cannot deny it."

"Oh, yes," Sanat Ji Mani said bleakly. "I know war."

"And you have led men in battle." He drank the last of his honey beer.

"Not recently," Sanat Ji Mani said, thinking back to his homeland when the Goths had come through on their way to Rome. That was the last time he had fought offensively, and it had left him filled with revulsion; Heliogabalus had ruled in Rome then, and had been incapable of mounting any defenses at the edge of the Empire, so it had fallen to the governors and garrisons to stem the tide: he had never again wanted to initiate a battle.

"But you know how, that is what matters," said Hasin Dahele, swinging around in his chair as two slaves came in bearing a brass platter piled high with goat and mutton, with half-a-dozen broiled fowl around the edges. A third slave followed with a large, flat basket filled with wide, soft breads shining with ghee. "Set it down, set it down," he ordered, gesturing to a place on the floor of the tent. "And bring cushions for me and my guests. And more honey beer." The slaves did as they were ordered, bowed and withdrew. "You know, you were right, Sanat Ji Mani," he went on genially as he left his chair and sauntered toward the tray with its steaming bounty. "You said I would need more slaves than I had planned to bring. You were right, and I was wise to listen to you. So you see, I do heed you."

"What can I be but honored?" Sanat Ji Mani said, putting his hands together and bowing.

"And you will help me with what must be done to conquer, and not just in the matter of bringing slaves along—incidentally, we have a great many more to take back with us, and I suppose they will slow us down—but in everything having to do with war." The Rajput stood uneasily, waiting for someone to bring his cushions. "How long must I wait?" he asked testily as the time dragged on.

One of the Guards set his lance aside and hurried to bring the cushions the Rajput had demanded. "If these are insufficient, O Exalted One, you have only to ask for more." He put the cushions down next to the platter. "I will try to discover where the honey beer is."

"Have some yourself," said Hasin Dahele magnanimously. "It is very good."

"When you have eaten and dismissed me, I will," said the Guard with a quick but hungry glance at the piles of food.

"You are very loyal," said the Rajput, dropping to his knees on the cushion. "He is loyal, do you not agree, Sanat Ji Mani?"

Knowing what the Rajput wanted to hear, Sanat Ji Mani said, "He is."

"And you know the importance of loyalty, Sanat Ji Mani," said Hasin Dahele, and roared with more laughter as he beckoned to Vayu Ede to join him.

Sanat Ji Mani remained where he stood, watching while the Rajput began to wolf down his food, using the bread to hold the meat. He was well-aware that Hasin Dahele was drunk, but whether on honey beer or triumph, Sanat Ji Mani could not tell.

Text of a letter from the Chinese pilgrim and spy, Lum, to the prefecture of the armies, currently in Hsi-an.

To the most honorable and esteemed Prefect of the Armies, admirable servant of the Wielder of the Vermillion Brush, this report from the city of Sindabur on the Arabian Sea, submitted most humbly to you for your assessment and evaluation.

The disruption this traveler has seen during the past year continues, but not with the same chaotic energy as before. Many people are still displaced and even as far south as this person has come, there have been others fleeing from the ruins of Delhi and the continuing fighting between the two men claiming the title of Sultan of Delhi, one of whom serves Timur-i and one of whom is the bin Tughluq. This person has not yet discovered which of them is the most supported by the Rajputs, as the regional Princes are known. If there is support given to either claimant to the Sultan's title, the power may shift quickly and with dramatic results. This is a happenstance that this person cannot anticipate or predict, there being too many possibilities to know which is the most likely. Whatever the result may be, it is clear to this person that there will be more fighting; until someone can take and hold the

Sultan's position, nothing will be settled. Had the Sultanate not been in decline before Timur-i came, the matter might have been more readily understood, but as there had been an erosion of the Sultanate for nearly fifty years, nothing could hold it together once Delhi was in ruins. Those regions that have broken away from the Sultanate may yet determine what becomes of Delhi and who rules there.

Trade in these western ports does not seem much hampered by the troubles in Delhi, but it is apparent in the market-places that many goods are missing because of the on-going struggle, and that most trade has been disrupted, although the slave-trade is flourishing, so much so that the Arabs no longer bring Slavs to market, but buy the captives of the Sultans and the Rajputs to be sold in the markets to the west. In time this will change, but for a while, the slave-trade will go from east to west across the Arabian Sea.

This person has seen many groups of people camping beyond the walls of towns and cities, scraping out a living from the menial work that is often left to those called Untouchables. In Delhi the Untouchables were not as apparent as they are here to the south, for apparently the Sultans did not require that all menial tasks—cleaning latrines, caring for the bodies of the dead—be done by these unfortunates. Here in the south, where the sway of the Sultans was less complete, the Untouchables continued in their appointed role. The people who have been shut out of their home cities and who have fled the on-going battles in the north are now little better than the Untouchables, except that they have some hope of improving their condition, which the Untouchables do not. This person knows that desperate persons do terrible things, and in a short time there may be uprisings among these homeless persons that will shake the fragile peace of the south.

Pursuant to that, as this person indicated, there are many Rajputs who are struggling to turn the collapse of Dehli to their advantage, for many of them now seek to establish borders for their Principalities and a few are trying to expand their territories while in the process. Every minor Princeling has been stirred by the disruption in the land, and many of them are seeking opportunities to improve their presence in the world. As an example, the small Principality, Beragar, has laid claim to all the lands between the Godavari and the Narmanda Rivers in the west where they define the highlands against the Ghats. The

Principality is small, but it is being said that the Rajput is ambitious and is attempting to claim a wider holding for himself while he has the opportunity. His is the Yadava region and as such, his people are diverse. He himself is said to be part of the traditional religion of the region, but to which of the many gods he is devoted, this person has not been able to discover. This person believes and reiterates that if the Rajput of Beragar has any success in his scheme more of the Rajputs will emulate him and there will be a number of small wars in the north and west of India, and that will bring about more disruption and confusion. If this upstart Rajput is unable to achieve his ends, then he may provide an example to others and lessen the upheavals that this person has observed in his travels.

This person most meekly requests that his family remain ignorant of what has become of him and in what enterprise he is involved. There has been shame enough brought upon them on this unworthy person's behalf and it would only add to their distress to learn what this insignificant person has undertaken.

With every assurance of this person's continuing dedication to the task with which he has been charged and with submission to the Will of the Vermillion Brush, at the Spring Feast of the Balance of Day and Night,

Lum

7

"Have you had any news yet?" Rustam Iniattir faced Rogerian, his large hands caught together; outside, Alexandria was being battered by a spring squall, rain coming in sporadic bursts, carried on capricious winds and accompanied by rambunctious seas.

"Come in, Rustam Iniattir, in the name of my master," said Rogerian, bowing in the Roman style. "No, I have heard nothing; I would send you word of it if I had."

"I had hoped you might have had some news by now," said Rustam

Iniattir as he shrugged off his cloak and held it out to Rogerian. His demeanor revealed his worry more than his words did. "Is there nothing?"

"Not yet." Rogerian took the cloak and hung it on a broad-headed hook near the door.

"I have been away from Fustat for a number of weeks," said Rustam Iniattir, allowing Rogerian to escort him into the house. "I had hoped that you might have learned something, and that your news had missed me." He paused on the threshold of the reception room, his eyes widening at the richness of the chamber; he stared at the opulence around him. "Sanat Ji Mani is a most . . . wealthy man," he said, breathing deeply at the sight of fine woods, silks and velvets, brass lamps, and Italian paintings.

"That he is. You saw his house in Delhi," Rogerian said, noticing how impressed Rustam Iniattir was.

"That I did, and I supposed that he had settled all his wealth there, and maintained less opulent establishments elsewhere; I see I did not grasp the extent of his wealth. This is beyond anything I . . . How can he maintain such luxury, in more than one house? He would have to have vast resources." He had lowered his voice and finally said, "I assumed he made a display in Delhi, to impress the foreigners who lived in the Street of Brass Lanterns and the Sultan's deputies. I am sorry that I did not appreciate the extent of his riches earlier. This is astonishing." He shook his head in continuing disbelief. "I had no idea."

"Why is that?" Rogerian asked, leading him into the reception room. "My master never made a secret of his wealth."

"No, he did not," said Rustam Iniattir. "I thought his generosity bordered on spendthrift, but I realize now that was not the case."

"He told you he could afford to do the things he did," Rogerian pointed out.

"Yes, he did. It was my doubt that made me question his wherewithal. I would have advised him to trade more extensively if I had known he had such a fortune to draw upon," Rustam Iniattir admitted.

"Not that his wealth can help him now," said Rogerian, motioning Rustam Iniattir toward a divan covered in Antioch damask. "If you will sit down, I will have refreshments brought to you."

The Parsi merchant complied, still staring at the finery he saw. "Is the rest of the house as grand?"

"Would you like to see for yourself?" Rogerian offered. "I will be delighted to show you all but my master's private apartments." He did not add that these contained not only Sanat Ji Mani's austere bed-chamber but his alchemical laboratory as well.

"That would be most kind of you," said Rustam Iniattir, relaxing on the divan. "I would enjoy seeing the house if it is all this wonderful."

"After you have had some refreshment, then, it will be my pleasure to show it to you." Rogerian inclined his head courteously. "Would figs and yoghurt be acceptable to you, or do you want something more? Would you want a substantial meal? I offer it in the name of my master, who would expect nothing less of me."

"A little bread in addition to figs and yoghurt would be much appreciated." He leaned back on the bolster of the divan and all but purred. "I thought that what Sanat Ji Mani had in Delhi was grand, but I see I was mistaken."

"My master has done well in his travels, at least he has in general. Whatever has befallen him now is not what has been usual for him." He thought back to Cyprus, Spain, Saxony, Poland, and China, recalling the hardships Sanat Ji Mani had endured in those places. As he spoke, he went to the side-door and summoned an under-steward, to whom he gave orders for food, then turned back to address Rustam Iniattir. "How is it that you have come to Alexandria? Your last letter said you were going to Al Myah Suways."

"I did go there, and I purchased two ships, a thing I could not have done without the good-will of those shipbuilders who have long been patronized by your master. I see now how he was able to assemble the fleet of ships he owns. I was unaware that he had eleven of them in the Arabian Sea and the Bay of Bengal. Eleven. I thought there might be five." He paused, gathering his thoughts, and then rushed on. "I had it in mind to offer the services of my ships if you should need them to bring Sanat Ji Mani here, but I am aware that they are unnecessary." There was a hint of chagrin in his tone, and a downward turn to his mouth.

"Who is to say that your ships would not be useful," said Rogerian soothingly. "I trust you were satisfied with the bargain you struck?"

"They accepted the endorsement he provided, as he told me they would, which enabled me to buy two large ships of a similar sort, for trading across the Arabian Sea. They are fine vessels, seaworthy and large, capable of carrying vast loads, which is why I am in Alexandria— to extend my business so that I may increase the amount of goods carried in my cargo holds between the Red Sea and the west coast of India: Hind." He took a deep breath. "I am always having to use new words for places, and for things. It is most disconcerting."

"I understand your confusion," said Rogerian, who had many centuries of the same experience.

"I have been accustoming myself to this new place, to the Mamelukes and Egypt—a most remarkable land, in its way. Nothing like what I have been accustomed to, but having merit." He pursed his lips. "I want to take a voyage up the Nile, when I have time enough to spare for the venture."

"It is a most interesting journey," said Rogerian, willing to let Rustam Iniattir set the direction of their conversation.

"You have made it?" he asked, a wistful note in the question.

"Yes; not recently." Rogerian inclined his head again. "There are many wonderful sights along the river: temples and pyramids and monuments that are as majestic as the Great Sphynx at Giza, above Fustat."

"Yes. I have been to see it, and the pyramids that stand by it. As impressive as anything I have seen in India, and unlike them; these dry lands with the past looming out of the sands, without forests or uplands or the trees that crowd the rivers of the southern coast . . ." His words drifted; he called himself back to attention with a wave of his hand. "Delhi was not so lush as the south, but it was richer than Egypt, and the people were as varied as the gods . . ." He coughed and pinched at the bridge of his nose. "That is all behind me. I remember to no purpose. Now that I have ships to call my own, I may extend my efforts to the Nile as well as other places," said Rustam Iniattir speculatively.

"It is a possibility, certainly," said Rogerian. "Once you have your markets established, you may want to cast your nets more widely."

"Yes. Well, it is the ships that make these things possible. In a year the vessels I have purchased will show their worth. It is a most promising venture for the House of Iniattir, and I want to show my appreciation for all that your master has made practical for me." Rustam Iniattir shifted on the divan as if it had suddenly become lumpy. "I am not one to take such generosity as my due."

"I did not think you were—nor did my master," said Rogerian, his faded-blue eyes glinting with amusement. "He told me from the first that you are a trustworthy man, and that you conducted yourself in an upright manner."

"That is a great compliment to me," said Rustam Iniattir, looking a bit embarrassed at such an encomium. "I had not understood that he thought so well of me."

"He would not have arranged for you to leave Delhi when you did if he did not," said Rogerian pointedly but with complete courtesy.

Rustam Iniattir nodded. "I supposed it was his way of protecting his wealth."

"Sanat Ji Mani has had his own ships carrying cargo for some years. His wealth was protected whether he, or you, left Delhi or not." Rogerian recalled the first purchase of Arabian Sea merchant ships, almost a century ago, and a faint smile creased his austere features. "He is a clever fellow."

"Not clever enough to leave with us," said Rustam Iniattir heavily. "I blame myself that he is missing. If only I had tried to persuade him . . ." He looked up at Rogerian. "How was I to know he would have no other chance to leave?"

Rogerian grasped his visitor's emotion, and tried to ease his guilt. "You are not to blame. He wanted us to leave so that he would not have to be hindered by our presence."

"Perhaps," said the Parsi. "And yet, I cannot help but feel if I had insisted, he might have come with us . . ."

"He would be glad to know you have done so well," said Rogerian, adding, "And what may I do to help you in Sanat Ji Mani's name? If your mission is for trade, I should probably tell you that he has more than twenty ships plying the waters of the Mediterranean Sea and the ocean beyond the Pillars of Hercules, carrying all manner of cargo." He gave Rustam Iniattir a little time to let this sink in.

"More than twenty?" Rustam Iniattir marveled.

"Four are in the harbor just now, if you want to inspect them," Rogerian offered.

"Oh, yes; I should like that very much," said Rustam Iniattir. "Perhaps later, when the rain has stopped." He shook his head slowly, incredulously. "I had no notion he had done so much, that he had so many enterprises."

"My master would tell you he has a restless mind," said Rogerian.

"If these are the fruits of restlessness, may I never repose again," said the Parsi with strong emotion. "I long to emulate him, to learn from him." He glanced around the splendid room again. "He lives as well as a Prince in this house."

Rogerian chuckled. "I know he would be honored by your attention."

"If only he were here," Rustam Iniattir added somberly.

"He will return, in time," said Rogerian.

"May your hopes be swiftly rewarded," said Rustam Iniattir. "He has far to travel."

"It is not the first time," Rogerian remarked.

"Ah, yes; he is an exile, even here," said Rustam Iniattir, pulling thoughtfully at his short-trimmed beard.

"His homeland fell to his foes many years ago, and he has been about the world since then," Rogerian told him, saying nothing of the thirty-four centuries Sanat Ji Mani had gone wandering. "Occasionally he returns there, but he never stays long."

"It is undoubtedly dangerous for him to do so," said the Parsi merchant, sighing. "I and those of my House know how it is to be shut away from home."

"Many have lost their homelands," said Rogerian. "I have not visited Gades—my native city—for a great many years."

"Are you also an exile?" Rustam Iniattir asked, mildly surprised.

"No," said Rogerian, and rose to go to the side-door where the under-steward and the senior cook waited, trays in hand. "Thank you," he said as he took the trays and brought them to the table at the far end of the divan on which Rustam Iniattir sat. "Your refreshments: figs, yoghurt, bread, and olive oil." He set the trays down. "I will bring you water or wine, as you wish."

"Wine is somewhat rare in this place," said Rustam Iniattir. "The Muslims do not drink it, and many will not sell it, either."

"That is their way; it is not Sanat Ji Mani's—he will provide his guests with the best he has to offer. The wine in this house is very good. It is from vineyards in Italy," said Rogerian, and did not mention that Sanat Ji Mani owned the vineyards.

"How splendid," said Rustam Iniattir, shifting in his seat to avail himself of the light repast. "Even absent, your master is an exceptional host."

"Enjoy your food, and with a good appetite," said Rogerian.

"That I will. And I will have some of the Italian wine, if you will bring it. I do not believe I have ever tasted any." He smiled quickly and broke off a section of bread, then dipped it in the bowl of olive oil.

Rogerian left Rustam Iniattir alone in the reception room and went along to the pantry at the side of the cavernous kitchen. There he took a bottle from the rack that held thirty of them, brushed the dust off, removed the sealing-wax from the bottle, and unstopped it. Selecting a cup of Venetian glass from the cupboard, he took them back to the reception room where he found his guest devouring the last of the figs. "I took the liberty of choosing a wine I thought you would like."

Rustam Iniattir looked up from the tray. "I am filled with anticipation; if the wine is of as high a quality as everything else in this house, I know I will be delighted," he said, an eager light in his eyes. "I have had the wine of Syria, and found it strong."

"This may be somewhat different, coming as it does from another land," said Rogerian as he poured the red fluid into the cup; he held it out to Rustam Iniattir, saying, "I am told this is a good example of what the vines produce."

Rustam Iniattir took the cup and drank, holding the wine in his mouth before swallowing. "Excellent," he approved. "I am most impressed."

"Then you may have three bottles to take with you when you go," said Rogerian, knowing it was what Sanat Ji Mani would do. "You said you would like to extend your trading; what have you in mind?"

Now that the intended purpose of his visit was before him, Rustam Iniattir faltered. "It probably will not seem much to a man with such extensive activities as your master has; it may be so minor an opportunity that it will not be worthwhile." He took a deep breath. "I thought that there might be some way to enter into a shared trading venture, something that would benefit us both," he said, a bit uncertainly. "I did not know that Sanat Ji Mani had so many ships, or traded so widely."

"Yes, he has ships," said Rogerian when Rustam Iniattir did not go on.

"I had thought he would be willing to do with ships as we have done with caravans," he said it without much emphasis, as if the finery of the house was intimidating him. "I also hoped he would be here: Sanat Ji Mani."

"I am authorized to act in his name, if that is what concerns you," said Rogerian. "I can make a contract that my master will honor."

Rustam Iniattir took another sip of wine. "It is not that I doubt you," he said as he put the cup down. "But the current circumstances are awkward, with your master being missing. You will agree that they are, will you not?"

"I agree they could be so construed," said Rogerian, watching Rustam Iniattir more closely than the Parsi merchant realized.

"Yes." He wiped his mouth with the edge of his sleeve. "Yes. I cannot think that it would be entirely correct to make such a contract, not until it is known if your master is . . . returning."

"You mean until we know if he is still alive," Rogerian corrected him gently.

Rustam Iniattir took more wine to cover his confusion. "You know Delhi was sacked and pillaged. Many were taken prisoner and many others were killed. How can you be sure that he escaped that slaughter?" Now that he had said it, he was appalled at himself; he stared at Rogerian as if expecting a rebuke.

"I am not sure," said Rogerian with a calm that made Rustam Iniattir more uneasy than before. "Yet I trust that he has won through." He did not add that Olivia had warranted to him that Sanct' Germain had not died the True Death, for that would require explanations he did not want to provide.

"What of the woman: Avasa Dani?" Rustam Iniattir asked suddenly.

"She has established a household of her own," said Rogerian, adding nothing more about the place.

"Ah. Just as well. With Sanat Ji Mani gone, her presence here could be misinterpreted." He gave a slow nod. "She must be eager for your master's return. A fortunate thing that fever spared her, in the end."

"She has asked when he might be expected," Rogerian said.

"A prudent question from a sensible woman. How long will you wait?" Rustam Iniattir asked, drinking the last of the wine in his cup.

"Ten years is what my master has stipulated in his Will," said Rogerian, still unflustered. "I must do my utmost to keep his affairs in order against his return, and that includes making contracts with merchants."

"I . . ." Rustam Iniattir hesitated and tried again, "I will have to consider my position before I say anything more."

"As you wish," Rogerian responded. "I know my master would welcome more dealings with you; your caravan endeavor has been most successful."

"And I would welcome an expansion of what we have done," said Rustam Iniattir. "But if Sanat Ji Mani remains missing, how are we to conduct business?" He sat back on the divan and mulled over the possibilities. "You may have the right to do business in your master's name, but how can you be certain he will approve what you have done? And if he does not approve, what will I be left with?"

"I cannot be completely certain; he always has in the past," Rogerian remarked. "I can offer only that assurance to you, and the pledge of the captains of his ships that they will abide by my orders in Sanat Ji Mani's absence."

"This is most difficult," said Rustam Iniattir, more to himself than to Rogerian.

"It may be," Rogerian agreed. "Still, it is the best we can make of an indeterminate situation; as long as he is missing and his fate unknown, I will look after his concerns, as he has charged me to do. If you decide you would prefer to deal with other ship-owners, I will see that you meet them, so that you can continue your business."

This surprised Rustam Iniattir. "Why would you do that, if it would put money in other men's pockets?"

"My master would still have his original contracts with you, so that if you prosper, he prospers," Rogerian explained. "It would avail him nothing to see your expansion thwarted."

Rustam Iniattir shook his head, perplexed. "Might I have a little more of that wine?" he asked, as much to gain a little time for thought as to have another taste of it.

"Of course," said Rogerian, and went to fill his cup. "It warms the heart on a chilly day."

"That it does," said Rustam Iniattir, and drank. As he wiped his mouth, he said, "In Delhi, I was a religious man; I kept the rites of my faith, and I was satisfied that Ormazd would triumph over Ahriman. Then I would have given some of this wine for Ormazd and the power of Light, with water for the world, as Zarathustra taught. But for the last year, I have not kept to the teaching as a pious man should."

"The last year has been a difficult one," said Rogerian.

"I fear it may have weakened my devotion." He said it as if confessing to a shameful secret.

"With what has transpired, that would not distress me," said Rogerian. "You have come through very difficult times, and many men's beliefs are changed during hard going."

"But my lack of trust may—" He stopped, trying to keep from saying more.

"Are you afraid you have put Sanat Ji Mani in danger because you no longer pray as you did at Delhi?" Rogerian guessed aloud.

There were tears standing in Rustam Iniattir's eyes. "Yes," he admitted, and lowered his head.

Rogerian sensed that he would have to go carefully with Rustam Iniattir. "Why should your gods protect Sanat Ji Mani when his own gods may have failed him?"

"But those are *false* gods, and Ahriman is mighty," said Rustam Iniattir. "Darkness rules this cycle, and without the devotion of the followers of Zarathustra, all hope will fade from the world."

"That is a bleak outlook," said Rogerian, "and a terrible responsibility for you to hold."

"Yes, it is," said Rustam Iniattir, and drank more wine. "I have never been to the caves in Persia where our faith was founded. I have never been to Persia. But I should have made a temple or founded a cave to worship in. I have money enough." He could not bring himself to look up.

"You also are in the land of the Mamelukes, and they might not readily accept your worship. They are willing to allow the Peoples of the Book to worship here, but you are not of their number." Rogerian waited while Rustam Iniattir thought about this. "To have you fined, imprisoned, or exiled would not be useful to you, or to Sanat Ji Mani. Perhaps your reticence is a gift from your Ormazd, to preserve you in this place."

"But if I lack faith, I am one with Ahriman," said Rustam Iniattir miserably. "I am part of the Darkness that is this cycle."

Rogerian thought about his own faded beliefs, and said, "If Ormazd is just and virtuous, he will not disdain what you have done; he will understand that the cycle was at work, not your lack of faith."

"But in this cycle it is most important for those who know the Light to serve it more zealously than when—" He drank the last of the wine. "If I cannot sustain my religion when I have been spared, what price will the world have to pay for my lapse?"

Rogerian did not quite laugh; he bit the insides of his cheeks to keep from doing so. When he could trust himself to maintain the gravity Rustam Iniattir's distress surely deserved, he said, "Is that it? You are abashed because you have not suffered more?" He saw the Parsi's slight nod. "What would your misery do to help my master? or the world, for that matter?"

"I have not deserved preservation," said Rustam Iniattir.

"Who among us does?" Rogerian asked. "This world is an aleatory place; some flourish who are despicable, some languish who are worthy of highest esteem."

"Because this is a cycle of Darkness," said Rustam Iniattir staunchly, trying to recover himself.

"Light or Dark, the meaning of it—if there is any—is beyond our understanding," said Rogerian. "And the gods, whatever they are, must know this and make allowances for it."

Rustam Iniattir sat very still. "I have failed my religion," he said as if pronouncing sentence.

"In time you may return to your trust in it," said Rogerian, aware that his guest was feeling the wine as much as remorse.

"I must hope I will," said the Parsi merchant. "There is so much to lose."

Rogerian wanted to assure Rustam Iniattir that he would not be held accountable for the fate of the world, but knew it would be useless to talk with him now; he bowed again, Roman fashion, and said, "If you would like to avail yourself of a moment alone, to think and to rest, I will be pleased to escort you to a chamber where you can withdraw and be alone with your thoughts. My master would extend the same opportunity to you, were he here."

Rustam Iniattir nodded. "I had not meant . . . My outburst was uncalled-for." He got to his feet a bit unsteadily. "You are right: an hour or so to clear my mind would be most welcome."

"If you will come with me?" Rogerian said, gesturing toward the corridor. "There is a withdrawing room just a few steps along."

"A most gracious courtesy to a guest," said Rustam Iniattir, trying to regain the polite demeanor he had had when he first arrived.

"It is what my master would do," said Rogerian, and opened a door on the other side of the corridor, revealing a room beautifully furnished with a broad couch, a writing table, and Sanat Ji Mani's red-lacquer chest. Elaborate wall-hangings depicting the seasons and made in France provided the principle decor, with milky light from clerestory windows to provide light for the handsome display.

"More elegance," said Rustam Iniattir. "I do not believe I have seen weaving like that before."

"The hangings would be thought sacrilegious by the Mamelukes, depicting human beings as they do. But within these walls we may show them safely enough." Rogerian bowed toward the couch. "Rest and restore your peace of mind. When you are ready, we will discuss business and I will show you more of the house."

"Thank you. I think I may have drunk the wine too quickly. I must ask your pardon for anything I might have said that offended you." He cleared his throat.

"You have not offended me, Rustam Iniattir, nor have you said anything that would spite my master." Rogerian backed out of the room, but did not close the door at once.

"You are good to say so," Rustam Iniattir told him. "And a short while for reflection should restore my mind." He made an apologetic gesture as he sank onto the couch. "I cannot tell you how—"

"You need not say anything." Rogerian assured him. "When you are ready, ring the bell you will find on the writing table and I will come."

"I will," said Rustam Iniattir. "I cannot imagine how I came to forget myself so . . . so heedlessly."

"No matter," said Rogerian as he closed the door. He stood in the hallway for a short while until he could hear Rustam Iniattir snoring, and then he went away to the back of the house to fetch parchment and ink, preparing to draw up the contracts that would expand Rustam Iniattir's trading empire into all the ports of Europe.

Text of a letter from Bhedi Tanka, military leader of Deogir to Rajput Hasin Dahele, carried by special messenger.

To the most Esteemed Rajput Hasin Dahele, Lord of Beragar and Ruler of Devapur, the greetings of Bhedi Tanka, Kshatriya Caste and military leader of the city and region of Deogir, lying to the north of your lands.

O most Worthy Rajput, it is with dismay that we learn of your adventures along the Narmanda River and we hear with alarm your stated intention of expanding your territory by moving to the north, which would infringe upon the lands held by my Puissant Rajput, who is master of this city and region as far as the Narmada River west to the Arabian Sea and east to the city of Asirgarh. These holdings are protected by a strong and ready army that would repel any attempt made against Deogir, by you or any other.

The reason I dare to address you is to let you know that your advances will be stopped, your men killed or castrated and sold as slaves to be sent far to the west if you should be so foolish as to enter my master's lands. Deogir is larger than Beragar and has access to the coast, which gives us many advantages that you do not enjoy. Therefore I urge you to consider the damage that will be done if you persist in your efforts.

Make no mistake, O Rajput: you will be defeated and your name will be infamous for generations to come if you challenge Deogir. Go

south of the Godavari, and be content with what your grandfather
has left to you. Do not continue on this course which must end in
catastrophe for you and all your people.
This at the first new moon after the Balanced Day-and-Night.
There will be no second warning.

Bhedi Tanka

8

A map was spread out on the table, and Hasin Dahele leaned over it,
a short rod in his hand which he used for a pointer. "This is where
we can cross the Narmanda; there is a bridge that has been used by
merchants and caravans for decades." His reception room was empty
but for the two of them and a pair of Guards at the far end of the
room; it was late afternoon and the day was beginning to cool, with a
breeze wandering in through the open windows.

"You will not find it easy to take your entire army over a single
bridge; it is a bottleneck, one that puts you at a tactical disadvantage
and could expose your army to all manner of assault that would sunder
your numbers and lead to their defeat," said Sanat Ji Mani. "You have
pushed your territory to the south bank of the Narmanda; be content
with that, and with the recognition of other Rajputs that your claim
to this territory is not to be questioned. You have shown that your
army is strong—why weaken it with hard campaigning and fighting?"
He turned away from the map. "Rajput, you will have opposition waiting for you if you insist on waging war."

"Do not tell me again to seek peace; peace will not bring me what
I am destined to achieve—what I deserve, and well you know it," said
the Rajput, standing up and glaring at Sanat Ji Mani. "I rely upon your
advice because I know you have experience of conquest."

"And I have found it to be a devastation and a waste," said Sanat
Ji Mani emphatically.

"Because you have no army to lead; it would be different if you did, I do not doubt," said Hasin Dahele, unconvinced. "If I put you at my side, in the van of my army, you will soon learn to love victory."

"I have no wish to fight with you, or any other army," said Sanat Ji Mani, thinking back to the many campaigns he had fought, and how little difference winning or losing had made. "Battle has brought me nothing but pain and loss, as it will bring them to you."

"The Gods have shown otherwise," said Hasin Dahele. "If I ignore Their course, I will lose more than war will cost me."

"How can you know?" Sanat Ji Mani persisted. "You have not put your gods to the test."

"No man may do that and be unscathed," said the Rajput brusquely. "They are not your gods; They are mighty."

Sanat Ji Mani indicated the regions marked on the map. "All the other Rajputs say the same thing, no doubt. You have my advice, however little it may be worth to you. You may use it or not: you rule here."

"And you do not wish to rule?" The Rajput was incredulous. "You, of all men?"

This time Sanat Ji Mani spoke directly. "Whatever you may think me, I have no wish for war, or conquest."

Hasin Dahele laughed aloud. "You still persist in your game: very well, you are nothing but a traveler on the roads, not quite a pilgrim and not quite a beggar. You are only a foreigner, a stranger in my country. Your plight is that of hundreds of others." He sighed. "I grow weary of this dissimulation, so I must prove that I can do all that you might do, had you the army to support you. When I have shown myself worthy, you will recognize my power and you will ride beside me in your right identity."

"My identity is Sanat Ji Mani," he said, knowing it was only one of many names he had used over the centuries, and that his name was the least of his secrets. "How can I be more than that? How do you think I have deceived you? Why should I wish to?" He waited for the answer, his senses alert, hoping that the Rajput had learned nothing of his true nature, for that would mean imprisonment at the least, and would expose Tulsi to greater danger than was already the case.

"You came here an outcast, as you yourself have admitted," said Hasin Dahele with feigned patience. "A *limping* outcast, a foreigner, not young, who is exiled, coming from the north, from outside of

Delhi. We all know what happened after Delhi. All the world knows how the men of Timur-i rebelled. Your servant was enough to give you away."

"Tulsi? How?" Sanat Ji Mani fought off the sudden fear that gripped him. "What has she to do with it?"

"She, too, is a foreigner, from Timur-i's army." The Rajput grinned as if he had made a point.

"Yes," said Sanat Ji Mani impatiently. "You knew that from the day I came here."

"And why was that? How could I know to look for you, and the woman with you? Why did I send my Guards to seek you out? You did not think it strange that I should ask my men to bring you to my palace, for my protection?" the Rajput asked, answering his own questions before Sanat Ji Mani could speak. "Vayu Ede said you were coming. Alvars are visionaries, and he has brought his vision to me. Because of him I expected you to be here, and here you are."

"Vayu Ede is a most capable man," said Sanat Ji Mani warily, "but he and I have never met until I came here; he did not visit me in Delhi. He was not with Timur-i's army. I did not know why you brought me here, and no one has been willing to tell me, although I have asked. You have told me before that Vayu Ede has visions, but what has that to do with me?"

"He promised you would come," said Hasin Dahele. "He said you would make me Ruler of the World."

"I?" Sanat Ji Mani shook his head. "I am an outcast as we both know. How can I do this thing?"

"You persist in your obstinacy," said Hasin Dahele, scowling.

"I have tried to maintain myself," Sanat Ji Mani corrected. "I have never represented myself as more than I am."

Hasin Dahele paced down the room, away from the trestle-table where the map was laid out. "Why do you not declare yourself? I have waited for months, and you have not been willing to reveal who and what you are."

"I am an exile. I wish to reach Chaul so that I might find a ship to carry me and Tulsi Kil across the Arabian Sea," said Sanat Ji Mani.

"And from there, to go to the western-most holdings of Timur-i, no doubt," said Hasin Dahele smugly.

"Why should I do that, if I am fortunate enough to get away from here?" he asked. "You have assumed things about me that are untrue."

"If you say they are, then I must accept it, for a while yet," said Hasin Dahele, sounding petulant. "You are a most difficult man, Sanat Ji Mani."

"It is not my intention to be," he said.

A vagrant gust of wind lifted the edge of the map, raising it into the air and skidding it along the trestle-table. Both men turned to look at it; Hasin Dahele hurried to put his hand on it to keep it from dropping to the floor. "You must come and give me the benefit of your experience," he said as he laid his sword on the map. "I am not done with you yet, or with planning."

"I have told you as much as I can," said Sanat Ji Mani. "If you want to extend your war, you must do it on your own counsel."

"There must be more fighting," said the Rajput as he studied the map again. "I cannot gain control of the coast if I do not act, and without acting, I might as well surrender to Deogir."

"Can you not keep within your region and govern it with care?" Sanat Ji Mani asked quietly.

"Would you do that, if Beragar were yours? Or would you fight? Would you broaden its frontiers? Would you try to bring it glory?" His challenge was hot-tempered and impetuous. "I cannot believe that you, of all men, would be content with half-measures when there is so much more to be had."

Sanat Ji Mani did not move from where he stood, six paces away from the Rajput, "I would seek to make Beragar prosperous, to secure its frontiers and to establish trade contracts with the other Rajputs whose lands abut on Beragar. I would make treaties to ensure peace and I would strive to avoid battles. That way all benefit, the people of Beragar most especially."

"You expect me to believe that?" Hasin Dahele exclaimed, rounding on him. "How can you speak so slightingly of me?"

"I intend no slight," said Sanat Ji Mani. "I am trying to keep you from damaging your people and yourself."

"By recommending being satisfied with what I have? You have the audacity to declare peace?" The Rajput was incredulous. "You have ruled an empire and you begrudge me one."

"I have not ruled an empire," Sanat Ji Mani said softly but with such intensity of feeling that the air seemed to shake with his words.

"Of course you have. It might not be as vast as you wish, but you have made your own," said Hasin Dahele.

"And what empire is this?" Sanat Ji Mani asked, appalled at what he was hearing.

"Why, *your* empire. Timur-i Lenkh's Empire," said Hasin Dahele in exasperation, and nodded fiercely.

"Timur-i's Empire?" Sanat Ji Mani repeated, dumbfounded.

"Have you another empire besides?" Hasin Dahele demanded. "Do not pretend innocence. I have known from the first."

"Known what from the first? this ridiculous notion?" Sanat Ji Mani still could not believe what he had heard.

"I was content to keep my knowledge to myself," said Hasin Dahlele, doing his best to excuse himself. "You cozened it out of me."

Sanat Ji Mani stood, transfixed by the ludicrous implications of this misconception. "Timur-i Lenkh? Why do you suppose that I—What has that to do with—" But even as he asked, he became cognizant of what the Rajput had assumed; much of his experience here, so puzzling before, now made a perplexing kind of sense: he knew what Vayu Ede had meant when he said *I know who you are*, which he had not been able to figure out until this moment. "How could you imagine I am Timur-i? That is what you believe, is it?"

"Of course. You need not deny who you are. I know you." Now that he had divulged his conviction, Hasin Dahele became less pugnacious. "I knew before you came that you would be here."

"But I am not Timur-i; I have never claimed to be," said Sanat Ji Mani, trying to keep his emotions in check. He spoke carefully, levelly. "How could I be? Timur-i is sixty-four, and he stains his hair with walnut juice. I am nothing like him. I am from the West, from mountains called the Carpathians. I lived in Delhi for a number of years, in the Foreigners' Quarter, and was taken prisoner by Timur-i when he sacked the city, as many others were. That is how I came to travel with his army; it was not any choice of mine." He spoke calmly, patiently, as if to a recalcitrant child. "Timur-i is a Turkish-Mongol. I am from other blood."

"You limp," said Hasin Dahele as if that settled the matter.

"I had a staple put through my foot to ensure I would not escape," said Sanat Ji Mani.

"Which you have conveniently lost," said Hasin Dahele. "I know those staples. How could you remove it?"

Sanat Ji Mani thought, trying to provide an answer. "It was done after Tulsi and I were separated from Timur-i's army."

"How? What smith pulled it out?" Hasin Dahele shook his head. "Enough mendacity."

"I do not lie. I am not Timur-i," said Sanat Ji Mani, realizing as he spoke that all protests were useless.

"It is to be expected that you will not want others to know who you are," said Hasin Dahele at his most reasonable. "I knew you would deny the truth; you must do so until you are satisfied that I am capable of succeeding you in conquering the world. I am willing to wait for your countenance. You need to be—"

Sanat Ji Mani dared to interrupt him. "I am not Timur-i. Believe this: in the West, I am called Franczesco Ragoczy of Saint-Germain. I have no army to command, and no empire. My country, from which I am exiled, is in Hungarian, Polish, and Wallachian hands, with the Ottomans of Turkey struggling to gain a foot-hold there."

"You must have a tale to tell, so that you can continue to refuse to acknowledge who you are," said Hasin Dahele. "I cannot force you to admit me to your confidences, not yet. And I will keep your secret."

"This *is* my confidence. I have no secret." Sanat Ji Mani's compelling dark eyes rested on the Rajput. "I am telling you the truth."

"I will show you that I deserve your heritage, and you will own me your heir," said Hasin Dahele, ignoring what Sanat Ji Mani had told him.

"*Look* at me," Sanat Ji Mani commanded, and the Rajput looked. "I am not a Turkish-Mongol. My people, some of them, have been called Etruscans," he said, not adding that they were the descendants of his Carpathian-dwelling tribes who had fled westward into Italy many, many centuries ago.

"You are a foreigner with dark hair and eyes, of middle years, and you limp on your right foot. You have come here, walking the roads and guided by your servant." Hasin Dahele smiled. "You will tell me, in time."

"I have told you," Sanat Ji Mani reiterated. "I am not Timur-i. He has gone back to Samarkand."

"Everyone knows that is not so; it is known throughout the world that Timur-i is an exile from his own army," said Hasin Dahele, a bit condescendingly. "He—I will say he rather than you—was overthrown by his jealous officers and left, abandoned, on the road with only one servant to care for him. He has suffered much, and it has taken a toll upon him. His eyes are failing, and so he cannot go abroad in the daylight without someone to lead him, and his skin burns. Of course he would deny who he is so that he would not become a captive, held hostage for his enemies." He favored Sanat Ji Mani with a serene smile. "Vayu Ede foretold your coming. I had only to set my men to look for you."

"And they found the wrong man," said Sanat Ji Mani. "I am not Timur-i. How many times must I say it?"

"Until you admit it is so, I suppose," said Hasin Dahele. "If you must continue this way, so be it. I will do all that I must to gain your support and acknowledgment."

"It will mean nothing," said Sanat Ji Mani.

Hasin Dahele laughed. "Do as you must. I will continue to plan my campaign, and you will see, when I am done, that I am a worthy successor and that I deserve to inherit your empire and all the world."

"I have no empire," Sanat Ji Mani said, knowing it was futile.

"No, not at present; I understand that. I shall help you to reclaim it," said Hasin Dahele, smiling confidently as he smoothed the surface of the map. "Then you will be pleased to name me your son."

"I want no war waged in my name," said Sanat Ji Mani, trying to find some means of turning the Rajput from his disastrous course.

"Of course not. That would reveal too much, and your army would come against me before I am ready," said Hasin Dahele. "I am going to push back our frontiers and then claim the west coast, and from there I will strike north. And you will come with me."

"And Tulsi?" Sanat Ji Mani dared to ask.

Hasin Dahele considered his answer. "I may permit her to accompany you, if you will give me the benefit of your advice." He stood still, his brows raised in speculation.

"I have little useful advice to give," Sanat Ji Mani said. "But if you want my opinions, you are welcome to them, so long as Tulsi is safe."

"And you believe she would be safer with you than staying here in the palace?" The Rajput shook his head. "If you want her to be protected, this is a better place than on campaign."

"Not for her. Someone has already tried to harm her." He said this bluntly, taking a chance that the attempt to poison Tulsi did not originate with the Rajput."

"What do you mean?" Hasin Dahele asked suspiciously. "Harm her in what way?"

"Someone attempted to poison her," said Sanat Ji Mani bluntly. "Fortunately she survived."

The Rajput's face darkened. "And I was told nothing of this? Why?"

Sanat Ji Mani took a moment to frame his answer. "If others in this palace believe as you do—that I am Timur-i—although I am not—one of your servants may have wanted to keep you from making common cause with me, and so tried to harm my companion as a way of protecting you."

"Or there might have been someone who is a spy for my enemies who sought to put us at odds, someone set to lurk in the palace and ruin the trust between us," said Hasin Dahele promptly. "That is much more likely." He put the tips of his fingers together. "Since I will have you with me, I will comply with your request and allow the woman to come with you. It will not be liked by many of my officers, but I will not have you distracted by concerns about her, as you might be if you are separated." He grinned suddenly. "So it is settled. You will campaign with me and I will make sure your companion remains with you. I will want to set out soon, for the rains will come and I must consolidate my gains before they arrive."

"It will be difficult to campaign at mid-summer," Sanat Ji Mani warned. "In this part of the world, the weather will work against you. The heat will make for hardships for men and animals alike."

"So it might. All the more reason to be away within a week." His eyes glittered with enthusiasm. "It will be a fine campaign. You will see."

Sanat Ji Mani could muster no exuberance at the prospect of war. "It will cost men and lives, animals, supplies and good-will. You will need to have barrels of water among your other supplies, or your men will not be able to fight."

"You have lost your zest from months on the road," said Hasin Dahele. "You will regain it once we have triumphed."

"And if you do not triumph, what then?" Sanat Ji Mani asked.

"You will withhold your sanction, and never acknowledge me," said Hasin Dahele in a tone that suggested that this was impossible. "But when I am victorious, you will declare me your rightful heir and Lord of all your Empire, and all lands that I shall add to that Empire."

Sanat Ji Mani shook his head. "I cannot do that," he said somberly. "I am not who you think I am, and anything I say in the name of Timur-i would be a lie."

"So you have told me already," said Hasin Dahele with a great show of forbearance. "I am willing to wait until I have shown that I am worthy to receive your—"

"It is not a question of worth," Sanat Ji Mani interrupted. "It is a question of misconstrued belief. You have put your faith in the visions of Vayu Ede, and in this instance, he has led you to error. It may be that he has gifts that reveal other matters of importance, but in this instance, he has stumbled."

"I know why you will not admit what we both know is true. Very well, I will abide by your reservations and I will not press you for any more commitment than what you have given. After we cross Narmanda, you will see that your Empire can be expanded and that I am the man who will be able to do it. My Gods have shown their favor by bringing you to me, and I will show my appreciation by enduring your demands. I should not be astonished that you would require more than my pledge to attain your grant of synodite." Hasin Dahele took a step back from Sanat Ji Mani. "I will convince you. That I vow, before all the Gods Whose influence has brought us to this place."

"What if you do not conquer the world?" Sanat Ji Mani proposed as if discussing birds or monkeys. "What then?"

"I cannot fail. The Gods have mandated my success," said Hasin Dahele. "As they mandated yours."

Sanat Ji Mani let the last go unaddressed. "But suppose men, not gods, should fail you: what will you do?"

"Oh, I will have the soldiers who could not do my bidding cut to pieces by those who obeyed, and their bones scattered to the corners of the earth," said Hasin Dahele with the nonchalance of one who has already decided.

"You will do the enemy's work for them," said Sanat Ji Mani.

"I will do the Gods' work," Hasin Dahele corrected him. "If you fail me as well, in triumph, I will have you scraped to death." He paused. "Do you know how it is done? The condemned is wrapped tightly in a net and everything that protrudes beyond the netting is scraped away with knives; the netting is tightened again, and the scraping is done again, and so on until there is nothing but bones, and then, what is left is dismembered."

Sanat Ji Mani listened to this in aghast silence; it would be an agonizing death, for only the destruction or severing of his spine would bring the True Death. "Why would you do this?

"I would do it if you fail to recognize me as your heir," said the Rajput with great purpose.

"To what purpose: I am not Timur-i," Sanat Ji Mani said with meticulous pronunciation.

"You will continue to say so yet a while; it is no more than what I expect," said Hasin Dahele. "I have said I will not object to it, for now."

"It will not change with time. I will not be anyone other than Sanat Ji Mani, now or in the future," he said. "You are too set on this tale you have accepted to comprehend that you are mistaken—Vayu Ede is mistaken."

"Call yourself what you will, I am going to reclaim and enlarge your Empire and you will one day own me as your heir." Hasin Dahele gestured his determination. "I have extended my generosity to your companion, to show that I am sincere in my goals. You will have to wait for the brunt of my campaign to see that I have the ability to do what I am sworn—and destined—to do. Neither you nor my soldiers can stop me from gaining what is mine."

"I am sure Tulsi and I are grateful," said Sanat Ji Mani, appalled by the Rajput's ferocity, and frustrated by his stubborn adherence to his conviction that Sanat Ji Mani was Timur-i.

"You are not now, but you will be, in time," said Hasin Dahele. "It may be best that you know now that I am conscious of you and your past. It will make things easier between us." He smiled with genuine pleasure. "You may want to go to your companion and tell her to prepare for travel. She will want to know that she is to ride with you."

"I probably should tell her to make ready," said Sanat Ji Mani with a slight emphasis on *should*, trying to imagine what Tulsi would say when she learned of the Rajput's beliefs.

"And assure her that if any more harm should come to her, I will punish the miscreant severely—also any spies that may be in the household." The Rajput grinned in anticipation. "Do not fret, Sanat Ji Mani, I will earn your high regard yet."

"There is no reason to," Sanat Ji Mani said fervently as he put his hands together and bowed.

"So you say, so you say." He waved Sanat Ji Mani away. "Well, go tell her that she is to go with us; give my servants a list of what you will require for campaign and it will be tended to. I will speak with you tomorrow evening." With that, he went back to studying his map.

Sanat Ji Mani left the reception room and hurried along the corridors to the apartment assigned to him and Tulsi. Every step of the way, he reviewed all that had transpired since they arrived in Devapur, and how puzzling it had been. Now that he understood the preposterous notion the Rajput had regarding him, Sanat Ji Mani realized that he had seriously underestimated their vulnerability. With such expectations of Sanat Ji Mani, there was no doubt that Hasin Dahele would demand his participation in his war, and would not be willing to accept anything less. He was frowning when he entered their room and discovered Tulsi in the middle of her evening exercises.

She looked up as Sanat Ji Mani came through the door. "More trouble?" she asked as she took her heels from behind her head and got to her feet.

"In some ways, yes. This is the heart of our trouble." He closed the door firmly and went across the room to the window. "And many lives are forfeit to the Will of the Rajput. Many lives, many more than ours."

"What do you mean? What does the Rajput want now?" Her voice was testy and she strode about the room, her apprehension translating itself into movement.

"He wants us to go on campaign with him," Sanat Ji Mani said.

"You expected that," she said, wanting him to reveal what was new in this regard; she had not noticed that Sanat Ji Mani had said *us* not *me*.

"Yes; I did." He inhaled deeply, the aroma of ginger and jasmine mingling on the evening wind. "And finally I know why."

Tulsi waited, then prompted, "Very well—why?"

"It seems," said Sanat Ji Mani remotely, "that Vayu Ede has had a vision, and Hasin Dahele believes the vision, no matter what I said to him."

"And that vision is—" Tulsi said impatiently, pacing back close to him.

"What it comes down to," said Sanat Ji Mani, "is that Hasin Dahele is convinced I am Timur-i Lenkh."

There was silence between them, Tulsi stood still, and then gave a crack of laughter. "You cannot mean it. Timur-i? You?"

"I have told him I am not, I have told him where I come from. It does not matter. He has accepted the vision and is certain that all he needs to do is conquer enough territory and I will declare myself to be Timur-i and make him my heir. We are not hostages. We are something far worse." Speaking this aloud made it seem more preposterous than hearing it from Hasin Dahele; Sanat Ji Mani gave a rueful chuckle. "I think I could have told him my true nature and he would have assumed it was only another ploy to keep from admitting my so-called real identity."

"But you would not do that?" Tulsi exclaimed, no hint of humor in her question. "You will not tell him you are a vampire."

"Of course not," he said, and added more gently. "I am relieved that you have refused a sixth embrace with me; we have hazard enough around us without that as an addition. I fear we will be under more extreme scrutiny now that the Rajput has informed me of his plans, and it is difficult enough as things are."

"I am not ready to—" She broke off, her manner apologetic. "I long for all you can do with me, with the pleasure you bring to my body, and I rejoice in your passion, but I cannot yet accept being made like you."

"Then you are right to refuse me," he said, his voice low and kindly. "I want no one to come to my life who is unwilling to have it."

"I do not know if I am unwilling," she said. "But I am not ready."

Sanat Ji Mani reached out to lay his hand on her shoulder. "Nothing will happen until you are," he promised her.

She was able to smile a little. "For that reason alone, I may be willing one day, but not now." Her blue-green eyes shone, partly in amusement, partly with unacknowledged tears. "And if you are supposed to be Timur-i, what must I be?"

"Apparently there is a story that many believe, that Timur-i has been cast out, abandoned with a single servant—"

"That tale is an old one," Tulsi scoffed. "I heard it four years ago at least."

"And you hear it again now: Hasin Dahele is positive that it is true." He moved his hand to caress her face. "I should never have brought you into this."

"You have apologized before," she said, dismissing his concern.

"Then I did not know the extent of the misconception under which we were laboring," he told her. "If only I could have discovered this earlier, I would have managed matters differently; I would have found a way to leave this place." He shook his head. "No. I learned the futility of second-guessing long ago. Had I known the Rajput's state of mind, of course I would have proceeded differently. But I did not know it."

"You have said that you suspected you did not know the whole of the situation, that there was more at stake than we assumed," she reminded him. "Does he *really* think you are Timur-i?"

"Yes, he really does," said Sanat Ji Mani, his shoulders drooping as if with sudden fatigue. "He will not entertain any other possibility. The more I deny it, the more certain he becomes that it is true."

"Then he is mad: he must be mad," she said.

"Perhaps. What matters is that he is Rajput and he is persuaded that he is destined to conquer all the world." He took a step back and sat on the edge of their bed. "We are to go with him on campaign."

"We—both of us," she said, to be certain she had heard correctly.

"Yes. I told him I do not want to be separated from you," said Sanat Ji Mani with a quick smile.

"And he agreed: I wonder why," she said, going quiet.

"He wants to keep my good opinion, I suspect," said Sanat Ji Mani.

"Or he wants us both where he can watch us," she said. "We may be hostages after all."

"That is another possibility," he agreed, and lay back, staring up at the ceiling. "So we shall make ready. And when we have the opportunity, we shall break away and head for the coast."

Tulsi came and stood over him. "Do you think he will permit that to happen?"

Despite his many reservations, Sanat Ji Mani maintained an optimistic expression as he told her, "I do not believe I will ask his permission."

Text of a letter from the merchant Kakar Kers to Vayu Ede.

To the most venerable and mystical Alvar, Vayu Ede, the submissive greetings of the Toda merchant Kakar Kers, who begs that the poet will read this account with understanding and regard for the intentions it represents.

In my travels from the coast, I have done as you have requested and taken time to observe other travelers on the roads. I have made note of how many men I have seen, and something of their nature, as you have asked me to do, and I now render the compilation of those observations to you, and ask that you recall your pledge that all customs taxation will be forgiven me for providing this to you. I am willing to do this but it is a risk and therefore I must have some form of recompense for my efforts. In this regard, I must tell you that there are still many men unsettled from the collapse of Delhi, who have been forced by circumstances to go about the roads of the world searching for a place to establish their businesses and families, more than two years ago, but fewer than last year. Those who travel now have fewer resources than those who were abroad last year; on the other hand, the current travelers have brought more things with them, their wealth being in possessions rather than gold, which is an advantage to traders.

I have been to Cambay and Chaul fairly recently and I can report to you that there is more unrest now in Chaul than there is in Cambay.

I have seen stricter discipline in Cambay, and higher taxes being imposed, but nothing so outrageous that merchants will avoid the place. Chaul, on the other hand, has lower taxes but far greater unrest. The situation there is still unresolved and for that reason, if no other, I have been wary of staying there too long, or becoming too heavily committed to trading from that port. I cannot guess what will transpire there in the next year, let alone for five years. I will decide if I am going to trade there again before too many months go by, for if I do not go there, I must select other markets or hurt my business.

The worshipers of Allah continue to exert their influence, but those following the traditional Gods are more inclined to keep to their own religions. Even those followers of Thomas have made their way as far as Chaul, and have put up their temple for worship. It would be possible for a just ruler to gain support in that place so long as he did not insist on imposing his Gods upon the people, who would not accept such limitation. The region of Chaul has long maintained its independence from the rule of Allah, and have therefore continued to allow many beliefs to be promulgated, so long as they are not exclusionary. Any ruler who did not tolerate these many forms of worship would be doomed from the first. I tell you for the sake of the Rajput, that keeping religion in the hands of the people is essential.

Also, as I have already informed you, there has been an increase in the flow of goods from north to south as those looking for a safe haven take all their belongings and set out for better climes. I have found many items of unusual design and rarity in market-places that do not often boast the remarkable; these are largely personal or family treasures, unique and prized, the last objects parted with in times of hardship. For that reason, I have spent more time in smaller cities and towns than I have in the past, to see what new merchants might be found in these markets; I want to see what is being offered for sale in these places. The most promising place has been Asirgarh, where I have found ivories and brasses from Delhi and fabrics from Assam and China. This is the result of many merchants coming south, and a shift in the routes traders use. How much this will effect the movement of goods, I cannot say, but for a year or two at least, I would reckon on these smaller markets to flourish while the larger ones are caught up in disputes.

It is my plan to go eastward until the rains stop me. Wherever I am when they come, there I shall remain until they pass. I will continue to gather intelligence in that place, and upon my return to Devapur, I will again report to you what I have seen, so that your master, the Rajput, may avail himself of the information. So long as I am excused the greater part of my taxes, I will serve you and the Rajput faithfully. If you should fail to demonstrate your appreciation, I know there are others who would be glad to have access to what I have learned.

Incidentally, it is rumored that the Rajput is going to cross the Narmanda and press into Deogir territory. If that is the case, be warned that an army is being assembled in the city of Deogir and that the soldiers are well-prepared to hold off any advance against them. For many weeks now there have been plans in motion to double the size of the supplies for the army and to secure all manner of metals and foodstuffs from the surrounding countryside so that the army will not have to forage over-much while on the march. Also, horses and asses are being commandeered from many of the people of Deogir for the purpose of fighting off any invasion. All this has taken place since the Rajput of Beragar pushed his territory back to the Narmanda River, for this has been seen as a sign that he is planning to encroach upon the region of Deogir itself. The Rajput would do better to strike out to the west than to go north, not only because there is more disorder in the west, but because he is expected north of the Narmanda River and not over the mountains to Chaul.

Submitted with my most sincere devotion to the cause of the Rajput's triumph, and with thanks to the Gods for his advancement, I look forward to the time that I may serve him in a more official capacity, as you have discussed with me, wise poet. I have told this to the scribe Sarojin, who has recorded all accurately, on pain of whipping for any mistakes.

Kahar Kers
Merchant

9

"We will use that pass," said Hasin Dahele, pointing to a gap in the peaks ahead of them. "The road is supposed to be good, and the weather is holding." He was beginning to look tired after ten days' travel; his dark-bay was fretful, pulling at the bit and fussing as the Rajput held him on short reins. The Rajput himself wore silks dulled by the constant dust of the road, making him appear less impressive than he had intended. Sweat left tracks in his face and under the arms of his pyjamas, his woven breastplate already chafing at the silk, fraying it at the neck and shoulder.

Beside the Rajput, Sanat Ji Mani did his best to keep in the shade of the umbrella held over him. Though he, too, was dusty, there was no indication of sweat on him or his dull-purple silk clothing. "It is a long distance to that pass, let alone through it. You will not accomplish the journey today, and possibly not tomorrow."

"Why do you say so?" Hasin Dahele asked imperiously. "My archers could be through the pass by tomorrow night."

"Possibly," Sanat Ji Mani allowed. "But your supply wagons and your elephants would not keep up with the archers, and that would divide your forces. If you take such a risk, you could be handily defeated by a smaller army."

"Timur-i divided his forces," said the Rajput in a critical tone. "His troops could cover vast distances quickly."

"That they could," said Sanat Ji Mani. "But not through mountain passes."

Hasin Dahele glowered at him. "His archers still moved swiftly."

"Timur-i had more than four times the number of horses you do, and could remount his soldiers frequently," Sanat Ji Mani reminded the Rajput. "This road is a hard climb, for all it is in good repair, and the horses will need to rest before and after they pass over the crest, unless you want to exhaust them so that they cannot be used in a fight."

"You think badly of my archers," said Hasin Dahele.

"No; I think any soldier fights better on a rested horse than on a tired one," said Sanat Ji Mani. "To say nothing of your elephants. Crossing the pass will be harder on them than the horses. You know that."

"They are sturdy beasts," said the Rajput mulishly.

"And sure-footed, but they do not often traverse mountain ridges, nor do they fight well on steep slopes," said Sanat Ji Mani. "They will need time to negotiate the pass, wide or narrow, or you will run the risk of injury to elephants and riders, as well as any unfortunate enough to be in their paths."

Hasin Dahele puffed out his cheeks. "As you say, they do not usually cross mountain ridges, and on flat land, their charge is generally unstoppable. You are right about the terrain." This concession annoyed him. "Very well. We will make camp at the base of the pass tonight and take all of tomorrow to get the army through; we should be able to accomplish that much. At least it is a broad pass, and not one like a goat-track, as some of the passes are."

"All the more reason to rest before going through," said Sanat Ji Mani. "You will have the opportunity to gather information from travelers from the west, and you can keep travelers from the east from going ahead of you."

"There may be advantages in that," Hasin Dahele mused. "I will consider this while we continue on toward the pass; how best to patrol the road and watch for any who might be spies. My scouts will bring me word of what is ahead at sunset." He coughed, swatting at the dusty air with his hand. "In the meantime, perhaps you should go to your woman's wagon and rest out of the sun. There are more red patches on your skin."

"I am aware of them," said Sanat Ji Mani evenly. "Thank you, Rajput. I will do that."

With a slow shake of his head, Hasin Dahele remarked, "I do not know how you led your army as you did with the sun burning you so badly."

"I have told you I did not lead an army," Sanat Ji Mani pointed out as he turned his dun mare and started back along the line of the army to the rear, his umbrella-bearer hurrying to keep up while his feisty roan mare fought to remain at the front of the march.

Tulsi Kil's wagon was in the middle of the ranks of vehicles, a small wooden carriage with high sides and a partial roof that was augmented with a double layer of heavy cotton cloth that covered the top and sides; Tulsi sat on the driving-box, handling the two mules pulling it with reasonable skill. She waved as she saw Sanat Ji Mani approach. "We have come far this morning," she called. "The Rajput is eager."

"That he is," said Sanat Ji Mani as he came abreast of the wagon. "I am going to get into the back and turn my horse over to this offi-cer"—he gestured toward the umbrella-bearer—"who can bring the mare back to me at sunset." For the sake of the young officer, Sanat Ji Mani repeated this in the Devapur dialect.

The umbrella-bearer looked relieved. "I will do that."

"Good. I am going to climb up beside my companion now, and you may take the mare." Sanat Ji Mani kicked his aching right foot out of the stirrup and swung his leg over in front, just brushing the mare's mane as he did. "Keep her walking at the same pace," he told the officer as he rose on his left foot and straddled the air between horse and wagon; a moment later and he had pushed away from the dun mare and onto the driving-box, facing backward but safe. He signaled to the umbrella-bearer. "She is yours until this evening. See she has plenty of water."

The young officer caught the reins and pulled the horse away from the line of carts, wagons, and larger vehicles—two water-wagons were drawn by teams of eight mules—and spurred toward the front of the army; the wagons kept on steadily and behind them shuffled the el-ephants.

"I thought you would be here earlier," said Tulsi, her gaze fixed on the blistered places on his hands and face. She had wrapped a length of cotton around her head and over part of her face as well as all of her neck. "Perhaps you should cover yourself more completely."

"I thought I would be here earlier, too, and the wagon-cover will shield me," Sanat Ji Mani admitted as he slipped behind her into the bed of the wagon. "This is much better."

"You are very white where you are not red," she told him as she leaned back on the driving-box in order to hear his response. "Does that mean you are weak?"

"I am tired," he said. "This heat is taking a toll on me."

"As it is on all of us," said Tulsi. "I never thought I would miss the desert, but after this, I do." She gave her attention to the mules for a short while, then said, "I suppose we will travel through the heat of the day?" It was more usual to rest, but Hasin Dahele had been determined to press on.

"I believe so," said Sanat Ji Mani, already beginning to drift into that torpid state that was his slumber. "He wants to cover as much ground as he can."

Tulsi laughed. "He will wear out his army before his first battle," she said with certainty. "His troops are not used to this pace."

"Nor should they be," said Sanat Ji Mani, and lapsed into semi-consciousness.

Tulsi, unaware that he could not hear her, went on. "These are not Timur-i's troops and they cannot move as his can." She waited for him to comment. "Sanat Ji Mani?" she called softly, and then smiled as she realized he was asleep. Holding firmly to the reins, she whistled to the mules to pick up their pace, and was intensely pleased when they minded her.

It was a long day, traveling at a rapid walk, dust rising in a vast cloud that marked the army's progress to anyone watching for a considerable distance. Twice there were short stops to water the animals, when riders and drivers could have water and lentil-cakes, but the Rajput was determined to reach the foot of the pass by nightfall and did not allow much respite from the grueling march. By the time the sun dropped to the edge of the mountains ahead of them, Tulsi was glad to have Sanat Ji Mani waken and take her place on the driving-box.

"Are you rested?" she asked as he gathered the reins into his hands.

"Enough to be hungry," he answered and added quickly, "I will find sustenance tonight, not from you. There are animals who can provide what I need."

She shook her head. "I wish I could be ready, but I am not. Your life is still too . . . too strange for me."

"Then you are right not to risk coming to it," he said with a swift, sympathetic smile. "It is difficult enough for those who seek it."

"I may yet regret my decision," she said.

"You have time to consider it still," he told her gently. "More immediately, I may have a plan that will get us away from this tomorrow."

She turned toward him, her eyes alight. "Tomorrow? Are we not supposed to go through the pass tomorrow? That is what the couriers were saying at our second water-stop."

"Yes, we are," said Sanat Ji Mani, "and that may provide us the opportunity we have been seeking."

"Tell me," she pleaded, wanting to hold on to his arm and knowing it would be improper to do so in this place.

Although no one around could hear them, or spoke the language they used, Sanat Ji Mani still lowered his voice. "There are two high valleys that comprise the pass ahead, that is, if the maps the Rajput is using are correct. If this wagon should lose a wheel on the climb to the pass, it would have to leave the road and then it would be forced to bring up the rear, behind the elephants. If we went slowly enough, we could drop far behind the army, and then we can ride the mules and take the other pass, the one south of us. It is narrower and steeper, but it is much nearer Chaul. From there we can find a ship and be on our way to Alexandria."

"Timur-i would kill those in wagons rather than leave them behind to fall into the hands of his enemies," said Tulsi, her expression dubious.

"Timur-i might, but Hasin Dahele would not," said Sanat Ji Mani. "He does not fear what is behind him, only what is ahead."

"And you think we could manage it?" she asked, trying to be convinced of his plan.

"I think we could, especially if more than one wagon lost a wheel, so that our predicament would not seem unique." There was a glint of intent in his dark eyes that caught her attention.

"Are you planning something more than a single accident?" She leaned forward to listen to him.

"I will not sleep tonight, so I may be able to go about the camp and work the wheels on a few other wagons and carriages; not too many, just enough so that one more will not be remarkable," he said. "We may also be able to delay our trouble until the others have occurred, and then we will have a better chance of success."

"How do you reckon that?" She rubbed her hands together and felt the grit that had accumulated there.

"If I can volunteer to help remount the lost wheel of another wagon, I can promise to attend to ours on my own," he said. "The soldiers will know I am able to do this, and we will drop farther back in the line by helping."

Tulsi nodded slowly. "It may work," she said. "It may be enough to get us away."

"So I hope," he said, and winced as a small gap in the mountains let through a brilliant shaft of sunlight. He tried to turn from it, but did not manage in time, and was left with a large patch of red on his forehead.

"That will be black by morning," said Tulsi. "Are you sure you should ride here before dark?"

"Oh, yes; I think I should be ready for my escort to appear," he said. "I wish I could have that umbrella right now." As quickly as the light had struck, it was gone. "Better," he said, doing his best to ignore the tenderness of his skin.

"Are all vampires so hampered by sunlight?" She sounded alarmed.

"When the soles of my shoes are lined with my native earth, or the floor of the wagon is, I am as sensitive as other men; sunlight would burn me eventually, as it does others, but it would be nothing like this. Without my native earth—well, you see." He lifted his hands; the red patches were almost black now and would begin to peel in a day or so.

"Where is your native earth? Have you none you can reach?" She was apprehensive, and it sharpened her questions.

"I had chests of it back in Delhi, but no doubt they are gone; everything else is. I should have two chests in a warehouse in Chaul, that will enable me to cross water without suffering too much discomfort. Without it, I would be incapacitated, with it I am only wretched." He managed an ironic smile.

"I saw you in the river," she said. "I thought you would drown."

"Alas, no," he said. "That would be too easy." He thought of his escape from the forest fire in Spain, when he had been bruised and battered for hours only to wash up on a jagged boulder far away from the flames.

Tulsi listened carefully, saying only, "Can you not resist it: what the water does?"

He nodded. "With my native earth, I can." Hearing his name shouted, he looked about and saw the young officer with the umbrella leading the dun mare. "I will have to go," he said to Tulsi. "I will find you after we have made camp tonight."

She held out her hands for the reins. "I will look for you."

"No; stay where you are. If both of us start searching, we may never find one another." He swiftly brushed a kiss on her lips, then rose on the driving-box, holding on to the frame to steady himself, and after steadying himself, dropped down into the saddle on the dun mare. "I will find you!" he shouted to Tulsi as he and the officer cantered off toward the front of the line.

Tulsi watched him go, distress showing in her features. She managed to wave but did not know if he saw it or not. Giving her full attention to the mules, she did her best to banish the worry that was growing in her. "There is nothing you can do about it now, in any case," she told herself aloud, in the hope that a stern delivery would bolster her mood, but she could not shake off the foreboding completely.

As Sanat Ji Mani approached the head of the line, he felt his right foot slip out of the stirrup. This did not make his riding much more difficult, for he had over three millennia of horsemanship behind him and could manage with far less. But the stirrup, a heavy, truncated triangle of thick metal, kept banging into his half-healed foot, and by the time he could pull the dun into a walk near Hasin Dahele, the wound through his foot was open again, and bleeding. He tried to conceal this as he bent in the saddle, caught the stirrup, and set his foot in place. Straightening up, he saw the Rajput was watching him critically.

"You are bleeding," said Hasin Dahele.

"It is nothing to bother about," said Sanat Ji Mani.

"Bleeding is always something to worry about, for it allows all manner of impure things to enter the body, as well as robbing it of strength," Hasin Dahele corrected him. "You have taken quite a chance with that injury." He raised his brows to add significance to his remark. "It is your weak foot."

"It is nothing," Sanat Ji Mani repeated. "I will put new wraps on it tonight."

"It will fester," said Hasin Dahele.

Sanat Ji Mani gave no response to the warning. "How much longer until you make camp?"

"You will be unable to travel," said the Rajput, unwilling to be put off.

"I doubt it," Sanat Ji Mani told him. "Now, about camp."

"It will have to be soon; the light is fading." He glanced up at the sky, already showing a scattering of stars against the evanescing sunset. "The scouts say there are wide meadows ahead. It will not be long."

"You will have to issue torches to your men if you wait much longer," said Sanat Ji Mani. "It is dangerous to cross unknown ground in the dark." He did not add that he saw almost as well by night as he did by day.

"I agree," said Hasin Dahele. "I was hoping we could move right to the foot of the pass, but I see it will not be possible." He signaled to the officer accompanying Sanat Ji Mani to close his umbrella. "I do not think you will need that until dawn."

"No. It is dark enough," said Sanat Ji Mani. "I will help to organize the camps, if you need such help."

"I would rather you tend to your foot. I do not want to run the risk of losing you to putrid blood. Care for the injury and rest yourself tonight, for tomorrow will make demands of us all." He motioned Sanat Ji Mani away, and went toward the white ass upon which Vayu Ede rode.

Watching him go, Sanat Ji Mani wondered why he had been summoned to the front of the line only to be dismissed. He rode to the side of the army, watching the companies ride by, some of the men lurching in their saddles, attacked by hunger and fatigue. He took advantage of this moment to assess the readiness of the soldiers and realized that most of them, although tired, were fit enough. He would have to try his ploy the next day. There would be no more opportunities to get away. As the columns began to turn and fan out to make camp, Sanat Ji Mani waited for the wagons to catch up, so that he might select the others to be disabled by the climb through the pass. At last he picked out the smallest of the water-wagons, a carriage filled with trunks and boxes containing clothing and armor, and a donkey-pulled cart bearing cooking pots and utensils for one of the cooks, who trudged along beside it rather than try to steer the donkey with reins. Those three, and Tulsi's wagon, would have wheel trouble on the next day. Satisfied that he knew what to do, he rode toward Tulsi's wagon and its pair of weary mules.

"I thought you would not come until later," she said as she saw him ride up; in the dwindling light, he seemed to be a bit of night arriving ahead of the dark.

"I have an injury; the Rajput has ordered me to tend to it." He rode to the back of the wagon, secured the dun's reins to the back support, then scrambled into the rear. Making his way to the front of the wagon, he called out to her, "We go over the pass tomorrow, as I expected. The Rajput is determined on it."

"And we will have an accident?" she called back, keeping her voice as low as she could.

"Yes. I will take care of that later, after midnight," he said as he emerged at her side. "Watch closely. We will be guided to a place to set up for the night."

"That I will," she said, and made a point of sitting up straighter to show how alert she was.

He lifted his right foot and looked down at the bloody leather of his boot. "Ah. I can see what bothered the Rajput," he said as he pulled off the boot with care and inspected the old injury; the wound through his foot had opened, not all the way, but enough to delay his healing by several months. He cursed in his native tongue, then noticed that Tulsi was staring at him in horror. "It looks dreadful, I know. But it is not dangerous, only inconvenient."

"It seems hideous," she said. "I thought you were improving. You said you were." There was an accusation in this last.

"I was. I am. It is much better than when I got the staple out," he reminded her.

"It made me sick to watch," she said quietly. "I do not like to think about it."

"Nor do I," he said. "I will have to wrap it tightly for a week or so, to keep it from opening any more."

"Do you think that will be sufficient?" She had to fight down the anxiety that was regaining a hold on her. "Can we manage our escape tomorrow?" The wagon lurched as she swung the mules off the main track to follow the other wagons to the place they would be assigned for the night.

"My foot should not stop that," he said. "The sun will be harder to manage than this injury." He was holding onto the seat as if the bumpy ride did not bother him. "In fact, we may be able to use the foot as a reason not to fix the wagon too quickly."

"You are a very wily man," she said, keeping her tone light. "No wonder the Rajput wants your advice."

"He wants it, but does not often take it. If he truly believes that I am Timur-i, he is behaving oddly." He noticed one of the officers directing them to turn aside and halt. "I think we have reached the halt."

"The mules will be pleased," she said, and pulled their reins to get them into position, then wrapped the reins around the splash-board and climbed down, reaching for their halters as she did. "Can you help me with the grooming?" she called up to Sanat Ji Mani.

"Of course," he said rather brusquely. "I will bring the brushes," he told her, reaching under the driving-box for the grooming supplies; with these in hand, he struggled to the ground, walking awkwardly, favoring his bleeding foot as he went to help unharness the mules.

By the time they were done and the mules were eating the handfuls of grain given to them before they were put on a grazing line for the night, the first wonderful odors of cooking were filling the air, reminding Tulsi that she was famished. She stowed her grooming supplies back under the driving-box, got out their cups and bowls from inside the wagon, and turned to Sanat Ji Mani, who was sitting on the ground, trying to tend to his foot. "I am going to get some food. Shall I bring some for you?" It would be expected of her and she had done it every night since the army had set off.

"Yes, if you would," he said, knowing she would eat it. "Not too much."

"As you wish," she said, but hesitated. "Do you have cloth to wrap that?"

"I do. Go along and get our meals," he said, glancing up at her with a generous smile. "I will have this taken care of by the time you return."

"Very well," she said, and set off toward the nearest of the newly blazing fires, prepared to wait in line for the shares of food being cooked. She wanted to stretch out her tired muscles, to do some of her tumbling tricks just to limber up, but did not: in the morning there would be a little time to exercise before beginning their day with the army—their last day with the army, she reminded herself, and did her best to feel encouraged. By the time she got back to the wagon, Sanat Ji Mani had his boot on once again and was practicing walking, trying to minimize his limp. "How does it feel?"

"A bit raw," he admitted. "But not impossibly so."

"Do you think you can make everything ready for tomorrow?" she asked as she sank down next to the wagon and began to eat the broiled lamb with the chickpea bread that had been the evening fare offered, along with hot, dark tea. "It may be difficult to accomplish."

"I must do it," he said. "When are we going to have another opportunity like the one we will have tomorrow?"

"I do not want to guess," said Tulsi, taking a long sip of the cardamom-spiced tea. "You may not have another opportunity before there is a battle, and then, anything might happen."

"So it might," Sanat Ji Mani said.

"Given what the Rajput thinks of you, he may well order you to the front of the army, to be beside him." There was bitterness in her voice, and an attitude of distress. "What can we do, if that is what the Rajput wants?"

"And probably will insist upon; Hasin Dahele will have his way," said Sanat Ji Mani, continuing to pace the small area between Tulsi's wagon and the next vehicle.

"Are you certain we will escape?" Tulsi's question came without apology.

"I hope we will," Sanat Ji Mani admitted.

"Hope," she echoed. "So you must tell me, what will we do if our plan does not work? Do you have another in mind?" Tulsi blinked her nervousness. "Is this our only chance?"

"There can be others, but they may require more planning, and more luck," he said.

"Then you have been thinking about alternatives?" She took a large bite of lamb and chewed with determination.

Sanat Ji Mani considered her question. "If it comes to that, we can always die," he said, so blandly that she stared. "You know, make it appear we are dead. It can be done. It is risky, but so is getting away on the mules."

She nodded. "I suppose you are right," she said, and was about to say more when the sound of approaching hoofbeats caught her attention; she saw that Sanat Ji Mani was standing still, his attention directed toward five approaching horsemen.

"Sanat Ji Mani," the Rajput called out. "I have been mulling over your injury, and I have decided to provide you an escort, in case you should need any additional help. These are Challa Bahlin, Sambarin Kheb, Garanai Kheb, and Kantu Asar. They will bear you company for as long as you may need them." He indicated the men behind him as he spoke their names. "I cannot rid myself of the notion that your foot will fester, and you will need to have men to do your bidding."

Sanat Ji Mani looked up at the Rajput. "Such attention is too much, Rajput. I have no need of the protection you offer."

"It is like you to say such things, to carry on in the face of injury," said Hasin Dahele. "But I cannot be as unconcerned as you, for I rely upon you for instruction. I will not neglect you; that would compromise my mission."

"You have your troops to think of first," said Sanat Ji Mani. "You will need to provide for them before you care for me, or any other advisors you may have." He kept his stance upright and his demeanor respectful, but watching him, Tulsi could see he was vexed.

Hasin Dahele laughed. "Two will be with you by night, and two by day," he said as if he had not heard what Sanat Ji Mani had told him.

"It is unnecessary," Sanat Ji Mani said with more force.

"It is my Will," said Hasin Dahele in a tone that ended the matter; he turned his horse abruptly, and rode away, two of the men following him, two remaining.

Sanat Ji Mani considered the men. "Will you remain far enough from us that my woman and I may be alone?"

For an answer, the two men repositioned themselves a short distance from the wagon, one by the grazing-line of the mules, the other beyond the rear of the wagon; they dismounted and took up their posts without saying a word.

Tulsi began to eat again, and managed to mutter to him, "I understood most of that: it seems we will have to die."

"Yes," Sanat Ji Mani agreed. "So it does."

Text of a letter from Rogerian in Alexandria to Atta Olivia Clemens in Rome; written in Imperial Latin.

To the oldest friend of my master, the greetings of Rogerian, with what little news as I have to impart.

Again, there is nothing to report from the lands of Hind, but that another small war may be underway in the western mountains of the central region, or so Rustam Iniattir's nephew Zal Iniattir has sent him word from the fortress-town of Asirgarh. If Sanct' Germain has been in that region, he may well be occupied with avoiding the conflict that seems about to erupt among the various people who live in those uplands. This is all conjecture, I grant you, and it is not unlikely that when he finally arrives here, or in Rome, it will turn out that he has been in China or Russia or some other place, making his way westward or eastward as the circumstances demand. But so long as Rustam Iniattir has heard this, I think it behooves me to pass it on to you, if for no other reason than to provide some notion of the difficulties that have arisen in that part of the world, and the consequent dangers such events can represent.

The business here continues to do well. I have entered into a formal trading agreement with Rustam Iniattir which I am convinced will be advantageous to my master when he finally returns. Rustam Iniattir is a prudent merchant with a clever eye to the market-places he can seek. I share his belief that there are goods from Europe that would be valuable in the East, and goods from the East that will be treasures in Europe. Whatever the case, if nothing else, this adds to the access Sanct' Germain has to the spice trade. His profits from pepper alone could be vast beyond reckoning, so long as the House of Iniattir maintains its position among merchants. I have agreed to carry his goods in Sanct' Germain's ships from Alexandria throughout the Mediterranean and Atlantic ports of call, and to allow him to purchase partnerships in three vessels, over time, so that his incentive to continue the association remains high.

Your admonition in regard to Avasa Dani was well-considered. She has her own establishment, at the edge of the Foreigners' Quarter, where she stands to be most successful with the least difficulties. I have paid handsome bribes to ensure her business will be undisrupted, and that she will not have to rely on the whims of patrons to gain the protection she requires in her chosen endeavor. She has employed fourteen women and plans eventually to have twenty in her household. She has set aside dowries for all the women and promised to find them suitable husbands when their days of employment in her house are at an end; for those who do not wish to be married, she has said she will provide all the trappings of widowhood and help the women to have their own households in another place, where no whiff of their former occupation can work against them. She is satisfied with her situation, and is content to remain as she is for the time being.

I have dispatched notice to all the captains aboard Sanct' Germain's ships and all the warehouse supervisors, to be alert for Sanct' Germain; I have provided two ways for them to be sure the man they have is the authentic Sanct' Germain, and have promised a reward to any of them who are able to assist him in coming to Alexandria or Rome. It may be an empty gesture, but I must do something, for sitting here waiting is taking its toll on me, and I would far rather attempt too much than do too little. He is not in Tunis or Spain now, but he might as well be. I am determined to aid him however I can. If you have suggestions of what more I can do, I ask that you send me word of them, and at once.

This, by my own hand on the 29th day of May in the year of the Roman Church 1400,

Rogerian

10

Crossing the pass had been grueling, requiring most of the day to accomplish; the heat had left the men and animals staggering, and the long descent was steeper than the climb had been. Nine men had fallen to their deaths, six of them taking their horses with them, as they tried to keep on the expanse of broken rocks that were the footing on the road just past the crest. The wagons had slithered on the polished stone, and the elephants had had to be led carefully across the swath, fidgeting every step of the way.

"We lost our chance," said Tulsi as she pulled her wagon to the side of the road as they made it to the first safe place; many other wagons were gathered there, more than half of them needing attention to wheels and harness.

"We have one remaining," Sanat Ji Mani reminded her; he was lying in the bed of the wagon, out of the inexorable sun; the skin had begun to peel off the backs of his hands and his forehead and cheeks had blackened.

"Do you mean dying? They are watching you constantly: how do you plan to convince them you are dead when you are not?" she asked, glancing around as if she feared being overheard by one of their escorts, although neither man spoke the dialect of Timur-i's troops.

"But I am," he said gently.

"Not like that," she said, unwilling to be cajoled.

"I do not know, yet. I have the glimmer of a plan, but nothing more." He pulled a length of heavy cotton over him. "I think my foot may provide the answer."

"Your foot? How?" Tulsi secured the reins, then prepared to get down to examine her mules. "Tell me when I return."

"Remember to check their legs for heat. They could come up lame if—" Sanat Ji Mani called after her.

"I will," she promised, interrupting him before she swung down to the ground, going to the mules and starting with the off-side one; the animal was sweating and fussing, still edgy from mincing across the slick slabs of rock. The off-side mule was the more fretful of the two, laying back his ears and champing at his bit as Tulsi began to check him over, noticing only that he was showing signs of over-exertion; although he had been standing for a while, the mule's breathing was still labored. The on-side mule was not in much better shape, being only a bit calmer than his partner; sweat flecked his coat and clung to the harness, and darkened his coat. He was fussy when Tulsi rubbed down his legs, seeking out hot tendons and joints; at one point he bared his teeth and tried to swing his head around to bite, but was thwarted by the harness.

"How are they?" Sanat Ji Mani asked as Tulsi came to the rear of the wagon, trying to get out of earshot of their escort.

"Worn out," she answered. "The on-side mule may have a splint forming. I will look again in an hour or so, to see if the bone is still tender."

"That could be a real problem," said Sanat Ji Mani as he listened to the shouts around them. "The Rajput does not have many mules to spare."

"No doubt he will find one for you," said Tulsi. "He does not want you to fall behind."

"You are angry," he said.

"Are you not?" she countered. "We are caught in a dangerous game. What will become of us when the Rajput decides that he has been fooled, and you are not Timur-i? Do you think he will forgive you your deception?"

"I have told him I am not Timur-i from the first he spoke of it," said Sanat Ji Mani, but in a tone that lacked conviction.

"Do you think he will remember? or care?" Tulsi demanded. "If you are going to get us away from here, it must be soon, before he has lost a battle and holds you accountable for it. And do not doubt that he will."

"I know you are right," said Sanat Ji Mani, his face set in strong lines of concern which she could hardly see in the gloom of the wagon's interior.

"Then what are we to do?" Tulsi left the question between them as she went back to the front of the wagon and signaled to the two officers escorting them. "This mule," she said awkwardly in the dialect of Devapur, as she touched the on-side mule, "hurt. He cannot pull. Get another."

The two officers exchanged wary glances, and one of them said, "You cannot be left alone."

"One of you go," said Tulsi, letting the words clunk together like the toys of clumsy children. "I will not move."

"If the mule is hurt, she cannot," said the other. "You go get a replacement and I will keep guard here."

"It may take a while," said the first. "I will bring the two Kheb brothers back with me, so we will be relieved for the night."

"Very good," said the second. "I will keep on guard here. There are other wagons here, as well, and it should suit the Rajput's purpose to have a soldier or two on duty."

"So it might," said the first as he prepared to start down the incline to where the greatest part of the army was regrouping after their harrowing day.

"Tell the Rajput where we are, and why," the second reminded him. "Do not leave it to some subordinate to do."

"I will," said the first, and sat back as his dark-chestnut began to pick his way down the hill.

"You should have another mule by sundown," said the second officer to Tulsi.

"Then we will stay here," said Tulsi.

"Through the night, of course," said the officer. "It would be too dangerous, trying to get down that road in the dark." He regarded Tulsi for a long moment. "You do not understand half of what I am saying, do you?"

Tulsi cocked her head. "The road is hard," she agreed as if trying to figure out the rest, which she comprehended perfectly.

"Yes," said the officer. "The road is hard." He dismounted and led his horse a short distance away to where a small rivulet sprang out of the rocky hillside. "Your mules will want water. Water," he repeated, bending to flick his fingers in the narrow stream.

"Yes," said Tulsi. "I will bring . . ." She mimed a pail.

"Very good," said the officer.

Tulsi pointed to the covered part of the wagon and, seeing the officer nod, climbed inside. "I am getting a pail for water," she said to Sanat Ji Mani. "He is a dunce, that one, thinking I know nothing more than a baby," she said in her own tongue.

"Which is what you want him to think," Sanat Ji Mani reminded her. "It suits your purpose to have him think you know less than you do." He watched her pull the pail from her chest of supplies. "You might take that smaller bowl, say that you need water for me."

She stopped and looked at him. "Why would I do that? You do not need water."

"If you say my fever is up, it would be useful," he added. "Tell him my foot has swollen."

Tulsi was still for a long moment. "I think I understand," she said, beginning to smile.

"Let him think I am getting worse, and that will help us." He touched her shoulder very gently. "Sound worried."

"I will," she said, beginning to enter into his intentions. "I will not say very much, just enough to cause a little apprehension."

"Very good," said Sanat Ji Mani. "You will do well."

"That is my plan; to do it well enough that he comes to conclusions I do not tell him to." She took her pail and a large metal bowl, then clambered out of the wagon and went to get water, returning a short while later. After she had given water to the mules, she climbed back into the wagon. "He listened," she said, almost grinning. "I did not say much, only that you were hot and your foot had started bleeding again."

"Did he ask you anything?" Sanat Ji Mani wondered aloud.

"Only: was I concerned," she said, and provided her answer before he could speak. "I said I was not; very curt and emphatic in my tone."

"And he will know that you are worried," said Sanat Ji Mani.

"Of course. He will think I am afraid for you, but do not want anyone to know I am." She sat down next to him. "Here is the water. What are you going to do?"

"Let a little blood get into it," he said. "Mine, not yours," he added hastily. "Then have you dump it where one of our escort can see it. Say nothing when you do, just dispose of it as if you do not want it seen."

She managed to contain an excited giggle. "This is fun. I like fooling them."

"Tulsi, be careful," said Sanat Ji Mani, thinking back to the punishments the Rajput had described to him: dismemberment of their escorts and the scraping through a net for themselves seemed far too real to lend much savor to their deception. "As preposterous as Hasin Dahele may seem, do not forget he is a powerful ruler and his whim is etched in stone."

"Is that why you want him to think you are dying?" Tulsi asked, her demeanor changing suddenly from amused to serious.

"It is a good reason, Tulsi; I do not want anyone hurt on my account. Yet I want to get us away from here, beyond the Rajput's reach." He laid his hand over hers. "In the morning, you will say to the escort that I had a hard night. Nothing more than that."

"All right," she said, a glimmer of her humor returning.

"Do not give them any reason to doubt you," he warned her. "We are playing a very desperate game."

"I will not forget," she told him. "I will give them no reason to think I am playing with them." She sat back. "I suppose you are going to unwrap your foot."

"I am," he said.

"A pity you have none of your medicaments left," said Tulsi, turning away. "It must hurt."

"Yes," he said, and did not add that none of the powders, tinctures, or ointments could provide him succor. "Water will at least get it clean."

"Is that desirable?" She was mildly upset at the notion.

"It is," said Sanat Ji Mani, and shifted to a position where he could pull off his boot again. "Do we have any more wraps like these?"

"A few," she said.

"Then be sure to throw these out along with the water, and tomorrow ask for more of them. The Rajput should agree to supply them." He tugged his boot off with some effort. "This must not happen too quickly. Tomorrow night you should say I am not improved, but behave as if I am worse."

She was listening closely now, her full concentration on him. "How long do you plan to languish?"

"Four days should be enough," he said. "I doubt there will be an opportunity to engage an enemy before then, and I do not want to have the Rajput be able to blame you, or those four men escorting us, for what becomes of me." He closed his eyes a moment, trying not to recall Hasin Dahele's causal bloody-mindedness. "You and I must make our plans in the next two days." He began to unwrap his injured foot. "Good. There is blood enough on these wraps. It should convince Hasin Dahele that something is amiss."

"And it is not?" she asked, looking at the bloody rags.

"No. You have seen how slowly I mend." He dropped the first bandage into the water. "I will heal."

"In time," she added for him.

"In time," he agreed, and began to remove the second wrapping.

She watched, revolted and fascinated. "What shall we do when you—?"

"When I appear to die?" he asked, continuing with his task. "Why, build a funeral pyre and set me on it. Just be certain the wood is very green and that there are oil-soaked cloths in amongst the wood as well, so that there will be enough smoke to let me escape without notice. Ask to light the fire yourself, as my companion. Also say you must prepare my body. They should allow you that." He put the second wrapping in the basin and began on the innermost bandage. "This is a little sticky."

"You can soak it off," Tulsi recommended.

"So I will," he said, moving the basin so that he could put his foot into it. "About the pyre: make sure it billows smoke. There must be a tremendous amount of smoke."

"There will have to be fire," she said, her spirits somewhat dampened.

"Yes, there will," he concurred.

"Fire is dangerous—deadly to vampires," she reminded him.

"That it is," he said. "If there were time before we reach an opponent, I might be able to think of something else; we will encounter foes very soon. We have passed enough villages that someone must have sent word to their Rajput that Hasin Dahele has brought his army through the pass. So it is safer to take a chance with the fire than waiting for battle or for the Rajput to turn on us." He gave her a long, steady look. "You do not want that."

"No," she said after a thoughtful silence. "All right. A pyre of green wood with oiled rags to make for more smoke. You will get away in the smoke. What of me?"

"Come with me," he said as if the answer were obvious. "We will take a horse—just one—and go toward Chaul."

"There will be much confusion, and the Rajput may not let me . . . He may not permit me to be near your pyre," she said.

"You have said you can leap through flames, that you have done it for Timur-i," he reminded her. "Then show your skill. Jump through the smoke, as if to die on the fire, but vault over and beyond, let the pyre lengthen your spring."

"Leap onto the fire? then off, through the smoke?" she asked, musing on the possibilities. At last she looked up at him. "Yes, I suppose I could—"

"Then you will seem to immolate yourself in grief," he said, smiling his encouragement. "They will not wonder what has become of you, for they will assume they know."

"It could work," she agreed after another short silence. "It is very dangerous, but it could work."

"Then make your plans, Tulsi," he said, and removed the last bandage from his foot. "We will have to act in four days, whether or not we are ready."

She nodded and studied him for a short while. "I will take the bowl now," she told him a bit later, and, taking it out of the wagon to dump it, realized she was now committed to their plan.

For the next three days, Sanat Ji Mani was thought to be getting worse. He did not leave the wagon when anyone could see him, his swift, furtive excursions limited to the darkest part of the night when he feed on the blood of animals, then returned to the wagon as silently as he had left. The black skin on his face peeled off and left pale, tender skin exposed, which made him look far more fragile than he was. When he was visited by the Rajput—very briefly during the afternoon water-stop near a small village which had sent food out in welcome—he made it seem that he had grown weak, struggling to speak, but insisting he was improving.

"It is a bad thing," said Hasin Dahele to Tulsi, speaking carefully so that she could comprehend him.

"It is," she agreed.

"He is very sick." The Rajput shook his head. "This is a bad thing, that he is so sick," as if repetition made his point more emphatically, afraid to use more difficult words with Tulsi, certain she would not understand.

"He is," said Tulsi. "Sick."

"The foot is worse." The Rajput stared at the wagon as if to tear off the cover.

"His foot is sick," said Tulsi. "Very bad."

"You must watch him, and drive very carefully," said Hasin Dahele, pretending to hold the reins. "Make it easy for him."

"The new mule is good," said Tulsi, as if she did not entirely grasp his meaning.

"Not the mule: Sanat Ji Mani. Use him well," said Hasin Dahele. "Tell me how he is every morning and every night. I must know how Sanat Ji Mani is."

"I will tell," said Tulsi, her palms pressed together and her head bowed.

"Before he dies, he must make me his heir, the Lord of the World," Hasin Dahele muttered, convinced Tulsi did not know enough of his tongue to understand what he said. "Before he dies, I must be recognized."

"He will live," said Tulsi, slowly and stubbornly. "He must."

The Rajput patted her arm. "Of course," he said, raising his voice. "Take care of him. See that he does not die too soon."

"I will," said Tulsi, and watched the Rajput stroll away, his head pensively lowered.

"He is convinced you are dying," Tulsi told Sanat Ji Mani a bit later that day; the army was coming to the end of its day's march and the pace was slowing. From her place on the box, Tulsi asked, "Will it be tomorrow?"

Chelsea Quinn Yarbro

"Yes. Mid-afternoon, I should think. Tell the Rajput not to stop until sunset, that I would not expect him to interrupt his campaign for me." He kept his voice low and sing-song, so that their escort would assume he had become delirious.

"I will," she said. "Sanat Ji Mani," she went on more tentatively, "there is one other thing. I do not know how to tell you, so I will say it directly: I have decided to stay as I am."

It took Sanat Ji Mani a while to respond. "If that is what you want, then it is my desire as well."

"You are not disappointed?" She sounded apprehensive.

"Yes, I am," he said. "But I would be far more disappointed if you let me love you a sixth time and came to my life unwillingly." He paused. "Will you still travel with me, away from here?"

"Of course," she replied, a thought too quickly.

Sanat Ji Mani lay still for a while, then said, "There will be a great deal of confusion tomorrow. Have you thought what we will do if we get separated at the pyre?"

She swallowed hard before answering. "You said we should take one horse," she pointed out. "That way we will not be separated."

"We should, but if it is not possible, then we need to agree where we will meet." Sanat Ji Mani kept his voice low and his tone kindly. "We may have to find each other later."

"Do you expect we will?" she asked crisply.

"I do not know what to expect, which is why we should be prepared for things to work out some way other than our plans," he said. "If we are separated, I will go to Chaul, to the warehouses on the harbor belonging to the foreigner Ragoczy. You will know them by the sign of the eclipse on the doors—a black disk with raised, open wings above it—and you will ask for me there. If I am not there, wait until the storms are finished, and then take one of Ragoczy's ships and go west, to the Mameluke Empire and seek out Rogerian in the city of Alexandria—"

Tulsi laughed. "Why would any of these people pay any heed to me? Would you, if I came to you saying that Sanat Ji Mani has said that I am to be given free passage to the Mameluke Empire? They would stone me from the door, and be right to do it." She turned around and looked briefly at Sanat Ji Mani. "This much I will do: I will go to Chaul. If I do not find you there after the storms have gone, I will make my way to Kiev, to find my father's family. Do not fret. I should be able to do that. If I reach the Arabian Sea, I should be able to reach the Black Sea. It is only a matter of finding a caravan that has entertainers; or a troupe in need of a tumbler." She said this as if it were a simple thing.

Sanat Ji Mani heard this out with dismay. "You have never met your father's family."

"All the more reason to find them," she said.

"You will have to pass through Timur-i's Empire," Sanat Ji Mani reminded her. "Unless you go east, into China and come through the Russian Principalities and Dukedoms."

"What does that matter if I cross Timur-i's land? Timur-i is still in Samarkand, they say, when they do not claim he is a beggar on the roads, or here. What would they care about a single female tumbler?" She kept the mules moving with a slap of the reins. "The team is tired, and so am I. I am glad this is going to end."

"Are you," he asked, the anticipation of loss sweeping over him.

She heard the sadness in his voice and added, "I do not mean you, Sanat Ji Mani. You have taken me away from a hard life—"

"And given you a harder one," he finished for her.

"No," she said. "I would never have known what it is to be able to make my own way in the world. I would have gone on believing that I could not manage without a troupe around me and a master to decide for me. I would have assumed that I could not fend for myself, or help another on my own." She saw that the wagons ahead of them were pulling off the road at the base of a bluff. "I think we are stopping for the night." She was busy with the wagon for a short time, finding a place for it, with room enough for a grazing-line for the mules. "You have given me . . . myself," she said, and prepared to begin their evening routine.

Sanat Ji Mani was silent while she got down from the driving-box, then he said, very quietly, "Thank you, Tulsi Kil."

"Tomorrow shortly after mid-day, I will send word to Hasin Dahele that he must attend you at once." She seemed not to have heard him thank her. "Then you may deal with him as you wish. I will ask that your funeral pyre be made tomorrow night, before the heat turns you rotten."

"A wise precaution, since I will not putrefy." He could feel her draw away from him, and it saddened him as nothing else she had done had.

"I think so," she told him before she took out the brushes to groom the mules.

The next day, she followed her plan to the last detail; she ordered one of their escort to fetch the Rajput, saying it was urgent. She had reddened her eyes by rubbing them and maintained a stoic calm that served to convince Garanai Kheb that something was very wrong; he rode off at a gallop and returned a bit later with Hasin Dahele, who brought his horse up beside the wagon.

"Is something wrong? Has he—?" He could not bring himself to ask the question.

"He is worse," said Tulsi, her voice so flat that the Rajput was afraid he had come too late.

"Can he speak?" He mimed a moving mouth with his hand.

"He talks," she said, and pursed her lips. "Very sick."

The Rajput made up his mind. "Take your wagon to the side of the road," he ordered, pointing, and added to the Kheb cousins, "Get this thing out of the way of the others. In shade." He pointed to a cluster of trees nearby where the undergrowth was thinner than in other places near the dusty, rutted road.

The escorts obeyed, taking the heads of the mules and tugging them out of the column of wagons and guiding them toward the trees; the wagon bounced and swayed, and with each movement, the cousins winced. As they drew up in the shade of the tree, Hasin Dahele dismounted and climbed into the rear of the wagon.

Sanat Ji Mani had made an effort to create a scene that would be fixed in the Rajput's memory; he had used charcoal mixed with berry-juice to darken the hollows of his eyes and to lend a subtle emphasis to the lines in his face. He had put a thin film of oil on his forehead and rolled a saddle-pad around his right leg to make it appear swollen under the blanket, and he had taken an old fowl-leg and put it under his cot to provide the unmistakable odor of decaying meat. His breath wheezed in his chest and he seemed to have trouble focusing his eyes.

Hasin Dahele crouched at the side of his cot. "This is a terrible thing, Great Lord," he exclaimed as he stared down at Sanat Ji Mani's supine figure.

"It is what comes to all men," said Sanat Ji Mani in a thread of tone.

The sounds of the army moving was all around them, the shouts of men and the neighing of horses, the blare of elephants, the braying of donkeys and mules, but all of them were as nothing to the two men in the wagon.

"But you—" Hasin Dahele shook his head. "The Gods sent you to me. How can they take you away again, before I have truly begun my conquests?"

"They are gods," said Sanat Ji Mani. He plucked at the blanket covering him with quick, febrile movements. "Do as my companion tells you when I am dead."

"Very well," said Hasin Dahele impatiently.

"Obey her," he insisted, grabbing for the grimy silk of Hasin Dahele's pyjama-tunic. "Swear by your gods!"

"If you will make me your heir, I will do all that she asks. Otherwise I will leave you beside the road for vultures." He glared down at Sanat Ji Mani. "Well?"

Sanat Ji Mani sighed. "If anyone is the heir of Timur-i, you are," he whispered. "You have made yourself worthy of that legacy."

The irony of Sanat Ji Mani's words was lost on the Rajput, who threw back his head and exclaimed. "I am! *I am the heir of Timur-i!*"

"Swear," Sanat Ji Mani demanded on what appeared to be the last of his strength.

"I swear. She will direct the disposal of your body." His concession was graceless, hastily given as if to show his lack of concern now that he had what he wanted.

"Then your gods reward you," murmured Sanat Ji Mani.

From her place on the driving box, Tulsi listened, astonishment tinged with repugnance at this display. She looked at the two escorts, who remained immobile, their faces set and their expressions stern. "Not good," she said in the language of Beragar.

The Rajput was getting out the back of the wagon, not caring about how he did it. As he reached the ground, he called to the escorts, "Get back in the line, at the rear. Stay with this wagon until he dies, then come and tell me." He remounted his dark-bay. "Oh, and do with the body whatever she wants, so long as it does not lose too much time. We have much to do!" His features set in a hard grin, he set his horse for the front of the lines, leaving Tulsi's wagon beside the road, under the trees.

Text of a letter from Zal Iniattir in Asirgarh to Rustam Iniattir in Fustat, carried aboard the Iniattir ship, *Evening Star*.

To the most fortunate, most esteemed, most capable merchant, Rustam Iniattir, the respectful greetings of Zal Iniattir from our House's center in Asirgarh, with apologies for the delay in sending you word of all that has transpired of late.

The height of the year is not far-off, and I am pleased to tell you that I have sent a caravan to the east coast, to the city of Rajmundri, for the purpose of gaining a foothold in the markets there. If we have stations here in Asirgarh and in Sirpur, it is useful to take advantage of trading in the Indian Ocean as well as in the various islands to the south. I have pursued other ventures as well, and I have reason to hope that within five years, your dream of a network of markets from the West to the East will be made real. So long as there are no more invasions, or trade routes are not compromised, we should continue to flourish.

But peace may be ending to the west of Asirgarh. The Rajput of Beragar has begun his campaign by moving north and west, which does not impose upon this city directly, but may interfere with our trading with the west coast, which is a great disappointment now that we have ships of our own to cross the Arabian Sea. War is never good for commerce, and if half of what is said of this man is true, we must be prepared to fend off worse than a few attacks on small villages. I have heard that Deogir is moving to intercept the Beragar army, which could mean fighting within the month.

I have hope of concluding an arrangement with Azizi Iniattir, who has been in contact with a merchant of Lhasa, calling himself Lonpah

ST' amloatohr; this merchant is a most enterprising fellow, with many interesting items to bring to market. Azizi Iniattir has initiated trade with this fellow and has recommended that I become part of their association, for the man appears to be able to handle goods enough to do business with all of us. If this continues to be the case, I will, of course, extend the markets to you; I do not imagine there have been many goods in the markets of Fustat that came from the Land of Snows.

It has been a profitable spring, I must inform you, one that has exceeded my expectations and that gives me optimism for the future. We have increased our goods in the warehouse we purchased by nearly fifty percent in the last four months. Much of what we have stored will be gone before the storms come, which is as it should be. We Parsi may have been driven out of our homeland because we continue to follow Zarathustra rather than later prophets, but we may yet make a place for ourselves in the broader world, and in a manner that does credit to all of us, as well as bringing good things to all of us.

I am pleased to say that I have found another wife and I am completing my arrangements with her family to bring her to my house. It will be a useful thing to have her here, for it will be to our advantage to have more children to run our enterprise as it grows larger. I am already considering sending one of my sons to learn to be the master of a ship, so that in time we may have our own Captains as well as the ships themselves. You may think this is too much, but I am certain that it would benefit our House to have a few men experienced with the seas to advise us, and to watch after our cargos as no one else could.

The signs are for heavy storms when they come, or so I hear from the herdsmen, who know how to read the sky and earth better than any priest. If that is the case, we should be sure our caravans are instructed to be cautious in their travels; I have already ordered many leaders to be wary of the weather, for it is better that they remain in a town for three months than that they be caught in tempests on the road, and lose half of what they are carrying, as well as ponies, donkeys, oxen, and camels. You may disagree with me, but I am sure that we are better served by circumspection than by rashness.

I hope this may be in your hands before the storms strike. If it is not, then I hope that you have good fortune and that after the dark of the year, you may show even more profit and trade than you have done so far, to the advancement of our fortunes and our House.

Zal Iniattir

11

Built at the crest of a small ridge, the funeral pyre stood out against the evening sky like a ruined temple. Tulsi had supervised its hasty construction, insisting the logs that formed its base be tied together with oiled rags; the four men who had been the escort for her wagon had obeyed her orders explicitly for fear of what the Rajput would do if they failed.

"Take him on a litter and put that on top of the pyre," Tulsi said as soon as they were done making the pyre and had returned to the wagon where Sanat Ji Mani lay.

"It is not very sturdy—the pyre is not," said Kantu Asar, pointing up at the pyre and shaking his hands.

"It is sturdy as it needs to be," she said, using their language with an ease that surprised them. "It will be ashes by morning, in any case."

"That it will," said one of them. "Is he ready to be carried? Are there any more rituals, or have you prepared him?"

"He is ready," said Tulsi, who had found washing and dressing Sanat Ji Mani's supposed corpse for burning an unnerving experience; he had looked so lifeless, so unnaturally still, his skin so waxen, that she wondered if he had actually slipped away from her. Only a covert squeeze of her wrist had reassured her and given her the inclination to go on, clothing him in pale cotton robes and leggings that made it appear his right leg was twice the girth of his left. The wrappings she had used would provide protection for his feet after he escaped from the pyre, and could be used to cover his skin to avoid sunlight. The thought of these things made her shudder, but she concealed her anxiety and stayed with the four men who had been her escort as they bore the litter through the camp and up to the pyre.

After the men set the litter on the pyre, they moved away. "Do you need a torch?" one of the Kheb cousins asked.

"I need something to light it with," said Tulsi, a bit sharply. "Is the Rajput going to watch?"

"No," said Challa Bahlin. "He will send Vayu Ede to observe for him. It is what the Rajput has declared."

"Because the Rajput has what he wants," said Tulsi, letting her bitterness show. "Very well. Bring me a torch as soon as Vayu Ede gets here." She glanced behind her, and saw that the ridge backed onto a defile with a trickle of water at the bottom of it. She gauged the distance from the ridge to the floor of the defile and decided it was worth the risk.

"Do you have any prayers to give?" Kantu Asar asked.

"I gave them when I prepared the body," said Tulsi, looking up at the still figure on the pyre: would this work? she asked herself.

"Then it is only a matter of Vayu Ede seeing," said Sambarin Kheb. He looked down at the camp. "They will watch when the fire is lit."

The other three made sounds of agreement.

"Be sure you stand well back. You do not want to be burned," said Tulsi, wishing she could limber up with stretches and jumps, but that, she knew, might reveal more than she wanted of what she was about to do.

"You will be in danger," said Garanai Kheb. "The fire—"

"That is my concern," said Tusli, her expression forbidding. "Do not linger; go down the hill, fetch me a torch, and wave to me as soon as Vayu Ede is here."

The men put their hands together and bowed as formally as they might have to an officer—a tribute none of them had ever before offered a woman—then turned away and did as she had ordered them; a short while later, Challa Bahlin returned with a lit torch which he handed to Tulsi in silence, then retreated down the slope, as hurriedly as he could without risking falling. A number of soldiers had gathered at the foot of the rise, curious enough to want to see the immolation.

Tulsi looked over her shoulder again, checking out the defile. It was deep enough to be dangerous in its way, but not so deep that falling into it was nothing less than suicide. She felt her body thrum with readiness. How much she wanted this to be over! "Where is Vayu Ede?" she asked the wind. "It will be dark soon." It was an effort to contain herself, for it would be so easy to set the whole pyre alight now, but it would dishonor the Rajput, and that could cause the soldiers to stop the burning. Shaking her head, she paced around the wooden structure to provide some outlet for the tension building in her. Finally the wizened figure of Vayu Ede emerged from the gathering crowd. He lifted his hands and began to recite some poetry that Tulsi had never heard before; she stopped still and let him go on. When he became silent, she went to the far end of the pyre, lifting her torch, and set it to the oiled rags holding the structure together.

At once the fire leaped up, stinking of oil and burning cloth; the green wood sputtered but was slow to light. Coughing in the billow of acrid smoke, Tulsi selected another large knot of fabric and lit it as well, sending a new mass of smoke into the evening breeze. Her eyes watered and she batted at the dark cloud as she tried to reach a third knot. The cloth caught fire and this time the wood began to crackle and hiss as the fire finally got hold of it. Now was the time. Tulsi flung the torch over the edge of the crest into the defile, and as it fell like a burning star, she sprang into the air and leaped atop the pyre, her hands raised so she might be seen. But her footing was uncertain and the cloth knotting the logs and branches together were burning brilliantly, and the whole of the pyre began to shift, the supports starting to give way.

There were shouts from below, and one of the four escorts started toward the pyre, only to be held back by his fellows.

With a moan, the pyre broke apart, most of it tipping toward her, away from the camp and toward the defile, the litter on which Sanat Ji Mani lay in a stupor sliding toward her. For a long, terrible moment, they teetered together, and then the pyre went to pieces, flinging Tulsi and Sanat Ji Mani backward into the defile with burning debris and charred branches falling with them. Cries of horror and dismay followed them down into the defile until they landed amid logs, branches, and scraps of burning cotton on the low-growing scrub that lined the shallow creek at the bottom.

The constellations of early summer told Sanat Ji Mani that it was after midnight when he finally opened his eyes. He smelled the residue of the fire around him, and he realized his clothing had been partially burned, leaving a stretch of his thigh exposed. As he tried to sit up, a sharp pain told him he had broken a rib, which explained why it had taken him so long to come to himself. It would be two or three years before the bone knit again; he had endured broken ribs before and knew what he would have to stand while it healed; he hoped he had enough cloth in the padding on his leg to wrap his chest. He had to wait while the dizziness passed, then he struggled to his feet, testing his right foot with care. Moving with great care not only to keep his balance but to go along silently, he began to search the defile, looking for Tulsi, his night-seeing eyes able to pierce the darkness as he made his way over the uneven ground and in among the bushes that crowded up to the stream. Knowing that he would have to find shelter before morning, he made his search diligently and swiftly, circling out from where he had come to, half-afraid that he might find her injured or worse.

Toward dawn he found an overhang that led to the small mouth of a cave. He hesitated before going in, for he knew he was in no condition to fight for the space with anything much larger than a mongoose. Finding a stone ledge just inside, he climbed onto it, easing himself down in order to minimize the hurt from his rib, and promised himself to search again at nightfall. He would be able to call for her then, for the Rajput's army would be gone. He tried to chuckle and winced instead at the thought that he was finally free.

With sundown came wakefulness and a new level of apprehension, for there was the smell of carnage on the air. Emerging from the cave, he prepared himself to find Tulsi's body, but although the odor of blood and feces was strong, he did not see her. Reluctantly he followed the smell to four carcasses, men who had died hideously, their bones exposed where scraping knives had gone as far as the netting that confined the men would allow. Their heads had been cut off and set up beside the remains of their bodies: Sambarin Kheb, Garanai Kheb, Challa Bahlin, and Kantu Asar stared with empty sockets that swarmed with insects at the partially reassembled pyre. Sanat Ji Mani put his hand to his face, knowing these men had died because he and Tulsi were not found. The only scrap of hope he took from these wretched remains was the certainty that Tulsi was not dead.

All through the next night he searched for Tulsi, calling her name and trying to pick up a trace of her; by the end of the night, he had to admit that she was gone. He accepted this with resignation, telling himself that she might have struck out for Chaul at once, for fear that the Rajput's men might search the defile, as he had seen they had done. In addition to the four pathetic carcases, he had seen the tracks of many men on the second night, and had supposed that there had been an enormous effort had been made to find them, or at least to determine what became of their corpses. If Tulsi had not lost consciousness, had been relatively unhurt, or had been truly terrified— she might have tried to rouse him and failed—she could have decided to press on as she said she would do. For the first time he regretted that she had chosen not to come to his life, to complete the blood-bond that would forever link them no matter how far apart they were. But she had chosen not to come to his life, and all he could determine was that he had no sense of her death. As he settled down for another day in the cave, he knew it was useless to linger in the mountains any longer; it was time to go westward, to the coast, and down the coast to Chaul.

It was difficult traveling alone: he was able to catch birds and small animals for sustenance, but there was no companionship, and he found his loneliness more intense than either his hunger or pain. In the short summer nights, he often waited on the outskirts of villages, not only to snare ducks and geese but to hear the sound of human voices. He fashioned a walking-stick out of a branch, and spent his dawns and sunsets carving Tulsi's face into it with the metal tongue of a belt-buckle he had found half-buried in the road, telling himself that he could use this likeness to show others when he searched for her in Chaul, not because he longed for her.

The first storms came almost a full month early, and his travel was slowed by wind and rain. He needed shelter more than ever now, for there was running water everywhere so that even at night he could find no relief from it. He was weak and exhausted, unable to travel far at night, and utterly helpless in the daytime. His journey was arduous, made more difficult by his growing concern that even if Tulsi reached Chaul, he would not be there in time to find her before she moved on to Lithuania and Kiev. By the time he reached the coast, he was desperate, and pressed himself to go farther each night, trying to take advantage of the lengthening darkness to cover as much ground as possible. His clothes by now were little more than rags, and he used what little cloth he had left to wrap his chest and genitals, and to put some protection on his foot. Although he was rarely seen, his injuries required care and he could not forsake the habit of modesty acquired more than thirty-four hundred years ago.

When he finally arrived at Chaul, he made for the docks where his warehouses and ships were. The night was far-advanced and only dogs and rats were abroad. He slipped through the streets he had learned many years before, past temples and market-squares, past fine houses and hovels, until the odor of the sea was strong in his nostrils and he could hear the sough and sigh of the waves, and the creaking of timbers from ships tied up at the piers. At last he had reached a haven; he found his warehouses and slipped in through an entrance he had made for his own use more than fifty years before. The hinges shrieked in protest as he swung back the hidden door far enough to allow him to get inside.

The aromas here were strong: pepper, ginger, cinnamon, cardamom, and coriander all vied for dominance in the air ; crates of the precious seeds, barks, roots, and powders were stacked against the walls and in clusters on the floor. At the point in the warehouse farthest away from the water were two ancient chests, banded in metal with his eclipse embossed on their ends, old and neglected in appearance: these were what Sanat Ji Mani sought, and to him they were more precious than casks of jewels and gold, for these contained his native earth. Setting his carved walking stick down, he worked the lock on the larger of the two, swung back the lid, and climbed in, pulling the lid closed on top of him. The annealing presence of the Transylvanian soil enveloped him as if in a maternal embrace, and he finally was able to rest.

He came to himself shortly after mid-day, when all of Chaul drowsed under the warmth of the brassy sun; he felt much restored, the pain from his foot and his broken rib had receded and he had regained a measure of his strength. Emerging from the chest with care, he pulled out a sack from the foot of the crate that contained clothing, weapons, his eclipse pectoral, and a small pouch of alchemical gold. Brushing himself clean of any smirches, he wrapped his chest and foot, then dressed in a kandys of black damask and leggings of heavy silk twill of dark, dull-red, and Russian boots with his native earth lining the soles. The fine fabric felt alien on his skin, and he suspected he still looked much the worse for wear. Taking up a dagger, settling his pectoral in place, its heavy silver links all but black with tarnish, and tying his pouch of gold to his sash, he readied himself to approach the factor who supervised his warehouses and shipping. He picked up his walking stick, ran his fingers through his hair and set off through the warehouse toward the front door.

The factor was dozing on a bench, a cup of strong, sweet tea standing half-finished on the arm of the bench; flies were already gathered on the rim. He blinked as Sanat Ji Mani approached him, as if uncertain if he actually saw someone or was dreaming. Slowly he sat up, his strong, dark visage registering his confusion. Belatedly he stood, put his palms together and bowed.

Sanat Ji Mani returned the gesture. "You would be Bhismali's son? I am the foreigner Sanat Ji Mani. You are my factor."

"Bhismali's grandson, Reverend Sir," said the factor, doing his best not to stare. "Oh, what a predicament . . . To meet you like this . . . I did not think . . . I did not know . . ." he stammered, trying to achieve the decorum their meeting demanded.

"I apologize for surprising you," said Sanat Ji Mani smoothly. "I have been traveling and have only just arrived." This slight mendacity did not trouble him; he went on smoothly, "It has been a hard journey."

"I should think so," said Bhismali's grandson, and Sanat Ji Mani could not help but wonder how he looked to deserve such a response. "Are you alone?"

"Alas, yes. There has been war to the north-east of here, and that made for difficulties," Sanat Ji Mani said.

"Yes. We have heard that the Rajput of Deogir defeated that upstart Hasin Dahele, and put his head over the gate of his city, where birds can pick it clean." Bhismali's grandson nodded his approval. "They say half the soldiers of Beragar are now Deogir's slaves."

Sanat Ji Mani was silent for a moment. "How do you know this?" he asked, knowing how quickly rumors could become accepted truth.

"Merchants from Asirgarh brought word of it, not ten days ago," said Bhismali's grandson. "I myself spoke with them, for they are part of the House of Iniattir."

"The House of Iniattir," Sanat Ji Mani repeated, and smiled.

"If you came through that fighting, it is no wonder you did not have an easy time of it," said the factor. "Everyone knows that there was fighting. There were many people on the roads, having lost their villages and their homes. Some of them still wander, and will for months to come."

"They have come here?" Sanat Ji Mani asked, thinking back to the many nights the roads had seemed empty; he had avoided villages and encampments, which, he thought, may have been a mistake—he might have learned something of Tulsi had he sought out other travelers. As he chided himself, he knew that such exposure was dangerous and that the chance of finding her by such random methods were slight, but he could not keep from thinking it might have worked.

"A great many; most have moved on, a few have gone back, now that it is over." The factor looked puzzled. "Surely you saw something of this."

"Yes," said Sanat Ji Mani. "But I did not realize how much of it was due to the fighting." He paused to consider. "And you are sure that the Rajput of Beragar is dead?"

"Yes. Everyone knows it is so, as everyone knows Timur-i is trying to attack the Land of Snows." The factor made a gesture to emphasize the obvious. "To think that you came through the fighting, though."

"Not quite through it," Sanat Ji Mani said.

"Then near enough to have trouble because of it," said Bhismali's grandson.

"It was difficult, and I fear that was my fault. Had I not been lax, we would not have been in danger; I hold myself responsible for what has happened." His voice changed, becoming more forceful. "My companion and I were separated; I had hoped I might find her here," he said as if a woman by herself were nothing remarkable.

"Her? You traveled with a woman?" Bhismali's grandson exclaimed. "Did you not have guards? Was it just you and the woman?"

"There were four guards," said Sanat Ji Mani. "All dead, some days ago." His dark eyes were deep and full of sorrow. "That is why I am most concerned for my companion." He held out his walking stick. "This is her likeness. She is from far to the north, with hair lighter than mine, and blue-green eyes, shaped like those of the Chinese."

"Um," said the factor, staring at the carved portrait. "I have not come across anyone who looks like this."

"She is a tumbler and an acrobat. Perhaps you saw her perform in the market-place," Sanat Ji Mani suggested.

"I am here when the market-places are active. My household tends to our purchases there." He contemplated the face on the walking stick. "Tall or short?"

"Not quite as tall as I am," said Sanat Ji Mani, knowing that she would be tall in this region. "Very strong."

Bhismali's grandson shook his head. "I know none such," he said. "Nor have I heard of any."

Sanat Ji Mani did his best to conceal his discomfiture, telling himself that this was just the first step in his search, that he could not expect to find her upon his arrival, not after they had been apart for nearly three months. "Well." He took back his staff. "I shall want to find her."

"Immediately?" Bhismali's grandson exclaimed.

"As soon as may be," said Sanat Ji Mani, fighting the sense of futility that threatened to overcome him.

"Where shall you want to look?" The factor was baffled but did his best not to show it.

"Everywhere in this city, and then north, along the coast, all the way to Cambay, if necessary." Sanat Ji Mani kept his tone level. "We will arrange matters shortly. For now, I must learn how trade has been and what news you have had from Alexandria."

"Ah, Alexandria," said Bhismali's grandson, nodding knowingly. "Yes. I have received regular messages from your factor there, Rogerian, who has been most concerned for your welfare. He has been diligent in maintaining your interests and expanding your markets; he has been dealing with Rustam Iniattir and his relatives most effectively. You and the House of Iniattir have made a fortuitous alliance that will continue to benefit you and them for many years to come. It was wise of you to enter into your trading with them." He was obviously far more comfortable discussing business than the missing woman; his eyes brimmed with enthusiasm. "I have records you may want to examine, all recorded on palm-leaves, as my grandfather taught me. He must have served your father; you cannot have been a merchant for almost fifty years. You do not seem as ancient as you would have to be." This last was dubious again.

"I do not look my age, I have been told," said Sanat Ji Mani smoothly. "If your grandfather trained you in his ways, then I will be satisfied."

"He did that," said Bhismali's grandson. "From the time I was very young. I have sworn to train my oldest son to take my place." He smiled. "You and your father have been most reliable, most honorable; my family is grateful to you."

"As I am to you," said Sanat Ji Mani, and glanced toward the warehouse. "Perhaps we can step out of the sun: as you see, I have been burned by it recently." Although he had not seen his reflection since he had awakened to vampire life, he could tell from the way his skin felt that his face was red and peeling.

Bhismali's grandson was chagrined. "I should not have kept you here. Of course we must go into the warehouse and I must show you all that has been done, what has been shipped from here, what is expected here, and the values of it all." He straightened up. "It will be a great pleasure for me to explain all that has been done. This warehouse is the older one, and the smaller. There is a newer and larger one on the next pier down."

"This is very good of you," said Sanat Ji Mani. "I received information about the second warehouse a few years ago, as I recall."

"It is a fine place. You will be proud," said Bhismali's grandson.

"No doubt I will," said Sanat Ji Mani, allowing the factor to escort him into the older warehouse. "Do you think it might be possible that this woman might have gone to the newer, larger warehouse?" He tried to make the question casual, but he could see from the expression on the factor's face that he had failed.

"It would be a most unsuitable thing to do," said Bhismali's grandson. "I cannot believe that any woman would do such a thing."

"She is not like your wives, or your daughters," Sanat Ji Mani said steadily. "She would not hesitate to present herself there, if that was where she was sent." But even as he declared this, he wondered if it was so. On her own in a strange place, Tulsi Kil might not behave as he expected.

"You may inquire there; it is your warehouse," said Bhismali's grandson in a manner stiff with disapproval. "But let us attend to this after I have shown you the records for the last several years. You will see that the disruption in the north has increased our trade, and as much as it damaged the markets of Delhi, it has brought more ships here to Chaul, and that has been fortunate for us. The Wheel turns for all of us."

"That it does," said Sanat Ji Mani, pleased to get out of the sun, although with his native earth in the soles of his boots, it no longer hurt him to be in the light. He went into the ante-chamber that served as a reception room and office, and gave his full attention to the records Bhismali, his son, and his grandson had kept for Sanat Ji Mani.

It was getting dark by the time he left to visit the larger warehouse; Bhismali's grandson had excused himself, saying he had duties to attend to at home, and promised to meet with Sanat Ji Mani the next morning. Sanat Ji Mani did not argue; he went along to the pier where three large warehouses sat, and approached the one with his eclipse painted on the side: Bhismali's grandson was right—the warehouse was half again as large as the older one. As he approached, two men with truncheons came up to him.

"Here. We will have none of that." The accent of the man who spoke was rough and his attitude surly.

"That is my warehouse," said Sanat Ji Mani mildly, indicating his eclipse pectoral and the painted symbol on the side.

"So you say," growled the second man, hefting his truncheon. "We want no thieves here."

"Neither do I," said Sanat Ji Mani. "If you are worried, would you take me to the factor. You may watch me at every step."

"Do you think—"The first began, only to be interrupted by the second.

"If we go with him both ways, and watch him, we can be sure he does nothing." He ducked his head, pleased with his cleverness.

"That we can." The first contemplated the plan and accepted it. "Yes. It will do."

"Have you had many thieves here?" Sanat Ji Mani asked as he resumed his progress toward the door to the warehouse.

"Since the fighting, yes. We have been kept busy," said the second man. "Ever since mid-summer, you would be surprised."

A sudden flare of hope went through Sanat Ji Mani. "And is this pier always guarded?"

"Day and night," the second man said. "Has been for months."

Sanat Ji Mani held up his walking stick, turning it so that the last afternoon sun struck the face he had carved. "Would either of you have seen this woman?"

The first man laughed. "What woman would come here?" He barely glanced at the carving.

The second man took the time to look at the portrait. "No. No one has come here with that face. A foreigner like that, we would notice, and remember."

They had reached the door to the warehouse; Sanat Ji Mani halted, saying to the two men. "Thank you. I shall not be long."

"We will watch for that woman, if you like," the second man volunteered.

Sanat Ji Mani gave a single nod, although he knew it would prove useless. He would search for her, but knew with a conviction almost as strong as the blood-bond itself, that he would never find her; Tulsi Kil had done what she had told him she wanted to do, back in the Rajput's palace in Devapur—she had vanished. "I will be grateful," he said, then scratched at the door before going inside.

Text of an account presented to Timur-i Lenkh in Samarkand.

To the favored of Allah, the Lord of the World, the Conqueror Timur-i Lenkh, the Triumphant, this requested information is being submitted in full submission and devotion to your Will; May Allah give you long life and a thousand sons:

Of the captives we took from Delhi, we have sold more than a thousand of them—1,268 to give the exact number—as was your order, the gold from which has been used to purchase supplies and food for your army. This money was sufficient to provide enough money to

*have three measures of gold still remaining, and set aside for the pur-
pose of purchasing food and supplies. Here in Samarkand, your most
wonderful city, we are amply cared for and there is no need to draw
on this money, so we have not done so; it is kept toward our next
campaign.*

*Of those remaining with the army, most are Muslims and have
made themselves part of your support forces for the good of our True
Faith. Among these 427, 118 have been executed for improper acts
over the last half-year, and their flayed skins left out as a warning to
others. Of the 309 left, all but six are fully assigned within the army,
most to the cooks and maintenance crews. They have shown themselves
loyal and deserve your good opinion.*

*The remaining six may give you some concern; to begin with, none
of them are Muslims, and their lack of religion is troublesome:*

*Abhu the metalworker has been willing to work in the smithy along
with our own men, and has not let his adherence to false gods interfere
with his labors. For now I would recommend keeping him where he
is and taking care to inspect his work to be certain he is not compro-
mising the quality of our weapons.*

*Iksander Mawan, the eunuch, has been most useful in keeping rec-
ords for us; he reads several tongues and that is a useful thing. While
I have reservations about him, I would recommend keeping him at his
books for a while, although I do think it would be best to leave him
here in Samarkand rather than take him on campaign; he is clever
enough and strong enough to be able to flee, which I fear he may do
if given the opportunity. The wound to his head has fully healed, and
it would be foolish to rely on his injury to keep him docile.*

*The soldier, Mutaz Shikhara, has been unreliable of late, filled with
dark thoughts and cast into lethargy; he is not a good man to send to
troops or into battle. Let him be given a simple task that gives him no
weapons, and perhaps he will cease to dwell in the darkness of his
losses; if he does not, then perhaps he should be sold. Since he has
done nothing against you or your rule, execution may not be called
for, but certainly he will never be a soldier again.*

*Nahar Erai, the shirt-maker, is a most useful fellow; he is willing
to ply his trade for as long as he is given meat and drink; he is not
loyal, but neither is he disloyal. He wishes only to earn his living, and*

I see no harm in him, as well as a great deal of use. So long as his fingers are nimble and his eyes do not dim, I would recommend keeping him with the army. He poses no danger to anyone, including himself.

Josha Dar is a puzzle, but a useful one. He has provided me with much useful information, all of which has been proven correct, and that inclines me to favor keeping him. But I cannot help being uneasy about him; there is something in his eyes that makes me question the reasons for his cooperation, and for that reason alone, I want to take time to observe him before giving a final recommendation to you regarding him. It may be that I am worried about nothing, but when a man is willing to betray his own people without reservation but will not pledge his dedication to a new master, I am not sanguine about him. For the time being, he is useful, but I fear he would make himself useful in the same way to anyone who would pay him, or keep him. Let me withhold my final decision regarding him for another half-year.

Timin Yamut, the leather-worker, has been growing sickly; he wheezes when he walks and his feet swell often. He has lost strength and his appetite is failing. The physicians tell me that he will not live long, and so there is no reason to recommend anything regarding him; his fate, as is the fate of everyone, is in the hands of Allah.

This is the whole of my report, and I present it to you with all humility. May it aid your deliberations, and may you grow increasingly wise from your contemplations.

Tolui Sati
Monitor of the Captives

At Samarkand on the Balance of Day and Night Toward Winter

EPILOGUE

Text of a letter from Avasa Dani to Sanat Ji Mani, written and received at Alexandria in June, 1401.

No, Sanat Ji Mani, I cannot see that any good would be served by our meeting again. I know your invitation was kindly meant, and I have received it in that spirit, but I am content with the life I have now, a life I know you have given me, and I do not believe that there is any purpose to our resuming our friendship now that I am of your blood.

It is gratifying to know your business with Rustam Iniattir and his House has done so well. I am pleased that you were able to gain something after your great losses at Delhi, and I thank you for the funds that success has brought to me. It is most generous of you to set aside five percent of your profits for my use. In time I hope I will have no need of them, but in case that does not happen as soon as I anticipate, let me express my gratitude not only for the money, but your understanding.

I was saddened to learn of your hardships after the destruction of Delhi; but, as you said yourself, many suffered far worse than you did, and you returned to this place to a thriving business, which is more than most were able to do. From what little Rogerian has told me, you have endured many adversities in the past and may do so again, so while I am distressed to know that you had difficulties, you are doubtless capable of dealing with all that is demanded of you. I will take you as an admirable example in times to come.

As long as the Blood-Bond tells me you still live, I will not fret on your behalf. Knowing that you are about the world is a comfort in itself, but as my life as a breathing woman is over, so is all but the Bond with you. While I know I owe you more than I will ever be able to repay, if you would continue your kindness to me, leave me alone.

Avasa Dani